THE
ACADEMY
JOURNALS
VOLUME ONE

GARRETT
ROBINSON

THE ACADEMY JOURNALS
VOLUME ONE
Garrett Robinson

The author greatly appreciates you taking the time to read his work. Please leave a review wherever you bought the book or on Goodreads.com.

Interior Design: Legacy Books, Inc.
Publisher: Legacy Books, Inc.
Editors: Karen Conlin, Cassie Dean
Cover Artist: Sutthiwat Dekachamphu

1. Fantasy - Epic 2. Fantasy - Dark 3. Fantasy - General

First Edition

Published by Legacy Books

To my wife
First and last

To my children
For continuing to teach me

To the Vloganovel crew
Who are bigger and better than ever

To my Rebels
It's been a wild ride, and it's only just starting

And to my wife
First and last

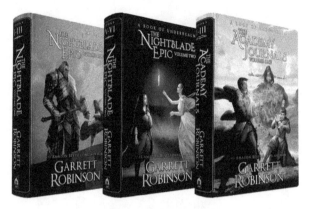

GET MORE

Legacy Books is home to the very best that fantasy has to offer.

Join our email alerts list, and we'll send word whenever we release a new book. You'll receive exclusive updates and see behind the scenes as we create them.

(You'll also learn the secret that makes great fantasy books, *great*.)

Interested? Visit this link:

Underrealm.net/Join

For maps of the locations in this book, visit:

Underrealm.net/maps

THE
ALCHEMIST'S
TOUCH

BEING BOOK ONE
OF THE FIRST VOLUME

OF THE
ACADEMY JOURNALS

ONE

THERE WAS A BLUE DOOR ACROSS THE STREET FROM THE TAVERN, AND no matter how hard he tried, Ebon could not stop himself from looking back to it every few moments.

To an unknowing observer, there was little to mark the door as special. Unadorned wood, painted blue, with a simple iron latch and no ornamentation. But everyone knew what lay behind it. Ebon did, certainly, and so his attention returned there, his gaze passing across it as if by chance before returning to the cup of wine in his hand.

It was easier to look at the blue door than around the common room of the inn where no customer would sit at his table. Indeed, they even avoided the tables next to his. Often Ebon felt the weight of a curious gaze upon him, yet when he tried to meet it the observer would turn away quickly, as though afraid of being caught. Only Tamen, sitting opposite, would look at him openly. But Tamen had nothing to fear from Ebon. Rather, it was the reverse.

It struck Ebon as a cruel joke. At home, he often had only a single wish: to be left alone. The wish was rarely granted. But now he would have given much for any companionship aside from Tamen's—and mayhap one type of companionship in particular.

His eyes darted away from the blue door again.

"The High King's Seat," he said, and drank from his cup. It was his third, or fourth, and a tightness had begun to form behind his eyes. "Long have I wished to see it, and yet now I wish they had never brought me."

Tamen did not answer. He only took a sip from his own drink, though it was much gentler than Ebon's swig.

"Mayhap I am greedy," said Ebon. "I wish for too much. Father has made it plain that I shall never attend the Academy. Yet still, when he told me I would accompany him to the Seat . . . still I held out hope."

The tavern was a bit quieter for a moment. Tamen's eyes flicked to one side, and then the other. "Mayhap it would be wise for you to speak more softly."

Ebon sighed and leaned back. "Wise. Who has ever called me wise, Tamen? If I were wise, I would be in the Academy. Or mayhap if I were in the Academy, they would call me wise. I feel it sitting there. Do you remember? We passed it in our carriage when we arrived. Straight past its wide front doors we drove, and then it was gone. Yet the place where it stands is forever burned in my memory. I feel that even after Father takes me home, I will be able to point to it."

"A sorrowful state of affairs indeed." But Tamen's words were accompanied by a rolling of the eyes, and Ebon knew the man grew weary of complaints.

Tamen was his retainer in name, but certainly not his friend. Not truly. Ebon knew the man's real purpose: a guard. If ever Ebon strayed from his father's wishes, thought to defy the will of his parents, Tamen would carry word of his misdeeds straight to them. He had done so often in the past. And then again, other times he had held his tongue. Ebon never knew which would happen on a given day.

His eyes strayed across the blue door before returning to his cup. He drank again. Did he wish to be left alone or not? Just now, he could not decide.

"What would my father say, were I to go to him and ask to see the Academy? Not to attend, but only to see it for myself. It would allow me to return home with some glimmer of a dream, some memory of the place I have longed for since I was a child. Would he deny me so small a thing?"

"Yes," said Tamen. It sounded as though there might be more to follow, but he left it at that.

Ebon nodded. "Of course he would. My father is not one to grant trivial boons. And no doubt even my presence at this tavern would strike him as trivial. 'Stand your lazy self, whelp,' he might say, as he likes to do, before commanding me to return home."

Again Tamen looked about the room, and this time his eyes flashed anxiously. "Keep your voice down."

Ebon sagged back in his chair. A spark of defiance flared in him, but he quickly extinguished it. What could he do? Make Tamen uncomfortable? Then the retainer would only speak to Ebon's father, and then Ebon might not be allowed to leave his room for a month. Mayhap longer. The vindictive will of Shay Drayden knew little of restraint.

He realized he was staring at the blue door and quickly turned away.

"I thought the Seat would be different," he muttered. "Not—not better, I suppose. But different. I thought that upon its streets, or in such a place as this, I might meet some chance stranger who would speak to me in ignorance of where I come from. Yet everyone here fears to sit beside me. They fear to sit within arm's reach. It is as though they can smell my family name upon me. Who here will even look towards our table? Even now, when I speak too loud because I have drunk too much wine?"

Several heads turned away from him, as though their owners knew they had been caught staring.

This time Tamen smirked. "At last you speak the truth. You *have* had too much wine. Mayhap it is time to think of turning our steps towards the manor . . . unless you have some other reason to remain."

This time it was Tamen who glanced towards the blue door.

Ebon's heart skipped a beat. But he would not let himself dwell on the thought that sprang to mind. Mayhap Tamen was hinting towards something, and mayhap not. Hope could be a cruel thing once taken away. Instead he leaned forwards, cupping his wine tighter and taking still another pull from it. Tamen leaned in to hear his murmur.

"Will my life always be this way, Tamen? Tell me true."

"You have asked me this before. How would you like me to answer this time?"

"Never does he turn his wrath on Albi. He looks at her as though her eyes are the moons. Yet we are almost of an age."

"Almost of an age. But not quite."

"Nor was I, once. Yet my life was the same even then. Shall I never be free of his scorn?"

Tamen pursed his lips and took a small sip of wine. "This may be of small comfort to you, but no one lives forever."

Ebon's jaw clenched, and he leaned away while draining the last of his cup. "That is a dark thought. You should not have said it."

Tamen shrugged and finished his own drink. "I mean no ill intent, and you know it. It is a truth none can ignore—neither the High King upon her throne, nor the wealthiest of merchants, nor the poorest beggar upon the Seat. Now, I would ask if you wish for more wine, but I think that would be very unwise."

"I would give anything not to be my father's son," whispered Ebon. He had not meant to say the words aloud, and he caught Tamen's eyes widening. But he would not shy away now. He pressed his fingers into the rough wood of the tabletop. "It is the truth. You know you would not trade places with me. Who would? Anyone who would desire my place thinks only of our family's riches. They spare no thought for the family itself."

Tamen stood abruptly. "We have been here too long, and you have drunk far too much. We must leave at once. Speak no more, or I will repeat your words."

Ebon grasped his hand, holding him in place. "Tamen, stop. Stop, I beg of you. I am sorry. My tongue runs too freely, it is true. Only . . . only this is unbearable. I know I cannot go to the Academy. But I . . . I only wish, for just a little while, that I could pretend I am not of the family Drayden. Can you find no pity in your heart for that?"

Tamen paused, and though his lips were pressed tightly together, Ebon thought he saw something soften in the man's eyes. He peeled Ebon's fingers away from his wrist.

"Mayhap I can find pity. But do not speak of it out loud. If you do, pity will not be enough to stay my tongue—and your father will not judge such talk lightly."

"Thank you," whispered Ebon.

Tamen leaned forwards over the table and fixed Ebon's gaze with his own. "Do you wish it in truth? To pretend you are not a Drayden?"

Ebon drew back, confused. "You know I do."

"Then follow your wandering eyes. They have rested often enough upon the blue door. Go there for a little while."

Ebon found his throat was suddenly dry. He wiped sweaty palms on the golden silk of his tunic. "You mock me. I tell you this trip is more pain than pleasure, and you mock me by dangling a wish before my eyes."

"Why would I mock you?"

"You would tell them. You would have to."

Tamen shrugged. "Why should I? There is no harm in such a thing. You may not believe me, Ebon, but I take no pleasure in the service I provide your parents. I am paid well, and so I do my duty. But I think this might be good for you. And for at least a moment, it might give pause to your endless whining. So I shall turn the other way—but just this once, do you understand?"

Ebon saw no hint of a lie in Tamen's eyes. He wanted to believe it. But how could he? How often had Tamen carried tales of his misdeeds straight to the ears of his father?

Yet never before had Tamen promised to keep such a thing secret.

His stomach did a turn. Darkness take them all. Even if Tamen did spread the tale afterwards, what could Ebon's father do? Lock Ebon up in his room—again? He might do that for any perceived offense. And yet Ebon would still have one happy memory of the Seat. No punishment could take that away.

He rose from his table and reached for his purse.

"Keep it," said Tamen, waving him off. "My coin is enough for these drinks, and you will need yours."

Ebon swallowed hard as he took the man's meaning. He turned to go, and the tavern's denizens turned their faces away as he passed into the night.

TWO

THE DOOR'S LATCH LIFTED LIKE A FEATHER, AND IT SWUNG INWARD ON well-oiled hinges that gave no sound. A heady fragrance rushed out to greet Ebon, nearly stopping him in his tracks. He could pick out fine, exotic perfumes from Calentin as well more familiar ones from his homeland of Idris; the unmistakable scent of Wadeland tea together with the cinnamon wine of Hedgemond. And under it all there was something sweeter, pungent but light, something that stirred his heart within his breast.

His knees had begun to shake. He forced them to move again and stepped across the threshold before his nerves ran out.

Here the lights were dim, even dimmer than they had been in the tavern. But the darkness seemed warm and comforting, inviting rather than ominous. Partly that was thanks to the fine music that floated on the air, the steady plucking of a harp that teased his ears like a whisper at midnight.

He turned to find the source of the sound and saw a harpist in the corner. One of the room's few lamps sat just beside her on a table, so that it looked as if it had been placed just to illuminate her. As he saw her clothes and the shape of her face, he realized with a start that she was a woman of Idris. But the light brown of her braided hair was rare in his homeland, as were her hazel eyes that glowed from the lantern.

Those eyes captured him for a moment as she met his gaze, though her fingers never faltered where they plucked at the strings. Ebon gulped and looked away before she thought he was staring, but he could not entirely turn from her. Instead he looked down, taking in her clothing. It was of a familiar cut, but he did not think he had seen anyone at home wear it quite so well. Her feet were bare upon the floor, resting against the harp's wooden base. He looked upon them for a moment and blushed before he could finally tear his gaze from her.

It was not until then that he realized there were many other figures in the room, men and women, all of them draped across chairs and couches that ran along the walls. Some studied him with curious little smiles, while others let their attention wander. Ebon gripped his trouser legs tightly as he realized that many of them were only half-clothed, and some less than that. Suddenly he did not know where to look, and his eyes darted wildly back and forth. But he was rescued as the house's matron arrived, smiling as she came to him.

"Good evening, young sir. How may the house ease you this evening?"

Ebon found that his tongue suddenly refused to work. As he tried to force the words out, he fumbled at his purse before finally producing a gold weight. "I have coin."

The matron's smile widened in amusement, but she was quick to take the coin from his trembling fingers. "Thank you. Is there any sort of girl you would prefer?"

He knew his face was the color of a beet. He looked down at his fine shoes and then around the room. He could scarcely see any of the figures in the dimness, a fact not helped by the fact that spots of light now danced before his eyes. He thought he might faint. From the corner of his eye he saw the harpist grinning, though she tried to hide it.

The matron seemed to misunderstand. "My apologies if I have made an assumption. Of course we have many fine men as well. I only meant to ask if you preferred a certain type of companion."

Ebon nearly choked. He shook his head quickly, but words would not come.

Her head tilted back slightly, and her eyes softened. "Ah. I may understand. Is this your first time, young sir?" At his shaky nod, she went on. "Your first time at a house of lovers, or . . .?"

"I have not—that is, I have never—"

She stilled him with a hand on his arm. "Forgive me for not realizing it at once. Worry not. We have some experience with such things, after all. But it is important that you know there are rules—very strict rules indeed, and behind them lies the weight of the High King's harshest law."

"I have heard something of them," mumbled Ebon.

She patted his hand. "Somehow I do not worry that you will break them. But I will tell you the most important one regardless: always you must obey the words of your lover. Only if you gainsay them, or act against their command, will you have anything to fear. Now, then. Would you prefer a recommendation? Sometimes that makes it easier."

Ebon hesitated, for in truth he had no idea how to answer her. His gaze wandered again and fell upon the harpist. She now looked demurely at the floor. But the matron seemed to catch his mind.

"Adara," she called out.

The girl's fingers ceased on the harp at once, and she rose from her chair. One of the men in the shadows took her place, and soon the chords rang out once more—though Ebon thought they were not quite as sweet, and he wondered if that was only his imagination.

As Adara approached him, it seemed that her beauty was magnified many times over. The sway of her walk stirred him in ways he was not overly familiar with, and she did not break his gaze, so that he found he could not look away. She said nothing when she reached him, but only took his hand and drew him towards the back of the room, where a blue silk curtain hung across a small doorway.

Beyond was a hallway that stretched in both directions. She took him left, and then around a bend that turned right, finally coming to a halt before a wide door. Ebon was thankful it was wooden, and looked thick—he had feared it might be open, or covered only by a sheer curtain. Adara lifted the latch and drew him inside, and then closed it behind them both with a soft *click*.

The room was well-lit, far better than the entry had been. Fine crafts sat upon shelves and chests of drawers, pots and urns worked in fine clay with handles wrapped in gold. But of course, Ebon's eyes were drawn to the bed that dominated the space. Its coverings looked even finer than those in his own room back home, though his came from all the considerable coin of his family. And this bed's legs looked far, far sturdier.

"You may sit," said Adara, waving a hand towards the bed. Ebon blinked for a moment before hastening to do as she said. He perched upon the edge of the bed and tried to find something sensible to do with his hands.

She smiled and shook her head. It made her braid sway back and forth, and he found himself captivated by her hair again. "That was no command. You will know a command if you hear it, though I do not suspect I shall have that need."

"Ah. Yes, I . . . thank you," said Ebon, immediately thinking that that was a stupid thing to say.

"Would you like some wine? It can bolster the nerves."

"Sky above, yes," said Ebon, never wanting anything so badly.

A fine golden pitcher sat next to goblets of silver, and Adara filled them both—though Ebon noted she filled one almost to the brim, and that was the one she placed in his hand. He drank greedily, recognizing the taste of cinnamon. He did not often care for cinnamon wine, but just now it seemed the finest thing he had ever drank.

Soon his cup was empty, and Adara took it gently to put on one of the tables beside the bed. Then she sat next to him, making the bed shift gently. He fought a sudden urge to edge away from her, wondering where it came from—especially since the greater part of him wanted nothing more than to move closer.

He realized she had not taken her eyes from his face, and he forced himself to meet her gaze again. She was not smiling, but neither did she look displeased. She looked only curious, as though she longed to know what he was thinking. Sure enough, she spoke at last. "Why have you come here tonight?"

Ebon gave a quick chuckle. "I should think that would be obvious. Why do most step within the blue door?"

"You know I mean more than that."

He looked at her askance, as his mind went to his words with Tamen. Yet she could not possibly know of that, or where he came from, or what drove him here.

To distract himself as well as her, he changed the subject. "Would you not like to know my name first, at least?"

"If you wish me to know it."

"It would not displease me."

"Then?"

"I am Ebon."

"Ebon. And have you a family, Ebon? Or are you a bastard?"

His nostrils flared for a moment. "I am a trueborn son."

Adara arched an eyebrow. "You speak as if it were some great shame to be a bastard. I take it you are from Idris, then?"

"And are you from elsewhere? You have the look of the women from my kingdom."

"My parents left there when I was very young. I was raised in Dorsea, where it is nothing special to be a trueborn child. Indeed, I think only Idris clings to the ancient tradition which shames bastards."

Ebon blew out a slow breath through his nose. "I am sorry. I did not mean to seem so . . . prickly."

That made her smile, and his heart warmed to see it. "Worry not. But also answer my question. You seem to think I shall forget it, but I will not. What drove you to open the blue door tonight, Ebon?"

You came here to forget you were a Drayden, at least for a while. He bit back the words on his tongue, though he wanted to tell her the truth. Yet what if she told others? It would not do for word to reach his father that he had visited a house of lovers. His wrath would be terrible.

Darkness take my father.

"I am here because I do not wish to be anywhere else. Wherever I go, I am my father's son, and none will let me forget it—him least of all. He has brought me here to the Seat, where I have long wished to go, and yet what can I do here? I remain in my room all day, only slipping out into the city when my mother tells me to do so and tells my retainer not to breathe a word of it to Father. Yet I cannot visit the Academy as I wish, for then he would hear of it, and I cannot even go to a tavern without its patrons refusing to sit with me, or speak with me, or even be within arm's reach. It is as though I walk draped in the curse of being a Drayden—"

He stopped short, looking at her in fear. But Adara shook her head gently and took his hand.

"I had guessed it already. Anyone in the front room would have known it at a glance. You need not trouble yourself. There are laws that you must follow while you are here, but we have our own code that we shall not break. No one will speak of your presence."

A great breath rushed from him, and in his relief it took him a long moment to realize that she still held his hand. Now she turned it over, its palm facing up, and she traced one nail across the lines of it. It sent a prickling feeling up his arm and into his chest, where it stayed and mingled with the comfortable warmth of the wine.

"You said you wish to visit the Academy," she said softly. "Why?"

"I have wished to go to the Academy since I was a child, and they discovered I have the gift."

Her eyes turned sharply towards his, and he saw a spark of excitement within them. "Are you a wizard?"

"An alchemist," he mumbled, blushing now for an entirely new reason. She looked at him as though he were some great champion of war. "But only by virtue of my gift. I have no training. I can do nothing."

She pouted. "You cannot show me even some simple spell? I should greatly love to see it."

He looked around. "Have you any water? I know only one spell— the one with which they test children, to see if they have the gift in the first place."

"I have no water. Only wine."

"I can do nothing with wine. I am sorry."

She smiled. "Then the next time you come, I will be certain to have water ready for you."

He looked down at his lap. "I shall not come here again. My family returns to Idris soon, and they will take me with them. But I would come if I could."

Her hand met his cheek, and she lifted his head until he looked into her eyes once again. Time seemed to slow for a moment, and he could hear his heartbeat thundering in his chest.

"Nothing is certain. If you have come here to forget your life outside these walls, then let us have a dream together: you, that you can
stay upon the Seat; and I, that you will visit me again."

He forced himself to laugh. "Those are pretty words indeed. I thank
you for them, though I know you must be bound to say what I wish
to hear."

She caught his meaning, and her eyes took on a wry twist. "You
think I mean to flatter you? I do not. Some lovers would do anything
to please their partners. I am not one such. If I tell you something, for
good or for ill, I mean it. That is one promise I will make now, and
keep always."

A voice at the back of his mind told him that even those words
were a lie, and yet Ebon believed her. And now she was so close that
her breath washed sweetly across his face, and he drank it in, even as his
hands rose of their own accord, and she pulled him closer to kiss him.

A short time later, they lay together beneath the satin sheets as
Ebon fought to reclaim his breath. Adara was curled up beneath his
arm, her head laying on his shoulder, her braid now undone to let her
hair spill across his meager chest.

"You must tell me," he said between heaving breaths. "Was I any
good?"

"Not at all," she said, stretching up to kiss him. "But that is all
right, for we have our dream. And in it, you will keep coming to see
me—and mayhap, one day, practice will see you perfect."

THREE

He woke with a terrible headache and the urge to vomit. Soon it grew too strong to ignore, and he fell from his bed to crawl for the chamber pot. Twice he retched, his face growing red. Then at last it poured out, thick and purple, full of the wine from the night before.

When it was over he rested for a moment, leaning his forehead on the chamber pot's chilly rim. At last he raised his head and looked around. The sight of his own room in the Drayden manor somewhat surprised him.

He remembered Adara—remembered her in vivid, lurid detail that even now made his stomach turn in knots—and he vaguely recalled leaving the house of lovers. He remembered returning to the tavern and ordering another flagon of wine. And there the memory faded.

The door opened without a knock, and Tamen came in with a warm, wet towel. He began to scrub flecks of vomit from Ebon's lips.

"I am fine, Tamen," said Ebon. But he put the lie to his words by clutching his forehead, where an iron spike seemed to be trying to burst from his skull.

"Of course you are," said Tamen, raising an eyebrow. He helped Ebon up and back to his bed, covering him with a sheet for decency. "I shall fetch some tea and empty your chamber pot before the whole manor smells of your insides."

He closed the door just a little too hard. Ebon winced at the sharp sound. Then he could do nothing but wait, until the door reopened at last and Tamen came to sit by his bedside.

"Here." With small brass tongs he held out a lump of sugar, which Ebon put on his tongue. Then from a saucer he served the green tea, not too hot, and Ebon groaned as its warmth filled him.

"Thank you," Ebon croaked, relaxing back into his pillows.

"You are only halfway to a cure. Now you must eat."

"Food is the last thing my stomach desires just now."

"And the first thing it needs."

"Leave me be, just a moment, I beg you." Ebon threw his head under the pillow to shield it from the sunlight coming through the window.

"I will not leave while you might still retch again. But I suppose I can guess from your current state that you enjoyed your evening?"

Beneath his pillow, Ebon could not keep a small smile from playing across his lips. "You cannot tell me I said nothing of it when I returned to the tavern."

He peeked out from his covers. A smirk tugged at Tamen's lips, and the man's eyes held a knowing glint. "You could barely speak. I have seen you drunk often enough, but not like that. It was all I could do to get you home."

Ebon's heart froze. "Tell me that my parents were not awake to witness it."

"Do you think I would have let them? Then their wrath would have fallen on me, not you. But they stayed at the palace late last night, and have returned there already this morning. You slept through their entire presence here."

That made him shoot up from beneath the pillow. He regretted the sudden motion at once. His hand went to his forehead with a sharp groan. "How long did you say they have been waiting? They must have risen early."

"Hardly. It is nearly time for midday's meal. You have slept long."

Ebon slumped back upon his pillows with a groan. He still did not know why his parents had brought him here. He hardly saw them, even to eat together. Why bring him just so that he could stay in the manor all day? If they had left him in Idris, at least he would have been free from Father for a time, with Albi for company.

He knew better than to voice these complaints to Tamen, of course. But at the thought of his sister, he lifted a weak hand. "Fetch me a quill and parchment. I should write to Albi."

But the retainer only folded his arms. "For what purpose? You will return soon, and then she will be alone no longer."

"We are to leave the Seat?"

Tamen rolled his eyes, as though it were Ebon's fault that his parents never informed him of such things. "As soon as they have concluded their business at the palace, which, sky willing, should be today."

Ebon's hand closed in a fist, scrunching his bed sheets. He forced himself to relax. "Then this trip was truly a waste. More than a week holed up in the manor, and for no purpose. My father—"

He bit the words off at once. *My father's cruel joke is complete,* he had almost said. But that would pass from Tamen's ears straight to his parents.

The retainer tilted his head as if curious, though he must have known that Ebon's next words would not have been courteous. "Do not regret your journey here too strongly. Just think: if you had been left home, a certain . . . opportunity would never have presented itself."

Ebon flushed. When he returned home and told Albi of the High King's Seat, last night would be one part of the story he would certainly leave out. But then a thought struck him. Had Tamen's leniency been at the command of Ebon's parents?

He dismissed the notion at once. They could have had no purpose for doing so. His father would never be so generous. Ebon's mother would sometimes grant him little boons, when she thought his father might not see it, but a visit to a house of lovers seemed a step quite too far.

Out loud, he said only, "I wish I were not going to be dragged off home again."

This time Tamen could not stop a wide grin, though he quickly hid it. "Still thinking of the blue door? Goodness. You must have had quite the time."

Ebon felt a mighty need to steer the conversation in another direction. "I should get dressed. Fetch me some clothes."

"Very well." Tamen rose, and from a cabinet by the window he produced a suit of fine yellow silk, tailored like all of Ebon's clothes to hug his thin frame. "But do not fret overmuch. One day, when you are head of the household, you can return to the Seat. The blue door will still be there."

"As will the Academy," said Ebon. "Mayhap I shall even enroll in studies."

Tamen snorted. "Forgive me if I am blunt, but that is a ridiculous thought. Children are expected to begin in their tenth year. If fate is kind to your father, you will not be head of the household until you have nearly reached your fortieth."

Ebon glared as the retainer laid his outfit at the foot of the bed. "I shall have no one to gainsay me. I could do whatever I wished."

Tamen turned sharply, throwing down the trousers in his hand. They fell in a rumpled heap atop the rest of the clothes. "No, Ebon, you could not. Even you are not so foolish. You will have responsibilities then, to your sister and to the rest of the family. Would you abandon that responsibility? I know you have no great love for our kin, but you should think at least of Albi."

"She could take charge in my stead. Indeed, I would welcome the shedding of that burden."

"Albi is not being groomed for the position."

Ebon spread his hands in a helpless gesture. "What grooming has my father given me, Tamen? I am forbidden from our trade meetings. I am forbidden from speaking to any members of the other merchant families. I have never even seen a member of the royal family. How does he expect me to step full-formed into his shoes, when I do not have the faintest knowledge of the leagues they have walked already?"

"And Albi? Could she manage better than you? I imagine she could do a fine job of directing a caravan, if pressed to it, and if she were surrounded by a staff of those who knew most of her business for her.

But she has received no instruction in such matters. You at least know something of the family's trade routes, our goods and services, and the relationships your aunt has worked hard to build across the nine kingdoms."

Ebon turned away. He wanted to shout, but Tamen was only an instrument, not the object of his wrath. The retainer's words were not his own, but came from Ebon's parents. Ebon wondered if Tamen believed them himself, or if he even cared.

In any case, the man's words were carefully chosen, for they reminded Ebon of his aunt Halab. Where Ebon's father was cruel at every opportunity, Halab had always treated Ebon with courtesy and respect, and mayhap even affection. In her presence, even Ebon's father seemed less harsh, less cruel, as though he did not wish to shame himself with ill conduct before his sister.

Yet still Ebon shied away at the thought of one day replacing his father. "Never do I wish to be involved in our family's trade," he muttered.

"Sky above," said Tamen, eyes widening in false shock. "Does the world exist to grant our wishes? If I had known that, I would have asked to be born a royal son."

There was a knock at the door. Ebon cocked his head at Tamen, but the man only shrugged. "Come," said Ebon.

It opened to reveal Mako. Ebon tensed, and Tamen grew very still.

Tall and very broad, but wiry, Mako was clad in a tunic of light grey, with sleeves to the elbows that revealed the designs tattooed on his forearms. Over that he wore a short jerkin of black leather. His trousers, too, were black, clasped at the waist by a belt with a silver buckle, and upon that belt hung a long and wicked dagger. His hair was cut so short it was almost stubble, and his hairline on both sides swooped up and away from his brows. Though his eyes often twinkled as though at some hidden joke, they were hard as steel, and couched in a face painted by many scars. Mako was in the service of the family, and though Ebon was not certain, he thought the man reported directly to Halab herself. He seemed to go from household to household, bringing messages and doing whatever might be required of him. But the simplicity of his duties did not hide the danger he wore about him like a cloak.

19

Now he strode into Ebon's room with a smile, and the smile widened as he hooked both thumbs through his belt. Though Ebon was still covered by a sheet, he felt utterly naked before Mako's keen gaze, and he had to fight the urge to cover himself. Then Mako took a deep sniff.

"A good morrow—or midday, as it were. And how fares the family Drayden's newest full-grown man?"

Ebon's eyes widened, panic seizing his throat. He shot a fearful look at Tamen, but the retainer shook his head.

"I said nothing."

Mako burst into laughter, a deep, ringing peal that surely thundered through all the halls of the manor. He bent partway over to lock gazes as though Ebon were a child, and then he slapped a hand against the leather pants that tightly gripped his legs. The sound of it made Ebon flinch.

"Sky above, the looks upon both of your faces are priceless. Fear not, little Ebon. I did not need any words from Tamen to smell the scent of your lovemaking. It is so strong that I imagine I could find the woman herself if I visited enough lovers upon the Seat."

"I . . . you are wrong," said Ebon, aware of just how weak his voice sounded.

Mako's chuckles died away, but they left behind his wide, toothy grin. "Save your terrified looks, little goldbag. If you fear I will tell your father of your—shall we call it an indiscretion?—then worry not. I have no interest in petty scandals."

"I say again, you are—"

Mako chopped a hand through the air, and Ebon's words died upon his lips. "I told you I will say nothing. And I did not come to sniff between your legs. Your mother and father require you for midday's meal."

"They sent you to summon me for a meal?"

Mako shrugged, his smile never leaving him. "And why not? I was to hand. I do not hold so high an opinion of myself that I cannot deliver a message."

So saying, he turned and left as quickly as he had come. Tamen went to the door and closed it, throwing the latch in place.

"Come, Ebon. You must ready yourself for the meal. And whatever else you can say about that man, he is right—we must wash that smell off you before you get within ten paces of your parents."

FOUR

Tamen had a steward fill a bath, though they had no time to heat it. Ebon shivered in the water, cold and brackish, drawn from the Great Bay. He spit it out quickly whenever it touched his tongue, despising the salty taste of it.

"Hurry, Ebon," said Tamen. "You know better than to keep your father waiting."

"I can scarcely move faster than I am." Ebon's voice came harsher than he intended, and thick with fear.

"Then this will have to do."

He leaped from the tub and began to dry himself. Tamen fetched some perfume and splashed it at his neck, his underarms, and his wrists.

"That is too much!" said Ebon. "I smell like a chemist!"

"Sky above, stop your bleating," said Tamen. He made a halfhearted attempt to swipe some of it off with a washcloth.

"Forget it. I must go anyway. My clothes!"

Tamen helped him dress in haste, shaking his head at Ebon's anxiety. But Tamen did not have to fear whatever capricious punishment Father would inflict if Ebon was late.

Soon he was running through the manor towards the dining hall. Fine tapestries fluttered on the walls in the wind of his passing, and he nearly bowled over the servants Liya and Ruba, who were dusting fine suits of armor mounted on stands. They cried out after him, but Ebon barely managed to call out "I am sorry!" as he fled.

He burst into the dining hall much faster than he had meant to, and the door flew around to slam into the stone wall behind it. Ebon froze on the threshold. His parents, Hesta and Shay, looked up sharply from the table, where they had already begun to eat.

"Did you have to run across all the nine lands to get here?" Though Ebon's father did not raise his voice, disdain dripped from each word, like rainwater sliding down the tiled roofs of home.

"I am sorry, Father," said Ebon, breathing hard. "I was in the garden when—"

But his father had already turned away to resume conversing with his mother. Ebon lowered his head, cheeks burning, and approached the table. A servant pulled out a chair. As he sat and scooted closer to the table, Ebon tried to edge away from where his father sat. But both his parents turned to him, eyes wide, and his father's lips curled with scorn.

"You smell like every courtesan on the Seat took a shit on you at once. Sit at the other end of the table before your stench makes me retch."

"Shay," said Hesta gently. Ebon's father shut his mouth with a sharp *click* of teeth and turned away.

Ebon rose hastily to follow the command. He did not sit opposite his father—that would no doubt be seen as a great slight, trying to claim the other end of the table. Instead he took the chair just to the left. A servant ran to put a plate of food before him, with seared pork and some strange vegetables he did not recognize. Ebon ignored the vegetables and tore into the meat, his stomach growling loudly. Almost from the moment the greasy meat touched his lips, he could feel his headache subsiding, and he sighed gratefully.

He glanced up towards the other end of the table, where his father was now complaining about some perceived slight he had suffered at the High King's palace. But Hesta very nearly ignored him, and instead looked at Ebon curiously. As her eyes played across his face, her brows raised slightly. Ebon ducked his gaze to focus on the meal.

Did she know? Could she see it somehow, or sense it in him? He dismissed the thought as ridiculous. Yet from the corner of his eye he could still see her studying him, only turning away to give his father cursory nods and sympathetic sounds at the most appropriate times. But then Shay's complaints grew in volume and energy, and Hesta finally turned to give him her full attention. Ebon vented a long sigh of relief.

His anxiety at his mother's lingering look turned his thoughts back to Adara. When he thought of the night before, he flushed. He could still see the light hazel of her eyes, feel her nails scraping his skin. He could almost sense the way she had—

Ebon had to shift in his seat. He found his attention dragged back to the conversation with his father as Shay raised his voice.

"The audacity she has, to keep us waiting for four days now, without *deigning* to grant us so much as a firm appointment."

"She is the High King, and we must serve at her pleasure," said Hesta, but her tone spoke only of full agreement with her husband.

"She is an arrogant sow."

Ebon's gaze jerked up at that, and even the servants standing at the edges of the room tensed. Shay ignored them all, while Hesta patted his hand reassuringly. He tore into his meal again, as though he had run out of fuel for the bitter fire that burned in his gut. The peace lasted only a moment, and then he slammed his cup on the table. "Wine!"

A servant scurried to obey. Ebon shook his head—slightly, so that his father could not see—and let his mind wander. His gaze fell upon the room's eastern wall, which was comprised entirely of glass doors that were now open. Through them he looked out across the Great Bay and its far reaches that vanished beyond the horizon. He had sailed those waters to get here, and would sail them again to return. It would be any day now, he imagined, unless his father extended the trip until they could meet with the High King.

Ebon would return to Idris, never having set foot inside the Academy. One day even the Seat would fade to a distant memory, until he could scarcely remember the manor where he now sat. Once again he found himself wondering why they had brought him in the first place.

Was the suspicion of his innermost heart right? Was this all some cruel new torture by his father? To dangle the Seat before Ebon, only to rip him away just as he began to love it? Then, for years to come, he could torment Ebon with the memory. *Do as you are told, boy, if you ever wish to return to the Seat,* he might say. *Speaking to a royal, were you? I had thought to take you to the Seat with me the next time I went, but you seem determined to prove yourself unworthy of that honor.* No doubt his father could come up with a thousand ways to phrase the same threat.

And though Ebon knew it was foolish, the most painful thought of all was that he might never again see the blue door. Or that if he did, in some far future year, he would not find a pair of hazel eyes behind it, waiting for him.

His mind was drawn back to the present as the hall's door clicked and swung open. Ebon looked curiously over his shoulder—and then he shoved back his chair, leaping to his feet with a cry of surprise. His aunt Halab strode through the doors, long golden dress sweeping behind her across the floor. Her hair, intricately braided and wrapped about her head like a crown, bobbed with each step, and she took them all in with sharp, dark eyes. Ebon's parents rose quickly in respect.

"Sister," grumbled Shay, stepping away from the table.

Halab went to him, and he kissed her cheeks before bending for her to kiss his forehead. Hesta came forwards more eagerly and wrapped Halab in a warm embrace.

"Sister," said Halab. Then she released Hesta and came straight to Ebon. He straightened with a smile as Halab stopped less than a pace away. "And look at you, darling nephew. You are a man now, and no mistake."

For a moment he quailed, for in his mind the words held another meaning. But he shook the thought away quickly—Halab had not seen him in more than half a year, and he had grown taller since then. He stepped forwards to kiss her cheeks, but she pulled him into a hug instead.

"None of that formality. My heart sings to see you."

25

"And you, Aunt." Then, just for courtesy's sake, he kissed her cheeks all the same.

"You are never lacking in charm. May I join you all for your meal?"

"Of course," said Shay brusquely. Quickly he went to scoop up his plate and move it to the next seat, and Halab sat at the head of the table. Ebon returned to his seat at the other end, but Halab stopped him with a sharp word.

"Nephew. What are you doing all the long way down there? Surely you were not banished for anything so trivial as the perfume you doused yourself in?"

Ebon froze, unsure of how to answer. He knew better than to speak ill of his father, especially with the man right there to hear it. But Shay spoke first, saving him from the dilemma. "He stinks worse than the palace."

"Yet family is family," said Halab. "Come, sit beside your mother, so that you may be as far from your father's delicate nose as may be."

Still uncertain, Ebon went to do as she asked, keeping a careful eye on his father. But Shay said nothing to gainsay his sister, though Ebon noticed his knuckles whitened where they gripped his silverware.

Meanwhile, a servant ran to fetch a new plate of food for Halab. The man's hands shook when he set the plate before her, and Ebon scoffed. The servants were too used to serving his father, and seemed not to know of his aunt's more genial nature.

Halab spoke around a tiny morsel of food. "How did you fare at the palace this morning?"

"The same as always," growled Shay. "She keeps us waiting in her halls, and will not even give us a time to return when we might actually speak with her. They claim it is because of the brewing trouble between Selvan and Dorsea, but I think that is an excuse. She thinks herself too high and mighty for us."

"She is the High King," said Halab, shrugging. One of her thin braids came loose and swung down towards her ear, and she lifted it carefully back into place. "We serve at her pleasure."

Shay snorted loudly. But Ebon noticed that he did not again slur the High King as he had done before.

"In any case, I had already heard something of your troubles," Halab went on. "I spoke with a friend at the palace—a very highly placed friend indeed. He has secured an audience on your behalf. Visit the palace at midday tomorrow, and you will find the doors of the throne room are open to you."

"Do you see, my love?" said Hesta. She smiled gratefully at Halab. "I told you that this would work out."

Shay kept his eyes firmly fixed on his plate. "Thank you for your help, Sister. That is most kind of you."

"Think nothing of it. I am confident the High King will speak on our behalf and secure our new trade route through Dorsea. Their border squabble is nothing of import, and certainly not to us."

His father's hands clenched harder. "Certainly."

Ebon smiled inwardly, but was careful to keep his expression impassive. He did not like to think what his father would do if he was seen snickering. But then Halab turned to Ebon, and he straightened somewhat in his chair.

"And what of you, Nephew? How have you enjoyed your time upon the Seat? I hope you have been able to experience all of the island's . . . oh, what word am I searching for . . . pleasures?"

Ebon blanched, but again he kept his mask of tranquility. "I have— that is, I have spent most of my time here, at the manor. But I have walked the streets once or twice, and found them to my liking. It is a grand city, to be sure." He knew he must not even hint that Shay had largely kept him confined to the manor.

Halab's brows drew close. "You have not wandered much? I thought you would eagerly poke your nose into every corner of the city. Surely you have visited the Academy?"

Ebon tried not to gulp, though his throat had gone dry. "No, I have not. It holds little interest for me." Those words nearly stuck in his throat, yet somehow he managed to make them sound earnest.

Halab glanced at Shay, but his eyes were fixed on his food. "That is unacceptable," she said lightly. "You must venture out upon the Seat. You are a Drayden, after all, and should know as much as you can of this place of power. I suppose I could show you one or two of my own favorite haunts . . ." She seemed to think for a moment, and then snapped her fingers at an idea. "I know. I will take you on a tour of the Academy myself."

The world stopped for a moment. Ebon could not move. His head, already aching, became light, and he thought he heard a high, thin whine at the edge of his awareness.

"Yes, that will do nicely," said Halab, and now it was as though she was talking to herself. "The dean is Cyrus, my cousin—and your cousin, too, Ebon, though more distant. Surely he would be only too happy to show his school to us. You may think it holds little interest for you, but I know you will love it. There you can find wizards of all four branches practicing their spells. Oh, flame and wind and weremagic and—yes, and alchemy. It is a sight to behold."

Ebon could not speak; he could barely breathe. He looked fearfully at Shay. Surely his father would not allow this. But his father still stared down at his hands. When the silence in the room stretched a moment too long, his gaze snapped up to Ebon, and he growled through his dark beard.

"Your aunt has asked you a question. Answer her."

Still Ebon could not force any words to come. In his heart he wanted nothing more than to go. But then he thought ahead. In a matter of days he would be leaving the High King's Seat, likely forever. Already he knew he would miss it, and would waste away days in Idris thinking of its clean streets and the high, pristine spires of its buildings. That pain would only magnify if he saw the Academy itself, for that was where his heart truly lay.

But then he thought further still. In Idris, his sister Albi would be waiting for him—Albi, in whom he had confided all his deepest wishes about his magic. He had spoken of it for so long, and in such warm terms, that she herself had come to dream of seeing it. If he went, he could return and tell her all about it. If he did not, Albi would not only be disappointed for herself. She would berate Ebon for years, telling him how he should have gone with Halab.

His hands steadied on the tabletop. "Thank you, dearest Aunt. It would be my pleasure to accompany you."

"Then it is settled," said Halab.

The dining hall fell silent. Ebon's father stabbed his knife savagely into his meat, and his mother dabbed gingerly at her lips with a napkin.

FIVE

Ebon had assumed they would take a carriage, but Halab surprised him by proposing a walk instead. "It is not so great a distance, and I would find it most invigorating," she told him.

As though he did not already know how far away it was. Ebon had memorized the streets between the manor and the Academy, though Tamen had never let him draw too close to the place.

Speaking of Tamen, Halab ordered him to stay at the manor, to give her some special time with her nephew. But she did bring Mako, and the man followed close behind them, almost within arm's reach, so that Ebon felt his presence no matter how hard he tried to forget it.

Just past midday, the streets were busy with all manner of folk going to and fro. There were no open markets in this part of the city, and so no vendors screamed their wares at passersby, but there were shopkeepers, and deliveries of food and drink passing by on wagons. Among the crowds, Ebon often caught flashes of red—either the red leather armor of constables, or the red cloaks of Mystics. These last he noted with some keen interest, for the order's strength had lessened in his homeland of Idris, and they did not often present themselves to his family. At least, not in any meetings that Ebon was privy to.

Halab soon noticed his wandering eye. "You find the Mystics intriguing, do you?"

"I suppose. It is only that they are very rare back home."

"That is just as well. They are a meddlesome lot. And they have no love for wizards, except those who wear the red cloak as well. That means they would have a particular dislike for you."

Ebon glanced at her with concern, but she laughed and gripped his shoulder before taking his arm.

"Sometimes I worry that you are too serious, though I think I may know the cause of that. It has not escaped me that your father puts great strain on you. You must forgive him for that."

He did not have the faintest idea how to answer. Even with Tamen gone, he had no wish to speak ill of his father, for Mako walked close behind them both.

She patted his arm gently. "I know it must be difficult to speak of. You need say nothing. And I take back my words—you need not forgive him. He has not forgiven you for some things in which you were blameless."

Ebon ducked his head, for suddenly his eyes stung. He spoke very carefully. "Momen's loss was a great pain to us all."

"It was," she said, patting his arm once more. "Come. It is far too pretty a day for such thoughts. And we are nearly there."

He looked up. There they were: the spires of the Academy's four wings, and in the center of them all, the great tower. High and mighty the place stood, nearly as tall as the High King's palace. But where the palace was laid all in stone of white and grey, with windows and bracings of gold, the Academy was of a stone so dark it was almost black, and its trimmings were in silver. Silver too were the banners that streamed from its many flagpoles, and all of them bore the simple white cross that stood for the four branches of magic, inside a white circle that was itself nested in an orb of black. Ebon had heard of the banner, but had never seen it until the day he had arrived on the Seat. Since then, it had remained ever in his thoughts.

Its size made it appear much nearer than it was, and still they had some distance to go. As they drew closer, Halab explained something of the place's construction. Many of the details Ebon already knew, knowledge gleaned from whispered conversations with servants who should have known better. Still he drank them all in, for he felt he would never tire of hearing tales of the Academy.

"Four wings it has, for the four branches, of course. But that is only a symbol, and the students are not kept to each wing according to their gifts. Rather, they are arranged by their age—or, I should say, their year of study. Now, do you see how high the walls are? They were built a good distance from the central building, the citadel, and there they have the training areas where more advanced students learn their arts. Though the walls are tall, they are never guarded. They are not meant to protect the Academy from attack, but to safeguard the city from the students. It would not do to have a young firemage blow himself up and take half a dozen nearby buildings with him."

Ebon laughed aloud at that, but Halab did not join him. He looked over to her, and saw that one of her eyebrows was arched.

"I am afraid that is no jest, nephew."

He blanched and looked away.

At last they drew near to the wide front door, set straight into the wall itself. The door was made of iron, dark and unpolished, as though crafted by a smith of little skill. But as he drew closer, Ebon saw that in fact the door was carved with innumerable small characters in some tongue that he did not know. Ten of them were as wide as his smallest finger, and they covered the door from top to bottom and from one side to the other, except on the trim, which was made of burnished brass. He tried studying the symbols for a moment, but they made his eyes hurt, and he had to look away.

Halab glanced back, and Mako stepped forwards to swing the huge iron knocker twice. It was wrought in the shape of a wolf that gripped a brass ring in fierce jaws.

For a short while, no one came to answer. Ebon shifted back and forth on his feet, though Halab seemed unperturbed. He was just about to suggest they knock again, when finally he heard a hideous iron screeching on the other side of the door. But it did not open; instead, a tiny metal hatch slid open at chest height. Ebon had not noticed the hatch before. Through the hole appeared a tiny, wizened old woman, who must have been standing on tiptoes and yet could barely see through the opening. Both of her eyes were wide and crazed, and one was completely white.

"What do you want?" the woman screeched.

Ebon's mouth fell open. Halab blinked and answered lightly. "Well met. I am here to visit my cousin, Dean Cyrus Drayden. He will be happy to receive me."

The woman studied them for a moment of uncomfortable silence. Then she vanished, and a moment later the hatch slid shut with another rending shriek of iron.

They stepped back, expecting the door to swing open. But nothing happened. Ebon looked uncertainly to Halab, and then to Mako. The bodyguard seemed faintly amused, and he kept his eyes fixed on the door. But Halab looked up and down the street in both directions, blowing a long sigh out her nose.

Just as Ebon thought she might knock again, they heard the heavy *snap* of a latch being thrown on the other side. With a bone-deep groan, the door swung in. On the other side was a short, portly man, thin dark hair clinging determinedly to a balding pate. He wore black robes of unremarkable fabric, but they were trimmed with golden brocade of fine make that caught both the sun and the eye as he moved his arms, which was often.

"Cousin Cyrus," said Halab, smiling graciously. "What a pleasure to see you."

"Halab, Halab," said Cyrus, stepping out to greet her. He took her hands in his and ushered her inside. "Come in, please. I offer my deepest apologies for the delay."

"Think nothing of it," said Halab. Then she turned to Mako. "Wait here for us."

Mako nodded and stepped to the side, facing out towards the street with his hands clasped before him. Ebon hurried after Halab as Cyrus drew her inside, and an attendant swung the door shut behind them with a *clang*.

Ebon froze, dumbfounded by the sight before him. The Academy's entrance hall stood at least ten paces high, its floor all black marble, thin white veins glinting with light from the many chandeliers hanging high above. A staircase with bronze railings swept up before them, seeming to promise the sky itself at the top, though Ebon could see it ended at a landing that went both left and right to vanish into hallways on the second floor. Other passages led off on either side of the stairway, while two doors stood closed at both ends of the great chamber. All the doors were wooden, but polished until they shone like metal, and everywhere were tapestries of glorious make. Ebon thought he recognized Calentin craftsmanship in their weave.

Students and instructors bustled about in all directions, like ants swarming through a hive, and none of them spared even a glance for Ebon and the others standing in the entryway. The illumination from the chandeliers was joined and strengthened by the sunlight from great windows set high in each wall, and they were made of colored glass that depicted many tall figures Ebon did not recognize. But they were beautiful, and clearly ancient, and he felt that the figures stared down on him in judgement as he stood beneath them.

"How do they light them?" he breathed, not meaning to speak aloud.

Cyrus snapped a glance at him and frowned. "Eh? What is that?"

"The chandeliers," said Ebon. "They are so high."

"Ah," said Cyrus. "The candles are placed and replaced by mentalists, and lit by elementalists, of course."

Of course. Ebon knew he might have thought of that on his own, were his father not so adamant about refusing to allow Ebon any knowledge of magic and other wizards. He gawked up at the chandeliers, his mouth open, and tried to imagine the wizards lifting and lighting the candles with their spells.

With a start he realized that Cyrus and Halab had almost vanished from sight, making for the passage to the right of the staircase. He scurried after them, barely able to tear his eyes from the windows high above. Quickly Cyrus took them down the hallway, past many doors on either side, until it branched right and he turned. At last he reached his destination: a door of iron not unlike the one in the front, and Ebon saw that it was worked all over with the same small symbols. It swung open easily at his touch, and they followed him inside.

They were in an office now—the dean's, Ebon guessed, for it was wide and well-lit and had a second half-floor reached by a narrow stair-case to the right. All sorts of artifacts sat on shelves along the walls, and many were strange to Ebon: crystal globes and metal orbs and rods of strange materials, beside and sometimes on top of many books that stood in great stacks in every corner. On the second floor were more bookshelves, and windows that let light come pouring in from outside. But Ebon noted that the books and the artifacts all seemed unused, for they were covered in a fine layer of dust.

"My heart sings to see you, Cousin," said Cyrus, going to Halab and kissing her on both cheeks before she kissed him on his forehead. "Again I must apologize for your treatment at the front door. Despite my years here, I have never succeeded in ridding this place of Mellie, daft old bat that she is."

"I hope you do not trouble yourself about it," said Halab gracious-ly. "Allow me to present my nephew, and your second cousin once removed: Ebon, Shay's son."

Cyrus regarded Ebon with a cool tolerance. "Indeed. Welcome, Ebon. You travel in mighty company."

He held forth a hand, and on it Ebon saw a ring bearing the cross-and-circle sigil of the Academy. For a moment Ebon was not sure how he was supposed to respond. After a moment that was just too long, he realized his mistake, and quickly leaned forwards to kiss the ring. Cyrus gave him a thin smile and turned away immediately.

"What purpose brings you here today, honored cousin? Is there any service you require of me, or anyone here at the Academy? Only name it, and it is yours."

"In fact, I am here for Ebon," said Halab. "Long has he dreamed of seeing the Academy, and as his family is busy in the palace, I thought to show him. Who better to introduce us to its labyrinthine halls than the dean himself?"

It looked to Ebon as though Cyrus tried to hide some slight dis-pleasure. "Indeed. Certainly I would be happy to—ah!" He turned to Ebon again, and now his eyes lit with recognition. "You are the trans-muter. Your father would not let you attend for schooling."

Ebon felt his cheeks burning, and he lowered his gaze to the floor. "Yes."

"A pity. And now you are . . . how old? Fourteen? Fifteen?"

"I have seen sixteen summers," mumbled Ebon.

"Sixteen!" The dean shook his head and pursed his lips. "Such a waste. Such a waste. But then, it is only transmutation. And better a glimpse of opportunity lost than to never know it at all. It will be my pleasure to show you my school."

He took Ebon's hand in his own, smaller, clammy one, and patted it. Ebon felt an urge to withdraw, but he did not wish to appear rude. The dean was looking at him like he was some boy whose legs had been cut off in a farming accident.

Cyrus opened the study door again and motioned them out. He made his way through the hallways, his steps sure, though Ebon was already lost in the massive place. Soon they stood in the entrance hall again, and once more Ebon was left to marvel at its craftsmanship.

"The student dormitories are near the top of the central citadel," he said, pointing up to where the staircase turned into hallways far above. "No need to visit them, of course, unless you like beds dressed in plain grey wool." He tittered.

"No, indeed," said Halab.

"Most of the classes are taught on the bottom floor, and here also are the kitchens and the dining halls. Come, let me show you where the students learn their spells."

He took them to the hallway left of the staircase. Doors lined the walls to either side, but Cyrus passed them by. "Instructor's studies," he said, waving at them dismissively. Soon they reached a set of double doors on the left, and Cyrus threw them open with a flourish.

Inside were many students sitting at long tables, and at the front of the room, a podium. Behind it stood a thin wisp of a man, clutching the wooden stand as though for support. He had wide eyes like an owl's, which blinked as fast as a heartbeat. His blinking sped still more at the sight of the dean.

"Dean Cyrus!" the instructor wheedled, leaping away from his podium as though from a coiled snake. He came forwards, wringing his hands together, mouth working as though chewing a tough bit of gristle. "What an unexpected visit."

"This is Instructor Credell," said Cyrus, putting a hand on Credell's shoulder, from which the poor man shrank witheringly. "He is the beginner's transmutation instructor—the man you would learn from, Ebon, if you were attending the Academy."

"Well met," said Ebon, holding forth a hand.

Credell stared at the hand with suspicion, then jerked his gaze up and tried to smile, but failed. "Are you a transmuter then? Fascinating! Where have you studied?"

"I am unlearned," said Ebon, feeling a familiar blush creeping across his face.

Credell blink-blinked rapidly with his owl eyes. "Oh, I . . . oh." Behind him, Ebon could see several of the students—all of them children far younger than he was—leaning to try and get a look at him.

"Mayhap we could leave these students to their studies," said Halab, giving the room a smile. "After all, they have much to learn."

"Of course, of course," said Cyrus, clapping Credell on the back until Ebon thought the instructor might fall over. "Carry on."

He stepped out and swung the doors shut again, whisking them a bit farther down the hallway to another set of double doors. Inside was a class of mindmages listening attentively to their instructor. The man's eyes glowed as he made a small iron ball dance in the air. Ebon stared in wonder, but to his disappointment the instructor lowered the ball the moment he saw the dean.

Then Ebon noticed something else intriguing: though there were surely more than a score of students inside, they all wore the same simple black robes. At first he did not know why that caught his eye, until he realized that he could not tell which students came from wealthy families, and which from poor. In his own household, even if he did not know all the servants by name, he knew them by their dress, just as he knew a member of his own family the moment he saw their bearing. Here, all the students were equal. He marveled at it, though only for a moment before Cyrus began to speak again, and Ebon had to pay attention to the name of the instructor as they were introduced to each other.

After a hurried explanation of the class, Cyrus pushed on to another room with another lesson, though Ebon could see no magic at play, and Cyrus did not say which branch the students were studying. They passed another room, and then another, as though Cyrus was in a hurry now and only wanted the tour to be over as quickly as possible.

Evidently Halab noticed Cyrus' haste, as well as Ebon's dissatisfaction, for she stopped the dean after he closed yet another set of classroom doors. "Good cousin, mayhap we could see the training grounds? I think my nephew tires of seeing so many classrooms that look the same." Then, before Ebon could claim in politeness that he was fascinated by the tour, she smiled at him and said, "And I think I agree with him."

Cyrus grew flustered and produced a silk handkerchief, with which he dabbed at his forehead. "Ah, of course, good cousin. The training grounds indeed—though be careful! They are not without peril."

"I trust your ability to protect us, dear cousin."

"Ah, I . . . ah, yes, of course. This way."

He set off down the hallway now, faster than before, until Ebon nearly had to jog to keep up with him, although Halab's long strides kept the pace with ease. After three turns that left Ebon utterly bewildered, he stopped at another set of double doors, these made of white wood. Cyrus hesitated only a moment before throwing them open.

Ebon's eyes burned at the sudden daylight, and he had to raise a hand to shield his vision. Once he could see, he found himself in a stone courtyard that extended many paces from the Academy until it ended at a grassy lawn that might have been trimmed with a barber's shears, it was so precise. And there, for the first time, he saw wizards using the full strength of their magic.

They had come upon a class of firemages, who bent flame and lightning in their hands before flinging them at iron figures set in the ground many paces away. One sent an infernal ball flying through the air to engulf one of these targets in flame. A short distance away, a girl Ebon's age drew water from a bowl, twisting it into swirls in the air before sending it shooting into the ground. Ebon thought that was the end of it, until a moment later the water burst from the soil again, erupting with a stream of earth to slam into an iron dummy's stomach.

"This is where the elementalists practice," said Cyrus, as though they needed the explanation. Ebon found himself rooted to the spot and scarcely able to hear the dean's words. "Let us move on to the mentalists—my branch, as it happens."

Halab had to prod Ebon's elbow before he moved, and then he quickly followed Cyrus. He saw now that they walked between two of the great wings of the Academy, and were moving from one to the other. As they went, Ebon could not take his eyes from the elementalists casting their spells. Each seemed more wondrous than the last.

There was another white wooden door set in the wall before them. Cyrus opened it to a short passage that cut straight through the wing and out the other side. Ebon stepped into the passage with a final, regretful look at the wizards behind him. But when they came out the other side, he found himself dumbfounded again—for here were mentalists, and if their magic was not so wondrous at first sight, when he looked closer he was even more overawed. For they raised plates of metal and heavy chairs with only their magic, so that it looked like some spirit caused the objects to move. Then the mentalists would drag them back and forth through the air, or make them spin. As Cyrus hurried them along, Ebon saw some students engaged in what looked like simple duels. They would throw things at each other—soft, straw-filled balls of cloth, not the iron weights he had seen at first—and the other student would try to halt the attack with their own magic. Sometimes it worked, and sometimes not; Ebon saw one student struck in the midriff by an attack, and she doubled over. It seemed the missiles were somewhat weightier than they looked.

They passed through another wing into another training area, and there he saw weremages. Some changed only the color of their skin, or the shapes of their faces, but Ebon saw some who turned into animals and back, as quickly and as naturally as he could change his own clothing. But Cyrus was moving faster now, and they stepped through one final passage into the last training area.

This one was smaller than all the rest, and looking up, Ebon saw that they were tucked in between the Academy's northwestern wing, the citadel's main entrance, and the wall. But Cyrus turned to them with a smile and gestured at the students gathered there, giving Halab a little half-bow.

"Here, I think, you will find something to hold your nephew's attention. Here is where the transmuters practice their craft."

Ebon looked at them in wonder. Some students sat cross-legged upon the ground, their palms pressed into the earth. Beneath them the grass roiled and shifted, turning now to wood, now to stone, and then back to turf, so smoothly that he could barely tell it was changing before it finished. There were iron dummies in rows, just like before, only now the students took the dummies into their hands and turned the metal soft, malleable, twisting them into different shapes, or posing them so that they looked like warriors in combat. Still other students dueled, like he had seen the mindmages doing before. Only these students would throw the cloth balls at each other with their hands, and the other student met the missile with palms open. The balls would turn to water at a touch, splashing harmlessly across the student's skin, or mayhap vanish in a puff of smoke.

Then Ebon saw one instructor standing far off to the side, with a student standing several paces away. The instructor held a bow and arrow in her hand, and the student watched intently.

Slowly the instructor raised the bow and drew, until the fletching rested against her ear, and then released the shaft.

Ebon cried out in alarm—but the student raised a hand as if to catch the arrow. When it struck her palm, it vanished in a puff of smoke, just like the cloth balls the other students used for their practice.

Ebon glanced at Halab. Even her brows had raised at that. Cyrus' smile widened. "A powerful bit of transmutation, that. Not one in a hundred transmuters can achieve such skill."

"Powerful indeed," said Halab. She turned to Ebon with a small smile. "So, my nephew? Are you glad to have seen this place?"

Ebon swallowed hard, forcing a smile. "Of course, dear Aunt. It is a wonderful sight. Thank you for bringing me here."

But in truth, his heart quailed. His steps came heavy and hard as he followed Cyrus back inside the Academy. He had seen the place he had always dreamed of, and he knew he would never forget it. Yet his dreams did not matter, for he would travel home all the same, back with his parents to Idris, likely never to see the High King's Seat again for decades, if ever.

Something of his mood must have shown in his face, for Halab stopped and turned to him. "Why, what is the matter, Ebon? You do not seem happy at all. Are you not glad to have come?"

"Oh, I am," said Ebon. He had no wish to seem ungrateful when Halab had done so much. "Only . . ."

She pursed her lips and patted his arm. "I think I understand your mind, dear nephew. Do not let yourself fall into despair. Not all paths are laid clear before us, and our fate is never set in stone."

"Of course not," he mumbled. But her words gave him little comfort.

SIX

When he returned to the family manor, Ebon learned from Tamen that his parents had at last gained their audience with the High King, and thus the purpose for their visit was fulfilled. So it was that the next morning he was in his room, despondent, while Tamen packed his things in preparation for the journey home.

"I wish you would cheer up," said Tamen. "You make for horrible company."

"Do you think it is that simple?" said Ebon. He picked at a loose thread in his pant leg, refusing to look up. "The place was glorious. I did not know that half the things I saw there were possible."

"No one forced you to go."

Ebon snorted. "Do you think I could have refused? I suspect this was all an elaborate torture. He has brought me here only to show me that from which he has kept me all my life. And my dear aunt—she thought to help me, to cheer me, but she has only increased my pain tenfold."

Tamen frowned and shook his head. "Mayhap it is for the best. Not even the very wise can see all ends."

"I see only one end before me, and it is one I do not wish to face."

Outside the window, the sky was bright blue with a few wispy clouds. They passed in and out of sight, moving quickly with the wind. Soon that wind would carry Ebon away on a ship, across the Great Bay towards home.

He had a thought and sat up, eyeing the door to his chamber nervously.

What if he fled? He could vanish into the Seat. Surely Father would not waste much time looking for him. Mayhap the Academy would take him, and he could begin his training, late in his life though it was.

But it was a flight of fancy. The Academy charged a tuition, and though he had some coin, he could not pay his way for long. Besides, if Shay did think to look for him, the Academy would be the first place to search. Ebon could well imagine his father's cruel sneer as he was dragged from his classes, not to mention the punishment he would face at home.

Soon all his things were packed, and Tamen summoned servants to carry them downstairs. Ebon forced himself to his feet and followed, moving slowly as though his shoes were made of iron. Many crates and bundles were stacked in the manor's front room, ready to be loaded onto carriages and driven to the docks. It seemed to Ebon that they were leaving with even more possessions than they had arrived with, though he had not seen his parents buy anything new.

He made his way out the front door and into the courtyard, and there he found a surprise: Halab had come to see them off. Beside her stood Mako, and in the middle of the courtyard was the main carriage, in which he would ride with his parents to the docks. They were present already, Shay engaged in some conversation with Halab, while Hesta stood quietly nearby. Ebon could not hear the words, but his father looked angry, and made many sharp gestures with his hands. But as soon as he saw Ebon he stopped, his face going stony, and he turned away from his sister.

Halab greeted Ebon with a smile. "Good morrow, my dear nephew. Did you rest well?"

"I did, Aunt," said Ebon. "I shall miss you dearly. The days will seem like years until you grace Idris with your presence again."

"Such manners," said Halab, going to him and taking his kisses on her cheeks.

"A silver tongue he has indeed," said Mako, grinning at Ebon over Halab's shoulder. Ebon tried to still a shiver of unease that ran down his spine. His aunt he would miss, but he was glad to be leaving Mako's presence, at least.

Then Halab drew back and looked past Ebon, to where Tamen held a satchel with some of his clothing in it. Her eyes widened, and her full lips parted slightly as she looked at Ebon again. "But Nephew, why does your retainer bring your possessions? You look as if you are making ready to leave."

Ebon stopped short, brow furrowing. "I am. Is our trip here not finished?"

"You cannot tell me you thought you were going back to Idris. Surely your parents told you that you are staying here?"

At first, Ebon could not put meaning to the words. He looked over Halab's shoulder. Father's face had darkened, his eyes drawn together in a squint while a vein throbbed in his forehead. But Mother had turned her face away from Shay, and upon her lips Ebon thought he saw a tiny smile trying to burst free.

"I . . . I do not understand," he said lamely.

Halab gripped his wrists tighter. "My dear nephew. How plainly must I state it? You will be staying upon the High King's Seat to attend the Academy."

His knees did not seem capable of holding him up, and he grasped for something to steady him. Tears sprang to his eyes, and his other hand tightened its grip on Halab's arm until he loosened it, fearing he might hurt her. He opened his mouth to speak, but a lump in the back of his throat prevented him.

It seemed Father had kept his peace as long as he could. He stepped forth angrily, spittle springing from his lips as he spoke. "If you think the Academy to be some lark, then you are an idiot. You are six years too late. You will look like an infant in a king's finery there. And never will you be a great wizard, no matter your foolish dreams."

Ebon choked back furious words, biting his lip to keep them from spilling forth. Halab looked back at her brother, and a cool anger smoldered in her eyes. But when she turned back to him, her expression was kind, and she squeezed his arm in reassurance.

"The choice is yours, of course. I would never dream of forcing you into such studies, if they are not what your heart truly desires."

"Show some wisdom for once in your life, and think ahead," snarled Shay. "What do you think you can still learn, now that you are nearly full-grown?"

Ebon looked at him and then back to Halab. His first instinct was to shout, with all his joy and fervor, that of course he would stay and attend the Academy. And yet, as they so often did, his father's words wormed their way into his mind.

What *would* it be like at the Academy? One thing was certain: he was here six years later than he should have been, and that would be plain to everyone if he attended.

If?

He had dreamed of nothing more for many years. Now that the gift was presented to him, would he shrink back from it? He had seen the Academy now and all that lay within its granite walls. And he knew he had never longed for anything so keenly.

"I wish to attend the Academy," he said, almost shouting it. Then he leaped forwards, forgetting all his courtesy, and squeezed Halab in so tight an embrace that he heard the air *whoosh* from her lungs. "Thank you, Aunt. Thank you. This is a gift greater than I could have dreamed."

"You are welcome, my dearest nephew," she said, gently patting his back. At last he released her, and she stood back from him. "Now you are under one obligation only: to make your family proud to have sent you. Can you do this for me?"

He refused to look at his father, and so kept his eyes on hers. "Yes. I give you my oath."

"I will remember it. Now quickly—say your farewells, for you should make your way to the Academy right away. I have sent word to Cyrus already, and they are waiting for you."

Ebon turned to look at Tamen. His retainer wore a befuddled look, as though he did not fully understand what had happened. He raised the satchel in his hand and lowered it again. But then a curious light shone in his eyes. He dropped the satchel and reached for Ebon's hand.

"I did not expect this."

Ebon clasped his wrist. "Nor did I. Are you happy for me?"

"I find that I am." His other hand came up to grip Ebon's shoulder. "Fare well. I shall tell Albi."

"Please do. And thank you." Ebon tilted his head, hoping the retainer heard the words he could not say. "For your years of service, and all you have done here on the Seat."

Tamen answered with a smile—and then they both jumped as a door slammed. Ebon turned to find the carriage door was shut, and his father was inside. But his mother waited for him by the carriage, arms wide, a pleased smile upon her face. He went and took her in his arms, breathing in the familiar smell of the perfumes she favored.

"Go and make me proud, my son," she said, scarcely speaking above a whisper. "I do not weep to see you go, for I know you are ready."

"Then you know more than I, Mother," said Ebon. "But Father . . ."

"Do not concern yourself over him," she said quickly. "I know you cannot see it, but he, too, knows this is best. And mayhap the distance between you will mend what time never could."

Ebon doubted that very much, but he forced himself to smile as he gave her a final kiss on the cheek. At last he turned to Halab, who stood there beaming at him. Mako stood just behind her, but Ebon tried to ignore him.

"Well, what are you waiting for?" said Halab. "Go, or they shall mark you tardy on your first day."

"Do well, little goldbag," said Mako. Ebon's skin crawled at his crooked grin. "I know you will be of great service to the family."

Ebon tried to keep his smile up for his aunt. But at the last moment he turned towards the carriage. Its door had a window, and though a curtain was drawn across it, the sunlight showed his father's silhouette inside. The shadow did not move, even as it grew silent outside the carriage, and the others looked at Ebon expectantly.

Darkness take him, then, said Ebon.

"Fare well," he said, and though he spoke to Halab, he knew his words would carry inside the carriage. "The next time you see me, I shall be a wizard."

Then he turned and strode from the manor's courtyard. He kept his pace measured until he was out of sight, but the moment he turned the first corner, he burst into a run.

SEVEN

B<small>Y THE TIME</small> E<small>BON REACHED THE</small> A<small>CADEMY HE WAS PANTING, AND HE</small> had to double over to catch his breath. Sweat made his tunic stick to his back, and immediately he regretted his flight through the streets. He did not wish to appear for his first day a stinking slob. But it was too late for such worries now. He stepped forwards and rapped sharply on the front door.

Unlike the day before, the response was immediate, and he cringed at the sharp cry of the door's hatch sliding open. There was the old woman Mellie, ghostlike eyes glaring out at him. Before he could so much as open his mouth she screamed "The Drayden!" and slammed the hatch shut.

Ebon cast a quick look over his shoulder. He had no wish for people to know his family name if there was any way he could help it.

The door clanged open, and Mellie waved him in with sharp, almost frantic gestures. She seized his wrist as he crossed the threshold. Her fingers were bony and frigid, but surprisingly gentle as she drew him up the great staircase that dominated the hall. Behind him he heard the door slam shut with a heavy boom. When he turned, there was no one there who could have closed it. A shiver ran through his limbs.

I am in the Academy now, he thought. It was a giddy prospect, and he fought the urge to burst out laughing.

Mellie took the stairs quickly, despite her age. Once they reached the top she whisked him off to the right, stopping at the first room they came to. Within were many shelves, running from floor to ceiling and covering the walls, and all of them filled with folded black robes. Mellie ran along the shelves, brushing each one with her fingers as though she could see them by touch, glancing back often at Ebon.

"How tall do you stand?" she snapped.

"I—just under ten hands," he said, squaring his shoulders.

"Hah! I will give my good eye if you are more than half past nine." Ebon barely kept himself from pointing out that if she already had an answer, there seemed little purpose in asking him the question.

Mellie went to a shelf and took one of the robes from it, and then shoes from another shelf. Without ceremony she threw them into Ebon's arms. He tried to catch them, but they came unfolded anyway, and one fell to the ground. He barely had a chance to scoop it up before Mellie had snatched his arm and drawn him out of the room again, screaming at him to *Hurry! Hurry!*

They did not have far to go; she took him across the hall, where he found a simple brick room and a large bronze tub. It was filled with water, and steam rose languidly from its surface.

"Clean yourself," said Mellie, thrusting a gnarled finger at the tub.

"I bathed just last night."

Mellie glowered and said nothing, only thrusting her finger at the tub again.

He sighed. There was a bench at one end of the room, and he carefully laid his new student robes upon it. Then he turned to Mellie, raising his brows.

"Be quick!" she snapped. "I do not have all day to deal with new arrivals, you know."

Ebon thought to himself that he did *not* know, since he had no idea what Mellie actually did here. But he did not wish to sound rude. "Are you going to leave?"

"Humph!" she said, placing her hands to her hips. "Do you fear an old lady leering at you? I will not leave the room only to have you take an hour to bathe yourself."

His cheeks burned. "I—I do not often disrobe before others."

She rolled her eyes. "Merchant children," she muttered. "If I turn my back, will that preserve enough modesty that you will get in the tub?"

"Yes—and thank you."

Mellie turned, and he hurried to throw off his clothes. The moment she heard the splash of water, she came and took the golden clothing he had worn from the manor.

"Wait! Where are you taking those?"

"To be burned, of course. No one told you? The clothes you bring here are destroyed. While you study here at the Academy, you will wear only your student robes."

"But those are expensive!"

Mellie held them up, appraising them with narrowed eyes. "I have burned far better. The king of Wadeland's second cousin came here wearing clothes worth enough coin to feed an army for a month." Then she vanished through the door.

After his surprise faded, Ebon found himself somewhat liking the idea of the fine tunic and trousers curling in the tongues of a fireplace. If nothing else, the unnecessary expense would no doubt rankle Father, if he knew. Ebon laughed at the thought and gave the bathwater a little splash.

When Mellie came back a short time later, her hands were empty. Ebon had finished bathing and had just dressed again by the time she appeared. Scarcely waiting for him to put on his shoes, she seized his wrist and drew him from the room.

Now they ran back down the main staircase into the great entryway, and then around to the right side, where he entered the hallway opposite the one Cyrus had taken the day before. He remembered the dean saying these were where the instructors had their chambers. Mellie stopped at the first door on the right and threw it open.

"New student!" she shrieked, and then scampered off towards the front hall again.

Beyond the door was a study. But this was no elaborate room filled with gilded ornaments like the dean's office. It was warmly lit by candles placed in the corners, and a soft green rug covered the floor. Bookshelves lined the side and back walls, and they were filled with books in perfect, neat rows. In the center of the room was a modest desk with a single leather tome on one side, and a stack of parchments in the center, just beside a pot of ink with a quill stuck in.

Behind the desk sat a woman of middle years. Her short, prim hair had once been flame-red, like a performer from Hedgemond that Ebon had seen in his youth, but now it was half grey. Light blue eyes fixed on Ebon's face with calm assessment. He noted that she wore dark grey robes, like the dean, but hers had none of the gold brocade that Cyrus had worn.

"Come in, please," said the woman. "And shut the door behind you, if you would be so kind."

Ebon stepped in, chiding himself for feeling so timid, and closed the door with a soft *clink*.

The woman sat back in her chair, sinking into its soft, stuffed leather. She studied him a moment more before gesturing with an open hand to one of the two wooden chairs opposite her. "You are welcome to sit."

He did, looking around the room with interest. Though he knew she was an instructor, he felt none of the discomfort he had felt in Cyrus' office. This place seemed warm and gentle, if not entirely comfortable. She let his gaze wander, her fingers steepled under her chin. When he at last turned back to her, she said no word, and only kept looking him over.

She must recognize me for a Drayden, he thought. Surely that explained her reluctance to speak. Ebon knew well how his family was regarded across the nine lands. Would that legacy follow him here? He had hoped to escape it at last, but now that hope seemed unlikely, or even foolish.

But when the woman spoke, it was not of his family at all. "How many years have you seen?" she said. "Fourteen? Fifteen?"

Ebon breathed a sigh of relief. But the question presented another problem, and he answered reluctantly. "Sixteen."

An eyebrow raised briefly. "Indeed? Well, no doubt you think that is a terrible burden to bear. Do not worry yourself overmuch. I had seen fourteen when I came here. Mayhap not so grievous a situation as yours, but an annoyance all the same. You will find it difficult at first, but not forever."

He sat a little straighter, surprised. "I am relieved to hear that."

"And your branch?"

Ebon blinked. "I am sorry. I do not understand."

"Of magic. What is your gift?"

"Oh!" said Ebon, clearing his throat. "I am an alchemist."

Her brows rose again, and this time they stayed there. "Indeed? I daresay we could use more of them."

His brow furrowed. "I am sorry?"

"Never mind. It is of little consequence. You should know, though, that your branch's proper name is transmutation, and you would do well to start using that name immediately. The same applies to the other four branches. We do not speak with the commoner's casual indifference in these halls."

He nodded thoughtfully, finding himself growing curious about her. "And you? What branch are you gifted with?"

She smiled at that. Then Ebon nearly jumped out of his chair, for her shape changed before him. First her eyes glowed, and then her hair grew grey and stringy as she shrank in her seat. In a moment Mellie sat before him, still regarding him from behind steepled fingers.

Frantically he looked over his shoulder to the door where Mellie had just left him. But the woman laughed and swiftly changed back. "I am not Mellie, boy. That was an answer to your question."

At last he understood. "You are a weremage."

"A therianthrope, but yes. Very good. And I have forgotten my manners entirely, or you have. Either way, my name is Jia."

He noted carefully that she did not give a family name. Mayhap she was a bastard, but mayhap that was custom here. He hoped so. "I am named Ebon."

"Ebon. A strong name. Well, Ebon, let us show you to your quarters."

He scooped his spare robes back up from where he had thrown

them in the other chair, and Jia stood to lead him from the room. Ebon remembered that the dormitories were on the second floor, and he expected her to bring him back out to the main hall to climb the wide staircase. But Jia led him farther into the citadel instead, where he soon saw another staircase leading up. This one was a spiral, and very narrow, so much so that he could easily touch both sides of it with his arms stretched out. Jia led him up, passing one landing but stopping at the second. They emerged into the hallway to find a door facing them just on the other side, and Jia led him within.

They entered a room with many chairs and couches set in small circles all about its edge, with a large open space in the center. But Ebon scarcely had time to study it before Jia took him to a door at the back. Through that door was a long, low room with many beds, along with cabinets and chests of drawers. She led him to a bed almost at the back and waved a hand at the cabinet beside it.

"Here you may store your spare robes," she said. "This bed is yours now."

Ebon looked around the room at all the other beds, wondering how many were occupied. "Is this where all the alchemists sleep?"

"No alchemists sleep here at all."

His cheeks burned. "I am sorry. Is this where all the transmuters sleep?"

She smiled warmly. "A quick student, then. The answer is no. The branches study together, but here in the dormitories you are arranged with the other students according to your ages."

That was a relief. Ebon had no wish to spend his days sleeping in a room full of children. But Jia must have seen the pleasure on his face as something else, for she fixed him with a stern glare.

"Do not look so excited. You should know that it is strictly forbidden for students to philander upon Academy grounds. This is a place of learning." Ebon's face grew beet red as he realized what she thought she had seen in his mind, but she pressed on before he could speak. "There are many places upon the Seat where you and the others may see to your needs. This is not one of them. Instructors walk the halls at night, and often inspect the dormitories. Keep yourself restrained while you are here, and if you require silphium, you will see to procuring it yourself. Is that very clear?"

"Yes," he said, voice strangled with embarrassment. "I assure you, I understand completely."

Jia lifted her chin, eyes softening slightly. "Good. Know also that fighting is forbidden, whether magical or otherwise. And *that* rule extends beyond the Academy's walls. Take some private duel out upon the Seat, and we will hear about it. If that happens, you will be expelled. Now then. You know where you will be sleeping, so allow me to show you where you will be studying."

She led him downstairs again, this time to the entrance hall and then down the hallway on the left. Soon they reached a door with iron bands that Ebon thought looked familiar. Sure enough, when she opened it he recognized the room where Instructor Credell taught beginning alchemy. But the room was empty now, and neither Credell nor his students were anywhere to be seen.

"This is your classroom," said Jia. "Your instructor is a man named Credell."

"I met him," said Ebon. He realized he had interrupted her, and lowered his gaze, blushing.

Jia did not seem annoyed, and only nodded. "That is good, since as you can see he is not here for an introduction. His students are dismissed just now, though they will return soon. In the beginning, your days of learning will be divided into two periods of three hours—one period before the midday meal, and one after. This is where you will study for the first period."

Ebon remembered the classroom full of young children with some despair, but he nodded at her words. "And my second period?"

"That is general study, and it takes place in the library. There, I shall be your instructor. Come."

She led him away, and Ebon thrilled at the thought that she would be teaching him. He had not liked the look of Credell, or the way the man seemed to flinch away from any word spoken above a whisper. Though Jia was a weremage, mayhap she could help him fill in the gaps in his alchemy, for he strongly suspected Credell would not.

The gaps in my transmutation, I mean. Ebon smiled to himself.

Jia turned this way and that, and soon Ebon was utterly lost again within the halls. When she saw him looking around, desperate for a landmark to locate himself, she said, "You will get lost often in your first days, and little will help to prevent it. Therefore we will not waste time teaching you where to find your classrooms, but rather how to recognize them. You can ask your fellow students if you have trouble placing yourself."

"Thank you," he mumbled, and abandoned trying to find some way to determine where he was.

"There are a some things you may try to keep in mind," she went on. "For example, the beginner's classes are located near the front of the citadel, while the advanced classes are towards the rear. Therefore you will move deeper and deeper as you advance in learning—except for your general studies, which are always in the library, and therefore always at the very back of the citadel."

Already his head swam. But it was clear she was trying to help. "I will try to remember."

She pursed her lips as though hiding a smile. "Mayhap that is not as helpful to a student newly arrived as I think. But here we are."

They had come to double doors of dark wood. Jia opened them, and he stepped inside—and then he froze, looking around in wonder.

Never before had Ebon beheld a sight like the library of the Academy. Never before had he imagined that so many books existed in all the world. He stepped just over the threshold to look up, for he could see at once that there was a second floor—yet as he craned his neck, he could see that in fact there were three, each one reached by a narrow iron staircase. Far, far above, the library's roof was a great yellow dome, worked of some substance like glass, but which cast a golden glow on the whole place. The glow was strengthened by glass lanterns set in many fixtures on the walls—no open flames were permitted, he guessed, for the safety of the books.

And books there were. He thought that there must be tens of thousands of them. The bottom floor where he stood had many tables laid out, and at each one sat one or more students with books laid open before them. Above, he could see more tables set against the railings, with more students reading more books. And yet the shelves seemed full to bursting with still more, and he could not see an empty space anywhere.

"Where . . ." he stopped, trying to collect his thoughts. "Where did they all come from?"

"All across the nine lands, and all throughout the long centuries of history," said Jia, and he heard the reverence in her voice.

"What knowledge do they hold?"

"All of it, I should not be surprised to learn. But you could spend five lifetimes here and not read them all, even if you did nothing else, and then you could never put such knowledge to use. I must admit to some small pleasure at the wonder I see in your eyes. Are you fond of reading, then?"

Ebon shrugged slowly. "I certainly enjoy it. And this . . . how could anyone see this place and not be struck by wonder? The dean took me through the Academy yesterday, but he never showed me the library. If he had, I would have called this the greatest wonder of the citadel."

Jia's lips drew into a thin line. "That does not greatly surprise me. Cyrus is not the most avid reader, nor was he even when he was a student here himself."

Ebon blinked. "You were here when he was a student? How can that be? You cannot have seen enough years."

It looked as though she was trying very hard to fight back a smile. "You will find that flattery has very little effect on me, Ebon."

He ducked his head at once. "I did not . . . I meant only that . . ."

She patted him on the arm. "I am mostly joking. Come. That is all you need to see today, and we should return you to your dormitory. You can return tomorrow, your first true day as an Academy student."

Quickly she brought him back through the halls to another spiral staircase leading up. This time Ebon recognized the staircase, and thought he might even be able to find it again, if pressed. That boded well. Once they reached the third floor she brought him to his dormitory and stopped at last before his bed.

"There is one more thing you should know. If you wish to send a letter to your family, you may bring it to me. I will see to its safe transport. The fee for a letter is a silver penny. But if you should wish to send a letter and do not have the coin, come speak with me, and I will see if there is anything that can be arranged."

Ebon blushed, for he had a thick coin purse in his robes—transferred from the clothes he had worn when he arrived, and always kept upon him in case of emergency. "I thank you for your consideration, but I do not think I shall have a problem with coin."

"I imagine that is true, for a son of the family Drayden."

A sudden chill flooded his bones, and he blanched as he looked at her. Wordlessly his mouth worked, trying to form some explanation. Jia smiled sadly at him, and then, to his surprise, she took his hand.

"You thought I did not know your family? It is written plain on your face, and your bearing, and your manner of speech. But if you think that matters here, you are mistaken. No one worth their salt cares for the name you and your kin bear. And the Draydens have produced many good wizards—sky above, one of them is the dean."

Ebon found words hard to muster. "But . . . but on the Seat, they . . ."

"I do not doubt that many on the street looked at you askance. But you will find—or you *should* find—that being a wizard is different. Many worries you have struggled with during your life will fade away during your time here. If they do not, then you are not learning all that you should. Do you understand me?"

He swallowed hard. "I am afraid not."

"Of course not. But you will. Your first class is tomorrow morning, two hours after the rising of the sun."

Then she left him, and Ebon stared after her, dumbfounded, as the dormitory faded to silence around him.

EIGHT

After Jia had gone, Ebon went to his cabinet and ensured his robes were neatly stacked. He doubted anyone would care how his cabinet looked, but he liked his things well ordered, and he no longer had Tamen to take care of them for him.

Tamen. Thinking of his retainer sent his mind spinning. Only a few hours ago he had left Tamen standing in the courtyard of the Drayden manor, and now he was in the Academy. He might see Tamen again someday, and then again he might not. Certainly it would be a long time, unless his parents returned to the Seat for some reason Ebon could not predict.

But when he thought of his parents, he thought of the closed carriage door and the shadow behind the curtain. That thought did not bear dwelling upon, and so he looked about the dormitory for something else to do. It seemed no duties were required of him, at least not until the next day. Mayhap he could inspect the common room, for he had only seen it twice, and both times in haste. He left his bed and walked the long aisle to the door leading out.

The common room was wide and tall, but somehow it maintained an air of coziness and comfort. He inspected again the plush chairs set all about the room and the fireplaces in either wall. Though it was late autumn, the day was warm, and so no fires were lit, but he did not doubt that they would give great warmth when winter's shroud descended upon the Seat. The walls were the same granite as the rest of the citadel, but they were hung with many tapestries of red and green and gold, and everywhere he saw the cross-and-circle of the Academy worked into the designs.

To his surprise, he noticed another student sitting in the common room. He did not remember seeing her when he had passed through with Jia. Mayhap she had come in only a moment ago—but then, mayhap he had missed her, for she sat quietly in the corner of the room and made no noise. Indeed, she did not even look up or appear to see him. Her hair was lank and black, her skin sallow, and dark bags hung beneath her eyes.

Slowly Ebon drew closer to her. Still she did not see him. She was holding something in her hands, and now he could see that it was a goblet of silver. Then, to Ebon's amazement, her eyes glowed with an inner light, and she pulled her hands away—but the cup stayed there, floating in midair.

She is a mindmage, he thought.

As the girl twisted her hands, the goblet began to spin. First it turned end over end, in line with the girl's nose. Then she concentrated, her nose twitching, and it began to twist in another direction at the same time. Her hands clenched, wiry muscles taut beneath the skin, and it spun in another direction entirely. It turned faster and faster, becoming a blur, and moving so fast now that Ebon thought it looked like a spinning silver globe, and not a cup at all.

Entrancement made him forget his fear, and now he walked eagerly over to her. He stopped just next to the arm of her chair, yet still she did not look at him. He waited a moment in silence, out of manners, and then gently cleared his throat.

"That is astonishing," he said, fearing his voice was far too loud in the stillness of the room.

The girl said nothing. Now he felt sweat beading on the back of his neck, and he pulled at the collar of his robe.

"I . . . I am Ebon. I am only arrived to the Academy today. How long have you attended?"

At last she looked up, meeting his brown eyes with her own, darker ones, though they still glowed from the use of her magic. Then her hands constricted, like an eagle's claws sinking into a rabbit's neck. The goblet abruptly stopped spinning, and it crumpled into a tiny ball of metal with a terrible rending noise.

Ebon jumped and turned to scurry hastily away. He found a chair at the other end of the room, blocked from sight by the furniture in between, and tried to sink into the plush cushions.

It was a little while before his heart slowed and his breath came easier. As the fright finally died in his breast, his fingers began to tap on the armchair. He looked about the room but could see no one else, nor could he hear the sound of anyone passing in the hallway. He could only feel the presence of the girl, as though her eyes were boring into his soul, despite the fact she could not see him.

Mayhap he had better practice his own magic. Soon he would be expected to perform it, after all, and he had not tried to use it in many years. Whenever Tamen caught him playing at spells, his father heard of it immediately. And he had never been allowed to meet another wizard, much less an alchemist.

His only knowledge of his gift was the spell he had done as a boy, when the Academy's examiner had come to see if he had the gift. Now he looked around and saw cups and a pitcher of water on a table nearby. Hastily he went and filled one, his movements quick, careful to keep his eyes from the corner of the room where the girl sat.

In his chair once more, he gently swished the water around in the cup before placing a forefinger into it. He stirred gently. It was neither cool nor warm, but the exact heat of the room itself. He closed his eyes and concentrated.

Hazy across the long years since he first heard them, the old wizard's words returned to his mind: *Feel the water. See it the way it truly is. And then change it.*

Ebon concentrated with all his might. His eyes squeezed shut so tightly that they began to pain him. But nothing happened. He opened one eye, just a crack, to be sure. But the water still sat lukewarm against his finger. The back of his neck prickled, and his forehead beaded with sweat. He thought he could feel something . . . something within him, yearning to break free. He reached for it, but the harder he grasped, the more quickly it slipped away.

A long, slow breath escaped him. He stopped reaching, stopped trying to know the unknowable power that danced at the edge of his awareness. Instead he thought only of the water. It grew before his vision, the goblet swelling until it took up all the world. Now even his finger was forgotten, except as the bridge that connected him to the liquid.

His vision brightened.

Ebon felt his heart hammer in his chest, but he forced himself to concentrate. Slowly his finger stirred, swirling in little circles and causing the water to splash against the cup's rim. But wherever he touched the water, it turned thick and soupy, until soon the cup was filled with an oil that resisted the turning of his finger.

With a gasp he sat back, leaning into the couch. His hand trembled as he lifted the cup again. Within, the water was a thick, oily soup.

He wanted to burst into laughter. It had worked. Years had passed since he had last dared to slip away from Tamen for long enough to try it. He thanked the sky above that he could still do it. What a bitter irony it would be to reach the Academy at last, only to find that he had lost his gift.

The door to the common room slammed open, and three students came storming in.

Ebon shot to his feet. Across the room, he saw the sallow-faced girl had gone. With a sinking feeling in his stomach, he realized he still held the cup before him. Swiftly he turned to place it on the table beside his chair, and then he straightened and wiped his finger against his robe to rid it of the oil.

A girl led the other students who had entered, and her gaze fixed on Ebon. She paused for just a moment, brows drawing close, and then she came to him. Her skin was dark, and her thick hair was cut just below her ears and intricately braided to frame her face, making her light eyes all the more captivating. She stopped before Ebon and put her hands to her hips, sizing him up. Though Ebon stood half a head taller than she, he felt himself quail in her presence—an effect greatly enhanced by the girl and boy who stood behind her, both of them several fingers taller than Ebon was. Though the girl wore the same plain black robes as any other student, her stance and the look on her face spoke plainly: here was a girl from wealth and power.

"Who are you?" she said. "I have not seen you before."

Ebon tried to speak, but coughed instead as spit caught in his gullet. He cleared his throat hard. "I—I am Ebon," he croaked. "I have only just arrived at the Academy today."

"Where did you train before? You cannot be sponsored by some lord. You are far too old. Did your family hire you some tutor?"

Ebon felt a burning all along his skin and knew his face must be dark as a well-cooked roast. "I have never trained before."

She stared at him for a moment, eyes wide, mouth open slightly. He could see in her face that she did not believe him. Behind her, the other students looked at each other askance. But then the girl's eyes darted past Ebon, to the wooden cup that sat on the side table. He tried to shift to the side, to block her view with his body. But her lips twisted in a cruel smirk, and she pushed past him to grasp the cup. Lifting it before her face, she dipped a finger into the crude oil.

"The trial spell?" she laughed. "That cannot be the only magic you know."

"It is," said Ebon, still flushed with shame. But now annoyance was blossoming to anger in his breast, and he spoke without thinking. "My father never wanted me to train, and if he caught me trying magic—"

The girl stopped him with a loud laugh, the others behind her snickering along. Then her eyes glowed white, and she snapped her fingers. A spark sprang from her hand and landed on Ebon's sleeve. He felt the heat of it immediately, and with a cry of dismay he tried to beat it out.

"Oh, does my flame bother you?" said the girl, laughing harder. "Here, mayhap this will help."

She threw the cup of oil on his sleeve. It doused the spark, but it also splashed across his whole body, soaking through until the cloth clung to his skin, cold and clammy.

"I have not seen a greater waste in all my years here," she said. "But

61

I suppose I am grateful. We have a jester back home, and I have missed having someone to amuse me. I am Lilith of the family Yerrin, jester, and I am most pleased to make your acquaintance."

Lilith dropped the cup and strode off through one of the dormitory doors—not the one that led to Ebon's room, he noted with relief. Ebon sat back down in the chair, not caring that his wet robe would soak into the cushions, and hung his head. No matter how hard he squeezed his eyes shut, he could not stop a tear of shame from escaping to run down his cheek.

NINE

When he had composed himself, Ebon retreated to his own dormitory and changed into a clean robe. Then he thought better of it and removed the robe, and once in his underclothes he climbed beneath the covers of his bed. He had no wish to meet any other students, especially not now. He had imagined the Academy would be better than his home. Here he thought to free himself from family obligation, from the infighting and politics that had surrounded him since he was old enough to understand them. But it seemed instead that he would face a whole new host of problems—or mayhap just Lilith, but she seemed trouble enough to last a lifetime.

Mayhap she will forget about me soon—especially once I begin to learn my magic, he thought.

You are a fool, came another thought. And for that, he had no retort.

Classes must have just ended, for soon other students came in from the common room, bustling with noise and conversation. Ebon ignored them all, and when they drew too close he pretended to be asleep. It was late in the afternoon, but still hours from nightfall, and Ebon spent them all in bed, curled up and pretending not to exist. It was a long time before he finally drifted off into a restless slumber.

When he woke, the dim grey shining through the window told him that dawn had not yet broken. He rose quietly, thankful that no one else had risen yet, and donned his robes. Then he made his way out of the dormitory, through the common room, where fires burned in both hearths, and down the stairs to the first floor.

The Academy was quiet and empty. Ebon felt as though everything around him had taken on a magical quality, otherworldly and not quiet real. It was easy to imagine, at least for the moment, that all the world had gone, and he alone was left to explore it. It made his feet itch to run about, his eyes seeking for cracks and corners.

Silently he padded down the passage to the entrance hall, afraid to make any noise too loud and break the spell. Though torches burned in sconces, and must have been lit by attendants, the place was empty so far as he could see. When he reached the hall he stood and, for the first time, looked freely upon the place.

The windows far above were just beginning to glow with dawn, and the staircase shone in the colored sunlight that came floating down. The bronze banisters glinted in his eyes, and he reached out for them. The metal was warm, though the rest of the air clung to night's chill. The stone steps were worn smooth from centuries of students' passing shoes.

He stepped away and went to the iron front door. It was still too dim to see well, so he pressed his nose quite close to the small symbols inscribed all over it. Now he saw that they were similar to regular letters, and yet somehow different. They were harsher, more angular, with no curves to be seen anywhere. Yet he could not read them, for the words were strange and ancient, and the more he studied them the more his head began to hurt.

"What are you doing?"

Ebon leaped half a pace in the air and came crashing down hard upon the marble floor. He scrambled backwards on all fours—and then stopped as he saw Mellie quivering above him. Her white eye was thrice its normal size, and the other one was squinted, a scowl warping her lips.

"Sky above," he muttered. "You frightened me."

"Next time do not bury your nose in an iron door," she screeched. "What in the nine lands were you looking at?"

Ebon shook his head and got to his feet, brushing dust from the seat of his robes. "The symbols on the door. Why? What does it matter?"

Mellie turned and put her own eye up to the door, looking for all the world as though she was noticing the symbols for the first time. Then she looked back to Ebon, blinked once, and stalked away. He sighed.

The entry hall was much brighter now. Soon the other students would come down from the dormitories to break their fast. Ebon had no great wish to be there when they did—especially since Lilith would be among their number. He thought he remembered where Jia had showed him the dining hall, but he went the other direction towards the classrooms. *Your morning classes will be in the first room on the left with an iron band on the door,* Jia had told him.

He found the door and opened it. The room was empty, and he paused on the threshold. A sigh escaped him as he thought of his frightened little mouse of a teacher, Credell.

Mayhap it will not be so bad as it seems, he thought hopefully. But he did not believe it.

Shutting the door behind him, he went to one of the benches at the rear. They were arranged in rows, all facing the front of the classroom, and each had a long table in front of it. He slid down the bench until he was in the farthest corner, where he could lean against the wall. There he sat, waiting for the start of the day, and his first class as a wizard of the Academy.

Somehow, it no longer excited him as much as he once thought it would.

Thankfully he did not have to wait as long as he feared. It was mayhap half an hour until the first other student arrived. She was a small, sharp girl with wild hair that stuck out all about her head like a halo. When she entered the room, she saw Ebon and stopped. For a moment she studied him, face pale, eyes darting about every so often. Then she leaned out the door and looked up and down the hallway before stepping back inside once more. Back and forth she rocked on her feet, from tiptoes to heels, mouth working as she tried to summon the courage to speak.

"I . . . I think you have come to the wrong room," she squeaked.

"I do not blame you for thinking so," said Ebon. "But this is where I am meant to be, though it pains me to say so."

The girl did not seem to have a ready answer for that. Once more she looked out into the hall, as though making sure she was not the one in the wrong place. Finally she came in and closed the door behind her, going to the opposite corner of the room from Ebon and sliding all the way down the bench, until she was as far from him as she could be. Ebon slouched against the wall. With every passing moment, it was harder to resist an urge to flee the Academy forever and catch the first ship back home to Idris.

Slowly the room filled up, students arriving one by one and filling the benches. Most of them looked to be eleven or twelve years old at the most—Ebon saw one who he thought might have been thirteen, but mayhap the boy was just tall. Each one stopped for a moment when they spotted Ebon. Many of them looked about the classroom as the first girl had, ensuring that they were in the right place. Soon most of the other benches in the room had been filled—but no one came to Ebon's table, or even to the other bench in his row, though it was across an aisle.

The time passed with intolerable slowness, until Ebon felt that half the day must be gone. At last the door creaked timidly open, and Instructor Credell entered. Once he had stepped inside he stopped, looking around the room with wide eyes as though he was surprised to find himself there. He did not seem to notice Ebon. After a moment's awkward pause, he gave a little jerk and scuttled to his lectern, gripping it for support. Again he stopped, this time looking across the students before him.

His eyes fell upon Ebon. He gave a little jump and a yelp, and his knuckles went white. His throat wobbled a bit, and a weak smile crawled across his lips as though it had been dragged there screaming.

"Ah!" he said. "Ah, yes. Er. Class, we have a new student. Greet our Ebon, of the family Drayden, will you?"

He waved a hand generally in Ebon's direction. Slowly the other students turned to look at him. Ebon withered, though he felt ridiculous at his embarrassment. These were only children. But in many of their eyes he saw fear, and knew it was fear of his family's name. He tried to smile, but was sure he summoned only a grimace.

"Ah," said Credell. "Yes. Well, we shall . . . ahem. We shall begin the day's lessons, then. Yes. You may all resume practice of your spells. I shall be around presently to instruct you. If you require help, raise your hand for assistance."

Awkward silence hung on the air for a moment, and no student moved. Then Credell flapped his hands, as though shooing a cat from the room, and the students broke into muted activity. Some went to retrieve wooden rods from a cabinet in the corner of the room, while others took hold of cups of water that already waited on the tables before them. Credell left his lectern and began to putter about the room, going from table to table and asking the students questions in hushed voices. Ebon could not help but feel that the instructor was very deliberately avoiding his gaze.

He shifted on his bench, unsure of what to do. All the other students seemed to know their business already. Ebon saw some of the children stirring the water in their cups and thought they must be practicing the testing spell. Others gripped their wooden rods, faces twisting as they concentrated. But he had no cup nearby to practice with, and he did not know what spell to cast upon the wooden rod, and so he stayed in his seat.

Credell moved through the room slowly, and seemed to move still slower the closer he drew to the back of the room where Ebon waited. Still Ebon forced himself to sit still; he had no wish to make a nuisance of himself on his first day. But when Credell finished with the table across the aisle, he spun and made for the front of the room. Ebon sat forwards in surprise. Quickly he leaned out into the aisle and thrust his hand in the air.

"Instructor Credell?"

The man leaped half a pace in the air and looked over his shoulder, face twisted as though in pain. "Ah. Er. Yes. Quite right."

He turned reluctantly and came back, each step as slow as though he was moving through water. But when he reached Ebon's table, a wide smile was plastered upon his face, looking as unnatural there as a mouse in a suit of armor. Ebon scooted aside to make room for him as he took the bench.

"Ebon," he said, voice quivering. "It is Ebon, is it not? I have such a terrible mind for names."

"It is," said Ebon. "What should I do?"

"Ah, yes, well," said Credell, fingers drumming on the table. "I was told you were never trained in transmutation, though I know that cannot be true, eh? A smart young boy like you." He chuckled and patted Ebon's shoulder. Ebon thought he could feel the sweat on the man's palms through the cloth.

"You were told the truth," said Ebon. "I know only the testing spell to turn a cup of water into oil."

"Oh, I am certain that is what you told everyone, eh?" said Credell, tapping his nose with a wink. "But I know what a curious mind can do. Worry not, for I will spread no tales of any spell I see you cast in this room."

Ebon blinked. "I think you misunderstand me. I could not practice any spells, even if I knew any, even in secret. My father kept a careful watch over me, and if I were to try . . ."

"Ah, well then," said Credell, shaking his head with a soft smile. "If you wish to keep up the pretense, I shall do the same. Anything for your honorable family."

"Instructor, I am *not* telling a tale. I want to learn. What must I do?"

Ebon felt his hackles rising as Credell gave him yet another broad wink. "Well, if you say you know nothing but the testing spell, then you had best practice it, eh? I will fetch you a cup of water."

He leaped from the bench as though stung by a bee and ran for the front of the room, soon returning with a wooden cup of water. This he placed before Ebon, and then stood hesitantly for a moment, looking down at him.

"Go on, then. I am sure you will make short work of it."

Ebon sighed and took the cup. He placed his finger within the water, trying to focus. Nothing happened. He frowned and concentrated, trying to reach for his gift as he had tried in the common room the day before. But now he could feel Credell's eyes upon him, as well as the eyes of every student in the room. They were all watching him, and he could feel their wonder at seeing this older boy try to perform the simplest of spells. He tried to force such thoughts from his mind, but they crowded back in until he could think of nothing else.

He slammed the cup down in frustration. Some of the water splashed out and onto his hand, and he shook it away angrily. "I told you, I never learned any spells. I was not even permitted to practice this one."

Credell shook his head with a kindly smile. But just as he opened his mouth to speak, the classroom door flew open. In strode the dean. He waddled in briskly and came down the aisle towards them, twisting to keep his belly from knocking over the students' cups upon the tables to either side. The other students froze the moment they saw him and drew away in fright as he passed by. Credell seemed to wilt like a flower thrown into a flame, shrinking into himself until he was as small and insignificant as possible. His watery eyes trembled until Ebon thought he might burst into tears. But the dean seemed to ignore the instructor utterly, his eyes fixed on Ebon.

"Ebon, my dear cousin!" he said, puffing mightily as he came to a stop before the desk. "How are you settling in here on your first day? My apologies—your second, I suppose." He chortled, thick jowls bouncing up and down as though he had made the wittiest of jokes. Beside Ebon, Credell tittered uncertainly.

Ebon tried to look anywhere else but at the dean. "I am well. Thank you for your concern."

"Of course, of course," said the dean, waving a hand magnanimously. From his tone, Ebon thought that in truth he could care less how Ebon fared. Most likely he was there only as a favor to Halab, but Ebon feared his presence would only make Credell behave even worse.

As though to put proof to the thought, the dean leaned over to look with interest at the cup that sat before Ebon on the table. His eyes narrowed, face twisting in a scowl.

"The testing spell?" he snapped. "Surely your time is not being wasted on so insignificant a thing. What is the meaning of this, Instructor Credell?"

69

He rounded on the poor man. Despite his frustration, Ebon felt only pity for the instructor. Credell retreated even further into himself, backing up until he stood against the wall, and his hands flew together to clutch each other at his breast.

"He—he said—he only knows the testing—" Credell tried to stammer.

"Only knows the testing spell? How preposterous!" blustered the dean. "I will not have you wasting my cousin's time on such tripe!"

Ebon spoke up quickly. "He tells the truth. I never learned anything but the testing spell. My father—"

The dean cut him off with a wave of his hand. "You need not trouble yourself to defend him, Ebon. Now listen here, whelp." He pressed forwards, and though he and Credell were of a height, the instructor had cowered so completely that he stood a head shorter than the dean. "I will not have you wasting Ebon's time. You will see to it that he learns his studies as quickly as he can, not squander his hours here endlessly repeating a spell that can be done by any child aged six summers!"

He turned on his heel and stalked to the front of the room, where he flew through the door in a rush and slammed it behind him. The *crash* of the door made Credell collapse at last, and he sank to the bench with a whimper. There he rested for only a moment before he seemed to realize that Ebon was still there. Then he leaped to his feet with a cry and rushed to the front of the room, where he cowered behind his lectern, refusing to meet the eyes of any of his students.

Every child in the room had turned their gazes upon Ebon, and he could nearly feel the terror radiating from them. It seemed the dean was not well-liked within the Academy walls, at least not by the students—and, if his behavior toward Credell was any indication, not by the instructors, either. Vaguely he remembered Jia's snide words about the dean the day before.

Even here, with his father halfway across the nine lands and drawing farther away each day, Ebon could not escape his family's name. He let his head sink until it rested on the desk and, closing his eyes, he wished he were back in his bed.

TEN

It seemed an eternity before a bell pealed and Credell called out that the students were excused for their midday meal. Almost before he finished speaking the words, the instructor was out the door like an arrow. The other students moved to flee just as quickly, but not faster than Ebon. In mere moments he was out the door and into the hallway. But the place was soon filled with bodies, students emerging from their classes all in a mass until he could hardly move through the press.

He spotted a door of white wood and remembered that those were the doors leading outside. The thought of open air, free from the crowd and the crushing weight of his embarrassment, suddenly seemed the greatest of luxuries. He shoved past several students to reach the door. Soon he was alone on the grassy lawn outside. Neither students nor instructors were there to disturb him, all having gone inside for their meal, and for a while Ebon simply walked through the gardens, closing his eyes and trying to forget the morning's disappointment.

He wished he had not come. For years he had thought the Academy would be a place of magic and wonder, where he could finally learn to harness the gifts that some fate had seen fit to bestow upon him. Yet thus far, if anything, the place seemed worse than Idris. At least in his family's manor he had Albi to visit and commiserate with. Here he had no one. And while the Academy itself was a beautiful place, and the High King's Seat rich in splendor and history, he found himself, for the first time, feeling a homesickness for the arid deserts of home. Were the sand dunes and the dry air really so bad? At least they were familiar. And at least there, though he was beneath his father's notice, still he was a child of wealth and power. Here he was nothing—or mayhap less than even that.

There was a stone bench nearby, and he slumped down onto it with a sigh. He hung his head so low that it nearly touched his knees, elbows grating against the rough fabric of his robes.

Could he still leave? Mayhap it was not too late. His parents would have left the island already, and mayhap Halab would have done the same by now. But he had some coin, mayhap enough to secure passage back home.

He thought of returning. In his mind's eye he saw himself walking through the broad front doors of his family's home, into the entry hall where Tamen would be waiting, no doubt wide-eyed with shock at seeing his master's return. And he thought of Albi's delight to see him, and his mother's warm embrace.

But the thought ran further, and he saw his father at the head of the dinner table, looking at him across a meal of meat pies and figs, silently gloating at his son's failure.

Ebon's hands balled to fists in his lap, shaking for a moment before he managed to still them. He felt the muscles in his jaw jerking as he ground his teeth together.

He would not return. That would mean that Father had won, and he could not bear such a thought. And he saw, too, the disappointment in his aunt's eyes when she found out. She had arranged all of this; certainly she had been the one to persuade his father to change his judgement. Always she had shown him nothing but kindness and compassion. He would not repay her by spurning her gift, by fleeing from his studies before they had truly begun.

Without meaning to, he shot to his feet. Mayhap he would fail in his training. Mayhap the Academy would throw him out on his ear, there to find passage home however he could. But he would not leave until then. Darkness take Credell, and darkness take the dean. Here, at least, he could practice his spells without rancor, at least if he kept himself from Lilith's sight. If the Academy could not teach him, then he would teach himself—or find someone else to do it. His heart burned at the thought, and it seemed for a moment as if he could cast a spell right then.

But his stomach rumbled loud in his belly, until he thought they might hear it inside the Academy's granite walls.

Ebon smirked to himself. He had skipped the morning's meal, and had not even had dinner the night before. If he wished to become a great alchemist, he would first have to eat.

He made his way back to the white door. Inside, the passageway was now empty. But Ebon could hear voices, drifting to him along the stone hallway, and he followed the sound. Soon he found the wide doors that led into the dining hall. The room was large, larger than he had anticipated, with a low ceiling and many benches laid out in rows. At the back was the food, served by attendants into simple dishes made of wood. Ebon did not see any sense of order to how the other students sat, except that students of the same age seemed to sit together. But there were many empty tables spread about the place. Quickly he made his way between the benches, thankful that everyone ignored him as he went. An attendant filled a bowl with stew and gave him the end of a bread loaf, and he made his way to one of the empty tables.

He ate voraciously, stomach gurgling in appreciation with every bite. Though it lacked the fine spices of the food he was used to, still after his long fast it seemed one of the better meals he had had in a long time.

When his bowl was empty he leaned back, sighing with relief. Idly he tore a piece of bread away and scraped at the leavings. His eyes fell upon his cup of water.

Mayhap he could practice. He looked around quickly. Though he saw no students using magic anywhere, he had heard no rule that it was forbidden. And he would need all the practice he could get, since Credell seemed too frightened of his family name to be of much help.

He took the cup and dipped his finger within. Slowly he stilled his mind, closing his eyes and trying to envision the water for what it truly was. He opened his eyes again and focused. Something tickled at the back of his mind. But the water remained water. Ebon stirred it with its finger, but nothing happened.

Ebon slammed the cup down, and it *clacked* against the table. Even the testing spell seemed out of his reach.

It is fine, he told himself. *You only need practice. Ten years you have been kept from your magic. You cannot expect to learn it in a day.*

"How go the spells, jester?"

His gut curdled at the sound of Lilith's voice. He turned to see her standing behind him, still accompanied by the two students he had seen in the common room next to the dormitories. The three of them held their meals in their hands, but the bowls were half-empty; they had been eating already, and had stopped to come torment him.

"Leave me alone," said Ebon. "I am in no mood for games."

"Oh, but what else are jesters for?" Lilith stepped forwards to sit beside him on the bench. The boy with her sat on her other side, while the other girl sat on Ebon's left. They shuffled slightly, pressing up against him, Lilith leaning close. "Are you finding your lessons difficult? How do you enjoy the other infants in your class? They must be keeping you good company, for I think you are of a mind with them."

Ebon ground his teeth together. Well he remembered Jia's warning that fighting among students was not tolerated. No doubt Lilith was thinking of this as well, and sought to anger him in order to get him in trouble. He would not give her the satisfaction.

Seeing his restraint, she leaned closer still, and her voice became silky smooth. "You know, do you not, that in truth your ignorance is no great loss? You would only be a transmuter, and what value are they? All know that elementalism is the strongest of the four branches. Mentalism is a close second, and therianthropy at least has some uses. But transmutation? What will you do, if you learn your magic? Will you become some nobleman's plaything in the outland kingdoms, turning water into wine for his court?"

The other two snickered loudly, drawing gazes from students at the tables nearby. Ebon felt his skin darkening as they looked at him, looked at Lilith, and then quickly looked away. He knew that look from too many years spent in his father's company: he was a mouse, and the favorite plaything of a tomcat, and they would keep their distance lest they get scratched.

I will show them who is a mouse, he thought wildly. His hands balled into fists on the table. Rules be damned, he would knock Lilith to the floor. Let her jeer at him then.

"What is going on here, Lilith?"

Ebon looked up to see Jia standing at the table. Her eyes were sharp and narrow, but they were looking at Lilith, not at him. Lilith and her friend shuffled slightly away from Ebon on the bench.

"Nothing, Jia," said Lilith, her voice light, unconcerned. "We are only welcoming the Academy's newest student."

Jia's voice took a quality Ebon had not heard from her before, and it bit like sharpened steel. "That is Instructor Jia to you, student. And I have no doubt how welcoming you can be. Take your greetings and yourselves and move them elsewhere, or I will see you scrubbing the dormitory floors."

Lilith ducked her head in acquiescence and made to rise. Her lackeys did the same. But as she made to stand, still bent over and facing away from Jia, she leaned close one last time to hiss at Ebon. "Keep your eyes open, little jester. You and I shall have such fun together."

Ebon swallowed hard as they left. Jia stayed put for a moment, watching them go. When she was satisfied, she looked back at Ebon. Still his fists were clenched on the tabletop, and now they were quivering. Shaking her head, Jia made to sit down—but Ebon leaped up in a rush, leaving his bowl and cup behind him as he fled the dining hall.

ELEVEN

EBON RAN THROUGH PASSAGEWAY AFTER PASSAGEWAY, AND SOON HE WAS hopelessly lost. He saw white doors and brown, rooms he thought were instructors' offices and rooms he was sure were classrooms. But he feared to pass through any of them, for he knew he would look like a fool. He had had quite enough of that for one day.

It was a long while yet before he must go to the library for his afternoon lessons. He slowed to a walk and let his steps wander, trying to get some sort of bearing on the halls and the manner in which they were laid out. Slowly he came to realize that the doors themselves were a sort of code. White wooden doors led outside to the training grounds and gardens. Doors with iron bands were classrooms. Double doors led to large rooms of special significance such as the dining hall or the library. When he saw some instructors disappearing into their studies, he paused and searched the doors for some identifying marks. Then he realized that their lack of ornamentation *was* their marker: a door of plain brown wood, undecorated, led to a study. All but the dean's door, of course, which had been made of iron. Ebon wondered why that was.

He found a staircase and took it up, looking for similar signals in the upper floors. But it seemed to him that the dormitory doors looked just like the doors to the studies, unless there was some other identifying mark he could not see. And every so often he came upon a door of ebony, or some other black wood. But all of the black doors were locked, and he had no faintest idea what might lie behind them.

Ebon froze in the hallway. He had entirely lost track of time, and now it seemed to him more than an hour must have passed. The afternoon classes had surely already begun.

He ran down the first stairwell he found and pounded through the hallways on the first floor. Now that he knew which doors led where, he was not quite so hopelessly lost as he had been. But still he did not know how to make his way deeper into the Academy, for he had no sense of direction. The halls were empty, so there were no students to follow or instructors to ask for direction.

At last he found a short hallway ending at two doors that looked very familiar. The library, or so he hoped. When he ran and threw the doors open, he nearly dropped to the floor in relief. Before him and above him the library stretched, vast and dusty and filled with the orange glow of the amber-colored glass in the ceiling far above.

Then he realized that he had come storming through in a rush, and much louder than he had meant to. The gaze of every student for thirty paces was fixed on him, all of them frozen in shock. And in the center of them all was Jia, one brow raised as she regarded him.

Ebon gulped and closed the doors behind him, as slowly and as quietly as he could manage. Only then did the students at last turn back to their books, though a few glanced up at him once or twice. Jia never turned her gaze. He made his way between the tables towards her, keenly aware that now he had sweated through the underarms of his robes. And he had not bathed that day, and had no perfume to wear.

"Well met, Ebon," said Jia. "I see you have found your way to the library at last."

He was grateful she did not bring up the incident at the midday meal. If she was content to forget all about it, Ebon was more than willing to do the same. "Yes, Instructor. I am sorry for being late. Still I have not learned my way about this place."

"I told you that I expected as much. Think nothing of it—though the citadel is large, soon you will walk these halls like one born to them."

He flushed, suppressing a smile, and looked about. Once more he was struck by the size and grandeur of the place. Though its three levels loomed over him, grave and solemn, still he found himself more curious than intimidated. "What . . . that is, what am I meant to do now?"

"Well, that depends. In the strictest sense, you are not *meant* to do anything, other than to enhance your knowledge in whatever way you and I deem best."

He blinked. "I do not understand."

"Come, sit with me." She waved him over to a table at the edge of the room, and moved to sit in a chair beside it. He took the one opposite her as she shifted the books between them so they could see each other.

"Do you know what you mean to do when you have completed your training here, Ebon?"

Ebon considered it for a moment, and then he shook his head. "I have never thought of it. Until two days ago, I never thought to set foot in the Academy at all. My father had long forbid it. Now it seems that all I can do is try to keep up."

"And you should. I have no doubt that that will consume much of your effort, especially at first. But you must begin to think upon this question at once, for its answer is the entire purpose of your study within the library." Jia leaned forwards, her gaze holding his. "Except for a very few, who stay to become instructors in turn, every wizard who studies here will go on to do something else in Underrealm. Some will serve as advisors in the courts of royalty or merchants. This is especially true of the commoners whose training is sponsored by a noble. Others will wander the countryside, using their spells for the benefit of the common folk. In either case, a wizard's purpose is to serve the nine lands. And therefore, the greater their knowledge, the better for all the kingdoms."

Ebon had never thought of this—not that he had had much cause to, never having been allowed to meet another wizard. "You make it sound like a great burden."

"It is a high responsibility—and one that not every wizard takes seriously. I hope that you will, Ebon."

"But I still do not understand, Instructor. What shall I study here?"

She leaned back in her chair, spreading her hands. "Whatever you think will serve you best, in whatever capacity you think you will find yourself after the Academy."

Ebon shook his head. "I have told you, I do not know what I shall do then."

"Well then, mayhap that should be your first goal: to decide. Do you have any interests already?"

Ebon looked away, studying his fingernails. He cleared his throat quietly. "Not any in particular."

Jia gave him a wry smile. "Your eyes give lie to your words, transmuter. Come now. What do you enjoy reading about? Many here enjoy herbs and healing. Others are interested in husbandry and the growing of crops. All are excellent areas of study, if you mean to travel about the nine lands and help others. So?"

Still he felt embarrassed. Throughout his life, a great many things had brought the sharp words and sneers of his father. But the sharpest and the cruelest were often in response to this love of Ebon's, which he had long since learned to keep well-hidden.

He spoke quietly, still uncertain. "I have often . . . that is, I would sometimes find myself reading a book of history. I enjoy tales of the past, of kings and the like who have long since died. Sometimes I would read of armies and battles, the rise and fall of kingdoms. I do not know why, but such tales always—they seemed to call to me."

At first Jia did not answer him. He felt sure she must be smirking at him. But when at last he raised his eyes to look at her, he saw a small but warm smile tugging at the corners of her mouth.

"That is a fine pursuit," she said. "The wisdom of the past can be of great help to us in the present, and lets us create better times to come."

Ebon smiled despite himself and turned away bashfully. "My father called it stupid. He said only fools spent their days living in the past."

"Your father sounds like the greater fool to me," she said snippily.

Though he had not spoken the words himself, still Ebon felt a little thrill, as though he and Jia had done some petty misdeed together. They shared a brief smile before Jia went on.

"I think you will find many helpful volumes here. After all, every book is history, if only it manages to survive the ravages of time for long enough. The older books are kept on the third level, as are the histories compiled by more modern scholars. Take that staircase just there, and then follow the walkway around to the southern wall. I will give you the name of a few volumes you may find helpful. Some are good to read all on their own. But you should start with one that may point you in the right direction. Read it first, and I think you will find yourself drawn towards others that may interest you."

She took a small scrap of parchment and scribbled at it with a quill from the table. After a moment she handed the scrap over to Ebon. The first title was underlined, and he read it aloud.

"*A Treatise on the Great Families of the Nine Lands, Their Origins and Lineage*. What is it?"

Her eyes sparkled as she regarded him. "The beginning of a great journey through the last many centuries, if I guess right."

TWELVE

WORDLESSLY HE STOOD AND MADE HIS WAY TO THE STAIRCASE SHE HAD shown him. It was wrought in iron and turned in a circle, one even tighter than the staircase from the Academy's first floor up to the dormitories. It ended at the second floor, and another nearby staircase led to the third.

On the third floor, the railing was eight paces away. He went to it to look over. His hands gripped the railing tightly, and he found it hard to breathe. He must have been at least fifteen paces in the air, mayhap twenty. The figures walking about the first level were now tiny; he could hide them with his thumb. His chest tightened as he turned away, moving closer to the wall.

The south end, Jia had said. He went there quickly, keeping his gaze from the railing. Soon he had reached it, and he scanned the shelves. Every book there was bound in leather, and they were of all colors and sizes. On the parchment, beside the title, Jia had scrawled the words: *Second shelf, third down. Red.*

He found the second bookcase, which had seven shelves. The third down was filled with many tomes, several of them red—but none of the titles scrawled upon the spines matched the one he had been sent to find. Puzzled, he looked at the parchment again. He had not misread it. The book was not there. There was one hole in the shelf, a space where a book might be, but nothing more.

Mayhap Jia had misremembered where the book was. Or mayhap it had been moved. He glanced at the other shelves quickly, but none of them held his prize. Then he moved to the next bookcase, and the next. Mayhap he had missed it. He went back and forth across all of them, finding every red book and reading the title carefully to ensure he had not made a mistake. Then he looked at the other colored books, too. Still nothing.

He ground his teeth. Mayhap he should find another title. But no, she had been very clear about where he should begin. He wondered for a moment if the missing book was some cruel joke by Lilith. He looked about, but he could not see her anywhere.

But his wandering eye did catch on something. At one of the tables, another student sat deeply engrossed in a tome. A stack of other books sat by the boy's left hand, and at the bottom of the stack was a red book. Ebon took a step closer. There, glistening with gold foil that had been worn off in places, he read the title: *A Treatise on the Great Families of the Nine Lands, Their Origins and Lineage.*

Ebon took another tentative step forwards. He tried to lean over, to place himself in the boy's field of vision. But the boy did not move. Another step. Still the boy read on, his nose only a few fingers from his book. He could not have seen more than fourteen years. His eyes, now squinting as he read, were close together, and his hair shone with a copper tint in the light of the lamps that hung on the library walls.

Though he felt at a loss for a moment, Ebon quickly chastised himself. The boy was just that—a boy, at least two years younger than Ebon was. All his attention was focused on his book, except when his eyes darted to the side to take notes with a quill. He was not even reading the book that Ebon needed.

"*Ahem!*"

He cleared his throat far louder than he had intended. Every student within ten paces jumped in their seats and turned to him with glares.

"Sorry! I am sorry!" he whispered, trying to reinforce the apology by waving his hands.

Slowly they turned back to their books. All but the boy with copper hair. Now at last he was looking up at Ebon. His blue eyes were wider than Ebon had at first realized, and now they seemed to take up the larger part of his face. His head was cocked to the side slightly, button nose reminding Ebon strangely of his sister Albi's, though otherwise the two of them could not have looked more different.

Ebon stepped still closer. Now he was at the table, standing above the boy. "I was told to read this book by instructor Jia," he said in a whisper. "Will you need it for much longer?"

The boy's gaze dropped to the book. "Yes," he said, and resumed his reading. His quill darted across the parchment.

Ebon stood stock still for a moment, unsure how to respond. At last he pulled out the chair opposite the boy and sat down. That drew the boy's attention again.

"I am sorry—mayhap I did not speak clearly. Jia told me to read the book. Might I use it—at least until you require it again?"

The boy blinked his blue eyes twice in quick succession, and then his brow furrowed. Again he looked at the book, as though he was hearing Ebon's words now for the first time. "Wait. You say that Jia told you to read it? It is a tome of history."

"I know," said Ebon. "I told her that was what I wished to read, and she pointed me this way."

The boy's eyes shot wide. "You asked to study history? Sky above, I cannot remember meeting another student who found it interesting." Then he drew back, looking suspicious. "Is this a jest? Are you playing some joke?"

"It is no jest," said Ebon, taken aback. "Why—why would it be?"

The boy sighed and shook his head. "Because older children always play jokes on me. And this is a beginner's tome. You are older than I am. Certainly you must have studied beyond it by now."

Ebon spread his hands. "I have not. I swear it. May I please borrow it? You may come and fetch me when you need it back."

Once again those blue eyes widened, and the boy leaned forwards, though his whisper only grew louder. "You *are* a beginner. How can that be? How old are you? I would guess at least sixteen."

Quickly Ebon darted a look over his shoulder, but no one had taken any notice. "Do you need to shout it?"

The boy only gave a little smile. "That settles it—certainly you are new here. Well, you are in luck, friend. I have read the treatise through and through, more times than I have kept count of. Jia told you, I imagine, that it is meant to point you to something else you might care to read?"

"She mentioned something of that sort. Why?"

The boy grinned. "Because I can tell you already what you should read instead—you will enjoy it far more, if you have any sense at all, which I suspect you do. It is a history of the Wizard Kings."

The room seemed to grow darker for a moment. Ebon felt the urge to look behind him again, but he fought it away. Even saying such words felt like a crime. "Do you mean this place has books about them?"

"I am not sure if it is even supposed to be here." The boy leaned forwards, his thin forearms pressing down into the book on his lap. "I found it one day, searching for something else entirely. It bears no title, either on its spine or its cover. I think the library's attendants simply missed it."

A secret book, possibly against the rules. Ebon found himself yearning to read it. He stuck out a hand across the table. "Then show me. I am Ebon, by the way."

"Kalem, of the family Konnel," said the boy. He reached out to grasp Ebon's wrist. "Come. I have hidden it away, to keep it from being found."

They stood, the red book forgotten. Kalem took his hand and dragged him away, down the walkway and around to the other side of the library. But he stepped far too close to the railing for Ebon's liking, and Ebon drew back.

Kalem blinked at him. "What is it?"

Ebon eyed the railing distrustfully. "I do not enjoy heights."

He thought the boy might laugh at him, but Kalem only gave a solemn nod. "I did not either. Then I spent three years on this floor of the library. The feeling shall pass in time, but for now we will walk closer to the wall."

So they did, until they reached the other end of the floor. There on the northern wall, Ebon found to his surprise that there were two passages leading into the granite. Kalem took him through and into a room that mirrored the library on the other side—just as wide, just as long, but with only a single floor below it. He realized that this second part of the library must extend back into the citadel quite a ways, until it butted up against the back walls of the dormitories.

"It is even bigger than I thought," breathed Ebon.

Kalem grinned back at him. "You had not seen this yet? Is it your first day?"

"My second," said Ebon. "How could so many books have ever been written? It must have taken a thousand scribes a thousand years."

"I do not doubt it," said Kalem. "Come."

There were far fewer people in this part of the library, and Ebon saw none at all on the same floor as them—all the students he could see were on the floor below. The lamps were less well-tended, and there was no amber skylight to fill the place with a warm glow, so that they passed from light to shadow and back again. In the farthest, darkest corner of the library, Kalem stopped at last.

"No doubt you received some training wherever you came from," said Kalem. "You can come here and do this any time you like. Only remember where it is."

So saying, he went to the narrow space between two bookshelves where the granite wall showed through. Placing his hands to the wall, he concentrated for a moment. From behind him, Ebon saw the glow of his eyes. Under Kalem's fingers, the stone shifted, turning liquid and sliding aside. When he took his hands away, a perfect hole, like a shelf, had appeared in the rock. Upon that shelf sat a book bound in blue leather. With careful, reverent hands, Kalem reached in to withdraw it.

"Here it is," he said. *"An Account of the Dark War and the Fearless Decree."*

Ebon shuddered as though an icy draft had blown down his back. "You say you found this shelf? How did you know it was there?"

Kalem shook his head quickly. "I found the book in the library. I made the shelf myself. It is no great feat, only you must remember to shift the stone back so that it does not crumble."

Ebon turned his gaze away. "I . . . I am untrained. My father never wanted me to learn magic. He only sent me here after my aunt convinced him."

Kalem's blue eyes widened and glistened in the lamp light. It shocked Ebon how expressive the boy's eyes could be, reacting often to even innocuous statements. "That is a great sorrow. Magic is a gift, and not one to be cast lightly aside. But come. You are here now, and have much interesting reading to do."

He led Ebon to a corner where a small table waited with two plush red chairs beside it. Ebon risked a look around before they sat, but still no students were in sight on their floor. Kalem saw his look, and his copper brows drew close together.

"Why do you keep looking about? No one is here to see us read it."

"It is not that. I only . . ." Ebon stopped. How could he tell this boy that already he was mocked for having to study with children, and he had no wish to give Lilith and her friends further cause to torment him?

But Kalem must have read something in his face, for once again he looked solemn and nodded. "I am young. You think I am a child, and do not wish to be seen with me."

"It is not that," Ebon said quickly, wishing he had been quicker to find a lie. "I . . . that is, a tome of the Wizard Kings . . ."

But Kalem waved him to silence. "Do not trouble yourself. I am well used to it by now. They placed me in a class more advanced than my years, for I learned my first transmutation lessons quickly. Now I am two years ahead. None of the other students in my class wish to spend much time with me, either. I am somewhat used to it." But despite the gentle words, Kalem avoided his gaze.

Ebon's attention caught on something else entirely, however. "Did you say you are an alchemist?"

Kalem blinked in surprise. "Are you indeed so unused to magic? Of course I am a transmuter—and you should not use the commoner's word for it, by the way. You saw me shift the stone. What else would I be?"

Ebon cursed inwardly. He should have recognized it at once, but he was unused to seeing such spells. "You and I share a gift. I am an alch—that is, a transmuter."

Kalem's mouth dropped open, his cheeks growing flush with joy. "Sky above. You are in Credell's class, then?"

"I am, sadly." Ebon shook his head and lowered his eyes.

"Sadly? What do you mean?"

Ebon shook his head and hit his hand upon the table, harder than he had meant to. "Credell seems terrified of me. He quivers too much to give me any sort of lessons. I only hope he gets over his terror long enough for me to pass beyond his class."

Kalem nodded sagely. "Ah, I see. I suffered much the same fate when I studied with him, though not so bad as you make it sound."

"Did you? Why?"

Once again the boy's cheeks flushed, and he lowered his gaze. "I imagine you must not know much of the kingdom of Hedgemond. We Konnels are of the royal family there, a smaller clan, yet still holding close to some power. You must be royalty as well if Credell is so frightened, though from your look I would guess you are from Idris. I suppose that makes us kin, though no doubt very distant?"

Ebon let that pass without correcting him. At last it seemed he had met a friendly face here, and he would do nothing to drive the boy away with the name of Drayden. And if he invited scorn by befriending Kalem, what of it? It seemed that to Lilith he was already a laughingstock, and to the other students he was someone to be avoided. Kalem's friendship could hardly hurt. "How, then, did you deal with Credell? For you said you took to your lessons quickly, or at least quickly enough that you eventually graduated his class."

Kalem did not seem to notice that Ebon had avoided his question. "I did the best I could, listened when he instructed the others, and practiced in my every spare moment. Once you pass the novice test, you will move to the second class."

"What is the novice test? No one made mention of it to me."

Kalem gawked at him. "Indeed? You must be of much higher birth than me, if Credell is that scared of you. The novice test is to turn a rod of wood into one of stone."

Now Ebon understood the wooden sticks he had seen in the hands of the other students in his class. "Turning wood to stone? Is that possible?"

"Have you really never seen such magic?" The boy smirked, but quickly hid it. "I am sorry. I cannot imagine what it must have been like for you, being so sternly kept away from what should have been a great joy."

"My father thought magic was . . . unseemly."

Kalem drew back and narrowed his eyes. "Are you—are you, by some chance, your father's eldest child?"

Ebon felt he had drifted upon some dangerous ground, but he did not know what it was. "I am. I had an older brother, but he was killed."

"You are the heir, then? The next head of your family?"

He swallowed hard, wondering how long he could maintain the deception of being royalty. "I am my father's successor, yes."

"Do you think your father meant to keep your talents hidden, and try to put you upon the throne?"

Ebon blanched. "No one would try to put a wizard upon a throne. That would invite the High King's wrath. You know this."

"I do," said Kalem, looking at his fingers where they toyed with each other in his lap. "Yet I have heard rumors that some have tried it. Always they are found and put to death, by the Mystics and the King's law both. Yet still some try."

"That was not my father's aim, I promise you. He would sooner see me in exile than holding any power, I think."

Kalem looked at him. "I am relieved to hear it, though it is a sad thing indeed. My father never had to worry about such—my sister waits to take his place at the head of the family, and I have two older brothers besides. Also, we are far removed from the line of succession to Hedgemond's throne. Sometimes I think my father scarcely notices me. And he is . . ."

He blushed and looked down. Ebon leaned forwards. "What is it? You may tell me."

The boy was silent a moment. "He is more concerned with our coin than with me, I think. We do not have the wealth we once did, and sometimes I have heard him and my mother speaking of what they might have to do if our coffers should run dry. I sometimes wonder if they will be able to keep paying for my teachings here. I do not know what I would do if they could not."

Pity flowed through Ebon, much to his surprise. Of all the many causes for concern his family had often given him, worry of their wealth was not one of them. It seemed that the Drayden accounts were bottomless. And with that thought, he had a flash of inspiration. He turned his chair to face Kalem and leaned forwards intently.

"Then let me make you this bargain, Kalem of the family Konnel. I will learn nothing while I am under Credell's tutelage. So you shall teach me instead. If you do, I shall give you a portion of my allowance. You can save it, and if your family cannot pay for your schooling, you will do it yourself."

Kalem looked at him, eyes shining. "You would do this? Why?"

Ebon shrugged. "Coin is of little concern to us. I am much more worried about how fast I shall learn my spells. It seems that each of us may solve the other's problem. What do you say? Is the bargain struck?"

Kalem grinned and thrust forth a hand. "It is."

Ebon shook his wrist. "Done, then. And I propose that we celebrate our pact. Let me take you out upon the Seat tonight, and we shall toast our bargain until we cannot see to find our way home."

The boy's smile vanished, and his eyes grew wide. "Do . . . do you mean to say we shall *drink?*"

Ebon smiled. "As an alchemist you may be the master, but it seems I have much to teach you as well."

THIRTEEN

They left the library the moment the bell rang. Ebon greatly wished for better clothes to wear out, but neither of them had anything grander than their simple black robes. But on the other hand, that meant there was no delay before their departure. He half thought that if Kalem were given any chance at all, the boy would turn tail and run as fast as he could.

"It is only that I have never had wine or ale before," Kalem said, as Ebon practically shoved him through the Academy's front door and into the street. "My mother and father viewed drinking much the same way your father, it seems, viewed magic."

"Then they are all wrong, though for different reasons," said Ebon. "There is much joy, and mayhap even some wisdom, to be found in the bottom of a cup, as you will soon learn. But we should find a place as far from the Academy as we can, so long as we can still find our way back."

They were not the only ones leaving the Academy. All around them, students in black robes flooded the streets, all of them seeming to have the same intent as Ebon: to forget the day's lessons and worries with the bounties of grape and grain. Ebon saw many taverns as they walked, but black-robed students entered all of them, and so he passed them by. Soon the streets thinned out, except for the Seat's usual crowds: tradesmen bringing their wares home for the day, and merchants and the nobility traveling here and there to attend parties and balls. It was a chillier day than the one before, and as the sun lowered, a brisk breeze snapped at their ears. Ebon put his hands in the pockets of his robes to warm them.

He found he was much more comfortable than the last time he had walked upon the Seat, when Tamen had been at his side and he had worried that any misdeed might be carried straight to the ears of his father. Now he spun as he walked, looking all about him at the buildings. Some were tall and mighty, and others were small and modest, but all felt warm and comfortable.

"The Seat is nothing like back home," he said, only half speaking to Kalem. "Even in the capital, all the buildings are made of white plaster, and they glare in the sun until they hurt the eyes. Everyone wears veils to protect themselves. Only the king's palace is different—lavish, built from stone and steel, and shining with gold spires and great domes. It is a pretty enough sight, I suppose. But I prefer the Seat."

"I still miss home," Kalem said quietly. "Our king rules from Highfell, and that is certainly no place so mighty as the Seat. Yet though the buildings are simpler, they seem more welcoming, and though the palace is nowhere near so grand as the High King's, still my breath was stripped away when I first beheld it."

Ebon looked at him in surprise. The boy spoke with surprising passion. Ebon wondered what it was like to be homesick—truly homesick, not like his earlier vague desire to flee the Academy back to Idris. He imagined yearning for the place from which you hailed, rather than for a few people whose company you enjoyed there.

They had not seen a black robe on the last many streets, and so Ebon cast his eyes about for a tavern. Soon he found one, a place with no door barring its entry and a wide window in the wall. He thought, with a flutter in his stomach, of the window through which he had spied a blue door. Had that really only been a few days ago? It seemed a lifetime. Well he remembered that place, far to the west of here, and in the back of his mind he decided that he might visit it again, if the chance arose. Had not Adara told him that she hoped he would return? They were the words of a lover, and mayhap spurred by coin. Yet now he could find out for himself.

But he drew his mind back to the here and now as he pulled Kalem towards the inn. "Come, we shall drink here. It seems a fine place—and just near enough that we shall not have trouble finding our way home."

"Are you certain?" said Kalem, looking up at the sky. "Already the day nears darkness."

"Then we shall walk home in torchlight. Come."

They stepped in through the door. Ebon was gratified to see that no one gave them a second glance. He still feared that Kalem might try to escape, so he kept his hand on the boy's arm on their way to the bar at the back of the tavern. There a stout man with great growths of brown hair on his cheeks surveyed them with a keen eye. His thick nose was red, and he wore an air that said he could be friendly enough, but would brook no disturbance of his domain. Ebon had seen it in many barkeeps over the years.

"Academy whelps," he said. "And not ones I have seen before."

Ebon felt a moment's trepidation. "Is our coin less welcome here than another's would be?"

The man shook his head. "Coin is coin. Only that boy with you looks a bit young."

"I will care for him," said Ebon, reaching into the purse at his belt. "And coin is coin, as you say."

He flipped a weight into the air, and the man caught it easily. His eyebrows raised slightly, and he bit down on the gold. "So it is, young master. They call me Leven, and I am at your service."

"Then let us have some wine, Leven; and make it something fine, from Calentin, but no cinnamon, if you please. I am Ebon, and my friend here is Kalem. I do not think we will drink enough for that weight tonight—but I ask that you do your best to help us try. If you do, I shall bring more of them."

Leven nodded and turned to fetch a flagon from a shelf. This he gave to Ebon, as well as two goblets of pewter—finer things than the wooden cups held by most of the tavern's other patrons. Ebon nodded his thanks and shoved his way back into the crowd, seeking an empty table.

Kalem was gawking at him. "A whole gold weight? That must be fine drink indeed."

"Not so fine as the price I paid," said Ebon. "But here is your first lesson of taverns, Kalem: pay the proprietor well when you can, and better than you should. If they are of a good sort, they will remember it when your purse weighs less. Now help me find a table—it is dim in here."

The boy gulped and nodded. At last Ebon spotted one in the corner—a low table, with benches set to either side of it, and both of them shrouded in darkness. It was perfect. Even if another student from the Academy were to come, he doubted they would see Ebon or Kalem sitting in the shadows.

"Here, Kalem. This will do nicely—ulp!" Ebon shot up in the middle of sitting down, for his rear end had struck someone.

"What do you want?" snapped a voice. Ebon peered closer, and saw bright eyes peering at him out of the darkness. He had guessed right about the shadows—the girl had been invisible, so complete was her concealment. Then he leaned closer, and saw that there was still another reason for it: as well as her walnut-dark skin, she wore the same black robes as Ebon and Kalem and had her hood up. Another student from the Academy.

"I—er, that is, I did not mean . . ."

The girl only stared at him, and to his relief Ebon did not think he saw much rancor in her eyes. "Did not mean to place your fat rear upon me? I should hope not."

Ebon swallowed. "I—we can find another table."

She studied him for a moment. Beneath the hood, her hair was the color of sun-dried wheat, but he could see that it was dyed that color, and cut in a short bob. Her light eyes were sharp, peering at him over a thin nose. Slowly those eyes turned downwards, spying the flagon in his hand.

"You could sit elsewhere. But then how could two whelps like you hope to drink all that wine?"

Ebon looked to his right. Kalem's eyes were fixed on the girl. Hoping her words were an invitation, Ebon nudged Kalem to take a seat on the other bench, and then slid in to sit beside him. The girl had a wooden cup before her, and Ebon carefully filled it before doing the same to the pewter goblets. Once the drinks were poured, he raised his and poked Kalem to do the same.

"To the hospitality of strangers in taverns," he said.

The girl neither answered nor raised her cup. Instead she threw the wine back in one long pull and clapped the empty cup down onto the table. Ebon hastened to follow her, but he could only drink half his goblet at once. Kalem seemed to have forgotten he was supposed to drink his at all.

The girl closed her eyes, running a tongue across her lips. "Sky above, that is fine stuff." Her eyes snapped back open, narrowing at them. "Fine indeed. The two of you are goldbags, then?"

Ebon balked. Mako, his aunt's guard, had used the same word, but he had never heard it before that, and had not wanted to ask the man for its meaning. But beside him Kalem blushed and ducked his head.

"We do not use that word where I come from," said Ebon, feeling the need to bolster the boy. "It does not sound very polite."

"That it is not," said the girl. She reached for the flagon and poured herself another cup, draining it in another long swallow. Ebon expected her to explain further, but she spoke no word. Kalem still had not touched his goblet. Ebon nudged him, and the boy took a tentative sip. His eyes widened, and he looked to Ebon.

"That . . . that tastes wonderful," he said.

The girl arched an eyebrow. "And this one is a goldbag whelp."

Ebon found his hackles rising, but he tried to stay calm. "If you intend to keep calling us that, at least tell me what it means."

But Kalem spoke before the girl could answer. "It is just what it sounds like. Goldbags—wealthy."

Ebon blinked. The girl leaned forwards, smiling at him, but not very kindly. "Wealthy, eh? I suppose some would put it that way. Some others would say greedy. Sitting in your palaces and manors, hoarding your gold. What do you lot do with all that coin, anyway?"

He held her gaze. "Just now, we pay for you to drink a fine Calentin wine."

She stared, and Ebon feared she might strike him—either with her first, or with magic, he was not sure, and did not know which would be worse. But then she burst out laughing and leaned back against the wall behind her.

"Fairly spoken, and more well-mannered than I have been. Never let it be said that only your kind are polite. I am Theren."

Ebon noted carefully that she did not give a family name, but he did not think it wise to ask why—he thought he could guess. "I am Ebon," he said, leaning forwards and extending a hand. "My friend is Kalem."

"Of the family Konnel," Kalem piped up. Ebon winced. Already the girl seemed irritated at their status. It seemed unwise to dangle their parentage before her eyes.

Sure enough, she sneered. "Oh, sky above, a *royal* goldbag." But when Kalem flushed and looked back towards his lap, she snickered. "Come now, child, I mean nothing by it. Goldbags are all alike to me—I think only you lot hold royalty in higher regard than the rest of us."

"You are a student, I can see," said Ebon, hoping to move the conversation onwards.

"As are you."

"Of what branch? And what year?"

"Inquisitive, are we? A mentalist, seventh year."

Ebon glanced at Kalem, and saw the boy looking at Theren with the same awe Ebon was certain must show in his own face. "You are nearly finished with your training, then?"

Theren shrugged. "Mayhap. They have not found a spell to teach me that I could not master. As long as they keep trying, I will keep learning, I suppose."

Ebon thought of the words he had had with Jia earlier. "And then? What will you do after? Surely your patron must be eager to have you back."

Her lip curled, and he knew he had made a mistake. "Of course you would assume I have a patron," she said. "But then again, a goldbag *would* think that a common girl could not be at the Academy without the help of some wealthy lord."

"I meant no offense." He did not break her gaze, hoping she could see his earnestness. "I am unused to the Seat, and unused to the Academy especially. It seems I have much to learn before I can even speak without making a fool of myself."

Her glower softened, and she turned away. "It seems so. And besides, you speak true. I have a patron, though I do not relish it. Not all of us have it so easy as you two, no doubt sent here with a mountain of your parents' coin to waste. Though I cannot complain at how you choose to waste it." She lifted her cup for emphasis, and then reached for the flagon again.

Ebon shrugged. "My family was not my choice, I assure you of that. Each life comes with its own struggles, and ours are no exception." She snorted. He ignored it, though it rankled him. "But if I am not fond of where my coin comes from, and if you and I both appreciate good wine, then help me waste it, I say."

She wagged a finger at him. "Now at last you speak wisdom. I suppose you are not so bad as all that—for a goldbag, at any rate. But if you mean what you say about being wasteful, we shall need another two flagons at least."

Wordlessly, Ebon reached for his purse and produced another gold weight. She rose and took it, studying it in the lantern light for a moment. Then she looked up at him once more.

"Very well, Ebon," she said. Ebon did not miss the fact it was the first time she had used his name. "Can you find it in you to forgive words harshly spoken? And you as well, Kalem?"

"Can you find it in you to get the damned wine?" said Ebon, smiling at her. "The flagon is nearly empty, and we do not have all night to drink."

Theren left them with a laugh. Ebon turned his smile on Kalem.

"I think I like her," said Ebon. Kalem did not speak a word, his eyes fixed on Theren from across the room. Ebon shoved his shoulder. "Leave off, little *goldbag*. If you stare any harder, your eyes may melt. Or mayhap she will melt them for you—can a mindmage do that?"

That shook Kalem from his reverie, and he glared at Ebon. "A *mentalist*, Ebon, honestly. And no, she could not—though I could, if I learned the spell to shift living flesh."

"You can turn stone and not flesh?" said Ebon in surprise. "But stone is so much stronger."

"Yes, and simpler. That is the key. Stone is much the same through and through. But our bodies are made up of so much—water, they say, and fire, and . . . well, flesh. That is why you are set to work upon a wooden rod. Wood, and all plants, are somewhere in between flesh and stone. It is easier to turn something complex into something simple than the other way around."

Ebon felt as though his head was spinning. "I fear I do not understand."

Kalem leaned forwards, eyes sparking with interest. Ebon had a feeling that the boy did not often get the chance to speak of such things with someone who cared to listen. "There are hierarchies, you see. Stone is one of the simplest, then wood, then flesh, to speak broadly. To turn wood to stone is easy. Flesh to stone is harder, but still easy for any second-year transmuter. Flesh to wood is harder still. Then stone to wood, stone to flesh, and wood to flesh. And then there is *shifting*. That is when you do not simply *turn* matter—you melt it, or turn it to mist, or make it vanish entirely. That is ... not *easier,* perhaps, but different, in a way many find easier to grasp. Do you see?"

Ebon did not see. In fact, Kalem had said *stone* and *wood* and *flesh* so many times that, together with the wine, Ebon was having difficulty remembering which word meant what. But just then, three black-robed figures strode through the tavern door, and Ebon's heart quailed as he recognized Lilith and her cronies.

Quickly he turned his head to the side, trying to hide his face.

"Shift yourself over," he said quietly. "Sink into the shadows."

Kalem blinked at him. "What? Why? What is it?"

"Those three who just entered, they are—"

"Is that my jester?"

Ebon groaned and looked up. Lilith wore a smile as she approached his table, standing there at the end of the bench so he could not rise without pushing her out of the way. Her companions stood behind her, still silent, arms folded as they looked down at him.

"Leave us be, Lilith," said Ebon. "What are you doing here, anyway?"

"I came seeking another, but now I think it would amuse me to drink with you instead. And may I remark how adorable it is to see you beyond the Academy walls with one of your classmates. He must be a first-year."

"I am not," said Kalem at once. "You have seen me before. I am in the—"

"Quiet, child," snapped Lilith, before turning her gaze back on Ebon. "I learned something of you today, jester. Do you want to know what it was?"

Ebon felt the blood drain from his face. He knew, or thought he could guess, what she was about to say. He had to distract her. "You know that if you fight me, neither of us will be welcome within the Academy again."

Lilith laughed at him, and turned to her friends. "Oren, Nella, did you hear that? My jester is worried for me. How kind of him to think of my education. But why would I fight you, little jester? You did not let me tell you what I had learned about you—Ebon, of the family Drayden."

Ebon glared at her. From the corner of his eye, he could see Kalem looking at him with wide eyes.

She smiled at Ebon's expression. "Yes, it was quite a shock. But I suppose it makes sense. A worthless student from a worthless family. Why did they send you away, jester? Had they run out of water for you to lick up from the ground?"

Before he knew what he was doing, Ebon shot to his feet, but Nella, the girl by Lilith's side, shoved him back down onto his bench. He tried to rise again, but found himself unable to move. His muscles strained against some unseen barrier. With wide eyes he looked down, but there was nothing there. Then he saw Oren's eyes glowing white, and he realized: this was magic.

Lilith leaned down, one hand resting on the table so that her face was only a few fingers from his. "What is wrong, water licker? Did no one ever teach you to deal with a *real* wizard?"

Ebon held her gaze, letting his hatred show. But then he saw movement over her shoulder: Theren, returning with two new flagons of wine. She stopped just behind Oren and Nella and glared. Then her eyes glowed white.

Lilith cried out as her foot shot up into the air behind her. Her head bounced off the table on the way down as she was lifted up.

The glow died in Oren's eyes as he turned in shock. An invisible force struck him in the chest, and he fell back against the wall. Nella spun in midair and fell next to him, and Ebon saw her grunting and straining against some hidden force.

Lilith's bonds slackened, and she crashed to the tavern's wooden floor. At once she shot to her feet, hands twisting before her as her eyes began to glow—but then she saw Theren and stopped. For a moment, all was still.

Then Leven the tavern-master was there, pushing himself into the space between Theren and Lilith, barrel chest blocking each of them from the other's view as he thrust his arms in either direction.

"All right, you lot have had your fun. No spell-casting is allowed in my barroom, as *you* know full well." He thrust a finger just under Theren's nose.

She smirked at him. "What spell-casting? The moment they saw me, they grew frightened and fell to the floor."

Lilith pushed forwards, but with a hand on her chest Leven stopped her. "That is enough. Leave here now, and mayhap I shall not send a letter to your masters."

The Yerrin girl glared at him, and then at Theren, but Theren's smirk only widened. With a huff, Lilith whirled and strode from the tavern—but not before she gave Ebon one last look of hate. Nella helped Oren to his feet, and they scuttled out the door after her.

The tavern had grown quiet as the fight broke out, but now slowly the other patrons turned back to their drinks and resumed talking. Leven watched as Lilith and the others left, and then turned his considerable girth on Theren, hands bunched to fists on his hips.

"You swore to me you would not begin another wizard's duel here."

Theren still held a flagon in either hand, but she swept one foot behind the other to dip in a low bow. "And it gives me great pleasure to have kept my vow. I did not begin a duel at all. In fact, to my mind, I ended one."

Leven shook his head. "I mean it, girl. I will not have you breaking more tables—not to mention my finest bottles."

Theren straightened and wiggled the flagons before his eyes. "Even if I have a new friend, who is willing to pay handsomely for such fine bottles?"

The alemaster shook his head, and his scowl weakened somewhat. But his voice remained stern. "Just remember: become more trouble than you are worth, and you will no longer be welcome here."

She stepped past him, planting a brief kiss on his cheek. "You have the heart of a king, Leven." But Ebon noted that that was no answer.

Leven walked away, and Theren resumed her seat across the table. She pushed one flagon towards Ebon and took a long pull directly from the other. "Well. It seems I misjudged you. If Lilith dislikes you so, you must be very nearly honorable—at least for goldbags."

Ebon shrugged. But Kalem had ducked his gaze, and at Theren's words he made to stand. "I should be returning to the Academy," the boy mumbled. "It is very late."

"Kalem, sit down," Ebon urged him. "Please. I am sorry, for I dealt with you dishonestly, though I did not lie."

Theren arched a thin eyebrow. "Oh? Dissent among the ranks?"

Ebon sighed and fixed her with a look. "I shall tell you as well, I suppose, since I would rather not anger you later, with your command of magic. I failed to mention my family's name earlier. But I am Ebon, of the family Drayden, and I hail from the capital of Idris."

Theren became very still, except for her fingers, which drummed on the neck of her wine flagon: *tap-tap. Tap-tap.*

"I am sorry," said Ebon, lowering his gaze now. "Only . . . only that name has plagued me all my life, and it seems that everyone I meet hates me because I carry it. I thought that here, where we all wear the same black robes, mayhap I could leave it behind. Yet I cannot. Lilith will not let me—and now, it seems, neither will the two of you. I should not have come here tonight." He made to stand.

"Oh, sit down," said Theren, eyes rolling. "Honestly, you wealthy ones are so prone to dramatics."

Ebon hesitated. Looking back, he saw Kalem still gazing at his own lap. After a long moment of silence, the boy finally looked up at him. "I thought you were royalty, like me."

"I am not," said Ebon. "Would you have befriended me, if you knew? I have not had a friend in many a long year. Forgive me, for I saw a chance at finding one, but I should not have lied to make it come true."

For a moment Kalem looked out the window, to the street where constables were just now coming around to light the street lamps. His hands twisted in his lap. "I suppose I can understand that," he said quietly.

Theren took Ebon's goblet and handed it to him. "Drayden or not, and whether you summon it by gold or by alchemy—only keep the wine coming, and you will have my friendship."

Ebon smirked, and he saw Kalem give a little smile. He took his seat, and together they raised their cups to drink deep.

FOURTEEN

WHEN HE WENT TO BREAK HIS FAST THE NEXT MORNING, EBON SAT at an empty table as he had done before. But soon, to his slight surprise, Theren came and sat wordlessly on the bench beside him. After a moment, Kalem sat on his other side. Theren looked none the worse for wear, but Kalem held a hand pressed hard over his blue eyes, and his coppery hair was greasy, as though he had yet to bathe.

"Why?" he muttered as he sat with them. "Why does it hurt so?"

Ebon smiled. "You have found the sweet pain of wine, my young friend. I fear that I did not watch you as closely as I should have. You drank too much for your own good."

Kalem peered at him from between his fingers. "Is it always like this? Do dragons scream within your head as well?"

"They do not, but then I do not think I drank so much as you," said Ebon diplomatically.

"You had more, and so did I," said Theren, missing his attempt at kindness—or mayhap not caring. "But we can hold our wine."

"Do not say that word," said Kalem, quickly pressing a hand to his mouth. "The very sound of it makes me want to vomit."

Ebon clapped him on the back, and the boy winced. "You should be proud you have not done that already."

"I have. Twice."

Theren had finished her food shockingly fast, and now she shoved the heel of her bread into Ebon's bowl to soak up some of his broth. "It occurs to me that after last night's fisticuffs, which I rather enjoyed, our conversation did not range so far as it might have. We seemed more interested in wine than words."

"Please, do not say that word."

Theren ignored him. "What did you do to invite Lilith's wrath, Ebon?"

Ebon shrugged, though secretly he was pleased that she no longer called him 'goldbag.' "I only met her the day before last. She seemed to hate me from the start, though as you heard, she did not learn my family's name until yesterday. Mayhap she only meant to mock me at first, because I . . . that is, I am . . ."

Theren frowned. "What is it? Come, spit it out."

Kalem looked at her, lips twisting. "He is untrained. His father never let him study magic."

Theren stared. "You cannot be serious."

"I wish I were not."

Theren's eyes glowed as she twisted a finger, and the empty bowl before her lifted up until it was standing on one edge. Spinning her finger in little circles, she sent it twirling on the spot, until it was only a blur before her. Ebon did not know if she did it to torment him, or only because her mind was working, but he wished she would stop it. "You mean to say that you cannot do even the simplest of magic? How did you learn you were an alchemist, then?"

"Transmuter," said Kalem.

"Wine," said Theren. Kalem groaned.

"I did the testing spell when I was a child," said Ebon. "But the moment my father learned the truth, he forbade me from ever trying it again. My valet was required to report it if I was ever seen trying a spell. I managed the testing spell again only two days ago, but when I tried it yesterday, it did not work."

"What did Credell say when you told him?" said Kalem.

Ebon stabbed his spoon into his soup, making some of it splash out on the table. "It was hard to tell around all of his gibbering. He is more frightened of me than he would be of a viper in his bed. At this rate I shall never be an alchemist."

Theren snorted. "Poor little goldbag. You know, do you not, that some of us do not have a family name to help us in our training here?"

He glared at her. "My name has not helped me at all. If anything, it has made things worse."

She dismissed him with a wave. "Spare me. The dean is a Drayden, and no doubt some distant cousin of yours." Then the glow faded from her eyes, and she leaned forwards with interest. Her bowl stopped spinning, and her voice dropped to a conspiratorial whisper. "Say. You could appeal to him for special permissions. We could leave the Academy after hours if we wanted. Mayhap you could have him speak to my instructor to teach me higher spells."

"You misunderstand his view of me," said Ebon. "He only sees me at all out of pompous vanity and some small sense of duty to my aunt. And his visit made Credell's treatment of me all the more difficult to bear."

Theren glared at him. "Poor little goldbag," she said again. She leaned back, her eyes glowed, and her spoon flew into her bowl with a little *clunk*.

Kalem watched her spells with a little pout. "I wish I were a mentalist," he said wistfully. "Or an elementalist, even. How wonderful it must be to have such power. Transmutation often seems the weakest of the branches."

Theren shrugged. "I will not deny that my gift can be amusing."

Ebon, too, was impressed by her effortless command of her magic. And watching her lift her bowl into her hands using only her mind, he was struck by an idea. "Theren—could you teach me?"

She blinked at him, the glow in her eyes dying. "Teach you what?"

"Magic. Kalem agreed to help me learn my spells, but you are more advanced than he. Mayhap you could even help both of us."

Kalem and Theren gawked at each other before looking back to Ebon. "Sky above," Theren said quietly. "Do you honestly know *nothing* of magic?"

He felt his cheeks burning, and he ducked his head. "I have told you as much already."

"You said so, yes, but . . ." Theren chuckled. "Oh, this is rich indeed. I was determined not to pity you, Ebon, but you test my limits."

Ebon leaned away from the table, folding his arms. He knew he must look like a pouting child, but he did not care. "Stop your mockery. Tell me what I said wrong."

Kalem put a gentle hand on Ebon's arm and spoke with a slow patience that grated on his nerves. "The different branches are utterly unlike each other. Theren could no more teach you magic than a bird could teach you to fly."

"I do not understand," said Ebon, brow furrowing. "Magic is magic. Does it not all come from the same source?"

Theren shook her head sadly as Kalem went on. "Mayhap, but it becomes different by the time we are able to use it. Elementalism is chiefly cast through speech, mentalism through the eyes. Therianthropy takes place in the mind, and transmutation is cast through the hands."

"But we all envision our spells as we cast them," said Ebon.

Kalem's lips pressed together, and he looked helplessly at Theren. Again she shook her head. "Yes and no. It is . . . well, it is difficult to explain, even for me. Even, I sometimes think, for our instructors. I can tell you only that once you have attained command of your gift, it comes ever more naturally. Likely you do not remember learning to walk, but you have seen babies trying to master it. They try and try, but they cannot keep their balance. Then, one day, they are able to take their first steps. From then on, they simply . . . walk. You do it without thinking now—but could you explain it to an infant?"

"And transmutation is to mentalism as walking is to a fish's swimming," put in Kalem, "or like a bird's learning to fly."

Ebon shook his head miserably. "I still do not understand."

Kalem put a hand on his shoulder and smiled brightly. "You shall. I will do my best to teach you. Soon you shall turn wood to stone as though it were pouring wine into a goblet." His face soured. "Ugh. I may need to retch again."

Ebon sighed. "I tried that this morning. I snuck into my classroom to fetch a wooden rod." He pulled it from his robes. "Yet it is still wooden, and I cannot seem to grasp the first thing about turning it otherwise."

"You will learn it soon," said Kalem.

"I hope so," groused Ebon. "It would be nice to have a victory, even one so small. My instructor is afraid of me, the dean only makes it worse, and for some reason I cannot comprehend, a Yerrin girl has decided to make me her own personal whipping-boy. Finding I cannot use magic after all would only seem to fit the pattern."

Theren's eyes glowed, and the rod floated from his grip into the air. She spun it before her eyes as she pursed her lips. "Well, I do not envy you. Learning my first magic after the testing spell seemed to take ages. But it came easier after that." The glow died away, and she caught the rod as it fell. She leaned forwards with interest, pointing the rod at Ebon like a baton. "Say. Mayhap we can solve one of your problems, at least. You have started some quarrel with Lilith, or the quarrel has come to you regardless. How should you like to repay her for shaming you?"

"Theren," said Kalem. His voice held a tone of warning. But Ebon leaned towards her, his interest piqued.

"I do not wish to invite the instructors' wrath for fighting," he said.

"*Fighting,*" said Theren with a quick shake of her head. "Sky above, nothing so crass. Only . . . she has the best of you in magic, yes? Yet you have strengths. Your family name is stronger than hers, and your pockets are deeper. And you have me." Her teeth flashed in a grin.

"Ebon, this is a terrible idea," said Kalem.

"You have not even heard it," said Theren.

"Say on, then," said Ebon.

"Not here." Theren looked about as though someone might be listening. "But let us gather after the day's studies, and we shall see what might be done."

"Why?" said Kalem, narrowing his eyes. "Why would you help him fight Lilith?"

Theren only shrugged. "She and I have had our own tussles in the past. Surely you can imagine how a girl like her might have more than one foe."

A bell clanged, reverberating about the dining hall. "Well, let us go to our classes," said Kalem. "This afternoon I shall do my best to help you learn your spells, and mayhap you will forget all about this foolish plan of Theren's."

"Fare well," said Theren. "I shall see you this evening. And know this, Ebon: I have not forgotten my plans for you. Some day soon you will speak to the dean on our behalf." She fixed him with a stern look and turned to go.

"She left her dishes," grumbled Kalem, scooping them up from the table.

Ebon realized later that he had not the faintest idea where to find Theren after their studies. But he need not have worried. When he and Kalem left the library at the end of the day, they found Theren waiting for them in the hall just outside. She stood on one foot and leaned against the wall, arms folded, but she straightened as soon as she saw them.

"There you two are. It took you long enough. Do not tell me you are bookworms as well as goldbags. I can only forgive so many flaws."

"Theren, I have been thinking," said Kalem. "Mayhap all that is required here is a calm, measured conversation with Lilith. I am certain that she and Ebon can work out their differences if only—"

She ignored him, falling into step beside Ebon and speaking so abruptly that Kalem fell to silence. "Allow me to instruct you in the manner of your revenge. I am quite proud of this idea. It relies for its success on the general prudishness of most goldbags, and particularly those of the family Yerrin."

"Prudishness?" said Kalem.

"You royal types are so concerned with concealing yourselves. The family Yerrin have adopted the affectation as well, mayhap because they aspire to your station," explained Theren. "Any commoner in the city or the forest thinks nothing of shedding some clothing on a hot day. But you would rather sit sweating in your carriages than reveal so much as your chest. In the highest circles, I am given to believe that being caught half-naked is the height of embarrassment."

"Well, certainly!" said Kalem indignantly. "You cannot tell me you would enjoy walking about naked. Our bodies are for spouses and lov-ers."

"Spoken like a true goldbag," sneered Theren. "And so does Lilith believe."

Ebon himself was not overly fond of being seen disrobed, except when it came to servants. But he said only, "I am listening."

"You should be watching instead. Lilith will be in the common room by now."

So saying, she led them on through the halls and up the narrow staircase towards the dormitories. When they reached the door leading to his common room, Ebon balked. But Theren gripped his shoulder with an easy smile.

"Now, then. All you must do is enter the room and speak with Lilith, and I will take care of the rest."

"You want me to attract her attention?" said Ebon. "I think she dislikes me enough as it is. She will set my robe on fire, if she thinks she can get away with it."

Theren shrugged. "Mayhap. But you will not have to suffer her torments long. I promise you that."

"Why will you not come with us?" said Kalem.

Theren's eyes hardened. "Because if she sees me enter with you, she might be less inclined towards torment."

"Oh, well, that *is* reassuring," said Ebon. "You mean to use us as bait."

"Come now. You may be a goldbag, but you do not strike me as a coward. Go, brave warriors! To battle!"

She opened the door and shoved them inside before slamming it behind them. The room was filled with students, some sitting in the chairs and couches, others standing beside them. The sharp noise of the door drew every eye, and for a moment the room was filled with perfect silence.

"Er . . ." said Ebon, his cheeks flushing. "Good evening."

"The jester has arrived!" Lilith's already too-familiar voice sang out from the other end of the room. "Fellow students, our evening's entertainment is here, and not a moment too soon."

She sat in a broad leather armchair, resting upon it as though it were a throne. Oren and Nella completed the picture, standing to either side of her like attendants. At her words, every student averted their gaze. Lilith was clearly on the hunt, and none of the others wished to become prey.

"Well met, Lilith," said Ebon. He wondered if he should go to her, or if he should act as if he were going towards his dormitory. Theren wanted him to speak to Lilith, but would it not be suspicious if he did so directly?

"And you have brought another plaything," said Lilith, nodding towards Kalem. "You must promise to keep him around. Two jesters are twice the fun, after all."

With a sigh, Ebon made his way across the room to her. Until Theren made her move, they would have to keep Lilith's attention. As they drew up before her, Kalem stepped forth and offered his hand. "Er, ah . . . well met. We have not been introduced. I am Kalem, of the . . ."

"Away, whelp. I saw enough of you last night—or at least, what little there is to see." Lilith waved a hand dismissively, and Kalem stepped aside as if she had moved him with mind magic. Her eyes fixed on Ebon. "So. Here he is. The jester of the family *Drayden.*"

She said the name loud enough to be heard throughout the room. From the corner of his eye, Ebon saw that the few students brave enough to look at him quickly turned away.

"I am no jester."

"Yet I find you laughable. And what other purpose does a jester have?" She smiled at him, and then at Kalem. "The two of you are a remarkable pairing. A royal son whose family has great power, and no coin. And a merchant son whose family has great coin, but whose power wanes across the nine lands. What a sight."

"You know nothing of my family," said Ebon, surprised at the fervor in his words. Anger made his stomach clench and the back of his neck prickle. He almost did not hear the sound of a door opening behind him, and then closing again quietly as Theren snuck in.

"Who does not know of the family Drayden?" said Lilith. "So dark and terrible a clan. Yet what have you lot done lately? You sit in your desert halls, planning trade routes and scrimping your coins. How the mighty have fallen. It is said that your grandfather ruled Idris with an iron fist, the royal family serving as his puppets. Your dear aunt must not have the spine for power."

"Do not speak of her," snapped Ebon.

At Lilith's side, Oren and Nella tensed. But Lilith only smiled. "I shall speak of what I wish. After all, we are friends here, are we not? Or at least, we are young people joined in mutual endeavor. To learn our magic. How fare your studies, by the by?"

Ebon's hands balled to fists. Were it not for Theren's command, he would have strode away to find comfort in solitude. Though Lilith sat and he stood, the scorn on her face made him feel as though she were looking down on him.

And then suddenly, she was. Without warning, Lilith's chair rose into the air. At first Ebon thought it was her doing, some trick of firemagic he had never heard of before. But the look of shock on her face soon told him it was otherwise. With a glance over his shoulder, he noticed Theren lurking in a corner, half-hidden behind a couch. Her eyes were glowing.

"What are you doing?" said Lilith. "Put me down at once!"

Ebon spread his hands, stifling a smile. "What do you mean? I know no magic. And I am a transmuter besides. Is this transmutation? If so, I have never seen its like before. Mayhap I have turned you into a bird."

The ceiling in the room was quite high, and now Lilith was very close to it. Then, the chair began to tip. Very, very slowly, it tilted forwards. Now every head in the room was turned towards her, watching as she scrambled to keep her seat. For a moment, Ebon was afraid she would fall to the stone floor. It would not be fatal, but surely it would injure her. But he reassured himself; Theren must know what she was doing.

"It is mindmagic!" cried Lilith. "I can feel it! Oren, stop them!"

"I cannot!" said Oren, whose eyes were glowing now. He ground his teeth in frustration.

"Which one of you is it?" said Nella. She went from chair to chair, seizing students by the front of their robes and looking into their eyes, searching for a glow. "When I find you, I will melt the skin from you!"

Then the chair flipped all the way over. Lilith barely held on to one of the legs, dangling there in midair. But then her feet lifted up, and suddenly she hung upside down in midair. Gravity did its work, and dragged her robe down around her shoulders, exposing her underclothes and a great deal of skin. Kalem yelped and averted his eyes. Throughout the room, reluctantly, students began to giggle. The laughter swelled, and soon was reverberating throughout the room and off the walls.

"What an audience I have tonight," said Ebon, turning to them all with a smile. "It pleases your jester very much to have brought you such mirth." He placed a hand to his waist and bowed, as fine as any courtier. The students only laughed harder.

"Put me down this instant!" cried Lilith. "Theren! Theren, I know it is you!"

She stopped moving through the air at once. Then, swiftly, she came back down. The chair turned over in its descent to land right side up. Lilith was not so lucky, landing hard—but not too hard—on her head. She shot to her feet and replaced her robes, her face a mask of fury. Quickly she made for Ebon.

Theren appeared as if from nowhere, standing beside Ebon with hands balled into fists. Kalem stood to his other side, though Ebon saw the boy gulp in fear. But fright, it seemed, was baseless; Lilith stopped a pace away, staring at Theren with . . . not hatred, nor even anger. Ebon recognized the look with a start, for it was the last thing he would have expected to see: sadness, along with a deep pain.

"You have a forked tongue, Lilith," said Theren softly. "And I care not what you do with it. But you will not use your magic against my friends again."

Oren and Nella came for Theren, but Lilith stopped them with outstretched arms. Her jaw spasmed again and again, but she spoke no word to Theren. Instead she turned her gaze on Ebon, and familiar hatred reappeared in her eyes.

"Until the morrow, *jester,*" she hissed. "You find yourself in fortunate company."

She spun on her heel and swept from the room. Oren and Nella followed after only a moment's hesitation.

The other students in the room turned quickly away. If Ebon had thought to earn more friends, those hopes seemed dashed. But Theren was smiling, and even Kalem wore a nervous little grin. That seemed enough, at least for now.

111

"I have not had such fun in months," said Theren, grinning. "Come, goldbags. Let us see if we cannot get ourselves a drink before nightfall."

FIFTEEN

They spent their time in the library the next day reading Kalem's hidden tome on the Wizard Kings. Or rather, Ebon read it while Kalem sat by and worked on his own lessons. Often Ebon would have some question about the text, and would ask Kalem. The boy's knowledge was incredible, and he would always answer Ebon with some tale from another of the library's volumes. Often Ebon would take down the names of other books that Kalem thought he should read, and soon his parchment was full of them. He looked upon the list with some dismay; it seemed half a lifetime's worth of reading.

When he tired of study, he would take out his wooden rod, and Kalem would try to teach him how to turn it to stone. But try as he might, Ebon could not summon the magic to do it.

"Take your time," Kalem told him. "It is only your third day."

"You do not understand," said Ebon. "As long as I am in Credell's class, my time here is wasted."

"I passed his class early, and yet still it took me half a year," said

Kalem. "You cannot expect to do it in a week, especially when you have never been allowed to practice before."

That day passed, and the next, and the next. Soon Ebon found himself settling into a comfortable routine—comfortable, at any rate, outside of Credell's class, although even that became more tolerable. The instructor still looked at Ebon with wide-eyed terror whenever he spoke or moved. But the other children seemed to forget their fear of him, since he did not do anything particularly frightening, and Ebon began to learn their names. The wild-haired girl he had seen on his first day was called Astrea, and she seemed to take a particular liking to him, though she still feared to speak with him. Often he would catch her staring from across the room, but she turned and blushed whenever he looked her way. Though Astrea looked nothing like Albi, his sister, still something in her manner reminded him of home. Whenever he could manage it, he would catch her gaze and stick his tongue out at her. She would giggle behind her hand and turn quickly back to her lessons.

Every afternoon, he would huddle in the library with Kalem. He would find tidbits from the history of the Wizard Kings that prompted him to start a catalog of other books to read. But in those tomes he would often come upon something that gave him some question, and then he would refer back to the great blue tome. He and Kalem spent as much time trying to learn spells as they did reading, though Kalem warned him often that they were supposed to use the time for studying, and Jia would be cross if she found out.

After two weeks, Ebon began to feel at home. When he thought back to his first two days, they seemed to have happened to someone else. Even Lilith's torments had lessened, though she still gave him an evil look whenever they passed each other in the hallways, and sometimes she jostled him in the dining hall when she walked by. But she gave him a wide berth whenever he was with Theren, which was often, and if Theren ever caught her nearby, she stared until Lilith scuttled away. Ebon suspected there was some history between the two of them, but when he asked Theren, she only shrugged and said, "Some, yes. She knows better than to create any more."

On some days, Ebon would sneak out of Credell's class and into the training grounds. The instructor could not possibly have failed to notice his absence, but mayhap he was relieved not to have the young Drayden in his classroom. Ebon knew he would get in trouble if he were ever discovered, but there were many hedges that ran along the Academy's wall, and he could go there to hide himself and watch the other students practice their spells.

Sometimes he watched the classes of the other three branches, the mindmages and firemages and weremages. But most often he went to the smaller grounds to see the alchemists practice. Their spells were less spectacular, not the sort of magic he often heard of in tales and the like. Yet Ebon knew, or hoped, that this magic lay in his future, and so it kept his interest better than any of the others. He did not see the student who had turned her instructor's arrow to dust, but he saw the others performing similar spells with the cloth balls they threw between each other.

When he watched the weremages, one instructor often caught his attention. He was a somewhat older man, black hair dusted with grey, and he wore his beard thick but trimmed close to his face. Ebon thought he had the look of one from Selvan. There was something familiar about him—but mayhap it was only because he looked so kindly. Always he spoke to his students in a calm and measured tone, and Ebon noted how he would show them a spell over and over again until they had learned it. Then he would leave them, but keep watch carefully from the corner of his eye. Ebon often thought wistfully how he wished Credell were such an instructor—but this man was a weremage, and could not have taught Ebon even if he wanted to.

One day he was in the library with Kalem. His wooden rod rested in his hands, and he tried to see into the wood, to change it. But he could not make it swell in his vision, the way a cup of water did when he cast the testing spell.

"Instead of seeing it, try to feel it," said Kalem. "Sometimes that works better."

"Of course I feel it," said Ebon. "I am holding it in my hands, am I not?"

"I do not mean feel it, I mean . . ." Kalem waved his hands about vaguely. *"Feel* it," he finished lamely.

Ebon's nostrils flared. "That makes it all much clearer. Quick, run to fetch Credell! I am ready for my test." He shoved the rod back into his robes. "Enough of this. I have found a book written by a member of my own family, many hundreds of years ago, and today I meant to start it. I will return in a moment."

He stood and strode away from their table, among the bookshelves that stood tall about him. The right section was easy enough to find, for he was now well practiced in seeking out the library's many works. Slowly he scanned the spines, looking for his book.

"How go your studies, goldbag?"

Ebon nearly jumped out of his skin, and he gripped the bookshelf to steady himself. When he turned, he could not believe his eyes for a long moment. Before him stood Mako. The man leaned casually against the bookshelf behind Ebon, the wicked knife at his hip shining as bright as the sparkle in his eyes. His thick, tattooed arms were folded over each other, but in one hand he held a book, which he had opened to the middle and appeared to be reading. With a start, Ebon realized that it was the very book he had come here to find.

"Mako? What are you doing here?" Something made Ebon's skin crawl, something more than his normal reaction to the man. How did Mako get to the third floor of the library without causing some sort of commotion in the Academy? Guests were not allowed to roam these halls unescorted. Yet no one else was in sight.

"Your lack of hospitality wounds me," said Mako, frowning. "It seems an eternity since last I was privileged to lay eyes upon you."

Ebon swallowed hard. "It has not even been a month."

"The days seem like years, and all that drivel." Mako slapped the book shut and made to return it to the shelf. But then he caught Ebon looking at it, and he held it up in mock surprise. "Oh, were you looking for this one? Here it is, young lord. Take it with my compliments."

"How did you know?"

Mako's too-friendly grin widened. "How did I know what, Ebon? There are far too many answers to that question for me to give them all here and now."

"Never mind. What do you want?"

"That question, too, comes with a host of replies. And why should I answer your question, when you have not answered mine?"

"Yours?" said Ebon, blinking.

"The first thing I asked you: how go your studies?"

Ebon looked about, unsure. "They go well enough, I suppose," he said. "Though I find it—"

Mako clapped his hands sharply, and Ebon's words died in his mouth. "Quite enough of that. I have come for another purpose. The family requires something of you."

The library was utterly silent about them. Ebon could hear his heartbeat thundering in his ears. "The family—by which I suppose you mean my father. What does he need?"

Mako looked down at the fingers of his right hand. His left drifted to the hilt of his knife, and Ebon's hands tightened on the spine of his book. But when Mako drew the knife, it was only to pick under his fingernails with the tip. It glistened in the dim orange glow of the library's lamps.

"What sort of question is that?" said Mako lightly. "He is your father, and the reason you attend the Academy at all. Are you not happy to fulfill his heart's desire, whatever that may be?"

"Of course," Ebon said quickly. The last thing he wanted was for Mako to run back to Father with tales of his ingratitude. "I only meant to ask, how may I be of service to him?"

"There will be a package left for you. Tonight, after the Academy's lanterns have been dimmed and that white-haired old bat no longer guards the front door. Too, there will be a special permission slip from your loving cousin the dean. It will allow you to leave the Academy."

Ebon's throat caught, and his voice grew weak, as though he were being strangled. "Leave?"

Mako took his meaning and grinned. "Not forever, boy—only for tonight. You must bring the package to the west end of the Seat, where you will find an inn called the Shining Door. A man there will recognize you, and you must give him the package."

"What is in it?"

"You need not trouble yourself over that."

"Could you not bring it yourself? This seems an awful amount of trouble." Mako's eyes went cold, and Ebon shivered. "I mean only that, certainly my father would like it to be done fast. It will be many hours until I can leave this place."

Still the bodyguard stared with ice in his eyes, though the grin never wavered. "He has patience enough for this. And besides, I am somewhat well known in that part of the city, and not in any way one would consider complimentary. But no one there will think you are up to anything nefarious."

"And will I be?"

Mako gave him a wink. "Why should you be? You are only delivering a parcel. If you get up to any mischief, it shall be on your own account."

Ebon felt as though the jaws of some unseen steel trap were closing about him. "But if I am doing nothing wrong, why must it be done so late at night?"

"Who would not enjoy a nighttime adventure? And you have the dean's special permission."

Ebon wanted to refuse. He wanted to tell Mako he would not do it, and that the bodyguard could deliver the parcel himself. How did he know that this was actually at his father's request? It might be Mako's own scheme, into which he meant to ensnare Ebon against his father's wishes. But Mako must have seen something of these thoughts on his face, for he sucked a slow breath between his teeth and shook his head.

"Ebon," he said genially. "Could you truly be so eager to disappoint your father? Halab may have spoken for you, but he could withdraw you on the slightest whim. Do this for him, out of respect and gratitude. He cares for you so very much."

The words carried no obvious threat, but still Ebon heard one. He could imagine being cast from the Academy, his tuition no longer paid, his allowance cut off, and he himself bundled into a ship bound for home. Again he saw in his imagination the triumphant sneer on Father's face as Ebon marched in through the doors of the Drayden mansion.

"Very well," said Ebon. "I will bring the package, if that is what my father wishes."

"He does," said Mako. He pushed himself off the bookshelf and gave Ebon a little bow—but Ebon thought he saw mockery in the gesture. He turned away from the bodyguard, opening his book as if he meant to read it right there.

"One more thing, little goldbag—do not look inside the parcel."

Ebon turned to look at him, but Mako had vanished. He leaned out to look around the bookshelf, but the aisles on either side were empty.

SIXTEEN

THE DAY ENDED QUICKLY—FAR TOO QUICKLY FOR EBON'S LIKING, FOR HE dreaded his errand. But soon the daylight had faded through the Academy's many windows, and he felt an uncertain anxiety settle about him. He sat with Kalem in the boy's common room—not the one outside Ebon's dormitory, for Kalem feared to go where the older children lived. Ebon had taken to visiting Kalem instead, three floors higher. The children here were of Kalem's age, and they looked at Ebon somewhat fearfully and left him alone. He found that he much preferred it that way.

As day turned to night at last and attendants came to light fires upon the hearths, Kalem began to yawn heavily in his chair. His eyes were bleary, and he rubbed at them. "I slept poorly last night. Or rather, I slept not enough. I became caught up trying a new spell my instructor showed me yesterday."

"Hm?" said Ebon, looking up. He had only been half listening.

Kalem looked at him oddly. "What has gotten into you? You are half bouncing in your seat, and I do not think you have heard a word I have said all night."

"It is nothing," said Ebon. "If you are tired, I will leave so that you may go to bed."

"I can stay up a bit longer, if you wish to talk. We have not tried your spell yet."

"I myself am weary." Ebon stood, and felt at once that he had done it somewhat too quickly. "I will make my way to my own room. Good night."

"Good night," said Kalem, yawning once more. He stood and retreated to his dormitory.

Ebon made his way quickly downstairs. Curfew approached but had not yet come, and so he was somewhat unsure what to do with himself. He did not wish to return to the common room outside his dormitory, for fear of meeting Lilith there. Instead he stole down to the first floor and made his way to the dining hall. Some spare loaves had been left out on the serving table, as they were each day, and Ebon snatched one up to tear into it. Something about his anxiety had raised his appetite.

He took the loaf with him as he went out through a white door into the training grounds. There was a stone bench he often liked to sit upon. He went there now, clutching his robes a bit tighter against the chilly night. The moons were just rising in the eastern sky, their glow drifting down to paint the grass in silver. The stars were bright that night, and Ebon watched them make their slow way through the sky. Soon it would be time, and he would have to go. But for a moment he could rest here on his stone bench, and pretend it was where he meant to spend the rest of his evening until he went to bed.

Voices sounded on the air, coming from around the corner. Without thinking, Ebon dove over the back of the bench and into the hedges by the Academy wall.

Around the corner came two instructors, obvious by their age even when the night turned their dark grey robes as black as a student's. Ebon recognized one of them: it was the kindly-faced weremage he would sometimes watch when he snuck out into the training grounds. The man walked with another instructor, one Ebon did not know by name, though he thought she might be a mindmage. They walked slowly, and their talk seemed without purpose.

But as they passed by, a curious thing happened. The weremage paused for a moment, and he turned so that he was looking straight at the spot where Ebon hid. Ebon's pulse raced so fast that he thought his heart might burst from his chest. But after a moment the instructor resumed his walk, taking two quick steps to catch up with his companion. Soon they had passed beyond the next corner of the Academy, and Ebon let loose a sigh of relief.

It was time, or past time now. He snuck out from the hedge, wolfing down the last scrap of his bread loaf, and made his way back to the Academy's entry hall. He half hoped to find Mellie standing guard there as she always was, but Mako had spoken true: it was a new woman, tall, thick, and matronly. Ebon had never seen her before. Her fat cheeks puffed as she stood to greet him. Under her arm was a parcel wrapped in brown cloth.

"You are the Drayden boy," she said. Ebon was unsure if it was a question, and so he did not answer. She shoved the parcel into his arms and led him to the front door.

"When you return, knock twice, then thrice, and I shall know it is you," she said. Then she very nearly pushed him out the door before closing it behind him.

Ebon sighed, looking up and down the street. A few figures moved about in the light of torches, but none seemed the least bit interested in him. He knew it was not unheard of for Academy students to go out after hours for one reason or another, but still he felt nervous, as though at any moment a constable would snatch him up and inquire about his business.

Quickly he set off into the streets. Then he changed his mind, thinking it might be better to stay out of sight as much as possible. Nearby was an alley that looked like it ran west for a ways. He made for it, blinking hard to help his eyes adjust as he slipped into shadow. But they did not adjust fast enough—he ran into another figure with a crash and a yelp.

"I am sorry," he stammered, stepping back into the moonslight. But then his eyes became accustomed to the darkness at last, and he recognized who he had run into: it was Theren. She looked just as surprised to see him as he was to see her.

"What under the sky are you doing here?" she said, sharp eyes narrowing.

"I might ask the same of you," he said defiantly, trying in vain to hide the parcel behind his back.

"And I will answer you readily. I am off to visit a house of lovers. Now it is your turn."

"I . . ." Words failed him for a moment. At last he found them, too late. "As am I."

"Truly?" she said, and he could hear in her voice that she did not believe him. "Then what is that package behind your back? It is too fat to hide, or you are too thin, I cannot tell which."

"It is nothing," said Ebon, trying to turn it sideways to conceal it better.

Her thin nose twitched. "Very well. Keep your secrets. It is no business of mine what a man does with his lover. But if we are of a purpose, then let us walk together. These streets are dark, and they can be dangerous."

Ebon scoffed. "Do not mock me by saying you wish for my protection."

"I would never dream of it. I mock you by saying that you require mine."

"I can fend for myself," he said, hoping she could not see his cheeks burning in the moonslight.

She thrust a finger under his nose, eyes alight. "Wait. I know what you are about. You have spoken to the dean, just as I said, and he gave you permission to leave the Academy."

"I did not! I . . ." He trailed off lamely, averting his eyes as he searched for an answer.

"I knew it." She folded her arms across her chest. "Yet you would not even extend me the same courtesy. I might have known better than to think a goldbag would help one so lowly born."

"Theren, I give you my word, I did nothing of the sort. I wish I were not here at all, and I—" He decided he must take the plunge. "I am not out to visit a house of lovers."

"Of course you are not. What, then?"

He looked over his shoulder and then back at her. "I was given a task. By my father. He wishes me to bring this package to an inn, a place called the Shining Door. The dean gave me permission to be out, indeed, but I did not request it. Nor do I wish to be here. I do not like anything about this."

"What is in the package?" She reached out a hand curiously.

Ebon snatched it away from her. "I am not allowed to look inside."

"How intriguing." To his shock, her eyes sparkled in the moonslight. "What is this? Some black business of your family's? Do you walk beyond the King's law?"

"I do not know," he insisted. "I only know that my father asked this of me, and he is the only reason I am at the Academy in the first place. So I mean to do as he asked and then promptly forget the matter entirely."

"An excellent plan," said Theren, drawing herself up. "And I shall come with you."

He balked. "No. You should not. Go to your lover, and pretend you never saw me."

She waved a hand in dismissal. "What pleasures could I find that would be grander than the intrigue of a midnight plot? Besides, what if you should find yourself in trouble? What will you do, turn water into oil and throw it in their faces? You need me."

"I shall not get into trouble. I am only delivering a parcel."

"So you think." She gripped his arm and dragged him into the alley. "Yet one never knows the perils that may lie in one's future."

He tried to think of how to dissuade her, but she pressed on so determinedly that he soon resigned himself to his fate. But he shook her grip off his arm and walked beside her in sullen silence. Theren, for her part, seemed to take this all as some glorious nighttime adventure, though to his relief she stopped asking him any questions.

As they neared the western end of the island, Ebon began looking about for someone to ask directions of. But Theren tapped him on the shoulder and pointed. "I know the Shining Door. It lies this way. Come."

She set off, and he hurried to follow her. Soon they found the place: a squalid little building tucked in between two larger ones. The thick beams that held up its roof were bent outwards, like a child taking a deep breath, or a body about to burst with pox. From the smell that drifted from its open front door, Ebon thought it was more likely the latter.

Inside, the common room was dim, and every conversation was muted. Many wary eyes glinted at them in the darkness. Ebon was acutely grateful for his plain students' robes; if he had appeared here in the finery to which he was accustomed, he would have feared to find a knife slid between his ribs, the assailant hoping to find a fat purse.

He wanted to leave immediately, but he forced himself to take another step beyond the threshold. His eyes roved about, seeking someone who recognized him. No one paid him any special attention at first, but then he caught sight of a sudden motion. In the back of the room, a figure beckoned him forth. Ebon did not want to approach, but neither did he want to be in this place a moment longer than he had to. With Theren by his side, he wove his way quickly between the tables until he reached the one where the figure sat.

It was a man, his skin pale to the point of being ghostly. This was certainly no man of Idris, and Ebon wondered why he would be in league with the Draydens. A thin mustache clung to his lip, dipping down into a sparse beard. His eyes were rat-like and flitted all about. His cloak and hood were blue, but his tunic and leggings were grey.

"You know who I am?" said Ebon, fighting and failing to keep his voice steady.

The man sneered and held forth a hand. Ebon gave him the brown parcel. The man quickly undid the string holding it shut and lifted a corner, peeking inside. Ebon craned his neck, trying to see, but the man drew it back.

"I was told you would come alone," he said in a rasping voice. He did not wait for a response, but stood quickly and left, making for the rooms at the back of the inn.

Ebon released a long sigh he had not known he was holding. "Let us leave this place, for I feel as though I grow dirtier the longer I remain." He nearly ran for the door, Theren beside him, and once in the open air he drank it in with long, deep breaths.

"Well, that provided no answers whatsoever," said Theren.

"I am glad," said Ebon. "The less I know of what just transpired,

125

the better, I suspect. If I could drink enough to forget it ever happened, I would."

"There might be time enough for that yet," said Theren. "It is not very late."

"The moons are halfway through the sky," said Ebon. "Let us return and sleep, or else tomorrow's classes shall be a torture."

"If you insist, alchemist. I will show you the way."

"You do not mean to go to your lover?"

She shrugged. "I think I have had thrills enough. She will still be there if I visit her on another night."

Ebon blinked at her. "She? Oh, dear. Should I have words with Kalem?"

Theren grinned at him, teeth flashing in the moonlight. "You do not mean he is enamored of me? Oh, the dear boy. Yes, do let him know that he would have no hope of turning my head, even if he were not so young."

Ebon shook his head with a little smile and followed Theren as she set off through the streets. They walked in silence, and soon Ebon found himself wondering what it was, exactly, that he had just done. He feared to know, and yet he found himself even more fearful of ignorance. Always he had taken great pains to avoid any inkling of his family's dealings. It was common knowledge that the Draydens were spice traders, but Ebon knew of his father's late-night meetings, of Mako's strange work that seemed to take him all across the nine lands. He saw the terror that shone in others' eyes when they heard he was of the family Drayden. Always he had shied away from such things. And now he suspected that, unknowing, he had been thrust straight into the middle of it all.

Theren must have entertained thoughts not unlike his own, for after they had walked together a while, she glanced at him. "Tell me true: what was that all about?"

Ebon sighed. "I said I do not know."

She shook her head. "You cannot mean to persist in that lie. I know only rumors of your family's doings, but if even half of them are true . . ."

"If you know only a rumor, you know more than I," said Ebon.

"Never have I involved myself in . . . in whatever it is my family does that makes others fear us so."

Theren scoffed. "More Drayden favoritism," she muttered.

"It is not," said Ebon, growing angry. "If you would for but a moment forget your abject, ignorant hatred of those who are wealthier than you, you might see that. I never wished to be my father's son."

"I cannot *imagine* such difficulty," said Theren. She feigned irony, but Ebon could hear true resentment lurking beneath it. "What anguish to ride in a golden carriage, hiding your face to avoid seeing the dark deeds that paid for it."

Ebon wanted to answer—or rather, he wanted to shout at her. But he was keenly aware that he might lose one of his only two friends at the Academy if he did. Besides, he did not quite know where he was, and did not wish to spend any time wandering lost on the Seat. So he walked beside her in silence, biting his tongue until it nearly bled.

Soon he saw the familiar shape of the Academy looming above the buildings before them. Though he knew he could enter the front door, he found himself curious about how Theren had snuck out. So when she turned left, he followed. She took him around the corner, where he found a small collection of wooden sheds pressed up against the Academy's outer walls.

Seeing his questioning look, Theren explained. "They keep brooms and such within, and use them to sweep the surrounding streets."

He thought she might enter one of them, revealing a hidden door. Instead, she stepped close to one of the sheds, eyes glowing. She crouched and leaped high in the air to land atop the shed. Again she crouched, lower this time, and gave another mighty jump. The Academy's wall stood ten paces high—she just managed to grip the edge of it with her fingers, and Ebon saw her eyes glow once more as she used her magic to climb up. She turned for just a moment and waved, a black shape against the stars, and then vanished.

"Well and good for her," Ebon muttered to himself. "But not for me, I suppose."

He trudged back to the front door and knocked upon it, twice and then thrice. After a moment it swung open, and the stern woman from before gave him a little nod. He ignored her, climbing the wide stairway quickly and making his way to his dormitory, where he dived beneath the covers and tried to forget the whole affair.

SEVENTEEN

By morning Ebon felt little better, and he was exhausted besides. Somehow he made it through his morning class, though often times he caught his head nodding. Once he barely snapped awake before crashing nose-first into the table. Credell could not have missed it, but the instructor, of course, said nothing.

Well, if I cannot concentrate, and Credell is too frightened to say anything about it, mayhap I should take advantage of the situation, thought Ebon. So he slid down the bench until he reached the wall, slouching against the stone. Soon the murmuring buzz of the other students lulled him into peaceful slumber, and he dozed comfortably.

It was a while later before he felt a tugging on his sleeve. He opened his eyes, expecting to see Credell—but it was Astrea, the young girl with the wild hair, her eyes wide as she stared at him. The moment he awoke she jerked her hand back from his sleeve.

"Class is over," she said softly. They were the first words she had said to him since the first day, when she thought he had come to the wrong classroom.

Ebon blinked hard and looked around. It was true. The room was empty. He had not even heard the bell ring.

"Thank you, Astrea," he said, and then yawned wide.

"I do not know why Credell is afraid of you. I like you."

Almost before the words had left her lips, she turned and ran for the door as though her life depended on it. In a moment she was gone. Ebon stared after her, blinking hard. But when he finally stood to leave, he found that he was smiling.

The dining hall buzzed with voices. Ebon stumbled between the other students, heading towards his usual table. Theren and Kalem were there already, and looked to be half done with their meals. Theren regarded him with a small smile as he sat, but Kalem's eyes were wide with questions.

"You are very late."

"I am," said Ebon. He spooned up a bite of soup with a grimace. They had had the same thing twice already this week.

"What were you doing?"

"Sleeping, as it happens," said Ebon.

Kalem blinked. He looked to Theren and then back to Ebon. "Sleeping? In your bed?"

"In my class."

The boy's jaw dropped, turning his face to a perfect mask of shock. He could not have looked more surprised if Ebon had changed to an Elf right before his eyes. "You . . . that . . . but your instructor!"

"Credell fears even to speak to me. If he tried to reprimand me, he might die of terror."

"The tragic life of a goldbag," muttered Theren, picking at her nails.

"Leave off, Theren," said Ebon. Her cheeks turned crimson, and she looked away.

Kalem had not recovered from his shock, and still gaped like a fish. "How could he let you sleep through his class?"

"What harm is there?" said Ebon. "It is not as though he teaches me anything when I am awake."

"Still . . . I can scarcely imagine it." Kalem shook his head—and then, after a moment, his eyes narrowed. "But why should you be so tired? You went to bed just as I did last night."

Ebon felt sick. He ducked his head, picking at his sleeve as though something upon it had suddenly captured his interest. "Yes, well . . . in fact, that is not quite what happened. I went out upon the Seat."

"We both did," Theren said brightly. Ebon wished she would keep her mouth shut. "Why not tell him what you did, Ebon?"

"I scarcely know myself. My father sent me a message, asking me to deliver a package to some inn on the west end of the Seat. He arranged special permission for me to be out after hours."

Kalem leaned forwards and spoke in a voice hardly above a whisper. "What was in the package?"

Ebon shrugged. "I was not supposed to open it."

"Though I greatly wanted to," said Theren.

"You went with him?"

"Not by intent. I pursued other interests, but we encountered each other upon the streets. He was so cagey about his purpose for leaving the Academy, I decided I should follow him and see what he was up to. But I learned nothing, for Ebon would not give me any answers."

Ebon felt his temper was dangerously close to breaking, and his weariness did not help. "I have told you—"

"Yes, you have told me," said Theren rolling her eyes. "No need to do so again."

"Well, I think you were both terribly idiotic," said Kalem, folding his arms across his chest with a scowl. "You should not have delivered the parcel if you did not know what was in it, Ebon. And neither of you should have gone wandering the Seat at night."

Theren shrugged. "I do it often. No one seems to mind."

"I doubt anyone knows that you do it," said Kalem.

"But that is saying the same thing."

"I would not have done it," said Ebon, speaking quickly before Kalem could think up another retort. "But my father is the reason I am here at the Academy. How could I be so ungrateful as to refuse to aid him?"

"But you do not even know what you did," said Kalem. "And forgive my saying so, but . . . but a favor for your family . . ."

Ebon looked angrily into his lap. "Say what you mean to say. A favor for my family is likely a dark deed. And yet what would you have done? What else could I have done?"

"You could have refused."

To Ebon's surprise, Theren spoke in his defense. "Mayhap we are trying overmuch to craft guilt out of innocence, Kalem. Ebon may be a Drayden, but he does not seem a bad *sort* of Drayden. What harm could come from a little parcel? And the adventure was somewhat amusing, at least."

"What harm? How can we know, without knowing what the parcel held? What if it was poison, or a dagger? Or . . . or even *magestones.*"

He said the word in such a hushed whisper that Ebon felt compelled to lean forwards. He looked to see if anyone else was listening. Theren's eyes grew dark, and she gripped Kalem's arm until he squirmed.

"Do not even whisper such things here, you fool!" she hissed.

"I do not understand," said Ebon. "What are ma—that is, what are those things you just named?"

"Of course you would not know," said Theren, rolling her eyes. "Tell him, Kalem—but *not* here, nor any place where curious ears might hear you. You two have your lover's nest in the library; speak of it there."

She released Kalem and left them. The boy stared sullenly after her, rubbing his arm where she had squeezed it. When he looked at Ebon, dark disgruntlement showed in his eyes.

"It is *not* a lover's nest."

Ebon could think of no words to cheer him up. It seemed to him that Kalem was right and Ebon was a fool. Yet even with that knowledge, Ebon suspected that one day his father would ask another favor of him—and he doubted he had the will to refuse.

"Come," he said quietly. "The meal is nearly over, and our next class beckons."

They cleaned their table and made their way into the Academy halls. Ebon's feet dragged with every step.

Once they had safely sequestered themselves on the library's third floor, Ebon leaned in close. "What are these magestones you spoke of before? Why did they bring such fear to Theren's eyes, when she fears almost nothing?"

Though there was no one in sight, Kalem still shushed him and looked around. "You should be very, very wary of speaking that word within these walls, even in the most shadowed whisper. Theren was right—it was foolish of me to say it in the dining hall."

"But what *is* it?" said Ebon, growing exasperated. "Or rather, what are they?"

"*They,*" said Kalem, taking great pains to avoid the word, "are black stones, or crystals, I think. I do not know where they come from—no one does, except those who sell them, and they have no wish to share the secret. Though they look like a shiny rock, they break easily in the hand or between the teeth. When a normal person eats one, there is no effect. But if a wizard should eat one . . ."

He fell silent, shivering, and once again he looked over his shoulder. Ebon shook him gently. "There is no one there, Kalem. You have looked at least a dozen times."

"Still I feel as though we are watched," said the boy. "Mayhap I am overly fearful. If we were found to be speaking of this, it would go ill for both of us."

"Well, finish the tale, so that we need never speak of it again."

"As you say. If a wizard consumes a magestone, their powers are increased manyfold. Even a modest elementalist could summon flames hot enough to melt stone, and an alchemist could turn a house to straw with a touch. If a wizard is mighty already, the stones can turn them nearly Elf-like in power. And some other, darker side of our magic is unlocked—for alchemists it is a corruption, like a plague we can imbue in matter that spreads to anything close enough. Whatever it touches withers away to nothingness, until the magic is spent. They call it blackstone."

Ebon had leaned forwards without realizing it, and now he was gripping the arms of his chair, as though his limbs had readied themselves to flee of their own accord. He forced his shaking limbs to relax.

"That sounds powerful indeed," he said. "But if it increases the strength of our magic, where is the great harm?"

"The stones do not only strengthen our gifts. They consume the mind as well. From the moment a magestone passes your lips, it fills you with an aching hunger for more. At first the craving is slight, just a tickling at the back of the mind. But if you deny it, it soon grows to a raging desire that will drive away all rational thought. Wizards who take magestone will kill to acquire more. They will cast aside all bonds of friends and family if only it allows them another piece. As long as they can keep up their supply, they may appear rational. But if for even a moment their store of magestone is threatened, they will destroy all the nine lands to secure it."

The library around them was utterly silent. Ebon let loose a long *whoosh* of breath. "Was that, then, the power behind the Wizard Kings?"

Kalem nodded slowly. "It was. There is an entire section of the blue book that speaks of it. You will read it before long. That is one of the reasons I am sure it is forbidden."

"But if you learned of it in the book, what of Theren? Surely she has not read the same words."

"She has not. But every student in the Academy knows of the magestones, or learns of them in time. It is strictly forbidden to speak of them, and so of course everyone does so. But if an instructor ever learns of such discussion, the punishment can be severe. Some students have been expelled."

"Just for speaking of it? That seems unfair."

"It may be, but then again, who wishes for students to graduate the Academy with a desire to find the stones? In fact the Academy's punishment may be considered light. If a wizard, having graduated, is found to have consumed magestones, the penalty is an immediate and messy death."

Ebon swallowed. "I will remember that. Where would you find magestones, if you wished to?"

Kalem's face went bone-white. "Ebon! After hearing my words, how can you ask that question?"

"I do not mean to go and secure some right this moment—or ever," said Ebon, frowning. "I only wonder, if they are forbidden by the Academy, and outside the King's law, then how do they even exist? They must come from somewhere—why does the High King not track down the source and wipe it out?"

"Why do you think I should know? The last I checked, neither of us were the High King's lawmen, nor seated at her councils."

Ebon smirked. "A fair point, I suppose, though wryly made. Very well. I still have a great deal of reading to do this day, and you have kept me at this discussion overlong."

"Do not let me stop you," said Kalem. He selected a book from their table and leaned back, waving a hand airily. "Go on about your business."

Ebon shook his head with a smile and rose to walk among the bookshelves. He was looking for a new tome, the biography of an ancient king of Calentin who many said was responsible for raising it to its present heights of culture and power. Soon he was lost among the shelves, peering at the books' spines in the dim light, here where the lanterns were often ill-tended.

"What a good little goldbag you have turned out to be."

The words nearly made him leap out of his skin. He recognized Mako's voice and ground his teeth together. When he turned, he found the man leaning against a shelf again, just as he had been last time. In his hand was a book, and Ebon knew without looking that it was the very book he had sought on the shelves.

"What are you doing back here?" Ebon whispered. "You must leave, before the instructors see you prowling about."

"Why should they eject me? Former students of the Academy are welcome to return at any time, if they seek some ancient wisdom in the library's vast wealth."

Ebon glared at him. "You never studied here. You are no wizard."

"Are you so certain of that?"

A shudder rippled through Ebon. What *did* he know of Mako? No, he had never seen the man use magic. But what of that? Only an overly boastful wizard would go about casting spells needlessly. Mako was many things—unnerving, overly friendly, and mayhap cruel—but he rarely boasted.

Mako was looking into Ebon's eyes now, and he smiled at what he saw. "Good, little goldbag. You are learning caution. Remember that our second thoughts are often wiser than our first, and the third are wisest of all—but the fourth bring only inaction."

Ebon shook his head, feeling as though he was ridding it of cobwebs. "Enough riddles. What do you want?"

"I wished only to congratulate you on the excellent service you rendered to your father."

"It was my pleasure to aid him." Ebon grimaced. Even saying the words felt like swallowing moldy bread.

"Yet you made a grave error. You brought your little mindmage lover for company."

Ebon gawked, his mouth working as he struggled for words. He was suddenly terrified for Theren. Mako did not truly care if they were bedmates. But if he knew that Theren had gone with Ebon, he knew she had seen the parcel.

Mako must have seen the terror in Ebon's eyes, for his grin widened. "Fear not, little goldbag. I mean your mindmage no harm. And I have not brought word of this to your father."

Ebon sagged against the bookshelf with relief. "Then why make any mention of it at all?"

"So that you know never to do anything so foolish in the future. I will keep only so many secrets on your behalf. If one of your little friends should accompany you again, they may find themselves drinking deep of the Great Bay's waters and making a little house of their own in its depths."

Ebon spoke through a throat of desert sand. "You mean to say, then, that my father will require more favors of me?"

"Dear, dear boy. Did you ever doubt it?"

"What was in the parcel?"

"You know better than to ask. You are happier without that knowledge; therefore remain ignorant. And the next time your father barks, and you jump to obey, leave your friends at home."

"I will remember."

"Good. Now return to your reading." Mako threw the book at him. Startled, Ebon barely caught it before it hit the ground. When he looked up, the bodyguard had vanished.

Fear had seized Ebon's limbs, and he found it hard to return to the table where Kalem waited. Now he knew what he had already thought—that Mako and his father were not done with him yet. Worse, he could no longer confide in Theren or Kalem, and would have to keep the truth from them. They might try to interfere; at least

Kalem would, and Theren might involve herself out of curiosity. That could spell their deaths.

Miserable and alone, Ebon left the bookshelves and made for the table.

EIGHTEEN

KALEM SEEMED TO SENSE THAT SOMETHING WAS WRONG, FOR HE ASKED Ebon many times that day what was troubling him. Ebon only shook his head and denied it, and after a while Kalem stopped asking. But he looked often at Ebon, his brow furrowed in deep thought, and he spent too long reading each page of his book.

After their studies, Theren met them in the hallways. "I have had a fine day," she declared. "Fine enough for celebration. What say the two of you to a night of drinks? I promise not to make you regret this one, little goldbag." She reached out and ruffled Kalem's hair.

He grinned, but Ebon's mood was still dark. "I have no cause to celebrate, myself. I think I shall remain here."

"No cause? Then come and drink until you find one. Come, dear Ebon. You are far too dour, and have been ever since last night. Together we can banish the dark thoughts that plague you. Tell him, Kalem."

Ebon barely kept himself from the retort that he was dour, in part, because of Theren's obvious distrust of him. She seemed polite enough now that she wanted him to pay for her wine. But before he could voice any such thought, Kalem looked at him doubtfully and shrugged.

"She may be right—it could help improve your mood. Answers can be quick to find if sought for by an easy mind, my instructor always says."

"That has the sound of fool's wisdom," grumbled Ebon. "But if the two of you insist, then I shall come with you."

"Excellent," said Theren, clapping her hands. "For in truth, I have no coin for wine, and need yours instead."

"Of course you do. How are you so impoverished already? Last night you had coin, at least, for a lover."

Kalem's face fell as he looked at her. "Ah . . . you are seeing a lover, are you?"

Theren gave him a little smile and ruffled his hair again. "I am afraid that was my aim, little goldbag. And for many months now have I enjoyed *her* company." She arched her eyebrow even as she stressed the word.

Ebon thought Kalem might grow even more distraught. But in fact the boy brightened, as though Theren had said more words that Ebon could not hear. "Oh! Oh, I see. Well. I am happy to hear it, then."

"I thought you might be. Come, wealthy patrons! Tonight we drink until our problems leave us at last!"

As she led them out of the Academy, Ebon drew Kalem back to whisper to him. "I had meant to tell you about her, but had hesitated, for I feared to upset you. Yet you seem cheered by the news."

Kalem shrugged. "And why not? I had thoughts of her, yes, but I thought it likely she would see me only as a child. But now I know that, even if I were older, things would be no different. It is not ill luck at the year of my birth, then, but another sort entirely."

Ebon frowned. "Still, ill luck is ill luck."

"My mind is eased regardless."

That made Ebon shake his head, even as Theren dragged them both into the streets. They made for Leven's tavern, passing through the usual flood of other students in black robes. But Ebon's thoughts kept up their endless wandering, mulling over Mako and his father and the parcel—and, more urgently, what they might ask him to do next. Once, he almost spoke of it to his friends. But then he cast a wary look over his shoulder, wondering if Mako lurked in some shadow, watching him. And, too, anyone on the streets about them could be one of Mako's agents, listening in to ensure that Ebon said nothing. Nowhere seemed safe anymore. Not even the Academy.

And then he thought of Theren, alone on the streets last night, and had an idea.

"I have changed my mind," he said, stopping in the street. "Forgive me, but I do not think I will drink with you tonight."

"Come *on*, Ebon," said Theren. "How will you deny me my right to a warm fire and flushed cheeks? And you seem as though a good drunkenness would do you well."

Ebon reached into his pocket and drew forth a gold weight. "Never let it be said I stood between you and a good flagon. Enjoy yourselves."

"Do not return to the Academy alone, Ebon," pleaded Kalem. "You should be with friends."

Ebon ducked his head, blushing. "I do not mean to return to the Academy."

Theren seemed to take his meaning at once, but Kalem's brow furrowed. He opened his mouth as though to ask a question, but Theren threw an arm over his shoulder and spun him around, marching him off down the street. "Come, little master. Our goldbag needs to be alone, and I can answer your questions without him." Soon they were out of sight.

Ebon was somewhat unsure of himself on the streets, but he knew his destination lay to the west, and so he headed that way. Soon he began to recognize a few of the buildings, and his steps came quicker and more certain. A few times he made a wrong turn and had to double back. But before very long he found himself on a familiar street, with a tavern behind him and a blue door just a few paces ahead.

As before, his throat grew tight and constricted, and he felt a tingling in his limbs. He looked down the street in both directions before chiding himself for being ridiculous. Who there would mind that he visited a house of lovers? He no longer had to worry about a retainer who might bring word of his deeds to his father, and no one else cared a whit.

He twisted the knob and opened the door.

Perfume, silk, and the strumming of a harp. Immediately his eyes went to the corner—but it was a man playing the strings. Ebon's heart skipped a beat. The house's matron arrived, sweeping up to him just as she had before, and wearing the same warm smile.

"Well met once again. How may we serve you this evening?"

"You remember me?"

She shrugged. "I have a gift for faces. Is there any sort of lover you are looking for tonight?"

Ebon licked his lips, for they had gone dry all of a sudden. "Is Adara here?"

Her smile widened slightly. "Of course." Turning, she beckoned, and from the shadows of the room's far corner, Adara rose at once. She had been sitting there all along, Ebon realized, and from the way she smiled as their eyes met, he suspected she had been watching him from the moment he stepped in the door. She wore Idrisian clothes, just as before, though this time the cloth seemed finer, and when the lamplight caught it, it shimmered. Too, she had a sheer blue veil over the lower half of her face. Though it did not entirely stop him from seeing her full lips, it drew his eyes to her own, where he found himself lost in wonder.

She took his hand. "Hello again, Ebon."

A short time later, she lay with her head on his chest, the two of them naked and nestled in the satin sheets of the bed. Ebon lay there silent for a long while, sometimes closing his eyes, sometimes opening them again. The quiet held only contentment. His troubles seemed far away, tiny things with simple solutions, only waiting for him to sweep them aside like so much dust. Adara must have sensed his desire for peace, for she said nothing, only traced her fingers across his chest in little patterns.

At last, Ebon lifted his head to kiss her. "I wish I could have returned earlier."

"As do I." She gave him a soft smile, and he returned it. They were lover's words, he knew, but that did not change the thrill they sent through him.

"How have I retained your lessons?"

"Not as well as could be hoped, but mayhap better than I expected." She smiled wider. "You must promise to let me teach you more often."

"I wish I could promise that," he said with a sigh.

She frowned. "What troubles you?"

He pursed his lips and looked away. She studied his face for a moment. He thought she might press him further.

Instead she pulled away, rising from the bed and going to a side table. His eyes were drawn to her movements and, if he was honest, her naked form. He watched as she brought him a pitcher and cup.

"I remembered what you asked for last time," she said. "I have kept these in my room ever since your first visit."

He sat up and looked inside the pitcher, and then he laughed. It was half full of clean, clear water. She smiled, eyes shining, and pressed it into his hands.

"Come. Show me a spell."

He shook his head, still smiling, and filled the cup with water. She took the pitcher back and put it on a table. He stirred the water, focusing on it through his finger. Kalem had practiced this with him often in the past few weeks, and now it came easily enough. The world grew brighter, and Adara gave a little gasp at the glow of his eyes. Soon the water was thick and soupy, and he withdrew his finger. The glow faded, and he handed her the cup.

"There. It is nothing very impressive, but it is magic nonetheless."

She took the cup gingerly and looked inside with awe, as though it held liquid gold. "That was wonderful to see," she said, her voice very small.

"Come now. Surely you know other wizards. I cannot be the only student of the Academy who comes here."

Carefully she put the cup down beside the pitcher. "You are not. But if the others wish to talk—which is rare—they only want to talk of themselves. They never offer to show me spells. And I rarely ask. I do not enjoy their company as I enjoy yours."

Lover's words. Yet still he smiled. "I only wish I had more to show you. I cannot learn my next spell, and I fear I will rot away in my class before I ever master it."

"What is it? Why does it trouble you so?"

He rose from the bed and went to his robe where it lay on the floor. From its pocket he drew his wooden practice rod. "I am supposed to turn this to stone. But for the life of me, I cannot seem to master the magic. I try and I try, but still it is made of wood, as you can see."

Sitting beside him, she ran her fingers over the rod. Her hand brushed his, making him tingle with delight. "Truly? You are learning to turn wood to stone?"

"I am supposed to. My friend Kalem says it is no great feat. He can do it in the span of a blink, though he is three years younger than I. It is the passing test of the first-year alchemist. Wood is the dead substance of something that was once alive. We learn to turn it to something that never lived in the first place. That which is alive is made of many things. That which is dead is usually much simpler. Kalem says that is the purpose of the test—not to see the wood for its complexity, but to envision the simplicity of the stone. But still I cannot do it."

She put her hand on his arm, running her nails along the skin. "I have faith that you will. It is only a matter of time. But I also sense that this is only one reason you look so concerned, and mayhap not the greatest reason of all."

He sighed, letting his hand fall to the bed. "You guess right. There is something . . . or some*one*, rather, who is much on my mind. I . . . my family has begun to give me errands. Only one, so far. Yet I fear more will come."

"What sort of tasks?"

"They had me deliver a parcel."

She giggled and stifled it behind a quickly raised hand. "That sounds like no dire deed."

"I do not know what was in it," he said. "But Mak—but the man who instructed me to do it is no man given to idle errands."

"Was it your father?"

He turned away. "I do not wish to speak of who."

"You may trust me."

"I do." He took her hands in his, and raised them to his lips. "Some might say it is foolish, yet I do. Only it troubles me. And it troubles my friend. She thinks I know more than I let on, and am withholding it from her."

"She?" Adara smiled broadly. "Ebon, if I were a jealous woman . . ."

"You need fear nothing of that. She prefers the company of women."

Her eyes flashed with recognition and—delight? Amusement? "Truly? Do you mean you have befriended Theren?"

Ebon rounded on her in surprise. "You know her? Wait . . . do you mean that you and she . . .?"

Adara frowned at him, and it seemed to Ebon that the affection in her eyes dampened. "I am not her lover. But Ebon, you should not be dismayed if I were. You do not hold any claim to me."

"Of course not," said Ebon quickly. "Only . . . I suppose I do not like to think of it."

She folded her arms. "You may as well. It is childish to do otherwise, and avoiding the thought may lead to darkness down the road. I have seen it before."

Ebon shook his head. "I am sorry. You are right, of course. Forget I made any mention of it at all."

Still she wore a little frown, but she relented and took his outstretched hand. "Very well."

He lifted her fingers and kissed them. "It is only that I am troubled. I do not know when Mako will return for me with some other task from my father, and I do not know what I will tell him when he does."

"You will do what he asks, of course."

He looked at her quickly. "You say it so easily. Does it not worry you?"

She shrugged. "Why should it? You only brought a parcel to someone in a tavern. If there is darkness in such an act, it comes before, or after, and is not your responsibility."

"Yet I bore the parcel."

She sighed and pushed his shoulders until he lay back upon the bed. Slowly, intently, she climbed atop him.

"Never do kings behead messengers for bearing words, even when those words displease the king. And if bearing such parcels keeps you upon the High King's Seat, and here in my arms, then I command you: bear them, Ebon. Bear as many as you must. Only do not leave me."

He found it impossible to muster any reply.

NINETEEN

THOUGH EBON'S FEARS HUNG DARK ABOUT HIM, IT SEEMED THAT FOR A time, at least, Mako and his father were finished with him. He saw nothing of the bodyguard as the days became weeks and true winter came to the High King's Seat. At home in Idris, the turning of the season had meant relief from unbearable heat; but on the Seat, Ebon had found autumn quite pleasant, whereas he now found himself chilled as he passed through the granite halls.

One day he entered the library for his studies and found Jia sitting at a desk on the first floor, reading a short letter. He gave her a wave, as he always did, but then he stopped. Jia was rarely jovial, but today she was more solemn than usual. Her face was grave, brows drawn together, and she hunched over the letter with worry.

Slowly he approached. She did not look up, or indeed seem to notice him at all. Soon he stood at the table, but she had not so much as batted an eye.

"Instructor Jia?" he said tentatively. "Is everything all right?"

She jerked in her seat and looked up at him. With a quick sigh, she folded the letter and tucked it away in a pocket before she stood.

"No, it is not," she said. "Yet it is nothing you need trouble yourself with. Do you require assistance?"

He shook his head. "No, Instructor. But what troubles you so? If I could help . . ."

"It is this battle in Wellmont. No doubt you have heard of it?"

Ebon frowned. "I have not. Wellmont—is that the city upon the border of Dorsea and Selvan? They squabble constantly. Surely it is no great worry."

"They do," she admitted. "But this seems to be something more grave. It has lasted longer than usual, at any rate. And even a border skirmish there would trouble me. I grew up in that city, as did a former student of the Academy, one who I cared for very deeply. The last I heard, she was stationed there, but I have not received word from her in months. And there is something else . . . something that happened in the battle . . ."

Ebon wanted to put a comforting hand on her shoulder, but it seemed inappropriate. Instead he merely stammered, "I am sorry to hear that. You taught this student weremagic?"

"I teach weremagic to no one."

He could not help a small smile. "Therianthropy, I mean."

Jia shook her head. "No, I was not her instructor. She was a mentalist. But never mind; this is nothing for you to worry over. We can do little about it in any case, here so far away from the fighting—and a good thing, too. Carry on with your studies, Ebon, and remember: wisdom in the right head may stop such wars before they begin. You should hold that endeavor as paramount, as should all people of learning."

"Yes, Instructor," he mumbled.

As he left her, he thought of the war, so far away, and wondered what it would feel like to have a loved one stuck in the thick of it. That thought drew him to his brother Momen.

He scarcely remembered when Momen rode away from home. Much clearer were his memories of the day they learned he had been killed. It had been a dark day, a day that seemed to go on forever, full of hurt and tears and hatred in Father's eyes. He doubted he would ever forget it; in fact a small part of him hoped he would not.

A thought struck him, and it seemed odd he had never thought it before. Ebon did not know how Momen had died. As far as he could remember, Idris had never been involved in any border wars with the three kingdoms next to it. Idris was a desert; it lacked the fair green lands that made Selvan so attractive a target. And the Camar, the royal family of Idris, were almost as fearsome as the Draydens. He had never mustered the courage to ask his father how Momen died, and now he likely never would. Mayhap Halab knew. He would have to ask, the next time he saw her.

Kalem was waiting at the table when Ebon arrived, and immediately he put down his book. "Let us see it," he said.

Ebon sighed and drew the wooden rod, handing it over. Kalem took a deep breath. His eyes glowed, and under his fingers, the rod turned to stone. He blinked, and it returned to wood.

"There. Did you feel it this time?"

Kalem had told him that wizards could sense other wizards using their spells if the magic was of an aligned branch. Weremagic and alchemy worked in tandem, he said, as did mindmagic with firemagic. Ebon could sense when a weremage or another alchemist was using their powers. Now, as he often had before, Ebon could feel a tingling on his neck and a turned stomach when Kalem transformed the rod. But it was no more help than it had been before.

"I sensed it, yes. But I still do not see how that helps."

"The feeling it gives you—try to emulate it. Try to recapture it when you cast your spell."

Ebon rolled his eyes and took the road. He tried to do as Kalem asked, picturing the tingling on the back of his neck and the vague roiling of his stomach. But that only distracted him from seeing the wood for what it truly was. Nothing happened to his eyes, and he soon cast the rod aside in frustration.

"It is no use. When I focus on the sensation, I lose sight of the rod, and when I think of the rod, I cannot think of the sensation."

"Just focus upon them both. It is quite easy."

Ebon thrust a finger under his nose. "If you tell me, even once more, that it is easy, I will—"

Kalem smiled and touched Ebon's robe. The whole sleeve turned to iron, and at the sudden change in weight, Ebon tipped over out of his chair. He yelped as he landed hard on his arm—but, as it was encased in metal armor, it did not hurt as badly as it might have.

"Change it back," he growled.

Kalem sighed and did as he asked. "Ebon, you grow frustrated too easily. A calm mind is the best facilitator of magic."

"I have few places to find calm in my life."

"Then I hope you are resigned to a life without spells," said Kalem with a shrug. "Because that is all you will ever have. When you struggle to clear your mind, let this encourage you: if you master yourself, wizardry will follow swiftly. Then all the physical world will be at your command; you will control earth, buildings, even the oceans and the winds. Is that not worth learning to cast aside fear and doubt?"

"What do you mean, the oceans and the winds? Those spells are of mind magic."

"*Elementalism,* Ebon. You could at least pretend that proper terms matter to you, for I can assure you they matter to everyone else."

"Elementalism, then," said Ebon through gritted teeth. "But you have not answered my question."

Kalem seemed to take this as an apology, for he nodded magnanimously. "I do not speak of elementalist spells like summoning water and wind. Those depend on motion. Our magic is the magic of change. You can turn water to oil easily enough. One day you will learn to change the air as well."

Ebon's curiosity was piqued. He had never thought of this before, nor seen an alchemist at the school do it. "How? What can you do with the air?"

"Some simple things," Kalem said with a shrug. "They teach more advanced spells in the next class. But I have learned the spell to make mist."

"Can you show me?"

Kalem looked surprised and more than a little pleased. He crossed his legs beneath him, and after a moment his eyes began to glow. Before Ebon's eyes, a mist seemed to spring out of nowhere, but as he looked closer he could see it emanating away from Kalem's body. Soon it filled the space all around them, spreading further and further until it reached the library's railing. The mist grew thicker and thicker, until Ebon could not see more than a few paces in any direction.

"That is all I can do for now," said Kalem. "My instructor says he could fill the entire Academy with fog, if he so chose. I do not know if I believe that, but then again, it is a very simple spell." He blinked, and the glow faded from his eyes. The mists rushed back and vanished, and the air was clear again.

"That is wondrous," said Ebon. "I would give much to be able to cast such a spell." He felt his own lack like an ache in his heart.

"You will learn it. In fact, it seems simpler to me than turning wood to stone. Air is a very simple thing. Not like wood."

"Mayhap I could try it," said Ebon.

Kalem looked uncomfortable. "I am not sure that is wise. They teach us our spells in a certain order, and they do so for a reason."

"What reason? If I can make mist, why should I not try it? Mayhap it will turn my mind towards other spells—even the spell for stone."

"Mayhap," said Kalem. "I suppose I cannot see the harm in it . . ."

Ebon closed his eyes and tried to envision the air around him. He spread his fingers until he could feel its coolness on his skin. At first he felt no different. Then he remembered how it felt when he turned water to oil. He did not picture the water in his mind so much as he *saw* it through his fingers. He tried it now, and soon it was as though he could see the air's tiny currents as they wove about him. He opened his eyes and focused. To his delight, the world brightened, and he knew his eyes were glowing. Thin wisps of mist sprang into being, twisting in little spirals about his fingers.

Joy shot through him, joy strong enough to break his concentration. The glow died, and the mists vanished. But rather than disappointment, he only felt his joy increase until he laughed out loud. "I did it!"

Kalem's grin matched his own. "You did at that. That seemed to come to you easily."

Ebon studied his fingers closely. He still felt that he could see the air's currents. "It was so much easier than the wood. I could see it as plain as the floor beneath my feet."

"As I said, air is simple. But still, even I did not learn mist so quickly. You should be proud."

"Have you ever used it? It seems to me that mists would be a powerful spell for sneaking about."

Kalem's face fell, and he looked to the ceiling as though for help. "Sky save me. Of course you would immediately think of how to use it for mischief."

Ebon gave his shoulder a little push. "Oh, calm yourself. I have no schemes to sneak about the Academy and wreak havoc. At least, not yet."

"You would find it a hard prospect even if you did. Any alchemist or weremage would sense what you were doing and put a stop to it."

"*Transmuter* or *therianthrope*, Kalem," said Ebon, wagging a finger in admonishment. "Honestly, you could at least pretend that proper terms matter."

Kalem scowled.

TWENTY

THE DISCOVERY OF A NEW SPELL, AND ONE THAT ACTUALLY SEEMED useful, filled Ebon's days with joy. Whenever he could, he practiced spinning his mists. When he grew bored in Credell's class, in between reading books in the library, in the common room outside his dormitory—all were perfect opportunities to steal away by himself and practice. And now he found himself wondering what else he might be able to learn. Suddenly his wooden rod seemed utterly unimportant. Oh, certainly he would need to turn it to stone one day—but why worry over it now, when he could learn other spells instead?

But not all his time was so joyous. Every so often, thoughts crept in of the parcel he had delivered for Mako and his father. Despite sharing his worries with Adara, and the conversations he had had with Kalem and Theren, he could not help but wonder what he was now involved in. If indeed he was part of some nefarious scheme, he doubted the King's law would care that he had not wished to be involved.

One morning he woke with an idea. He toyed with it all through

Credell's class, turning it over and over in his mind. By the time of the midday meal, he knew he had to bring it to Kalem and Theren.

"I have been thinking hard," he said, as soon as they were all seated in the dining hall. "And I want to know what was in the parcel."

"I am sure we would all like to know," said Kalem. "But that carriage, as they say, has driven on already."

"Mayhap not for good."

Theren leaned in, eyes alight. "My dear goldbag. You cannot be proposing what I think—no, what I *hope,* you are proposing."

"Mayhap," said Ebon with a grin.

Kalem looked back and forth between them, utterly lost. "I do not understand. What do you mean to do?"

"I shall return to the inn where I brought the package. If the man is still there, I mean to find the package and learn what was inside it."

Kalem could only gawk. "You cannot be serious."

"He is, and it is glorious," said Theren. She laughed out loud and slapped her hand down on the table. Many students looked over in shock, but she ignored them. "My dear little goldbag. I take back all the nasty things I ever said about you. Well, not all of them, but the greater part of them at least."

"You will help me, then?"

"She will *not,* because you will *not* do this mad thing," said Kalem. Though he whispered, it was so loud and harsh that Ebon doubted it did much to hide the words. "You do not know what you are involved in. You could be killed."

"I doubt that. The man we saw is some agent of my family's. He would not dare raise a hand to me, for then he would face their wrath—or at least my aunt's, for I doubt my father cares whether I live or die."

"You do not know that," said Kalem. "What if he hired your family to do this thing for him? If they are in his employ, and not the other way around, that is a very different situation."

Ebon scoffed. "My family, playing the part of lackey to some man in a rotten hovel of an inn? That is hardly likely."

"You are quick to say so, yet what if you are wrong? It could go ill for all of us."

"All of us?" said Ebon with a smile. "Do you mean to come with us, then?"

"Say you will, little goldbag," said Theren, shaking Kalem's shoulder. The poor boy flopped all about as though he were a rag doll. "It would not be a proper adventure without you."

"I do not *want* it to be a proper adventure!" whined Kalem, shoving her hand away.

Ebon leaned in closer. "Think, Kalem. You have heard rumors of my family's doings, have you not? It seems I am being drawn into them, though I did not will it. Will you not help me fight off their influence? I do not mean to grow up and become another agent of whatever mischief my father wishes to get up to."

"Then leave it behind," said Kalem miserably. "Refuse to follow his orders, and keep your nose out of whatever is happening."

"Too late for that," said Theren. "His nose is already well stuck in."

"And I cannot refuse him," said Ebon. "He will withdraw me from the Academy. Mako said as much."

Kalem seemed to know he was defeated. It made him sullen, and he folded his arms in a pout. "This is a terrible idea."

"Mayhap, but it is the only thing I can think of to free myself. I see you as a friend, Kalem. A true friend. Will you help me?"

The boy rolled his eyes and looked around. "Of course I will. You idiot."

Ebon and Theren cheered as they embraced him.

That night, Ebon met his friends in the hall outside of Kalem's common room.

"All right," said Kalem, looking thoroughly disgruntled. "If we mean to go through with this mad scheme, then let us get on with it. How do you mean to sneak out?"

"Theren has a way."

"And I shall not leave you behind this time," she said with a grin. "But I do not think all three of us can approach the wall without being seen."

"You need not worry about that," said Ebon. "I have learned a new spell."

He focused on the air around him, and the world grew brighter. Mist sprang from his skin, swirling about to surround him. Soon he could not see the others, though he could still sense them standing close. His chest swelled with pride—but then he heard Kalem and Theren burst into raucous laughter through the mist, which they swiftly hushed.

"What?" said Ebon. "What is it?"

"Ebon, you look ridiculous," Theren managed to choke out. "Stop that foolish spell at once."

He did not understand, but he let the image of the mist slip from his mind. The world darkened, and the fog receded. Kalem still clutched a hand to his mouth, his eyes bugging out from laughter, and Theren's dark face had darkened further as she fought to remain silent.

"Do you not think the Academy's attendants would notice a perfectly student-sized cloud of mist scuttling about the halls?" said Theren. "It practically held to your limbs. You were as inconspicuous as a two-mast ship falling through the ceiling of the High King's palace."

"It looked like this." Kalem's eyes glowed, and mist sprang into being around him—but it held only a few fingers away from his skin, so that he was like a little boy made all of fog. He crouched and slunk down the hallway in a low run, head swinging back and forth as though looking for pursuers. Theren clapped both hands to her mouth again and nearly fell over laughing.

Ebon's cheeks were burning, and he looked down at his shoes. "Stop that. It is easy enough for the two of you to mock me; you have been here for years."

Kalem let the mists die away, and Theren put a comforting hand on his shoulder. But they could not hide the glints in both their eyes. "Indeed, it is unfair," said Kalem. "I am sorry. And you should be very proud of how quickly you have learned the spell for mist. But on this outing, at least, I think I should be responsible for concealing our escape."

"Very well," grumbled Ebon. "Then let us get on with it."

He led them through the halls and then down the wide staircase to the front hall. Mellie was there by the door. She straightened in her chair and fixed them with wide, suspicious eyes. But Ebon only gave her a little wave and turned around, heading back down the hallway to the white doors leading outside.

"Turn left," said Theren. "We should leave by the eastern doors, for I need to use the sheds."

Ebon did as she said, and soon they had reached the training grounds outside the citadel. A few other students stood here and there in pockets, scarcely visible in the dim light. There, too, Ebon saw Jia and the other instructor he had often seen on the training grounds, speaking with each other as they strode down a path.

"We shall have to wait for Jia and Dasko to pass," muttered Kalem. "They are both therianthropes; if I cast my mists now, they will detect it."

Dasko. So the instructor had a name.

Jia saw Ebon and gave him a nod, which he returned, but the two instructors took no other notice of them. Soon they had vanished around the corner of the citadel. Ebon waited a few moments just to be safe, and then he gave Kalem a nod.

The boy's eyes glowed, and mist filled the air all about them. Ebon heard a few muted sounds of surprise from the other students in the training grounds, but he and his friends were already running for the wall. He would have run straight into it if Theren had not stopped him with a quick hand. She guided them all until they stood by the wall together, huddling against it in the fog. A few paces away, Ebon saw shacks built against the inside wall, perfect mirrors of the ones on the outside.

"I will go first," said Theren. "The sheds are easy and will give you a sense of how to make the landing. If I am atop them first, I can help steady you. Then we get to try the wall—that will be the fun part."

"I doubt it," said Ebon. He remembered the sickness in his stomach when he had stood upon the library's third floor balcony and shuddered.

"Up we go, then," said Theren. She crouched, eyes glowing, and then with a leap she vanished into the air.

Ebon gulped hard. Then he felt something under his arms where they joined the shoulders. He looked down, but there was nothing there. *Theren's magic,* he realized. Steeling himself, he jumped as high as he could.

An unseen force gripped him, throwing him through the air. Then he was coming down, the shed roof beneath his feet. It came too quickly, and he fell with a crash. Soon Theren had gripped his arm and hauled him up.

"All well?" she said.

Ebon nodded, a bit shaken. A moment later, Kalem came flying through the air to land beside them both. The boy's eyes still glowed from holding the mist in place.

"The next leap will be harder," Theren warned. "Be ready to grip the wall with all your might."

Again she leaped first, the glow of her eyes vanishing into the mist above them. Again Ebon felt unseen hands holding him up. He crouched as low as he could. For a moment he could not will himself to move.

"Ebon?" said Kalem.

"A moment." Ebon took two deep breaths. "Sky above, protect me."

He leaped.

This time he rocketed through the air, the mist stinging his eyes so that he had to close them. Then the cold against his skin vanished. He opened his eyes to see the top of the wall rocketing towards him.

He could see he would not clear it.

Panic froze his limbs. But then his chest struck the wall's lip, and on instinct he reached forth to seize it. His elbows barely cleared the edge, and his shoes scrabbled uselessly against the wall as he tried to help himself rise the last pace.

"Ebon!" Theren fell to her knees and reached for him just as Ebon lost his grip and fell into empty space.

For an instant, time stopped. He could see the world in perfect detail: the horror in Theren's face, plain despite the glow in her eyes; the rough texture of the wall sliding away under his hand; his robes fluttering in the air that rushed past him.

But then Theren's hand closed over his wrist, and he slapped against the wall hard enough to knock the breath from him. Theren swung him one way, then another, and her eyes glowed brighter. He felt another unseen push, and an invisible rope tugged him atop the wall.

He collapsed on his back, panting, clutching the granite beneath him until it scraped his fingers. Theren must have thought he was hurt, for she knelt above him and looked into his eyes.

"What is wrong? Are you injured?"

Ebon could not speak, but he shook his head. She grinned at him.

"I would wager you never thought the Academy would be like this, goldbag. Come. Kalem is waiting, and likely wondering what we are up to."

She stood and went to the edge. Ebon closed his eyes, willing the world to stop spinning.

"Aieee!"

Kalem screamed as he landed beside Ebon. He cleared the lip easily and landed facedown. Like Ebon, he seized the wall's top as though he might never let go.

"My apologies," said Theren. "You are much lighter than either of us. I may have brought you up too quickly."

"Yes, you may have," said Kalem, voice shaking.

"I cannot go back down," said Ebon, voice breaking on every other word.

"What?" said Theren.

"I cannot do that again. I cannot move. Please. Please, I cannot."

Kalem pushed himself up to a sitting position and looked ruefully at Theren. "He deals poorly with heights. I had forgotten."

Theren shook her head and rolled her eyes. "Come now, Ebon. It is only a little jump. Going down is much easier, for I do not have to lift you—only stop you from falling to your death."

Ebon's limbs shook harder. Kalem, still sitting, slapped Theren's leg. "Leave off, Theren! Can you not see you are frightening him?"

"It is not her, Kalem," said Ebon. "Look how high we are. I was mad to think I could do this."

Kalem came crawling to Ebon's side. "Come, Ebon. You must go down, one way or another. It may as well be on the outside, rather than into the training grounds again."

"I cannot move. Tell one of the instructors I am here. They can lift me. I care not if they punish me, or even expel me. I *cannot* move, Kalem."

Kalem frowned and put a hand on his shoulder. "But you can.

Because you must, and because you were right before. Your family has some evil work afoot. We can put a stop to it, but not without you. Come, my friend. Sit up, first. Then we will take the next step."

Sit up. That seemed easy enough.

Ebon took another deep breath and forced his hands to slide across the stone until he could lift himself. Soon he was half-sitting, though still he tried to keep himself low to the stone.

"Good, good," said Kalem, speaking softly. "Now. Theren will go down first, as she did before. And I will be here with you until you are ready."

Theren shook her head, but she did as Kalem said, stepping off the edge of the wall and vanishing into the darkness. The only thing they could see of her was her eyes, faintly glowing in the darkness ten paces below.

"It is so far," Ebon said, trying not to wail.

Kalem squeezed his shoulders. "You can do it. Come now. You are older than I am."

"That only means I am larger. What if she should drop me?"

"You heard her—going down is much easier than going up. If it helps, I will push you."

"If you do, I will pull you with me."

They both chuckled, though Ebon had to force it. "All right," said Kalem. "Whenever you feel yourself ready."

Ebon slid closer to the edge of the wall. It was just there now, right beside his hand. He did not even have to jump. He could simply fall. His heart still hammered in his chest, and spots of light danced before his eyes. He thought he might faint. *That would get me off the wall in short order,* he mused. The thought summoned a bitter laugh.

He slid his feet over the edge and pushed off.

Panic seized him again—but this time it did not matter, for Theren caught him. He could see her as he drew closer, the glow in her eyes brightening, hands held up. The closer he fell to the roof of the shed, the slower he moved. By the time he was two paces above her, he was no longer even afraid, for he moved slower than a brisk walk. He came down upon the roof easily, but still his nerves made him fall to his hands and knees.

"Did I not tell you?" said Theren. "Easier than going up."

"You were right," said Ebon. He forced himself up and embraced her. She started in surprise, but hugged him back after a moment. "Thank you."

"Yes, well," said Theren, clearly uncomfortable. "Leave off, or our little alchemist will dive into the abyss without me to catch him."

A moment later, Kalem was down. He and Theren jumped easily off the shed roof. Ebon elected to climb down, hanging from the edge before dropping to the street. Then they ran off, and soon the Academy was out of sight.

They had come over the east wall, and so they ran in a wide loop until they were heading west again. As they went, Kalem looked about in excitement. His young face glowed with a silver tint in the moonslight.

"This is terribly, terribly stupid of us. We could get in a great deal of trouble, or even be expelled from the Academy. It is all rather exciting."

"I fear we have proven a poor influence on our young friend, Ebon," said Theren, teeth flashing in the dark.

"Mayhap, but mayhap he shall be better for it. You are a bit prudish when it comes to rules." Ebon ruffled Kalem's hair. Kalem batted his hand away.

"Leave off. You speak as though you have done this often, instead of once, and then with special permission from the dean."

"Lucky for you both, then, that I am an old hand at this," said Theren.

"How many times have you snuck out?" asked Kalem.

"You mean this month?"

Ebon shook his head and smiled. In truth he was far more worried about this excursion than he had been the last time he was in the city after dark. But now the journey was his own choice, and besides, he had his friends with him. That was more comforting than ignorantly doing his father's bidding.

Before long Theren had led them to the Shining Door, which looked every bit as dirty and irreputable as the last time. "Don your hoods," said Ebon. "I would not have anyone here recognize Theren and I from when we came before."

"They will see our students' robes," said Theren. "That may be more than clue enough."

"That we cannot help."

With their hoods raised, they entered the inn. Almost immediately, Ebon felt Kalem draw closer to him. The patrons in the common room gave them evil looks. With their hoods up, gazes lingered a while longer as some tried to see their faces. Ebon ignored them as he made his way to the back, where the innkeeper stood with his hands spread on the counter.

"Well met," said Ebon, trying to deepen his voice. "We seek a man who roomed here, or mayhap rooms here still. He had a thin beard and Elf-white skin. When last I saw him, he wore blue and grey."

"I may know many men," said the innkeeper. "And it does me no good to discuss any of their business. Shove off."

Theren tensed beside him, but Ebon put a hand on her arm. From his purse he drew a gold weight, sliding it to the barkeep. The man eyed the coin for a moment, but he did not move. Ebon sighed and extracted another, placing it beside the first. "That is all you will get, and is more than a fair price for loosening your lips."

The innkeeper scowled, but he took the coins and tucked them into his pocket. "The one you seek is not here at the moment, though he still holds a room."

"What use are those words?" snapped Theren.

"They are the only ones I have."

"What room has he taken?" said Ebon.

The innkeeper pointed to the hallway leading to the back. "First on the right."

Ebon withdrew another coin. *No matter my allowance, at this rate I shall soon be a pauper.* "For your willing assistance," he said. If the man caught the irony in Ebon's tone, he did not show it—but he took the coin.

They moved towards the hallway, Ebon in the lead. But before they reached it, Kalem tugged at his sleeve. "What do you mean to do?" he whispered.

"Search the man's room."

"Are you mad? What if the innkeeper is wrong? What if he is here, and even now slumbers within?"

"Well, if he is slumbering, then we shall have no trouble," said Theren brightly.

"Unless he wakes. Or unless he does not slumber, and is sitting there waiting in lamplight for some foolish Academy students to come bumbling to their deaths!" Kalem's voice rose with each word until he was nearly screeching, though still in a whisper.

"Our only other choice is to turn back and make for home," said Ebon.

"That seems an excellent idea."

"For cowards," said Theren.

"I am going," said Ebon. "Kalem, if you wish, you may withdraw. We shall find you on the street in a moment."

Kalem looked as though he might, but then he looked around. Many eyes were now upon the three of them, for they stood near the center of the room.

"Oh, very well," he muttered. "Only I think this is the height of idiocy, and speaking of the two of you, that says quite a lot."

They reached the door. Ebon pressed an ear to it for a moment, but he could hear nothing inside. He turned the latch and stepped through. The door gave a long *creeeak* as it swung slowly open. There were no lanterns within. The only light came from the common room itself, and that was too dim to reveal anything.

He squared his shoulders and took another step in. The room was dead silent. Theren and Kalem's footsteps sounded like thunder as they came in after him and swung the door shut.

It took a moment for his eyes to adjust, and even then they could not see into the shadowed corners. But faint moonslight through the cracks in the drawn shutters revealed a dirty, unkempt bed and a single chest of drawers. There was a lamp on the floor by the bed, and for a moment Ebon thought to light it. But that might be folly; what if the man returned and saw the light glowing beneath his door?

"Look quickly," he said. "The package was soft, wrapped in brown cloth, and tied with simple string. I think it was mayhap two hands wide. Find it, if you can, or anything unusual that might have been inside it."

They set about their search. Theren moved to the bed, lifting the straw mattress and the pillow. Her nose coiled in disgust. Ebon understood why as he dropped to the floor and searched under the bed's frame—the floor smelled of something untoward, a smell he could not place and did not like. But there was nothing underneath, except some rubbish of paper that held no words.

But from the chest of drawers, Kalem whispered, "Ebon."

Theren went to him at once, and Ebon joined her a moment later. In the bottom drawer of the chest was the brown cloth parcel. Ebon recognized it at once.

"That is it," he said. "Open it."

"Why should I?" said Kalem, voice shaking. "You open it."

Ebon reached for it with shaking fingers and undid the string. The brown cloth fell away. But in the darkness, he could not see what lay within. He reached for it and drew it out, holding it under the moonslight.

It was a tabard, that was plain: white with gold edges, and large enough to be worn over a suit of plate armor—or mayhap chain, if the wearer were particularly large. It covered chest and back and upper arms as well, and a lifetime of wealth told him the cloth was very fine. But more importantly, upon the breast was displayed a sign: a four-pointed star with a red gem in the middle. Ebon knew he had seen it before, but it took him a moment to place it. When he did, his heart skipped a beat.

"The High King's sigil," breathed Theren.

"This is worn by the palace guards," said Kalem. "I went there once. Every one of the High King's personal guard wore a tabard of just this make."

"Why would I have been asked to deliver this? And to a man like the one we saw, in such a flea-ridden place?" said Ebon.

"Mayhap there is more to be found," said Theren, and she returned to the drawer.

But just as Ebon was about to join in her search, a sound made him freeze. The door's latch turned, and before he could tell them to hide, it flew open. There in the doorway, wreathed in the lamplight from the room beyond, stood the pale man with the thin beard.

TWENTY-ONE

KALEM GAVE A SHARP CRY AND STRETCHED OUT HIS HANDS. HIS EYES glowed, and a thick mist filled the room. At the same time, Ebon leaped forwards to drag Theren back from the chest of drawers. Together the three of them pressed back into the room. Ebon did not know what to do, but he knew that trying to escape through the door would mean capture.

Together the three of them pressed back into the room. Ebon did not know what to do, but he knew that trying to escape through the door would mean capture.

Theren tore from his grasp, and he lost his grip on Kalem. Then a form came forwards through the mist, wiry hands grasping at empty air. The pale man.

He seized the front of Ebon's robe and dragged him in. Even so close, the mists were too thick to see his face.

"Help!" cried Ebon. He tried to strike the man, but found his wrist caught in an icy grip. His assailant's skin was cold and clammy, his arms all wiry muscle.

The other hand released Ebon's robe. Then Ebon heard a *snikt*—a drawn dagger. The steel flashed in the mist as it came up, ready to plunge into Ebon's heart.

Something invisible struck the man. His head flew back, and he dropped the blade. His ankle flew high, flipping him upside down. Ebon had seen it before when Lilith had attacked him in the tavern. It was Theren's magic.

"Run!" she cried.

Ebon ran for where he thought the door was. But he misjudged and struck the wall instead. A small form crashed into his back—Kalem. Ebon grabbed the boy, and together they pressed through the door into the hallway beyond.

Theren was there, but she did not waste time with words. Together they fled through the common room. The innkeeper cried out, but they ran on, heedless. Soon they were in the cool, clean air of the streets beyond, but they kept running until they had left the Shining Door far behind.

At last they stopped in an alleyway, far from any main street. Kalem collapsed against a brick wall, sliding to sit on the filthy ground. Eyes closed and head thrown back, he cast down his hood.

"Did he see us?" said Theren. "Does he have our description?"

"Our hoods were raised," said Ebon. "And though he held me by the wrist, I could not see his face in the mist. I think we are safe."

Kalem's panting slowed at last. His gaze fixed angrily on Ebon. "Safe? You nearly got the three of us killed!"

"How was I to know he would return while we were in his very room?"

"How could you simply assume he would not?" said Kalem. "He meant to murder us. What if he had? Can you imagine your parents receiving a letter that you had been killed upon the Seat?"

Ebon felt his cheeks burning, and he looked down at his shoes. The street was silent for a moment. "My father would read the letter and then most likely throw it in a fire. I doubt he would even tell my mother."

"I came from an orphanage in Cabrus," said Theren. Her voice was nearly as quiet as Ebon's. "No one there would care. My patron would

164

see it as an inconvenience. Then she would find another wizard to do her bidding."

Kalem's mouth hung open, but no sound came out. He looked back and forth between them and then dropped his own gaze. "I . . . I am sorry," he said. "I had not thought . . . that is, I thought only of my own parents."

Ebon shrugged. "Who could blame you? I, too, considered only myself. It was thoughtless of me to bring you here."

Theren pulled the boy to his feet and gave his shoulders a little shake. "Do you jest? We might be dead if not for our brave Kalem here. Your mists were exquisite."

Kalem still looked abashed, but he gave a little smile. "I panicked. I hardly knew what I was doing."

She smiled. "Better a fool who does the right thing than a wise man who does the wrong, I always say."

Their somber mood lifted somewhat, and Ebon gave his friends a smile. But then he frowned again. "I only wish we had learned more. I wonder what he had that uniform for."

"There I may be of some help," said Theren with a wide smile. "For I found something else, just as our unwelcome guest arrived."

Her hand vanished into her robes. A moment later she drew forth a parchment and unfurled it. It was a map of the Great Bay and the High King's Seat, with marks and symbols scrawled all across it.

They made their way back to the Academy as quickly as they could, and Theren helped them over the wall once more. Again Ebon found it a harrowing experience, but already it was easier than the last time.

After sneaking into the citadel, they went to the common room outside Kalem's dormitory. The younger children had all gone to bed, and they huddled together over a table to study the map by firelight.

The Seat itself took up most of the map, though Selvan's coast was depicted to the west. The docks on the east and west ends of the island were drawn in more detail than the city itself. Near the western docks, many ships had been drawn in dark blue ink, while near the eastern dock were more ships drawn in red. From the High King's palace were drawn lines in blue and red, tracing through the city and out to the docks to meet the ships of the same colors.

"What does it mean?" said Kalem softly.

"I do not know," said Ebon. "It looks like a route from the palace to the docks, to ships waiting."

"It could be," said Theren. "But look here."

She pointed, and Ebon saw a smaller drawing that had escaped his notice. To the south of the eastern docks, on the very southeastern tip of the island, was a smaller ship—more of a boat. A rough cave had been sketched around it, and they were both enclosed by a red circle.

"None of this means anything to me," said Ebon. "I know little of ships and sailing."

"Yet the drawings seem more concerned with the island than with the boats," said Theren.

Kalem's expression became grave. "Mayhap this is some plot. Have you heard the tale of the Lord Prince in his youth? Some bandits captured him and hid him in their forest stronghold, where they hoped to extract a mighty ransom from the High King. This may be some plan to do the same again, or something similar, at least."

"I have heard that tale," said Ebon. "But it would be foolhardy now. His guard has been vigilant ever since. And he was captured upon the King's road, not within the palace itself."

"A brash plan may succeed where a more timid one fails, if only because one's foes do not expect it," said Theren.

"And mayhap it is not the Lord Prince," said Kalem. "Mayhap it is some other member of the royal family. Mayhap some king or young prince from one of the outland kingdoms. This is an ill finding. We should tell one of the instructors so that they may warn the palace."

Theren cuffed the back of his head. "Think. How could we tell them we came by this information? What is your plan? I can imagine your words to Jia. 'Pardon me, Instructor, but I snuck out of the Academy after nightfall and found a plot to capture one of the royal family. Or I think I did—you see, I am not sure *what* I found, in truth.' You would be put on the first ship home before you could finish the words."

"Yet great disaster might be averted," said Kalem. "We do not have to tell them it was we who found this map. We could leave it where they could find it and let them deduce the rest for themselves."

Ebon sat scowling down at the map, only half hearing his friends. Finally he spoke in a low murmur. "We do not know what this means. We do not even know the full extent of our own ignorance, for this may lead to some other truth we cannot imagine. What if this is nothing evil after all? What if the man is an agent of the High King herself, carrying out some order?"

Kalem frowned, and a moment passed before he answered. "Ebon, I can see why you would wish to believe that. It would mean your family plotted nothing untoward and that you were blameless in following your father's order. Yet I think it is dangerous to so easily believe that is the case."

"How else can you explain his uniform?" said Ebon. "Surely those cannot be obtained from just any clothier. Mayhap he is in hiding, until he leaves upon his mission and must reveal himself to be the High King's agent?"

Theren and Kalem looked at each other uncertainly. After a moment they shrugged.

"I think we should rest," said Ebon. "Whatever the truth behind this map, it would be foolish to act too quickly upon guesses. The hour is late, and our minds may be befuddled. Can we agree upon that, at least?"

"I suppose so," said Kalem doubtfully.

Theren let loose a mighty yawn. "I call those words wise. Very well. I am only glad we have had another night of excitement. We should do it more often."

"We should *not*," muttered Kalem.

Ebon rolled up the map and tucked it into his sleeve. Then he paused a moment before speaking, and he had to duck his head before he could. "I wanted to thank you both, by the by. For coming with me. I would have died were it not for you."

Theren flushed and looked away. "Well, you would not have been able to go were it not for me. I think that may balance things out."

Kalem smiled at her, and then at Ebon. "I believe that what she meant to say is, 'You are welcome.' But now I truly must go to bed, or I will fall asleep in my chair. Good night."

"Good night," said Ebon.

Kalem rose and went to his dormitory. Theren followed Ebon out, and silently they descended the stairs toward the older students' dormitories. But when they reached the bend in the hallways where they were meant to part, Ebon stopped her for a moment.

"I thanked you already. But I feel I owe you an apology as well."

That took her aback. She smiled slowly. "Why? You have done me no harm."

"No true harm, mayhap, but I have sometimes been impatient, or thoughtless, or simply stupid. Yet you have never abandoned me."

Theren shrugged as though bored. "You have not given me sufficient cause yet, I suppose. And besides, I have already said I find you a decent enough sort. For a goldbag."

Ebon stepped close and took her shoulders. He kissed one cheek, and then the other, before stepping away again.

"What was that?" she said, eyes narrowed in suspicion. Her hand twitched, as though she restrained herself from rubbing at her cheek— or mayhap striking him.

"A greeting, and a parting, for dear family and friends," he said. "The custom of my kingdom—though one in which I am ill practiced, for there are few who I hold dear enough to earn it."

Theren's jaw clenched, and she did not answer. To his surprise, Ebon thought he saw her eyes glistening. But she only said, gruffly, "Well. A bit more kissing than I am comfortable with, but then your kingdom is very strange. Good night. Goldbag."

She turned and quickly made off down the hall.

TWENTY-TWO

OVER THE NEXT FEW DAYS, EBON MET WITH HIS FRIENDS AT EVERY OP-
portunity. During meals they would sit together and discuss the map.
Every afternoon, Ebon would pore over it in the library with Kalem.
Yet no matter how they tried to read the markings, they could find no
further meaning in them.

Once, Ebon went to Jia and asked her if there were any special significance to the colors of red and blue when used in mapmaking. She
looked surprised at the question, and launched into some explanation
of how farmers used them to mark the rotation of crops through the
seasons. Though Ebon knew at once it had nothing to do with his own
map, he found himself forced to sit and listen to the lecture.

After he finally escaped and returned to Kalem, he slouched in his
chair. "I feel nearly dead from boredom. I can think of nothing but cotton and wheat and the best dates for planting them. Only I have them
mixed up, and would likely try to grow cotton in the dead of winter."

Some days later, the three of them sat huddled together at the midday meal. All were silent, staring into their bowls with no new ideas

springing to mind. Ebon had thought for so long upon the map that he imagined he could see it splayed out on the table before them.

"There is something we might do," said Theren slowly. "Though I doubt Kalem will like it."

"With such an introduction, how could I refuse to hear your plan?" said Kalem, rolling his eyes.

"We could go to the docks and see what we might find to explain the marks," said Ebon.

Both Kalem and Theren gaped at him, but Theren spoke first. "That is just what I meant to say. How did you know?"

"I have thought the same thing myself," said Ebon. "I did not mention it before now, because I thought that if even you had not spoken of it, it must be a terrible idea indeed."

"It is!" hissed Kalem, leaning forwards. "It *is* a terrible idea, and you must put it from your mind immediately! Already you have nearly gotten us all killed. Do you wish to risk our lives again?"

"I know no other way to learn the truth of the map," said Ebon with a shrug.

"And this is entirely different besides," said Theren. "Before, we went in search of a man who we knew—or at least suspected—was up to mischief. Now we are only going to see the docks."

"Mayhap we could go there during the daylight hours, to further reduce any danger," said Ebon halfheartedly. But he knew it for a poor idea, and he saw the same thought in Theren's expression.

"That would likely teach us nothing at all," she said. "Whatever this plot may be, we are unlikely to find it laying plain for us to find. If dark deeds are to be done, wisdom says they would be done in the dark."

"Another nighttime adventure, then," said Kalem. "Well, you may count me out."

"Dear cousin Ebon! Might I have a word?"

The voice shocked them out of their hushed conversation. Ebon looked up to find the dean standing over their table. He and Kalem froze. But Theren only leaned back carelessly, eyeing the dean with casual disinterest.

"Dean Cyrus," stammered Ebon. "Forgive us. We did not see you there."

"Please. 'Dean Cyrus' sounds so formal. 'Dean' is sufficient. Now, about that word . . .?"

The dean looked pointedly at Kalem and Theren. Kalem took the hint at once and leaped from the bench as though he had been stabbed. In a moment he had vanished among the other children in the dining hall. But Theren only looked to Ebon, brow arched in question. He nodded. She removed herself from the table, though much more slowly than Kalem had.

Dean Cyrus took a seat opposite Ebon. He had no food with him, and he leaned forwards on his elbows with a friendly smile. Ebon was keenly aware of the effect it had on the other students nearby. They seemed caught between wanting to watch and wanting to be as far from the dean as possible. He saw many students leaning away in their seats, as though they found even a few extra fingers of distance more comfortable.

"So. How go your studies, Cousin?"

"They progress well, Dean." It was a lie, of course, but Ebon well remembered how Cyrus had treated Credell when he thought the instructor was not teaching Ebon quickly enough.

"I notice you are still in Credell's class."

"Yes, and he is working hard at my instruction," said Ebon earnestly. He tried to smile but was afraid it came out as a grimace.

"Clearly not hard enough," said the dean, sounding annoyed. "A bright boy like you, and especially one so old, should have graduated his class already. I imagine he has you fooling about with that wooden rod trick?"

"Yes, Dean," said Ebon, ducking his head.

"Such a simple spell. The basest alchemists can perform it. Some students come to the Academy already having learned it from a wizard in their homeland. You should be well past it already. I shall have to speak with Credell."

"I assure you that is not necessary, Dean," said Ebon in desperation.

Cyrus waved a hand airily. "Think nothing of it, my boy. Your loyalty is admirable, but you owe nothing to an instructor who does not give you enough attention."

Ebon wanted to sink through his seat and into the stone floor. But he said only, "Yes, Dean."

"Now, then. What of our dear family? How fare they? Have you had any words with Halab recently?" The dean leaned forwards, his fingers spreading across the tabletop, and Ebon caught a curious light in his eyes.

Now we come to it—the true reason for this visit. Ebon knew full well that the dean cared little for his studies. But he could not imagine why he was interested in Ebon's correspondence with the family. Unless . . .

Ebon's heart quailed with terror. Mayhap the dean was in league with his father, in whatever plot centered around the Shining Door. Mayhap they suspected Ebon had been the one to attack the man at the inn, and now the dean was here to investigate the truth.

He chose his words carefully. "I have not spoken with Halab, nor with any other of the family, since I arrived here, Dean." *Other than Mako,* he thought. But if he was right, and this visit was about the happenings at the Shining Door, then Cyrus would already know of Mako's visits. And if he was wrong, Ebon doubted the bodyguard would appreciate a loose tongue.

Cyrus' eyes glittered. "Oh? Are you certain? Have none of them written to you? You may tell me, of course."

"They have not, Dean. Honestly. Mayhap . . . mayhap they have been too busy to write."

Come to think of it, it was odd that he had not received a letter. Father would never have sent one, of course, but enough time had passed that Albi could have. Then he realized that he himself had not yet written home, and his ears burned. It had been nearly two months since he left home. Albi would likely be furious with him.

The dean smiled and shook his head. "Oh, Ebon. You cannot think me so simple as all that. If anyone in the family has told you something you do not wish to relay, let me rid you of your fear: I am fully informed of all goings-on back in Idris. I only thought we might combine our knowledge and see what we could surmise from it. I would be especially interested in correspondence with Halab, for she has not answered my letters in some days now."

Days? That meant Halab was still on the Seat. If she had returned to Idris, Cyrus would not have expected a response for weeks.

"I have not written Halab," said Ebon. "Though you have reminded me that mayhap I should, to thank her for sending me here. It was only by her grace that I was able to attend."

The dean's mouth twisted, becoming something sour and foul. "Yes. Grace, indeed." Then he leaned back, taking on a crafty look. "Well, we might speak of something else. Have you learned any . . . *other* . . . spells? That is, spells other than what Credell has tried and failed to teach you?"

Ebon swallowed hard. He thought of the mists Kalem had taught him to spin. Did the dean know of that? How could he? Had Ebon broken some rule without knowing it?

He realized he had taken too long to answer, and spoke in haste. "No, Dean. I have learned nothing else. I am trying to focus on Credell's teachings."

Cyrus leaned still closer. "Come, Cousin. I was a student here myself once. I know students will often pass knowledge to each other of new spells they have learned. Has one of your alchemist friends taught you anything new? Mayhap that young copper-haired boy who was just here?"

Ebon swallowed hard. "Kalem said it is unwise to learn our spells out of order. I have tried to persuade him, but he has only instructed me in the spell that turns wood to stone."

Cyrus' expression darkened. His voice dropped to a whisper, one that Ebon could barely make out. "You would not do well to lie to me, boy. You could scarcely have a worse enemy in the Academy than the dean."

Ebon's pulse sang in his ears. His throat had almost gone too dry to speak. "I am not lying, Dean."

For a moment they sat there, staring at each other. Then, abruptly, Cyrus leaned back.

"Hm. Very well." He folded his hands into the sleeves of his robe. His brows drew close, lips pressing into a thin line. "I understand the urge to guard your friends' secrets. As for our family, I ask you this: should you hear from Halab again, please come and tell me at once."

"I will, Dean," said Ebon earnestly.

Cyrus stood quickly and swept off, leaving Ebon wondering as to his meaning. He knew only one thing: the jaws of the trap were closing still, and he could not think how to free himself.

TWENTY-THREE

THE NEXT DAY, EBON WAS SLUMPED AGAINST THE WALL IN CREDELL'S class. He watched the instructor go back and forth through the classroom, giving the children advice and answering their questions. Just now Credell was beside Astrea, the wild-haired girl and the closest thing Ebon had to a friend here. The girl seemed to be on the cusp of transforming her wooden rod. Often Ebon had seen her eyes glowing with her magic, the wooden rod swirling beneath her fingers. But when she stopped, she still held only a wooden stick. Credell was turning the rod from wood to stone and back again before her eyes, explaining it to her with murmured words that Ebon could not hear.

It made Ebon's heart ache. Credell was not a bad instructor in truth, for Ebon could see how gently he dealt with the young children. Yet he still could not speak to Ebon without shaking, nor provide any answers to whatever unseen barrier stood between Ebon and his magic.

A knock came at the door. Credell's head jerked up at the noise, and for a moment he only stared. Then his gaze flitted to Ebon, eyes filled with fear. Ebon shrugged.

Credell rose and went to the door. He ducked his head outside to speak with someone Ebon could not see, and when he closed the door he held a message in his hand.

"Er . . . ah . . . Ebon, of the family Drayden," Credell stammered. "You have a visitor. She awaits you outside the Academy. The dean has given you permission to go."

Ebon started in his seat. A visitor? Who would visit him here on the Seat? It could not be his father, for Credell had said *she*. And if Ebon's parents had returned, his mother would never visit him alone. For a moment the thought of Adara flitted through his mind, but he dismissed it as foolish.

Then it came to him in a flash. He shot from his seat and ran from the room, ignoring Credell, who flinched as he passed by.

He burst from the Academy's front door into the street. There she stood: Halab, wearing fabulous golden clothes interwoven with threads of real silver. She turned at the sound of the door opening, and as her gaze fell upon Ebon, she spread her arms.

"Dearest nephew," she said.

"Halab!" Ebon cried, throwing himself into her arms. They embraced for a long moment, and then he remembered his manners. He pulled back, kissing her first on one cheek, and then another. She placed a gentle hand to his cheek.

"Even now you have not forgotten courtesy. I am glad, for you are a long way from home."

"My heart gladdens to see you, dearest aunt," said Ebon. To his great surprise, he found tears springing into his eyes, and against his will they leaked down his cheeks. "I have missed you most terribly. As well as all of the family," he added hastily.

She arched an eyebrow, as though she knew he thought of his father. "Indeed? Then I am only sorry I have not visited sooner. I have arranged for us to spend the day together."

"Truly?" said Ebon. He glanced back at the Academy's front door. "I . . . well, then I am most grateful."

"Oh? Do you not enjoy your studies?"

"Of course I do," he said. "I cannot tell you how much joy I have found here."

"I hope you will tell me all about it," she said, putting his arm in hers as she led him off down the street.

Tell her he did, for nearly two hours as they made their way through the roads of the Seat, apparently without any aim or destination. He told her of the library's many wonders, and of Kalem and Theren, and even Credell, though he left out some details of the instructor's craven nature. Of course he said nothing of his adventures beyond the citadel's walls, and especially nothing concerning Adara. He doubted Halab would disapprove, but he knew his father would, and some whispered word of it might reach home. *Best to keep that to myself*, he thought.

By the time he had finished his tales, his throat was raw from talking. Halab had nodded and made little noises of appreciation at just the right moments. When at last he dwindled to silence, she chuckled and shook her head. "Had I known you would take so well to the Academy, I might have spoken to your father years ago. And yet, in another sense, I think you arrived here at precisely the right time."

Ebon was about to ask her what she meant, but she jerked his arm to the left and down a side street. "Quickly. This way. We do not want to miss the beginning."

"The beginning of what?"

But before she could answer, the thunder of trumpets and bells tore the air asunder. The sound made Ebon nearly jump out of his skin, but Halab stood steady, as though she had expected it. Looking around, Ebon realized they stood scarcely a street away from the High King's palace. They were at the mouth of a main thoroughfare where it met the Seat's greatest road, the one that ran straight west and east from the palace to the wide gates at either end of the island. A crowd had formed around them. As Ebon looked up at the palace, resplendent in white and gold, its great gates began to swing open.

An army marched forth. First Ebon saw many soldiers on horseback, their mounts' hooves dancing gaily as they bounced in parade march. Behind these came more on foot, striding easily even in full plate. All of them wore tabards like Ebon had found in the Shining Door: white with gold edges, and the four-pointed star in the center. The sigil of the High King.

After a time, the High King's army had passed. But after them came still more troops. These were tall and stern, their finely-crafted armor polished until it shone, throwing the sunlight in Ebon's eyes. And all of them wore red cloaks, though their hoods were cast back.

"They are Mystics," said Ebon, voice hushed in wonder.

"Indeed," said Halab. "This is the greater part of all the Mystics here upon the Seat. They march at the command of the Lord Chancellor himself, and he at the command of the High King."

"But where are they going?"

"They go to join the war in Wellmont, in the southwest of Selvan. Or, it is more correctly put, they go to put a stop to it. The High King has at last decided that this border squabble is unseemly, and aims to halt it by strength of arms."

"Can she not simply command them to cease their fighting?"

"Oh, dear nephew. The minds of kings are stern and stubborn and difficult to sway. She might issue such a command, of course, but Dorsea might not listen. And even if they did, resentment would burn like a bonfire in their hearts, only to erupt again into war, and mayhap a worse one. At times, soft words may serve for diplomacy. But a wise ruler knows when to use an ironclad fist instead. Come."

Though the march was not yet over, she turned and led him away. Ebon cast one last look over his shoulder at the red-cloaked soldiers marching by, but they were soon lost to sight through the crowd.

She led him unerringly through the streets, and soon he recognized where they were: the neighborhood that surrounded the Drayden family manor. Before long he saw it, standing two stories above the surrounding buildings, its stones painted gold like their homes back in Idris. His steps faltered, and he felt as though a cloud had passed over his heart.

"Come along now," said Halab, tugging at him playfully. "Your father does not wait within. Today it is only you and I."

He smiled and tried to deny that that had been his thought, but she waved him to silence. They found the gates open and waiting, and when they climbed to the smaller dining hall on the fourth floor, a feast had been laid out for them. From the way it steamed, Ebon guessed it had been hastily uncovered the moment they had arrived.

His weeks at the Academy had nearly caused Ebon to forget how well his family ate. He feasted on lamb and figs and fine spiced soup, and salad dressed with oils that teased his tongue delightfully. Though he never went hungry at the Academy, now he ate like a man famished. When at last he could not down another bite, he sighed contentedly and sank back into the plush cushions of his chair. Halab had finished some time ago, and now she watched him over steepled fingers, a small smile playing across her lips.

"Should I investigate the Academy for starving you?"

"Not at all. It is only that they have so many to feed, and cannot prepare the food so fine as our servants can," said Ebon. "I am ever grateful, and will remember this meal for many months to come."

She reached for her wine goblet and took a delicate sip. That reminded Ebon of his own cup, and he took a deeper pull. "Remember it indeed, and in good health. And now, my nephew, tell me. You have spoken much of your time at the Academy. Have you enjoyed your time here, and your new friends? Truly?"

Ebon frowned. "Of course. Does it seem otherwise? I am happier here than ever I was at home."

Her gaze was fixed on his, and her eyes had grown sharp. "Yet it seems to me I hear something behind your words, some source of discontent that troubles you. Do my senses deceive me?"

He balked at that. She was right, of course. But how to tell her of the errand he had been sent on? Though he felt that he owed his father little in the way of loyalty, still he did not wish to trouble Halab with such matters. Shay was her brother, and it was not well to speak ill of kin to kin.

Halab sighed and put down her goblet. "I see you do not deny it, but are reluctant to speak of it, which I understand. Let me, then, hazard a guess, for recently I have spoken with Mako."

Ebon knew the blood must have drained from his face, and fear put a tingling in his fingers. If Halab knew what Ebon had been up to, mayhap she meant to withdraw him from the Academy. Was that her true purpose here?

But Halab pressed on before he could answer her. "He has told me that your father sent instructions, through Mako himself, to deliver a parcel for him. I know nothing more than that, for neither did Mako. Is this true?"

"Yes, Aunt," said Ebon. His voice betrayed him and broke.

She leaned forwards and patted his hand. "There, nephew. Do not worry yourself about such things. Though we may never know the truth behind your errand, do you truly believe your father would use you for some evil end? Surely you cannot think *that* badly of him."

"Of course not, Halab," said Ebon. The words sounded hollow even in his own ears, and from the look in her eyes, she heard it.

"Shay has always enjoyed his little schemes, even when we were children," she said. "They may be cloaked in secrecy, but they are always harmless. And if he should send Mako to you again, you should not hesitate to obey him. After all, it is by your father's grace that you are able to attend the Academy at all. I spoke on your behalf, of course, for he did not welcome the idea. But if Shay insists, he could withdraw you from the Academy and have you brought home. I do not believe either one of us wishes that."

"No, certainly not," said Ebon, shaking his head quickly.

"Good. Then serve your father as he wishes you to. It is a small price to pay. Now. I have had the gardeners carefully tending the roses, and they have bloomed most admirably for winter. Let me show them to you."

Ebon rose to follow her down and into the garden. But though he smiled and spoke with her through the day, as the sun gave way to dusk and then to moonslight, he thought hard upon her words, and wondered when Mako might come for him next.

The next day, as soon as Ebon could find Kalem and Theren together in the dining hall, he told them what had happened. At first they were both keenly interested in the High King's army marching forth, but as he went on to tell them of Halab's words, their moods dampened. Kalem looked only bemused, but Theren looked troubled.

"I take this for good news," said Kalem. "If you have done nothing wrong, then you have nothing to fear."

"A foolish notion," said Theren. "Many heads have rolled free from bodies that committed no sin. I take this as a sign that something evil has indeed transpired, and your aunt seeks to distract you from it."

Kalem looked confused. "I thought you said your aunt was one of the kind ones in your family."

"She is," said Ebon. "No worse than me, certainly. Therefore I think you are half-right, Theren. I think my father works some dark plot, but keeps it concealed from her. She is, mayhap, *too* loving, and cannot imagine any dark motive on his part. I only wish I knew what he is up to."

"You do not suppose anyone in your family knows what we have done?" said Kalem, voice quivering. "If that truth becomes known, I do not think that any of us will remain students here for very long."

"If they knew what we did and meant to expel us for it, it would have happened already," said Theren.

"Unless they cannot prove it," said Kalem.

Theren scoffed. "Since when have the rich needed proof or just cause to punish those who displeased them? Certainly they would not hesitate to cast me from this place, though I do not doubt Ebon would remain."

Ebon frowned. "What? Why me?"

She rolled her eyes. "Come now, goldbag. You are a Drayden. The dean is a Drayden. He has even begun to take meals with you. Surely you cannot still think to deny you have his favor?"

"He has not 'begun' to take meals with me," said Ebon angrily. "He ate with me once, and only to obtain information. I tell you, my family cares nothing for me—except Halab. Why do you still take me for a favored son?"

Theren shrugged. "All sons are favored whose cribs are lined with gold."

Ebon slammed his bowl down. The tables around them grew silent. "I think I have had quite enough of your small-minded scorn, Theren." He stood and swept away, leaving his dishes behind.

Let her clean up after me, for once, he thought.

TWENTY-FOUR

THE NEXT TWO DAYS WERE TERRIBLE, AS HE WAS FORCED TO AVOID Theren in the dining hall and in the passageways of the Academy. Whenever he saw her heading towards him, he would turn away and hurry past her without speaking. Theren seemed content to ignore him as well, though he thought he saw her smirking whenever he happened to glance her way.

He still spent his time in the library with Kalem, for he had no gripe with the boy. Kalem seemed nearly as miserable as Ebon. Again and again he urged Ebon to reconcile with Theren. Only to himself would Ebon admit that he was sorely tempted; Theren and Kalem were his only friends here. But no matter what they went through together, it seemed she would never see him as anything more than some rich and pampered child, worthy only of her scorn. It seemed that nothing he said would convince her of the truth: he only wished for his family to leave him alone.

Where once he had visited Theren and Kalem in the common room outside of Kalem's dormitory, now he spent most of his evenings wandering the training grounds. They were expansive enough that he could go for hours without seeing another soul, if he was careful. There were hedges and bushes, planted for the purpose of separating different training grounds, into which Ebon could lose himself easily.

As moonslight lit the grounds on the second day since his fight with Theren, Ebon was sitting on a bench near the Academy's outer wall. It was nowhere near the sheds Theren used to sneak out at night—he had made certain of that. He rested upon a bench, leaning back against the granite wall and picking at his fingernails. But his eyes saw nothing, for his thoughts were far away; he thought of Albi back home, of the subtle scorn in Theren's eye when he saw her now, and especially of Halab and Mako and his father.

A sound drew his mind back to the present: the snap of a twig in a nearby bush. His gaze drifted to the sound, and he sat forwards. "Who is there?"

No answer came, but he thought he heard the rustling of leaves. His pulse quickened, and he pushed himself up from the bench. His hands clenched to fists, but he hesitated. Mayhap he had not heard anything after all, and was now being ridiculous. This was the Academy. Who would attack him here?

An unseen force picked him up from the ground and launched him through the air. He slammed into the outer wall. All his breath left him in an instant as he fell to the grass.

Before he could find his feet, the unseen force struck him again. This time it was a hammer blow to his face. His teeth stabbed into his upper lip, and blood spattered the granite wall.

"What—" he managed to stammer, before another invisible blow struck him in the gut. He cried out, tears spilling unbidden from his eyes. At last he recognized it for mind magic.

Theren?

It seemed impossible. She was angry with him, but not this angry.

The force lifted him up to press him against the wall, and this time it held him there. Though glazed eyes he looked down. But it was not Theren before him. It was Cyrus.

"You saw her," rasped the dean. Though his eyes glowed, Ebon could see his fury in the twist of his brow. "You saw Halab. You spent the better part of a day with her, and yet you did not tell me."

Until this very moment, he had utterly forgotten the dean's request to inform him of his dealings with the family. Now his mind spun, confused, clouded by pain.

"I . . . what?" said Ebon.

He flew a pace away from the wall and then came crashing back. His head struck the stone hard, and stars exploded in his vision.

"Worthless whelp. Did I not tell you? Did I not ask you, ever so kindly, to tell me if you spoke to our family? Yet you disobeyed. I will be kind no longer. I knew you were in league with them. Tell me why they have cut me off. *Tell me!*"

Again he slammed Ebon into the wall. Then, abruptly, the invisible strings vanished. Ebon fell forwards, so senseless that he could not even break his fall with his arms. The grass cushioned his landing, but still it felt as though he had been punched in the chest. Barely able to see, he pushed himself up to his elbows.

"She told me nothing," he said, voice coming thick and bubbly through the blood that gushed from his lip. "She said nothing of you. I do not know what has—"

Magic seized all his limbs at once. He rose into the air. Not too high—no doubt the dean feared to lift him into view of any other students who might be in the training grounds—but Ebon knew he could go much, much higher if Cyrus wished it.

"You lie," he hissed. "You are in league with them. You were sent here to spy on me!"

"I was not," Ebon said, sobbing now. "I do not know why I was sent here. Halab said nothing to me of you. I swear it. She only asked after my studies."

"Tell me the truth, or I will throw you over the wall and let you splatter to soup on the pavement beyond!" said Cyrus. "This is your last chance. Tell me what you and Halab spoke of."

"I swear it! I swear it to you!" cried Ebon. His guts churned in shame, but he could not stop himself from crying, crying as he had not even when he was a little boy, when word came back that his brother Momen had been killed in some far-off land, far from home, far from family. Now Ebon knew he faced the same fate.

For a moment Cyrus studied him, face contorted in fury. Then he relaxed. He lowered his hands from where they had been twisted to claws before him, and the glow died from his eyes. Ebon crashed to the grass again and lay there shaking.

"A pathetic boy you prove indeed," snarled Cyrus. "No subterfuge can be that complete. I wager if I stepped closer, I would smell that you have soiled yourself."

Ebon gave no answer, but only pressed his face deeper into the grass, groveling. He waited for Cyrus to speak on, but no words came.

After a time he looked up. The dean had gone, vanishing into the darkness that even now deepened in the garden. Letting his face fall again, Ebon wept until his tears had soaked the ground, mingling with the blood that still flowed freely from his mouth.

He heard quick footsteps growing louder, and in a moment hands seized his shoulders to roll him over onto his back.

"No! No, please, I swear I know nothing!"

"Shush!" said Theren—for Theren it was.

She dragged him up to sit and pulled him close. There she held him, uncaring of the blood that soaked into her robe as she pressed his face into her shoulder. "Shush," she said again, and rocked him like a mother rocking a babe. Ebon clutched her like a solid wall in an earthquake, and his weeping redoubled.

It was a long while before his tears finally subsided. When they did, he sat back. To his shock, he saw Theren, too, was weeping. She tried to hide it at once, swiping her sleeve across her cheeks, but he could see where her tears had left their marks, and could just see the red of her eyes in the moonslight.

"I saw him," she said, her voice shaking. "I saw it all. Forgive me, Ebon. I wanted to intervene, but I was so afraid. He is the dean, and I . . . forgive me."

She clutched at him again, and he found himself comforting her in turn. "I forgive you," he murmured. "I would have been just as scared."

"But you are not even trained," she said. "Mayhap I could have staved him off. If he had tried to send you over the wall, as he said he would, I would have torn down the Academy to stop him."

"I know you would," he said, pushing her back and looking into her eyes. "I know it. You are my friend, after all, are you not?"

In frustration she pounded his chest with her fist, but gently. "A terrible friend I have proven to be. Too craven to stand in your defense, and too foolish to believe what you said about your family."

"Ah," said Ebon, forcing himself to smile. "So at last you believe me when I say I am no favored son of the Draydens?"

"I should say so." Despite herself she laughed, and then swiped at her nose with her sleeve. But then her tears welled anew, and she looked away from him, as though she could not meet his eyes. "Ebon, I wanted so badly to help you. But I would have been expelled."

"Yes, you would have," he said. "As I said, I might have done the same as you."

"No, that is not all I mean," she said. "Ebon, leaving the Academy would be the worst thing that could happen to me. I fear it more than death itself."

Ebon frowned. "Why?"

She stood rather than answering, and then helped Ebon to his own feet. With his arm over her shoulder she led him to the bench nearby, and together they sat. Still she said nothing, not for a time, at least. Her hands were pressed together before her eyes, and she slid them against each other slowly. Her gaze was somewhere far away, as Ebon's had been before the attack.

"When I discovered my gift," she finally said, "I was living on the streets of a city called Cabrus."

"That is in Selvan, is it not?"

"It is, and no decent place for an orphaned girl. I fled the orphanage when I was young, for the matron there was cruel to us. But on the streets I found someone far worse; a weremage who killed any homeless girls who came into her clutches. I avoided her as long as I could, hoping to one day find passage from the city and escape her grasp at last. That is when I learned of my gift, and before long, word of it reached my patron.

"She is a woman named Imara, of the family Keren, and I think she earnestly believes that all things in Underrealm exist to serve her—either to be amusing, or to be useful. She saw me as some mix of both. She tested me to confirm my gift, and then she offered her patronage. I accepted, though I disliked her greatly, for my only other choice was to remain in Cabrus and someday die. And now, if I ever return to Dorsea, I will be her lackey for the rest of my days."

"Can you not earn your way out of her service one day?" said Ebon. "There are laws."

Theren shook her head. "Spoken like a true child of wealth," she said. "Laws can be bent, if not broken outright, and the wealthy have perfected the art. I could try to flee her service, of course. But if Imara is spoiled and vain, she is also spiteful, and full of wrath for those who wrong her, whether she imagines it or not. And so I remain here. I only . . . it is a terrible excuse, yet I only wanted you to know why I did not try to stop the dean. He would send me home . . . home to *her.*"

Ebon looked down at his hands, which gripped each other so tight that the knuckles were white. It seemed terribly unfair. Suddenly, even his own family seemed less onerous than Theren's circumstance.

"I wish I could help you," he said. "Only I do not know how. My family *could* help, of course—our coin purses are deep enough to pay off your service easily. Yet my father would never agree to it."

His father. Thoughts of Shay, of his whole family, whirled in Ebon's head. He still felt fear of them, yes, but now that was overshadowed by anger.

Ebon's silence had never been enough for them. Obedience had never been enough. Still they all despised him, except Halab, and Albi, and mayhap his mother. He had followed their unfair, uncompromising rules all his life, or tried to—and despite it, Cyrus had very nearly killed him.

He would never be free of them, unless he acted.

His hand moved of its own accord, gripping her arm hard. "Theren. Come with me. We must find Kalem."

"What?" she said, frowning. "Why?"

"Trust me. But you will have to help me walk."

He threw an arm across her shoulder again, and together they hobbled into the Academy, making their way towards the younger children's dormitories. They were careful to avoid any instructors, for Ebon had clearly been beaten and did not wish to explain why. Soon they were in the hallway outside Kalem's common room, and Theren left Ebon leaning against the wall while she ducked in to fetch the boy.

When Kalem came out, his eyes fell upon Ebon and shot wide. "Ebon!" he cried. "What has happened to you?"

"Do not worry yourself," said Ebon. "Only come with us."

They made their way to the stairwell, stopping in between floors and sitting together on the steps. Ebon knew their voices might carry far on the stones, but then again they would be able to hear anyone coming.

"My father is up to something," he said. "I did not wish to believe it at first, but now I know it must be true."

"How?" said Kalem.

"Because of Cyrus' actions. It was he who did this to me, Kalem. He knows something is afoot, but he thinks it has to do with Halab. Yet she, too, is being deceived by my father."

"Very well," said Theren. "I could have told you as much, and I tried, but—" Ebon gave her a hard stare, and she subsided with a gulp. "In any case, what do you mean to do about it?"

"I mean to search the docks, as we both said. We must, for it is the only way I can solve all our problems at once. If I can find some proof of my father's plans—"

"You can bring it to the constables," said Kalem.

Ebon shook his head with a grimace. "No. Then blame might fall upon my whole family. But I could speak with Halab. There will never be a better time. She is here on the Seat, and my father is far away in Idris. Halab knows him only from their youth together, and will not believe me without firm evidence. But if I bring it to her ..."

"She can address the situation on her own," finished Theren. "That seems wise. Mayhap she could have a stern word or two with Cyrus, as well." Scowling, she cracked her knuckles against each other. "Or she might let me do it."

"I have no doubt she will put him in his place," said Ebon. "But I have not told you all. If Halab deposes my father, I shall be head of my household. Then our gold shall be mine to spend as I wish."

Kalem frowned, but Theren's scowl twisted to a smirk. "A goldbag in truth. I suppose I do not object if you buy finer wines, as long as you continue to share them with me."

Ebon shook his head slowly. "I would not waste wealth on such

187

petty things, Theren. In fact, I would give my seat up to my sister, once she came of age. But first, I would purchase your contract away from your patron. As I said, it would solve *all* our problems—not only my own."

Theren went very still. She blinked hard, tilting her head back and forth—not quite a shake of the head. "You need not—that is not—"

"Come now," said Ebon, spreading his hands. "What use is gold without a proper reason to spend it?"

"Thank you," she whispered. "You are a truer friend than I have been. If this is your aim, I am by your side."

Kalem still looked doubtful. "This seems a shaky plan at best. It relies overmuch on luck. What if there is nothing at the docks?"

"Then we shall think of something else," said Ebon. "But we must do something. It was easy to be complacent before, but Cyrus has shown us we must act. If he, the dean, is so frightened, then something dark indeed is about to take place. You are a royal son, Kalem. Will you not act for the good of the nine kingdoms?"

The boy stared at his feet. "I think you overestimate the situation," he muttered.

"But mayhap not," said Ebon. "Please. We cannot do it without your mists."

"Very well," said Kalem. "I will help."

"Good. We should all rest well, for we make our move tomorrow night."

TWENTY-FIVE

Ebon took a long bath and went to bed the moment he was done. When he woke he felt refreshed in mind, but rest had made his whole body sore from its injuries. Gingerly lifting his robes, he saw that bruises covered most of his body, and the back of his head was still tender. But whether by design or by fortune, the dean had left his face unmarked except for the deep cut inside his lip. Though he walked tenderly through the day, neither instructors nor students gave him a second look or seemed to see that anything was wrong.

He ate his midday meal with Theren and Kalem. They spoke only a few muted words as they ate, and made no mention of the evening's plan. Ebon thought his friends must be anxious—he himself was more than a little afraid. But he also felt a curious resolution. For once in his life he felt as if he were taking a stand against his father. That more than made up for his bruises and aches.

They made for the city streets as soon as the afternoon's studies had ended, taking a moderate supper at Leven's tavern. The plan was to stay out past curfew, rather than waiting for nightfall before sneaking out.

Theren would have to help them scale the wall when they returned, but Ebon was happy to avoid doing so on their way out, for he still did not enjoy being flung through the air.

As daylight began to fade from the sky, Theren led them east at a rapid pace. They had to cross most of the island, and so they wasted little time talking. By the time they reached the eastern wall, it was nearly time for the gate to be shut for the night. Though the guards would have let them pass through to the docks, Theren had warned them against such a course. The guards would surely take note of three Academy students passing just before nightfall, and word might have made its way back to the citadel.

Therefore they drew to a stop between two houses a stone's throw away from the wall, and there they waited for the moons to rise. The gatehouse, a massive structure wrought partly in iron, stood nearly seven paces high. But when the guards lowered the gate at last, Ebon saw that there was a man-sized door in it. That was where they would make their exit.

"I have only snuck out once," said Theren. "It was difficult, but this time the mists should make it easier. I will distract the guards. Kalem, cast your spell once they are away from the gate."

Kalem nodded mutely, his wide eyes shining in the moonslight. Ebon could see the fear in the boy's face, but for once he made no complaint.

Theren raised her hands, and a glow sprang into her eyes. Ebon could see two guards, one to either side of the gate. They clearly did not anticipate any trouble, for they both leaned against the wall in positions of easy rest.

Ebon did not see Theren move, but suddenly both guards pitched forwards as if pushed. They caught their feet and put hands to swords as they peered into the darkness.

"What was that?" said one.

"I do not know," said the other. She squinted down the street. "Who is there?"

Theren shoved them both again, this time away from the gate. Again they stumbled, and this time one of them fell to the street.

"It is some spell!" he said. The air rang as he drew his steel.

"Once more, and then it is your turn, Kalem," murmured Theren.

Her hands twisted, and the guards stepped still farther from the portcullis. Mist sprang to life and flooded the street, thick and soupy.

Theren gripped Ebon's arm and pulled him forwards, and he in turn dragged Kalem. The guards both shouted in the fog, but their voices were several paces away. Together the three friends reached the wall and edged along it until they found the portcullis.

The door had no lock, only a heavy latch that kept anyone outside from opening it. Ebon lifted the latch as quietly as he could and rushed through the door. Theren and Kalem came only a half-step after, and Theren closed the door behind them. They raced from the gate as fast as they could.

The stone road soon turned to old, weather-beaten wooden planks. Theren pulled Ebon and Kalem to the side, where great stacks of crates and barrels stood in rows. Once they had vanished among the cargo, Kalem let his mists fall away. They had reached the docks.

"A fine job," said Ebon.

"It will be harder to get in, but not by much," said Theren. "I can lift the latch from outside."

"Excellent," said Ebon. "Let us be quick, then."

He withdrew the map from his pocket. They spread it out where the moonlight fell down between the crates, studying it in the pale silver glow. The docks were drawn in some detail, and they could see where the ships had been etched. Both were to the south of where they stood now.

"Let us go south," said Ebon, "and see if we can find where these ships lay."

"Very well, but be careful," said Theren. "Look."

She leaned beyond the crate and pointed. Ebon and Kalem followed her outstretched finger. There in the moonlight they could see a figure, and Ebon barely made out the hardened red leather of the man's pauldrons. A constable.

"Likely there are more, but we can avoid them if we are careful," said Ebon. "Kalem, if they should spot us, you will have to hide us."

He made to lead them on, but Theren waved him back. "You are still tender from your injuries," she said. "Let me go first."

So saying, she set off among the cargo and down the dock. They had many stacks to hide behind, but between each one they had to make a harrowing run across open space. Every time they did it, Ebon was sure they would be caught. But Theren always timed their runs well, so that no constable was nearby. Before another hour had passed, they had moved far down the docks until they reached the first spot marked on the map.

"Here we are," said Ebon. "Now let us see what may be seen."

Together they leaned out to peer into the night. But Ebon's heart fell almost immediately. There were two docks before them, each large enough to hold a vast ship. But both lay empty.

"What does that mean?" said Kalem. "The ships are clearly drawn right here."

"I do not know," said Ebon.

"What of the other ship on the map?" said Kalem. "Will that dock be empty, too?"

"I do not know, Kalem!" hissed Ebon. "The only way to find out is to move on."

He caught Theren's eye in the moonslight. She was looking at him doubtfully, brow furrowed in worry.

"There will be something," he reassured her. "There must be."

"But what if it already happened?" she said. "Whatever was plotted, we may have missed it."

"Then we are wasting our time," he said. "But at least we tried. And we can think of something else."

She sighed and led them off down the docks once more.

Before they had even reached the second marking on the map, Ebon had a sinking feeling. No ships loomed out of the darkness above the stacks of cargo. When they arrived, it was the same as before: two spaces ready to hold grand ships, but now empty. There was nothing there. Their venture had failed.

"The same again," said Kalem. He frowned for a moment and then tilted his head at Ebon. "Mayhap that in itself is a sign? Why should these spots be empty? I mean these precise spots. Mayhap the signs on the map mean something other than what we thought."

"We saw many empty spots along the way," said Theren. "I doubt it means anything sinister. Ebon, what say you?"

But Ebon was frozen. The spots marked on the map were empty, yes. But there was a ship just next to them. It was a small vessel, with only a single mast and space to carry mayhap a dozen passengers. But there were people milling on the dock beside it, and he recognized two of them.

"Ebon?" said Kalem.

Ebon waved him to silence. He leaned forwards, hands gripping the edge of a crate tightly.

Yes. It was them. Liya and Ruba, two of the servants from the Drayden family manor upon the seat. He had almost bowled them over as he ran for the dining hall, the morning after his first night with Adara. Now they carried satchels that looked very much like traveling sacks. They vanished beyond the edge of the ship.

"I need to get closer," he said. "I need to see those people just there."

"Why?" said Theren.

"Just get me closer."

She sighed and looked up and down the dock, but there were no constables close by. Quickly she stole across the planks, and now they were more exposed than they had been at any point along their route. Ebon followed quickly, and Kalem came just behind. Now they were only a few paces away from the figures boarding the ship.

"Be quick," said Theren. "We could be seen far too easily here."

Leaning out once more, Ebon saw that he had been right. Yes, Liya and Ruba were there. And now they stood among a crowd of others he recognized. There were the manor's cooks and cleaners, the gardeners and the stable boy. Ebon was so surprised at the sight that he nearly called out to ask what they were doing, and only stopped himself at the last moment.

"It is them," he whispered. "All the servants from our family manor. They are leaving."

"What?" said Theren. She stopped surveying the docks and looked at the people boarding the ship instead. "What do you mean, all of them?"

"Every one," said Ebon. "I do not recall a face from the manor that is not here before us now."

"But where is your family?" said Theren. "Surely they would not stay to manage the household themselves. Unless . . . have they run short on coin? Mayhap they could no longer pay these servants, and are sending them home."

Ebon snorted. "Not on your life. No, they are being sent away."

"To Dulmun?" said Kalem.

Ebon blinked at him. "What? No. They would be sent to Idris. Why would you say that?"

Kalem pointed to the front of the ship. A green pennant hung there, with the sigil of a white wave breaking across it. "That is a ship of Dulmun," he said. "It is of their king's own fleet."

"Mayhap they hired it," said Ebon.

"They could not," said Kalem. "The king's ships never work for hire. They sail only at his personal—"

"You there!"

The shout made them jump. They whirled to see a woman in red leather armor standing only a few paces away, hand on her sword hilt.

"What are you three doing?"

Ebon glanced over his shoulder. The manor servants had heard the constable, and were looking in his direction. If even one of them recognized Ebon, he and his friends were doomed.

"Run!" he whispered, and shoved the others forwards.

They tried to dodge past the constable and run back the way they had come. But the woman was too quick, and moved to blocked their path. They turned and ran the other direction.

"There are other piers running back to the shore!" cried Theren. "Make for one!"

But looking ahead of them, Ebon saw they were too late. Another constable had heard the commotion and was coming for them now. His sword lay bare in his hand, its steel glinting in the moonlight.

"The cargo!" said Kalem. He ran for the stacks of crates. Ebon and Theren followed a step behind. The constables shouted as they gave chase.

But as Kalem wove through the stacks of crates, Theren's eyes glowed, and she threw her hands wildly from side to side. Barrels swayed where they stood, and then came crashing down to block the pathways behind them.

The constables' angry cries faded as they reached the western edge of the docks. But there were still ten paces of black water between them and the shore.

"Theren, can you carry us across?"

"Are you mad? I can hardly lift you to the top of a wall."

"I may . . . I may have something, said Kalem, though his voice shook. "Theren, could you lower me to the water?"

"No time!" said Ebon. He threw himself to the edge of the dock, grunting at the flare of pain from his bruises. The tide was high, and the water was only a pace away. "Give me your ankles!"

Kalem crawled to the edge and over, with Ebon and Theren clinging to his legs. His robes fell down around his shoulders, so that his underclothes were exposed.

"Not one word, from either of you," he snapped.

"Be silent and hurry," said Theren. "They are getting close." And indeed, Ebon could hear the constables' voices carrying above the crates and barrels, moving around the stacks of cargo towards them.

Kalem reached out his hands until they touched the water. At once, a wave of ice spread from his fingertips. Out and out it spread, until a small platform of ice stretched out for many paces in all directions, securing itself in place by wrapping around the poles of the docks.

"All right!" he squealed. "Let me go!"

They did, and he came down on the ice on hands and knees. He crawled forwards, spreading the ice before him a pace at a time. Ebon and Theren scrambled to climb down from the dock behind him.

But just as Ebon had almost reached the ice, he heard a triumphant cry. Something snatched at the back of his robes. He barely twisted his neck enough to see the constable behind him, one gloved fist holding Ebon's robes. Her sword was held high, ready to strike.

"Let him go!" Theren's eyes glowed, and her hand cut through the air. The woman's head snapped back, and her grip fell away.

Ebon crashed onto the ice. He crawled as quick as he could, just behind Theren.

"Thank you," he told Theren, voice shaking.

"Better than my showing against the dean," she said with a faint smile.

They were halfway to the shore now. Again Ebon heard a cry behind him, but this time much farther away. He glanced back. The constable Theren had struck still lay senseless on the dock, but the other had arrived at last.

The man ran for the dock's edge and gave a mighty leap out onto the ice. But when he landed, it cracked beneath him, and he sank into the water with a yelp.

Ebon froze—but then he saw the man's head break the surface, and his limbs flailed wildly as he fought to remain afloat. At last he got hold of the ice, and there he clung, sputtering and trying to spit the seawater from his lungs.

Ebon and his friends reached the shore and climbed the steep slope leading up to the city's wall. They made their way north until they had reached the eastern gate again. But before they could reach it, Theren reached out and snatched Kalem's cloak to pull him to a stop.

"Wait. We should not go inside yet. There is still the marking to the southeast to investigate—the small boat drawn near the cave."

"You *cannot* mean to go there, too." Kalem's voice rose to a shout. "This is twice now we have nearly gotten ourselves killed, and twice too many. I will not do it again!"

"But we did *not* get ourselves killed," said Theren. "And now they will be searching the docks for us, while we will be on the Seat's southern edge. We will be safer than ever before."

"Nothing about this is safe!" said Kalem, stamping his foot. "If you wish to go running about on more misadventures, then please yourselves. I mean to return to the Academy, now, without any delay. And if you will not come with me to sneak in, then I will march straight back to the gate and knock upon it, and I will not care if they punish me."

Theren's eyes flashed, but Ebon put a hand on her arm. "Leave it, Theren. I do not think I could last much longer in any case." The crawl across the ice had made his aches and pains worse, and he now found it difficult even to walk. "We can always return another night, when we have rested."

"Yes, and when Kalem has had time to find his courage again," muttered Theren.

Kalem folded his arms. "Call me a coward if you wish, but you know I am right. If there are guards posted where the small boat is drawn, they will be more vigilant now, not less. And Ebon looks as though he might collapse."

"I might, at that," said Ebon.

He smiled, trying to ease the tension, and reached out an arm for Theren. She slung it over her shoulder and sighed.

"Very well," she said. "Only something in my heart tells me the danger grows greater, not less, the longer we take to discover whatever is going on."

"Be that as it may, we must take a little longer yet."

They walked north again at Ebon's nudge, making for the eastern gate.

TWENTY-SIX

By the time Ebon sat for the midday meal with his friends, he had come to deeply regret their excursion. Now his bruises felt crippling, and his limbs hesitated before obeying his will. He sat hunched over his food, barely able to eat, while Theren and Kalem spoke animatedly about the map.

"Mayhap the blue markings to the west were the right ones, and the red were only a decoy," said Theren.

"But why?" said Kalem. "What purpose for the difference? Mayhap they are both clues, and we simply do not understand what the different colors mean?"

Theren sighed. "I think we will have little luck with guesses. We will only find more answers if we look for ourselves."

"You say that as if it is some simple thing," grumbled Kalem.

Ebon sat silent, staring at his food. His friends had not cared overmuch about the Drayden servants stealing away on the ship, but Ebon's mind had been heavy all morning. Halab had said she was here for family business. This must have been what she meant.

The family was withdrawing from its property on the Seat. He could not imagine why.

And another thought grated at him; Halab had spent the whole day with him but had said nothing of this. Had she not imagined that he might come to the manor, visiting it after his study hours? How did she think he would feel, arriving to find it empty, or mayhap even sold to some new owner?

It felt as though his family had abandoned him in truth. That would not be such a terrible prospect coming from Father—or at least it would be no surprise. It was different with Halab.

A black-robed figure stopped beside the table. Ebon looked up to find Lilith looking down at him, smirking. Oren and Nella stood beside her, as always. Ebon barely managed to restrain a groan.

"Well met, jester," said Lilith. She looked to Kalem. "And jester's monkey."

Ebon noted that she utterly ignored Theren.

"What is it, Lilith? I have little patience for jibes today."

"I had heard you went and watched the High King's armies march forth. Did any of your kin march with them? Three wizards of Yerrin are in her ranks."

"I do not know," said Ebon. "If any of my family are soldiers, I have not heard of it."

"Of course you would not have," said Lilith. "Not all families are as proud of their members as Yerrin. Not all families have cause to be."

Ebon scowled, and was surprised at himself for doing it. No matter how little love he had for his family, Lilith somehow made him wish to defend them.

"And are your family taking you on holiday as well?" she went on.

He blinked. The question seemed to come from nowhere. "What? Holiday? No. Why?"

"Winter approaches. My parents are traveling to Feldemar to welcome it, and they are taking me with them. Mayhap the family Drayden is too poor to take such holidays? Or mayhap they *are* taking one, and have simply forgotten you."

Ebon's hand clenched to a fist on the table. Theren shifted on her bench. "Leave off, Lilith," she said.

Lilith's eyes flicked to Theren, but only for a moment. "Well, I must away to prepare for the voyage," she said. "Enjoy your time trapped here in the Academy, jester. When I return, I shall be sure to regale you with tales of my travels."

She sauntered off, out of the dining hall and into the Academy. Oren went with her, while Nella remained, finding a table in a corner by herself.

"That one is simply insufferable," muttered Kalem.

"Her boasting does grow tiresome," said Ebon. "Though in truth, with all we have seen and done in the past weeks, her torment somehow rankles less."

"At least she has given us one piece of the puzzle," said Kalem brightly. "I would wager that that is why your household staff were readying to leave. Your family must be taking a journey for winter, just as hers is."

Ebon was taken aback. "You think she was correct?"

"Why else would they have been loading themselves upon that ship?"

He realized that Theren had not spoken since Lilith left. Her sharp eyes roved across the dining hall, her short bob of hair swinging into her face as she looked back and forth.

"Theren?" said Ebon. "What is it?"

"There are no Yerrins in the dining hall. There were two missing from my class this morning, which I thought was curious." She stopped looking about and leaned forwards. "Are there other Draydens enrolled in the Academy just now? Are they still in their classes?"

Ebon shrugged. "Not so far as I know. It is only me. And the dean, of course."

Her eyes grew dark, and she looked away. Ebon knew she was thinking, as he was, of Cyrus' attack in the training grounds. They ate the rest of their lunch in silence.

Before sunrise the next morning, a hand slapped over Ebon's mouth, jarring him awake.

His eyes shot wide, and he struggled to rise from his dormitory

bed. The barest grey glow drifted through the window, casting his assailant as a shadowy figure. Powerful arms dragged him from his bed,
still wrapped in a blanket, and pulled him through the door in the
back of the dormitory. His screams were muffled under the clutching
hand, and no one heard him. He tried to fight, but his injuries kept
his movements weak. The hand pinched his nose and mouth until he
could hardly breathe.

Once they reached the hallway, he was pressed roughly against the
stone wall. There in the torchlight, he at last caught sight of his attack-
er's face.

Mako.

Ebon froze where he stood.

"Good morrow, little goldbag." Mako's voice was a dagger sheathed
in silk. "My apologies for awakening you so. An urgent matter presses,
and I could not wait for you to come to the library."

Ebon only stared at him, eyes wide with fear. His heartbeat would
not stop thundering in his ears, and it sounded like the march of a
giant.

"If I remove my hand, will you promise not to scream?" said Mako.
"If you do, I cannot bring you the message I came to deliver, and that
would be very bad for both of us."

Slowly, Ebon nodded. Mako peered into his eyes for a moment. He
must have seen what he wanted, for at last he removed his hand.

"What do you want?" said Ebon. Fear and the last groggy remnants
of sleep made his voice hoarse and raw.

"I might ask you the same, goldbag. You must want something—or
else you would not have returned to the inn with your friends after
I warned you not to. And you certainly would not have gone to the
docks the night before last. That was foolish indeed."

Ebon's knees went weak. He would have fallen to the floor if Mako's strong arms were not still pressing him to the wall. All his misdeeds
were known. Surely Mako would bring this to his father, and then
Ebon would be sent home. Or worse, Mako might tell the dean. Then
Cyrus might seek to finish what he had begun in the training grounds
and leave Ebon's cooling corpse in some dark gutter.

Mako chuckled. It grated from his throat like a panther's growl.

"Do not look so frightened. Whether you choose to believe it or not, I am actually somewhat fond of you. I warn you that I know these things not because I mean to tell our family, but so that you know you have been careless at a time when you should be more careful than ever."

"You speak in riddles," said Ebon, trying to sound brave. "Say what you have come to say, and then leave me be."

"Spoken like a true little lord. As, indeed, I hope you shall be one day. But that will never happen unless you heed these words: leave the High King's Seat at once."

Ebon balked. "What? Why?"

"You must trust me. I have learned things, things I should have known long since. Waste no time. Bring your friends with you, if you must. But make for the nearest boat you can find, or crawl upon the ice like you did at the docks. Only leave this island behind you, or face your death."

"Without knowing why? I am not your puppet, Mako."

"I could issue it as a command, if you wish."

Ebon remembered Halab's words. "And would that command come from my father, or from you?"

Mako only grinned. His teeth flashed red in the torchlight, as though they were drenched in blood. Ebon quailed, but forced himself to remain steady as he gave a grim smile.

"You say nothing because there is no strength behind your words. I may be forced to play into my father's schemes, but not yours."

"No strength, you say? I know what you have been up to in the dead of night, Ebon. I could reveal it all to your father, or even to dear Halab. What would you do if she withdrew her support? Do you really think you could remain at the Academy? Yet I have chosen to tell you first. Why would that be, unless I had some liking for you?"

"I can think of many reasons."

"Yet you do not voice them. Trust me in this. Leave the Seat."

Ebon only glared. Mako met his gaze for a moment, and Ebon thought he saw earnestness in the bodyguard's eyes. But then the man's lips twisted in a familiar smirk, predatory once again. He drew back and vanished around the corner. Ebon watched him go, shaking.

TWENTY-SEVEN

THE DAY BEFORE, EBON'S INJURIES HAD KEPT HIM FROM DRESSING FAST enough to eat in the morning. Now he rushed to don his robes despite the pain and hobbled down the stairs as fast as his legs would carry him. Because Mako had startled him awake so early, he arrived at the dining hall before all but the very first students. There he waited, pacing, until Kalem arrived at last.

"Kalem!" he said, gripping the boy by his robes. "We must find Theren. Something is happening."

"What do you mean?" said Kalem, eyes wide.

"I do not know exactly. But we must find her."

"We should wait outside her dormitory."

Ebon nodded, and they set off through the Academy. His pain spiked with every step, but Ebon forced himself to move on. They climbed the stairs to Theren's room and waited outside her door. Students emerged and gave them curious looks before brushing past. Finally Theren appeared, still rubbing sleep from her eyes.

"Theren, come quickly," said Ebon. "I must tell you and Kalem something."

Her brow furrowed. Ebon took her sleeve and dragged her down the hallway until they found a secluded corner where they would not be disturbed.

"An agent of my family came to me this morning. He warned me to leave the Seat at once."

"What? Why?" said Kalem.

"He would not say. But he said it was a warning."

Theren's face went Elf-white.

"I do not understand," said Kalem. "Does some danger await you within the walls? Mayhap he knows of some plot by the dean to attack again."

"He said I could bring you with me, if I wished," said Ebon. "Why would he say that, unless—"

"I know why," said Theren. "The Seat is going to be attacked."

Ebon and Kalem stared at her. The hallway fell to silence.

"What?" said Ebon at last.

"Think, Ebon. Lilith and the other Yerrins have fled. I spent the rest of yesterday searching around. Many children of other wealthy families have fled as well. Mayhap they know what is coming, or mayhap they only heard some dark rumor of a coming storm. But they have taken their children and fled. Your manor staff have been removed. You thought it was by your aunt, but it could just as easily have been your father. Something is coming, something powerful enough to endanger every soul upon the Seat."

Ebon shook his head quickly. "No. That would be treason of the highest order. My father may have concocted some dark scheme, but that is a step too far, even for him."

"How else do you explain it?" said Theren. "Why else would they be fleeing this place like rats from a ship?"

"But my parents have not sent for me," said Kalem, frowning.

"Forgive me," said Theren. "But you have told us already that your family's star has fallen. And they are from Hedgemond, an outland kingdom. I doubt they would have heard any rumor of whatever doom is coming."

"Think, Theren," said Ebon. "If what you say is true, then I am part of it. I did my father's bidding, and if his scheme was to attack the Seat, then I played a role."

"You did not know what you were doing."

"I did *not* lend aid to an attack on the Seat," Ebon snapped. He realized his voice had grown far too loud, and he went on in an urgent whisper. "Others may look upon my family with fear, but not even the rumors of our deeds are that black. Besides, if they were part of this plot, then why would my father leave me here?"

But before the words left his lips, he knew the answer. And Theren and Kalem looked at him with such sadness in their eyes that he felt tears welling up in his own.

"No!" he cried, no longer caring who might hear. He thought he might be sick. "No, you are wrong. My father lost one son already. He would not sacrifice the only other one he had."

Except that he cared, truly cared, when Momen died, he thought. *Do I think he would feel the same way about me?*

"It is the only thing that makes sense," Theren said quietly. "What better way to prove your father's innocence than the fact that his own son died in the attack? It is a perfect deception."

"If it were my family's plot, Mako would have not have found out at the last moment, as he told me. He would have known from the first." Ebon felt desperate now.

"Unless he lied," said Kalem. "Or unless it was kept from him, as well. The fewer who know the secret, the fewer to let it slip."

Ebon turned and leaned his head against the stone wall. The earliest chills of winter had seeped into it, and it calmed him like a piece of ice held to a fevered forehead. He took a deep breath. Still he would not believe it. His father did not—*could* not hate him this much.

Ebon would not listen to the voice in the back of his mind, the voice that said *Yes, yes, Ebon. He could. Of course he could.*

"I will prove you wrong," he said. "The map is some smaller mischief, already played out."

Kalem looked at Theren uncomfortably and then back to him. "Ebon . . ."

"No. No more words. I will show you. We leave, now."

Ebon marched off down the hallway. He tried to tell himself that he did not care if they followed, but in truth his heart flooded with relief when he heard their footsteps behind him. Together they stormed down into the entry hall. Mellie sat in a chair by the front door, her head nodded to her chest in sleep. Ebon broke into a run and threw open the door, bursting out into the streets beyond. Kalem and Theren followed just behind him. They heard Mellie's squawk as the old woman was startled awake. But before she could react, or even call for help, the three of them had vanished into the streets.

"Well, now we have earned ourselves trouble indeed," groused Kalem.

"I do not care," said Ebon. "This ends now. I am tired of skulking about in search of answers."

His bruises were forgotten now, and he found it easier to walk than he had for days. Indeed, Kalem had to scamper along to keep up with him, and even Theren's long legs swung mightily to match his pace. Ebon eschewed stealth and took the main road east. After a time they were forced to walk around the High King's palace, and then only a short distance remained to the east gate.

Ebon had a moment's trepidation as he approached it. But the gates stood open, and travelers came in and out of it at their will, for it was not heavily guarded during the day. Still he threw up his hood, and Theren and Kalem followed suit as they emerged into the open air beyond. A wave of sea breeze struck them, salty and sweet and carrying the cries of gulls. A morning fog lay upon the Great Bay, a fog thick and tall enough to hide all sight of the horizon, but it ended half a league from the dock's edge. An itch sprang to life on the back of Ebon's neck, but he dismissed it as impatience.

"We will search the southeastern marking on the map first to see if the boat and cave mean anything," said Ebon. "If I am right, I wager we will find an empty cave, its boat long gone. Just as the ships on the dock were gone."

But glancing back over his shoulder, he realized Kalem had stopped short. The boy stood just outside the gate and off to the side, his eyes fixed on the Great Bay. As Ebon looked closer, he noticed Kalem's hands were shaking. Theren, too, had seen him freeze.

"Kalem?" she said. "What is it?"

"The . . . the fog," said Kalem. His voice quaked. "Ebon, can you not feel it?"

Ebon glanced at the fog, confused. "I see nothing."

"Do not look," said Kalem. "Feel."

Ebon closed his eyes and focused. Then he felt it—the tingling on the back of his neck. It was no trick of his mind, but the same sensation as when Kalem spun mists close by.

"Sky above," he whispered.

"What?" snapped Theren. "What is it?"

"That is no morning mist," said Kalem. "It is the work of alchemists—a host of them."

Horns blew on the wall, startling them. And then as they watched, hearts sinking with horror, a host of ships sailed from the mist, drums pounding with war.

TWENTY-EIGHT

EBON WAS FROZEN. THE SIGHT OF THE FLEET SAPPED HIS COURAGE AND his will, so that he felt like one of the training dummies in the gardens—mute, lifeless, unable to move. And above them the horns continued to blare, now joined by bells and the shouts of guards as they saw the ships coming at last.

"What should we do?" said Kalem. "What is this?"

"An invasion," said Theren. "And look at the pennants. Those are Dulmun ships."

"But what do we do?" said Kalem again.

"We must go," said Ebon. "Now!"

His shout finally put life back in their limbs, and they burst into a run. But Ebon and Theren went in opposite directions and crashed into each other.

"Where are you going?" said Ebon.

"Where are *you* going?" said Theren. "That map showed a boat on the southeastern end of the island. It must be for escape. We can use it."

"She is right," said Kalem. "If it is still there, which it may not be. But what other choice do we have?"

But Ebon placed a hand on each of their shoulders to still them. His hands shook, but he forced himself to stand as strong as he could. "I cannot come with you."

"What?" said Theren. "Why not?"

Ebon thought of the Academy, of its thick granite walls and the three floors of its library. He saw Jia and even cowardly Credell. And he thought of Astrea's tiny face, her wild hair that stood out around her head like some hat from one of the outland kingdoms. "The Academy. If indeed my family had some part in this, then I had a hand in it as well. I must go and try to save whoever I can."

"But they are on the west end of the island. They will have plenty of time to escape, for they can run to the western . . ." Kalem's voice trailed off, and his wide eyes grew even wider. "Oh, no."

"Another attack?" said Theren, coming to the same thought. "From the west?"

"Coming from Selvan," said Ebon, nodding. Terror made his voice shake, and tears leaked from his eyes. "The attack will come from both east and west. The Academy will try to get the students out, and they will march straight into the enemy's waiting blades."

Theren stamped her foot and looked away. "You are right. Darkness take us."

"I . . . I will come with you," said Kalem, squaring his shoulders and trying to stand taller.

"The two of you could make for the boats," said Ebon. "I only go to deliver a message. One can do that as easily as three, and this attack is my fault, not yours."

"I went with you to the Shining Door," said Theren.

"And I . . . well, I would not go off on my own, letting you walk into peril," said Kalem.

Ebon swallowed hard against a sudden lump in his throat. "Thank you. But we have tarried too long. Hurry!"

They ran for the gate. Even as they passed through it, it had begun to lower. Just before it closed, Ebon took one last look behind him. Through the portcullis, he saw that the ships were drawing close. Upon their decks were arranged row after row of warriors, all wearing the green and white of Dulmun. Then the iron gates outside swung shut, blocking the portcullis and the ships both.

Not everyone outside had made it into the city before the gates shut. Ebon and his friends fled from the wails that came over the wall.

Ebon ran as fast as he could, and Theren and Kalem lent their hands in support when he needed it. The main road across the island had turned to chaos, with nobles and merchants alike looking about them in terror, unsure of what threat lay beyond the walls. They all seemed half ready to flee, yet they held fast, as though they waited for something to save them.

"Dulmun attacks!" cried Ebon. "Defend the walls or flee to your homes! The Seat is under attack!"

The others took up the cry, and it spread through the streets. Almost immediately he regretted opening his mouth, for the already-thick crowd became a congealed mass of bodies, heaving back and forth as everyone tried to go in all directions at once.

"Come! This way!" Theren led them off the street into the alleys. There they found the way was clearer, and they made good time. Before long they passed the High King's palace on the right, and before much longer the Academy loomed tall and dark before them.

They turned towards the main road again, where lay the front door. Just before they reached it, they heard a great *THOOM* from the west. The sound and force of it stopped them in their tracks. Ebon tried to see the source through the crowd, but the bodies pressed too thick.

"Up!" said Theren. A wagon full of hay sat nearby, and together they climbed atop it. From on high they saw that the western gate lay in ruins, and the portcullis had been raised. Troops wearing blue and grey poured through the gap, slaughtering all in their path. A chill ran down Ebon's spine as he recognized their blue-and-grey clothing—the same colors as the man at the Shining Door to whom he had delivered the parcel.

"Those are no soldiers of Selvan," said Kalem.

"Come," said Ebon. "Into the Academy."

They ran across the street and threw open the door.

The entry hall was full of people, students milling about in confusion while instructors tried to maintain order. More students were filing in from every hallway and down the main stairs. Ebon spied Jia in the press. She stood in the center, directing the other instructors to gather their students and make ready to leave. Ebon ran to her.

"Instructor," he said. "You have received word already?"

"Ebon, rejoin your class," she said briskly. "Obey your instructor's orders. No need to worry, we are leaving by the western docks."

"The docks are taken," he said. "An army has just broken the gates. Even now they are on the streets."

Jia's face became grave, and she looked away. "That is ill news. Curse the dean for his cowardice." Her eyes sharpened as they met Ebon's. "Forget I said that. Those words were spoken in anger."

"What did the dean do?" said Theren.

Jia gave her a wary look. Ebon spoke up instead, trying to feign concern. "Please, Instructor. He is my cousin."

"He is nowhere to be found," said Jia. "I sent for him as soon as I heard, but he does not appear to be anywhere within the Academy. Mayhap he is at the palace on business. It is no matter. There are other ways off the island. Instructors! We make for the south wall! Now, proceed through the front door, as quickly and orderly as you can!"

The students pushed past them in a rush, barely restrained by their instructor's barked commands. Kalem stepped close to Ebon. "Do you think the dean received word of the attack?"

"I doubt it," said Ebon. "From what he said when he attacked me, my family has removed him from their counsel. Most likely he heard the same warning as the rest of the Academy and put the pieces together, just as we did. But never mind him. We must help in the escape."

In a great mass the Academy students flooded the streets, turning east and then south, making their way to the walls. Ebon looked all around and at last spotted instructor Credell. The man shivered with every step he took, and his wide eyes swept about like a sow being led to slaughter. Yet he kept his students about him and ushered them along with the others. Ebon found himself admiring the man for not having fled already.

"Ebon!" Astrea's small, piping voice cut through the din, and she threw herself through the crowd to clutch at Ebon's legs. "Ebon, what is happening? Why are we leaving?"

Ebon scooped her up, though the pain of his bruises nearly made him cry out, and held her on his hip as he kept walking with the crowd. "It is nothing to fear, Astrea. Some soldiers have come to attack the island, but our instructors will keep us safe."

He only wished he believed that himself.

"Where do they mean to take us?" said Theren. "There is no gate in the southern wall. There are towers and places to climb down, but I think that would take too long."

"Jia must have some plan," said Ebon. "We have to trust her."

By the time they reached the south wall, the sounds of fighting pressed close on all sides. Ebon could hear the clash of steel to both sides and behind them as well. But he had not yet seen any of the combatants. The procession stopped at the wall, all the students clumping together in a mass.

Jia barked commands. Some instructors separated from the crowd and went to the wall. Ebon saw Credell join them. Then he realized that all the instructors were alchemists, and some of the older alchemy students had joined them.

"They mean to—" Kalem began.

"I see it," said Ebon. "You should help them."

Kalem looked uncertain for a moment, but Ebon gave him an encouraging nod. The boy scampered away to join the others at the wall.

As one, the alchemists stepped forward and placed their hands to the stone. Their eyes glowed, and the light of it joined together until it seemed a hundred torches shone upon the wall. Slowly at first, and then faster and faster, the stone beneath their hands began to shift. It spread out and away, above the alchemists and to either side.

In a few moments it was done, and a wide door had appeared in the wall, as neat and as smooth as if it had been carved there in the first place. The alchemists stepped back, the glow fading from their eyes.

"Instructors!" said Jia briskly. "Bring your students through the wall and lead them west. At the docks we will capture ships to bring us across the water."

"Instructor," said Ebon quickly. "What about the rest of the island?"

He saw her eyes waver for a moment, but the thin line of her lips remained firm. "Our duty is to the students. We must see them to safety or lose the next generation of wizards in one fell swoop."

Ebon's throat went dry, but he nodded.

Then someone gave a great shout, and they all turned to look. From the streets to the west poured men in grey and blue uniforms, steel swords bared and glinting in the sunlight. With a battle-cry they fell upon the students trying to flee through the wall.

The instructors leaped forwards to defend their charges. The attackers were driven back in a hail of flame and thunder and invisible blows that sent them crashing to the ground. But they were many, and they pressed forwards with fervor, until soon they had almost reached the mass of black robes.

Then Ebon saw weremages in battle for the first time. Jia's skin rippled as muscles formed beneath it, and hair sprouted all over her body. Her grey robes melted into her skin. In a moment a bear stood where Jia had been—but a bear larger and more fierce than Ebon had ever seen, almost twice as tall as he was, and its claws were long and glinted like steel.

With a heart-stopping roar Jia launched herself into the fray, ripping into the soldiers like an axe through kindling. They cried out in terror as they fell before her. All around, other weremages joined in the attack, until soon blood ran freely on the street.

But they were still few, and some of the blue-clad soldiers edged around them, seeking the students. One came straight for Ebon, and he backed up quickly.

Theren stepped forwards, and an invisible blow hammered the woman into the ground. Her sword went skittering across the pavement, and Ebon picked it up with shaking fingers. He had learned some sword fighting at home, but had never used such a heavy blade.

Another soldier charged, heading straight for Credell's class. The children recoiled and screamed as Credell tried to place himself in front of them.

Ebon struck wildly, giving the soldier pause as he avoided the blow. But the man took only a moment to recover. He swung with practiced ease to bat Ebon's blade out of the way. An overhead strike came quickly, too quickly for Ebon to block it—but then Credell was there, his hand raised to catch the weapon. Ebon cried out a warning—but the moment the blade touched Credell's fingers, it turned to water, and splashed harmlessly across them both.

The soldier stood dumbfounded for a moment, until Credell leaped forwards and seized his throat. Iron rippled out around his fingers, transforming both cloth and flesh until the man's whole neck had been turned to metal. He fell to the ground, unable even to gasp, eyes bulging from their sockets as he fought desperately for life. Credell stepped back, staring at his own hand in horror, shoulders quivering.

"The children," said Ebon. Credell did not hear. Ebon shook him. "The children! Get them through the wall!"

Credell shrank from the words and the sight of Ebon's face, but at last he nodded. He turned and ushered the children onwards with quiet words. Ebon turned back, seeking Theren and Kalem.

Before he found them, he saw Nella. The girl stood near the edge of the crowd of students, her eyes flying wildly about in fear. A soldier in blue leaped forwards through a gap in the teachers, trying to attack the students. Nella screamed and tried to reach for her magic. Her eyes glowed, and flames sprang from her fingers. But they guttered out almost at once as she lost her concentration.

The soldier pressed forwards, sword jabbing for her gut. Nella tried to step back, but tripped upon her own feet and fell.

Ebon sprang and swung. His sword struck the soldier on his breastplate, and the man stumbled back. Ebon held the sword forwards like a spear, while with his other hand he reached down to drag Nella to her feet. But he had only a moment before the soldier recovered. Ebon barely managed to parry a blow.

Nella found her strength, and this time lightning arced forth. It seized upon the soldier's metal armor and set his limbs to spasms. He collapsed in the street, shrieking, while Ebon and Nella backed away and into the crowd.

Ebon turned to her, and she met his eyes. He saw fear in her gaze—but also confusion, as though she could not understand why he was there.

"Are you all right?" he said.

She nodded. "Th-thank you."

Ebon dropped his gaze and turned away, seeking Theren and Kalem once more.

At last he found them at the rear of the procession, helping to guard the other students from attack. At least Theren was fighting—Kalem stood behind her, eyes glowing, but he could not find a place to strike. Ebon knew the boy's magic was still young, far weaker than Credell's. He could not use it without placing himself in striking distance.

Theren suffered no such restrictions. No soldier could come close. She battered them back with unseen force. The glow in her eyes was like an inferno, and her hands were twisted to claws as she lashed out again and again. But then the instructor beside her took an arrow to the throat and fell to the street. Theren's eyes returned to normal for just a moment as she looked down in horror.

"I am here," said Ebon, stepping in beside her to fill the gap. "Keep your eyes to the fore. He is beyond your help."

Her eyes glowed as she touched her magic again, but her voice shook when she answered. "What do you hope to do with that little pigsticker, goldbag?"

Ebon had to laugh. "Not much. But mayhap I can take a blade instead of you."

"See that you do." She struck at another soldier, knocking him away.

Their foes were finally forced to retreat under the onslaught, ducking behind the edges of buildings and hiding from sight. Many of their corpses lay littered about the street. But Ebon also saw bodies in black robes, and more in the dark grey of instructors. He was relieved to see that Jia was not among them—she had retaken human form and was once more directing the withdrawal.

Now the last few students were passing through the doorway that had been carved in the wall. A few more instructors held back, hands held up warily and eyes glowing in readiness for another attack. Ebon's eyes roved, searching for danger.

But then, between several buildings and at a great distance, he saw a flash of dark grey.

An instructor?

He took a cautious step forwards, squinting. The figure passed into view again.

Not quite an instructor—the dean. He was fleeing south and east, away from the fighting, and away from the rest of the Academy. But it was not the sight of Cyrus that stopped Ebon's heart. It was the girl at his side: a girl in fine blue robes and soft shoes. A veil covered the bottom half of her face, but he knew her at once.

Adara.

"Ebon, watch out!"

In his distraction he had stepped into the open. Two soldiers in blue sprang from behind a shop. They came for him, while a third fired an arrow from behind them.

Ebon flinched as it struck him—only, it did not strike him at all. It froze in midair mere fingers away, and then Theren was there by his side.

Before he could so much as raise his heavy sword, she battered one of the soldiers aside. But the other struck too quickly, and his sword tore into her arm. Theren cried out and fell to the ground.

With a scream, Kalem leaped forth. He seized the man's breastplate, and it turned to stone. The man swayed back, off balance. Theren fought to her knees and punched the empty air. As though she had struck the man himself, he flew up and off his feet, crashing into the archer. They landed and lay still.

"Theren!" cried Ebon, falling to his knees beside her. "I am sorry. Are you all right?"

"It is only a scratch," she said. But she grit her teeth hard, and her face had gone pale.

"Come, let us get you to safety," said Kalem, helping her the rest of the way to her feet. Ebon lent her a hand—but his eyes had turned to the east again.

He could no longer see the dean, but he had seen which way they were going.

He looked back. The last students were gone, and the instructors after them. Kalem was helping Theren through the wall, and Jia was there, the last to leave.

She looked past them for a moment and saw Ebon. Their eyes met. Her brow furrowed, and she opened her mouth to call to him.

Ebon whirled and vanished into the streets, chasing after the dean.

TWENTY-NINE

There was no fighting in this part of the city, and so Ebon was able to move quickly. Before long he spotted Cyrus again. The dean walked fast, but was not quite running. Adara walked freely by his side. Every once in a while Cyrus would take her arm, but to steady her, not to drag her along. Ebon guessed that he had already threatened her to get her to come with him.

He still carried his blade, but he did not know what to do with it. He was not willing to kill the dean, even if he doubted Cyrus would show him the same courtesy. But Ebon had to know where he was taking Adara, and for what purpose. Did he mean to flee the Seat? Or did he have some deadlier goal in mind? Ebon only knew that he could not abandon Adara to Cyrus' company, for the dean had shown himself to be half a madman already.

Before long Cyrus reached the wall, and now he moved along it as though searching for something. They passed some towers with doors leading in, but Cyrus passed them by. Ebon doubted the dean would enjoy the idea of climbing down with a rope. *He probably thinks it beneath him,* Ebon thought bitterly.

At last Cyrus reached a tower and went inside. Adara followed close behind. Ebon thought it looked just like the other towers, and so for a moment he waited and watched. But when neither of them reemerged, he stole forwards to the door.

It opened easily, and he poked his head inside. There was only a nondescript guardroom—yet in the floor a wooden hatch lay open. Stairs led down into the darkness, and no torches lit the way.

Ebon gulped. But Cyrus and Adara must have gone into the hatch; there was nowhere else to go. He crept to the edge of the hole. He could see to the bottom of the stairs, where a stone corridor ran away beneath the ground.

There was nothing for it. He took one step down, and then another. His sword shook in his hand. When he reached the bottom, he had to put a hand on the the wall to guide himself. But fortunately the passage ran straight and true, and he was able to edge his way along without much trouble.

Suddenly there was a terrible, shuddering groan, and Ebon ducked back. But then he saw a light far, far ahead—the bright blue light of day. He had to squint against it for a moment. Two figures appeared in silhouette and then vanished, leaving the door open behind them.

Ebon moved faster now that the way was lit. Soon he saw that the passageway ended in a door leading outside. There was a small platform, and steps heading up to the left. But beyond the platform was only empty space, and he could hear the roar of waves.

When he reached the end, he could see why: he had emerged into the cliffs on the south of the Seat. Along the island's southern coast, sheer rock faces provided no easy way to climb down and reach the water. The stairs to his left lead back up the wall to the top of the cliffs high above. Cyrus was nowhere to be seen.

Ebon climbed the stairway. There was no handrail to steady him, and so he leaned against the cliff wall. Once he reached the top, he spotted them again: Cyrus in his dark grey robes trimmed with gold, and Adara in blue. He began to run, for they had built quite a lead. They made for a break in the cliffs far ahead, which opened like a rent cut by some great axe.

He began to close the gap, but not quickly enough, for they reached the lip long before him. But just as they reached it, Adara happened to glance back over her shoulder. She froze in shock, her mouth falling open in a perfect circle.

"Ebon!" she cried.

He stopped short, now ten paces away. The dean turned in surprise. When he saw Ebon, he gave a small smile. But then Adara broke away from him and ran for Ebon, and Cyrus' lips twisted in a scowl. He reached forth a hand, eyes glowing, and unseen bonds snatched Adara where she stood. She turned her head back to him with a frown.

"What is the meaning of this? Release me at once."

Cyrus shrugged and obeyed her. But she did not run for Ebon again, and the dean looked at him with a sneer.

"Why have you followed me, boy? Should you not be with the rest of your sheep?"

"What are you doing with Adara?" said Ebon. He tried to keep his voice steady, as well as the sword in his hand. "Leave her be."

"Leave her . . .?" Cyrus threw back his head and laughed. "You foolish boy. She is coming with me, away from this place. I have hired her."

Ebon could not put meaning to the words for a moment. When he finally looked at Adara, he saw she wore a sad smile. "Is this true?"

"I am a lover, Ebon," she said. "I told you once not to dwell on the others I spend my time with."

"But with *him?*" cried Ebon. "You do not know what a monster he is."

He took a few cautious steps forwards. Now he and Cyrus were only a few paces away from each other, and Adara to the side between them both.

Cyrus waved a hand. "Save your whimpering. I know now that I struck at you in error. Our family has abandoned you here to your death, as they have done with me. But you should count yourself fortunate to have found me. I will let you come along if you wish, for I could use a servant as I travel."

"Servant? For you?" Ebon's hands shook, not with fear now, but with rage. "Do you think I would lift so much as a finger to help you? You nearly killed me."

Adara turned to Cyrus, fixing him with a steely gaze.

"I thought you were in league with our clan," Cyrus snapped. "But they have outwitted us both, and used us as pawns. Now we have only one chance: to flee to the outland kingdoms where no one will find us. I have paid for Adara's entertainment, but I can take you as well. You will need my protection."

"I need *nothing* from you!" cried Ebon, taking another step forwards. He still held his sword, and was almost angry enough to use it. "I would not accept any gift from you, no matter how freely given. I would take my chances against all the wildlands between Idris and Calentin before I took one step by your side."

Cyrus sneered. "How dramatic. Very well. Come, Adara. We will leave this simpleminded fool to his own devices."

"No," said Adara. She folded her arms. "I will not go with you."

Something evil flashed in the dean's eye. "What?"

"You heard my words. If you attacked him, then you and I are no friends. You will go on your way without my companionship."

"Friends?" Cyrus jeered. *"Friends?* You are a lover. I have paid you already. Now come. Your guild's rules are very strict, after all."

"Take your coin and be damned, you bleating steer." From her dress Adara pulled a handful of coins and flung them at his feet. "The King's harshest law is strict as well, and very clear. I will not take one step by your side more than I wish to."

Slowly Cyrus' face twisted into a mask of fury. A glow crept into his eyes. "You are mine until I say otherwise," he hissed. A hand leaped forwards, shaped like a claw, and Adara cried out as she was hoisted in the air. "Always you whine about your wish to see me cast some spell. Well, here is your spell, woman. Do you like it?"

"Stop it!" Ebon raised his sword and attacked. But the dean stretched out the other hand and caught him, too, with magic. Though only a pace away, Ebon was frozen still, unable to move a muscle.

"What do you hope to do with that, boy?" said the dean, chuckling. "Your gift is an utter waste. Look at how you squander it, batting at me with steel. You have not even begun to glimpse the power of magic, and you never will. Your father was right to hold you from the Academy."

While still holding Adara suspended, he pushed with his power, and Ebon was thrown upon his back. The sword flew from his hand across the dirt. Then Ebon flew upwards again and came crashing down on his face. The pain of the last beating redoubled, and he cried out.

"Whimper and whine, little pup. You refuse my hospitality? Very well. I will not bother to kill you, for you will die here regardless. And what would the family think if I slaughtered one of our own?" Then he gave a cruel smile. "Although mayhap your father would reward me if I rid him of his worthless son."

The dean loomed over him now. The glow in his eyes brightened, until Ebon could not look into it for fear of being blinded. The force holding him against the ground increased, pressing him down, down into the dirt, crushing the breath from his body. He fought for even a death gasp.

His head twisted as it was shoved into the ground, until his eyes fixed on Adara. There she hung, watching him die, weeping in fear. No, not fear, he saw, for her eyes never left his. She wept in grief. Grief for him.

Something rose within him, like the whisper of a familiar voice he could not place. The world grew brighter, though he knew not why. Was this what it was like to die? A bright light seeping into the world, banishing the shadows and turning the sky to a blinding fire?

No, came the whispering voice. *It is your magic. Your eyes are glowing.*

Ebon looked at his hand. It twisted where it was crushed against the dirt. He could feel the power emanating from it, the strength of his will turned to wizardry.

With a cry he reached out despite the crushing force. His fingers clutched at Cyrus' ankles.

Ebon felt the cloth beneath his fingers, and the flesh beneath the cloth. Through his fingers he *saw* them—saw them as they appeared, and then saw them as they truly were, all the fibers and tissues and specks of dirt. Their essence was laid bare before him, awaiting his command.

Change it.

His eyes flashed brighter, and Cyrus' feet turned to stone.

The force pressing Ebon into the dirt ceased. He looked up. Cyrus' face was frozen in a mask of horror. Then he screamed, a horrible, screeching wail that cut through the air and turned Ebon's stomach. Frantically the dean tried to take a step backwards, but now his feet were weights he could not hope to move. He wavered.

Ebon heard quick footsteps running towards them. Adara came from nowhere, and with both hands she shoved Cyrus in the chest.

The dean tumbled backwards, struck the edge of the cliff, and slid off it.

Ebon scrambled forwards to look over the edge. Cyrus plunged, still screeching, into the water of the Great Bay. He vanished into the waves.

A long moment passed while they sat there, looking at the spot where Cyrus had vanished. The water churned, with not so much as a ripple to mark his passing.

Then, Adara reached down and took Ebon's arm. She helped him up, clutching him tighter as he nearly fell back to his knees.

"Are you all right?" she said quietly.

"I am hurt," he said. "He attacked me once already. This time it was worse."

"I will help you walk," she said. "But first, this."

She seized his face and pulled him in for a deep kiss. Ebon melted into her, and it was as though a great weight rose from his shoulders. When she was done she pulled back, leaning her forehead against his, and he joined her in closing his eyes.

"I am sorry," she said. "I did not know."

"You could not have," he said. "But come. We must flee. The Seat is lost."

She helped him hobble to the edge. There he saw a staircase leading down, and far below a cove was waiting. In the wall of the cliffs was a cave, wide and dark, and a crude wooden dock had been built into its edge. Tied to the dock were three small rowboats.

"The final mark on the map," said Ebon.

"Hm?"

"Nothing."

With Adara's help he lay in the bottom of one of the boats. Then she cast off the dock tie and began to row, and slowly they pulled away from the island.

"South and west," he said. "We must make for the coast of Selvan, but not where the invaders might catch us."

She nodded. "Who are they? What do they want?"

"I do not know," he murmured. "I only wish I had discovered them sooner."

Her eyes grew distant, looking past him and above him to the island they had left behind. "I doubt you could have prevented it," she said quietly.

Though it was a great effort, Ebon lifted his head. Behind them the Seat was burning, burning with the fury of the sun, and black smoke drifted towards them on the wind. Tears spilled freely down his cheeks, and neither of them dared to speak as they left the flames behind them.

EPILOGUE

THE BUILDINGS THAT LINED THE STREETS WERE BLACKENED AND RU-
ined, for the fires had run amok across the whole of the Seat. Ebon did
not guess that more than one building in four could be salvaged. The
rest would have to be torn down and rebuilt.

Only two structures on the Seat had withstood the sacking: the
High King's palace, bloodstained but unbroken; and the Academy,
whose thick granite walls even the fury of the attackers could not cast
down.

The invading armies had left before the sun set on the day of their
attack. The fleet of Dulmun sailed east, returning to their kingdom.
The blue-and-grey clad soldiers, who some were now calling Shades,
vanished into the forests of Selvan. Rumors about the reason for their
retreat abounded, and Ebon wondered if anyone would ever learn the
truth.

A voice inside told him that someone already *did* know the truth,
and that they were of the family Drayden.

For a week, the students and instructors of the Academy had stayed in Selvan, under the hospitality of that land's king. But when the attackers did not return, and the High King's armies marched hastily back from the war in Wellmont, they had prepared themselves to return home.

Now they stood before the Academy. Ebon stood amid the other students, and in a ring about them were the instructors. Every eye was turned skywards, where the peaks of the citadel loomed above them like an angry father—or, mayhap, like a tired old aunt, welcoming her nephews and nieces into her home, though she was weary to the point of death.

"It has not been touched," said Kalem, voice hushed in awe.

"Good," said Theren fervently. Her arm was still in a sling from her wound, though she swore every day she was going to throw the thing in a rubbish heap.

Jia stepped forth and threw open the front door. Slowly, and without a word, they all filed in.

"You!" shrieked a voice, the moment Ebon stepped inside.

He looked over in surprise. There was Mellie, sitting in her old chair by the front door as though she had never left. "You left without permission! You and your friends!"

Ebon could do nothing but smile. Jia arched an eyebrow. "Mellie, do you mean to tell me you stayed?"

The little old woman blinked up at her through watery eyes. "What is that supposed to mean? Where else would I go?"

Jia only shook her head and led them inside.

Once they had assembled in the entry hall and the doors had closed again, Ebon felt a curious peace settle over them all. Within the citadel, they could not see the destruction that had swept the Seat. The hall was unchanged, and he suspected that the dormitories and the classrooms would be the same.

"Students," said Jia. "Students, assemble. Together, please. *Quiet!*"

Her final bark threw them all to silence, and every eye turned to her.

"Now," she went on. "A terrible tragedy has befallen the High King's Seat. Thank the sky, the Academy suffered less loss than we might have. But all of Underrealm is reeling from this attack, and I will not bandy words with you: these are uncertain times. Many of you will likely be called home by your families. Try not to blame them if they do so. They seek only to ensure your safety."

Ebon felt eyes upon him. He looked to his right, and through the crowd he saw Lilith staring at him. The moment he met her gaze, she ducked her head as if ashamed, but then quickly looked back at him defiantly. He turned away.

"Now, Dean Cyrus of the family Drayden has been missing since the attack. It is presumed he fell in the fighting. We will respect and honor his noble memory."

Kalem snickered. Theren elbowed him hard. But Ebon flushed deep crimson. He had not told his friends what happened to Cyrus. Only Adara knew the truth. He wondered if that would always be the case.

"With the Academy resuming its normal operations, a new dean is required. And it is now my duty to present him to you. He is an accomplished wizard, who I am certain some of you will already have heard about. Please show him your utmost respect."

She stepped down from the stairway. A man went to take her place. He was thin and gaunt, and his black hair hung limp and stringy about his face, almost reaching his shoulders. He had a grim look, with thin lips pressed tight together and dark eyes that held neither humor nor warmth. And yet Ebon thought he felt something noble in the man, something in his bearing that commanded respect and attention, like a general returned home after a lifetime campaigning—though this man looked to be hardly older than Ebon's father.

"Well met," he said, his thick, rich voice rolling forth to echo around the entry hall. "I am Xain, of the family Forredar, and I pledge myself to your learning, and your safety, for as long as duty may require of me."

THE MINDMAGE'S WRATH

BEING BOOK TWO
OF THE FIRST VOLUME

OF THE
ACADEMY JOURNALS

ONE

Once, a new instructor at the Academy would have been the talk of the school for days, but now the count of corpses made her unremarkable.

Indeed, Ebon only knew about Perrin, of the family Arkus, because he was to be her pupil. A woman named Lupa had once taught second-year alchemists, but she had perished in the attack upon the High King's Seat, falling beneath the blades of the grey-and-blue-clad warriors who had struck from the west, who some said were called Shades.

In the weeks since that battle, Ebon was surprised to see how quickly the Academy had resumed its routine. But repetition could not entirely wipe away the memories. Meals were now muted affairs, and students whispered to each other beneath nervous eyes. Too often, instructors mistakenly called upon students whose seats were empty, and classrooms fell to mournful silence. Too often, Ebon passed other students in the common room, tucked into a corner chair, weeping beyond comfort at the loss of a friend.

Too often, Ebon's thoughts drifted back to the day of the attack, and he saw flesh turn to stone beneath his fingers.

The High King had tripled the guard upon the Seat, and watch-fires never ceased their burning in the towers that looked west and east across the Great Bay. The larger part of the Selvan army was now stationed upon the island. Once that would have filled it to bursting, but now there were many empty buildings to house them. Droves of students had been called home despite the increased guard, their parents no longer confident in the strength of the Academy's granite walls. This despite the fact that the Academy had largely been untouched in the fighting. Only one other structure had stood so firm: the High King's palace, bloodstained but unbroken.

"I heard that the High King slipped through the Shades like a thief in the night and led the escape to Selvan's shores," Kalem murmured. He, Ebon, and Theren sat in the nearly-silent dining hall, eyeing their food without eating it. The boy's copper hair stuck out in all directions, for he had roused late that morning.

"And the Lord Prince with her, thank the sky," said Ebon. He had heard the same tale. These days, rumors flew like wind through the Academy halls. It had begun to weary him. He picked at a stain on the table, causing grime to collect beneath his fingernail.

"Thank the sky," echoed Kalem, who seemed not to notice Ebon's mood.

"If you say so," said Theren. She rolled her shoulder and slowly moved her arm in a wide circle. It had been injured in the attack and was only recently free from its sling. Sometimes it still pained her. "Yet she could not stop the sacking of the island, and still she has not struck back against Dulmun. Her flight could be taken for cowardice."

Kalem's hand tightened to a fist, and he glared at her. "You would rather she had fallen in the palace? Then Dulmun would have won, and there would be no rebuilding now. The nine kingdoms would be in chaos."

Theren tossed her short bob of hair. She had not renewed its dye in some time, and her dark roots were beginning to show. "Dulmun *did* win. And do you mean to say that the kingdoms are not already in chaos? Half seem to waver on the brink of joining the rebellion."

"If the other kings have no wish for war, that does not make them cowards, nor traitors." Kalem lifted his chin, freckled nose twitching. "And besides, we from Hedgemond have pledged our strength to the High King."

"Your kingdom sits a half-world away. It could not be farther from the war," said Theren. "Not for nothing is Dulmun's army so feared. If your king shared a border with them, he might not be so eager. I fear the others will join Dulmun before taking up arms against them."

"Hist now," said Ebon, stabbing a spoon into his porridge. "I grow weary of war talk."

But that was not the truth. Ebon hated any reminder of the Shades' attack. Not because of the carnage they had wrought, but because of his own battle, alone save for Adara, on a cliff at the Seat's southern shore. Again his mind showed him flesh turning to stone. The porridge soured in his mouth.

He had not told his friends the truth of that day. Instead, with Adara's help, he had concocted a well-crafted lie. For how could he tell them that the day the Shades attacked the Seat, he had killed the dean—*former* dean, he reminded himself—and his own kin besides?

That truth would not go over well with the King's law or the Academy's faculty. Neither, Ebon suspected, would his friends find it easy to forgive.

"What else would you discuss?" said Theren. "War is all about us."

"Yet it need not consume our lives," Ebon said. "We still have our studies. Today I shall finally leave Credell's class behind."

"And you have my congratulations," said Kalem. "Almost any instructor would be better than he has been to you. If Lupa were still alive, I should say you would be lucky to fall under her tutelage."

The boy fell silent at the mention of Lupa, his eyes cast down. Theren put a hand on his shoulder, but furtively, as though it were an inconvenience. "Try not to dwell on such thoughts. Let us be grateful for those of us still here."

"As long as we *are* here," Kalem muttered. He froze and darted a quick look at them, as though the words had been an accident.

"What do you mean?" said Ebon, frowning.

"Nothing," said Kalem, staring very hard at his breakfast.

Theren narrowed her eyes and then reached over to pinch the back of Kalem's neck, as though she were a mother cat and he her kitten. "Kalem. What troubles you? Tell me now."

"Ow!" Kalem cried out, batting at her hand. "Leave me be, witch."

Ebon leaned forwards. "Tell us, Kalem."

Kalem sighed and looked at them uneasily. "It is nothing. I will make sure it is nothing. It is only . . . my parents wish to bring me home. Back to Hedgemond."

"What?" said Ebon, eyes widening. "You cannot leave!"

"That is what I have told them," said Kalem. "And so far they have listened. It is only that . . . well, after the attack on the Seat . . . they no longer consider it safe."

"But only the parents of the smallest children are withdrawing them," said Theren scornfully. Then she gave Kalem a sidelong glance. "Although, now that I think of it, your size—"

Kalem swung a fist, which she easily blocked. Ebon gave her a dirty look. "Stop it."

She grinned. "I am sorry. The temptation was too great."

"In any case," Kalem continued, still glaring at her, "thus far I have managed to convince them I am safe here. Indeed, I feel safer at the Academy than I would in my family's own home, what with the war brewing."

"And does your family agree?"

"For now, at least," said Kalem softly. "I am not leaving just yet."

"I wish others' parents would pull them from the school," muttered Ebon. Across the dining hall, Lilith's malicious gaze had caught his eye.

Something had changed in Lilith since the attack on the Seat. Before she had seemed to take Ebon for a joke and had mocked him with open scorn. But now she seemed truly hateful. He knew not why she despised him so, nor what he could do to mitigate it—and he feared what might come of it if he did nothing.

Theren followed his gaze to Lilith, and her countenance grew hard. Turning back, she leaned in close to speak in a low voice. "That reminds me. Have you heard about the vaults?"

Ebon frowned, but Kalem leaned in closer. "I have heard only a rumor."

"It seems something was stolen from them," said Theren. "Though we are not yet certain if it was taken during the attack, or some time after the students returned to the citadel."

"That is like what I heard," said Kalem. "But why do you say *we?*"

"Did you not know? I conduct my servitude in the vaults."

Kalem's eyes widened. But Ebon raised a hand to stay them both. "A moment. As far as I am concerned, you are both speaking in tongues. What servitude? And what are these vaults you speak of?"

"Every student in their sixth year embarks upon servitude in the Academy," said Kalem. "It is meant to teach us the value of simple work in the service of others. Also we are paired with advanced wizards with many years of experience, so that we may learn from them."

"And what are the vaults?"

"They are rooms buried deep within the Academy's bowels," said Theren. "Within them are contained magical artifacts of thousands of years of history. Some predate the Academy itself."

Ebon opened his mouth to ask another question, but Kalem spoke first, and eagerly. "What was it that the thief stole?"

"An artifact, but which one, we do not know," said Theren. "I have spent the last several days trying to find out. But I cannot find the records for the room where the theft occurred."

"What are these artifacts?" said Ebon. "What do they do?"

"Wizards of great power can imbue objects with magical qualities," said Kalem. "These can perform some small bits of magic even without a wizard's power. Some are little more than baubles. But others, especially older ones, often carry the power of the Wizard Kings."

"And that is what made me think of the theft when you were staring your daggers at Lilith," said Theren. "You see, she—"

But just then, the bell tolled, signaling the start of morning classes. Theren looked across the dining hall, where Lilith was collecting her dishes for the kitchen.

"Damn. We should speak more of this, for there is much to tell. This afternoon, in the library." She shot to her feet and scooped up her plates with a simple mindspell, suspending them in the air as she weaved her way through the dining hall.

"The library? But . . ." Kalem's voice trailed away, for she was already gone. He and Ebon rose more slowly, scooping their dishes up with their hands. But as Ebon found his feet and turned, he ran hard into another student, and all their dishes fell to the stone floor together.

"Sky," spat Ebon, trying to brush remnants of egg and porridge from his sleeve. Then he looked up and blanched. He stared into the dark eyes of a girl he had met before. He had seen her in his common room on his first day in the Academy. When he had tried to befriend her, she had crushed an iron goblet before his eyes.

"I am sorry," stammered Ebon.

"Why should you be?" said the girl, her voice an apathetic monotone. "It was an accident. I was behind you anyway."

Her eyes glowed, and Ebon braced himself for a blow. But instead, his dishes sprang up from the floor and into his hands, while the girl's flew into her own. She sauntered off without a word. Ebon let out a sigh.

Kalem snickered beside him. "I was afraid you would soil your underclothes. Why are you so afraid of that one?"

"I met her the day I arrived. She was . . . much less friendly, then. She crushed a goblet of iron like it was parchment, and I thought I saw ill will in her eyes."

Kalem shrugged. "Well, she is a powerful mindmage, and no mistake. Isra, I believe her name is. But she is not so fearsome as you make her out to be. And after the attack on the Seat, I think any ill will between students has fled the Academy's halls."

"Not so with Lilith."

"No, I suppose not."

They shuffled with the other students towards the kitchens to discard their bowls, and then the assembly passed muted and mournful into the halls. Theren joined them outside the dining hall, and just before Ebon left for the first-years' classroom, he gave his friends a wan smile.

"Wish me good fortune," he said.

"You do not need it," said Theren. "Or if you do, then you should not be graduating in the first place."

"That is not helpful," Kalem said, scowling at Theren. "Good fortune, Ebon."

TWO

OLDER STUDENTS PEELED AWAY AS EBON MADE HIS WAY TOWARDS CRE-
dell's class, and the crowd around him grew ever younger. He quite looked
forwards to having older classmates soon. Credell's students were all first-
years, children of ten or eleven. The next class would bring only one year's
improvement, but Ebon hoped he would look a little less out of place.

He reached Credell's classroom and stepped through the door. The
instructor had not yet arrived, but many students had, and in the front
row he saw little wild-haired Astrea—the only student in his class to
befriend him. She brightened at the sight of him and waved eagerly. He
gave her a small smile and waved back, ruffling her hair and making her
giggle as he made his way to the back row of benches.

More first- and second-years had been withdrawn from the Academy than from among the older children. Astrea was one of only six
left in the class, besides Ebon himself. It made him wonder why they
did not combine this class and the next into one. But then he realized
Credell would teach him for two years if that were the case, and he
shuddered.

Credell arrived at last. He gave the room a quick look, his eyes lingering for a moment upon Ebon. Since the attack on the Seat, Credell's fear seemed to have lessened somewhat. Yet still the instructor jumped when Ebon spoke too loudly or moved too quickly.

"Well, ah, class. Ahem," said Credell. "Normally I would have you all resume your lessons. But today we have a matter of ceremony we must attend to first. Ah, er . . . Ebon, would you please approach the front of the classroom?"

Ebon slid down his bench and went forwards, acutely aware of the other students staring at him. Many of them had been there months longer than Ebon, and he could feel their awe that he had graduated so swiftly. He wondered if he would have been ready for this first test so quickly, if it had not been for Cyrus.

Credell held forth a wooden rod, careful not to brush Ebon's fingers with his own as he handed it over. Ebon turned to the class, holding the rod high. He felt the grain of it beneath his fingers, the tiny ridges and valleys of its form. In his mind's eye, he peered *into* the wood itself, seeing its true nature, the countless tiny parts that composed it—

—*his hand wrapped around Cyrus' ankle, the spark of power within him, flesh turning to stone*—

—he squeezed his eyes shut, shaking his head to banish the images. They faded, but reluctantly. The rod was still wooden. Now Credell and the students were staring at him expectantly.

Ebon drew a deep breath through his nose and released it slowly from his lips. He focused on the wood again.

And then the room grew brighter—or at least it appeared to, for Ebon's eyes were glowing. He saw the wood for what it was. And then he changed it.

Pure, simple stone, grey and lifeless and solid, rippled from his fingers. In a moment it was done, and the rod had been turned. Around the room, children reached up to scratch at their necks, or shook their heads as though repulsing a fly. Ebon knew they could sense his magic, though many of them had not yet learned to use it themselves. Wizards could always detect spells from their own branch, or from the mirror branch.

"Well done," said Credell, his relief plain. Clearly he was as eager to be rid of Ebon as Ebon was to leave the class. He reached out and awkwardly patted the boy on his shoulder. Ebon returned the rod. With a flourish of his fingers, Credell turned it back into wood.

"Class, you have borne witness. Ebon has mastered the first test of the transmuter, and has moved beyond us. Rise now, and let us escort him to his new instructor."

The children rose silent and solemn, filing into a line in the room's center. Credell led them into the halls. They passed several doors—the first-year classes of the other branches of magic—before reaching one where Credell stopped. He tapped out a trio of soft knocks.

"Come in!" commanded a woman's voice, thick and rich and full of power. Credell nearly dropped the rod in fright, so sudden was her call. But he swallowed hard and opened the door. Ebon followed him inside.

This room had a window overlooking the training grounds, and for a moment the morning's light made Ebon blink and shield his eyes. Once they adjusted, he looked about. The room was much the same as Credell's: two files of benches stretching from the front to the back, every one with its own desk, and a handful of students scattered among them. But many bookshelves were lined against the wall with the door, filled with thick leather tomes of every description. Ebon was surprised. He had not seen any other classrooms with bookshelves. He had thought the Academy's books were all harbored in its vast library. The thought of yet more things to read set his head spinning.

Then Ebon looked to the front of the room, and his heart skipped a beat. There behind the lectern was, quite simply, the most massive woman he had ever seen. Her shoulders seemed to stretch as wide as Ebon's arm span, and though the ceiling was at least a pace above her head, her stature made it seem that she might bump against it. Huge hands gripped the lectern's edges and nearly enveloped it, and her dark grey instructor's robes strained mightily to contain her frame. Her eyes seemed small compared to the rest of her ruddy features, yet they sparkled with interest even when the sunlight missed them. Ebon thought this woman looked nothing like a wizard, but rather a mighty warrior of campfire legend, stripped of armor and shrouded instead in cloth, against which her body tried to rebel.

"This is the new one, then? Well, come in, boy. I am Perrin, of the family Arkus. Let us get your test seen to, for I was just introducing myself to the other students."

"Erm . . . ah . . . yes," said Credell, quaking as hard as he ever had when confronting Cyrus, the former dean. "E-E-Ebon, here you are. T-take it."

Ebon took the wooden rod, which Credell had extended in trembling fingers. He brought it to Perrin and waited.

"Well? Go on. You have done it once already—or should have, before you were brought here."

Ebon nodded, at a loss for words. He turned to the class and held the rod aloft. This time, shock at Perrin's appearance kept his thoughts from drifting to Cyrus. His eyes glowed, and stone rippled along the rod.

"Good!" said Perrin. She clapped her hands, and the sound was like thunder. "And can you change it back?"

The blood drained from Ebon's face. "I—what? No, I only—"

"Oh, calm yourself," said Perrin, waving him off. "I only asked from curiosity—it is not a requirement. Now, be seated quickly. Or, no, that is not right. Remain here. There is the ceremony, is there not?"

She stepped out from behind the lectern—revealing boots that Ebon could have fit both feet into—and approached Credell. The craven little instructor quailed as Perrin thrust the rod towards him.

"Do you vow that you have instructed this pupil to the best of your ability, in judgement as well as in skill?"

"I . . . I so vow," whimpered Credell, taking the rod. He made a brave, but ultimately futile attempt to straighten his shoulders. "Do you vow that you will continue his instruction, in judgement as well as in skill, to the best of your ability?"

"I so vow. Now, as I said, I have scarcely been able to speak to my new students. If you do not mind."

Perrin reached out and threw the door open. Then, quickly—but not unkindly—she ushered Credell's class through it. Ebon caught one last glimpse of Astrea waving him a happy good-bye before the door shut between them.

"Well, then. Find yourself a seat. There are many open benches—

too many, it is a tragedy to say. Sit near the front, for I shall have to work with you first, or else you will no doubt wander like a hatchling without its mother."

Ebon nodded and made for a seat. One bench in the second row was entirely unoccupied, and he slid onto it. Perrin returned to the lectern and cleared her throat into a meaty fist.

"Now, then. Welcome, ah . . . hrm. What was your name?"

"Ebon, of the family—" He stopped short. He had not meant to mention his family name. But now Perrin was peering at him, and he could feel the other students' curiosity at his pause. He gritted his teeth. "Of the family Drayden."

If Perrin thought anything of it, she gave no sign, though Ebon thought he felt several students stiffen. "Well then, welcome, Ebon. I will say to you what I told the class before your arrival: I do not know you, and you do not know me. Yet I knew something of your former instructor, Lupa, for she was only a few years behind me when I myself studied here. A good woman. But you are left with me, for which I apologize. You deserve someone wiser, more powerful in transmutation, and certainly a good deal more patient. Those things I cannot promise you. But this I can vow: I will do my best to make of you what I can, and help you along your road to knowledge. And I can promise you what the High King Enalyn, sky bless her name, has promised us all: I will keep you safe with my every breath. I will serve you to the limits of my power. And I will—"

A sharp rapping came at the door, and Perrin stopped short. She glowered, hands gripping the lectern tighter for a moment. "Come in, and be quick!" The bark in her voice made every student in the room jump.

The door swung open, and in swept the Academy's new dean, Xain of the family Forredar. He was a lank man and sun-pale under his dark skin, with thin black hair hanging down to his shoulders. His dark grey robes bore no ornamentation as the former dean's had, and yet somehow Xain looked far more impressive in them. It was something in his eyes, Ebon decided. They were haunted, yes, and yet they bore also a steely resolve. Though his frame was slight, and could have appeared frail, there was a set to his shoulders that spoke of grim determination.

It was a moment before Ebon realized that Xain was not alone. Beside him was a boy who could not have been more than ten years of age. Ebon wondered if he was a new student at the Academy—until he saw the boy's dark eyes and pinched nose. They were the same as Xain's. He had to be a relation, mayhap even his son.

Though Perrin had answered gruffly at Xain's knock, she now beamed a warm smile. "Good morn, Dean Forredar. We are honored by your presence."

"No more than the Academy is honored by yours, Perrin. Instructor Arkus, I mean. Forgive me—my tongue has nearly forgotten the Academy's courtesies."

He stepped forwards and extended a hand. Perrin clasped his wrist firmly. "And mine the same. Though no great surprise, considering the years."

Xain nodded and turned to the class. His tone grew brisk, though not entirely unfriendly. "Greetings, students. You know who I am, or something of me, at least. But I would wager you have had little chance to know your new instructor, and thus you cannot understand the honor you have been granted. Perrin of the family Arkus is as good a woman as I have ever met. I hope you will afford her your utmost attention and your most earnest effort."

"The dean is far too kind," replied Perrin, stifling a smile. "Though I will not deny you should heed his advice, if ever you wish to pass this class. And who have you brought with you? This cannot be little Erin."

"It is, though not so little anymore." Xain beckoned the boy forwards. Erin came timidly, balking at the instructor's great size. But Perrin stooped until she was nearly at eye level with the boy and gravely reached for his hand.

"It is my pleasure to meet you, young sir. And my heart is gladdened to see you by your father's side again."

Erin smiled bashfully. "Thank you, madam." His voice was so soft, Ebon could hardly hear it from where he sat.

"I did not mean to distract you all," said Xain, his eyes roving the room. "I am only showing him about the Academy and could not pass without stopping to see you. I expect you—"

Xain's glance fell upon Ebon, and there it stopped. He grew rigid

240

as a board, hands tightening to fists by his sides. Ebon felt hot blood flooding his cheeks, though he knew not why.

"You there," said Xain, nearly spitting the words. "What is your name?"

"E-Ebon, Dean Forredar."

"Your family name," he snapped.

The color that had flooded Ebon's face drained away at once. "I am of the family Drayden, Dean."

Xain gave no answer. But his hand went to Erin's shoulder and drew him close, as if to shield him. A moment longer he stared, and Ebon could not mistake the look in his eye: hatred, fiery and pure, more so even than Lilith had shown. Then at last Xain turned away.

"Good day," he said tersely, and swept from the room with his son in tow.

Slowly, every eye turned to Ebon in wonder. Even Perrin gave him a hard look. Ebon's gaze fell to his desk, and he stewed in a shame that he did not understand.

THREE

THE REST OF THE MORNING CLASS PASSED QUICKLY, IF UNCOMFORTABLY.
Ebon tried to pay attention as Perrin laid out the studies he would need
to complete, and he retrieved a book from the shelves at the instructor's
commands. But though he sat for hours staring at the first page, the
words had become a blur before his eyes. He could see only Xain's dark
gaze, gleaming with unknown malice.

When at last the bell rang for midday meal, Ebon shot from his
bench. But just as he reached the door, Perrin bellowed to stop him.

"Ebon! Return your book to its place on the shelf."

Ebon turned sheepishly to do as he was bid. Several other students
had been about to leave their books out as well, but quickly they scrambled to return them. Though he might have imagined it, Ebon thought
he felt Perrin's careful eye upon him as he returned the book and fled
the room. Only then did he break into a run, flying through the citadel
towards the dining hall.

He found Kalem and Theren standing in the food line and fell into
place beside them. He had little desire to eat, but neither did he want

to be alone. Something of his mood must have shown in his face, for Kalem frowned in concern.

"What is wrong? You look as though you woke this morning to find yourself a wizard no longer."

"Oh, it is no great matter," said Ebon bitterly. "Only that the new dean seems to despise me even more than the old one, and just as with Cyrus, I have no faintest idea why."

"What?" said Theren, arching an eyebrow. "What do you mean?"

Ebon told them all that had happened, doing his best to convey in words the hatred he had felt in Xain's eyes. Kalem shook his head mournfully.

"That seems ill fortune. I wonder what it is all about?"

But Theren rolled her eyes. "I think you may be imagining things, Ebon. It seems far-fetched that he could so quickly detest you. Though I have no doubt he will learn to, once he knows you better."

"This is no jest," said Ebon irritably. "You doubted me when I told you of Dean Cyrus' treatment. Do you recall how that turned out?" His body still bore the fading bruises from when Cyrus attacked him.

As Theren's eyes fell in shame, Ebon's guilt grew in response. She felt remorse that she had let Cyrus strike Ebon with his mindmagic. But she did not know what Ebon had done to the dean on the day of the attack. That secret was his alone—and Adara's, of course. His mood softened at that thought.

"I apologize," Theren said quietly. "If you say that is what happened, I believe you."

"Think nothing of it," Ebon muttered, unable to meet her eyes.

"If Xain indeed has animosity towards you, there must be some reason," said Kalem. "I will see if anyone knows what it might be. In truth, I know little of the man, beyond the fact he is favored by the High King herself."

"I shall ask about as well," said Theren. "Though I do not have many friends."

At the front of the line, they fetched their food and sat to eat without speaking further. But Ebon's appetite had gone from little to nothing, and he could not force himself to eat much of the soup. He gnawed at his bread instead, chewing until it was a soggy mess in his mouth.

Theren scooped up the last of her soup, slurping it noisily, and then shoved the bowl away. "A fair meal today. I think they have started cooking better since we returned to the Academy. No doubt in an attempt to raise our spirits."

"Or they are more liberal with their spices, since they have fewer mouths to feed," muttered Kalem.

Theren snorted and punched his shoulder. "Still such dark words! That sounds like something I might say. Here is something that might cheer you: I have changed my schedule. Hereafter, I shall spend my afternoons in the library with you."

Kalem grinned. "So that is why you said we would speak in the library this afternoon. I had wondered."

Ebon, too, found his mood lifted. But then a thought struck him, and he frowned. "I thought you were no fan of book learning."

"Of course not," said Theren, pursing her lips. "I am not joining you because I wish to study with you, but because I do not want my afternoons to be so incredibly dull."

Ebon and Kalem stifled groans as they looked sidelong at each other. Ebon would be glad for Theren's company, but he enjoyed the peace of his time in the library. Many hours had he and Kalem whiled away, tucked into their armchairs with books of ancient lands and Wizard Kings.

"Well, we will certainly enjoy your presence," said Kalem. But Ebon could hear that his heart was not in the words.

"Of course you will," said Theren. "And that reminds me. This morning we were speaking of Lilith, and of the theft in the vaults. I meant to tell you that—"

Someone stopped behind Ebon, abruptly enough that their shoes squeaked upon the stone.

"The vaults."

Ebon turned. Behind him stood Credell. The thin-faced, wheedling instructor wore a vacant look. He turned to them all, his eyes fixed on Theren. "The vaults," he repeated.

"Yes, Instructor?" She raised her eyebrows. "My servitude is in the vaults. What of it?"

"I had almost forgotten." Credell's voice was absent its customary shake, and his nervous tics had disappeared. "I must enter the vaults. Give me your key."

Kalem looked uncertainly at Theren. She met the boy's eyes and gave a barely perceptible shrug. "Instructor, I have no key. It is only given to me during my servitude, and only when I must enter the vaults themselves."

"The vaults," he said, more urgent this time. "I must enter them. Give me your key."

Now Theren was growing exasperated. "I do not have one," she said, very nearly snapping at him. "Besides, you are an Instructor. If you have Academy business within the vaults, you can enter them your-self. Egil will admit you. But I do not have the key."

Her last words crackled, and Credell jumped at last. He blinked twice, and then looked down as if noticing Ebon at his elbow for the first time. He drew back as if from a viper, wringing his hands just under his chin.

"Ah, yes, of course," he stuttered. "Of course you have no key. Silly of me. I had forgotten. I do not know why . . . why I thought you . . . er, I am sorry. Good day."

He turned and left, winding away through the tables. All three of them kept their eyes fixed upon his back until he was out of sight.

"That was most odd," said Kalem.

"Bizarre," agreed Theren. "I wonder if he is all right. After the at-tack upon the Seat, I mean. War can break one's mind, they say."

"He seemed well enough the past few days in class," said Ebon qui-etly. "That was unlike I have ever seen him . . . and yet, not worse. He was less frightened. More sure."

"Mayhap he is finally growing a spine." Theren shrugged and seemed to dismiss the matter. "In any case, I was speaking of the theft."

"Of course," said Ebon. "What news have you?"

"Well, few students perform their servitude in the vaults. But Lilith is another."

"The both of you?" said Kalem. "I am amazed the Academy is still standing, if the two of you have been in such close quarters so long."

Theren glared at him. "I can control myself when I wish to. And besides, we are rarely present together. The caretaker, Egil, almost never requires two students at once."

"Yes, well and good about all of that," said Ebon, waving her words aside. "But what of Lilith? What does she have to do with it?"

"I have had a thought brewing," said Theren. "Mayhap it was some member of the Academy's faculty who carried out the theft. But it could also have been a student. And if it were a student, who better than one who performs their servitude in the vaults? Such a one would know better than any other how to do it."

Kalem looked at Ebon, his brow creased with doubt. "That seems a far reach, Theren. What student would dare risk such a thing? Even Academy faculty might think twice about trying to breach the vault's defenses."

"Yet many of us are more powerful than our instructors," said Theren. "I am stronger than any mindmage here, especially now that Cyrus has vanished. Lilith is at least as great as any firemage on the faculty—though, I say that without knowing the new dean's measure. He may be a great firemage, for all I know."

Talk of Cyrus had begun to make Ebon uncomfortable, so he steered the topic away. "I hear little evidence beyond 'It could be so,' Theren. And I do not know if even that is true, for Lilith was far away when the attack occurred. How could she have carried out such a theft from another kingdom?"

"She said she left the Academy, yes," said Theren. "But what if she lied? What better alibi?"

"Ebon is right," Kalem said. "If that is your only proof, it is flimsy indeed."

Theren frowned. "It is at least a place to start."

"To start what?" said Ebon.

She looked at him with wide eyes, as though the answer was obvious. "Why, to find the thief, of course."

Kalem gawked. "No. No, we are not engaging in another mad scheme, Theren. If the theft is indeed a matter of great worry, then let us—"

But just then the bell rang, and the dining hall filled with the sound of scraping benches as students stood from their meals. Almost chipper, Theren jumped up to bring her dishes to the kitchen. Kalem growled and followed her.

Ebon went with them, but he stopped and looked over his shoulder one final time. Credell stood in the doorway of the dining hall, looking about with a faraway gaze. One hand stole up to scratch at the skin beneath his collar. He shivered as though cold and then vanished into the hallways.

It is no matter, thought Ebon. *You have left his class, and he is no longer your concern.*

Yet a chill crept up his spine as he followed his friends to the kitchen.

FOUR

Later, in the library, Kalem and Ebon introduced Theren to their nook on the third level. Predictably, she seemed to think it boring. She dragged another chair over to join them and draped her feet across the table in their midst. Kalem snatched books from beneath her shoes with a scandalized expression, and soon both he and Ebon were grinding their teeth as they tried to read, for Theren seemed far more interested in talking. Though they tried to give her only short, one-word replies, and thus dissuade her from speaking, Theren refused to take the hint.

Soon Ebon felt himself at the breaking point. He leapt to his feet and scuttled away towards the bookshelves, muttering something about finding another reference book for a report he was writing for Instructor Jia.

Once safely ensconced in the bookshelves and out of earshot of Theren's endless chatter, Ebon sighed in relief. Leaning around the shelf's edge, he saw Theren still going on animatedly to Kalem, while the poor boy shoved his nose very nearly into the spine of his book. Ebon chuckled and ducked out of sight.

"How heartwarming to see the three of you united in your pursuit of wisdom."

The words made Ebon jump, but then he recognized Mako's voice. He softly chuckled and turned to find the bodyguard behind him, leaning against one of the shelves. Mako was clad all in black, black shirt beneath an even darker leather vest, and tight leggings that paraded his wiry muscles. Black, too, were the scabbards at his waist, where his long and cruel daggers rested.

"Mako. It has been some time since last you visited me."

"Well, war blazes across Underrealm." Mako waved an airy hand. "I have been here and there and most places in between."

"And now you return. To what do I owe the honor?"

"To this," said Mako, reaching within his vest and producing a letter.

Ebon shook his head and took it. He had never fully understood Mako's role within the Drayden family's business, and it still confounded him every time he saw the bodyguard running messages like a simple courier. The letter bore his family's seal, and Ebon's heart skipped at the thought that it might be from his father. But no, Shay Drayden had a personal seal. Ebon peeled the letter open.

Dearest Brother,

There are not words in all the tongues of the nine lands to describe how angry I am with you. Why is it that the first letter I received from you did not come until the High King's enemies had invaded the Seat? Two months you had to write me a letter, and yet you did nothing. You are an inconsiderate lout and a brute besides.

That said, I am, of course, so very glad to hear you were not harmed in the fighting. But only one way may you retain my good humor towards you! If you write me back, at once and without delay! I know <u>nothing</u> of your time at the Academy so far and it is <u>unbearable</u>.

Of course, your letter may very well find me upon the road, rather than at home. For yes, we are traveling, dear

249

*brother! Even now, we make ready to travel to the Seat
to visit you. (Well, we do not come only to visit you, but
of course we will visit you while we are there.) Are you
not excited? It will be wonderful to see your face again,
inconsiderate and selfish as you might be.*

*Write me at once, dear Ebon. Send it back with Mako
if you can, but send it quickly in any case. And be ready
to visit me on the Seat, for I have a thousand and one
questions.*

*With love,
Albi*

Ebon was weeping almost from the moment he recognized his sister's frenetic scrawl upon the parchment, and he laughed with every
insult, for he could almost hear the way she would deliver them. Her
nose would be scrunched up tight, as it was when she grew angry or
excited, and her brow would be furrowed, and she would plant her fists
on her hips just so, moving them only to brandish them before his nose
as if ready to strike him.

But though his heart sang at the thought of seeing Albi again, it
darkened, too, at the thought of his family. If the Draydens were returning to the Seat, his father would be there as well. Shay had been
against Ebon's coming to the Academy from the first. Might he use the
attack as an excuse to withdraw him?

Ebon turned to Mako. "Albi says they are coming to the Seat. Do
you know when they will arrive?"

"Some time before Yearsend, certainly," said Mako.

"But that is just around the corner."

"Of course it is." Cruelty lurked in Mako's grin, buried behind an
indifference that Ebon thought must be feigned. "That means they will
be able to celebrate the holiday in your company. Mayhap they can
even meet your little Academy friends—though no doubt there are
some other, more private friends you would rather keep hidden." His
grin widened.

Adara sprang to mind, and Ebon felt color in his cheeks. "I . . . am surprised they would wish to visit the Seat so soon," he said, changing the subject for his own benefit as much as Mako's distraction. "Many think it dangerous here. Some parents are even bringing their children home."

"The attack upon the Seat was a tragedy, no doubt."

"As you say. But that begs a question: how did you learn of it in time to warn me?"

Mako shifted on his feet, uncrossing and recrossing his arms through a moment of silence. "How do you think I learned of it, little Ebon?"

Ebon felt his pulse quicken and his breath came shallow. "Did you hear of it from someone in our family?"

Mako snorted. "A Drayden? No. This may shock you, Ebon, but I have friends outside our clan. Well, I say 'friends,' of course, though they might not agree. But in any case, brigands and ne'er-do-wells are of a kind, and through us news may travel from one end of Underrealm to the other, faster than a bird's flight."

That was not quite an answer, Ebon realized. "Did the family Drayden have aught to do with the attack?" he pressed. "I . . . just before that day, Cyrus confronted me in a rage. He seemed to think Halab was plotting—"

"If he spoke those words, then he was a fool in truth," said Mako vehemently. "For years I called him scum, and untrustworthy. Halab would not listen. She tried so hard to see the good in him, when I knew there was only pettiness and selfishness and greed. Mayhap even a touch of madness."

Ebon thought of when Cyrus attacked him in the garden, and a phantom pain flared into his ribs. Then his thoughts went to their battle on the cliffs, and he shuddered. "You may be right about that," he murmured.

"To accuse Halab was to prove his ignorance. There are reasons for that, which I cannot explain now, though mayhap the day approaches when I shall. Your father, on the other hand . . ."

He trailed off, and when Ebon looked up he saw the man regarding him with a keen glint in his eye. "What of him? He was the one who had me deliver the parcel to that inn upon the Seat. Are you saying that played some role in the assault?"

Mako laughed, but softly, for they were still in the library. "Your question is absurd. Not because of its premise, but because you think I would tell you if you were correct."

"That is no answer."

"It is not meant to be." Mako pursed his lips at Ebon's scowl. "Oh, very well. Enough games. You wish for more certainty? Then think upon what you know. Cyrus was a madman. Quite useful to the family, yes—yet prone to baseless fears of being undermined."

"Then he was lying."

"The family Drayden had an agent at the height of power within the Academy. The dean has the ear of the High King herself, and a place upon her council. Would your father leave such a resource upon the Seat to die?" His dark grin returned. "You, mayhap, he would allow to perish. But not Cyrus."

"Very well," Ebon muttered. "I believe that—not for your words, but for the truth you speak of my father."

Mako gave a mocking bow. "You are too gracious, little lord gold-bag."

Ebon felt as though a great weight had lifted from his shoulders. If the Draydens had no hand in the attack, then he had played no part by delivering that parcel for his father. But with that worry removed, Ebon's thoughts ran to a more pressing concern.

"I must ask you something else," said Ebon. "What do you know of the Academy's new dean? The replacement for Cyrus?"

The bodyguard's countenance darkened, his upper lip curling in a snarl. "That meddlesome fool. You would do well to stay away from him."

"That choice may not be mine. He has seen me already, and from the moment our eyes met, I felt that he hated me. His malice was like a physical thing, reaching out to grip my throat."

Mako snorted. "How poetic. Yet if I were there, I might not doubt your words. Xain of the family Forredar has much cause to hate the family Drayden. And as it happens, your woes with this dean stem from his troubles with the former."

Ebon blinked. "With Cyrus? What has he to do with this?"

"Everything. You know the dean spends much time within the

High King's court. Upon a time, Xain was often in that court as well, along with another mindmage of our clan: a man named Drystan, who you would never have met. Always Drystan and Xain were at odds, for both were powerful wizards of mirror branches, and Xain always gave counsel against Drystan's advice. They had been rivals even from their Academy days, yet it was not until they were both grown that their rivalry blossomed into violence, invited by Xain's own arrogance. There was a duel—a wizard's battle. Drystan received aid from Cyrus, and another, still more powerful wizard. When the duel was finished, someone lay badly hurt, but it was neither of the contestants. Xain's magic spun out of control, striking a bystander with no stake in the fight. The victim was a distant kin of the High King herself."

The blood drained from Ebon's face. "That is no small crime."

"No indeed. Constables and Mystics pursued Xain from the Seat and across all the nine lands. But now, for reasons beyond understanding, the High King herself has pardoned him. Something to do with this war that now engulfs Underrealm, though I have not learned any details. And now that he is ensconced in power again, he hates the family Drayden. He blames us for his own failures, his own weakness. Thus if you have earned his ire, I warn you: hide. He is an eagle, and you are a mouse. Do not provoke him. Do not even speak with him if you can help it."

"I have no wish to spend any more time with him than I must," said Ebon, shivering. But he was thinking of Xain and Cyrus and their duel. What might Xain think if he knew Ebon had killed Cyrus in the end? But now Mako was looking at him keenly, and he forced himself into a steady calm. "But this is an unreasoning cause for hate. I am not Cyrus. What happened to Xain had nothing to do with me."

Mako shrugged. "You are a Drayden, even if not by your choice. Every great family has some dark deeds to their name. And your best intentions do not pardon the actions of your kin."

Ebon sagged against the bookshelf, his head lolling back to strike the leather spines. Another dean whose hatred of him he could neither explain nor hope to alleviate. His life seemed a sad mockery, a jester's play. His hands clenched at his sides.

Mako, for his part, seemed to be reveling in Ebon's discomfort.

He smiled again and then straightened. "Well, I came only to deliver a letter. Now I must be on my way. Unless you wish to reply to Albi?"

"It would take me time. I will send it by regular courier. I am grateful for the letter—and for the truth about Xain."

"It was my pleasure, truly," said Mako with a flash of his teeth. But then his eyes drifted past Ebon, and he grew somber. "As for your other question—about the attack on the Seat. You know the Draydens are not the only wealthy family in Underrealm."

He nodded, his gaze still fixed on something over Ebon's shoulder. Ebon turned. There, a few shelves away, was Lilith, half-hidden by gaps in the books.

Ebon turned quickly to Mako. "Are you saying Yerrin was behind the attack?"

Mako shrugged. "I know nothing for certain. Only it seems unlikely that Dulmun and the Shades could have staged such an invasion without the coin of a great merchant house. I will say this: if Halab commanded me to investigate the attack, that is where I would start my search."

And Theren had believed that Lilith might be behind the theft in the vaults.

Mako turned as if to leave, but Ebon reached out and gripped his arm. It felt like iron. Mako glanced down at Ebon's hand. Ebon gulped, trying to hide a tremor of fear.

"Thank you. I have not had the chance to say that since you saved my life. I may owe you the very beating of my heart, along with the lives of my friends. I have not always thought highly of you, but I see now that that was my mistake."

Mako looked almost startled, which in turn surprised Ebon; the bodyguard rarely showed anything other than contempt and condescension. But his wide grin slid back into place after only a moment, and he flicked two fingers in dismissal. "That is no mistake on your part. Few think highly of me, especially among the wise. And if I saved the lives of some within the Academy, well, then, it was an accident. I had only hoped that you would be around a bit longer, at least. You are so amusing, after all."

He stepped around the corner of the bookshelf and vanished.

FIVE

EBON RETURNED TO KALEM AND THEREN IN THEIR ALCOVE AGAINST the wall. Kalem appeared to have given up trying to read. He leaned back with his chin in his hand, listening to Theren as she went on about some new spell she was trying to master. They both looked up at his approach.

"Thank the sky," said Kalem. "It is my turn to go and look for a book."

"What do you mean?" said Theren, frowning. "You cannot tell me the two of you do not enjoy my company. I have changed my entire class schedule for you."

"Theren, I come here to *read,* not to *speak,*" said Kalem.

She seemed about to reply, until she looked up and saw the concern in Ebon's face. "Ebon? What is it?"

Ebon glanced up at her, and then over his shoulder where he had been speaking with Mako. He shifted on his feet, the letter from Albi crinkling in his hand. "Er . . . my family is coming to the Seat," he said, holding the parchment aloft.

Both his friends grew solemn. "Well. That is a pleasant surprise," Kalem said, with visible effort.

"Oh, do not be an idiot, Kalem," said Theren. "When will they come?"

"Some time before Yearsend. But in fact, that is not what troubles me." He sank into a chair between them, his mind racing at how he might tell them without revealing Mako's involvement. "I have been thinking on what you said before. About Lilith being the thief who robbed the Academy vaults."

"Yes?" said Theren, sitting straighter. "Do you believe me now?"

"Let us say that I did," said Ebon. "What would we do about it? What do you know of Lilith?"

Theren frowned. "What makes you think I know anything of her? She is a goldbag, like any other. Well, besides the two of you, mayhap."

Ebon rolled his eyes. "I mean, how might she have done it? Where might she have hidden what she stole?"

Kalem spoke before Theren could answer. "I do not understand, Ebon. Why have you changed your mind so suddenly? Just this morning you agreed with me that there was little evidence pointing to Lilith."

"I have been considering the possibility," Ebon said, hearing Mako in his mind. "And I think it is unlikely that Dulmun would risk open war against the High King, even with the alliance of these Shades—whoever they are—unless they also had the support of one of the great families. A royal family, for your strength of arms, or of a merchant family, for the depth of our purses."

"But there are dozens of merchant families across Underrealm," said Kalem.

"Few have purses deep enough for a civil war," said Theren, leaning forwards in excitement. "Only Drayden or Yerrin could do it. And Yerrin removed their children from the Seat during the attack, while you and Cyrus stayed here. I think I see your mind, Ebon."

Kalem shook his head. "All of this is still only conjecture. And I ask you both again: even if you are right, what do you mean to do about it?"

"To expose her," said Ebon, leaning forwards. "Think of it. If we can prove the Yerrins had something to do with the attack—and the theft within the vaults—they would face the High King's justice. Dulmun would lose a powerful ally and be forced to surrender before this war has truly begun. Does your loyalty towards the High King not demand this of you?"

He thought he might have convinced Kalem, for the boy paused with a frown. But when he finally answered, he was angrier still. "No. This is a mad scheme. Where do you even get such thoughts, Ebon? And do not tell me they came from that letter."

"I have been thinking on this, as I said," Ebon muttered.

"I can see the lie in your eyes, Ebon. I have seen it there before. Can you not even trust me with the truth?"

Now even Theren was looking at Ebon askance. So he sighed and looked away uneasily. "Very well. When I went to fetch a book just now, I was visited by Mako, my family's bodyguard, of whom I have spoken before."

"Here?" said Kalem, his voice shrill. "In the library? In the *Academy?* How did he enter?"

"I do not know. He seems to come and go as he wishes."

"He has been here before?" said Kalem, nearly shouting.

Now Ebon was growing angry. "Yes, and somewhat often. What of it? Mayhap Cyrus permitted it, and he has heard no different from Xain. Or mayhap he knows a way in and out of these walls that no one else is privy to. What matters is not how he came to tell me, but *what* he said."

Theren seized Ebon's knee, gripping it tight enough to make him wince. "Did he tell you Lilith had something to do with the attack upon the Seat?"

Ebon looked away uncomfortably. "He . . . not exactly. It is rarely so plain with him. But he did say that if he were to investigate the attack and the theft in the vaults, he would begin his search with the family Yerrin."

She released his knee, but only to slap his leg. Ebon grunted and rubbed at the spot. "I knew it!" Theren hissed, her voice shaking. "She must have used her time in the vaults to scour the records for the artifact her family wanted. In exchange for helping Dulmun in their assault, they would have access to any artifact they desired within the vaults. Her family must be putting her up to it."

"Understand that Mako did not *say* any of this," said Ebon. "It is only a theory, for now, and we must carefully consider our steps before taking them."

"Only a theory, you say? But I am certain of it. It was a Yerrin plot, set in motion months ago."

"Yet what would they earn from this?" Ebon asked. "Do we believe they would risk the fall of an entire kingdom for a handful of magical trinkets?"

"Some of those 'trinkets' hold power beyond reckoning," said Theren. "And what does Yerrin care if the kingdom of Dulmun should stand or fall? They are not royalty. Their business will go on, and their wealth will accumulate as it has for countless generations."

"Very well," said Ebon. "If we consider ourselves correct, and that Lilith was the thief, what now? How can we prove it and expose the Yerrins?"

"We could follow her."

Ebon and Theren went still, staring at Kalem in amazement. He met their wondering looks with tight-pressed lips and eyes smoldering in anger.

"I am surprised to hear that from you, Kalem," Ebon said carefully.

"Are you?" said Kalem. "If it is true—and if your family's spy says it might be, mayhap we should listen—then Lilith must pay. All the Yerrins must. How many empty chairs are in the Academy? How many lecterns require new instructors? And if the invasion was a tragedy, the coming war will be far, far worse. If blame for that may be laid at Yerrin's feet, then let it be laid, and let them pay the price."

Theren snorted, but Ebon could see admiration in her eyes. "You sound like one of the kings you scorned earlier, eager for war."

Kalem shook his head. "I have no wish to fight," he said, more quietly now. "I only want proof. If we can get it, then let us do so—but in secret, and without recklessly endangering ourselves, or I will not help you. Then we can take what we have learned to the Academy's faculty, or mayhap to the constables. Let them deal with the criminals. If we can do that . . . well, then mayhap my parents will no longer wish to bring me home."

They all fell silent. Then Ebon rested a comforting hand on Kalem's shoulder. "No doubt you are right. If we are all of us resolved, we should start immediately. We shall follow Lilith's steps outside of class, as close as her shadow. If Yerrin should plot against the Academy again, we three will be first to know."

They spent the rest of their afternoon in studious silence. Theren even stopped trying to speak to Ebon and Kalem while they read. But when the day's final bell tolled, they stacked their books upon the table and made quickly for the halls. Ebon tried to spot Lilith on their way out, but either she left as soon as the bell rang, or she was lost somewhere in the crowd.

Only moments passed, however, before Theren summoned them with a sharp whistle. There was Lilith, heading towards the dormitories. Her lackeys, Oren and Nella, had joined her from their classes, and the three of them walked in step. Ebon and Kalem moved to close the gap between them, but Theren gripped their arms.

"Not too close," she said, bringing her mouth to their ears to be heard above the crowd. "We do not want them to think we are following."

Once Lilith reached the stairs, she led the others up. The older students' dormitories were nearest the bottom, so they left the staircase almost at once to enter the common room. While Lilith went into her dormitory, Oren and Nella remained behind to keep watch.

"What do you suppose she is doing in there?" whispered Theren.

"Nothing good, I feel," said Ebon. "If she does not emerge in a moment or two, one of us should sneak—"

But then Lilith reappeared in the doorway, and the words died on his tongue. She had changed from her plain black student's cloak to a finer one trimmed in dark green brocade. He had never before seen her in specially tailored student robes—indeed, he would have thought it was against the rules.

Lilith swept past Nella and Oren, who hastened to fall into step behind her. Ebon and his friends followed all the way back to the library, where she swept in through the wide doors.

"I have never thought that Lilith was the studious type," said Ebon. "And if she is studying, why should she go to change her cloak?"

"Do you wish to wait here and wonder? Only one thing will reveal the truth." And so saying, Theren pushed through the library doors. Ebon and Kalem traded a final worried look before running behind her.

Inside it was silent. Only a handful of students were in view, puttering about the shelves with candles or lanterns now that the sun was fading from the skylight above.

"There." Kalem pointed, and Ebon's gaze followed. He saw a number of students sitting near the library's rear, and Lilith was among them.

"Let us get closer," said Theren.

They stole off to the right so they could wend their way through the shelves towards the gathering without being seen. As they drew near, they slowed their pace until they were moving little faster than a crawl. At last they stopped behind a thick shelf and leaned around the corner to watch.

About a dozen students had gathered to meet with Lilith. They had arranged armchairs into a circle with some tables set about for refreshments—cheese and bread, and many flagons of wine. They spoke lightly and laughed often, drinking freely; Ebon noted that some already had ruddy cheeks and noses. He could catch snatches of conversation, of lessons learned and spells mastered, of which instructors were kind and which cruel. But Lilith was silent and cold, positioned as if at the head of an invisible table, and her eyes were grave as they stared into nothing.

"What is she brooding on?" wondered Ebon.

"More to the point, what is this gathering all about?" said Kalem. "Why would they meet in the library if not to study?"

"Not everyone enjoys books as much as you and Ebon, Kalem," said Theren.

Ebon looked about the room with a frown. "No, he is right. If they do not wish to study, they could meet in the city. There are inns and taverns aplenty with better refreshments than they have here. So why the library?"

Theren's brow furrowed. But after a moment, Kalem snapped his fingers. "What else might they find in a tavern?"

Ebon blinked. "I know not what you mean. Noise? Distraction?"

"Near enough to the point. Other people. Whatever they are discussing, they do not wish to be overheard."

"But that is silly," said Theren. "There are other students here, in the library. Sky above, *we* are here, and can hear them."

"*We* came looking for them, and can only hear their words because we are eavesdropping. Who else would be here now, except students who enjoy learning more than an evening spent with friends? Bookish children, as you might call us, Theren. And look: none of those will draw within a stone's throw of this gathering of merchant children and nobles who bully them."

Ebon looked and saw that Kalem was right. Some students there were indeed, pulling tomes from the shelves to study by candlelight. But they all steered well clear of Lilith's party. If he had happened to be here for other, more innocent purposes, he would have done the same.

As if in answer to Kalem's words, Lilith stood abruptly from her chair. The other students went silent after a moment, looking up at her expectantly.

"We must invite more to this gathering," she said. "The goldbag society must grow. We will reach out to every merchant's child. Every royal son and daughter."

"Hear hear," said one of the students, raising her goblet with a prim smile. "Though I am nearly scandalized to hear you use that uncouth term. Goldbag. Honestly. Such a weak word, if truly they mean it as an insult."

"Surely you do not mean everyone, Lilith," said Oren with a nasty grin. "Not that Drayden whelp, at least." He gave a laugh and looked around. The other students tittered in approval. But Lilith fixed him with a steely gaze.

"Every merchant's child. Every royal son and daughter."

Oren's face fell. "Even Ebon?"

"*Every merchant's child.* The goldbag society must grow. We must invite more students to this gathering."

"All right, Lilith, we have heard you," said Nella. She shook her head with a weak smile. "Sit and drink. You are drawn tight as a Calentin bow."

Lilith shuddered, shaking her head as she placed a hand to her brow. "Yes. Yes, very well. Only do not forget."

She took her seat again and gratefully accepted the wine that Nella pressed to her before leaning back into her cushions.

Ebon turned to the others. Kalem's face was scrunched up as he peered at the gathering. But Theren had gone stony, her hands balled into white-knuckled fists.

"Every child of merchants and royalty, is it?" said Theren. "Such petty, small-minded revenge. How very like her."

"What do you mean?" said Ebon.

Theren tossed her head. "Do you not see, Ebon? She is forming this little gathering of children with wealth and power. Sky above, she is even willing to mend her bridges with you. And why?"

"I do not know," said Ebon, frowning. "I myself have no wish for such a mending."

"Of course not. Yet she aims to beguile you. Because one day you will rule over your family and its deep reserves of coin, as Lilith will rule hers. What an alliance that could be. And if she sat at the head of your group of Academy friends . . . well, think how amenable you might be to any favor she might ask."

"I would never do her any favors, nor would I join this little cabal," Ebon insisted.

"As I have said already, I *know* you would not," said Theren. "I am angry at Lilith, not you. *Think*. She knows we three dislike her. We have confronted her in the past. And what does she think of to solve this problem? Division. Seducing the two of you while she leaves me out in the cold."

"You may overestimate our importance," mumbled Kalem, eyes at his feet. "I would be surprised to know that Lilith thinks much of us at all, let alone enough to concoct such a scheme as that."

"Neither of you has known her as long as I," said Theren darkly.

"Look!" said Ebon, pointing. "Where is she going?"

Lilith had stood and begun to move away, but when Oren and Nella made to rise with her, she waved them down. "I must use the privy," she said, and swept off, drawing her black cloak tight. Her steps were brisk and clipped, and she stopped only once, to look back over her shoulder when she reached the library doors.

Ebon shared a look with his friends. "The privy, she says?"

"I doubt it," said Theren. "Let us go."

"But do you not think—oh, never mind," grumbled Kalem, for they had started off without him.

By the time they reached the hallway, Lilith had almost vanished, but they spied her just before she turned a corner. They hastened to follow down another two halls—but when Lilith reached the turn to the privies, she passed it by. Again Ebon, Kalem, and Theren shared a silent look before running behind her. She reached one of the white cedar doors that led out, and then again glanced down the hallway in both directions. Ebon and his friends were only saved because Lilith looked the other way first, for they dove into an alcove before she could turn back to see them. Once they heard the door swing shut, they ran after her again.

The night air outside was wonderfully cold upon their cheeks, for inside the citadel Ebon had begun to sweat beneath his cloak. Snow had yet to fall, and so they could keep their steps silent upon the soft grass as they followed Lilith deep into the Academy's training grounds. She took an odd path, weaving through bushes and hedges first one way, and then another.

"Has she seen us following her?" said Kalem.

"I do not think so, for still she moves slowly," said Theren. "She could be lost, but more likely she is taking precautions."

But even as she spoke, Lilith turned the corner of a great hedge and broke into a run, her steps fading towards silence.

"Go!" said Ebon. They sprinted for the end of the hedge and came into the open. Lilith was nowhere to be seen.

"Split up!" hissed Theren. She ran off.

"Theren!" said Ebon. He could follow her, but it would be a waste. He ran straight, and Kalem scampered to stay at his heels.

"How do you know she went this way?" said Kalem.

"I do not," growled Ebon. "I am hoping."

The hedges formed into a sort of maze in this part of the garden, but they could see a fair distance in every direction. Ebon thought he could hear running footsteps around every corner. Whenever he wondered if they were only in his mind, they came again, and Kalem would seize the sleeve of his robe. Then they would run pell-mell to catch up, only to hear the steps fade and vanish again.

"Darkness take her," said Ebon. "She must know we are here."

"Hold!" said Kalem, gripping his arm.

They went deathly still. Footsteps on the other side of the hedge continued for a moment before petering to nothing.

Kalem met Ebon's eyes in the moonlight. The boy's were wide and frightened, but then, Ebon guessed that he must look much the same.

They crept along, Ebon's steps slow and soft as a field mouse. He heard one sharp step on the other side of the hedge. It sounded like a stumble. He looked at Kalem again and received a nod. Lilith was sneaking along beside them.

Then they heard murmuring voices from the other direction.

Ebon whirled. Kalem barely stifled a cry. From the other side of the hedge came the sound of running. Lilith was trying to flee, taking advantage of the distraction.

"Catch her!" Ebon whispered.

"I think I can—" Kalem's eyes began to glow. He stepped towards the hedge and held forth his hands. Where he touched the shrub, it hissed and vanished into steam. Leaping forwards, he cleared a tunnel through the plants—only for Ebon to hear him give a muffled cry from the other side.

"Kalem!" Ebon barely kept his voice muted as he bounded forwards through the bush. On the other side were two dark figures. He flung himself at the taller one, tackling it to the ground.

"Get off me, you idiot goldshitter!" hissed a familiar voice.

"Theren?" said Ebon, for indeed it was her. He pushed up and away, holding out his hands. "I . . . I am sorry, I did not know—"

"Leave it," she growled. "And help me up."

He hastened to take Theren's hand and pull her to standing. "We heard you and thought it was Lilith."

"I heard you and thought *you* were Lilith. When I heard those voices, I thought she was trying to escape."

The voices. Ebon waved at his friends for silence. Together they crept towards the gap in the hedges that Kalem had cleared. The voices were still there. Two of them, both hushed.

264

"That must be Lilith," whispered Kalem.

"Aye, and one other," said Theren.

"It is a good thing they did not hear us," said Ebon. "Now, if we can see who—"

But there came rustling steps on the grass, and the trio threw themselves behind a rosebush. Lilith emerged from the garden into the moonslight. Her eyes were fixed straight ahead, and her steps were steady. Had she glanced to her left she might have seen Ebon, but she did not waver on her way back to the citadel.

"After her," said Theren.

"In a moment," said Ebon. "First I would like to know who she spoke to."

"Her accomplice means nothing. We are following Lilith."

"It will be but a moment." Ebon did not wait for an answer, but slipped around the rosebush and into the hedges. Here the plants formed a sort of fence around a small yard with two stone benches. Ebon had come here on occasion, when he wished to be alone with his thoughts. He reached a narrow gap in the hedge, pressing himself up against it to peer inside.

He could see no one.

Ebon turned to find Theren and Kalem eyeing him expectantly. He frowned, shaking his head. Theren pushed past him to see for herself.

"Theren, wait!" Ebon grabbed for her sleeve, but she cast him off. Ebon flinched as she stepped into the open. But nothing happened. Slowly, he straightened and joined her.

No one was there. The benches were empty.

"Who was she talking to?" Kalem asked.

"They must have slipped away," muttered Theren.

"Our eyes were upon the exit the whole time," said Ebon. "They could not have left without us seeing it."

Theren snorted. "This is the Academy, Ebon. A weremage could have turned to a snake and slithered away, a mindmage could leap over the hedge. A firemage—"

A child's piercing scream rang out from the citadel, cutting her words short.

Shock froze them. Then Ebon cried "Lilith," and ran, while the others hastened to follow. Together they burst through the white cedar door and flew through the halls, towards the screams that grew louder and more terrified the closer they drew.

"We make for the vaults," said Theren as they ran. "Something has happened. Lilith must—"

They rounded the final corner and froze, struck dumb at the sight before them. In front of a great iron door lay Instructor Credell. His eyes were no longer anxious and shifting, but vacant and staring up at the ceiling, as blood spilled from his slit throat to pool around his body.

SIX

FOR A MOMENT EBON COULD SEE NOTHING BUT THE BODY. CREDELL'S face was Elf-white, marked only by the dark blood that had spattered his skin as it spurted forth. That blood ran thick and slow now, soaking into his hair and robes. Ebon thought of the day the Seat was attacked, and that Credell had been bloodstained then, too, fighting to defend his students from the Shades in an uncommon display of courage.

His students. Astrea. *Darkness take me,* thought Ebon. For there she was: little Astrea, cowering against the wall. She was screaming, still screaming, and he realized it had been her voice they had heard from the garden. Her feet scraped the floor and her hands dragged at the stone wall as though she wished to burrow into it and away, but she could not remove her eyes from Credell sprawled on the floor.

Another student stood beside her, holding her in a tight embrace—Isra, the girl he had run into in the dining hall that morning. She held Astrea tight, her face held to the girl's, whispering comfort into her ear. Some other students stood about as well, drawn by the commotion just as Ebon and his friends had been—but all, like Ebon, were frozen in fear.

He forced himself to move, crossing the hallway towards Astrea. He knelt before her, placing his face in between her and Credell's corpse.

"Astrea. Astrea!"

She stopped her screaming long enough for her wild eyes to find his. It took a moment for her to recognize him, but when she did she flung herself forwards, wrapping her arms around his neck. He turned so her face was pointed away from Credell. But then, to his surprise, Isra reached out to drag Astrea backwards. She knelt to hold the girl as Ebon had done. Her eyes were wide, her face even more gaunt and pinched than usual. Astrea gripped her hard, tears soaking the older girl's robes.

"What happened?" said Theren.

For a moment Isra seemed unable to speak, only looking up and blinking. At last she shook her head and stuttered, "We—we were walking. Together—the two of us. We found him here, like this."

"Who else was here?" said Theren. "Was it Lilith? Did you see her?"

Ebon frowned. "Theren."

Isra only blinked, still in shock, and her hands tightened on Astrea's shoulders.

"What is going on here? Stand aside, all of—oh, sky above. Back. *Back!*"

They turned to find Jia. Her light skin had grown paler still, and she stood before the students, waving them back from the body. Instructor Dasko arrived a moment later. He stared at the body a bit longer than Jia had, but then he joined her in ushering the students away.

"Sky above, Ebon, get that child out of sight of him!"

Jia's sharp rebuke jarred him from his thoughts. Crimson blush crept into his cheeks that he had not thought of it. Quickly he went to Astrea, guiding her down the hallway. Isra kept a tight grip on the girl's shoulder, but she did not stop him. They halted around the corner as Astrea collapsed to the stone floor. Isra sat beside her, one arm still wrapped protectively about the girl's shoulders.

Heavy, thudding footsteps sounded down the hall, and Perrin came into view a moment later. She caught Ebon's eye and tossed her head. "What is all this commotion for?"

Ebon pointed down the hall. "It . . . Instructor Credell, he is . . . they found him . . ."

Perrin's face grew solemn, and she broke into a heavy jog. Though she vanished around the corner, Ebon could still hear the sharp hiss of her breath when she saw Credell. Then her booming commands rang forth, ordering students to draw away from the body so the instructors could do their work.

"Are you all right?" Ebon winced at once, hearing how foolish the question sounded. "Would you like some water? Or anything else from the kitchens? I could fetch something . . ." But Astrea only shook her head, eyes fixed sightlessly upon her feet.

Theren drew close, and pulled Kalem in as well. "It was Lilith," she murmured. "It must have been. She slipped away from us so she could do this. I knew we should have followed her."

"Murdering an instructor?" said Kalem. "That is madness. She could not. And besides, why would she?"

"The vaults, of course," said Theren, frowning. "Did you not see the door where Credell lay? That is the entrance."

Kalem balked, sharing an uncertain look with Ebon. But sharp, clipped footsteps down the hallway distracted them, and they all turned to see Jia approaching. She swept her gaze across them, lips pursed.

"Did anyone see what happened?"

"No, Instructor," said Ebon. Astrea shook her head.

"Who arrived first?"

"Them—Astrea and Isra, I mean, or at least they came before we did," said Theren. "But Instructor, in the garden we saw—"

Jia silenced her with a raised finger, and then went to kneel before Astrea and Isra. She took the younger girl's hands in her own, pressing them gently together. "Astrea," she said softly. "It pains me greatly that you saw that. I am sorry to ask, but it may help us—did you see anything? Anything at all that might help?"

Astrea shook her head, eyes still saucer-wide. Isra gripped her tighter. "We were together, Instructor, walking through the hall. We found him just as you saw him."

"Is that true, Astrea?" The girl nodded. Jia sighed and stood. "Thank you both. Isra, please see Astrea to her dormitory, and wait with her in the common room until I can visit you. Do you understand?"

Isra nodded and stood. But before she could leave, Theren sprang forwards to take Jia's sleeve.

"Instructor. We may have seen something that could help. Moments before we heard Astrea scream, we were following Lilith in the gardens. She spoke with someone out there, though we could not see who. Then she eluded us, vanishing from sight. It was only moments later that they found Credell's body."

Jia frowned. "Why were you following her? What do you mean, she *eluded* you?"

"She snuck away. She stepped out of sight so that we could not follow her."

Ebon had grown more uncomfortable with Theren's every word, and now he took her by the arm. "Theren, that is not exactly what happened. Instructor, we were following Lilith, but she did not know it, and she did not try to evade us. She went into the Academy while we stayed behind."

Theren's eyes upon him were full of fury and hurt. "But it *was* before Credell was killed," she insisted.

Jia glared, folding her arms across her chest. "Theren, I know something of the feud between you and Lilith, but accusing her of murder is far beyond reason, even for you. Unless you have something more substantial than this—"

"I have not accused her!" cried Theren. "I have only told you what I saw. Is it not at least worth questioning her?"

"Little more than any other soul at the Academy," said Jia. "Many were surely alone when—"

Abruptly she stopped talking and drew up straight, folding her hands together before her. Ebon *felt* a presence behind him and turned. There stood Dean Forredar, imposing in his robes of office, his dark eyes fixed on Ebon.

"Son of Drayden," he said, his voice dripping with scorn. "I am not surprised to find you present in such a commotion."

"Dean," said Jia gravely. "Instructor Credell has been found dead. I will show you the body. Dasko and Perrin have cleared the students out of the hall."

That gave Xain pause, but only for the space of a breath. "Did any witness what happened?" he said, never taking his gaze from Ebon. "Were you there, son of Drayden?"

Fear mixed with anger in Ebon's breast—fear of Xain's reckless malice, and anger at the injustice of it. "No, Dean. I was in the garden with Theren and Kalem."

Xain looked to Ebon's friends. Theren nodded, and Kalem said, "It is true, Dean."

"Several other students reached the body before Ebon and his friends, Dean," Jia added. "We had just begun to question the students when you arrived."

Xain looked from her to Isra, who met his gaze with one of equal steel. He shrugged and pushed past Ebon, who was forced to step aside. Jia followed him around the corner. Ebon had almost decided to go with them when he heard many footsteps coming down the hall from the opposite direction. In a moment, Lilith appeared. Behind her were the students she had gathered in the library.

"Lilith!" Theren's voice rose to a furious shout. "What have you done?"

The students stopped, and Lilith glared back. "What are you talking about, Theren? We heard a tumult and came to see what it was."

"You lie." Theren stepped forwards. Ebon gripped her arm, and Kalem took the other. "We know what you did, Lilith."

"And what exactly is that?" Xain's voice rolled through the hallway, freezing them like mindmagic. The dean swept forwards, Jia at his side, and both came to a stop between the two groups.

Jia spoke first. "Lilith, can you account for your whereabouts this evening?"

Lilith blinked, brow furrowing with doubt. "I . . . I was in the library with my friends."

"We saw you!" cried Theren. "We saw you in the garden, Lilith. And then you came back into the citadel, just before Credell was killed."

Beneath her dark skin, Lilith went grey as ash. "Killed? I . . ." She swallowed, looking at the others beside her. "I only stepped out to get some air, and then I went straight back to the others. They were there, and know I am telling the truth."

"She is," said Oren immediately. But on Lilith's other side, Nella hesitated. It was only a moment before she nodded in assent, but Ebon noted it.

"Very well," said Jia. "Then we are done here. All of you, return to your rooms. Ebon, if you would, look in upon Astrea in her dormitory. I will be there as soon as I can, but I want to ensure she has friends about her. She is far too young to have witnessed something so wretched."

"I will, Instructor." Ebon noted that Xain had fixed him with a dark look, and did not seem pleased to see them go. But again he turned without speaking, and Ebon hastened away before they could be recalled.

The students with Lilith were silent. Theren gave them all dirty looks as they went, and once the hallway branched off, she dragged Ebon and Kalem in another direction. Out of earshot, she pressed them both into an alcove.

"Lilith *must* have had something to do with this. I know it."

Kalem frowned and looked down at his feet. "I am not so certain."

Theren opened her mouth, but Ebon jumped in before she could speak. "He is right, Theren. We cannot know anything for certain. We only lost sight of her for a moment. How could she have killed him and then returned to the library so quickly?"

"It was not such a long distance," said Theren. "I think that, after she lost us, she made for the vaults. But she came upon Credell, killed him, and then ran for the library as quickly as she could before anyone could see what she had done."

"But why?" said Kalem. "For what purpose?"

"For no purpose," said Theren. "He must have surprised her. Do you remember this morning, when he asked for my key to the vaults? Credell never enters the vaults, but some business must have called him there. Lilith did not expect that, and so when he saw her, she panicked."

Ebon looked down the hall, towards where Lilith and the others had vanished. He gritted his teeth and shook his head. "I do not know, Theren. Lilith has been cruel to me since the day I arrived. But a murderer?"

Theren scowled. "I do not think she is some vile killer who sits about plotting the slow, torturous deaths of others. But I know she is

272

ruthless, and ambitious, and tied closely to the dark dealings of her family. The Yerrins may hold no candle to the family Drayden, yet it is known that they, too, will kill any who stand in their way."

"But Lilith is scarcely more than a girl," said Kalem. "We all are."

"You mean *you* are," said Theren. "She is on the cusp of her eighteenth year. More than old enough to act as an agent of her house—and indeed, I believe she may be. She might not have wished for Credell's death, but she had a hand in it nonetheless."

"If what you say is true, I am more fearful than before," said Kalem. "I want to prove the guilt of those who had a hand in the attack. But if the Yerrins will kill to protect the secret, might we not die ourselves? And our new dean is out for Ebon's blood. If we try to investigate, we may land ourselves in even greater danger, or be expelled. And from outside the Academy, we can do nothing."

"If we remain, but do nothing, then what does it matter if we are expelled or not?" said Theren. "Underrealm itself is in danger. Do you think we can attend our studies for the next few years and hope the war will pass us by?"

Kalem fixed her with a hard look. "I think it is easier for you to say that than for us. You have completed your studies, and everyone knows it. If you left now, you would be a full-fledged wizard, whether or not you had the Academy's blessing to practice. Ebon and I have not that luxury. You ask us to risk all our learning, many years more of education, trying to prove guilt that may or may not exist."

Theren had no answer for that, and looked uneasily away from them both. "Do you feel the same, Ebon?"

But Ebon scarcely heard her. His thoughts were far away, upon the southern cliffs of the Seat, where Cyrus' flesh had turned to stone under his hand. He felt as though he stood upon those cliffs again. He could step forwards, plunging himself into the abyss with no hope of return. If he joined Theren in her hunt for Lilith, he could be expelled, or die—or be forced to kill again. But if he stayed his hand? If he shut his eyes and feigned ignorance of the dark clouds swirling about the Academy? Then others might perish, and if Ebon did not kill them, still he would bear the guilt of it.

"Ebon?" said Theren.

"I do not know. I do not know. I have no wish to be killed or expelled in a hunt for the truth. But neither do I wish to sit and do nothing, when it may lead to the deaths of others like Credell. I know not what to do."

"That is hardly helpful," said Theren, snorting. "Choosing to do nothing is still a choice."

"I do not wish to do nothing," said Ebon. "Yet I fear to do *anything*. I . . . how can I explain it, when I do not understand it myself?"

"Ebon, stop being a coward and—"

"Leave off, Theren." He pushed her away and strode down the hallway without looking back, for he knew he would find her glaring at him in anger. Cyrus' face flashed before his eyes again, and then again, and the former dean's dry, crusted lips whispered the word *murderer*.

He shivered, hating himself for his indecision. Yet how could he ease his mind? To whom could he speak?

The answer came in a flash. Only one person would understand. Only one soul could hear him freely.

Adara.

SEVEN

IT WAS FAR TOO LATE TO CONSIDER LEAVING THE ACADEMY TO SEE HER, and the instructors were all on high alert after Credell's murder. So Ebon did as he had promised and went to Astrea's dormitory to visit her. But he found Isra sitting in the common room instead. She looked up as he entered. Her eyes were vacant.

"Is Astrea here?" Ebon said, keeping his voice hushed. The common room was empty save for the two of them.

"She has gone to bed," said Isra.

Ebon nodded. "I should do the same, then. As should you, I suppose. Do you . . . do you wish me to walk you back to the dormitories?"

Isra scowled.

He raised his hands at once. "I only mean . . . it must have been terrible. To find . . . to find him."

She seemed to consider that for a moment. "I suppose it was terrible," she murmured. Lifting a hand, she showed Ebon her fingers. He could see them twitching. "See? My hands are shaking."

"Who could blame you? I can only imagine what it has done to Astrea."

Isra lowered her hand and looked at the dormitory door mournfully. "I wish she had not seen him," she said, voice scarcely above a whisper. "She has always been so fragile."

"You have known her long, then?" said Ebon.

Her eyes flashed. "I am not here to swap tales with you, goldbag."

Ebon ducked his head. "I am sorry," he muttered. "Good eve."

He returned to his dormitory and went to bed at once, hoping his thoughts would be clearer in the morning. Instead he lay awake for hours, wrestling with thoughts of Cyrus and Credell. Both had made his first few months at the Academy terrible, though for very different reasons. And now both were dead. He fell asleep seeing their faces, their lifeless eyes staring into his own.

A dark mood had settled over the Academy the next morning, like a funeral pall thrown over all who dwelt within. The dining hall was somber, and no one dared speak above a whisper. Ebon found Kalem and sat with him, neither saying a word. Theren arrived soon after, and though she sat with them both, she did not meet Ebon's eyes.

"I did some asking last night, after . . . well, after," she muttered. "Nothing was taken from the vaults. Credell must have happened upon Lilith as she was trying to get in, not out."

If she did not wish to discuss their argument from last night, Ebon was happy enough to oblige. "That is good, I suppose."

"Not good for Credell," said Kalem.

Ebon looked away. Then his eye caught on something strange: a white tabard amid the sea of black robes. He looked about the room to find more of them; soldiers in white and gold, and all bearing swords and shields.

"Who are they?" he said, pointing.

Theren and Kalem raised their eyes, and Kalem's mouth fell open. "The High King's guards. What are they doing here?"

"No doubt they were sent to aid the Academy's defenses after the murder," said Theren.

Despite himself, Ebon laughed. "What do they hope to do? Have they forgotten this is a school of wizards? Their blades and armor will help them little against all but the youngest of students."

"Mayhap they think the murderer was no wizard," said Kalem. "After all, Credell was not killed with magic, but by a dagger to the throat."

They fell silent at that. Credell's sightless eyes danced in Ebon's vision again, and then his face turned into Cyrus'. Ebon's breath came harsh and shallow, and lights danced at the edge of his eyes.

"Ebon, what is wrong?" said Theren. "Your face is pale."

"I need . . . I need to walk. I need air." He stood, and they made to follow, but he waved them back down. "No, thank you. I would rather be alone. I will find you later. In the library, mayhap."

His friends settled back into their seats, though Kalem clearly wanted to come. Ebon left the dining hall, nearly stumbling against the door on his way. The hall was cold, colder than he remembered—or mayhap it was just that the dining hall had grown too warm. He pressed his hand against the frigid stone to steady himself.

He must see Adara.

Now? he thought.

Yes. He could not attend his studies like this. Half of him wanted to vomit, and the other wanted to return to bed, to curl in a ball and never rise again. If he could not unburden himself, he feared his heart might fail him.

His mind made up, he went quickly to the Academy's wide front hall. His heart crashed in vicious thunder at his temples as he entered the open space with its vaulted ceiling—but then he sighed in relief. The sharp old caretaker, Mellie, was not standing guard at the front door as he had feared she might be. It was a bald man instead, with a crooked back and rheumy eyes, who Ebon had heard was named Cratchett—some old wizard called back to duty long after his prime to fill one of the many sudden vacancies in the Academy's staff. He wandered about his post, eyes seeming to catch nothing at all. Ebon waited until he had rounded the corner before running out the front door into the street.

He gave silent thanks for the well-oiled hinges as he swung the door shut behind him. Sticking his hands into either sleeve against autumn's chill, he set off into the streets. The air bit briskly into his skin, even through his thick robe, and he hurried his pace to get the blood moving. He thanked the sky that it had not yet snowed, though clouds crowded above, making him anxious. Quickly he turned his steps west and north, winding his way through the city to where he knew a blue door was waiting.

All about him, the Seat was bustling. Soldiers patrolled the streets, wearing different colors: the white and gold of the High King, the blue and white of Selvan, and the Mystics' red and silver. But, too, there were masons and carpenters aplenty, for buildings across the island were in need of repair. Dulmun had wreaked terrible havoc across the city, as had their allies, the Shades. Houses and shops and taverns alike had been torn asunder, and now, if the owners were still alive, those structures were being rebuilt. The air rang with hammer beats, and the songs of saws, and choirs of shouting builders. After the tragedy, the new activity joined into a chorus that lifted the heart, and yet it held also an undertone of urgency. War was upon Underrealm now, and if it had not yet blossomed to its full fury, not a soul upon the Seat doubted that it would, given time.

When at last he reached his destination, Ebon ducked into an alley and looked furtively about. Most upon the Seat knew that Academy students were not allowed out until evening, and he had no wish for word to be sent back about where he had gone. But no one seemed to pay him any mind. So he slipped from the alley and across to the blue door, entering as quickly as he could.

There were not so many people lounging about the front room as when Ebon had first come. No doubt some had fallen in the fighting, while others had left the Seat. But Ebon guessed that the blue door saw its fair share of customers these days; not only would many seek comfort after the attack, but the Seat now housed soldiers from across the nine kingdoms. His stomach twisted at the thought that Adara might be occupied already—but then he saw her in the corner playing her harp. She flashed him a wide smile, and he returned it. Then the matron swept forwards to greet him.

"Good day, sir. Do you wish to visit Adara?"

"If she will see me." Ebon reached for his coin purse, but the matron waved it off.

278

"I do not doubt that she will. But you have not yet used up all your last payment."

Her gaze slid past him. Adara stood at once and approached, leading Ebon to her room by the hand. Inside, she gripped his robes and pulled him close for a deep kiss.

"I have sorely missed you," he said, holding her out by the shoulders to look at her.

"And I you. But what are you doing here now? It is the middle of the day."

"I had to come. My heart is in turmoil, and my mind will offer no rest."

Her hands slid down his chest, her smile coquettish. "Then it will be my pleasure to soothe you."

"I . . . that is not what I came for."

She cocked her head, though her smile did not wilt. "I never thought to have you refuse me."

That made him chuckle. "Nor did I ever expect to. But I came because there are things I must speak of. And they are . . . they are things I can say to no one else."

The smile faded, and her eyes grew solemn. "I think I see your mind. Come, then. Sit and speak. Will you take wine?"

"Please."

She fetched him a cup and poured one for herself as well. He took a deep drink and then stared at his hands in silence. Adara said nothing, only waited patiently, soft eyes never leaving his face. He wanted badly to tell her of the thoughts that plagued him, but now that he was here, his tongue felt thick and limp in his mouth.

"My family is coming to the Seat," he said, because that, at least, was easy to say.

"And are you pleased?" she said, her tone very careful.

Ebon shrugged. "Mayhap. I shall see my sister again, and that is a joy. But my reunion with my father shall be . . . not quite so happy, I fear."

She placed a hand on his knee. "If he should trouble you, I will always be here to help you forget."

"That would be most unwise," Ebon said quickly. "I would be foolish to visit you while my father resides upon the Seat. No doubt he will have me watched. He might scorn me if he learns I am visiting a house of lovers, and that I could bear. But then he might go further, seeking to visit some sort of harm upon you."

Adara's eyes hardened, and her lips drew tight. "He would not dare raise a hand against a lover. The King's law protects us."

"Nothing so brazen." Ebon shook his head. "He is a snake, and could devise any manner of trouble for you."

Some of the fire left her. "I will take you at your word. Worry not— if you cannot see me while your family is upon the Seat, I will still be here when they leave. And yet . . . forgive me for saying so, Ebon, but this is not why you have come to see me today, and you are only wasting time by not speaking of it."

He dropped his gaze, staring at his hands where they fidgeted in his lap. When he spoke, his voice was far smaller than he had meant it to be. "No, it is not. I . . . I cannot stop seeing . . . that is, remembering what happened."

"I understand," she murmured. "It was no happy memory."

"That was the first day I saw someone killed—and then in the same day I, too, struck a death blow."

"You are blameless. Had you not . . . done what you did, he would have murdered you instead."

He winced. "And yet."

She nodded slowly. "And yet. It may be the truth, but I know that makes it no easier to bear."

His throat grew dry, and so he drained the cup. She went for the pitcher, but he shook his head. "No more. At least not yet. There is something else . . . something I have thought of often since the attack. Had I not seen the two of you slipping away through the city, you would have gone with him."

Adara's eyes grew sharper. "Ebon, I have told you—"

"No, forgive me," he said hastily. "I did not mean that as it sounded. I understand that you are a lover. And you had no knowledge of Cyrus other than his custom, I imagine. What I mean is . . . had I not come after you, he would have taken you from the Seat in safety. He only hurt you after I attacked him. Without me, you would not have been harmed."

"Oh, Ebon," she said, softening. "Does that truly worry you? I am glad you came when you did. I knew Cyrus for a snake, but not the extent of his treachery. I thought he could remove me from the Seat in safety, and so I went with him, planning to leave his company in the first town we reached. But if I had known he ever laid a hand upon you, I would not have taken a single step by his side." She cupped his cheek with her hand, and brushed her fingers to push a lock of hair behind his ear.

Lover's words, he thought. And yet, when she had learned the truth, she *had* rejected Cyrus. It sent his mind reeling, but he could not waste thought on this now. He had come here to speak, not to wrestle with his feelings for Adara—though already he suspected that they were stronger than might be wise.

"I think of him often," said Ebon. "I see his face, frozen in that death scream, and I hear him as he plunges into the Great Bay. In my dreams he visits me, and in my waking hours his wail is like a far-off thing, drifting to my ears through the windows, and I can neither escape it nor speak of my troubles. How could I look Kalem or Theren in the eye if they knew what I had done? Yet sometimes I wish to tell them, if only so I need not bear the burden alone."

"You cannot tell them. You must not."

Ebon raised an eyebrow. "Why so adamant? They are my friends. They would not betray me to the constables."

Adara pursed her lips and took another sip of her wine. "The King's law would justify what we did, were the constables or the Mystics to know. It is not the King's law we must fear. It is your family. No matter the justification, how do you think your father would react if it were known that you killed a scion of the family Drayden?"

Ebon's hands trembled at the thought. "My friends would *never* tell my family."

Her eyes grew mournful, and she put a hand on his. "I know Theren well enough. She would understand. I know she had no love for Cyrus. But Kalem . . . understand that I have not met him. Yet he is a royal, and thus holds a greater regard for the King's law. He would not tell your kin. But he might tell the constables, and then word of it would reach your family regardless. I cannot believe a royal would be satisfied until the matter was brought before the law."

Ebon's brow furrowed. He wished to deny Adara's words. And yet, it *did* sound like something Kalem would do. The boy would wish the matter resolved to the satisfaction of himself, the King's law, and likely some within the Academy. Then word would surely reach his father. The thought made him cringe. Ebon could only imagine what might happen to him then.

Some of his worry must have shown in his eyes, for Adara gripped his hands tighter. "I see your fear. Do not let your heart be troubled. We need fear nothing, for your family will never learn the truth."

"But then what am I to do? I may keep the secret from my family and the King's law, and even my friends, but I cannot keep it from myself. And it is my own mind that plagues me."

"Then take comfort in me." Adara gently pulled him close, planting a kiss on one cheek, and then the other. "Tell me of your worries and your fears, and let me dispel them." Her kisses fell to his neck as her hand slid across his chest.

Ebon gulped. "That is an attractive prospect, to be certain." He drew back and met her eyes. "It will be as you say, at least for now. But you might not feel the same if you could only get to know them better—or Kalem, at least, since you know something of Theren. What if we spent time together, all of us, beyond the blue door?"

Adara frowned, and in her eyes there was a worry Ebon could not place. "Are you certain that is wise? If your father is having you watched . . ."

"He would not do so yet. Not until he reaches the Seat. And it would gladden my heart to have you all together—you three, who I love most in this world."

He blushed and looked away, for that seemed a foolish thing to say. *She is a lover,* he reminded himself. He had known that when first he came to see her, and every time since. Why, then, was it so hard not to think of Adara as something more? He did not see her as *his,* certainly . . . and yet, whenever he thought of her, it seemed to him that each belonged to the other.

Then, to his surprise, Adara's hand was on his cheek, and she turned him to face her. Softly, she said, "If it would ease your mind, then gladly will I meet them." Her hands fell to push him onto the bed, and then she was atop him. "After all, it is my duty to ease your burdens."

His only reply was to kiss her.

EIGHT

Some hours later, Ebon sat drinking in a tavern a few streets over from the Academy. Soon the bells would ring for the midday meal, and he might slip in through the front door unnoticed. It was not uncommon for students to take their meal in the city, and he could merge with the crowd without drawing much attention. Some gave him odd looks as he waited—his Academy student robes were out of place in the tavern before the midday—but after his visit to Adara, he was unable to summon much concern.

"You must learn to wash the smell off, little goldbag."

Mako's growling voice nearly made Ebon choke on his wine. The bodyguard had appeared at his elbow without warning. Now he pushed Ebon aside and slid onto the bench beside him. Ebon was glad to see the man, but he could not stop a nagging thought, warning him that Mako had blocked his exit.

"Mayhap I shall bathe instead of eating."

"You had better. You smell more like your lover than yourself." Mako's teeth appeared in a cruel smile—though Ebon did not find it quite so frightening as he once had.

"How did you know to find me here?"

"I did not. I had planned on visiting you in the library this afternoon, and was waiting for my chance to slip inside the citadel. Only by chance did I enter this place to find you waiting for me instead."

"Waiting for you?" said Ebon, chuckling. "I knew not that you sought me."

Mako's smirk widened, and he motioned to a barman for ale. But then his face grew solemn. "You should have guessed it after what happened in the Academy last night. I had to come to see that you are all right."

Credell's corpse flashed in his mind, and Ebon shook the thought away. "I am whole. It is kind of you to worry, but I was nowhere near the murder."

"That is not what I have heard. It seems you were one of the first to arrive after the body was discovered."

"One of the first, but not *the* first. Credell was already cooling and beyond any help when I got there."

"Do you know aught of what happened? Have you learned anything since?" said Mako. Ebon looked around with discomfort, but the bodyguard set a steady hand on his shoulder and grinned. "No one gets close enough to listen in on me, boy. Not without my knowing it. Speak."

Still Ebon hesitated a moment before answering. "We were following Lilith just before it happened. She was sharing wine with friends, and then she went out into the gardens. We thought she was alone, but then we heard her speaking to someone."

"Who?"

"We do not know. We tried to find out, but Lilith left, and her friend disappeared. That is when the screaming started, and Credell's body was found."

Mako drummed his fingers on the table but never took his gaze from Ebon. His ale arrived, and he took a deep gulp. "It seems there is a strong case to be made for Lilith's guilt."

"Mayhap," said Ebon, nodding slowly. "Yet we lost sight of her for only a moment."

"Much can be done in a moment. A moment is longer than I need to cut a man's throat, I promise you."

Ebon shuddered and looked into his wine cup. "You think she did it, then?"

"I think more and more signs point that way. If Lilith had a hand in the theft from the vaults, or in Credell's death, it seems the family Yerrin stands much to gain."

"The artifacts, you mean? That was Theren's guess."

"The family Yerrin thwarts us in many things, and seeks ever to expand their influence. If they had even a handful of the more powerful artifacts in the Academy's bowels, Drayden's star might wane. Do not shrug—you might not care for your father's ill fortune, but I would wager you care for Halab's."

Ebon flushed. "Of course I wish no harm upon her. And what is more, if it is true that Yerrin played a role in the attack upon the Seat, then I have no wish for their future success. They must be brought to justice."

Mako smirked. "How very noble of you. I think you will have ample opportunity to catch her and expose the truth."

"Why?"

"She has stolen from the vaults already, but now she has killed Credell before their doors. Why? Why would she have been there, if not to steal again? She was thwarted this time by Credell, but that does not mean she will give up. Keep following her, Ebon. Catch her in the act, and you shall have your justice. Mayhap you shall even have it before another corpse is on our hands."

Ebon frowned into his cup. "I hope so."

"We will speak more of this later. I have not only come to ask you about Credell's murder. I bring word from the family."

Ebon sighed. "What is it this time?"

"They will arrive to the Seat upon the morrow, and hope you will join them in the manor."

A shiver rippled through him, sliding down his back from the base of his skull. He tried to hide it, though Mako's glinting eyes said he had failed. "I will, of course. You may tell them."

"I shall. And that brings this conversation to an end—and just in time."

Before Ebon could ask what the bodyguard meant, the Academy's bells began to toll, signaling the end of morning classes and the serving of the midday meal. Ebon gaped. "How did you . . .?"

Mako pointed to the rear of the tavern. On a shelf behind the bar sat a large hourglass. The tavern's owner turned it over even as Ebon watched.

"I am no wizard, little Ebon, though the look on your face was a delight. Often simple observation serves better than magic. I wish you well in your quest for the truth—only take care, and do not place yourself in danger you cannot get back out of. It would have been a tremendous waste of my effort to save you from the attack on the Seat only for you to die now."

"I will keep that in mind," said Ebon, giving him a wry smile. "I would hate to see your effort wasted."

Mako laughed, tossed a gold weight on the table for the drinks, and slipped out the door.

NINE

STUDENTS WERE ALREADY POURING OUT INTO THE STREETS BY THE TIME
Ebon reached the Academy's wide front doors. He waited until a sizable
crowd was pressing through and then slipped inside between them.
Mellie was back on watch, and she fixed him with a suspicious glare as
he passed by. But he escaped without incident, and she did not call after
him. He rounded the corner of the first hallway and pressed himself
against the stone, letting out a long sigh of relief.

"Ebon!"

He very nearly jumped out of his skin at the shout. There was Perrin, her massive frame trundling down the hallway towards him, brows
almost joined as she frowned.

"Instructor Perrin," stammered Ebon. "I—that is, I—"

"Stow it." She folded her arms and peered down at him through
narrowed eyes. "Did you not think I would notice your absence? An
empty seat is a tad conspicuous, especially so near the front."

Ebon bowed his head. In truth he had not thought overmuch about
it—Credell had been too terrified to say anything of the many times

288

Ebon had vanished from the classroom. "I am sorry, Instructor. I was only—"

A massive hand clapped down on his shoulder, squeezing tight—but not painfully. When he raised his eyes again, Ebon found Perrin looking back at him with soft concern.

"You do not need to tell me where you have been. Last night was a terrible tragedy, and none could fault you for needing to clear your mind after what you saw. Only next time, tell me."

He ducked his head again, but this time in shame. She thought he was upset over Credell's death. And Ebon supposed he was, but that was far overshadowed by his worries about Cyrus, and Lilith, and now his family's arrival upon the Seat. What did it say about him that he had so little concern for the death of his first instructor at the Academy?

But he could say none of this, of course, so he only mumbled, "I will remember, Instructor. Thank you. And again, I am sorry."

Perrin clapped his shoulder again—Ebon thought the spot might bruise—and left him. Ebon shuffled towards the dining hall, trying not to feel so wretched. The moment he stepped inside, Kalem and Theren leapt up from their seats and came to him.

"Where were you this morning?" hissed Kalem.

"I made a wager with him that you went to see your lover," said Theren with a grin. "Tell me I am a gold weight richer."

"You are." Ebon could not help matching her smile. But Kalem drew back, his eyes filled with reproach.

"Ebon, what possessed you? No one minds you having a lover. But leaving your classes to visit her?"

"My thoughts would give me no peace," said Ebon, frowning at him. "You cannot tell me your mind is inured to the sight of corpses, even after the attack on the Seat."

Kalem had no answer for that, and he lowered his eyes. But Theren took their arms and pulled them both towards the door. "Enough of that. Come to the library, Ebon, for we have something to show you."

"What is it?" said Ebon. "I have not even eaten."

"I took a roll for you." Theren produced the mangled, squished thing from her pocket and shoved it into his hand. Ebon grimaced. Soon they whisked him into the library and up the stairs, where they huddled in their third-floor corner. Kalem went to the wall and put forth his power, and the stone shifted to reveal his secret cubbyhole. He drew an old tome of plain brown leather, unadorned, with no title on the cover.

"I found this book," said Kalem.

"In the library?" said Ebon, raising his eyebrows. "Wonders may never cease."

"It was hidden," Kalem said, scowling. "It was covered in dark and dust behind a bookshelf."

"Most likely it fell," said Ebon. "What of it?"

Kalem looked at him, almost haughty. "Ebon, I know nearly every inch of this library. The shelf was flush to the wall until, at most, a week ago. Someone wanted to hide this book."

Theren took the book to show Ebon. "They wanted to hide it because it is from the vaults."

Ebon recoiled. "Do . . . do you mean it is enchanted?" He swallowed hard, wondering if he should run.

She rolled her eyes. "It is not from *within* the vaults, you craven. It is a logbook. A very *old* logbook."

Ebon relaxed and, after a moment, leaned forwards to look at the book with fresh interest. "But why would it be here?"

"Why, indeed? Especially one so ancient. It is centuries old, and at first I doubted it could have any unchanged entries."

"What do you mean?" said Ebon.

"When an item comes to the vaults, we enter it in a new page on a logbook, with the room's number noted here." Theren pointed to the top right corner of a page, where a number had been scrawled and then crossed through with a red X. "Once all the entries have been crossed out, the logbook is retired to the archives. This book is from hundreds of years ago. The entries should have been replaced with other artifacts. But one—"

Ebon pointed to the entry on the open page. It described a cloak of green cloth and the enchantment placed upon it. "A spell of warding? What is that?"

Theren glanced at it. "Look here—runes of silver sewn into the collar and imbued with mentalist spells. They infuse the cloth with power so that it protects the wearer with magic. Though the cloak would still be cloth, and therefore light, it would protect you like a shirt of mail. Although see here." She pointed to the bottom of the page, where a note had been added: *Verified to be drained upon the twelfth of Yunus, Year of Underrealm 823.*

"Drained?" said Ebon. "What does that mean?"

"Any wizard can put some of their magic into an object," Theren explained. "A sword imbued with elementalism may burn with fire at a word, or, as with this cloak, mentalism may make objects much stronger than normal. The magic will leach out with time, often in the course of a day or so. But if runes are carved or woven into the object, they can be made to hold the magic for longer—or, in the case of some mighty Wizard Kings, forever. That is why these artifacts are kept within the vaults and out of reach until their power fades. It was a command issued long ago, around the time of the Fearless Decree. The King's law says no wizard may sit a throne, and a king with enough enchanted objects is as good as a Wizard King."

"Enchanted objects are outlawed, then?"

"Yes and no," said Kalem. "Many can be found throughout Underrealm, and some wizards will make small enchantments for everyday use. The Mystics do not concern themselves with such trifles. Only objects of great power are controlled. The lord chancellor of the Mystics is the final authority on which artifacts must be kept within the vaults, and which are not worth the trouble."

"One entry in that logbook remains," said Theren. "One artifact that is still within the vaults—or was, until it was stolen."

Ebon flipped through the pages to find the entry, glancing at the other listings as he did. There was a sphere of gold, bearing runes like those on the Academy's front door. The text said that, with the right words, it could erupt into a giant ball of flame and consume everything nearby before returning to its original shape. The next page described a circlet that let the wearer vanish from sight. He turned page after page, reading about each artifact in turn. Some held power he could scarcely imagine, while others seemed only to have a practical, everyday sort of use. It seemed different lord chancellors of years past had had very different ideas of what sort of enchantments should be protected within the vaults. But all the entries were crossed out with a red X—until at last he found the one that was not.

> *The Amulet of Kekhit*
> *This amulet of crystal is bound in gold and depends*
> *from a chain of silver. Its dark powers were hers, and show*
> *no signs of decay despite the many centuries since it was*
> *pried from her long-rotting bones in the southern reaches*
> *of Idris.*
> *Added to the vaults upon the 10th of Arilis, Year of*
> *Underrealm 194*

The artifact's name had two lines drawn in red ink beneath it, but nothing more was said of its properties. There was a crude sketch of the amulet; the crystal was shaped like an arrowhead, pointing down and away from the wearer's throat. Ebon flipped to the next page, but it was only the logbook's next entry.

"This amulet—that is what was taken?" said Ebon.

"I am sure," said Theren. "See where they have drawn a line beneath it? They must have planned this for some time."

"I fear I do not understand what it does," said Ebon.

"Nor I," said Theren. "But it is crystal, and therefore it must be powerful. Nothing holds magic so well as crystal. This *is* the missing logbook. When I could not find the entry of what had been stolen, I thought it was a clerical error. But it was here, in this book, which someone stole. And there is something else. Keep turning the pages."

Ebon did, and soon came upon where some leaves had been torn from the book. One remnant had some smudged writing near its spine, but he could not make out what it said.

"Why are these pages torn?" said Ebon.

"More artifacts—likely more they plan to steal. Mayhap they tore the pages out to better keep the secret and then tried to hide the tome."

"Why not destroy the book, rather than hide it?" said Ebon. "It seems it would hardly have been missed if you did not know where it had gone."

Theren shrugged. "Mayhap the thief meant to take the amulet and then choose other artifacts to steal later. Or mayhap they meant to destroy it, but they were nearly discovered holding it and concealed it in haste. Who is to say?"

"Should we tell Jia? Or the dean?" said Kalem.

"No. I will arrange for it to be found in a way that leaves us all blameless. Hopefully they will read through the pages and realize what has been taken."

"But still we know nothing of the amulet's powers," said Ebon.

"We have a name," said Kalem. "Kekhit. We must discover who she was. She sounds familiar, but I cannot place her. Doubtless we will find something in *An Account of the Dark War and the Fearless Decree.* I will start searching at once."

"If only there were more than one copy," said Ebon, shaking his head. "I would like to help in the search."

"We know she lived in Idris and was long-dead by the year 194," said Kalem. "The two of you should search for more books from that time. Who knows but that you may find the truth before I do."

Theren gave a long-suffering sigh. "Does it matter if we know what Kekhit's amulet does? We know Lilith has stolen it and that we must reclaim it from her. The amulet's enchantments do not seem important."

Kalem frowned. "We still do not know for certain that Lilith stole the amulet."

Theren glanced over his shoulder, and her eyes hardened. "We could always ask her ourselves."

They followed her gaze. There was Lilith, a few dozen paces away and heading straight for them. Ebon tried to speak a word of restraint, but Theren leapt from her chair and strode forwards to meet her. Kalem and Ebon scrambled to follow, flanking her on either side as she and Lilith faced off. Ebon realized that he and Kalem probably looked a great deal like Oren and Nella when they stood like bodyguards by Lilith's side. That was not an entirely comfortable thought.

"Good day, Lilith," said Theren evenly. "How odd that you should seek us out, for I have had a mind to speak to you as well."

Lilith stared, blinked, and then turned her gaze to Ebon.

"Good day, Ebon. I hope you have been well. Some friends and I have been congregating here in the library after the Academy's hours, and I was wondering if you might like to join us." Slowly she turned to Kalem. "You, too, would be most welcome, Kalem of the family Konnel."

Ebon blinked. He gave his friends a sharp look, but they both seemed equally mystified. He cleared his throat, drawing Lilith's attention back to him. "We have questions for you, Lilith, as Theren said."

Theren's eyes had grown dangerously narrow. "Where were you when the Seat was attacked?"

For a moment, Lilith said nothing. Then she shook her head, as though the thought were distressing, before finally turning to Theren. "What do you mean? I was home in Feldemar. You already knew that. All of you did." She gave three sharp blinks and returned her attention to Ebon. "What say you, son of Drayden? We would be most privileged by your presence—by both of you. We call ourselves the Goldbag Society, after all." Her lips twisted in a small, self-deprecating smile.

Theren's breath came quicker. She took a half-step forwards. Ebon wanted to place a hand on her elbow, but he was suddenly afraid she might strike him. "Your petty arrogance does you no favors, Lilith. Why did your family draw you home to Feldemar just as the Seat was attacked?"

Lilith focused on her again, brow furrowing as though it were a great inconvenience. "I . . ." She shook her head. "What are you saying? Do you mean to say I had something to do with the attack?"

"I said nothing of the sort." Theren's smile grew cruel. "But now that you mention it, is there any truth to such a thought?"

Again Lilith shook her head, her eyes growing sharp and focused. She took a step back, staring at Ebon and Kalem as though seeing them for the first time. "I cannot believe this. I do not know what foolishness made me invite you to our gatherings."

Theren stepped forwards as though she would catch Lilith by the hand and prevent her escape. "You did not answer me. Why did you mention yourself in connection to the attacks, Lilith? What are you hiding?"

Lilith was shaking with rage—but, too, her eyes were hurt as they stared into Theren's. "That you would think such a thing of me shows your ignorance. I was devastated when I learned of Dulmun's treachery.

Until we learned what had happened, I wept every day for fear that my friends and classmates—and yes, even you—might have perished in the fighting."

"Sentiment is an ill look for you," spat Theren. "Like an adder wrapping itself in feathers and calling itself a songbird."

Again Lilith retreated—this time in earnest, turning away. But she stopped after a few steps and gave them a withering look over her shoulder. "Call me an adder, then. But call me also a fool for thinking your death a tragedy."

She swept off, and for a moment Ebon thought Theren would pursue her. He seized one elbow, and Kalem the other, and they half-dragged her to their chairs in the corner. But when he looked back over his shoulder, he saw Lilith was looking at them again. Fury twisted her face, and angry tears wet her cheeks. At last she turned and ran away, vanishing among the bookshelves.

By the time they returned to their chairs, Theren was shaking. She rounded on Ebon and Kalem. "That manipulative little sow. I know she had something to do with the theft, and there is a fast way to prove it. We must get into the vaults."

"Get *into* the vaults?" said Kalem, his eyes wide. "You are mad. We could be expelled."

"Not if they do not catch us. And if we visit the room where the amulet was stolen, I will know for certain whether it was Lilith who did the deed."

"How?" said Ebon, shrugging. "What do you hope to find?"

"Every wizard has a . . . a sort of signature," said Theren. "Think of it like handwriting. An imprint upon the spells they cast. One wizard who knows another well can read the signature. If I can investigate the vault where the artifact was taken, I can tell if it was Lilith who stole it."

"Spell-sight? That is a wildly inaccurate practice, and prone to errors," said Kalem. "Every instructor speaks of its unreliability. No king's court will accept such as testimony, except in some of the outland kingdoms."

Theren slapped her hand on the back of a chair. "I know Lilith's mark. I will know if it was her."

A moment passed. Ebon cleared his throat and then quietly said, "What do you propose to do?"

She gave a thin-lipped smile. "I can sneak into the vaults with Kalem. After I conduct my search, Kalem can shift stone and tunnel our way out."

"Only Kalem?" said Ebon. "What of me?"

Theren shook her head. "Forgive me for saying so, but you could do nothing to help. You do not yet command the magic required to aid our escape."

Ebon gave them both an uneasy look. Then he stepped away from the chairs, to the corner where the wall sat exposed between two shelves. He reached out and set his hand on the stone. Magic coursed through him. The stone melted and warped beneath his hand, folding away to reveal the hidden shelf where Kalem stowed books he wished to keep secret.

Theren's brows arched. "You have learned to shift stone?"

"Ever since the attack on the Seat," Ebon said, forcing his thoughts away from the sound of Cyrus' scream.

"That is often the way of it—once the first step is taken, the rest come easier," said Kalem brightly. "I knew nothing of this, Ebon. Congratulations—you are learning far more quickly than I did."

"Only because I am six years older," said Ebon. "And I cannot put the stone back, only push it away."

"I can replace it," said Kalem. "And this will make the tunneling faster."

"You are interested in the plan, then?" Theren grinned. "This may work after all. Two alchemists to aid our escape, instead of only one."

"You mean transmuters."

"I mean be silent, Kalem."

"When do you propose we act?" said Ebon.

Theren pursed her lips. "We can do nothing tonight. It would be best to avoid the vaults until Sunday. The Academy will be on holiday, and I will be performing my services. Lilith will not. The days between now and then will give me time to prepare."

Ebon sagged, for a thought had struck him. "Very well," he sighed. "If we must."

"What troubles you?" said Kalem.

"It is my family," said Ebon, lowering his gaze. "They arrive upon the Seat on the morrow."

"How could they interfere?" said Kalem. "There is no way they could know what we mean to do."

"Of course not," said Ebon. "But my father will no doubt have some torment for me, in one form or another."

With an encouraging smile, Theren clapped his shoulder. "Try not to worry overmuch. If you should be drawn away Sunday night, I believe Kalem and I can manage without you."

Kalem straightened and reached for his book. "And in the meantime, we still have work to do. Who knows what we might learn before then if we find out about this Kekhit?"

Theren sighed and stood. "Very well. We are bound for the bookshelves after all, Ebon, though it pains me as a woman of action."

Ebon joined her, and together they returned to the shelves, searching through spines in the library's quiet.

TEN

THE NEXT MORNING, EBON SAT IN CLASS WITH PERRIN BESIDE HIM. The poor bench groaned and creaked under the woman's mammoth weight, and Ebon held himself ready to leap out of the way should it snap to kindling beneath them. Perrin had already gone about the class and set the other students to their tasks before coming to him.

"We did not have time yesterday, but now you will learn your aim while under my tutelage," Perrin began. "You had one spell to master before you graduated your first class. Here, you will have three."

"Three?" said Ebon, dismayed. It had taken him two months to turn wood to stone and pass Credell's class. He did not relish the thought of taking more than half a year to graduate from this one.

"Three to pass, though I expect you to learn many more while you are here. The three tests are these: to turn your stone rod back into wood, which is harder than you might expect; to turn a flower to ice without changing its shape; and to turn obsidian white."

The last one made Ebon blink in surprise. "Changing a stone's color? That cannot be harder than turning stone to wood."

298

"It is far, far more difficult," said Perrin gruffly. "Matter has many properties. Some are simpler than others. Color is one of the strangest."

Ebon snickered, but stifled it quickly as Perrin's eyes narrowed. "My apologies, Instructor. It is only that I do not take your meaning. Color is color."

"Oh?" said Perrin. "Tell me, what is stone?"

He blinked. "It is . . . it is rock. The stuff of the earth. It comes from the ground and the mountains."

"And what is wood?"

"The stuff of trees. You cut them down and take them apart, and there is your wood."

"And what is green?"

Ebon blinked. "I . . . it is the color of grass, and leaves. It—"

"No. Those are things that have the color green. But what *is* green? A leaf may *look* green, but that does not mean it *is* green. What is color itself? You know, do you not, that there are those who cannot see colors, or to whom different colors look alike? People who see no difference between green and blue?"

"Yes," said Ebon, nodding slowly. "I know this."

"If they do not see the green in a leaf, does that mean the leaf is no longer green?"

"Of course not," Ebon said, irritated. "It is only something wrong with their eyes."

"Who is to say? Who is to say that we do not imagine the green in the leaf, and they see it for its truth? Who is to say that the color I see when I look at good tilled earth, is not the same color you see in a cup of wine?"

Ebon shook his head. "That is ridiculous. I know what I see. Anyone does, if they are not mad."

"Ridiculous, you say?" Perrin smiled grimly. "Mayhap you are right, mayhap not. But you are a student, and the purpose of the student is to ask questions—not assume you know the answers already. You say you know what you see? Let me show you something."

She placed her hand on the table. Light flooded the room as her eyes glowed with a furious luster, brighter than any Ebon had seen. He focused on the hand—and then, suddenly, it was not there. It did not fade, nor wisp away in smoke. It simply vanished. Ebon jumped up with a cry.

"What happened?" Perrin spoke through gritted teeth, forcing each word from her mouth. "Why are you frightened?"

"Your hand!" said Ebon. "It . . . it is gone!"

"It is not," said Perrin. "It is there. I feel it. I am moving my fingers now."

"But I cannot see them!"

The glow died in her eyes, and her hand reappeared. She flexed her fingers, curling them into a fist before reaching towards Ebon. He withdrew, frightened. She only wiggled her meaty fingers. "Go on. Take my wrist."

Slowly, tentatively, Ebon did. Her hand enveloped his, gripping him firmly, solid, present—*real*. Ebon shuddered. As he looked about the room, he saw that the other students were looking at them both with awe. He turned back to Perrin. "How did you do it?"

"It is difficult to explain. Except that there is something—the air, is how I perceive it—that controls how you are able to see my hand. I can twist it so that it shows you nothing. And so my hand disappears." Perrin looked around the room. "That is a powerful spell of transmutation—rarely can a wizard master it. And before you go thinking wild thoughts of my strength, take note that even such a small illusion required all of my concentration. There are transmuters in Underrealm who can make their whole bodies vanish. But if you never reach such skill, do not count yourselves among the weak. It is a rare ability. Also, you should all be working."

The other students hurriedly dove back into their books and spells.

Perrin turned her gaze on Ebon again. "Color is not nearly so hard. Yet it is far, far more difficult than simply changing the substance a thing is made of. You have learned to turn wood into stone. But with color you must go deeper, smaller, until you can find the thing that makes a stone appear grey—or black, in the case of obsidian—and turn it white instead."

"I understand," said Ebon, slowly nodding.

"Of course you do not," said Perrin, smiling a little. "Not yet. That is why you are in my class. Though unless I miss my guess, you wish you had passed it already."

Ebon looked away. "Is it so obvious?"

"Do you think you are the first student to arrive late at the Academy? When I attended, our oldest student had seen more than twenty years. Though I would wager she faced less jibes than you, seeing as how she could tweak the ears of most children."

That thought made Ebon smile. "Thank you, Instructor."

"You are welcome. Now, fetch your book again. You will find many bits of wisdom that should help you master your first test."

Perrin rose, the bench screaming in relief, and moved on to the next student. Ebon went to the shelves to find his book. But once there, he looked over his shoulder at Perrin. The instructor was a giant, and often impatient. Yet there was a deep-seated kindness in her heart that made Ebon feel safe in her care. And certainly she was a far sight better than Credell.

He felt a stab of guilt at that thought and turned back to the bookshelf.

Soon Ebon had found the book and returned to his seat. The spine cracked as he laid it out and began to read. He quickly lost himself in the words, spelled out in careful, tiny script by some transmuter of ages gone, which spoke of the properties of different types of matter. Many of the terms whisked around and about in his mind, spinning until he felt dizzy. But he squeezed his eyes shut briefly and pressed on, determined to learn what he could.

The time whisked away as he lost himself in his studies, hardly mindful of the students practicing their magic around him. But after a time his attention was dragged away from the pages as the door to the classroom clicked and swung open. Ebon looked up to see Dasko, one of the advanced weremage instructors, a man with grey-flecked black hair whose beard was trimmed close. When Ebon had fled Credell's class in the mornings, he had often seen Dasko teaching students upon the grounds. The instructor's gaze went to Perrin, to whom he beckoned.

Perrin frowned and excused herself from the student she was speaking to. When she reached the door, Dasko did not bother to lead her outside, but spoke quickly in whispers. Ebon dropped his gaze to the book so he did not appear to be eavesdropping, but he leaned as far forwards as he could, cupping his left hand across his cheek so he could surreptitiously plug one ear. Still he could hear little more than snatches. "*. . . the artifact . . . pendant . . . another vault . . .*"

The whispers stopped abruptly. Ebon could not help himself; he looked up. Dasko's eyes were fixed upon him, and he quickly looked back down. But the instructors did not resume speaking. Ebon let his eyes wander, so it looked like an accident when he eyed the door again. But Dasko was still watching him, and now Perrin was, too.

"Ebon," said Perrin. "Come here, if you would."

The class went deathly silent. Ebon's ears burned, but he tried to feign indifference as he stood and approached the instructors.

"This is Instructor Dasko." Perrin's voice was low, betraying nothing. "He brings a message from Instructor Jia. She wishes to speak with you."

That took Ebon completely unawares. "Jia? What for?"

"I imagine she will tell you. Off you go—but once you are done, return without dallying."

"Of course." Ebon followed Dasko out into the hallway. The door closed behind them with a sharp *click.*

ELEVEN

DASKO LED HIM ONWARDS, THOUGH EBON WELL REMEMBERED THE WAY to Jia's study. What could this possibly be about? Dasko and Perrin had said something about the vaults. But why should they think that had anything to do with Ebon? It seemed impossible that they could have discovered what he and his friends planned for Sunday.

He thought of Jia and Dasko standing over Credell's body, and his stomach wrenched. They must be investigating the murderer.

The day the Seat had been attacked, Jia had seen him flee from the other students. That had been explained, with Adara's help, but mayhap she still regarded him with some suspicion.

But she could not possibly think he was involved with Credell's death. She had been one of the few people at the Academy, instructor or otherwise, who had been kind to Ebon from the moment he arrived.

Dasko spoke suddenly, surprising him. "You are Ebon, of the family Drayden, are you not?"

"Yes."

303

"I am Dasko. I have seen you about the Academy, of course, though it was not until recently that I learned your name."

"Ah," said Ebon uncomfortably, not sure what response was expected of him.

Dasko turned to regard him keenly. "Now is an ill time, for Jia awaits you. But I had wondered if, on some occasion, I might speak with you privately."

Ebon swallowed—he hardly thought that instructors needed permission for such a thing. "Of course. I am at your service."

"Excellent. Soon, then. Here we are."

And indeed they were. In his surprise, Ebon had lost track of their progress, but now they stood at the door that led to Jia's study. Ebon gave Dasko one last, awkward nod, which the man returned before striding away through the halls. Then Ebon lifted a hand and knocked.

"Come in," said Jia from the other side. Ebon turned the latch and stepped within. "Ebon. Excellent. Please come and have a seat. Would you like a cup of water?"

"Now that you mention it," said Ebon, realizing that his throat was as dry as the deserts of home. "But I can pour it."

"Do not be silly. Sit." She rose and went to the side table, poured two wooden cups, and placed Ebon's in front of him before returning to her seat. But when she caught sight of his face, she must have seen how frightened he was. "Did Dasko not tell you why I wished to see you?"

The bluntness of the question took him by surprise. His skin crawled beneath his robes. "No, Instructor."

She looked skywards. "Blast that man. Doubtless he did not think of it, and has forgotten what it was like to be a student. You are not in trouble."

Ebon could not help it: he let out a loud bark of laughter, nearly choking on his water. He put the cup down and coughed, and then sank into the cushions while pounding on his chest.

Jia graced him with a small smile, though she hid it quickly. "I imagine you were worried."

"I may have been," said Ebon, his voice hoarse with choking.

Her smile died. "Well and good. But this is still a matter of gravest importance. I must ask you some questions, and it is imperative that you are absolutely honest."

Ebon sat up straighter. "Of course, Instructor."

"Tell me again what happened when you left us on the day the Seat was attacked."

His heart quailed. He had guessed wrong. This was to do with Cyrus, not Credell. She had said he was not in trouble, so she did not suspect him of anything. But still this seemed a dangerous line of questioning.

"I thought I had explained that already."

"Tell me again. The whole of the tale, from beginning to end."

Shifting in his seat, Ebon repeated the same lie he had told her before, when he and Adara had landed on the shores of Selvan and then made their way to the other refugees. It was a lie Adara had helped him craft. In his ear he heard her voice as though she were speaking to him now.

They must believe your reason for leaving them, and so it must be something you would do—good-hearted, if mayhap a bit foolish.

"After the blue-clad soldiers attacked us in the streets, I thought I saw someone running close by. They wore black robes, and so I thought a student had become separated from the group. I chased after them."

"Which was—"

"Foolish, I know," said Ebon, ducking his head. Hopefully she would think it was shame at her chastisement rather than at the lie he told. Again he heard Adara's soft words.

The best lie is rooted in truth, yet you can make no mention of me whatever. Therefore I shall be someone else—someone who will speak to the truth of your tale, if I ask them to.

"But still, I did it. And when finally I caught them, I found only a woman in a black dress who had fled the fighting. I tried to return with her to the other students, but you had already left through the wall. I followed the trail to the docks, from which you had already sailed. There was a small rowboat that had been cast off from its ship and was nearly too far from the docks to reach. I dove into the Bay, swam to it, and rowed back to her. Then we set out for Selvan."

"The woman's name?"

Mitra.

"Mitra. She told me she was a handmaiden from the palace."

Jia sighed and leaned back, steepling her fingers. "Very well. We have spoken with the woman, and she tells the same tale. I am sorry I had to ask again, but the dean insisted."

A wave of relief washed through him, though he tried to hide it.

Jia looked away for a moment and then leaned forwards again. "Ebon, tell me one thing—and no matter your answer, I vow to you that I will not be upset. Do you swear that you did not return to the Academy at any time during the attack?"

His heart skipped a beat. "No, Instructor. I mean, yes, I do swear it. I did not return here." Then he hesitated. He had no wish to further this line of thinking—and yet, he had *not* returned to the Academy, and could hardly say anything to incriminate himself. So he pressed on: "Why do you ask?"

She regarded him carefully. "Have you heard any rumors floating about the halls of late?"

Ebon blushed. "Mayhap. Something to do with the vaults."

Carefully she folded her hands on the desk. "Yes. I would ask you *never* to repeat such rumors. They do no one any good, though of course all our attempts to quell them have only redoubled them. But yes, something was taken from the vaults. Already we sought the thief, of course, but Instructor Credell's death has given the search a fresh urgency. Whoever broke into the vaults may have had something to do with the murder. So I will ask you once more, and then leave it alone. Did you return to the Academy during the fighting? If you saw anything—anything at all—it could be the kernel of information that helps us discover the thief's identity—and mayhap the murderer's."

Ebon understood at last, and relaxed. They were questioning him not about Cyrus, but about the theft—and not because he was a Drayden, but because he had become separated from the group. He could answer honestly and with a clear conscience. "No, Instructor. I swear it—I left the Academy when you did, and returned with you. I know nothing of the vaults. I am only relieved you do not suspect me of the theft."

Jia smirked. "Oh, there was no question of that. The vaults are protected by incredibly powerful enchantments and—you will forgive my saying so—you were only a first-year transmuter. We know without doubt that you had no hand in the theft itself."

Ebon laughed wryly, and it earned him another smile. "Mayhap this is the first time I am gladdened by my own lack of power."

"Not for long, I think. Under Perrin's able tutelage, you should progress through your lessons most quickly."

He sat up. "I will return to class and attempt to prove you right."

"Not just yet," she said, holding up a finger. From a drawer in her desk she withdrew a slip of paper and handed it to him. "A missive, sent for you."

Ebon frowned—and then he recognized the Drayden family seal pressed into the wax that held the parchment closed. He blanched.

Jia's eyes hardened. "Is everything all right?"

He tried to force a smile. "Fine, Instructor." He took the letter and cracked the seal. There in his mother's thin handwriting was a simple note:

We have arrived, and await you in the manor.
—Hesta

Carefully he folded the letter and stowed it in a pocket. His throat was suddenly dry, and he took another sip of water.

"Ebon, you look troubled. Tell me what is wrong."

"It is my family," Ebon said reluctantly. "They have arrived upon the Seat."

Jia leaned back in her chair, letting a few heartbeats of silence stretch between them. "I see. Far be it from me to pry into your affairs, Ebon. But I hope you know that you need not visit them if you do not wish to."

Ebon gave a wry smile and shook his head. "If I did not, they would send someone to fetch me."

"The family Drayden is powerful indeed, but their reach does not penetrate the Academy's walls." Ebon heard steel hidden in her words—not anger at him, but an unyielding promise of strength. "Especially since Dean Cyrus was lost. Stay if you wish, and I vow that no one will drag you forth."

Her conviction, and the kindness that rested behind it, brought a lump to the back of his throat and made his eyes smart. But he wondered if she would speak so confidently if she knew of Mako, who seemed to appear and disappear from the library on a whim. "I thank you, Instructor. And if it were only my father who wished to see me, I might do as you say. But it is my mother as well—in fact, the note came from her—and my aunt Halab, who has always been kind to me. And most of all, my sister, Albi, who I have missed the longest. No. I will go to see them, though the good will be tarnished by the bad."

"As you wish. You may go now, if you like. I will send a note along to excuse you from the day's classes. As I said, discuss the vault with no one."

"I will not, Instructor."

She gave him a sharp look, eyes glinting. "Not even with Theren and young Kalem?"

Ebon swallowed and looked away. "I . . . of course not, Instructor."

Her pursed lips made him wonder if she believed him. "Hm. Well, if you should think of anything else that might help . . ."

"I will tell you at once, Instructor," said Ebon. "And . . . thank you."

He left her and made for the Academy's front door, shaking his arms as he went, for a thrill of fear still coursed through him.

TWELVE

EBON STOPPED IN THE FRONT HALL. HE HAD MEANT TO GO STRAIGHT into the street and make for the manor. But now he wondered if he should go up to his dormitory and change into fresh robes. His hands shook no matter how he tried to rid himself of his anxiety, and his breath came so shallow that it set his head to spinning.

He heard his father's voice in his mind. *Coward. Sniveling coward.* And indeed, he felt himself on the verge of tears. Self-loathing filled him at the fear that blossomed in his breast, and yet he could not dismiss it.

What did he think would happen? Did he think his father would strike him? Harm him? Try to kill him, even? No, certainly not. Especially not if Halab were there, which she would be. Would Shay try to remove him from the Academy? Ebon doubted it, for he could have done that by letter—and again, there was Halab. She would object, and Shay would not gainsay her.

Mayhap Ebon only feared the look in his father's eyes—the hatred he knew he would find there, and the scorn.

He forced himself to square his shoulders. Never mind going upstairs to change. He had no other clothes—only his student's robes were allowed in the citadel. He could don a fresh set, but why? It would make no difference to his father. Let Shay see him with some of the day's dust upon him and with palms smudged with ink from his books. Ebon was a wizard now—or at least he was studying to be one. Shay could face that truth or fly into a rage at it, but it would change nothing.

He went to the Academy's wide front door. Mellie stood there, and Ebon made to stop and explain. But before he could, she reached over and opened the door without saying a word. He stared for a moment, confused, but then shook his head and left. He had long ago given up on trying to make sense of the mad woman's actions.

Winter had come at last to the High King's Seat, and snow fell gently from the grey above. Though clouds covered the sky, they were thin, and so the sun still shone through them, lighting the island in its glow. The snow muffled all sound, so that the clattering of construction and the rumbling of wagon wheels sounded distant, like a city observed from atop a mountain.

Ebon had retrieved his overcoat from where it hung outside Perrin's classroom, and he wrapped it tighter about himself. His hood helped keep his hair free of the falling snow. Quietly he murmured thanks that the streets were clear, for his shoes were not meant to wade through deep drifts. Servants of the High King had been about, their horses dragging great plows that pushed the snow off and into the gutters.

Back home in Idris, the cold had sometimes been worse than this. But Idris was a desert, and never saw snow. Some thought that meant the land was gentler, but in truth it was the opposite. Here in the green lands, the earth itself resisted any changes in weather. When the day was hot, the ground held that heat so that evening took longer to cool the air. And when the sun rose in the morning, the trees clutched at night's chill and sent it wafting along on dawn's breezes.

In the desert, change came fast and harsh. The sun's absence turned night into a frozen void where one could die from exposure in no time. And daylight's baking rays were reflected by the sand itself so that travelers were roasted from above and below. All life and society in Idris were tailored around the desert's merciless nature, from the homes to the horses. Despite the snow that dusted him now, Ebon found this land far gentler, and felt grateful for it.

He had thought the road to the Drayden manor would seem longer, with the dread of his father looming over him. But in fact, it seemed far too short a time before he stood outside the gates, hands shoved under his arms to protect them from the chill. He hesitated before stepping forwards, keenly aware that he could still turn around and go back to the Academy. Certainly his family would fetch him, one way or another, but it would stall the reunion for at least another day.

But then he thought of his father the last time they had seen each other. It had been in the courtyard, the very one before which he now stood. And without saying farewell, his father had hidden within a carriage, concealing his face in the curtains, too ashamed to so much as glance at his only living son.

Ebon's heart burned. *He* was not the coward. That epithet belonged to his father.

He stepped forwards and pounded on the iron gate.

A hatch slid open, and a yeoman peered out. "Master Ebon," grunted the man. "You are expected. A moment, my lord."

The hatch screeched shut, and then the gate groaned as men dragged it open. A slight wind wafted out from the courtyard through the gap, making Ebon blink. When the gate was open, he saw the courtyard was filled with wagons. Trade goods to be sold upon the Seat, Ebon guessed—spices, most likely. He trudged through the snow, for here there were no shovels or plows, and through the front door.

No one waited for him in the front hall, nor on the high landing that overlooked it. The staircases were empty, and no servants could be seen moving through the adjoining hallways. But Ebon heard voices from the upstairs common room, and then a light laugh that sent his heart racing: that was Albi for certain, though there was something different about her voice.

Excitement seized him and banished thoughts of his father. He leapt up the stairs two at a time, hand gliding on the rail as a smile forced itself across his face. Feet pounding on the stone, he ran like a child down the hallway and threw open the door.

There they sat—but not for long, for as soon as they saw him they all rose to greet him. Halab caught his eye first, her beaming smile warming him to the heart, and then his mother, who rushed forwards to embrace him. But she was overtaken as a short, plump figure threw itself past her and into Ebon's arms, clutching his neck and crying delight into his ear.

"Ebon, you useless, horrible, *horrible* . . ." Albi's words vanished, replaced by sharp sniffs as she choked back tears.

He held her, arms locked as though he might never release her—though he did, when Hesta arrived and demanded a free arm to hug her with as well. Albi drew back a step, looking up at him with shining eyes.

"You have grown taller," she said.

"I? It is you I can hardly recognize." He laughed and hugged her close again.

But then a shadow darkened his mood, for a man stood up behind Halab. Ebon braced himself—but then he looked again, for it was not Shay who stood there, but a man he did not know. A man of the family Drayden, certainly—he had the eyes, the stolid brow. Doubtless some cousin or uncle of Ebon's. But another glance around the room confirmed it: Shay was nowhere to be seen. And then, in the room's deepest corner, Ebon saw Mako was here as well. The bodyguard leaned against the wall, a sarcastic smile playing across his lips as he watched Ebon.

Hesta must have seen the confusion in Ebon's expression, for her lips tightened. "Your father was caught up in business the very day we left Idris to come here. He was forced to stay home."

Ebon looked at Albi. "I . . . I thought from your letter that he would be here."

His mother looked as though she thought he had gone mad, but Albi gave a sad smile of recognition. Another would have thought Ebon was disappointed that Shay was missing, but Albi would know how overjoyed he was. "He, too, thought to visit. His decision to stay was made at the final hour."

"It was all quite sudden, but nothing to concern ourselves with," said Halab, who had now approached to stand behind Hesta. Ebon's mother and sister drew aside in deference. "Well met again, my dearest nephew. My heart has been fairly sick in your absence."

Ebon kissed one cheek and then the other, gripping her shoulders tightly. "Dearest aunt. How I have missed you."

She turned and gestured to the couches surrounding the hearth, where the fire still burned. Together they crossed the room—but they halted before taking their seats, for the man still stood there, looking at Ebon with something very much like a glare.

"Doubtless you remember your uncle, Matami—brother to your father and I." Halab inclined her head. "He came in Shay's place."

At hearing the name, Ebon found that he *did* remember. He had met Matami once or twice, although the last time was quite some years ago. "Of course," said Ebon, bowing deep. "Well met, uncle. It has been a long time."

"Indeed it has." Matami gave a loud sniff and turned away, returning to his seat. Albi met Ebon's gaze and playfully rolled her eyes. Ebon barely managed not to laugh out loud.

He took an armchair between Halab and Hesta. Albi left her chair and sat on a rug at his feet, her head leaning on his knee. "So, Uncle Matami," said Ebon. "What business do you conduct for my father here upon the Seat?"

"Nothing you need concern yourself with," said Matami, each word terse and clipped. But when Halab gave him a sharp look, his jaw tensed, and he continued. "I mean only that you are a student of the Academy now, and doubtless the family's business would strike you as uncommonly dull."

In fact, Ebon thought he might be right—but he almost wanted to inquire anyway, only to prove Matami wrong, for he found himself with an immediate dislike for the man that only grew with every passing moment. But over Matami's shoulder, he saw Mako snickering while sipping his ale. Ebon's mood lightened at once, and he suppressed his own smile as he gratefully took an offered goblet of wine.

Evidently Halab was still dissatisfied with Matami's answer. "No need to be so brusque, brother. Matami is here to escort the wagons in the courtyard—doubtless you saw them when you arrived—as well as the goods inside. They are spices for the High King's palace."

"Spices?" said Ebon. "That many wagons full will surely fetch a fine price."

"They do not mean to sell them," said Albi, sounding annoyed. When Ebon looked down at her in surprise, she sighed and looked skywards as though searching for strength. "They bring them as a *gift*. Something to ease negotiations for a new trade route through Wadeland. I see only wasted riches. That many wagons would fill our coffers to bursting for a decade."

"And the new trade route will fill them for a century," Halab chided. "Dear niece, this is a lesson you must learn well: today's wealth is well spent if it earns tomorrow's fortune."

Again Albi looked at Ebon and shook her head, and again he had to stifle his laugh. Halab suppressed a smile.

"I see your secret, scornful looks, girl," she said, delight dancing behind her words. "I will attribute it to youth, rather than disrespect. You are wise beyond your years, but life will bring you more wisdom still."

"As you say, dear aunt," said Albi. "But now that Ebon has arrived, may we eat? I fear I will simply *starve.*"

"Of course." Halab motioned to the servants standing near the door. "We will take our supper now."

They rose and went to the dining table at the other end of the room. The last time Ebon had eaten here, they had sat at a high table and chairs, after the fashion of the Seat and most other kingdoms. Now the dining table had been replaced with one in the Idrisian design, a low table with cushions all around it upon which they could sit cross-legged. One by one they settled in. Halab gestured for Ebon to sit by her right hand at the head of the table, with Hesta to her left. Albi quickly seated herself beside Ebon while the servants brought dishes and trays of food. Matami did not look pleased to be shunted down near the other end of the table, but he took his seat beside Hesta without comment.

Ebon's mouth watered at the smell of roasted lamb. It was placed at the table's center, and before him were set small plates of figs, light crackers, and chickpea spread mixed with many fine spices. Liya, one of the household servants, leaned over him to fill his goblet with wine.

"Thank you." Ebon reached over to lift the goblet and make it easier for Liya to pour. But she recoiled with a sharp hiss of breath, and wine spilled from her pitcher. Ebon yanked his hand back before it got soaked, and the wine splashed on the table instead.

"Liya!" said Halab sharply. "What is the matter with you?"

Ebon looked up at her. The serving woman's face was filled with fright—far more than seemed appropriate in response to Halab's mild rebuke. "I am sorry, mistress. I will fetch him a new place mat immediately."

She ran from the room and soon returned, replacing Ebon's mat as quickly as she could. Hoping to dispel the awkwardness, Ebon met Albi's eyes and made a face. She giggled.

Soon the dinner had been served, and the servants withdrew. Ebon dug into his lamb, savoring the way the sweet, tender meat broke apart in his mouth. He was unable to help himself from letting out a small groan of delight. Albi nearly choked on her food as she giggled again.

"Do they starve you at the Academy, my son?" Hesta smiled from across the table. "You sound as though you have not eaten since we saw you last."

Ebon shook his head. "The Academy takes excellent care of us, Mother. Only, they must serve so many, you understand, and their cooks cannot hope to match the skill of ours."

"And do you find yourself missing all the trappings of home? Your family has never kept you wanting for luxury, dearest nephew." To Ebon the words sounded almost like an accusation, but Halab smiled to soften them.

"I have grown used to life within the Academy. It is only now that I realize how different things are from the way they were in Idris."

"And your studies?" said Hesta. "Are they going well?"

Ebon smiled, trying to make it look modest. "Well enough. I wish I were moving faster. But I did complete my first class in two months when it should have taken a year." A thought came to him, sudden and perhaps mad, but he went on with it. "I could show you a spell, if you wished. A small one only."

Albi's eyes shone, and Halab gave an indulgent smile. But Mother's eyes widened, and for some reason she looked at Matami with what looked like fear.

"If you wish," said Halab. "Only do not put a hole in the table, please."

"Of course not," said Ebon, shaking off his worry at Mother's expression.

He picked up an empty wooden cup from the table. Focusing, he called forth his magic. The room seemed to grow brighter as his eyes glowed.

Stone rippled out around his fingers, turning the wood, until the spell was finished. He placed the cup, now wholly stone, back on the table with a small *thunk*.

Albi squealed with delight. But Matami was glowering down at his food, and his cheeks grew darker by the moment.

Halab's eyebrows raised. "That is most impressive. I knew when I sent you there that my faith in your wits would not be misplaced."

"*My* instructors also say I am a quick student," said Albi, beaming. "Since you left, Ebon, I have been learning all sorts of new things, from accounting to history to everything in between."

"I have noted you show particular interest and skill in the courts of the nine lands," said Halab with a gentle smile. "That subject is complex and intricate, and ever-shifting, yet it is one of the most valuable things any merchant could know."

Ebon frowned slightly. His father had never permitted him to learn much about the other kingdoms. It seemed he was fearful that Ebon might seek a better life, mayhap someplace where he might be permitted to learn his magic.

Now Halab cast her bright smile to Albi before turning to place her hand upon Hesta's. "Bright minds run in the family, it would seem. I can only imagine your pride."

"What mother could wish for more than to see her children succeed?" said Hesta. Yet it seemed to Ebon that some worry still hovered about her. Matami had stopped eating entirely.

It felt as though the wind had fled from Ebon's sails, though he knew that was foolish. He had thought Halab and his mother would wish to speak of him, not Albi. After all, they saw her far more often. And sky above, he had performed magic! Was that not more impressive than the knowledge of courtly graces?

He took another sip of wine, trying to dispel such thoughts, and replaced the goblet on the low table. He was reminded of the table that had been there before, and that cast his mind back to the night he and his friends went to the eastern docks, where they saw the manor's servants stealing away on a ship like thieves, taking the furniture with them.

Carefully he drummed his fingers on the wood, trying to appear nonchalant. "I notice many things in the manor have been replaced. The furniture, the tapestries and rugs. Even these dishes look new. Were things lost in the attack upon the Seat?"

Halab's happy smile dampened, and she glanced at Hesta for a moment before sliding her eyes quickly away. Hesta looked down into her lap, suddenly fidgeting with her napkin. But Matami had looked up at last, and now he fixed Ebon with a withering glare, so furious that his brows nearly joined to one above his eyes.

"I only learned of this after the assault," said Halab. "But Shay decided to redecorate. He had everything removed from the manor and brought back to our estates in Idris, to be replaced with new things. He said he wished to rid the manor of its western trappings and make a home in the proud tradition of Idris again."

Clearly Albi did not know the source of Halab's sudden anxiety, but she caught the room's mood. Her eyes roamed from one face to the next but found no explanation. For his part, Ebon felt a tingling on the back of his neck; a heightened sense of awareness seemed to have come over him, bringing a roiling in his gut and a light-headedness that sharpened his thoughts.

"It is very fortunate," he said carefully, "that my father did so just before the Seat was attacked. Imagine the damage if all our possessions had been here when Dulmun sacked the island."

Halab's worried frown deepened—and Ebon saw that she looked at Matami for a moment before averting her eyes.

"Most fortunate indeed," said Halab.

Matami had not taken his eyes from Ebon's for so much as a moment. "We should all be blessed with such fortune," he growled. "It is a sign of some higher favor. Not like the Yerrins, whose home was demolished in the attack. Pompous fools." He drank deep of his wine.

"We are fortunate," Halab repeated. "Indeed, when I heard of the attack—after I learned that you had survived, Ebon, for of course that was my greatest worry—I grew concerned that this manor might have fallen. Only then did Shay mention what he had done."

The table went quiet as she sipped gingerly at her wine. Ebon glanced across the room to where Mako still leaned against the corner wall. The bodyguard fixed him with a hard stare, and there was a glint in his eye that did not come only from the fireplace. Ebon wondered if Mako was thinking the same thing as him.

Just then, there was a soft knock at the door. "Enter," said Halab, and a courier strode in, wearing the white and gold of the High King. She dropped her missive into Halab's hand and withdrew without a word. Halab glanced at the paper before looking up and giving them all a smile.

"We have been summoned to the palace," she said. "They have offered us an audience faster than I thought."

She stood, and the rest of them hastened to join her. Hesta and Matami went to Halab's side. But before she left, Halab went first to Albi and then to Ebon, giving each child a long embrace.

"You will likely be gone before we return," she told Ebon. "You must visit us again while we are still here. And if you have friends at the Academy, you must bring them, for we would all like to meet them."

"Farewell, my son," said Hesta. "It has gladdened my heart to see you again."

"And you, Mother." Ebon hugged her tight, inhaling her sweet perfume. He had not known how badly he missed it. "I will see you again soon."

They left. The moment the door shut behind them, Albi whirled to Ebon and seized his hands.

"Finally!" she said, laughing. "I thought they would *never* leave. Come now, Ebon. I want to hear everything—and I want to tell you everything I have been up to, as well. But first, you must put on some *proper* clothes."

Ebon looked down at himself, feigning insult, though he could not hide his smile. "Proper clothes? What is wrong with my Academy robes?"

"Do not pretend to be simple," she said, pushing his shoulders. "Go! Fetch yourself something more fitting to your station, and then let us walk in the garden. It is beautiful, more so with the snow, and not so smoky as it is inside."

"As you wish, my lady." Ebon bowed low, which earned him another slap on the arm, and then he left to find himself some new clothes.

THIRTEEN

Ebon climbed to the second floor and made for his room, but when he reached the door he paused. Its fresh-cut planks and shining varnish spoke of new carpentry. He looked across the hall. The opposite door was not so new, but it bore a small scorch mark near the stone floor.

So. The attackers had gone through the Drayden manor. And Shay's "fortunate" decision to empty the place of their possessions had likely saved the family much coin. The armies would have rushed through the rooms and found nothing to steal. Likely they had destroyed the door to Ebon's room out of spite, or mayhap frustration.

Then he opened the door and found that it did not lead to his room at all. Instead he found a sitting room. There was a bookshelf at one end, some tapestries on the other walls, and a single armchair beside the fireplace. His bed was gone, as were his bureaus and chests. The one mark he had left upon this house, scrubbed away like a recalcitrant stain.

Ebon swallowed past a suddenly dry throat and stepped back, closing the door softly. Quick footsteps down the hallway drew his attention. It was Liya, the servant who had spilled his wine at dinner. She looked up and saw him just as he saw her. Her steps faltered.

"Liya," he said, forcing his voice to be calm. "Do I still have any clothes here? Have they been put somewhere else?"

She looked back over her shoulder, shifting on her feet as though she might run. But then he saw her take a deep breath, composing herself by the time it escaped her lips. "Yes, milord," she said timidly. "This way, please."

He followed her down the hall and around the corner. There was another wooden door, just like the one that had once led to his room. She opened it to reveal a storeroom. Crates and barrels lined the walls, stacked in neat and orderly rows. Atop one stack was a chest with a lock, but he could see from the way the lid was ajar that it had not been secured.

"If milord will help . . .?" Liya took one end of the chest, and Ebon hastened to take the other, and together they brought it down to the floor. Ebon swung it open to find a familiar sight—the fine golden silks he had grown up wearing.

"Just what I wanted. Thank you, Liya."

"Of course, milord." But Liya would not meet his eyes, and it seemed she wanted to leave the room but was unsure how he might react.

"Liya," he said, frowning. "What is it?"

Her eyes widened, and she clutched at her dress with her hands. "Nothing, milord."

"You are afraid. Of what, I do not know, but of something, certainly."

She shook her head quickly, too quickly to make her words ring true. "I am not, milord. I swear it."

Ebon found himself growing exasperated. "Tell me the truth, at once. I may not rule this household, but I am nephew to the one who does. Out with it, or Halab will know the reason you withheld yourself."

Her olive skin went pale. "No, milord! Please, please not that. It is . . . it is only that . . . we are all grateful to see you alive, young master. And you must understand; we were ordered to leave the Seat. We never meant to leave you behind."

Ebon balked. The thought was so strange that for a moment he could not react. When he did, it was to laugh. "Liya, of course I know that. I never thought you meant to abandon me."

He stepped forwards, reaching out a comforting hand for her arm. That was a mistake. She shrieked and drew back. She hesitated, but then fear got the better part of decorum, and she fled through the door back into the hallway.

Staring at his hand, Ebon felt realization crash upon him like a wave from the Great Bay. His magic. She feared his magic, as though with a simple touch he might strike her dead. The thought was so simple-minded and foolish that he wanted to laugh. But the fear in her eyes had been real enough.

Was that what the servants of the Drayden household thought? That he had become some dark wizard of evil, and would return to them like some lesser Wizard King? A tyrant whose commands were to be obeyed without question?

Why should they think otherwise? You are your father's son, after all.

He forced such dark thoughts away. Darkness take her. He was scarcely even a member of this house any longer, and its servants could think of him whatever they wished.

The golden silks felt glorious, and Ebon worried that he might smudge them with his ink-stained fingers. But he had no time to bathe, so he closed the door and changed anyway. When he was done, he looked down on himself in wonder. Once, garments such as these had been part and parcel of his everyday existence. Now they seemed like the height of unnecessary opulence. His Academy robes were of cloth so rough it was almost burlap. But rather than feeling more comfortable, this outfit felt too smooth, like a slithering serpent sliding along all his skin.

He shook off the sensation and made his way downstairs. The back door stood open, letting the cold air flood through the bottom floor. Ebon closed it behind himself as he stepped into the gardens. There was Albi, waiting for him with her coat pulled tight about her and a fur hood covering her head. But there, too, was Mako, standing aloof a pace or two from the girl, arms folded and bright teeth bared in a grin.

Albi turned. "Ebon!" she said, relief plain in her tone. "How wonderful you look. Much better than those drab black rags. Come."

She took his arm and very nearly dragged him away through the gardens. Ebon got only a glance behind them at Mako. The bodyguard's grin widened, and he gave Ebon a mocking wave with two fingers before retreating into the manor.

"Thank goodness," said Albi in a hushed tone. "That man has always terrified me."

"Mako?" said Ebon, raising his eyebrows. "He used to make me uneasy, I will admit. But terrifying? I think you exaggerate."

He felt her shudder where their elbows were locked. "I mean it. He seems to view everyone as a meal about to be devoured. If I could do any more to avoid him without being rude, I would."

Ebon thought of the room upstairs, the terror in Liya's eyes when she looked at him. His mouth twisted. "Mayhap you do not give him enough credit."

She snorted, but said nothing more. Ebon turned his gaze away from her out to the garden. The manor had been built upon a sizable plot of land, as far as property went upon the Seat, though compared to the Academy it seemed a cramped patch of dirt. Many of the plants were dead to winter's cold, but plenty of evergreen trees had been put about, and their verdant branches showed stark against their light dusting of snow. The plants were strange to him, and familiarity had not lessened their oddity. What scrubs grew in Idris were thin, small, and hardy. They bore the night's cold as well as the day's heat, but that was because they were small and self-contained. These pines and the live oak at the garden's center were like grand old men who refused to cow before winter's stormy assault, and Ebon felt like a child in their shadow.

Albi gripped his arm tighter. "I have missed you so much, dear brother." Then she drew back her other hand and struck him in the chest as hard as she could.

"Ow!" he cried, rubbing at the spot. "You have a strange way of showing it."

"How could you fail to write me?" she said, pouting. "I did not receive so much as a hasty scribble until the Seat was attacked, and we all feared you might be dead."

323

"I doubt you *all* feared it," said Ebon, thinking of his father. But her scowl deepened, and he spoke hastily to avoid another smack. "I am sorry. Of course I should have written you. But even before the island was attacked, my days were much occupied with fear and danger."

That earned him a snort. "You make it sound *quite* dramatic."

"In truth, it was," said Ebon. "Indeed, I almost died more than once."

He spoke in earnest, but Albi only laughed. "Oh, Ebon. Do not think to wheedle out of this with outlandish tales. Only promise to write me more often in the future, and we may leave it at that."

A part of him was irked, for he had thought he might confide in her, at least, the way he did with Kalem and Theren. But then again, there were things that had happened in the months before the attack that he wished to tell no other. So he simply said, "I promise."

"Good. Now, tell me of your magic! After so long, I can only imagine how pleased you must be to put it to use. I thought I would simply *die* of delight to see you cast a spell."

He smiled. "It is a greater pleasure than I can say. I am only a simple beginner yet. But still . . . the power . . . sometimes I cannot believe it."

"Show me again," she said, eyes dancing.

Ebon looked about them on the ground and found a small branch, about as long and thick as his index finger. He stooped to retrieve it, and then concentrated. His eyes brightened, and stone rippled along the branch until it was all grey. Releasing the hold on his magic, Ebon placed the branch in her trembling hand.

Albi did not speak for a long moment. Her mouth parted in a silent circle. Then she gripped the branch in both hands and tried to break it. She strained, but nothing happened.

"It is stone through!" she whispered, as though someone might be lurking around the corner to eavesdrop. "Did you turn it all the way? And the cup?"

"Every part of them both," said Ebon, not modest enough to hide his smile.

Albi clapped her hands once and laughed. She tucked the branch into a pocket in her cloak. "I will hold this always as a keepsake. And to think you learned this after only a few short months. As I said before, I have proven to be a quick study as well—and in more things than book learning." Her eyes danced, and she leaned in closer to speak in a false whisper. "I have had a romance, you know."

Ebon nearly froze, a flush creeping up from his collar and into his cheeks. "A . . . you what?"

"Oh yes, a very passionate one," she said, giggling as her blush matched his own. "Such a charming, handsome boy. We stole many kisses here and there, in dark corners while I was visiting his family with Mother. But sadly, he was royalty. After a time I felt I had to ignore him and rebuff further advances, because after all, his family would never allow us to be wed. Still. If I seem a bit womanlier to you, that is no doubt why."

She gave a self-satisfied little smile and smoothed the front of her dress, though Ebon saw no wrinkles. *Womanlier?* he thought. True, Albi had grown what seemed an incredible amount for the few short months since they had seen each other, and she carried herself with a more mature air than before. But Ebon thought of his own dalliances with Adara, and the crimson deepened in his cheeks.

"Why, Ebon!" she laughed, mistaking his look. "I do believe I have embarrassed you."

Should he tell her? Of course not. Albi might keep some of his secrets, but only when she thought they were important. She would see nothing wrong in his visits to Adara, and so she might make mention of them to Shay. That could be a disaster.

He forced a tight smile and said, "I did not know you had such a rebellious streak within you, dear sister."

Another flashing smile answered him. "I know. I feel so *scandalous.* And we had to keep ourselves so carefully hidden, for it was the first time I was permitted to join Mother and Father on a caravan excursion. First we traveled north to the capital, and then west to explore the new route we wish to . . ."

On she went, telling him about the trip, her first with their parents where she actually had a role to play. The story was all too familiar, for he had gone on a few such excursions himself. Now that he was no longer there to attend them and learn the family's trade, he supposed it was only natural that they would bring Albi along in his stead.

With a shock he realized that that life was slipping away from him, and he did not want it to. Mayhap he had never wanted to follow in his father's footsteps, transporting spices across Underrealm to fill the family's coffers. But long years had let him grow somewhat used to the idea, and now he realized it might never be. What would he do when he graduated from the Academy? He had asked Theren that question often enough, for she was on the cusp of having to make that decision. But he had rarely thought of the answer for himself.

And as his thoughts ran further, he realized suddenly that the answer did not concern Albi at all. She did not care if he finished his training and returned to the family's business, or went off into some other kingdom entirely—so long as he wrote her, most likely, and visited on occasion. He could hear it in the way she spoke of her exploits with the caravan, and as he thought back, in the way she had turned every conversation away from him and to herself instead.

Had she always been so vain? And, a far more perplexing thought: had Ebon been the same when he was in her position?

He thought of Liya's face in the storeroom earlier, and how it had filled him with annoyance rather than compassion. His mood darkened further.

"—and do not hate me for saying so, but Father's mood has been much gentler since you entered the Academy, and I think especially so since now I will be the head of the family."

Albi's words snapped his attention back to the present. He stared at her for a moment, letting the words play back in his mind so that he could understand them. And yet still they held no meaning. Albi seemed to recognize that she had said too much, for she looked at him wide-eyed, and her mouth worked as she fought for some explanation.

"What do you mean?" But he knew the answer even as he asked.

"I mean only . . . Ebon, please, do not be angry with me."

The pain in her eyes, the sorrow for him, sealed the knowledge in his mind. Shay did not only mean to remove Ebon from the family's business dealings. Ebon's inheritance, his role as the future head of the family, was now forgotten, like a nightmare fading in daylight.

Had Father made the decision the moment Ebon joined the Academy, out of spite for losing his son to the fate he had always hated? Or had he concocted the plan for other reasons? Had he removed Ebon from his inheritance in the same breath he had ordered the Draydens' possessions removed from their manor upon the Seat?

Did Shay remain home in Idris because business held him? Or mayhap because he was ashamed to face the son he had left on the Seat to die?

From nowhere, a laugh bubbled up in Ebon's breast. It erupted before he could stop it, and he was glad to learn that it was hearty and cynical, rather than desperate.

"Ebon?" said Albi, still looking at him fearfully. "What is it?"

"Nothing," said Ebon. For truly, that was what he faced. His father's motivations did not matter, because Ebon never needed deal with him again. He was cast out from the family, from its business, and from his role as its future patriarch. Halab would always give him her favor, and that was more than enough.

How often had he wished, as a boy, that he did not bear the name Drayden? In effect, that was what he faced now.

"Nothing," he said again. "It is only that I made a wish when first I came to the Seat, and that wish has come true. Mayhap I should have been more careful in making it. But then again, mayhap this is all for the best."

She still looked at him askance, clearly unsure, and likely now worried that his thoughts were addled. He gave her the most reassuring smile he could muster, and once more took her arm. "Come," he said, pulling her along. "Tell me more of your trip. I want to hear everything."

FOURTEEN

They walked in the garden and spoke until Albi said she was too cold, and then they sat together and spoke near a hearth inside the manor. And as before, Albi spoke mostly of herself, and all that she had done since last she saw Ebon, and some things she had done before, and whenever Ebon spoke of himself she barely nodded before relating it to another of her stories. Soon he stopped trying, and simply listened. Despite the dark cloud that had been cast over his thoughts, it *was* good to hear what Albi had been up to in his absence.

At last Albi yawned and said she might nap, for they had traveled long to get here and had only arrived the night before. The afternoon was now winding on, and the faint glow of the sun through the clouds was edging towards the western horizon.

They stood together, and Ebon gave her one last hug. "I cannot tell you how glad my heart has been to see you again, dearest Albi."

"And you, Ebon." She gave him a gentle slap on the arm, not nearly so hard as before. "But if you ever forget to write me again, I will return to the Seat with an army of sellswords."

"I will remember."

She made for her bedchamber, and Ebon for the storeroom where his Academy robes waited. He found them neatly folded and stacked. Mayhap Liya had done it, in some sort of apology for her earlier conduct. Or mayhap it had been another passing servant. It did not much matter, he supposed.

His Academy robes felt much more comfortable, and he sighed with relief once changed. He had no wish to stay for another encounter with the servants, so he went downstairs and to the front door—but there he found Mako waiting, leaning on the wall and picking at his nails with his long, silver knife.

"Greetings, young lord," said Mako, with a curious amount of courtesy. "Might I walk you back to the Academy—at least for part of the way?"

"Certainly," said Ebon, and gestured for Mako to join him. He said it lightly enough, but in truth his mind was already racing. Mako never spoke privately for idle purpose.

The streets were soft and muted about them, and there were no passersby. But still Mako waited until they were a long way removed from the Drayden manor before he spoke his mind. He looked both ways cautiously and stepped closer so that Ebon could hear his growling murmur. "Did you notice that your uncle did not seem pleased to see you?"

"I did. But if he is my father's brother, I count it as no great surprise."

"Yet his scorn for you was not the only strange thing. Did you note his response when you asked questions about the manor being redecorated?"

"I did, and I thought it odd," said Ebon carefully. "It does not seem my uncle has any great affection for me. What did you make of his mood?"

Mako did not answer directly, but chuckled and said, "His ire should strike you as nothing new, when your father has hated you all your life."

Despite himself, Ebon felt his ears burning. His jaw spasmed, but he forced himself to speak anyway. "Do you bring up his odd behavior for a reason, or not? You already told me that our family had nothing to do with the attack upon the Seat."

Mako seized Ebon's throat in an iron grip and dragged him from the street into an alleyway. There he shoved him against the stone wall of a building, bringing his own face to within an inch of Ebon's. His breath smelled of something rancid, though it was hidden by mint.

"Still your witless tongue in the streets, you goldshitting little fool."

Ebon glared over Mako's hand. But he knew the bodyguard was right, and that he had been foolhardy to speak so openly. Anger had provoked him. And now it made him drag Mako's hand away so that he could whisper, "Mayhap if you ceased playing games and said what you meant to say in the first place, I would not be so tempted to speak out of turn."

Mako did not glare at him, but neither did he wear his usual self-effacing smirk. His eyes were pits of ice, and that ice penetrated Ebon's soul, such that fear seeped in at the frayed edges of his anger. Though he could not see it, he was well aware of Mako's hand hovering at the hilt of his long, cruel dagger. The white of his scars fairly glowed against his dark olive skin.

But when Mako spoke, it bore none of the frigid tone that his look promised. "I did not tell you the family was blameless in the attack on the Seat. I told you I did not *learn* of the attack from a Drayden."

His hand left Ebon's throat, and Ebon slumped back against the wall. Though he hated to look weak, he reached up and rubbed his neck ruefully, for he thought a bruise might form. "I do not understand the difference you mean to imply."

"Mayhap Matami indeed had something to do with the attack, and your father as well. Mayhap they kept the truth from me. I assumed they would not—after all, they could hardly ask for a better agent to help with such a plan. But then, long has your father been uncomfortable with the favor I have shown you; and that favor comes because Halab does the same, which he also resents."

Ebon released a sigh, and it crystallized to mist in the frigid air. "You mean they may not have told you because they feared you would warn me."

Mako nodded. "Just as I did, the moment I learned."

A long silence followed. Ebon stared at his shoes and tried to wrestle the feelings battling in his breast. This day was one for hard truths, and each had struck him like a blow: first, that his father would not even come and see him on the Seat, so ashamed was he of Ebon's enrollment in the Academy; second, that he had been robbed of his inheritance, which would now pass to Albi; and finally, now, the possibility that his death had been planned by his father all along, mere collateral damage in the wake of some grand scheme that spanned all of Underrealm.

But one thing troubled him. Shay was not the master of the family Drayden. "Halab directs our family, not my father. She would never have had anything to do with the vile treason of Dulmun."

"Certainly not," said Mako. "That is plain, if for no other reason than that you were left here on the Seat. Halab has always loved you better than Shay has."

"And because it would be the very highest of crimes against the High King."

Mako raised one eyebrow and shrugged. "As you say. But if what we have begun to guess at is correct, I believe we are looking at a plot by Shay, and possibly Matami, operating without the knowledge of Halab."

Ebon quailed at the thought of him and his friends slipping through the Academy grounds at night, and what they had planned for this Sunday. "So Lilith is innocent?"

"Impossible." Mako shook his head and turned to pace back and forth. But he stopped himself almost immediately, and went to the mouth of the alley to lean against the brick wall opposite Ebon. "Yes, impossible. Or so I think. Shay and Matami could never concoct such a scheme on their own. They would need help within the Academy. They might have thought to use Cyrus, but he was always an untrustworthy sort."

That made Ebon's heart skip a beat. He licked his lips. "Was? You speak as though you are certain he is dead."

Slowly, Mako's eyes turned to him, and once more they were pits of ice. "Are you not certain yourself?"

Ebon was glad he had put his hands in his pockets, for they were shaking like an old man's. "He might have fled the Seat. That is what some say."

"Some say foolish things." Mako spat, the saliva sinking into a wet hole in the snow. "In any case, Shay and Matami would not have brought him into their conspiracy, for he would certainly have told Halab. They must have seduced Lilith instead—or, mayhap, they are working with higher contacts in Yerrin, and Lilith is in the employ of those contacts."

He pushed off from the brick wall. Again he paced, now holding a clenched fist to his chin, tugging on it as though he pulled an invisible beard. "Yes. Yes, that would make sense. They think to make a play for greater power. By this temporary alliance with Yerrin, they think to increase their own standing."

Ebon was still shaking from the dark truths Mako had hinted at before. Could the bodyguard possibly know what had transpired between Ebon and Cyrus when the Seat was attacked? It seemed impossible. But in any case, the best thing was to draw the man's mind elsewhere. "Why? For what ultimate end? We have never had love for Yerrin."

Mako met his gaze. "To take Halab's place at the head of the Drayden family. In exchange for Yerrin's help to get there, Shay and Matami will promise more favorable relations with Yerrin once in power."

"But . . ." Ebon shook his head, unwilling to believe it. "But what would happen to Halab?"

The bodyguard's nose flared slightly. "Nothing that I would allow, I promise you that."

Still Ebon did not want to think it could be true. "But this would not help the family. Already we are stronger than Yerrin. It would weaken us, and strengthen them."

"Yes, it would weaken Drayden—but it would strengthen Shay and Matami in the process," said Mako. "They would sacrifice the family's power to enhance their own. It is the opposite of what Halab would do. And that is why they think she must be removed."

His voice rang with finality. Ebon squared his shoulders. "You are certain of this, then?"

"Rarely am I certain of anything, nor should you be. Yet it seems the likeliest thing."

"We must catch them."

"I shall work on that. You must focus on Lilith." Mako put a firm hand on Ebon's shoulder. "Catch her in the act, Ebon. Have her dragged before the King's justice and put to the question. She will expose those in her family giving the orders. They in turn will expose Shay and Matami, if indeed they are involved in this plot."

"Then I will expose her," said Ebon.

"Good." And just like that, as though he were done casting a spell, the ice faded from Mako's face, and his sardonic smile flew in to replace it. "I think you and I shall form a fine team, little goldshitter."

Ebon smiled grimly. "I think I prefer goldbag."

"I knew you would say so. Until we meet again, then. Good fortune this Sunday."

He stepped around the alley's corner, and when Ebon stepped around to follow him, Mako was gone. But then Ebon heard a scrape from up above, and he looked up in time to see a leather boot vanish over the edge of the tile roof.

At last I have caught him in the act. Not a spell after all.

It was only then that he realized Mako had wished him good fortune on Sunday, though he had never mentioned the plan to break into the vaults. Ebon's gaze jerked back towards the sky, where the bodyguard's boot had vanished.

FIFTEEN

EBON RETURNED TO THE ACADEMY JUST BEFORE THE END OF THE AF-
ternoon's study. Quickly he made his way to the third-floor alcove,
where Kalem and Theren listened with rapt attention to his account of
the afternoon's doings—including his conversation with Mako.

"You told him about our plan?" said Kalem, voice edging towards panic.

"I did not," said Ebon. "He has . . . ways of learning such things. I
long ago gave up trying to understand it."

"I think you should try again," Kalem shrilled. He must have realized how loud he sounded, for he looked anxiously over his shoulder
before going on. "One whisper of our plot in the wrong ear, and we
could all be thrown out of the Academy for good."

"He means us no ill will," said Ebon.

"Not that you know of."

"I know it."

Theren slapped her hand against the table. "Enough of this. There
is nothing we can do about it now. But I have had an idea—one I think
may be more important, and a relief to you besides, Ebon."

He frowned. "What do you mean?"

"You think Shay and Matami may have had something to do with Lilith's scheming because they stand before your naked eyes," she said, speaking quickly in her excitement. "Yet I have another idea. One that would make more sense, if you would rather not believe your own father has turned kinslayer. What if the Drayden helping Lilith has been someone else entirely?"

Ebon and Kalem exchanged an uncertain glance. "Well, spit it out," said Ebon. "Though I do not see how you could know my family better than Mako and I."

Her grin widened. "You do not see it, do you? And that is why it is the perfect deception. It is not your father, or your uncle. It is Cyrus."

Kalem's eyes widened in recognition. But Ebon felt a void open in the pit of his stomach, a void that sucked in his fears and anxieties and anger and spit them back up as raw, red shame burning its way to his heart.

What could he say? How could he refute her idea, which he knew for a fact to be wrong, without confessing his crime? Ebon had had his doubts when Adara insisted that he must keep Cyrus' death a secret. But whether or not he could have told them before, he certainly could not do so now.

"I . . . I find that hard to believe."

"That is what makes it so perfect," said Theren, smiling in triumph. "We know he hated you. And we know that, at the end, he blamed your family for cutting him out of their plots and schemes. He fled the Academy in terror, and he knew that if he returned, he would be tried and found guilty under the King's law, then to die a slow death under the knives of Mystics. So instead, he thinks to amass power for himself by collecting artifacts from the vaults of the Academy. He knows them better than any. And he might have enlisted the help of the family Yerrin, for certainly he would not have gone to his kin, who he thinks betrayed him."

"This does make sense, Ebon," said Kalem. "I might never have thought of it, but Theren is right—that is what makes it such a devious scheme."

"He was scum, Ebon." Theren's cheeks spasmed as she bit them, her lip curling in a snarl. "You know that better than most."

At last Ebon saw why Theren had seized upon this idea and why she believed it so strongly. Cyrus had attacked Ebon upon the Academy's grounds, and she had watched, afraid to intervene. Still she blamed herself for the beating Ebon had taken, and now she thought she saw a chance, however small, at redemption.

"Tell me," she said. "I have given you several reasons it could be true. Tell me one piece of proof against it."

Ebon raised his hands, gesturing helplessly as he said the only thing he could. "I cannot. But even if it is true, still we must catch Lilith."

"You are right," said Theren, her savage grin widening. "Sunday night cannot come fast enough."

The next few days passed far too slowly, like leaves clinging stubborn to a tree, and with Ebon wishing all the while for Sunday night to be over and done with. Certainly sneaking into the vaults would terrify him, but it could not be worse than the waiting.

Sunday after dinner, Ebon met Kalem in the halls near the library. They stood awkwardly with their arms folded, leaning against walls and trying not to look suspicious. Finally Kalem threw his hands up in the air.

"Where is she? I am beginning to have doubts about this whole thing."

"Only now?" said Ebon. "I thought you doubted it from the first."

Kalem only glowered, and when he spoke it was not to answer. "What if we cannot escape as she planned? She says enchantments keep us from tunneling in, not out. How would she know? She is no transmuter."

"You mean alchemist."

"I mean alchem—" Kalem stopped short, his eyes narrowing.

Just then they heard the rumbling of iron wheels, and soon Theren appeared from around the corner, pushing a mammoth wooden cart that looked like it might fall over. It was swathed with many blankets.

"There you two are," she said. "Well, here it is. Our manner of entering the vaults."

"Would you like to say it louder?" said Kalem, looking about nervously.

"Oh, calm yourself. And climb aboard." Peeling back a few of the blankets, Theren revealed a lower shelf of the cart, built just above the wheels so that, with the blankets laid down, no one could tell it was there at all.

"You mean to sneak us in on this thing?" said Ebon. "I feel as though I have taken splinters just from looking at it."

"I am sorry—did you expect a cushion?" said Theren. "Sit, little goldbag, and be grateful."

Ebon was not grateful, but he sat, and Kalem climbed in beside him. Theren threw the blanket back down so that they were hidden. Ebon and Kalem looked at each other nervously as the cart began to roll on.

They stopped after a few moments, and there came the creaking of a large door. There were two, Theren had told them, before they reached the administration room. Within it was a closet in which this cart and many others were kept, where she would stow them until she was ready to move on. At the creak of the second door, Ebon held his breath; now they were no longer alone.

"Good eve, Egil," said Theren brightly.

"Hello, my friend," came an ancient and creaking voice. "Stay awhile, and listen. I have found an account of something most interesting."

"I am afraid I cannot," said Theren. "I have yet to complete my entries for the day. Another time, mayhap."

"Ah. Very well, then. Another time."

There came the sound of another, much smaller door, and the cart rolled forwards again. The second door shut, and they found themselves in utter darkness.

"This must be the closet," whispered Kalem.

"I think so." Ebon risked peeling back one of the blankets and peeking out. Slowly his eyes adjusted to the scant light from under the door. They were indeed in a closet, filled with more carts like the one upon which they sat. He slid out and onto the floor as silent as a mouse, and Kalem quickly followed. Together they stole over to the door, where candlelight illuminated them from below and cast Kalem's eyes in shadow.

There was nothing to hear, other than the thin scribbling of quills on parchment from Theren and Egil, and Egil's persistent cough. But Ebon knew there was another person in the room—a palace guard standing at the vault's main door. He wondered suddenly if they should stay in the cart. What if the guard thought to investigate the closet?

He was just about to reach for Kalem's shoulder and say as much, but then in the room beyond, Egil dissolved into a fit of hacking coughs. They went on and on, until Ebon could fairly hear the phlegm splashing out of the old man and onto the table. He cringed.

"Egil, are you all right?" Ebon heard swift footsteps as Theren went to his side. "Quick, run and get him some water."

"You get it," came the voice of the guard.

"I cannot—I am in the middle of my forms, and if I stop now I shall have to start over. Run to the kitchens. It will not take you a moment."

There was silence as the guard hesitated. But then they heard hasty footsteps as she left, and then a few sharp slaps as Theren pounded Egil on the back. Soon the coughing died away, and with effort he spoke in a rasp.

"I am all right. I am all right. Thank you, Theren. Drat these fits. They are coming more and more often. Not long now."

"Do not be so morbid, old man."

He chuckled. "You are a good child, Theren. Thank you. You should get back to your forms."

"They can wait a moment. And besides, *you* should be going to bed. It is late, after all."

"Mayhap you are right. But I have not finished this page—"

"The page can wait. You need your rest. Come on, off you go."

Another croaking chuckle. "Very well. You will make a fine mother one day, if you wish it—or you can simply continue to baby me."

"As long as you will let me. Good night."

"Good night."

Slow, shuffling footsteps receded. Then Theren ran to the closet and threw it open.

"We must hurry. That took far longer than I thought, and we have little time."

Ebon and Kalem leapt up and followed her to a wide, iron door on their left. Theren threw the latch and flung it open, ushering them inside before closing it once more. Immediately she set off at a run down the hall, torches flickering to either side at the wind of her passing.

They had no time to gather their bearings, but as they ran, Ebon noted their surroundings: thick wooden doors in rows to either side, each set in a stone arch with a pointed peak. Torches lit the place well, but left every corner flickering in shadow. The ceiling was oppressively low compared to the Academy's usual spaciousness, and he found himself ducking with every other step. And something else was odd. His skin had begun to crawl from the moment he set foot in the vaults, hair rising on the back of his neck as though some danger pursued him.

"This place gives me an ill feeling," he said as they ran.

"It is the enchantments," said Theren. "They are worked into every door, but only wizards can sense them. They are the artifacts' greatest protection."

"Not very good protection if we strode in so boldly," Kalem pointed out.

"They are for the rooms, not the halls themselves," said Theren. "The rooms are where the darkest secrets are kept."

They turned a corner, and then another. The itching under Ebon's skin increased until he wished to stop and claw at himself. Then Theren skidded to a stop, so quickly that Kalem and Ebon slammed into her from behind. There before them was a door—or rather, a frame, for the door was gone.

"Here it is," said Theren. "This is the room from which the artifact was taken."

"Well then, search for Lilith's spell-sight," said Kalem.

"I will," said Theren, glaring at him. "You go to the corner and keep a lookout."

Kalem ran off, grumbling. Ebon lingered as Theren fell to one knee and ran her hands along the edges of the doorframe, eyes glowing.

Curious, he leaned over to look past her and into the room. It was a plain space, no more than four paces to a side, made of the same black granite as the rest of the Academy. But the floor was polished white marble, and in the center of the room sat a table of silver that stood on a single leg. The table lay bare. Looking still closer, he could see all sorts of designs traced into it. They looked familiar, but he could not place them—until he remembered the same sort of designs worked into the Academy's front door.

Theren looked up for a moment, following his gaze. "They are sigils of enchantment," she said. She turned back to the door, but kept speaking. The soft glow of her eyes lit the iron framing under her fingers. "Meant to protect Kekhit's amulet from thieves, but in some cases they protect anyone present from the power of the artifact."

"I should like to learn enchantment, if I can," said Ebon.

"I wish you good fortune," said Theren. "There are few who teach it. Fewer still among alchemists." Then her hands fell, and the glow faded from her eyes as she hung her head. "Damn it. Darkness damn it all."

"What?" said Ebon, stepping forwards quickly. "Is it her?"

"No. I was certain it would be, but it is not." Theren looked up in regret. "I am sorry."

Ebon muttered a curse. "And you do not recognize it as anyone else?"

"No one that I know of. It is partially obscured, though done in haste. I only know that it is not Lilith, and that I know for certain."

Just then, Kalem came running down the hall towards them. "Someone is coming! We must flee!"

"Who is it?" said Ebon.

Theren gripped them both by the arm. "Never mind that—*run!*"

She took her own advice, and they were quick to follow. Turn after turn she led them down, until Ebon was lost. Every hallway looked the same. Once he was sure they passed the same open door where they had started, but that was impossible. At last they found a place with a sort of alcove, in which rested a small iron bench.

"Here," she said. "Under the bench. It is the most likely place to be overlooked. And they will no doubt have lost us by now."

Kalem fell to his knees, and the hallway flashed white with the glow in his eyes. Stone melted away beneath his fingertips. Ebon knelt beside him and did his best to help. "Who was it?" he said through panting breaths.

"I could not see," said Kalem. "As soon as I heard their footsteps, I ran as quickly as I could."

SNAP!

The air crackled with power. The stone, which only a moment before had been flowing like water, snapped back into place. In an instant, the wall was just as it had always been. Ebon and Kalem looked at each other in confusion—but then Ebon felt Theren's hand tugging him up by the shoulder, and he rose to stand beside her. Before them stood Xain, eyes dark with fury, and Jia, with a white glow fading from her eyes.

SIXTEEN

Jia marched them through the halls towards the dean's office, one hand on Theren's shoulder and the other on Ebon's. Kalem followed meekly to the side like a beaten dog. Xain was just beside them, his footsteps silent.

When they reached the door, Jia released Ebon's shoulder to open it. Ebon began to step in, but she jerked him back. Xain hesitated half a moment before entering first, as though he had not expected such deference. He swept over to his desk and sat in the wide, plush chair. Jia nudged them forwards before taking her place at Xain's side. Ebon approached the desk meekly, eyes on his feet, and Kalem beside him; but Theren carelessly threw herself in one of the chairs.

"Stand, Theren," snapped Jia. "This is not some casual visit."

Theren obeyed without question, her expression calm. Standing beside Ebon, hands clasped behind her back, she spoke first. "You should let the two of them go. All of this was my idea."

Jia scoffed. "Even if that were true—and I have my doubts—they

342

would be guilty for following you. We do not teach our pupils to blindly follow every mad suggestion that comes their way."

"I forced them to do it," said Theren. "I said I would spread their darkest secrets through the school if they did not do as I asked." Ebon risked a glance in her direction, but she kept her eyes on Jia.

"Oh?" Jia arched an eyebrow. "And what dark secrets are those?"

Theren spread her hands. "They did as I asked."

Xain had stayed silent and moved not a muscle. His hands gripped the arms of his chair, and Ebon might have thought the dean was not even listening to the exchange—and mayhap that was true, for his eyes never left Ebon's face.

But Theren's casual indifference had struck a nerve in Jia, and she slapped her hand on the desk. "This is not some jest, Theren. You know the vaults are forbidden to students except in performance of their servitude, and you know *why*, better than most who study here. And as an aside, you have utterly disregarded the entire point of your services, and from this point on, you will help clean the privies instead."

Theren did not even blink. "That seems fair, Instructor."

Jia's nostrils flared. "There will be more punishment than that, I can assure you." She turned to Ebon and Kalem. "And the two of you. What were you thinking? Theren has some history of getting into trouble, but both of you are from proud families. I had hoped you might have some positive influence on her, not the other way around."

"I have told you it was my idea," said Theren, speaking before Ebon could reply. "I have learned to read the signs of other wizards. I noticed while filling out my logs that something had been taken from the vaults, and I thought I might be able to discover who."

"Spell-sight," Jia said with a snort. But then her eyes sharpened. "You did not sense anything, did you?"

Ebon thought he saw the corner of Theren's mouth twitch. "No, Instructor."

"And the two of you? What was your role in this foolery?" Theren opened her mouth again, but Jia raised a single finger and silenced her. "I have heard quite enough from you. I have directed my question at Ebon and Kalem."

Kalem looked uncertainly at Ebon. Ebon squared his shoulders.

"Theren said she could use our help after she had searched for the . . . the signs of the other wizard's power, or what have you. We were meant to use our transmutation to leave the vaults."

"So that you would not be detected. How fortunate for us, then, that someone had already warned us you might be trying to sneak inside. Students always seem to think that rumors only fly into their ears and not into ours."

At first Ebon was confused, but then he realized: *Lilith.* In anger at their argument, Theren had said she would prove that Lilith was the thief. Lilith must have guessed at their intent to sneak into the vaults and gone running to Xain or Jia. That explained how they had been found so quickly. Theren's cheeks flushed red, and she ducked her head to hide the fury in her eyes.

Xain moved for the first time, pushing back his chair and then standing to lean over his desk. Still his gaze was fixed on Ebon, who looked at the floor again.

"I do not believe you," said Xain softly. "I think this was a plot by the Drayden boy."

Ebon felt the blood drain from his face.

Theren opened her mouth again, but Xain spoke first, and sharply. "Be silent. I speak not to you, but to him. What say you, Drayden? Do you deny it?"

He could not raise his eyes. He did not know what to say. If he denied it, he condemned Theren. If he admitted it, though it was false, he would take the blame upon himself.

But then Theren scraped her shoe upon the floor and cleared her throat. She had taken the blame from the first. Hopefully she had some sort of plan. So Ebon raised his head and met Xain's eye. "The truth is as Theren told you."

"You lie. It is plain to read in your voice, as well as your eyes. Gather your possessions. You are banished from the Academy."

The world spun beneath his feet. A high whine sounded at the edge of Ebon's hearing. His hand shot out to grip Theren's arm, a desperate attempt to steady himself. But then Jia cleared her throat.

"Dean," she said quietly. "The Academy's rules do not provide for such a punishment. Not unless you believe their intent was to use the vault's artifacts to wreak havoc upon their fellow students—and then you would have to expel all three of them."

At that, Xain hesitated. He straightened slightly, sweeping his gaze to Theren, and then to Kalem. His jaw worked, muscles spasming under the skin. But at last he sat, leaning back in his chair and propping his chin upon his fist. "I have half a mind to," he said, but the fire was gone from his tone.

"Consider yourselves lucky we did not flood the hallways with flame, as is our right," said Jia. "And consider yourselves on notice, as well. You will *all* receive punishments for this, and if you should do anything so idiotic ever again, I shall banish you myself. Do you understand?"

"Yes, Instructor," they mumbled in unison.

"Very well. Come."

They left the room on Jia's heels. Once in the hall, they all turned their steps towards the dormitories—but Jia snapped her fingers and pointed. They paused, but when she did not move, they quickly followed her directions. She took them down the hall around the corner, where she stopped and glowered at them with arms folded.

"What in the darkness below possessed you?" Her voice was now filled with a much greater fury than she had shown in Xain's office. "That was by far the most foolish thing I have seen any student do in all my days here."

Ebon's face burned. Xain's hatred was easy to bear, for he knew it was rooted in a falsehood. But Jia's fury was righteous, and he knew it. "We are sorry, Instructor. It will not happen—"

"Again? It certainly will not. If it does, I promise that expulsion will be the *least* of your worries. How could you do this, Ebon, after we spoke in my office? And you, Theren." She rounded on the girl. "Do not think I am unsympathetic to your situation. But also, do not think I would hesitate to throw you out of this place on your ear, no matter where you must go afterwards."

At last Theren showed her shame, cheeks darkening as she averted her eyes. Ebon stared at her in wonder. So Jia, too, knew the tale of Theren's life outside the Academy, and the home to which she loathed the thought of returning. But he had little time to think on it, for Jia turned to him and Kalem.

"I spoke no falsehood concerning your families. Your lineage has its share of stains, Ebon, but I thought you might wish to cleanse them. This is not how you go about it. And Kalem—you are *royalty*. Did you spare a single thought for how you would shame your king, if I were to send him word of his cousin behaving like a common thief?"

To Ebon's shock, Kalem burst out crying and hid his face in his hands. Jia stopped her tirade at once, and though she tried to keep her stern demeanor, her eyes softened. Tears spilled freely between Kalem's fingers to drip on the stone floor, and he scrubbed at his nose with the back of his sleeve.

"I did!" he sobbed. "I did think of it. But . . . it is only that I cannot stand it anymore. The sights we saw out on the streets. The instructors who were killed, and the students as well. And now Credell, who taught me only a few years ago. I see his face. I see *all* their faces, in my dreams, and sometimes with my waking eyes. I only . . . I only wanted to *do* something. Something to help. What if they come back for us?"

Jia's face transformed to a vision of perfect shock, but no more so than Ebon. He realized his mouth was hanging open, and he closed it with a snap. Then he elbowed Theren so that she did the same. Jia turned to them.

"Is this true? Is that why you embarked upon this mad scheme?"

"Yes," said Theren. "I told you I wanted to see if I could learn who had broken into the vaults. I suppose that was only half the truth. I thought . . . I thought that mayhap it might help defend the Academy. Somehow. It was a foolish thought, I know. If only there were something I could do . . . that *we* could do." She raised her eyes to the sky, blinking hard as though fighting back tears. Ebon bit down on his tongue to keep from laughing, and kept his eyes on the floor to hide the smile.

Kalem's sobs redoubled, and he lurched towards Jia, wrapping his arms around her waist. She started, hands drawing back. But after a moment she lowered one to his hair and patted his shoulder awkwardly with the other.

"Will Dulmun come back, Instructor?" said Kalem.

"They will not," she said softly. "They know that if they should try, the High King has now gathered much strength upon the Seat to repel them. And the instructors will keep you safe, besides. Now stop crying. It is unseemly for a son of royalty."

Kalem nodded and sniffed hard, stepping back and swiping at his nose again. Ebon reached out and draped his arm across the boy's shoulders. He looked plaintively at Jia. "He has been inconsolable since the attack, Instructor. We have tried our best to comfort each other, but we all bear the same scars. We only thought that taking action—*any* action—might do us all some good."

Jia sighed. "I suppose I understand, at least in part. But you must never do anything like this again. If you find your thoughts so occupied, you may always come and talk to me, or whichever Instructor you prefer. We are here to help you, and to protect you. You must let us do both, or we shall indeed be in far greater danger."

Ebon nodded quickly. "Of course, Instructor. I understand. And we will not try anything of the sort again."

"Promise me."

"We promise," said Theren vehemently.

Jia waved her hands quickly. "Then be off with you. It is nearly time for bed."

They turned and made off down the hallway. As soon as they had rounded the corner, they broke into a jog, and then a run once out of earshot. They did not stop until they reached the foot of the stairs leading to the dormitories.

"That was a brilliant performance," said Theren.

Kalem looked at them both. His eyes were still tearstained, but he wore a broad grin. "It was, was it not?"

Ebon shook his head. "I wish you had done it in front of Xain. His judgement is far harsher."

"Did you see the hate in his eyes? He would have shown no pity. Not like I knew Jia would."

Theren snorted. "Remind me never to believe a word that comes out of your mouth, Kalem."

They all burst out laughing.

SEVENTEEN

THE MOMENT EBON ENTERED THE DINING HALL THE NEXT MORNING, he felt many eyes upon him. He stopped in the doorway, looking at the other students in confusion—but the moment he looked at the students watching him, they quickly turned away. Some whispered to their friends behind their hands and turned back when they thought he might no longer be looking.

He moved forwards again, frowning—and then it dawned on him. Word must already have spread of their exploits in the vaults. These were not looks of fear, or scorn—most were curious, and mayhap some even admired what he had done. A grin tugged at the corner of his mouth, which he quickly tried to suppress.

Ebon reached the line of students who awaited their meal. There, just two students ahead of him, was little Astrea. Her frizzed hair stuck out even more than normal, as though she had not taken much care to brush it that morning.

"Astrea," said Ebon. She did not move. He tried again, louder. "Astrea!"

She turned to look at him, and a chill struck his heart. Great bags hung beneath her eyes, which were bloodshot, and her skin was paler than could be explained by long hours of study. It did not seem she knew who he was at first, for she had to blink twice before recognition dawned in her eyes.

"Ebon," she said, trying to smile. She stepped out of line to join him. Her thin arms wrapped him in a hug, but it was a half-hearted thing.

Credell's death must have struck her far harder than he had thought. Guilt coursed through him, for he had not once gone to check on her since they saw the body. She was only a child. He opened his mouth to ask her how she fared, but then thought better of it. Instead he patted her hair and said softly, "I have greatly missed seeing you."

"I have missed you, too. But I will soon graduate into your class."

"Thank the sky," said Ebon, giving an exaggerated sigh. "I need you to teach me. Perrin is a fine woman, but she does not understand the intricacies of my mind as you do."

That earned him a small smile, which warmed his heart to see. "I do not think your mind is very intricate."

Ebon clutched at his chest. "You wound me." She giggled, and his smile broadened. "I hope you have been spending time with your other friends. I know they are not so entertaining as I am, nor as clever, nor handsome. But none of us should spend our days alone, especially now."

It seemed she understood his true meaning, for her eyes clouded. "I have been spending time with my sister," she said softly. "She has been a great comfort to me."

He frowned. Then he remembered the night they had found Credell—the older student, Isra, kneeling beside Astrea and holding her away from the sight of the corpse. "Isra? She is your sister?"

Astrea shrugged. "In a way. We both come from an orphanage in Feldemar. Or we did, until our sponsor found us. I suppose we should say we are part of her household, now."

"I did not know," Ebon said quietly. The thought that Astrea was an orphan, bright-eyed and kind as she was, saddened him greatly. He tried to imagine himself in her place. She must have loved Credell very much, for he was always kind to the other students, and never feared them as he had Ebon. And now he was gone. No wonder Astrea looked so worn. Ebon wondered if he could even keep attending class every day, were their roles reversed.

Astrea looked down at her shoes now, and her chin had begun to tremble as though she might cry. Quickly Ebon put a hand to her shoulder and smiled. "I cannot wait to study with you in Perrin's class. There are three spells to learn before you can pass the second year. One is to change obsidian's color to white. I have never heard of such a thing."

She blinked, banishing tears as he drew her interest once more. "I know," she said, and then leaned in to whisper. "I have even been trying to practice the spell. Let me see if I can . . ."

Her brow furrowed, and she put one of her fingers to the edge of the wooden bowl. For a heartbeat, light flashed into her eyes and then faded. When she withdrew her finger, the spot was a shade lighter.

Ebon gawked. "That is incredible, Astrea. But how can you be so far advanced, and still not perform the passing spell for the first-year class?"

Astrea shrugged with a self-conscious smile. "Some wizards take more easily to one spell than another. But I am almost done with the testing spell, too. I meant it when I said I would join your class soon."

They had reached the table at last. Attendants scooped porridge into their bowls, and they made their way through the dining hall towards their friends. When they reached the center of the room, Astrea gave Ebon a final smile.

"I will see you soon," he promised.

"And I you," she said, wandering off.

Kalem was waiting at their table when Ebon sat down. "Good morn," he said, speaking around cheeks filled with food.

"Good morn," said Ebon. "Did you have as much trouble sleeping as I did?"

"I cannot know, for I was not there. But most likely, yes. I kept starting awake with thoughts that Dean Forredar might change his mind and expel us after all."

"I thought he might abduct us in our sleep, and have us thrown into the Bay," muttered Ebon. That, indeed, had plagued his nightmares. He had seen it, like the day he had fought Cyrus on the cliffs, except that he was Cyrus and Xain was the one on the ground. The dean gripped Ebon's ankles and turned them to stone, and then he was falling, falling into the ocean, where dark waters swirled around him and crawled down his throat.

"But morning has come, and still we reside within these walls," said Kalem. "I, for one, am grateful."

"And I," said Ebon. "But we must decide what to do next."

Kalem fixed him with a glare. "Ebon."

"Come now, Kalem. A thief is still on the loose, and a murderer. And we know Lilith must have been the one to tell the instructors what we were up to. It is another sign of her guilt."

Leaning forwards, Kalem spoke in a harsh whisper. "And what do you mean to do about it? I mean to do exactly what we should have done from the first: *nothing*."

"You were eager enough to pursue Lilith before. What of her guilt? What of the family Yerrin's treason against the High King?"

Kalem shook his head. "I was a fool before, and so were you, for agreeing to Theren's scheme. We are Academy pupils, Ebon, and hardly advanced in our training. We only barely escaped with our skins intact. We have landed ourselves in as much trouble as I have ever been, and I will not do anything to make it worse."

Ebon opened his mouth to answer, but then he heard raised voices a few tables away. He turned and saw Astrea standing beside the table where she had been eating, facing another student her age. Ebon recognized him as a boy named Vali, a weremage, and one of Astrea's friends. But now the boy stared at Astrea with cold eyes while her face contorted with tears. It was her voice Ebon had heard.

"What do you mean?" said Astrea, shaking. "You are not making any sense."

"I am not your friend." Vali's voice was odd, monotonous. "I do not wish to see you."

"We are in the library together every day, you idiot," said Astrea, her voice cracking.

"I am not your friend," Vali said again, and then turned to leave her. Astrea burst into tears and slumped back down to her bench.

Something was wrong. Ebon frowned, trying to place it. He took a step forwards—but before he could go to Astrea and comfort her, the dining hall door burst open.

Theren flew by him in a rush, her face twisted in rage. Ebon and Kalem glanced at each other and then scrambled to follow. Soon they were a half-step behind her. Finally Ebon saw where they were headed: Lilith, sitting with some other seventh-years. Her back was to them, so that she was unaware of Theren approaching from behind. Too late, her cousin Oren looked up and saw them. He tapped Lilith on the shoulder to warn her. But Theren was already there, snatching Lilith by the back of her robe and dragging the girl to her feet.

"You flap-mouthed sow!" she cried, shoving Lilith back so that she nearly fell across the table.

Oren leapt forwards, trying to shove Theren away. She caught one of his wrists and twisted it, kicking his leg as he recoiled in pain. He fell back, his rear striking the bench hard. Lilith's friend Nella stood to the other side, but she seemed reluctant to enter the fray. Ebon realized her gaze was on him. When the Seat had been attacked, she and Ebon had stood together against the Shade soldiers. Now they looked at each other uncertainly, neither willing to leap in on behalf of Lilith and Theren.

But the girls did not need the help. Lilith had found her feet, and she stared daggers into Theren's eyes. Theren's nose was less than a finger's breadth from Lilith's, and she matched the girl's stare with equal hatred.

"You were a fool to go along with the Drayden boy," said Lilith.

"Do not dare to point fingers." Theren shoved her again. Oren shot to his feet, but he seemed reluctant to take another trouncing from Theren. "No one would have known if you had kept your fat lips together. Have you forgotten all the things I might tell them about *you?* One stray whisper—"

"You should be thanking me. Now you have been kept out of his schemes—whatever they might be." Lilith looked past Theren to glare at Ebon. He tried not to shudder. "You have called me an adder, but you ignore the snake in your own pocket."

The students all around were on the edge of their seats, some with their mouths hanging open, as though they could not wait for the argument to burst into a fight, mayhap one of spells. Cautiously Ebon reached out and took Theren's arm.

"Come, Theren. Leave her be, and get some food in you."

"Yes, heed the words of a sniveling Drayden," sneered Lilith. "Only do not be surprised or come running to me when you find his knife between your shoulder blades."

Theren had drawn back a step, and though her fists were shaking at her side, her face was an impassive mask. "You are the one who has shown herself faithless, and not for the first time."

To Ebon's shock, Lilith grimaced in obvious pain. Her eyes glistened, though he could not believe there might be tears in them. "You have tried endlessly to paint me as an agent of evil. It will never work, and that infuriates you. One day you will see how wrong you are. I only hope it will not be too late."

She turned sharply, robes flapping out like a cloak, and resumed her seat. Oren still gave them a sullen look, while Nella breathed an audible sigh. Theren looked as though she might push the matter, but Ebon and Kalem took her arms and turned her gently away. They made their way back to the table and sat, while nearby students discreetly averted their eyes.

"Here," said Ebon, pushing his plate in front of her. "I was finished anyway."

Theren stabbed the gruel with her spoon but did not scoop any to eat. Kalem was staring down at his hands, mouth working as though searching for words to say.

"We might have gotten away with it," said Theren. "Damn her."

"All ended well enough," said Ebon. "It is done."

"So I should forget it?" said Theren. "I will not. She must have had something to do with the theft. Why else would she have warned Xain?"

"To spite you, or mayhap for pure mischief," said Kalem. "You said yourself that you could not sense her power in the vaults."

"Mayhap she learned to hide it." But even Theren did not sound convinced by her own words.

"You spoke of things that you know about her." said Ebon. "Why do the two of you hate each other so? Her loathing of me, I understand. My family and hers have—"

Theren shot to her feet and stalked away from the table, leaving Kalem and Ebon to eat their breakfast alone.

EIGHTEEN

FOR MANY DAYS AFTERWARDS, THEY HAD TO REMAIN ON THEIR BEST behavior. Jia, or mayhap Xain, must have passed word to their instructors. Ebon found that Perrin now watched him closely, and was reluctant to let him leave class for any reason, even to visit the privy. When they met and studied each day in the library, Kalem and Theren told him that their classes were much the same. Under such careful watch, it was impossible to continue searching for the thief who had broken into the vaults.

Since Shay had not come with the rest of his family, Ebon did not fear to see Adara, and so he visited her every other day or so. Upon one such visit he at last arranged for her to meet Kalem and Theren for dinner. They decided to see each other upon the last day of Febris, the eve of Yearsend.

Astrea soon graduated into the second-years' class with Ebon, performing the same graduation ceremony as he had. Ebon was surprised to find her presence a great comfort, for he had not had any luck making friends among his new classmates. Though he was unable to speak with her often, or for very long, she would always smile at him as they passed each other in the classroom—though he could see how tired her smile had become, for she went about her days haggard and careworn, showing a glimmer of life only in his presence or Isra's.

After sneaking into the vaults, Ebon often felt that the eyes of all the faculty were upon him, especially Xain's. But in a way that was a blessing, for it made him focus upon his studies, and under Perrin's tutelage he found a renewed passion for learning that he had not felt since before the Academy. Credell's sniveling had made him doubt he would ever become a true wizard. But now his childhood dreams were rekindled, and they burned twice as bright. Often he would study halfway through the midday meal, poring over a tome until his groaning stomach forced him to leave.

In addition to studying books, he was thrilled to be practicing his spells. Now that he could shift stone, Perrin encouraged him to do it a bit every day. Shortly after the incident in the vaults, Perrin presented a small wooden box and set it on the desk. It was less than a handbreadth wide, and hollow, yet it had been filled with stone in some manner Ebon did not understand. That is, until Perrin placed her fingers upon it, and the stone began to shift and ripple like water. "Practice moving the stone out of the box. That should be easy enough. But then—and this shall be the hard part, at first—put the stone back in."

Ebon soon learned the truth of her words. Shifting stone away from him was simple: he touched it, and it radiated from his fingers like brushing away dust. Yet whenever he tried to put it back into place, the stone rippled away from him and around his skin. He could not try for long without growing frustrated.

"This is often the way of it for transmuters," said Perrin. "When first we learn to shift stone, or anything at all, we can only push it away like an infant batting at a coin held before its face. Eventually they learn to take hold of things and move them where they will."

Ebon glared when she said that, not sure he enjoyed being compared to an infant. Fortunately for him, there was much else to learn.

Before the attack on the Seat, Kalem had taught him to spin mist from the air. Now Perrin let him practice it in the classroom. The first barrier, and the greatest, was learning to spin it more than a few inches from his body. Theren and Kalem had laughed when he first cast the spell, for the mists clung to him and made him look like a man made of smoke. Try as he might, Ebon could not seem to push the mists farther out. When he attempted it, they simply vanished to nothing.

"You are thinking with your skin," Perrin told him. "Your own magic is a conduit. You cannot turn all the air in a room to mist just by touching it—that would require you to be as large as the room. You must learn to see the mists you have created as an extension of *you*. Follow it out from yourself in your mind's eye, and turn the air it touches into still more mist."

Ebon felt his head spinning, but he tried it anyway. Mist clung to his hand, and he focused until he could *see* the mist, hovering in the air, clinging to his skin. Then he tried to feel the air beyond it, but he saw only darkness. He grit his teeth and thought harder. The mist vanished.

"No, *use* the mist. It is not your tool; it is a part of you."

"I am trying," said Ebon.

Perrin sighed and stood. "Practice will help. You remember how much easier your testing spell became after you cast it for the first time. They will all be like that, for a long while at least. And then, one day, your mind grows used to the process, and learning new spells is no longer so taxing."

Ebon crossed his arms on the table and rested his chin upon them. "And when will that happen? After my fortieth year?"

Perrin slammed her meaty hand on the table. Ebon jumped and sat straight on his bench. "None of that," said Perrin. "You will learn nothing by moping. You will learn only through effort. Now try it again."

Day after day Ebon struggled with his mists. Perrin spent more and more time watching him, lips pursed and brow furrowed beneath her massive shag of hair. Each time he became aware of Perrin's gaze, Ebon's concentration began to waver. Soon the thin fog he had managed to wrap around his arm would vanish entirely. Then he would groan with frustration and fight a mighty urge to flip his table over.

"Mayhap it would be good to distract yourself with another lesson," said Perrin one day.

Ebon frowned. "Another one? I have not mastered the mists yet, nor shifting stone. Would it not be better to focus on them rather than take on another spell?"

"Some instructors might say so, but I call them fools. Sometimes it is better to pursue many things at once. With each spell we flex a different part of our mind. Each may teach us something of the other. Yes, if you sit there and try endlessly to spin your mists, you may learn it faster than if you practice other spells in between—yet I think you will learn all of them faster if you practice all of them in turn, and change between them to freshen your mind."

Ebon had never heard of learning this way, but he was willing to try; he thought he might scream if he had to spin mists even one more time. "Very well. What am I to learn?"

"What do you know of defensive magic?"

Ebon's eyes widened. He remembered the day he toured the Academy. Upon the training grounds, he had seen students of all the four branches practicing their craft. And where the transmuters had been practicing . . . "I have seen alchemi—that is, transmuters, turn arrows to dust in mid-flight."

Perrin chuckled. "You are a long way from that, I am afraid. Indeed, that spell is like invisibility—only a handful of transmuters are capable of learning it. But the simplest magical defense is stopping another wizard's spells. That is far easier than halting a physical attack—and far safer to practice, as well. What have you learned of the four branches and their relationship to each other?"

"Not as much as might be hoped, I am sure."

"Each branch has its mirror," said Perrin. "Mentalism to elementalism, transmutation to therianthropy. A wizard may dispel magic of their own branch, or of its mirror."

Ebon shook his head. "What do you mean, dispel? All of this is strange to me."

Perrin smiled. "Spin your mists."

Ebon frowned and reached out a hand. His eyes glowed, and a thin fog sprang to life to wrap around his arm. But then Perrin's eyes glowed in answer, and there was a *snap* on the air. Ebon felt his connection severed, and the mist vanished. He gawked at his arm, now laid bare.

"That is what I mean," said Perrin. "You can stop the spells of another wizard if you learn to sense them being cast."

"I can stop other alchemists from using their magic?"

"And weremages as well." Perrin leaned forwards with a smile, her eyes alight with interest. Ebon noticed that she had said *weremages,* not *therianthropes,* and had not corrected his use of *alchemists.* "Weremagic is our mirror branch, and our spells are intricately tied to theirs."

Ebon did not say it aloud, but he thought of when he had snuck into the vaults. He and Kalem had been burrowing through the stone to escape, when there was a snap, and the stone had reverted back to its true form. When they had turned, they had seen Jia with her eyes glowing. Now he realized that she had dispelled their magic.

"I see," he said, nodding slowly. "That makes sense to me. Alchemy and weremagic are of a kind. They both turn things into something else—a weremage changes their own body, and we change that which we touch. Firemagic and mindmagic are similar in that they both exert power outside of the wizard."

Perrin grimaced. "That is too simple a way of putting it, but you have the idea. And that is why you should be wary of battling a mindmage or firemage. Anyone with a degree of skill could strike you down before you could get close, where you would be able to defend yourself."

With a sick lurch in his gut, Ebon thought of Cyrus atop the cliff overlooking the Great Bay. "I will keep that in mind," he muttered.

Perrin must have noted Ebon's somber tone; she frowned, but she let it pass. "Well, to practice a counterspell, you shall need a spell to counter. Astrea, come here, if you please."

Ebon looked up with delight as Astrea rose from her desk and came to join them. She frowned as Perrin directed her to sit on the bench beside Ebon. The instructor then produced a wooden rod and placed it in the girl's hand.

"Take the other end of the rod, please, Ebon," said Perrin.

He did, though he felt just as confused as Astrea.

"Good. Now, Astrea, I want you to change the rod to stone, just as you did for your testing spell. Ebon, you must feel her magic as she casts it, and try to stop her. Now, begin."

Astrea looked at Ebon, and he back at her, and he knew that neither of them had the faintest idea what Perrin was talking about. They shrugged at the same time and giggled. Then Astrea began to concentrate. Her eyes glowed, and Ebon felt a familiar prickling along his spine—the sense that another transmuter was using their magic in his presence.

Slowly, stone rippled along the wooden rod towards Ebon's fingers. He narrowed his eyes, trying to sense the stone as it turned. But he could only see the material itself, and not the magic acting upon it. In a few moments it was done; the rod had turned to stone, and Ebon released his grip with a sigh.

"Let me turn it back," said Perrin, reaching for the rod. But Astrea withheld it from her.

"I can do it, Instructor," she said meekly. Her eyes glowed once more, and the rod rippled back into wood. Perrin gave an appreciative smile, and Ebon sat gaping.

"I did not know you could turn the rod back into wood, child," said Perrin. "That is most impressive."

Astrea only shrugged. "I learned that spell before I could do it the right way. Everyone says I was supposed to learn wood to stone first."

Perrin shook her head. "That is the way of magic. Some wizards take to some spells more easily than others, and in truth there is no 'right' way to learn. You should take pride, for that is one of the testing spells to graduate this class."

"Even I have not learned it yet," said Ebon, giving her an encouraging smile.

Astrea smirked at him, though it was half-hearted. "That is not a surprise. You are brand-new to the Academy."

Perrin's laugh rang through the room, making the other students pause at their desks. "I will leave the pair of you to practice. Remember, Ebon: search for her magic, and stop it with your own."

She went off to the next student whose hand was raised. Astrea turned the rod to stone again, while Ebon tried in vain to keep the wood in place. After a few attempts, he still sensed nothing. He dropped his hand from the rod with a frustrated growl.

"I am sorry," Astrea said quietly. "I will try to slow my spell."

"No, it is certainly not your fault," said Ebon. "It is mine. Perrin gave me this spell because I had grown frustrated with the others, and yet it turns out I am no better at this one."

Astrea gave him a small smile. "I have enjoyed my other spells. Have you learned to shift stone yet? I cannot seem to do it."

"Yes," said Ebon, not without some small degree of pride. Then, thinking that might have sounded boastful, he added, "Of course, I can only shift it away from myself. I cannot control it enough to put it back inside the box."

"Nor can I," said Astrea. Then her mood dampened, and a shadow seemed to swallow her features. "My friend Vali told me his second-year lessons were beastly. Though he is a weremage, and I know our spells are not the same."

Vali was the boy she had had the row with in the dining hall. Ebon forced a smile, hoping to turn her mind away. "I am certain you will pass this class before I will—likely before the year is behind us. No doubt I will be an old man, my beard hanging to the floor, before I finish, and you will come back to the Academy to visit me."

She tried to smile, but her chin trembled as tears filled her eyes. "I do not understand him. Vali, I mean. First he told me he wanted nothing to do with me. But just this morning he came to me and said he did not know what he was thinking, and that of course he has always been my friend. I cannot make sense of it. I saw the look in his eyes then—it was as if he did not know me."

Ebon sighed. He should have known it would be foolish to try and distract her. First the death of her instructor, and now this—not to mention the attack upon the High King's Seat. She was only a child, and it made him heartsick that she had suffered so much in so short a time. Gently he put a hand on her shoulder.

"Sometimes people grow apart, Astrea. It cannot always be helped. And you should not try too hard to remain close to someone who does not see your worth."

His soft tone broke her; she sniffed hard and swiped at the tears that leaked from the corners of her eyes. "Too many have gone and will never return. I do not want to lose anyone else."

"I am here, and you will not lose me," promised Ebon. "Indeed, you would be hard pressed to get rid of me. And you have Isra. I do not know her well, but from what I have seen, I do not think she plans to leave you any time soon."

Astrea scooted forwards and hugged him. Ebon held her tight, patting her hair as tears soaked his robes. Over her head, he saw Perrin watching the two of them. For an instant he feared she might rebuke them for talking when they should be studying. But instead, she nodded and gave him a sad little smile.

These days we must all take care of each other, Ebon thought.

When Astrea had composed herself, she shifted away and retrieved the wooden rod. Ebon took the other end with a smile. "Come, wizardling," he said. "Do your worst."

She did, now with the hint of a grin.

NINETEEN

THE NEXT DAY WAS THE LAST OF FEBRIS, AND THE EVE OF YEARSEND.

It was the day Ebon would take Kalem and Theren to sup with Adara, and his nerves tormented him throughout his morning classes. His distraction must have shown, for Perrin barked at him more than once, telling him to keep his mind on his spells. The moment the midday bell rang, Ebon made for the dining hall, gobbled his meal, and then spent the rest of his spare time out upon the grounds. He shook his hands often as he walked, letting them chill in the freezing air, hoping to untie the knots his stomach seemed determined to twist itself into.

While he paced, he saw a curious thing: the boy Vali, Astrea's former friend, was out walking alone. His arms were crossed over his chest, and he shivered, but it seemed to Ebon that it came from more than the cold. Too, the boy's face was haggard and careworn, his cheeks gaunt, eyes darting in every direction. Ebon felt a twinge of pity. Mayhap the boy was consumed with guilt for the way he had treated Astrea. These days were dark, and worked in strange ways upon the mind. He hoped the two of them could find a way to reconcile.

But then Vali passed, and Ebon thought of his dinner with Adara. Again he grew anxious, and Vali was quickly forgotten.

Free study in the library was no better. Ebon sat staring at the pages of his book, his eyes unfocused and unseeing. Every so often he would shake his head as he came out of it, but then a moment later his thoughts returned to wandering. After a time, Theren leaned back in her chair with an exasperated sigh.

"Sky above, Ebon. Why are you so troubled by tonight's meal? You have *lain* with the woman. A meal with her cannot be this terrifying to you."

Ebon started at Theren's frankness and looked over his shoulder, but they were alone. Kalem was off somewhere among the bookshelves, searching for a mention of Kekhit. He frowned at her.

"I am not 'terrified.' I am only a bit nervous. Mayhap I am afraid you and Kalem will embarrass me."

Theren arched an eyebrow. "You forget I know Adara already, Ebon. If she did not wish to see me again, she would not have accepted your invitation."

He glowered at that. Then a thought struck him. He spoke carefully, trying to appear nonchalant. "Theren . . . when you say you know Adara . . . how did the two of you—"

She silenced him with a sharp look. "I know what you are asking at, Ebon. And you ought to know better. If Adara and I met as lover and guest before you knew her—or even after—that is none of your business."

Ebon swallowed. "That *is* how you know each other, then?"

Her eyes hardened. "I have said neither yes, nor no. I have said it is none of your business, and you do yourself no favors with such thoughts. She is a lover, Ebon. She may have known me, or any other here in the Academy, or upon the Seat. It is none of your concern."

"I know that," said Ebon hastily. "I do, it is only . . ." He hesitated, searching for the right words. He looked around the edge of his armchair to ensure Kalem was still safely stowed among the shelves. When he spoke, he could not meet her eye, but stared at his fidgeting hands. "I know it is foolish of me, Theren—trust me, I know it. Yet . . . I catch myself wishing I were more than her guest. Certainly I feel as though

364

she is more than my lover. And sometimes I see in her eyes . . . I do not know, for I *have* heard many things about lovers' words. But I think she may feel the same about me, or at least something similar."

Theren did not answer for a long moment, and as Ebon raised his embarrassed gaze, he saw something horrible: not anger, nor even irritation, but pity. She shook her head and closed the book in her lap, which she had only been half-glancing through anyway. Then she leaned forwards until their faces were level and gently placed one of her hands on his.

"Ebon," she said carefully. "Your thoughts wander a road that will only end in heartsickness. A guest's dealings with a lover can be many things, and all of them wonderful. But it is never anything more than it is, if you take my meaning. And if there is no honesty between you and her, then your time together will end in darkness, and sooner rather than later."

He shook his head quickly, smiling even though he did not feel like it. "Of course I understand that. It was foolish of me to speak. Forget I said anything."

"Do not be dishonest, Ebon. With me, or with her. Speak to Adara. She must hear your thoughts, and you must hear her answer. Dancing around it will only make things worse."

"Of course," Ebon repeated, and forced himself to chuckle. "Forgive me. I was foolish to trouble you."

Theren looked as though she was about to say more. But her gaze drifted over his shoulder. Ebon followed it to Kalem, nearly running as he came towards them, hoisting a book like a trophy over his head.

"I have found her!" he said in a shouted whisper, as though he wanted to crow but was afraid to disturb the library's peace. "I have found Kekhit!"

"Be silent!" said Theren sharply. Though no one was close enough to hear, Ebon understood her caution. The last thing they needed was for some instructor to hear them discussing the Wizard King whose amulet had been stolen from the vaults. "Sit down and tell us what you have found, but keep your voice hushed."

Kalem nearly leapt into his armchair between them, flipping the book open to a page he had held with his thumb. "Here she is. I had been searching in ancient histories of Idris, but none bore mention of her. At last I realized that many tomes from before the Dark War had been lost, and such histories would not help us. Then I thought to look in accounts of the Dark War itself. By the account of that logbook page we already found, Kekhit died long before that time, but if she was as powerful as she seems, I thought there might be mention of her—like an echo of her power reverberating down through the centuries, having finally faded away before we were born."

"Very poetic," said Ebon, arching an eyebrow. "Now, stop regaling us with your brilliance, and tell us what you have learned."

Theren hid a smirk as Kalem scowled. But the boy lowered his eyes to the page and held his finger against a passage. "Here it is. This says she was an ancient Wizard King of Idris, and a being of unstoppable power. She could hide the glow in her eyes when she cast her spells, so that her foes had no warning of her attacks. Her magic could strike whole armies dead, and she once captured a dragon and forced it to serve as her steed, when wyrms were not so uncommon in Underrealm."

Ebon's eyes widened at the thought: a wizard riding through the sky upon a dragon's back, raining death and fire from above. But Theren snorted and rolled her eyes. "Nearly every ancient Wizard King has some such tale. By the time of the Dark War, men were wiser, and history better kept. Then there were no more such tales. The thought of riding a dragon is a flight of fancy and nothing more."

Kalem shrugged. "You may be right. There are more accounts of her strength, though I will not trouble you with them now. But one thing is interesting; some say she was Elf-touched, for it is said she lived for four hundreds of years."

Theren laughed out loud. "Four centuries? Nonsense."

Ebon might have believed the dragon, but now even he had to shake his head. "That is impossible, Kalem. There are Elf-touched who walk the nine lands even today. But they live their spans and then fade like all the rest. Elves do not grant everlasting life—that gift is theirs alone."

Kalem gave them both an exasperated look. "I am not vouching for the author's integrity," he snapped. "I am only relaying her words. Now, do you wish to hear about Kekhit's amulet, or not?"

Theren and Ebon leaned forwards together. "The book speaks of it?"

"In fair detail," said Kalem. "It seems Kekhit enchanted many objects with dark and eternal magic. Of all the artifacts she imbued with power, none have lost the strength of their spells. Chief among them was her amulet, which she wore always, and never let another lay a hand upon it. It allowed her to transcend all other Wizard Kings of her time, giving her the strength to cast darkfire without the use of magestones."

Theren's face blanched, and she drew back in her seat. But Ebon looked between them without understanding. "What is darkfire? I have never heard of this."

Kalem's face grew solemn, and he leaned in to speak quietly. "You remember when I told you of the power of magestones? And how a transmuter who consumed them could cast a spell called blackstone?"

"I do," said Ebon. "It is a sort of corruption, is it not?"

"One that destroys anything it touches," said Kalem, nodding. "Darkfire is similar. It is a flame, blacker than the darkest night, and it will burn steel and flesh like parchment. It cannot be put out once it is started. Water cannot douse it, nor can it be suffocated. It burns until it peters out, utterly consuming everything in its path."

Ebon felt a tingle creeping along his skin. His mind's eye filled with visions of melting flesh and bone, and he thought he might be ill. "That is horrible," he said, and the words cracked. He cleared his throat to strengthen his voice. "Can magestones grant no powers but those for evil?"

"None," said Theren, shaking her head firmly. "It is the same for all the four branches. To mindmages, magestones give the strength of mindwyrd. It gives us a voice of command, so that we may order anyone to do what we wish, and they have no choice but to obey, even once they are out of our sight. It is a perversion of our natural power; with my magic, I can move your body easily enough. With magestones, I can take command of your mind, so that your body enforces my will."

The library seemed to have darkened around them. Ebon shook the feeling off. "And weremages?" he said, fearing the answer. "What does it do to them?"

"It is called hellskin," said Kalem softly. "They become twisted monsters, like demons of the darkness below. Their shape depends on the weremage and their strength, but their skin is always covered with jutting horns and barbs, and their strength is unmatched by any natural creature. In their hellskin form, weremages are impervious to magic, and the greatest among them can tear armies apart with their bare claws."

Ebon felt the blood drain from his face. Theren saw it and smirked. "Now do you understand why the Academy so stringently bans any discussion of magestones? Many of us react as you do now, terrified and afraid for our very souls. But some students hear such tales and can only think of the power magestones would grant them."

"I want nothing of such power," said Ebon quickly.

"Then you are surprisingly wise. But what else does the book say of Kekhit, Kalem?"

"That is all. But still, that is a great deal more than we knew before."

"So the thief's plot may have something to do with darkfire," said Theren, eyes sharp. "And we know they are a firemage as well."

"Like Lilith," muttered Ebon.

"Exactly."

By unspoken agreement, they rose from their chairs. "Where did you find that book, Kalem?" said Ebon. "It seems we have much more to learn, if we mean to save the Academy."

TWENTY

DESPITE THEIR EARNEST SEARCH, THEY FOUND NOTHING THE REST OF the day. Ebon half wanted to spend the evening in the libraries to continue the hunt, but at the same time, he had no desire to miss their dinner with Adara. And so, reluctantly, they left the library and made ready for an evening upon the Seat.

Some days ago, Ebon had asked Theren to recommend a fine tavern for their meal, and she had spoken of a place called the Sterling Stag. She had only been there once, but it had served the finest food she had ever tasted. When Ebon asked her how she had afforded such a meal, she glowered and told him to mind his own business.

Before they left, Ebon bathed and dabbed on a bit of perfume he had bought some time ago and kept hidden in the chest at the foot of his bed. Finally he met his friends in the hall and set out with them into the streets. Kalem had washed as well, and had even combed his hair. To Ebon's great surprise, even Theren had prettied herself up for the occasion, with two thin braids running back along her temples to join a tail into which she had woven back her hair. When she caught him staring, she gave him a pointed look, and he quickly turned.

Snow had at last come to the Seat, and now it drifted down gentle and lazy upon the air, dusting across their skin and catching in their eyelashes before melting. They had to draw their hoods up against the chill, and each wore the simple black coats given to students in wintertime. Kalem kept looking at all of them nervously, lips twisting one way and then another.

"Our student robes look a bit . . . plain, do they not?" he said, brushing at his legs as though they were dirty.

"It is a great honor to study at the Academy—or so I have been told," said Theren.

"We look presentable enough. Do not worry." In truth, Ebon's words were for him as much as for the boy, for he found himself more nervous than he had thought he would be. Theren saw it, and she frowned.

"Ebon, you should not be this anxious."

He scowled. "I am not anxious. I only wish for the evening to go well."

"I know it. I will be on my best behavior."

"And I," said Kalem, but his voice cracked.

Ebon's favorite haunts were all to the west of the Academy, and the Drayden family manor was due east, but the Silver Stag was to the southeast, and so he was walking along unfamiliar streets. But Theren knew her way, and she led them without pause. As they neared the High King's palace, buildings grew ever finer. More were made of stone, and so bore less damage from the attack upon the Seat. Second floors, and even third, became more common, and the walls were often painted in bright colors. One place looked familiar, and Ebon realized his aunt Halab had taken him there when the High King's armies marched forth from the palace. But Theren turned away, and after only a few more blocks, they stood before a grand two-story building with a stag painted in silver upon the door.

"Here we are."

"Well, let us not stop," said Ebon. "Most likely she has arrived already." But he did not take the first step.

"Indeed. We should not keep her waiting." But Kalem, too, remained frozen.

Theren smirked and shook her head. "You are hopeless, the both of you." She seized their arms and pulled them forwards, nudging the door open with her foot before half-tossing them both within.

At once Ebon thought it must be the friendliest tavern he had seen on the Seat. A bright buzz of conversation hung in the room, and no one spared them more than a curious glance before returning to their meals. A crackling fire burned in the hearth and flooded the room with warmth, which was strengthened by the many lanterns that hung low on the walls, so that the place was as well-lit as though it were daylight. Ebon saw no others in Academy robes, not even instructors. Instead there were many people with fine clothing, dresses and tunics and pants all woven with the most expensive silks. A dozen perfumes wove a wreath of heady odor, and he drank it in with a long breath. They scanned the room, searching for an empty table, but before they found one, the tavern's matron approached.

"The grandest of evenings to you, young ones. I am Canda, and master of the Stag." She was a burly woman, and tall, and gave them a look that was both polite and appraising. "I hope I give no offense, but I must tell you that the price of board here is more than you might be used to. Have you the coin to pay for it?"

"We have," said Ebon proudly. "But there is a fourth in our party who may have arrived already. A woman of Idris?"

"You mean Adara?" Canda beamed a sudden smile. "Forgive me, young masters. She did not tell me you were Academy students, or I would have brought you to her at once. She waits at your table. Let me show you the way."

Canda set off through the room, leaning back and forth as she wove through the tables, and Ebon followed with Kalem and Theren close behind. A moment later he saw Adara. Tucked in behind a table in the corner, she was resplendent in yellow silk trimmed with gold. With a start he realized she had worn the gold for him, for it was the color of the family Drayden. He flushed, even as she caught his eye and they traded a grin. She rose at once and came around the table to greet them.

"Adara, it is my pleasure to introduce you to Kalem of the family Konnel," said Ebon. "You already know Theren."

"Indeed. Well met." Adara leaned over to kiss Theren's cheeks.

"Idrisians," said Theren, rolling her eyes. Ebon elbowed her. "And well met, of course."

Adara smiled and then turned to Kalem. "And it is my pleasure to make your acquaintance, young lord."

She made as if to give him the same greeting as Theren, but Kalem drew back, shifting on his feet. "Er . . . ah . . . I am sorry," he mumbled. "In Hedgemond, it is . . . that is, such a greeting . . ."

Adara nodded at once. "I am unfamiliar with Hedgemond's customs," she said easily. "My apologies if I was unseemly."

"Not at all," he said, shaking his head.

Ebon stifled a grin as Adara turned to her chair. He took his seat beside her, with Kalem at his other hand and Theren to Adara's right.

Canda smiled. "Tonight's meal is a fine roast of beef, and a salad prepared in the manner of Idris, with vinegar at Adara's request. I also have some figs, if you would like them."

Ebon smiled at Adara, and her eyes glinted with delight. "That sounds wonderful," he said. "And wine as well, please, for all of us."

Adara raised a finger. "Mead for me."

Canda nodded and drew away. Ebon looked to Adara with surprise. "Mead? I thought you took wine."

"I do, when I am with the guild, for they choose what drinks to provide. When it is not my coin, I am not choosy. But wait a moment—you have hardly given me a proper greeting."

She slid her hand across his cheek to the back of his head and pulled him in for a deep kiss. When finally he drew back, Theren was looking discreetly away; but Kalem was staring with eyes wide and mouth open. It was a moment before he came to his senses and blushed. Adara cast her gaze upon him with a smile.

"I apologize again, young lord, if we have given you further cause for embarrassment."

"I should be the one to apologize," mumbled Kalem. "I am your guest. It is only that I am unused to such things. Forgive me."

"Think nothing of it."

Just then, a girl came by with their wine. Kalem drained one cup quickly and then refilled it from the flagon. Theren raised her eyes at him. Adara sipped at her mead.

"Very fine," she said, licking her lips in satisfaction. "You made a fine choice in this place, Ebon."

"You may thank Theren. It was at her advice. Where did you learn to drink mead? It is not common in either Idris or Feldemar."

"But I have not been to only those kingdoms. I left Feldemar in my youth and dwelt for a time in Dulmun."

That darkened their mood, and they fell silent. Ebon and Kalem looked down at the tabletop, and even Theren picked with her fingernail at the edge of her cup.

"My apologies," Adara said softly. "I spoke without thinking. I did not mean to silence a pleasant conversation."

"It is nothing," said Theren. "You cannot be blamed for the war Dulmun chose to wage upon us."

"They have always been a proud people," said Adara. "Though I am as shocked as anyone at their revolt, they are mayhap the least surprising kingdom in which to find such treachery—for they are, after all, descendants of Renna Blackheart herself. I am only glad no others have joined them."

"Not yet," said Theren. "But few are willing to wage war against them, either."

"Hedgemond is willing," said Kalem.

Ebon was scarcely paying attention to the conversation, for he was deep in thought as he looked upon Adara. It surprised him, though he knew it should not have, that he had never learned of her time in Dulmun. There was still much of her past he did not know. It bothered him, though he knew it should not.

Adara caught him staring. She gave him a small smile and a peck on the cheek. "Enough of darkness. Let us speak of something more pleasant. What have the three of you been up to? It has been some days since Ebon and I spoke."

Theren's mouth twisted. "That subject is not much brighter than the other. We have found nothing of use, only dark words of peril."

Kalem looked wide-eyed at Ebon. "She knows of the theft from the vaults?"

Ebon nodded. "Of course. That is the least of the secrets she carries."

"Indeed, I had heard before Ebon told me. The Academy is a wonderful place for many things, but keeping secrets is not one of them." Adara smiled and placed a hand over Ebon's. "But what are these dark words you spoke of?"

"We think we may have found what was stolen from the vaults," said Ebon. "An amulet. One of immense power, though we know not what it does."

Theren leaned in and lowered her voice. "It belonged to some Wizard King of ages gone by. One named Kekhit."

Adara shook her head. "I have never heard of her."

"She is a thing of ancient times. She may even predate the years of Underrealm," said Ebon. "Now we are searching for any tale of her, some history that might help us understand what the amulet might do."

"I have been doing some searching of my own," said Adara. "I will spread word of this and see what may be learned from those who help me."

Ebon frowned. "What searching?"

Theren gave him a crafty smile. "Do you know nothing of the guild of lovers? They are a meddlesome lot."

Adara gave her an admonishing look before turning back to Ebon. "Different houses and members within the guild maintain close contact with each other. Our clients' secrets are never shared, but some information may be passed along, if it does not violate trust. Since you first told me of the theft from the vaults, and then of that ghastly murder, I have had friends searching for any sign of the culprit."

Ebon's stomach lurched, and he spoke soft but urgent. "Adara, that may be folly. If anyone were to learn of your prying . . ."

"They will not," she said, raising an eyebrow and smirking, as though Ebon were both very sweet and very foolish. "The guild looks after its own. In any case, I have learned nothing certain about the theft. Though I have heard many other whispers. It seems there is a girl skulking about the Seat. She wears black robes, like a student of the Academy."

Theren looked at Ebon. "A girl? What did she look like?"

Adara shrugged. "No one has gotten close enough to see. But she has spent much time around the northern end of the Seat, and after curfew."

Ebon raised an eyebrow at Theren. "That sounds like something you might do, Theren."

She frowned. "Since the attack I have been unable to sneak out. The sheds to help me are gone, and the instructors have placed new enchantments upon the walls, and reinforce them often. And besides, I have no business in the north. It could be Lilith."

Kalem sighed. Ebon shook his head. "But for what purpose, Theren? If you think she is the thief, why would she spend time in the city?"

Theren glared, but she had no answer. Adara quickly went on to fill the silence. "Whoever she might be, she is only one of the figures now skulking in shadows. Ebon, your family's man, Mako, has been poking his nose all about the island."

Ebon shrugged. "That is nothing unusual for him."

"His activities have greatly increased," said Adara. "That man's heart is as dark as a sky without moons. Do not trust him."

"Mako warned me the day the Seat was attacked, and that saved our lives," said Ebon, somewhat surprised to find himself defending the bodyguard. "If he is crafty, and somewhat caustic-tongued, that does not mean he is rotten through."

"The deepest rot is the hardest to see," said Adara. "I do not mean to tell you what you should do—only that you should be careful."

Gently she touched his cheek, and his irritation faded. Theren smirked and shook her head, but Kalem lowered his eyes and flushed with embarrassment. Ebon gave him a pat on the shoulder. "There there, little lordling. You will soon be a man grown, and may yet become used to those who do not hide their affections."

"I did not think my presence would cause you such discomfort, Kalem." Though she had been easy enough twice before, now it seemed to Ebon that he heard annoyance in Adara's tone. "I know Hedgemond is no place like the Seat, or Idris where Ebon and I hail from—yet I had not thought it so bashful a kingdom as you make it out to be."

"It is not that," mumbled Kalem. "It is . . . it is only that . . . well, you are very pretty, and . . . womanly."

Adara's irritation vanished at once. She laughed lightly, spurring Ebon to chuckle. "I shall take that as a high compliment, good sir, since I know that many fair ladies must have visited the courts of your family. Have I mayhap taken for discomfort what was, in fact, curiosity? If you should ever wish to step beyond the blue door, I am well familiar with the lovers in the various houses upon the Seat. I assure you I could find a suitable partner from among them for you."

Kalem's face went beet-red. "I . . . I thank you for the offer, but no. I do not think I would enjoy such a thing."

"I must heartily disagree," said Ebon. "I myself found it most enjoyable." Adara smiled and placed her hand on his thigh beneath the table.

"Oh, I am certain it would be a pleasure," said Kalem. The red of his face deepened as he heard his own double meaning. "But . . . I have a hope that one day I will find one whom I love, and that my first tryst might be with her. I do not wish the one without the other, if you understand me."

"I do indeed," said Adara softly. "And I praise you for knowing your own mind so well. It is not common, especially among men so young, if you will forgive me for saying so. Many never think upon what they truly want, and such a thing always leads to tears. For many, love is a necessary part of intimacy. For others, the two are close friends, often present together, but not always. It is better to know which is true for you before engaging in either."

Kalem bowed his head and said nothing. Theren leaned away in her chair, throwing an arm over its back. "I myself have always known which was which. To my mind, anyone who thinks they are one and the same is a fool." She gave Ebon a hard look, and he glared back.

But Adara only cocked her head. "I do not know if that is true."

As if to prove Theren wrong, Ebon reached down to where Adara's hand rested in his lap, and scooped it up in his own. Without thinking, she laced her fingers through his, and he kissed the back of her palm. "I think that a night in bed may not always be a night in love," he said softly. "And yet, sometimes, one may lead to the other, so that love springs forth unbidden."

The words sounded foolish in his own ears as he said them, and he half expected to receive one of Adara's sharp, exasperated looks. But she smiled instead, a soft and gentle smile, hinting at nothing, promising so much. He had never known how much hidden meaning was in her eyes until then, when all pretense seemed removed, and he could peer deep into her heart for the first time: pure and unadorned and revealed at last.

She leaned in close, and in a murmur so low only he could hear it, said, "Sometimes love springs forth indeed."

Lover's words, came the whisper in his mind. But he could not stop the thrill in his heart.

TWENTY-ONE

THE REST OF THEIR DINNER PASSED LIGHT AND FAIR, AND AFTER THEY finished eating Kalem returned to the Academy with Theren. But Ebon and Adara stepped beyond the blue door, and he lingered there longer than he should have, so that by the time he returned to the streets he had to hurry home for fear of missing curfew. Upon a time that would not have troubled him, but now the Academy was strict about such things, and besides, he was still closely watched after his adventure in the vaults.

He was only a few streets away when the sun vanished behind the western buildings. He picked up his pace, intent on reaching the Academy before dark. But as he cut through an alley between two busy thoroughfares, a hand swept from the shadows and dragged him towards the wall.

The hand clamped over his mouth, silencing his sharp and sudden cry. His every muscle tensed as he readied himself to fight, to cast a spell, to do something—but then he recognized Mako and scrabbled to drag the bodyguard's hand away from his mouth.

"There are other ways to get my attention," he groused. "You frightened me half to death."

But then he paused, for Mako was looking all about him, peering over both shoulders as though expecting to see someone lurking, waiting to strike at them both. A *crack* around the corner made the man jump, though Ebon recognized it as the sound of a barrel falling from a cart. This was so unlike Mako's usual conduct that Ebon was shocked into silence.

"I have found something most interesting, little goldshitter. But we must act quickly if we are to take advantage of it."

Ebon frowned. "What is it? What did you find?"

"You know I have my ways in and out of the Academy—ways that allow me to pass through the citadel unseen, to visit you, and to see what may be transpiring within its walls."

"I do, though I know not how, exactly."

"Nor should you." Mako smiled for the first time, and Ebon found that strangely comforting. "Some knowledge is dangerous for others to have. Suffice it to say my pathways take me through nooks of the Academy that are seldom seen. Yet it seems one such nook has been visited by another."

His fingers fished in a pocket on his black leather vest, and from it he drew a piece of parchment. This he unfolded and held before Ebon.

"Do you recognize this?"

Ebon frowned—but only for a moment before his eyes shot wide with shock. It was a page torn from a vault logbook. From the yellowed edges, and the fact that the paper had been torn out, Ebon would have wagered it came from the same logbook they had found in the library, where they had learned of Kekhit's amulet.

"Where did you get this?"

Mako cuffed his ear and snarled, "I told you, in one of the Academy's hidden passages. You are not seeing what is important. Look again."

Ebon scanned the page and read:

*This globe's origins are unknown, though it has passed
from hand to hand through the centuries, and many
Wizard Kings used it. Likely one of them created it. A*

mentalist or elementalist who speaks the word—then there was a word that was all inked over, as though some later cleric had sought to obscure it—shall cause the globe to erupt with terrible energy, killing all nearby, but sparing the caster. This is a mentalist enchantment, and summons no fire or thunder.

The learned scholar will recognize this as a common enchantment in elder days of both mentalism and elementalism, but this is one of the more powerful examples found to date.

Ebon shuddered at the thought of what such an artifact could do in a crowded room. Unbidden, his mind showed him an explosion in a classroom, and he pictured the broken bodies left in the aftermath. But then he saw what had caused Mako such distress: words in red ink, drawn near the bottom of the page and underlined twice.

30 Febris

He stared at it for a moment. "The Eve of Yearsend. What do you mean for me to see about it? It is today's—"

Realization struck him like a hammer blow, and his knees went weak. Mako saw it. His grin widened and turned cruel.

"You see it now, do you not, goldshitter?"

Ebon snatched the page and threw the bodyguard's hand from his shoulder. He began to sprint from the alley towards the Academy, but Mako seized him and dragged him back around.

"Let me go! I must warn them!"

"Warn who? Think, boy. What do you mean to do with what we know?"

Ebon blinked at him. "Catch Lilith, of course."

"But catch her doing what, exactly? Show your instructors now, and doubtless they will post guards around the vault. Lilith's name is not on that page. As it stands, she is blameless. You will not prove her guilt unless you find her with this orb afterwards, for now you know what you are seeking."

Ebon shook his head at once. "No. I will not let her steal it. I must catch her in the act. Last time, an instructor lost his life, and there is every reason to believe that may happen again."

Mako frowned, but he must have seen the resolution in Ebon's eyes. "Very well. Hurry then, goldbag, and pray you are not too late. I have heard no tumult in the Academy yet, so there may still be hope. But where will you say you found this page?"

"I know not," said Ebon, wanting to run. Even now he was wasting precious time. "Where did *you* find it?"

Mako shook his head. "A fine attempt, but I am not so easily fooled. Say you found it under a hedge in the garden. Here." He took the page, dropped it under his boot, and mushed it about with his heel. It came up grimy and torn in the corner. "That will help the lie. Now go!"

Ebon turned and sprinted for the Academy's front door.

His shoes pounded on the stone floors of the hallways, and the slapping sound ran on ahead of him, echoing all around so that it sounded as though an army ran beside him.

But no. No army. Only me, and mayhap too late.

At first he thought to make for the vaults, to catch Lilith on his own, but almost at once he realized the folly of such a plan. She might have Kekhit's amulet, and therefore power beyond reckoning—but even at her weakest, she was far more than Ebon's match. So he ran instead for the instructors' offices.

Halfway there, he rounded a corner and nearly ran into Theren. Eyes wide, she opened her mouth to ask him a question. "No time!" he cried, wheezing and short of breath, and ran on. She caught up a moment later, running by his side.

"Where are you going?"

"Jia. Lilith is about to strike."

Her eyes narrowed as she doubled her pace. She reached Jia's office before he did and threw open the door for him. They practically fell in across the doorstep. He thanked the sky above, for Jia was there at her desk with Dasko. Both instructors looked at them wide-eyed in shock.

"What is the matter?" said Jia.

"Instructor," said Ebon, wheezing as he thrust forth the logbook page. A fit of coughing claimed him, but he choked out his words. "I found this. The vault thief—they mean to strike again. Tonight."

He thought she might look alarmed, or mayhap frightened, but she glared at him instead. "Ebon, you were specifically warned to stay out of—"

"No!" cried Ebon. "I found this in the gardens by chance, I swear it. Just look, Instructor!"

Dasko had taken the page from Ebon, his eyes scanning the text. He took Jia's arm, and she met his eyes. For half a moment they stared at each other. Ebon held his breath.

THOOM

A blast rocked the Academy, thundering through the halls. A chorus of screams followed it.

Jia and Dasko fled the room, forgetting all about Ebon, who followed at once. On he ran, though Jia screamed at them to stay back, to return to their dormitories. On, past the students who stood mute and terrified, torn between curiosity at the commotion and fear of another attack, and mayhap a corpse awaiting them all. On, with Theren beside him saying "Not again, not again, sky above, please," a terrible whimper made all the worse coming from her.

Another boom rocked the hallways, and more screams told them which way to go—though of course they did not need guidance, for they knew it came from the vaults.

Just before they rounded the corner and reached the entrance, Jia and Dasko's eyes glowed white, and the two wizards transformed. Jia's robes sank into her flesh, and hair sprouted all over her body as she turned into a massive bear, its head nearly striking the ceiling. Dasko had become a beast of the far northern jungles, a catlike creature with a huge mane of golden fur.

Together they roared, loud and terrifying enough to make Ebon's heart skip a beat. Almost he stopped in his tracks, for his limbs had seized up, but he forced himself onwards. Theren had not abandoned the chase, and her eyes glowed as she reached for her magic. He would not abandon his friend, nor his instructors, though he did not know what he might do to help.

They crashed through the first door and into the vault's office. The last time Ebon had passed through it quickly. He remembered the two high, tall windows in the walls. They were open now, their shutters flapping. He remembered the wide wooden desk where Egil worked, and the several smaller desks around the room's edges.

But now his eyes were drawn to the student hovering in the air ten feet off the floor. A maelstrom poured through the windows, becoming a funnel of destruction that whipped him about. A lanky towheaded boy, eyes wide with pain and fright. Astrea's friend, Vali.

And Vali screamed as magic crushed the life from him.

Horror-struck, Ebon was so focused on Vali that at first he missed Lilith. Then he saw her standing near the vault's entry. The door listed open. Lilith's eyes glowed as she held her hands high, commanding the squall. She grimaced as she shouted at Vali: "Stop it! Stop it!"

Theren gave a wordless cry as her eyes sprang to light, and she leapt forwards to fight Lilith's magic. Jia and Dasko stormed ahead, one of Jia's massive paws catching Lilith in the chest and flinging her to the ground. Dasko planted a clawed foot on her abdomen. But Lilith managed to keep an arm raised, and the glow in her eyes did not die. Her lips quivered with words of power.

Ebon searched the room for something, anything to do. He saw a number of other students who had gathered at the commotion—Lilith's friends Oren and Nella were there, and some other members of the Goldbag Society. Isra was there, her dark brown eyes wide and staring, horror-struck, at Vali suspended in midair.

Ebon leapt forwards and pushed the three of them to draw their attention. "Use your power! Stop her!"

Oren blinked without understanding, and Isra did not even look away from where Vali hung in the air.

Ebon shoved Oren harder. "Stop her!" he cried again, pleading.

As though waking from a dream, Oren shook his head. He nudged Ebon aside as light sprang into his eyes. Nella, too, shook off her horror, and her eyes glowed.

But it was too late. With a cry, Lilith's arm fell to the stone floor. Vali screamed as the wind blasted him towards the wall. He struck the stones with the force of a thunderbolt.

A wet *snap* filled the air.

He crashed to the ground, head lolling to the side at a hideous angle.

The room fell silent for a long moment. Then a piercing scream stabbed the quiet behind Ebon.

He turned, and his heart broke.

There, in the vault's outer doorway, stood Astrea, clawing at her cheeks and neck as her wail rose higher and higher, until it seemed to be the only thing in the world.

"Get her out of here!" Jia had taken human form again, and she waved a sharp hand at Ebon as she spoke. Shaken from his inaction, he went forwards to take Astrea's arm and pull her from the room. Isra darted to his side and reached down, sweeping Astrea up into her arms.

As he stepped out through the door, he took a final glance back. Lilith had been seized by the instructors and several students. Someone had made a gag from a torn piece of robe and wrapped it around her mouth. She stood staring after Astrea with wild, sightless eyes. Theren stood to the side, stricken with horror.

Then the door closed behind him, and there was only Astrea's scream. He tried to put a comforting hand on the girl's arm, tried to speak words of peace. But Isra had very nearly enshrouded the girl, and her eyes filled with raw fury whenever Ebon tried to reach out.

"Astrea," he said, trying to avoid Isra's hateful glare. "Astrea, it is all right. It is all right."

"It is not all right!" Astrea screamed, slapping at his hand. "He is dead!"

"Go away," Isra hissed. She turned back to Astrea, holding her closer, murmuring to her. Ebon barely made out the words. "Be calm. Be calm. Breathe deeply, and put Vali from your mind."

Astrea's breath came ragged, sucked in and pushed out between her teeth. Her hands shook where they clutched at Isra's robes. But slowly the tears stopped pouring from her eyes. Slowly her look grew far away as she focused on Isra's words. Her breaths grew deeper. Calmer.

"There," said Ebon quietly. "Good. Well done."

"I told you to leave us," said Isra. She released Astrea and stepped towards him, pushing him hard in the chest. "You filthy goldbags. Can

384

you not leave us alone? Can you create nothing but blood and suffering?"

Ebon blinked at her. "I . . . I had nothing to do—"

"Be silent!" Isra cried.

Her eyes blazed with light. Fear seized Ebon's heart as an unseen force hoisted him a foot above the stone floor, and he knew it was her magic.

"You never fail to find ways to kill us without blame. How many died in the attack on the Seat? Who started this war? Who will die on its battlefields? Not you, goldbag."

He tried to speak but could not. Some students stood within sight of them, but they were frozen in horror. Ebon swallowed hard and tried again.

"I want nothing of this war," he said, every word quivering. "I am sorry. I know not what madness seized Lilith, I swear it."

For a moment she only stood there, chest heaving with her breath. But then she let the glow slip from her eyes, and Ebon fell to the floor, only just managing to keep his feet.

"Leave," she rasped, and then turned to Astrea, who clung to her once more. "Leave, goldbag. You can do nothing to help. You can only hurt."

Ebon wanted to answer, but had no words to do so. Instead he turned and moved off down the hallway.

TWENTY-TWO

EBON WOKE TO A DARK DAY AT THE ACADEMY.

It was the first day of Yearsend, but there was no celebration. Ebon was grateful that classes were suspended for the holiday, for he could not imagine trying to sit in Perrin's classroom and read tomes of magic.

Instead he, Kalem, and Theren went out into the gardens. Many students had chosen to remain inside, for it was now the dead of winter, and so they were alone among the hedges and bare rosebushes. For a while they said nothing, listening only to the crunch of their shoes in the snow, watching only the mist of their breath upon the air. Ebon had his hood up against the weather, as did his friends, and so they rarely even looked at each other.

"She stole more artifacts from the vaults," Theren said at last. "From what I can tell, the count is more than half a dozen. I no longer serve in the vaults, but I spoke with Egil, and he let it slip. She must have gone back and forth a few times, emptying rooms until Vali . . ." Her words tapered off.

Ebon shrugged his shoulders, hunching them as though against a bitter wind. He could scarcely close his eyes without seeing the boy's head twisting to the side and hearing the snap of a neck. Credell's death, at least, had happened out of sight. And he was an instructor. To murder a child so young . . . it made him heartsick to imagine the letter that must have been sent home to Vali's family.

Lilith had been dragged off and delivered to the Mystics. They would not kill her at once, though the penalty of death was certain. First they would try to learn where the stolen artifacts had gone. He had been there when they took her away. Before they managed to gag her, she had muttered, "He was supposed to join us," over and over again. As she passed him in the hall, she had still been trying to repeat it around the cloth that gagged her.

"Credell was a tragedy," said Theren, the words quivering. "But had I ever imagined she might kill a boy so young, I would have stopped her. I would have snapped her neck mys—" Her voice shattered at last, and she hid her face behind her hood, her shoulders shaking with sobs. Ebon had only seen Theren weep once before, and like then, it was an unnerving sight. He and Kalem looked away, feeling suddenly awkward.

Footsteps crunched across the snow towards them, and they looked up, grateful for the distraction. To Ebon's surprise, it was Dasko. The instructor came forwards with his hood up and hands tucked into sleeves, shielding them from winter's chill. He stopped a few feet away and nodded to each of them in turn.

"Well met," he said softly. "I had hoped . . . I am sorry I could not come and see you earlier, Ebon. But I wondered if I might still speak with you, as I requested some time ago? I would not think to trouble you now. But mayhap after the Yearsend feast?"

Ebon glanced at Kalem and Theren. "Of course, Instructor."

"Very good." But Dasko remained, fidgeting with his hands and tugging on his thumbs. Then his head jerked up, and he winced.

"That is only part of the reason I have come. I must discuss an unpleasant bit of Academy business. Might I . . .?"

He waved a hand. Ebon glanced at Kalem and Theren, and then stepped away with Dasko. The instructor's grey eyes wandered for a moment before he spoke to Ebon in a low murmur.

"Last night . . . I know that after you left the vault's office, you and Isra had words."

Ebon's ears flushed with shame. "We did," he muttered.

Dasko's frown deepened. "We know she struck at you. With her magic."

"I cannot blame her for that," said Ebon. "What we had all seen . . . and then, I would not leave her and Astrea be when she asked me to."

A sigh slipped from Dasko. "Then you do not wish to punish her?"

Ebon blinked, looking at him with wide eyes. "Punish her? No, of course not. Sky above, how could I think to do so?"

The instructor's shoulders sagged, and he ran a hand through his hair. "Thank goodness. She broke the Academy's rules. If you wished it, you could ask for punishment to be meted out. But I am greatly relieved you have no such wish. You are right that last night would have put a terrible strain on anyone, and for Isra in particular." He shook his head.

Curiosity poked at Ebon despite himself. "What of her? I have never thought she viewed me very highly."

"Indeed not," said Dasko. "It is not a happy tale, and mayhap it is not mine to tell. But it might shed some light on her actions, and since you have shown her mercy, I see no reason not to tell you. Isra was sent here an orphan, as was Astrea."

"I heard something of that from Astrea herself."

Dasko grimaced. "She likely did not tell you—mayhap she does not even know—why Isra came to that orphanage in the first place. But her parents were killed by the royalty of Wadeland."

A chill crept up Ebon's spine. "What? Murdered?"

The instructor looked away. "As with many things, the truth is not so simple. Her father was crushed under the prince's carriage. When her mother sought recompense, the king tired of her pleading and had her executed."

Ebon stared at him. "But that is monstrous. The King's law—"

"Provides for no such thing, I know," said Dasko. "The king of Wadeland is foul indeed, but the High King cannot interfere with every injustice across Underrealm. Especially when no witness remained to bring word of this misdeed to her."

"I cannot believe . . ." Ebon shook his head, afraid he might be sick. The way Isra spat every time she said the word *goldbag*—at last he felt he understood.

"I told you it was no happy tale," Dasko said quietly. "But I have taken enough of your time. Be with your friends, and be grateful you are all whole. Also, I have this for you."

From an inner pocket of his robes Dasko produced a letter and placed it in Ebon's hands. Ebon broke the Drayden family seal and unfolded a letter from Halab, inviting him to the manor for lunch to celebrate the holiday.

Hot fire burned in his veins, and he could not stop his hands from shaking. Lunch with his family would mean he would have to see his uncle, Matami, and Matami might have been involved in Lilith's crimes. That truth might come out as the Mystics questioned Lilith, but then again it might not. From what Ebon knew, the Mystics were not seeking accomplices, but only where she had taken the artifacts. The thought of sitting across from Matami's haughty, smirking face for an entire meal made him want to melt a stone and throw it in the man's eyes.

He forced himself to stay calm. Matami's presence might be un-bearable, but it would be good to see Halab and his mother, and espe-cially Albi. "Thank you, Instructor. May I send a reply?"

"Of course." From a pocket, Dasko produced a bit of charcoal and gave it to him.

Ebon walked back to Kalem and Theren. "I am invited to a meal with my aunt. When last I saw her, she invited me to bring any friends from the Academy I might wish. What say you? Will you come with me?"

They both nodded, so Ebon scrawled his answer on the parchment and handed it to Dasko.

"Very good, Ebon. We shall speak on the morrow." He gave Kalem and Theren a small nod before leaving.

"What did he have to say to you?" said Theren. "You spoke longer than I thought you might."

But Ebon had no wish to speak of Isra's story, which still turned his stomach. He only said, "In her anger, Isra used her magic upon me last night. It was a small thing, and no harm came of it. But Dasko wished to make sure I did not want to see her punished. I told him of course I did not. It is Yearsend, after all. A time for forgiveness."

"Yearsend," said Kalem with a sigh. "It seems such a hollow thing. Who can care for a holiday now?"

"Mayhap we need it," said Ebon. "Something to take our minds from the darkness we have borne witness to. What better for the purpose than a celebration?"

"Midday meal in a goldbag's manor, and the Yearsend feast for supper," said Theren. "Fine distractions indeed. Yet I do not think they will rid me of the darkness."

"Try to let them," said Kalem. "It is not as though we can blame ourselves for what happened."

Theren chewed at her cheek. "We knew what she was up to. We might have done more to stop her."

"You did all you could—we all did," said Ebon. "We were very nearly expelled because of it."

But Theren only shook her head and looked away.

An hour before midday, they went to their dormitories. Now that Ebon knew Shay would not be in the Drayden manor to see him, he took a bit more care to wash away the stains of the Academy. He bathed, donned fresh robes, and dabbed on a bit of perfume. The hourglass in the common room told him he was running late, so he hurried to the front hall. Theren was already waiting, and it seemed that she had done nothing special with her appearance. Kalem joined them soon after, scuttling down the stairs and still trying to fix his mussed hair with his fingers.

The streets did much to lift their spirits, for they bustled with Yearsend celebrations. Those outside the Academy cared little for what took place within its walls. They caught many friendly smiles, and soon Ebon found himself returning them. Some vendors gave away little sweetmeats without asking for coin in observance of the holiday, and horses and carriages were a bit more considerate of passersby on foot. Many musicians played as they walked, singing fine songs while they strummed at lutes and small hand-harps. Soon Ebon and Kalem were laughing as though it were a day like any other. But Theren's mood only darkened the further they went, and after a time she rounded on the others with a snarl.

"How can you giggle to each other so? As though you are little children."

Kalem stopped in his tracks, frowning. "We are only trying not to dwell in darkness, Theren."

"Look around you. Darkness is everywhere, and we cannot help ourselves but dwell in it." She folded and then unfolded her arms, fists bunching as though she wanted to strike at the air itself. "I hope they drag the truth from Lilith on the tips of sharp knives. May she lead them straight to her accomplices—and for my own satisfaction, I hope it *is* that worthless ferret Cyrus. Nothing could make me happier than to see that dung heap die the slowest of deaths."

Ebon lowered his gaze to his shoes so Theren could not see his sudden discomfort.

Kalem shook his head. "Mayhap she will. Mayhap not. In any case, whoever her accomplice is, they have lost their way into the Academy. They have no choice now but to slink away into the darkness, never to return."

"You may believe that," said Theren, scowling. "I am not so sure. Cyrus may try to strike again."

"Mayhap."

They reached the Drayden manor soon after, much to Ebon's relief. They stopped before the wide front gates as Ebon knocked. As they waited for a guard to open the way, Ebon glanced back at his friends. Kalem inspected the place appraisingly, but Theren stared wide-eyed. Ebon smirked.

"Are you overawed, Theren? This is not so great a building as you seem to think. After all, you dwell within the Academy."

Theren jerked her gaze from the manor to glare at him. "You think rather highly of yourself for one born into such wealth through no fault of your own."

Ebon chuckled. Just then, a guard opened the hatch and saw him, and soon the gate swung open. They stepped through the gap as soon as it was wide enough, and Ebon led them through the courtyard towards the manor's front door.

"What is in these wagons?" said Kalem, pointing at Matami's trade wagons, which were still out in the open.

"Spices and other trade goods for the High King," said Ebon.

"That many wagons filled with spices?" said Theren, gawking again. "But that would be worth a fortune."

"And now you know why our coin purses are so deep. Here we are."

Ebon opened the front door and led them inside. The entry hall was bright with many candles and torches lining the walls. Someone must have notified Ebon's family of their arrival, for they found a reception waiting: Halab, Hesta, and Albi.

"Dearest nephew," said Halab, coming forwards to give Ebon a tight hug.

"Dearest aunt," said Ebon, kissing her cheeks. "Allow me the pleasure of introducing my friends."

But she interrupted him, smiling at them each in turn. "There is no need. I know their names already. Welcome, Kalem of the family Konnel. The honor of your house is well-known throughout the nine lands. I have had many favorable encounters with your kin, and I look forward to many more in the future."

Kalem's mouth opened slightly, though it seemed he was lost for words. Theren rolled her eyes and folded her arms. But then Halab turned to her and gave a deep bow.

"Well met, Theren. Tales of your prowess as a mentalist have reached me even here in my manor. I am graced by your presence, and ever grateful for the friendship and kindness you have shown my nephew. I worried greatly for Ebon when he stayed here upon the Seat, for he had neither family nor friends to look after him. You have my thanks for being part of the remedy."

Theren seemed as flustered as Kalem. She cleared her throat and looked about uncomfortably, before trying to mimic Halab's bow. "It was . . . it *is* my pleasure, I suppose, milady. Though friendship might be a strong word, for sometimes it seems I only get him into trouble, and he only gets me out."

Halab laughed, so warm and hearty that every face in the room burst into a smile. "What else are friends for, dear girl?" She stepped forwards to embrace Theren, and then Kalem. But when she drew back from the boy, he flushed and, stepping forwards, kissed her first on one cheek, and then the other. Halab went stock still in shock, and Ebon's eyes widened.

"I have heard that that is the proper greeting in Idris," said Kalem, mumbling and keeping his eyes lowered.

A slight flush crept into Halab's cheeks, but her tone maintained nothing but grace. "It is, son of Konnel—though, normally, it is reserved for family greeting family, or for very close friends indeed."

Ebon tried desperately not to burst into laughter, for Kalem's face went so red it was nearly purple. He jerked and twisted, trying to stammer out an apology, but his voice shook so hard he could not get out so much as a word. But Halab only laughed again, and this time they joined her.

"Worry not, my friend." Ebon put a comforting hand on Kalem's shoulder. "Your intent is welcome, even if your knowledge is lacking."

Halab then waved an arm to beckon Hesta and Albi forwards. "Allow me to introduce my sister by law, Hesta, Ebon's mother, and Albi, her daughter, Ebon's sister."

"Well met," said Hesta, bowing. Albi joined her a half-moment later, for she was giving Theren an appraising look. But when she rose from her bow, she gave Kalem a wink. "Will you try to kiss my cheeks, Kalem? We shall have to see if I try to stop you."

Kalem's blush deepened. Halab arched an eyebrow, while Hesta slapped her daughter's wrist. "Albi! That was ill said. It is not seemly to embarrass a guest in our home."

"I did not mean to embarrass him, mother," said Albi, and this time her wink to Kalem was broader. "Who says I spoke in jest?"

"Albi! If you cannot compose yourself, you may take your supper alone," said Hesta.

"Forgive my niece," said Halab, giving her a steely look. "She nears womanhood but does not yet know what to do about it. In time she may yet learn to behave as befits her station."

Finally Albi wilted. "I meant no offense," she said, lowering her gaze. "Forgive me."

"Think nothing of it," said Kalem. "After all, I have embarrassed myself far worse already."

"That you have, my friend." Ebon laid his arm across the boy's shoulder. "But the day is yet young, with much time to redeem yourself. And I smell lamb."

Lamb it was. Halab led them to the dining room, where the meal had already been laid. There, waiting for them in an armchair, was Matami. He rose as they entered, giving Ebon a curt nod.

"Nephew."

"Uncle. My friends, Theren, and Kalem of the family Konnel."

He nodded without speaking, looking at them as though they were pieces of dung he had just noted on the bottom of his shoe. Then they sat to eat.

Again Ebon thought he might melt from the fine taste of the food, with each bite seeming more delicious than the last. Beside him, Kalem closed his eyes often, rolling the food around on his tongue.

Theren showed no decorum whatsoever. She moaned anew with every bite, and her lips smacked loudly, for she chewed with her mouth open. Ebon had never noticed it before; in the Academy's dining hall, there was so much bustle amid the hum of conversation that such a thing could go unremarked. He wondered if she had eaten this way in the Sterling Stag, and how he could have missed it. It made him more and more uneasy, and he kept trying to nudge her under the table, but she ignored him. Across the table, Albi stared at Theren with wide eyes, utterly scandalized. But Matami's scowl grew with every wet smack of Theren's lips.

To their credit, Halab and Hesta were the picture of decorum. They ate primly and quietly, and if they noticed Theren's atrocious manners, they gave no sign. Once she had eaten her fill, Halab dabbed at her lips with her napkin and turned to Ebon. "Troubling news has reached me, nephew. It seems that tragedy has struck the Academy again."

The room's mood darkened at once. Even Theren ceased her loud chewing. "It has, Halab," he said quietly.

"What happened, exactly? Word does not reach my ears so quickly without being twisted in the mouths of those who bring it."

"There is a student—or there *was*, I suppose I should say. It seems she was stealing things from the vaults beneath the Academy."

"Vaults?" said Albi, perking up.

"Rooms in the basement, protected by magical enchantments," said Kalem. "Inside there are powerful artifacts that grant the owner abilities akin to wizards, or else strengthen the magic of wizards who hold them."

"How fascinating," said Albi in a voice of silk. "Thank you, Kalem." She smiled sweetly, and Kalem gulped.

"Her name was Lilith, of the family Yerrin," said Ebon. "Last night, she was caught in the act of her theft. The student who caught her was . . . that is, she . . ." He could not go on, and let the words subside.

"She killed him," said Theren, voice clotted with fury. "Just a boy. Younger even than Kalem."

"Such a tragedy," said Albi. "But what more can one expect from a Yerrin? They have always been a treacherous clan."

Ebon fixed her with a look. "Her cousin, Oren, fought to stop her. He pitted his power against hers, and though he failed, that does not lessen the effort."

"Were you there, my son?" Beside him, Hesta's eyes shone as she regarded him.

Ebon frowned. "Yes, Mother. But I was unharmed. She struck only at Vali."

"How horrible that must have been," she said, shaking her head. "I am so sorry you had to witness it."

Her hand held his tightly, thumb caressing his palm. A sudden lump formed in his throat, and he blinked back the smarting in his eyes. He could not remember the last time his mother had touched him so, for he never saw her without his father, and Hesta knew well that Shay would scorn them both if ever he found his wife coddling their son, as he saw it.

"We are whole," he said, placing his other hand over hers. "That is all that can be asked. Others are not so fortunate."

"And may you ever remain so, now that the criminal faces the King's law." Halab raised her goblet. "To those in the darkness."

"To those in the darkness." Around the table they raised their cups and drank deep.

TWENTY-THREE

TALK SOON TURNED TO LIGHTER MATTERS, AND IT WAS NOT LONG BE-fore the meal was done. Halab excused herself. She and Hesta had some business in the city, but she promised she would return before long. Matami vanished without a word. Ebon wondered whether he ought to leave the manor with his friends, but before he could, Albi bounced to his side and seized his arm tight.

"Well, brother, what say you? Shall we walk in the garden again? This time there are more of us, and mayhap this company is more interesting as well." She fixed Kalem with a coquettish smile. The boy blushed and stared at his shoes.

Ebon tried to hide a frown, but did not entirely succeed. "I suppose so. But let us show my friends the manor first."

"Oh, what greater pleasure could there be?" said Theren, rolling her eyes. "I have often longed to explore the dwelling of wealthy goldbags."

Albi gasped. But Ebon shook his head ruefully. "Try not to mind her. I have had to grow used to it. There are many in the Academy who

396

resent us for our coin. Some of the other merchant's children, or children of nobility, wear the term 'goldbag' like a badge of honor."

"Well," said Albi, looking at Theren askance. "I do not know that I wish to get used to it. But come. Let us show them about."

And so she and Ebon took them room to room, showing them the fine craftsmanship of the furniture and the artistry of the tapestries and paintings. Kalem was most interested. Ebon knew the boy's family had fallen upon hard times, and likely he now walked among more wealth than he had ever seen. What was more, Albi would often take his hand briefly as she pulled him from room to room, or press up against his arm as she pointed out a particular detail in a painting, so that Kalem grew ever more flustered as they went, and tried with increasing difficulty to keep his eyes on the manor itself. Ebon soon found himself frustrated with Albi's obvious flirting, but worried that if he mentioned it, it would only get worse. She had always loved to tease him.

Theren seemed impressed at first, but quickly became bored. Soon Ebon practically had to drag her from room to room, following behind Albi as she grew ever more relentless in her advances towards Kalem. At last he felt he had to end it. He interrupted her just as she was explaining the history of a painting hanging in the main hall.

"It has grown too warm and stuffy in here," said Ebon, fixing her with a sharp look. "Why do we not step out into the courtyard to cool ourselves?"

Albi glowered. "I suppose, if my brother is uncomfortable."

"He is," said Ebon. "Come."

Outside, the frosty air was indeed a welcome relief from the heat of the manor's fireplaces and torches. Ebon sighed, watching his breath waft up into the grey sky. Before them lay the wagons, arranged in neat rows, canvas roofs covered with a light dusting of snow.

"When does Matami mean to bring the wagons back home?" said Ebon.

Albi turned from Kalem, whose eye she had been trying to catch, to stare daggers at him. "Who knows, or cares? He will take them home when he leaves the Seat. I have heard it will be soon, but nothing more exact."

Ebon frowned. A thought tickled the back of his mind—something important that he could not place. Something about the wagons, full of spices for the High King, soon returning home to Idris. All under Matami's command . . .

It came in a flash. If he and Mako had been right in their suspicions, Lilith might have been in league with Matami and Shay. Now she writhed under the knives of Mystics who sought to learn where the artifacts had gone.

But what if they lay before Ebon's very eyes?

Albi was caught up in some whispered conversation with Kalem. Ebon snatched Theren's elbow and drew her aside.

"What has gotten into you?" she said, shaking her arm from his grip.

"The artifacts. What if I was right before, and Lilith was in league with my uncle? If she stole the artifacts and brought them to him, and he means to take them back to Idris . . ."

Ebon trailed off, letting his eyes rest upon the wagons. Theren followed his gaze, and then gave a start. "You think they are here?"

"They could be. Who would think to look for them? He could have done it under my aunt's very nose, planning to bring them home to my father."

"There is only one way to find out for sure." Theren gripped his arm, dragged him towards the wagons, and opened one of the back flaps. But the wagon held nothing.

"Search the others," said Ebon. They split up and went wagon to wagon down the line. But one after the other was empty.

"What are you doing?" Albi appeared at his elbow, and was now looking at him as if he were mad.

"Where are the spices?" said Ebon. "All the goods you brought from Idris? They are not here."

"Of *course* not," said Albi, rolling her eyes. "We have delivered them already and are waiting for the wagons to be refilled before leaving."

"Are they *all* empty?" said Ebon. "Has anything come in, mayhap, to bring back to Idris? Anything recent?"

Albi looked skyward in thought, and then opened her mouth to reply.

"What in the darkness below do you wretches think you are doing?"

398

Matami pounded through the snow, approaching them with fury blazing in his eyes. He seized Ebon's shoulder and shoved him away from the wagons.

"Leave off!" cried Theren, going to Ebon's side. She scowled up at Matami, who tried to loom over her, though he was only two fingers taller. He raised a hand to strike her, but that was a mistake. Theren's eyes flashed with light, and she put forth a hand. Matami reeled suddenly, struck by an invisible force. Albi screamed.

"Guards!" cried Matami. "Take her!"

Drayden men in chain shirts, holding spears and with swords on their belts, streamed into the courtyard from the manor and the gatehouses. But they balked upon seeing Ebon there with his friends.

Matami seized one of the guards by the arm and shoved him towards the children. "I told you to take her! Vile little witch—you shall be flogged for this, and the boy as well." His sharp, dark eyes fixed on Ebon. "And you would be wise never to return, nor should you have come today. Spare the family further disappointment from any association with your feckless, worthless self."

Still the guards seemed reluctant to move. Theren's hands remained raised, and her eyes held their powerful glow. "I see only one worthless wretch here. Why do you not try to take me yourself? You call Ebon a disappointment, but at least he is no coward."

Matami bared his teeth, and he turned to the guard beside him, grasping for the man's sword.

"Stop this madness!"

Halab's shout pierced the courtyard, ringing in Ebon's ears. He turned to see her behind them, standing in the gateway leading to the street. But she did not meet his eyes, for she never removed her furious gaze from Matami.

Ebon's uncle blinked, and his hands froze halfway to the sword. "Sister," he rasped. "These three—"

"Silence your weeping sore of a mouth." Halab came forwards, pushing the children firmly aside to stand before them. A finger pointed at the guard beside Matami, who straightened to attention at once. "You there. Jarrah, is it not?"

The man bowed at once. "Yes, my lady."

"Strike my brother in the stomach, and do not be gentle."

Matami's mouth gaped in protest. Jarrah hesitated only a moment, but then he saw the resolve in Halab's eye. He turned, driving his mail-covered fist into Matami's gut. Matami gasped, his breath leaving him, and fell to his knees in the snow.

"Get him up," said Halab. Jarrah dragged Matami back to standing. "And now put him back down."

Again Jarrah punched Matami, and this time the man whimpered as he fell to all fours in the snow. Ebon winced, averting his gaze. But beside him, he saw Albi watching their uncle with her chin held high, eyes bright, a grim smile playing at her lips.

Halab stepped forwards and seized Matami's collar, dragging him back to his feet and staring into his eyes. He could not meet her gaze, but turned every which way to avoid her.

"Sister," he said, still gasping from Jarrah's blows. "I only—"

"You are only a sniveling, spineless wretch," said Halab. "You dare to call my dearest nephew worthless? Know this: I value his life more than yours by a wide, wide margin. His friends are my guests—*my* guests, *Matamiya,* and yet you dared to order violence against them. Thank the sky my guards are wise and did not follow your madness. Even our servants prove they are worthier than you."

She released his collar, folding one hand into the other and twisting the ring on the middle finger of her left hand. Matami sagged in relief, probing at his tender stomach. But then Halab removed the ring, and struck him in the eye with her own balled fist. He cried out and fell again, clutching at his face.

"I have always been able to tumble you, and I see nothing has changed," said Halab, her voice dripping with scorn. "Were you anyone but my brother, I would throw you to the King's law, or mayhap mete out her justice myself. Never lay eyes upon my nephew again. Now begone."

Matami reached up towards the guards, seeking their help to stand. But Jarrah and the others stepped away, lifting their gazes from him in contempt. So he scrabbled on the ground until he could stand and then, without a backwards glance, slunk away between the wagons. But from the moment she banished him, Halab turned away, ignoring him, and she looked upon the children with sorrow. Absentmindedly, she shook out the fist with which she had struck Matami.

"Dearest nephew, and you, my guests. I thank the sky above that I returned when I did. This was unforgivable."

"Matami's conduct, mayhap, but not yours, dear aunt," said Ebon.

"He is right," said Kalem. "Think nothing of it, I beg you."

There was a moment of silence. Then Ebon drove a sharp elbow into Theren's ribs. "Ow! Oh, er . . . it is no great worry. I could easily have bested him in a fight."

"You should never have needed to," said Halab, shaking her head. "This is my household, and his dishonor falls upon my own head."

"You cannot be responsible for Matami, Halab," said Albi, smirking. "He has always been such, or at least as long as I have known him."

Halab sighed. "He has never enjoyed being the youngest of us. It clouds his thoughts, leading them to anger more easily than is desirable. I assure you, his intentions are not so bad as they seem—though of course, intent matters little when one's conduct is so wretched."

Kalem stepped forwards and gave her a bow. "I hope I do not speak out of turn, madam—but for me, he is more than overshadowed by you, in whom intent and conduct are united in honor, and both warm the heart."

From the corner of his eye, Ebon saw Theren roll her eyes. But Halab put a hand to her breast, cocking a head as she smiled down at Kalem.

"Now here is one whose courtesy cannot be held in too high of esteem, and whose silver words could charm the heart of a carrock. I thank you, Kalem of the family Konnel, and am reminded of my own words, when I looked forwards to more favorable meetings with your family. From this day forwards, I shall call no meeting more favorable than ours."

The boy flushed and retreated behind Theren's shoulder. Ebon smiled at Halab. "Now we must be going, dearest aunt. The day wears on, and the Academy holds a Yearsend feast."

"You cannot leave after this," said Halab. "I had meant to attend business in the palace, but I will postpone it. We can hold our own feast to atone for today's unpleasantness, though it will be on short notice."

"Please do not trouble yourself," said Ebon. "Dark times have fallen upon us all, and nowhere more so than in the Academy. But now that they have passed, it would do us well to draw together and spend this Yearsend in each other's company, so that the healing of our hearts may begin."

Halab inclined her head. "Your words are wise, dearest nephew. Already you have learned much at the Academy, and you do our family a great service. I hope we may see each other again soon."

"Of course we will." Ebon stepped forwards to kiss her cheeks. "Farewell."

Kalem held forth a hand. But Halab used it to pull him close into an embrace, and then did the same with Theren. "Visit whenever you wish. I am at your service, and the manor is yours."

Theren raised an eyebrow. "And what of the goblets and silverware within the manor?" Ebon snatched her sleeve and dragged her away.

Albi said her farewells last, primly shaking Theren's hand and giving Ebon a hug. But Kalem she kissed on the cheek, much to his embarrassment. "I hope to see you all again soon," she said, though she never took her eyes from Kalem's.

They left at last, setting out into the streets and winding their way back towards the Academy. As the manor vanished from sight behind them, Theren was first to break the silence.

"Your aunt was a kind and honorable woman. I have heard very different things about the Draydens. If they were all like her, I imagine your family's name would be no terrible thing."

"You are right," said Ebon. "I have been disliked all my life because of my family name. Halab has been my only consolation. I think she tries to guide my kin in the right direction. But they resist her, as Matami clearly shows."

"She is not the only one," said Kalem. "Your mother also was very gracious, and your sister most polite." His cheeks reddened again, and he avoided their eyes.

"Polite indeed," said Theren, smirking as she pushed his shoulder. "And you were most charming in turn. See to it that you do not charm yourself into her bed."

"*Theren!*" cried Kalem, looking as though he might be ill. "She is a child."

"She is nearly a year older than you."

"*I* am a child!"

But Ebon ignored them both, for his thoughts were preoccupied by what Kalem had said. Yes, his mother had been kind to his friends. Yet throughout his life, she had never been kind enough to protect him from his father. Never did she participate in Shay's cruelty, but she never spoke against it, either. Today she had been concerned at the thought of Ebon witnessing Vali's death. Did she not realize that that had disturbed Ebon nowhere near as much as the hatred and scorn of his father?

Theren seized his sleeve, startling him from his thoughts. He blinked as he looked at her. "What?"

She pointed past him. "There. Look at that cart."

Ebon followed her finger to a wooden cart down the street, loaded with several crates. Beside it walked a man in dark grey instructor's robes, while two of the High King's guard flanked the cart on either side. And looking closer, Ebon could see that the instructor was Dasko.

TWENTY-FOUR

"THAT IS DASKO," SAID KALEM.

"Hush!" said Theren. "We can see that. Get out of sight."

"Why?" asked Ebon. But she and Kalem were already scampering behind the edge of a nearby shop, and so he followed. The alley they ducked into stank, and Ebon covered his nose with a sleeve, reluctant to touch anything. "Theren, what are you doing?"

"Are you not curious what Dasko is doing out here, or what is in the cart beside him?"

"Curious? Certainly," said Ebon. "But not enough to skulk about like some thief."

"I want to follow him," said Theren. "It is the first day of Yearsend. Why is he not on holiday?"

"A student died only yesterday, Theren," said Kalem quietly. "No doubt the faculty have much to look after."

"This far into the city? No, there are too many questions. Come, and let us have answers."

Theren darted out from the alley, for Dasko and the cart had turned

404

down a side street. Ebon and Kalem hastened to follow. From building to building they scuttled, keeping always in the shadows, though in truth Dasko and the High King's guard did not seem overly cautious. They never looked about—and why should they? They were in the middle of the street. It was not as though they moved in secrecy.

Soon Kalem grew impatient. "This is folly. Clearly they are up to nothing nefarious, and the Yearsend feast will be starting soon."

"Leave if you wish," said Theren. "I mean to see where they are going."

Kalem clearly considered it, and Ebon was almost tempted. But just as he had resolved to leave, the cart pulled to a stop, and the guards took position at its rear. It had halted in front of a modest stone dwelling, two stories like the Drayden manor, but nowhere near as lavish. But Ebon noted that none of the other buildings on this street had doors accessible from this side—their front entrances were all on other sides, other streets. It gave the home a sense of isolation, and there were few passersby.

Theren drew them farther out of sight into the alley. "Sky above," she breathed. "Why are there so many guards?"

Ebon blinked, for at first he could not see what she was talking about. But then he looked again. There were two more guards from the High King's palace, one at each of the building's front corners. Near the home's front door stood two figures in regular clothing—yet when Ebon looked closer, he recognized two instructors from the Academy, neither wearing their traditional dark grey robes. Then Theren pointed to the roof, and Ebon saw two red hoods silhouetted against the sky. Mystics, standing guard from on high. Bows were slung on their backs.

"What is Dasko doing?" said Ebon. "What could possibly justify this many guards?"

"Never mind their number," said Kalem. "Why three different groups? What would the High King, the Academy, and the Mystics all wish to guard?"

"What indeed?" grated a harsh voice just behind them.

Ebon jumped and turned around, heart in his throat. There behind them stood Dean Forredar. Kalem gave a little squeak, and Theren's face grew stony. But Xain ignored them both, instead casting all of his ire upon Ebon. Ebon, for his part, tried to match the wizard's gaze.

"Why are you skulking about here, Drayden?"

"We are on our way to the Academy from my family's manor."

"Yes, your manor," Xain sneered. "I know it is close by. That is why I chose this place for my home. How do you like it?"

Ebon glanced over his shoulder, at a loss for words. "Your . . . home? This is where you live?"

"I am only recently returned to the Seat, and have been searching for a suitable dwelling. When I found this one, I knew I had to have it—so close to the Drayden manor, where I can keep an eye upon the scheming of your kin. Keep foes closer than friends, as they say."

"It seems a sturdy house," said Kalem, his voice cracking.

Xain ignored that. "I have a warning for your family, Ebon. Tell them to be on watch, for they are being observed. Too long did they plague me when last I dwelt on the Seat, and too long did they keep me gone after they drove me out. Now I have returned, and I have the High King's favor. The days of their power in Underrealm are numbered."

"I had nothing to do with whatever quarrels you had with my family," said Ebon. "I mean you no ill will."

"Ill will? What does your will matter? You have been raised as one of them. Doubtless you have joined their schemes without even realizing it. So whoever your master may be, tell them what I have told you."

"I have no master." But even as Ebon said it, he thought of the task Mako had given him, the counterfeit uniform he had delivered in the dead of night. He shook the thought away. "Nearly all of my kin hate me anyway."

Xain looked to Theren and Kalem then. "As for the two of you— you would do well to quit this boy's company. No matter what he has told you, you cannot trust a Drayden. Walk by his side, and one day you will find yourselves alone and friendless, betrayed in pursuit of some long-festering scheme."

"I can choose my friends for myself," Theren snapped.

Kalem raised his hands, palms outward. "I think tempers have run high. Certainly there is some sort of common ground—"

Light snapped into Xain's eyes, and he raised a hand. "Begone," he growled. "And if I catch you skulking about again, I will not be so lenient."

Theren raised her own hands in response, but Ebon seized her arm even as her eyes glowed to meet Xain's. "No, Theren."

He pulled her towards the mouth of the alley, refusing to meet the dean's eye. At first Theren resisted, but in the end she let herself be pulled along. Once around the corner, they broke into a jog, and then a sprint once out of sight of Xain's home.

After a few streets Ebon felt safe enough to stop. He bent double, hands on his knees, while Kalem sank to the ground, his back against a stone wall. Theren scarcely seemed winded, and she glared back the way they had come, fists on her hips.

"Why was Dasko there?"

"Did you not understand even that much?" said Kalem. "He was helping Xain move into his new home."

"I know that is what they were doing," said Theren. "But why *Dasko?* He is an instructor at the Academy. Any number of day laborers could be hired, if Xain needed to move a few crates."

"It is likely they are friends," said Kalem. "I know Xain and that new instructor, Perrin, attended the Academy together. Dasko seems of an age with them. It is not Dasko's presence that intrigues me, but that of the other guards."

"I think I know something of that," said Ebon, for he had just remembered his conversation with Mako. "Xain performed some great service for the High King, for which she honored him greatly. It is why he was allowed to return to the Seat after my family drove him out, as you heard him say. The guards must have been posted by the High King."

"She could command the Mystics *and* instructors from the Academy to join her own guards," said Theren, nodding. "That makes sense. But what threat does she think Xain faces? What threat does *he* think he faces? Surely he is not afraid of Ebon's paltry might—though I mean no offense by that."

Ebon raised his eyebrows. "No, clearly not."

Kalem pushed himself up from the ground. "Well, we will do ourselves no good sitting here wondering about it. And now my robes are soaked by the snow. Come, let us return home, before I catch my death of cold."

"Xain is a firemage," said Theren, laying her arm across Kalem's shoulders as they set off together. "You could return and ask him to dry you out with his flames."

Ebon shook his head and went after his friends.

TWENTY-FIVE

THEY GATHERED IN THE DINING HALL FOR THE YEARSEND FEAST SOME time later. The food had been laid out and hidden beneath white sheets held up on wooden frames, concealing the meal from view. But the sheets could not mask the smell, which wafted through the hall and set every mouth to watering.

The instructors' table stood at the head of the hall. Xain sat in the place of honor with his son Erin beside him. Once the hour struck, Xain stood and raised a goblet of wine. Everyone quieted, and he waited a moment in silence. When at last he spoke, his thick voice filled the room's every corner, thrumming in Ebon's breast.

"Since the time before time, Yearsend has been an occasion for joy. We herald the passing of another year of our lives, and the sky's bounty that has allowed our survival. But that celebration is always tempered by mourning, for we acknowledge those who have gone to the darkness below, and thank them for their gifts in life. This year has given us more cause for mourning than most. Many have been lost, and some greater than others."

His next word cut short in a choking sound, and he bowed his head. The hall was deathly still. Ebon, Theren, and Kalem looked to each other uncertainly. The silence lasted only a moment, but when Xain raised his head, his cheeks were wet.

"Some give their lives that we might go on. Others give their lives that we might find redemption—they bring us back from the darkness, though we stand on its brink. Still others give their lives to time's natural sway, and then our mourning is not so bitter. But worst of all are those who are taken without reason, claimed by the madness of a sick mind, or by the treachery of a kingdom breaking its vows. Often we seek explanation. It is rarely to be found. We can only honor the dead, who we shall never see again."

Another pause. Ebon heard many students in the hall hiding their sniffles, while others sobbed openly. Xain raised his goblet higher.

"To those in the darkness."

Every cup lifted. "To those in the darkness."

They drank, and then the first course was brought round the tables.

That evening's Yearsend feast left nothing to be desired, fulfilling every wildest tale Ebon had ever heard of the celebration's splendor upon the Seat. Throughout each year, the Academy had to serve hundreds of students three times a day. While the food was wholesome and hearty, it was rarely delicious. During Yearsend, it seemed, the cooks aimed to make up for all the rest of the year's plain fare. There were fine roasts of meat, of boar and beef and lamb, flavored with wonderful spices, served tender enough to fall off the bone. They were joined by crops from all across the nine lands, so that the students had chickpea spread and figs from Idris, and then at the next table, buttered yams and yellow rice from Calentin. In the center of the spread was a table filled to bursting with desserts, where honeyed confections of every type were piled high, and students were free to take what they wished. Wine was also served, although this was held by the cooks, and only given to students who were old enough, and even then withheld if they thought a student had had too much. The last thing the Academy needed was a drunken brawl with hundreds of young wizards who had yet to fully command their powers.

Again and again Ebon went to the serving table to load his plate with more food, again and again leaning back on his bench and clutching at his belly, afraid it would burst. At last he gave up, leaning heavily on the table, sipping lightly at the last of his wine. Kalem's head was nodding beside him, and across the table Theren was licking honey from her fingers.

"A particularly fine feast this year," she said, and gave a loud belch.

"I will not say it is the finest food I have ever eaten, yet I would count this as my favorite meal," said Ebon. "Rarely in my life have I been able to take such a meal with friends, rather than a father who made my life a torment."

"Hmmm?" said Kalem, looking at them sleepily. "Ah, yes. A fine feast indeed."

Theren chuckled and shook her head. But then Ebon felt a hand on his shoulder and looked up to find Dasko standing over him.

"Good eve, Ebon. Have you enjoyed your feast?"

Ebon nodded. "Very much so, Instructor. I hope you have as well."

"Indeed. Might we still take that walk, as I requested?"

"Of course." Ebon stood, but then he looked to his friends.

Theren waved him off. "Go. I should get this one to bed." She pointed to Kalem, who seemed in danger of falling asleep and drowning in buttered yams.

"Good night, then," said Ebon. "I will see you upon the morrow." And he set off through the dining hall after Dasko.

Dasko led him through the hallways and out a white cedar door into the training grounds. The moons lit the night well, and torches mounted along the citadel's walls helped them pick their way forth on the garden path. The instructor did not speak immediately, but let the night's silence rest, occasionally looking up at the stars as they shone bright in the sky.

"I have only been an instructor here for a few years," Dasko said at last. "I studied here in my youth, of course, but that was long ago. I feel as though I have been rediscovering the place anew. It is certainly a different experience, being an instructor."

Ebon blinked and then frowned. "I imagine it would be."

Dasko sighed. "My apologies. I am not certain how to say what I mean, and so I prattle about inconsequential things. That, and not my preoccupation with Lilith's crimes, is what kept me from speaking with you before today."

He stopped, and Ebon halted beside him. Again Dasko looked up at the stars, his jaw working.

"Before I returned to the Academy, I was a mercenary," he finally said, his voice so soft that Ebon leaned closer to hear it. "I fought for a sellsword army that marched across the nine lands. We served with many great families, both merchant and noble. And in one campaign, I served your family. The Draydens. That is when I met your brother."

Ebon felt as though someone had struck him in the gut. He had scarcely thought of Momen since first he came to the Academy. Indeed, ever since his brother's death years ago, Ebon had tried to avoid thinking of it at all. He felt suddenly light-headed.

"Momen and I became fast friends after our first battle together," Dasko went on. "When you came to the Academy, I hardly noticed you, though sometimes a thought tickled my mind. Then, after the attack on the Seat, Jia was frantic, because you had been separated from the rest of the students. Though we eventually found you, her mention of your name was what let the pieces fall into place—Ebon of the family Drayden, younger brother of my friend Momen. During all the time we served together, he would speak of you more often than anything else."

A gasp escaped before Ebon could stop it. His eyes burned, and he turned away, swiping at them with the back of his sleeve. The air felt suddenly frozen, and he raised his hood against it. Dasko took his shoulder gently and guided him towards a stone bench. Ebon sank onto it, hiding his face in his hands and trying to master himself.

"I am sorry to resurrect grief," murmured Dasko. "I did not mean to bring sadness, but advice."

"What advice?" said Ebon, no longer caring at how his voice broke. He found himself growing angry with Dasko—angry that the man would presume to speak of his brother, who he could not have known half so well as Ebon.

"Before Dean Cyrus fled the Academy, it seems that you and he had little love for each other," Dasko said carefully.

Through his grief, Ebon's heart skipped a beat. What did Cyrus have to do with anything? "He was not overfond of me, no."

Dasko looked him in the eye. "Was that because of some personal disagreement between the two of you, or because of some more general schism between you and the family Drayden?"

Ebon shrugged and looked away. "I know not what you speak of."

"I think you do," said Dasko. "Momen often felt the same way— never comfortable in the company of his family, and always burdened by their reputation, which as you know is fearsome. Always he wanted to cast off their name, and something tells me that you may be similar."

Though he would have been loath to admit it, a thrill trickled through Ebon's heart. He never knew Momen had felt the same way about their family. "Even if that were true, what do you expect me to do? I was born a Drayden. I will die a Drayden."

"Yet you need not live your life under the suspicion of others. You must know that Dean Xain thinks ill of you for no other reason than your family's name. I know it cannot be easy to shed that shadow when everyone you meet can see only the darkness it wraps around you."

"And what can I do about that? In truth, I am used to it. I have little choice but to duck my head and hope to go unnoticed."

"But you have been noticed, Ebon," said Dasko, leaning forwards. "Xain does not wish to admit it, but the other faculty know you suspected Lilith from the first. And you may have helped expose her earlier than she would have been otherwise. Soon the Mystics will have wheedled the artifacts out of her. Because of you, the Academy now takes steps to ensure the artifacts will be safer in the future. You should be proud of that, at least. And you owe nothing of that to your family."

"Pride in myself helps nothing. Certainly not Xain's view of me."

"That is what I mean to say. You have helped, whether he sees it or not. Continue to do right, but not in the hope that Xain will love you. Your kin have wounded him, and that wound may never heal. But do it because of the people you may help along the way. That, I think, is what Momen would do."

Ebon stood from the bench, glaring at him. "That is too far."

"I am sorry," said Dasko, standing and bowing his head. "You are right, I presumed too much. Yet I only say what Momen told me on occasion: that he wished to return home and help you, for he knew life with your father would be harder once he had gone."

Though he held his scowl, Ebon felt some of his anger dampen. Momen could not have known just how true his words would prove. He turned away from Dasko, loosing a breath into mist upon the frigid air, and steered the conversation in another direction, hoping to ease the burning in his heart.

"You said they have not yet drawn the truth from Lilith? I had not thought it would take this long to find the artifacts she stole—especially the second time, for she did not have long to hide them."

Dasko shrugged. "She must have worked quickly. It will not be long. The Mystics are . . . very persuasive when they wish to be."

"Will they kill her?"

"Not the Mystics, no," said Dasko softly. "But once they have recovered the artifacts, they will turn her over to the constables, who will put her to death under the King's law."

And there might vanish any hope of learning Lilith's link to Matami or Shay. Ebon ground his teeth in frustration. It seemed that she would suffer for her crimes, but that the conspirators behind her—and he was sure such conspirators existed—would escape, for no one seemed to be looking for them.

Yet, mayhap if Ebon could speak to her . . .

His heart raced. What excuse could he invent? No one would believe he and Lilith had ever been friends. But there was Nella. Ever since the attack on the Seat, she and Ebon had been . . . if not friendly, at least cordial. Yes. It might work.

He turned back to Dasko. "I wonder . . . I know her crimes were terrible. And Lilith and I had a grudge from the moment I arrived here. Yet there are those who never had the chance to say farewell, and if Lilith will never return, it seems cruel to deny them that opportunity. I am close to one who is dear to her."

Dasko nodded, cutting him off. "Theren. I know."

Ebon balked. Theren? How could Dasko ever think Theren and Lilith were friends? Yet the certainty in the instructor's eyes was unmistakable. Ebon nodded and quickly continued. "Just so. Could it be arranged, do you think, for us to visit Lilith? I wish for my own sort of peace with her, and I know Theren desires the same."

The instructor frowned. "I do not know if that would be wise,

Ebon. For one thing, she will not be the same as when last you saw her. The Mystics are never kind to their prisoners. And they will likely be reluctant to have her speak with any outsider. *I* know your character, but they will not."

"Please, Dasko," Ebon begged. "Help me with this, so that this chapter of our lives may be left behind us. I promise we will urge Lilith to tell them what she knows. And the sight of a friendly face may pry loose what the blades of the Mystics cannot."

Dasko's frown deepened. But he looked away in thought before nodding. "Very well. I will see if I can arrange something with Jia, if it is that important to you—and, mayhap, as some token of payment for the ill will borne against you here at the Academy, which you did not deserve."

"Thank you, Instructor. If given the chance, I promise I shall not waste it."

"I believe you," said Dasko, shivering suddenly. "And now let us return to the citadel. I am not yet an old man, yet I find myself less resistant to the chill than I was in my youth."

They made their way back to the Academy and parted once within, heading off to their beds. But Ebon lay awake for a long while, thinking of Momen and Lilith and Theren.

TWENTY-SIX

The next day, Ebon wanted to tell Theren what he had asked Dasko about their visiting Lilith. But his courage failed him every time he sought to speak, and so the day passed without her knowing. The second day was the same, and the third. At last he decided to tell her when the moment seemed right, and not before. After all, there was every chance that the Mystics would not allow Lilith to see them at all. What good could come, if that were the case, from telling Theren?

So they spent the first three days of Yearsend in calm and rest. All day Ebon was with Kalem and Theren, either in the Academy or out upon the Seat. Though studies were suspended for the holiday, they spent a few hours each day in the library. Kalem still searched for more lore concerning Kekhit, and Ebon helped, but it was a half-hearted quest now. Lilith had been caught, and whatever mischief she had plotted with Kekhit's amulet, she could not hope to accomplish it now.

They spent their evenings in the dining hall or out upon the Seat, telling each other tales or listening to musicians fill inns with their splendor. Ebon felt a sense of peace he had not felt in a very long time.

True, there were rumblings that the High King was readying her armies to make war on Dulmun at last, and whispers about the nine kingdoms—how some were on the cusp of joining the war, while others were on the cusp of joining it on the wrong side. But all was peaceful on the Seat. Even war rested during Yearsend.

It was a leap year, and so they had a fourth day of holiday to enjoy. The dawn came bright and cold, and they lounged in the library for most of it. Ebon had received word that his family would be hosting some royals. Halab had given him the opportunity to visit the manor, but had not required it, and so he had declined. He had attended such dinners before, and knew he would be bored to tears. So in the morning he sent word to Adara asking if she wished to meet in the evening, and by the midday meal she had replied that she would be delighted. She had even painted her lips and pressed them to her letter, which Ebon laughed to see.

As the sun began its long march towards the horizon, they left the Academy and made for the western end of the Seat. Kalem hummed aimlessly as they went, and Ebon drank deep of the crisp air. But Theren scowled as she walked, and after a while gave Kalem an irritated look.

"Cease that humming. Soon studies will resume. Let us have a proper period of mourning, at least."

Ebon stifled a grin. "All good things end, Theren."

She pushed him, nearly making him stumble into the snow. "Yet you need not remind me. Do you know how my mind grows numb, studying my lessons when my skills are so far advanced?"

"And doubtless your humility troubles you greatly, as well," said Kalem, wide-eyed and innocent. Quickly he ducked Theren's swinging fist.

They made for Leven's tavern, the place where they had first met, and one of their favorite haunts on the island. It was far enough removed that there were rarely other students about—but this time Ebon ran into Isra at the door. He did not see her coming out as he entered, and their shoulders struck each other. She glared at him, and he ducked to avoid her dark, intense eyes.

"My apologies," he said.

She did not answer him for a moment. Then at last she said, "Well? May I pass?"

417

Ebon blushed, for he had not realized he was still blocking the door. "Of course, of course," he said, stepping aside. She made to move past him, but he spoke quickly before she could go. "How is Astrea?"

Isra met his gaze, now with softer eyes. "Well enough. I am taking care of her."

"Thank you," said Ebon. "I will try to spend more time with her once classes resume, to help ease her mind."

To his surprise, Isra's face hardened. "I hardly think that would help."

Ebon frowned. "What? I—"

"Everyone knows you have been meddling about the Academy. Who is to say you did not provoke Lilith? She is another goldbag, after all, just like you."

"You speak strong words about something you do not understand," said Theren, giving the girl a scowl. "Ebon is nothing like Lilith."

Isra snorted. "Easy words for you, who may dip your hand into his pocket to pay for fine food and drink. A goldbag's friends defending a goldbag. Yet you, too, will suffer in their war."

She turned and left them. Theren made to follow, but Ebon seized her arm. "Let her be. We are all distraught after events of late. Some show it differently than others."

"I would like to show her something, certainly," Theren growled. But she let Ebon bring her inside.

Leven hailed them the moment they entered the bar, and they waved back from the doorway. Their table was empty, and they made their way towards it. But then Ebon noticed that at one table sat Oren and Nella, Lilith's companions. They were together in a corner, shoulders hunched over their drinks, neither of them speaking. Their eyes wandered, and Ebon could not help feeling that they looked somewhat lost.

"Give me a moment," he said, letting Theren and Kalem go on without him. He crossed the room until he stood by Oren and Nella's table. Nella gave him a courteous nod, but Oren only glowered up at him.

"My condolences for what happened to Lilith," Ebon said softly. "That cannot be easy."

Oren's brow furrowed deeper. "Get away from us, you sniveling little—"

"Oren!" Nella cut him off. They matched glares until Oren relented, taking a sip from his cup. Nella looked back up to Ebon. "Thank you. But I do not believe Lilith could do this."

"Times are strange indeed," said Ebon. "Many have revealed in themselves things we can scarce imagine."

"You mistake me," said Nella, frowning. "I mean I *do not* believe Lilith could do it. She is no monster. I know it. I—" Her voice broke, and she looked away.

Ebon stood uncomfortably for a moment. Then he tossed a gold weight upon the table. "Have yourselves a fine bottle tonight."

Oren glared. "We do not need your coin, Drayden."

"I know you do not need it. But I wish to give it. You may choose not to believe me, but her fate brought me no joy. Good evening."

He backed away. For a moment he thought Oren would throw the coin at his face. But Nella picked it up, nodding her thanks, and then waved down a barman. Ebon crossed the room and joined his friends at their table.

"And why did you feel the need to take your life into your hands?" said Kalem, looking across the room in fear.

"They have lost a friend," said Ebon quietly. "If you think they do not feel the pain of that, just as we would, you misunderstand them."

"Their friend is a murderer," said Theren, glaring into her cup of wine.

"I think there is more to it than that," said Ebon. "That is why I want to talk to her."

He spoke the words without thinking, and caught himself too late. His eyes widened. Theren's look sharpened at once, though it took her a moment to understand. When she did, she leaned in to whisper.

"You mean to speak to Lilith? What madness has taken you, Ebon?"

"I need *both* of us to speak to her. We know, though no one else wants to admit it, that Lilith could not have worked alone. I could still have traitors in my family, and they must be exposed."

"You want *me* to come with you?" Theren leaned back and folded her arms. "Never. Not though my life depended on it. I have no wish to lay eyes upon her again."

"Not even if it might save more lives? Even now the artifacts may be on their way across Underrealm. The criminals behind the theft are at large, and no one is yet safe."

Theren glared, but Ebon met her gaze and did not waver. Kalem looked uncomfortably between them. "Theren, it could help," he said. "And besides, if you are so angry with her, you will never get a better opportunity to say so."

"You will never have another opportunity at all," said Ebon. "Once they find the artifacts, Lilith will be put to death."

Theren blinked and looked away. "Very well. If only to help you, and because of my failures to do so in the past."

"Thank you." Ebon put a hand on Theren's. "I will not forget this."

"You had better not," she said, sighing. Then her eyes slid past him, and brightened. "But forget all of that now. Someone has arrived."

Ebon looked over his shoulder to see Adara stepping through the front door. She wore new clothes, or at least ones he had not yet seen, colored violet and trimmed in black. Ebon and Kalem stood to greet her, Kalem blushing furiously.

"Good evening, Theren, and to you, Kalem," said Adara. She smiled, and then drew Ebon in for a kiss. "And good evening to you, my love."

He grinned back at her. "A good evening it is, now. Please, sit. We have ordered a fine bottle for ourselves, and Leven knows to bring you some mead."

"Thank you," she said, sliding down the bench. He took his place beside her. Leven soon came with the mead, and together they raised a glass.

"To Yearsend," said Ebon. "A more eventful year I have never seen."

"To Yearsend," they said, and drank. Kalem's eyes kept darting to Adara and then away again, his fingers fidgeting with his cup.

Theren raised an eyebrow. "What has you so anxious?"

Adara laughed lightly. "It seems I have made the son of Konnel uncomfortable again. I chose to wear his family's colors tonight."

"Aha," said Ebon. "Kalem, you did not tell me."

"It is only that I was surprised," said Kalem, his eyes on the table. "And it has . . . er . . . well, it has made me think of someone else."

"Oh?" said Adara. "Has the young lord at last found a spark to ignite a flame within his heart?"

"Nothing so grand," said Kalem, but his cheeks had gone bright red.

Ebon frowned, but Theren laughed. "We visited Ebon's family only a few days ago. His sister Albi took quite a liking to our little noble-born friend."

Adara looked to Ebon, and when she saw the look of annoyance on his face, she giggled. "Look at the dutiful brother, holding back such stern words."

"I have no words," said Ebon, hiding his face behind his goblet. "Albi's doings are none of my concern."

Theren snorted, while Adara hid a smile. But then she leaned forwards, and in a low voice said, "When you sent your letter this morning, Ebon, I was most glad. I have heard something more from the other lovers. It seems many Academy instructors and other faculty have been seen along the east end of the Seat, though no one knows quite what they are doing."

Ebon nodded slowly. "We saw something of this already. The new dean, Xain, has moved into a dwelling there, and it seems the High King has placed a guard around his house—though I know not why."

Adara frowned. "That hardly seems to account for it. There have been many goings-on—far more than could be explained by one man taking residence in a new home."

"We were there," said Theren, shrugging. "We saw them bringing in his possessions."

"Well, that is not all," Adara went on. "That Academy student has been seen about again, the one I spoke of before. Only this time they were spotted to the east, in the same area as the dwelling you speak of."

Ebon shook his head. "That does not matter now. Lilith has been caught, and is in the care of the Mystics. You will not see her skulking around again."

"The student was seen only last night."

They all went very still. Ebon, Kalem, and Adara shared a look. "Last night?" said Ebon. "But Lilith was captured four days ago."

"Then it is not Lilith lurking about," said Adara.

Theren stared down at her hands. But Kalem shook his head. "And we never had any reason to believe it was, if you think about it. Likely it is someone causing harmless mischief—mayhap going to see a lover, as you do, Ebon."

"Yet I always return before curfew," Ebon muttered. All this talk of Xain's home and the skulking student had brought it back: the itch in his mind he had felt in his family's courtyard, like something heard and then forgotten. And now the image of Xain's home joined his scattered thoughts.

He started in his seat as he suddenly felt someone at his elbow. Looking up, he found Oren standing over their table. The boy's dour expression had gone, and he smiled down at them magnanimously.

"Greetings, Ebon and Kalem. Ebon, I am sorry for speaking angrily before. My mind is much preoccupied these days."

Ebon looked to Theren uncertainly. She broke off from glaring at Oren just long enough to give Ebon a steely look. "Worry not overmuch," said Ebon carefully. "These are strange times."

"Indeed. That is why I have come. I thought you and Kalem might wish to join me in the library. A number of us gather there in the evenings to share wine and conversation. We call ourselves the Goldbag Society." He chuckled and shook his head. "Every merchant's child. Every son and daughter of royalty."

A chill crept down Ebon's spine. He looked past Oren for Nella, but the girl was nowhere to be seen. "That . . . that was Lilith's gathering," he stammered. "But she is gone."

Oren shook his head. "I have taken her duties in running the group. Your company would be most welcome—as would yours, son of Konnel."

Ebon could see that Theren was about to do something foolish, so he quickly cut her off. "I thank you, Oren, but I will decline. I have friends to spend my evenings with already."

But Oren frowned at Theren. "She is no merchant's child. No son or daughter of royalty."

Theren shot to her feet. "I have had enough of this, and more besides. Leave us. You were not invited here, and they have already said they do not want to join your goldshitter club."

Oren did not move. Instead he glared at her, planting both fists on the table. "They *must* join."

"We *must* do nothing," said Ebon, growing irritated. "Leave us be, or—"

Light flooded Oren's eyes as he reached for his magic. But Theren struck first, not with a spell but with her fists. One hand chopped hard at Oren's throat, and the other struck him between the eyes. He fell back with a cry, his head striking a table on the way to the floor. He rolled over onto his stomach, groaning, while Kalem shouted and gripped Theren's arm to keep her from going after him.

Ebon was standing, unsure of what to do. But when Oren turned back to them, the glow had gone from his eyes. Instead they were wild and wide, turning in all directions. At last he focused on Ebon, mouth twisting in hate.

"I know not what I was thinking," he spat. "To have you and this whelp of a boy would shame us all."

"I am glad you have seen reason," said Theren, her voice filled with steel. "Now begone, or next I will use my spells."

Oren fought to his feet and swept away, weaving between tables and bursting through the tavern's door. What few curious eyes had found them slowly drifted away. Ebon took his seat, as did Theren, who was still fuming.

"That was most odd," said Adara, still looking in the direction Oren had gone.

"Mayhap you can tell your lover friends about it," said Theren. "More whispers to slither across the Seat."

"Theren," said Ebon, frowning.

"It is all right, Ebon." Adara put a calming hand on his arm. "He was beastly. I am sorry it tarnished what was a most pleasant evening."

Ebon smiled at her. But Theren snorted and stood from the table. "The night is still young. I shall see you back at the Academy. Just now I find I need something more than wine to soothe me."

She flung the tavern's door open and left. Kalem frowned. "Do you think she will seek Oren, and try to finish their fight?"

Ebon shook his head. "Theren is hot-headed, but even she is not so foolish. I believe she makes for a house of lovers."

Kalem blinked and sank back on his bench. "Ah. I see."

"Speaking of which," said Adara, her hand sliding onto Ebon's leg. "Theren was right about one thing: the night is yet young."

Ebon smiled, but then he paused. He looked at Kalem, raising his eyebrows. Kalem rolled his eyes.

"Oh, go on. It is the eve of the new year, after all. I shall go spend mine alone, in the library. Only do not leave me to pay for the drinks. My allowance is late, and it has been scant besides."

Ebon threw a gold weight onto the table, and then he and Adara stole off into the night, making for the blue door to the west.

TWENTY-SEVEN

CLASS BEGAN THE NEXT DAY, AND IT SEEMED EVERYONE IN THE Academy was all too eager to throw themselves into the business of learning once again. Ebon hoped that Yearsend had been a healing time for them all: a time to reflect upon their tragedy, to wrestle with their feelings, and then to put sorrow behind them. Now life could go on as it had before, and everyone seemed eager to embrace it.

But three days later, Ebon received a sobering reminder of the Academy's losses, though he did not recognize it when first it came. A messenger in dark grey robes came to the door—one of the Academy faculty, bearing a scrap of parchment that bore only a few words:

> *Please come and speak with me. You are still not in trouble.*
> *Jia*

That made him smile. He showed the note to Perrin, and she waved

425

him off before resuming her lessons with Astrea, who these days barely looked up from her desk.

When he reached Jia's study, Ebon was confused to find Theren already waiting. Jia waved him towards an empty chair, and he sat.

"I have spoken with Dasko since you made your request, and also with an old friend in the Mystics. She has secured their agreement to let the two of you see Lilith."

Theren had been scowling since before Jia began speaking. Now she opened her mouth to speak, but Ebon saw the fury in her eyes, and interrupted her.

"Thank you, Instructor. It will do us good, I think, to see her."

Jia looked bemused, knowing something of his feud with Lilith. And she was no fool—she likely knew something of Theren's feelings towards Lilith as well. Yet for some reason, she had arranged the meeting anyway. He would not squander this chance, for he might never have another opportunity to learn the truth of Lilith's motives.

But before she answered him, Jia grew solemn once more. "You must understand something before you go to see her. Lilith has been put to the question since she left us—more than half a week ago, now. Do you understand what that means?"

Ebon understood only too well. He swallowed hard. "Yes, Instructor." Theren nodded grimly.

"She will look much the worse for wear, to say the least, for still she withholds the location of the artifacts she stole. You have been allowed to see her on one condition: you must make an attempt, at least, to draw that information out of her. Those artifacts cannot remain outside the Academy's control."

"We understand, Instructor."

She softened. "And one more thing. When you see her . . . you must understand that the Mystics' questioners take no pleasure in what they have put Lilith through, nor in the further action they must take if you fail. It is their duty. And it is in the service of the Academy's safety—as well as the safety of all the nine lands."

Ebon bowed. "Yes, Instructor." From the corner of his eye, he saw Theren hesitate.

"Lilith will die, then? It is certain?"

Jia's lips twitched, and for a moment it seemed to Ebon that her eyes shone. But she blinked, and the moment was gone. "Yes," she said flatly. "She killed another student. We all witnessed it."

Theren's throat worked, eyes wandering as though she had not heard Jia's words. She nodded, but would not meet the instructor's gaze.

Jia stood to lead them out of the Academy and into the streets, making her way towards a tall stone building a few blocks distant. Ebon had passed the building a few times, but had never learned its purpose. As they came to a stop before its doors, he realized it must be a station for constables, for two of them stood in their red leather armor before the door.

Inside, the broad front room held more of the lawmen. But in the back corner were a pair of Mystics, both of their cloaks drawn about them. One, the taller of the two, had his hood down. The other had their hood raised, covering their eyes, and what little Ebon could see of the face was covered by still more red cloth, like a mask drawn over their features. He felt a little thrill of fear as Jia led them forwards.

"These are the students," she said gently. "The ones to see Lilith."

The taller Mystic said nothing, but only looked down at his companion. The shorter one spoke, and the voice, though raspy and harsh, revealed its owner to be a woman. Still he could not see her eyes. "You mean to see the murderer, Jia."

"Yes," said Jia softly. "The murderer."

The Mystic's head jerked towards the door behind her. "She is in there. We will be just outside, ready to act if she should try to harm you."

"Lilith will not be able to harm me," said Theren, eyes flashing.

"Can you now?" The Mystic erupted in a hideous, bubbling laugh. "Somehow the spirit in your words tells me you are no liar. Are you a firemage, then, the same as she?"

Theren frowned. "A mindmage."

"Still better, or so I have always said." Again came that laugh, sending shivers along Ebon's arms. "Well, you have come for a purpose. See to it."

The Mystic pushed open the door. Theren did not hesitate, and pushed in at once. But Ebon looked at Jia uncertainly until she ushered him on with a wave of her hand.

There, sitting and chained to a table in the room's center, was Lilith. Ebon did not recognize her at first, and thought they must be in the wrong room. The girl's hair had been cropped close to her head. Her limbs were pale and gaunt, and though she still wore the black Academy robes they had brought her here in, now they were covered with filth and matted with blood. Blood, Ebon guessed, from the cuts that covered her body. They were on her fingers and her hands, her ankles and feet. They had left her face free from cuts, but not from bruises, which welled up her cheeks and eyelids until she looked a different person.

Ebon threw a hand to his mouth, suddenly nauseated. But almost worse than her wounds was the look in her eyes. They were wide beneath the swelling, roving wildly in every direction. They must have been starving her, or else she would not eat, for her body had wasted away. She murmured and whimpered and grunted in an unending stream of unintelligible words as though she were half-mad.

The sight of her froze Ebon in his tracks. Beside him, Theren looked just as horror-struck. But Lilith did not even appear to see them.

Theren started when Ebon at last put a hand on her arm. He led her forwards, and they took their seats across the table from Lilith. Ebon leaned over, trying to put himself in the girl's line of sight. But her eyes moved with him, and away, so that he could not meet her gaze. He wanted to speak, but knew not what to say. To his shock, Theren was shaking beside him.

"Lilith?" Ebon said softly. "It is Ebon and Theren."

"Why?" said Lilith, the word snapping like a whip from amid her mutterings.

Ebon looked at Theren, and she back at him. Then he leaned forwards. At least she knew they were here. "Lilith . . . we have come to speak with you. We want to know why . . . why you killed Vali. And Credell."

She slapped her palms on the table and then winced at the sound of it. *"I did not kill Credell!"* she rasped, looking him in the eyes for the first time. But then she looked away again, eyes roving across the walls. "I did not kill Vali either. I do not think I did. I wanted to help him. To save him. He was supposed to join us. The goldbags. I asked him."

Theren sat up straight, sudden anger flashing in her eyes. "You asked him to join your little club, and killed him when he refused?"

But at Theren's cry, Lilith retreated into herself. Her wrists were chained, but she pulled them as far back as she could, and drew her knees into her chest, whimpering.

Ebon placed a hand on Theren's arm. "I do not know that that is what she is saying," he whispered. "Or that she truly understands what we are asking."

"I do," insisted Lilith, whispering without looking up from beneath her close-cropped hair. "I do."

He leaned in across the table, keenly aware that the Mystics were just outside and could likely hear every word. "Lilith. Were there others involved?"

Lilith chewed at her nail. She had already bitten it away, and blood sprouted from her skin beneath her teeth. "I did not kill any others. *I did not kill Credell.* I did not kill . . . I hope I did not kill Vali."

"What do you mean you *hope* you did not," said Theren. "We were there, Lilith. We saw you."

Ebon waved her to silence. "I do not mean more victims, Lilith. We know there were no more. I mean others you were working with. Other conspirators. Can you name them?"

Lilith shuddered in her chair. "I . . . there was another. Another. I cannot say."

"Please," said Ebon. "Please, Lilith, tell us. If we find them, we can find what was stolen."

She stopped moving, and when her eyes met his, they were clear as fresh water. "And what will happen to me then?"

The room went still. Theren looked away. Ebon shook his head. "Then, at least, the pain will end."

Lilith burst into tears, burying her face in her arms on the table. "It is not fair. Not fair, not fair. I do not want to die. Do not want to die. I cannot remember the face of the other. And I do not want to die."

"I doubt Vali wanted to die," spat Theren. But it seemed to Ebon that some of the venom had seeped from her tone.

That only made Lilith recoil further. Ebon could feel her slipping away. He scooted forwards in his chair. "Is it worth it, Lilith? Staying alive, only to suffer more of this pain?"

She curled up in her chair again, rocking back and forth. "I do not want to die. I cannot remember. I did not kill Credell. I do not want to die."

"Please, Lilith. Where did you take the artifacts? Tell us that, at least."

There was no answer, and from her fevered mutterings, he knew none would come. Ebon sighed and stood, pushing his chair back. Together, mute, he and Theren left the room. The Mystics stood solemn outside, heads bowed. Jia must have seen failure in their expressions, for she looked at them with sad eyes.

"It was good of you to try," she said softly. "We should be going."

She took them outside the constables' station. But Theren's legs shook beneath her, and she gripped Ebon's arm for support. When Jia turned to see what was the matter, Theren forced a smile. Ebon could see the tears shining in her eye, threatening to spill forth.

"I wonder if I might walk back alone, Instructor? I need more air to clear my head."

Jia frowned. But Ebon met her gaze. "I can remain with her. I, too, would not mind some time out of my classroom."

"Of course," said Jia, nodding. She gave Theren a final, mournful look, and then slipped away through the city streets.

At once Theren staggered off, away from the street and down an alley between two buildings. Once in the shadows she began breathing hard, her shoulders heaving, little screams of frustration bursting forth every few moments. She turned to the brick wall beside her and struck it with her fist.

"Theren!" cried Ebon. "Theren, stop it!"

She ignored him and struck again. Her eyes burst into white light, and her magic spilled forth. A chunk erupted from the wall with a *crash*, and a shard of stone grazed Ebon's cheek, flinging him to the ground.

"Stop it!" he screamed.

At first he thought she did not hear him, for again she punched the wall. But then she stopped and turned, leaning back against the brick with her eyes closed as she faced the grey sky.

"What is the matter with you?" said Ebon. "You act as though you have been seized by madness."

Theren shook her head, eyes still closed. "I suppose I have, after a fashion. You have asked me often before why Lilith and I hate each other so. Or I suppose I should say, why I hate Lilith, for she has never returned the courtesy. It might have been easier if she had."

Ebon pushed himself up from the ground, trying to dust the mud from his sleeves. With a finger he gently probed his cheek, and it came away with a small streak of blood. He pressed the cut hard with his palm. "Speak plainly, Theren."

"We were lovers once."

That was somewhat more plain than Ebon had intended. The air went very still. She gave a deep sigh and then at last opened her eyes to meet his gaze.

"Lilith and I. For almost three years, before the two of us knew much of what we were doing."

Ebon blinked, shaking his head. "You . . . you and Lilith? But you have hated goldbags since even before we met. It is . . . I do not understand."

"I hated them, it is true. Yet you and Kalem have earned my trust, for you are not like most of them. Neither was Lilith, once. She was only a child, or scarcely more than one. And of course we were not in class together, but we studied together in the library, and we spent time together in other places. I learned another side of her, and it was one I came to love dearly. She felt the same. But then, as we both grew into adulthood, she began to act more like the rest of her kin. The family Yerrin is not so dark as your own, but neither are they gentle folk. And Lilith was a favored scion of their house, unlike you, who have long had cause to take issue with the evils of your clan. Lilith embraced them instead. And so I knew I could be with her no longer. She never forgave me for leaving—but I think her feelings for me never faded, as mine did for her."

"But . . . but you were so eager to prove her guilt," said Ebon, shaking his head. "How could you . . .?"

Theren blinked hard, fighting to hold back her weeping. "I thought her family was behind it. I thought to prove it, and thus to show her—

to show Lilith—that they had no love for her in their hearts. At last I thought she might see the folly of her ways. I did not know she had been seized by this madness. And now Vali . . . that poor boy . . ."

She turned away.

So much seemed clear to Ebon now that had been strange before. The way Theren had always hated Lilith, beyond logic or reason. The way Lilith would never fight back, no matter what Theren did to her.

"It must have been terrible for you. Seeing her do that."

Theren choked on a sob and tried in vain to turn it to a barking laugh. "It was. For many, love is a cruel and unkind mistress, and never more so than with Lilith and I."

"Love, you say. Do you love her?"

She shrugged. "Who knows? I think it is better I do not, for her time in this world will soon be ending."

"Yet often love springs forth unbidden."

Even through her tears, Theren smirked. "This is not some Elf-tale between you and Adara, Ebon. This is life, and life is cruel. Lilith embraced its cruelty, and now she will pay the price."

Once, Ebon might have been secretly pleased at the thought of Lilith's death—not that he wished her such harm, but that she would no longer torment him. But now, its inevitability only made him feel hollow.

He reached out a hand for his friend.

"Come, Theren. It is cold out, and the day is only just beginning. Let us leave the streets, and try to leave our troubles as well."

"I do not think it shall be as easy as that." But she took his hand and let him draw her away from the wall, and together they made their way back to the Academy.

TWENTY-EIGHT

The memory of Lilith in the constables' station haunted Ebon for the next few days. Often he would catch himself thinking of her in class, when Perrin's sharp rebuke would bring him back to his spells. Or he would sit in the library, staring at the same page for nearly an hour. At last he would realize that he was not seeing the words on the page at all, but Lilith's wild, darting eyes.

Her madness struck him as odd. He knew that torture could do strange things to a mind. Lilith's frantic muttering and wordless rocking in her chair seemed like something more than that. But he had no idea just what it might be.

Fingers snapped before his eyes, bringing him back to the dining hall where he ate with Kalem and Theren.

"Ebon," said Kalem. "What is the matter with you? You have not spoken since we sat down to eat, nor have you touched your food."

"I am sorry. My thoughts these days are troubled. What were you saying?"

Kalem sighed and turned away. "Oh, nothing of great import. But *you* had better treat your classes with better attention. I hear Perrin has half a mind to kick you back to the first-years' class."

Ebon chuckled. "She did, until yesterday when I managed to shift stone back into the box." It had almost been an accident, but still he had done it; after shifting the stone from the little wooden cube, he had managed to scoop it all back in. When he tried repeating the spell, of course, the stone had splattered all over the place, but at least he had done it the once.

Theren was silent beside them, glaring down into her oatmeal, sullen as she had been since their visit to Lilith. Ebon had come to regret bringing her along. He was glad to know the truth of her relationship to Lilith, but it was obvious she had been greatly disturbed by what they had seen.

When their meal was over with, they made for the hallways. Theren struck off on her own without a word, while Kalem ruefully shook his head and bid Ebon farewell. He headed for Perrin's class, but soon a sharp whisper stopped him. He rounded and saw Oren lurking in an alcove.

Ebon glanced up and down the hallway in both directions, suddenly unsure. He wondered if this might be some trick—especially since he did not see Nella, who he trusted more.

With a frustrated growl, Oren seized his sleeve and dragged him down the hallway, ducking out the first white door they found and emerging onto the Academy's grounds. Quickly he hauled Ebon to the great outer wall, stepping into a hedge where no one could see them.

"What is this about, Oren?"

The boy's eyes were wild. "I have heard you saw Lilith."

Relief flooded Ebon, and he loosed a sigh. "Oh. Yes, I did. But you could have asked me that in the hallway."

Oren ignored him, seizing the front of his robes. "How is she? Are they treating her well?"

Ebon gave him a quizzical frown. "No, Oren. They are not. She is a murderer, and being put to the question for . . ."

He stopped, for he could not tell Oren about the artifacts. Then he took another look at the boy and realized there was something odd about him. His hands spasmed where they held Ebon's lapels, and every muscle in his face was twitching. His eyes darted every which way, not seeming to search for anyone coming near, but simply out of an inability to sit still. Gaunt was his face, drawn thin as though he was starving. It had only been four days since Ebon had seen him last, but the change in his features was startling.

"Are *you* all right, Oren?"

"Of course I am," Oren snapped. "I am not the one under the knives of the Mystics."

"You do not look well."

"*I am fine!*" cried Oren, shaking him. Ebon seized his wrists and tried throwing him off, but Oren had the grip of a madman.

"Fine, then," said Ebon through gritted teeth. "Let me go. I have told you what I saw."

"Lilith could not have done it, Ebon. She *would* not. And *could* not. I know her. She is my cousin. We have spent all our lives together. She is no murderer, I tell you."

Ebon felt himself soften. He put a hand on Oren's shoulder. "I was there, Oren. You and Nella tried to stop her. And we all saw what she did to Vali."

"She did not," said Oren, shaking his head. "She was . . . that was . . ."

"I am sorry," said Ebon. "But at least it is over."

"*She did not!*" Oren shoved Ebon away, and light sprang into his eyes. He held out both palms, and flames erupted in the center of each. Ebon raised his hands to shield his face, terrified.

But then the flames winked out as quickly as they had come. Oren stared at his palms, horrified.

"I did not mean . . . I would never . . ."

Ebon tried to answer, but Oren ignored it, turning away. He wandered slowly off, still staring at his hands, muttering *I would never, I would never.*

A thrill of fear coursed through Ebon, and he made his shaky way back to Perrin's class.

The next day, Ebon was practicing his counter-magic again. He sat opposite Astrea on the bench, each of them holding one end of the wooden rod. He could tell her heart was not in it, and yet still he could do nothing to stop her.

"Try again," he said. "I think I am ready."

Astrea sighed. Her eyes filled with light, and she pushed stone up along the wooden rod. Ebon's own eyes glowed in response. He sought for the stone, trying to stop it. He could *almost* see it, *almost* glimpse the particles of stone sliding along the wood. But they were surrounded by some sort of glow, and he could not see through it to the stone beneath.

Soon it was done, and Astrea held up the stone rod with a sigh. Ebon growled in frustration. But then he thought again about what he had seen. He squinted at the rod, and a careful smile stole across his face.

"Try it again."

"Ebon, I am weary of this."

"Please, Astrea. I have just thought of something that may work."

She sighed, changing the rod back to wood, and then placed the other end in his palm. Once more her eyes glowed, and stone rippled along the rod.

Ebon focused on the glow. He saw it sliding along the wood, transforming it piece by piece. But now, rather than trying to stop the stone, he seized the glow, and . . . *squeezed*.

Snap

The magic winked out of existence. The light vanished from Astrea's eyes, which widened as she looked down at the rod. Ebon laughed and held it aloft. It was made of wood, with not a spot of stone to be seen.

Across the room, Perrin straightened from where she was teaching another student. "Have you done it at last, Ebon?"

"I have, Instructor!" Then he heard his own crowing and cleared his throat. "That is, with Astrea's help, I believe I have learned my first bit of counter-magic."

Perrin thundered to the front of the room and then waved Ebon to join her. "Ebon, tell the class what you have learned."

Ebon held up the rod. "When Astrea first turned the rod, I could see only the stone turning the wood. But I could not stop it, and so she always bested me. But at last I learned to look for the magic itself.

It appeared as a glow, surrounding the stone as it moved along the rod. When I focused on the glow rather than the stone, and stopped it, her magic failed."

"And that is the answer," said Perrin. "Only through practice and concentration can we see magic clearly, and that is what lets us defend ourselves against it. Magic appears differently to some—many see it as a glow, the way Ebon does. Others see it as a rippling in the air, or a fine dust swirling about. However we see it, it is not *until* we see it that we can learn to control it. The heart of transmutation is to see the *thing* for what it is, and change it. In counter-magic, you must see the magic itself. Though this is not one of your passing lessons for the class, it is nevertheless an important one. Take pride that you have learned it."

Ebon beamed. The other students wore expressions ranging from interested to disgruntled. Back on the bench, Astrea seemed numb, and had not lifted her gaze from the desk. The sight dampened Ebon's spirits.

The bell rang for the midday meal. Ebon looked uncomfortably away and made for the door. But outside it, to his surprise, was Dasko. The Instructor pushed himself away from the wall with a nod.

"Ebon. I had wondered if we might walk together before lunch?"

"Certainly, Instructor." Ebon bowed.

Dasko nodded again and waved Ebon down the hallway, towards a white cedar door leading back out to the gardens. For a moment, he was reminded of his encounter with Oren. But the warm sun outside dispelled such uncomfortable thoughts, though it fell on a world still covered with snow.

"I heard through the door that you have learned your counter-magic. That is a fundamental of magic that some wizards do not grasp until years later in their educations."

Ebon shrugged. "I have the advantage of being older than most of my peers."

Dasko shook his head. "It is not only that. Magic is something ethereal and ephemeral. It is change itself. That is why so many wizards struggle to move from their testing spell to other spells, but learn much faster once they have passed that first step. Too many wizards focus on the thing before them: the wooden rod, or for therianthropes, the color of our skin; the stone the mentalist tries to lift, or the spark the elementalist seeks to summon. They do not learn to see the magic itself, the pure force of alteration that influences all the world."

Though he nodded, in truth Ebon's head had begun to spin. Dasko laughed and clapped his shoulder.

"Momen used to wear the same expression when I spoke to him of magic. A man of action, your brother was. Do not trouble yourself with my words. They are certainly too heady for a student in a second-year class. They will make more sense in time."

"Of course, Instructor. But none of this is why you came to see me, unless I miss my guess. What can I do for you?"

Dasko held his smile, though it lost some of its spark. He looked ahead at the path as they walked. "I thought to ask about your visit with Lilith."

Ebon studied the ground. Oren's interest made some sense to him, but now Dasko? It seemed Ebon and his friends were not the only ones who wished for more of an explanation of the recent tragedies. "Did Jia tell you nothing?"

"Nothing much. She was not in the room, or so she said, and so details were hard to come by."

"It was . . . terrible. She seemed mad, as though her deeds had driven her mind to ruin. Or mayhap it was the torture. She recoiled at the slightest sound, and her body was an awful mass of bruises and wounds."

"You say she acted mad?" Dasko's eyes lit with interest. "How, exactly?"

Ebon frowned. "I . . . her eyes darted all about, and her fingers would not stop twitching. She chewed at them, though they bled and must have pained her greatly. She reminded me of a trapped animal—desperate to escape, but only hurting herself more."

Dasko frowned, stroking his close-trimmed beard with one hand while slowly nodding. "I see. That is interesting, to be sure."

"I do not understand, Instructor. Can you not go see her yourself? Surely you do not require permission, as Theren and I did."

"My duties here have prevented me," said Dasko, looking away. "As well as certain other duties I have been asked to perform, outside the Academy's normal hours."

Ebon remembered him unloading crates from the cart into Xain's home. But surely the dean must have moved in by now. Mayhap Dasko was one of the instructors required to stand guard. "I see. Then, may I ask why this interests you so?"

Dasko quickly shook his head. "Do not trouble yourself over it. It is only that I have been wondering something. I knew Lilith, you see. She attended the Academy before I came here as an instructor, and we had more than one occasion to share time. She could be . . . very difficult as a student. Yet I would never have taken her for a killer."

That reminded Ebon of what Oren had said the day before, and what Nella told him in the tavern on the final day of Yearsend. He frowned.

Crunching footsteps approached, and Ebon looked up to see Jia strolling towards them as though by happenstance. But from the careful look in her eye, and the slight flush in her cheeks as Ebon saw her, it took but a moment to realize she sought them. When Dasko turned back, the smile tugging at the corner of his mouth confirmed it.

"I . . . hope you will excuse me, Ebon. Instructor Jia and I had meant to meet each other over the midday meal."

Ebon nodded quickly—too quickly, and he felt foolish. "Of course, Instructor. Do not let me intrude, or keep you from your duties."

Jia took Dasko's arm, and he led her off through the garden. Ebon made for the dining hall, unable to banish a secret smile.

TWENTY-NINE

LATER, IN THE LIBRARY, EBON SAT WITH KALEM IN THEIR ALCOVE. THEREN had not joined them for the midday meal. Now it was some time into the afternoon's study period, and still she was not with them. They read together for some time, until at last Kalem looked up from his book.

"Do you think she is all right?"

Ebon shrugged. "Why should she not be?"

Kalem frowned and returned to his book. But only for a moment, for they both heard pounding footsteps moving along the library's third floor in approach, and looked up to find Theren running full tilt towards them.

In a flash they were on their feet. But looking behind her, Ebon saw nothing wrong. She was not being chased, other than by the curious looks of other students disturbed by her flight. And the look on her face was not one of terror, nor anger, but of fierce joy. She seized the front of Ebon's robes and shook him, her voice quivering in excitement.

"I do not think Lilith did it," she said, speaking fast. "I know who it was."

Ebon blinked, trying to pry her hands from his body. "Calm yourself, Theren. Everyone is watching."

"Who cares? Lilith is innocent."

Finally he removed her hands from his lapels. "Come, Theren, sit, and tell us what you mean, from the beginning."

She growled, but she took her seat between them. Ebon took one last look over his shoulder. The few curious onlookers turned back to their books.

"Now, what do you mean by this, Theren? You were there, as I was, when Lilith killed Vali. We both saw it, as did many others besides."

"No," said Theren, vehemently shaking her head. Then she paused. "Well, yes. We did see that. But I have thought much, and have had an idea: *mindwyrd.*"

Kalem's eyes widened. But Ebon frowned. "I do not understand."

"Mindwyrd," said Kalem. "Do you remember? It is the power mentalists gain when they consume magestones—the power of command, so that anyone who hears their voice must obey."

"Exactly," said Theren. "If someone had Lilith under the control of mindwyrd, they could have forced her to do what she did. Lilith would have obeyed without question, for she would have had no choice."

But now Kalem shook his head. "That may be possible, Theren. But do you honestly believe someone in the Academy could be using magestones? Surely someone would have noticed by now. The wizard's eyes turn black instead of white for more than a day after the stones are consumed. Lilith killed Vali nearly a week ago. If she was involved in Credell's death, it is many weeks. How could black eyes have gone unnoticed for so long?"

"What if the wizard is not in the Academy?" crowed Theren, far too loud. Ebon shushed her, and she glared at him, but still she lowered her voice to a whisper. "It could be someone beyond the citadel walls. Someone who sent Lilith in to do their dirty work each day, and then made her return to keep the mindwyrd strong, for it will fade if the victim's contact grows stale."

"It is possible," said Kalem. "But even if we acknowledge that, what then? Again, we have an idea that something *may* be true, but no evidence to prove it."

"But we may," said Theren. "I have heard tales of the effect mindwyrd has on its victims. They say it drives them half-mad, as Lilith was when we saw her in prison. She was haggard, her face gaunt and her eyes filled with insanity. These are only rumors, though—that is why I need your help. If we can find proof here, in the library, that these are symptoms of magestones, we can prove her innocence—or at least cast doubt's strong shadow upon her guilt. And once we have done that, I believe we can work towards proving who held her under mindwyrd while she committed her crimes: Cyrus."

Ebon froze. His mouth opened, but he could not summon words. *No. No, no, no, Theren.*

Kalem arched a brow. Theren leaned towards him, speaking faster. "Think. He fled in terror from the attack on the Seat, and he knows that if he returns, he will be branded a traitor and a coward. Doubtless he could have kept running, to find some hovel in an outland kingdom where he might spend the rest of his days. But Cyrus was always a greedy steer. I think he returned and worked his mindwyrd upon Lilith to steal the artifacts for him. Then he could retreat to some outland kingdom to live his days in wealth and power. Mayhap he might even try to take a throne, establishing himself as a new Wizard King."

"That would be foolish," said Kalem, shaking his head. "No one would stand for it. The High King would cast him down at once."

"He could take a new name, so that no one would even know he was a wizard," Theren argued. "And the High King is embroiled in a civil war. What attention could she spare for some usurper on the other end of Underrealm? It is the best possible time for such a scheme."

Ebon had to speak, but he shook with fear at the knowledge of what he must say. "Theren," he began. "This is . . . I am sorry, but this is not—"

She scowled at him, jaw working. "Ebon, I know I have given Lilith no end of grief while you have known me. But I have mocked and derided you and Kalem as well, and yet I know you are not murderers. Lilith is the same. She is vain and small-minded, but she is *not* a killer. Since Credell's death, I have told you how I could not believe Lilith was capable of such an act. Mayhap some part of me—some hidden part I did not wish to acknowledge—saw the truth, even when my eyes could not. I am certain of this, Ebon. Cyrus *must* have done it. He has been influencing her with—"

"I killed Cyrus."

Her words snapped to a halt. She and Kalem went still as statues. The boy jerked in his seat—back, as though he meant to stand, and then forwards again.

"What . . . what did you say, Ebon?"

Ebon could not lift his gaze from his lap. In a whisper he said, "It was the day the Seat was attacked. You remember when I ran off from the group. I told you, and everyone else, that I thought I saw an Academy student fleeing the battle. In truth, I saw Cyrus, and Adara was by his side."

Kalem frowned. "Adara? Why would she . . .?" But Theren looked at Ebon with pity, and Kalem's words faded to nothing.

His cheeks burned, but he forced himself to speak on. "I caught them upon the southern cliffs of the Seat. There, where that little cove had been marked on the map we found, was a boat that Cyrus meant to escape in. I confronted him, for I thought he was kidnapping Adara. It turned out I was wrong, but he grew wroth and attacked us both. He nearly killed me, and with his magic he throttled Adara as well. In my desperation, I found my magic. I turned his feet to stone, and then Adara cast him into the Great Bay, where he sank and drowned."

Theren sagged in her seat, placing one hand to her forehead. Kalem stood, hands twisting at his sides. He turned as if to walk away but paced behind his armchair instead. Ebon felt wretched.

"Darkness take it all," Theren murmured.

"I am sorry," said Ebon. "I should have—"

She shook her head. "No, Ebon. I do not blame you. I even see why you did not tell us. It is only . . . it means Cyrus is not behind this."

"It could be someone else," Ebon said. "Some other wizard manipulating her—"

"They would have to know the Academy."

"What if it was someone in the family Yerrin? Someone who first gleaned information about the vaults from Lilith, and then held her in mindwyrd when she refused to help them on her own?"

"The family Yerrin deal in magestones, or so it is said by many," said

Theren. "But they never consume the stones themselves. Magestones are a slow poison of the mind. Yerrin knows this better than anyone. No agent of that house would risk themselves. Cyrus was the only person who made sense."

Ebon stared at his shoes again. "Still. There could be someone," he murmured.

"I suppose there could," said Theren. But she sounded utterly defeated.

Kalem had gone still behind his armchair, head bowed. Ebon looked up at him. "What are you thinking?"

The boy shrugged. "What is there to think, Ebon? I know not what to say."

"I imagine you are angry."

"Angry? I . . . I do not know. We are friends. But this . . . this is wrong."

Theren sat forwards. "It was in defense of his own life, Kalem. You knew Cyrus—"

Kalem gave her a hard look. "If that is true, he could have told the story. The King's law would have protected him."

"The King's law, mayhap," said Ebon quietly. "But my family? Never. You know the King's law matters little to them. Mayhap Halab would have forgiven me. And I can never guess at Mako. But my father . . . my father would never have stood by. It would have been the excuse he long hoped for. He would have killed me."

"Mayhap. Mayhap not," said Kalem. "You could have figured out some way. Something. *Anything,* rather than keeping this deed in the dark. Sky above, Ebon, you could have told *us.* We could have thought of something—or agreed to keep it secret. Together. But this? I cannot abide by it."

He stepped out from behind the chair and made to leave. Ebon stood. But Kalem only gave him a sad little smile.

"I will not tell anyone what you did, Ebon. You need not fear that. But in the last few months I have grown to love you, mayhap more dearly than my own brothers at home. I thought we had grown to trust each other."

"We do," said Ebon. "I do."

"How can you say that? Were our positions reversed, what do you think I would have done?"

Ebon found it suddenly hard to speak. But he forced the words out, hearing the tears lurking within them. "You would have told me."

Kalem left. Ebon watched until he was out of sight among the shelves and then sank back into his chair, head in his hands.

THIRTY

Kalem did not eat with them that night or the next day. During breakfast and the midday meal he sat pointedly at a table far away, and did not so much as glance in Ebon's direction. When it came time to study in the library that afternoon, he was nowhere to be found.

Ebon thought of finding another place in the library to study so that Kalem could have his nook. After all, he had been there long before Ebon, and had shared it when Ebon came to the Academy. But Ebon still held some hope that Kalem might forgive him, and if that happened, he wanted to be where the boy could find him easily.

But the afternoon's free study passed, and there was no sign of Kalem. When Ebon and Theren went to the dining hall and fetched their suppers, they saw him sitting many tables away. Still he would not look in their direction.

So they ate, neither of them speaking. Now that he had told his friends, Ebon felt terrible that he had kept the secret from them for so long. But also, the weight of Cyrus' death seemed to have mostly fled.

When alone, or in a quiet place, or trying to drift off to sleep, he no longer saw the scene playing out in his mind.

That was little comfort, though, when he had to bear Kalem's hatred instead. And he was not the only one who harbored a strong resentment for Ebon. Whenever he chanced to look at the head of the dining hall, Ebon saw Xain staring daggers his way. That was nothing unusual, mayhap, but today his anger seemed to have gained a particular intensity.

"Mayhap he heard about our visit to Lilith," said Theren, after Ebon mentioned it. "I have noticed him giving me a dark glare as well. I do not think he appreciates our meddling, as he no doubt thinks of it."

"At least with her capture, I no longer have to worry about him thinking I am the killer."

Theren shrugged. "Do not worry about that. I am certain it is only a matter of time before he finds something else to blame you for."

That forced a chuckle from him, though his smile quickly vanished. "Even though the threat is over, I still feel its shadow hanging over the Academy. I thought it would have dissipated by now. No one seems fearful. Only sad."

"Of course they are," muttered Theren. "We have all suffered loss. I only wonder if the pain will ever fade."

Ebon saw Astrea sitting at a table with others, yet still seeming so alone as she stared at her food. Isra was beside her, but even that could not bring her any cheer. Likely this darkness would accompany the rest of her life. For how could it ever be healed? Who could explain to a child so young why Lilith had done what she did? Especially when no one knew her ultimate aim?

"For some, I doubt it," he said sadly.

Theren must have misunderstood, for she patted his arm to comfort him and said, "Kalem will forgive you. He only needs time."

Ebon looked back at his food. "I do not know about that. He holds honor highest of all virtues. More so than you, and certainly more so than me."

"Do not be so certain. He values friendship greatly, as well. And you must remember, Ebon: before meeting us, Kalem had only a few friends. He gave himself to us fully, for we went through much together in the days before the attack. After that, to learn you did not trust him . . . but give him time, and I think he will understand why."

"It is not that I did not trust him! I only . . ." But he stopped and hung his head. How could he defend himself? If he had trusted them, he *would* have said something.

The doors of the dining hall flew open, slamming into the walls on either side. Ebon turned his head to look, and his eyes shot wide.

There in the doorway stood Oren, chest heaving, shoulders hunched together, hands formed to claws. His eyes were wild, scattered, searching everywhere. He was muttering something Ebon could not hear, growing ever louder until they could finally make out the words.

"In my head, in my head. Cannot get her out. Always there, in my head. Always *whispering.*"

At the head of the hall, the Instructors shot to their feet. Some began to come forwards. But Oren's eyes finally fixed on Ebon, and he pointed with a shrill scream that stopped everyone cold.

"You! You know! You know she did not do it!"

Ebon's mouth worked, but he could say nothing. Theren stepped around the table to stand beside him, her lips set in a grim line.

"You know! You know she is in my head! *Whispering!"* Oren screamed.

Then he flew into the air.

Ebon flinched, for he thought Oren was leaping for him. But the boy had been hoisted up by his neck. He froze ten feet up, feet thrashing for purchase. A gurgling burst from his throat as he struggled for breath. For a horrible moment Ebon thought it was Theren acting in his defense. But her eyes were not glowing, and she looked just as frightened as he was.

He seized her robes. "Look for the caster!" he hissed.

She understood, and together they turned in a circle, searching for glowing eyes in the hall. But the press of students was too tight, and now they were milling about, some trying to get farther from Oren, others pressing closer in fascination. There was Nella, pushing forwards, trying to help her friend. Kalem stood frozen in horror. Isra could not take her eyes from Oren even as she dragged Astrea away—Astrea who wept silently, still numb, her face a dead mask. But nowhere could Ebon see the glow of magic in anyone's eyes.

But then came the instructors, now forcing their way through the crowd. They leapt forwards, hands high, and Xain was at their fore. He gritted his teeth, muttering words of power through them, fingers twitching as he sought to bring Oren down from the air. Instructors of mentalism and elementalism stood beside him, trying to dispel the force that held Oren aloft. Those instructors who could not help tried to control the students instead, some of whom had begun to panic. They were guided away from Oren's swinging form, to the edges of the room and out of reach.

"Get him down," growled Xain. His blazing eyes swelled until they lit the space all around him like a burning sun. "Damn it, get him *down!*" Theren leapt to his side, unleashing her power to help.

Oren jerked, moving towards the floor in fits and starts. But too late. All around the dining hall, cutlery flew into the air—knives and forks, all spinning in languid circles.

Suddenly they tore through the room like a cloud of wasps. In a storm they struck Oren, impaling him in a thousand places. Some struck the students behind him who had tried to flee the hall.

Then the magic ceased, and Oren slammed to the ground, his eyes staring sightless.

Everyone began screaming at once—the students who had been struck, now lying on the floor with steel protruding from their skin, and all who had witnessed it, who now pressed for the dining hall's door like a panicked mass of beasts. Perrin bellowed, trying to restore order and direct the flow of bodies by placing her massive frame in the way. Jia stared horror-struck at Oren's corpse on the stone floor, but soon shook herself to awareness and helped the other instructors manage the frenzy.

A hand seized Ebon's collar and threw him back. It was Xain, eyes filled with malice.

"He said you knew. What did he mean? Speak, or I will roast you."

"I know nothing," Ebon choked. "I swear it!"

Light blazed in Xain's eyes, and blue fire sprang up around his palm. "Why did he name you?" he snarled. "The magic that killed him had the strength of magestones behind it. Where are they?"

The dean was crazed. Blood filled the corners of his eyes, mayhap from the effort of trying to save Oren, or mayhap from pure rage. But then something struck Xain from nowhere, and he flew away. Ebon jumped, backing into a table. Theren stepped in front of him, eyes still glowing from the spell that had batted the dean away.

Xain shot to his feet, eyes blazing with light. A gust of wind blasted from his hand—but Theren raised her hands to meet it. The spell stopped cold.

She struck, and Xain was forced to take a step back. Gritting his teeth, he countered with a stronger gale. Again Theren batted him aside, the wave of her hand almost flippant.

Then a brown shape seized the dean, and Ebon recognized it as Jia's bear form. She turned partway back to human, but she kept her size, so that she stood many hands taller than him. Her body bulged with muscle, and she was taller and broader even than Perrin. She dragged Xain up until he was forced to stand on his toes, and when she spoke, her voice was a raging growl.

"Master yourself, Dean. Ebon had nothing to do with this. Mentalism killed Oren. You must have felt that when you tried to stop it."

Xain's breath heaved in ragged gasps. He stared her in the eyes before his gaze slid past her to Ebon. Even as he watched, the rage in the dean's eyes cooled to ice—though that made it no less terrible, and in fact Ebon found himself more afraid than before. With a jerk, Xain threw off Jia's hand and stalked from the dining hall.

Most of the students were gone by now. Someone had fetched a tablecloth and covered Oren's body. Slowly Jia resumed her natural form. She stared at the bloodied cloth on the ground for a moment before going to Ebon. He met her eyes and saw sympathy within them.

"Are you all right, Ebon?"

He nodded weakly. "He did not harm me. Not in truth."

She shook her head slowly. "You did not deserve that. But in addition to his . . . relationship with your family, the dean has a particular distaste for those who would use magestones. It does not excuse his conduct, though it may help you to understand it."

Ebon's eyes were fixed on the cloth covering Oren's body. "What happened to him?"

Jia only shook her head. But Theren spoke softly. "It was mindmagic. I could sense it, but I could do nothing to stop it. It was power like I have never felt—not only strong, but somehow corrupt. If it is true what Xain said, that that was the strength of magestones, then I now know why they are such a great evil."

"I searched for the black-glowing eyes," said Ebon. "But I could not see them. No one was casting a spell upon him, save you and the others who tried to save him. Certainly I saw no black magelight. The murderer must have been skulking out of sight. Mayhap they were outside in the hallway, or in a nearby room."

Scowling, Theren shook her head. "That is not how mentalism works. It needs line of sight. The murderer was in the room. You must have missed them in the crowd."

Jia looked just as frustrated. But then she froze, and a look of horror fell across her face.

"Instructor? What is wrong?" She did not answer, and terror bloomed in Ebon's breast. "Jia?"

At last her eyes found him. He saw her tears welling forth.

"Lilith," she whispered, and then turned to bolt for the door.

Ebon and Theren looked at each other for half a heartbeat, and then ran after Jia as fast as their legs could carry them.

THIRTY-ONE

It took some time to secure Lilith's release. Jia's friend was not there, and at first the other Mystics would not take her word. They said that Lilith was held on the command of the dean, and only his command could release her. She had to send a messenger to get a letter from Xain. At first she wanted to send Theren, but the girl refused to leave the prison until Lilith left it as well. Then she wanted to send Ebon, but quickly thought better of that.

At last a messenger was sent, and one as well to the family Yerrin. Lilith's parents arrived first—both of them merchants in fine green cloth trimmed with silver, whose faces were a heartbreaking blend of sorrow and relief. Theren greeted them awkwardly, and introduced Ebon—but they had little attention for anything other than the door leading to the jail cells. So Ebon and Theren stood off to the side, trying not to look at the Yerrins.

"I forgot to thank you for helping me in the dining hall," Ebon muttered after a while.

"Think nothing of it," said Theren. "Xain was wrong to act as he did."

"Wrong or not, you were glorious," said Ebon, shaking his head. "I knew something of your strength. But to defeat the dean himself so easily . . ."

She shrugged. "Likely he withheld his strength. He did not wish to harm me, but only to get through me so he could reach you. He did not even unleash flame."

Ebon gripped her shoulders and turned her to face him. "You are a boastful person by nature, Theren, and only modest when you know you have no reason to be. It does not suit you. You may have saved my life, and we both know it. Accept my thanks."

Her jaw tightened as she fought a smile. "Still your flapping lips, Ebon. You are so dramatic."

He sighed and shook his head before pulling her into an embrace. She did not return it, but neither did she push him away.

When Xain's decree finally arrived, it was delivered by none other than Nella, who greeted Ebon with a stiff nod.

"I heard what was happening and insisted on bringing this myself," she said.

"We came as quick as we realized the truth." Ebon looked away, for he felt too ashamed to meet her eyes. "It was our fault this happened to her in the first place."

Nella did not seem to want to look at him, either. "This is the second time you have proven yourself to be not entirely a bastard." He gave her a quick look, but saw her wearing a small smile, which he easily returned.

After reading the letter, the Mystics sent two constables into the prison to fetch Lilith from her cell. They all had to wait far longer than made sense to Ebon—surely the prison could not be so vast that it took this long to fetch her.

But when Lilith finally arrived, he thought he understood better. She could barely walk, and was mostly carried by the constables who held her arms. She looked far worse than the last time he had seen her—the swelling in her face had receded, but black bruises remained, splotching her already-dark features like grisly birthmarks. The cuts on her hands and limbs had multiplied, and her lips were bone-dry and cracked. The fireplace lighting the station's front room cast her face in hideous shadows and made her look like a demon of the darkness below.

Jia and Lilith's parents moved to help. But Theren was faster. She seized Lilith with a piteous cry, wrapping her arms around the girl in a tight embrace. Lilith's arms fumbled and grasped, as though she could not see Theren and was trying to feel for her presence. But once her arms were draped over Theren's shoulders, she held her tight as she could, and tears leaked from her wild, wandering eyes.

"Forgive me," Theren murmured into her shoulder. "Forgive me, please, for I will never forgive myself." Lilith's eyes still stared into an unknowing distance, but her fists tightened on Theren's cloak.

Then Lilith's parents were there, and they helped the girls hobble awkwardly towards the door. Jia stood back so as not to intrude. As they passed Nella, Lilith reached out a tentative hand, and her friend gripped it tight. But Lilith would not release her hold on Theren.

Before they stepped out into the cold, Lilith's parents helped her into a cloak, lined with fur to protect against the chill. It seemed Lilith hardly noticed them as they put it on. But just before they led her outside, she blinked and looked around. Her eyes rested first on Theren, and then on Nella.

"Where . . . where is Oren?" she croaked.

Everyone was deathly silent. Tears streamed from Jia's eyes, though her face did not twitch.

Ebon stepped forwards, unable to meet Lilith's gaze. "Oren fought for you," he murmured. "He never believed—not for one second—that you were guilty. He gave his life trying to make the rest of us see it. I wish I had listened sooner."

Lilith's eyes filled with tears. Her hands twitched, as though she were grasping for something that was not there. Her parents bowed their heads and then went to help her outside. But she seized at Theren all the more tightly. "No," she whimpered. "No, no, no. Do not make her leave me. Do not make her leave me alone."

Theren met their stares. One after the other, they nodded. And so Theren was the one to help Lilith out to the street where a carriage waited for them. She climbed in with Lilith, soon followed by her parents. As the driver readied the horses, Theren thrust her head out the carriage window.

"I will return soon." She held out a hand, and Ebon gripped it tightly. "Keep yourself whole."

"I will," said Ebon. "See to her."

Theren nodded. The driver switched the horses, and the carriage set off down the street, leaving Jia, Nella, and Ebon to watch it go. Once it was out of sight, Jia turned to them.

"Now we should return, for there are many in the Academy who still need our help."

Nella nodded and set off down the street. But Ebon stayed where he was, staring at his feet. Jia cocked her head at him, waiting until he met her eyes.

"If it is all right, Instructor, I would rather not return just yet. I feel the need to stay in the open air a bit longer. To clear my head."

She studied him long enough to make him wonder if she knew the truth of his mind. At last she nodded. "Very well. Only do not stay out past your curfew."

"Thank you, Instructor."

She gave a final nod, and then went off to follow Nella back to the Academy.

Ebon turned his steps west, seeking the blue door.

Though she greeted him with startled delight, Adara could see at once that something was wrong. She drew him to her room as quickly as she could. He tried to give her a smile, but it was a broken thing. She sat him at the edge of her bed and held his hand.

"What is it? What is wrong?"

"There has been another murder," Ebon managed to whisper.

Her brow furrowed. "I thought Lilith had been caught."

"Lilith was not the murderer."

"Oh." It was a tiny sound, full of understanding. "Do you wish to speak of it?"

"Yes." But then he said nothing.

She waited a moment before tracing a finger along his neck. "Do you wish to do something other than speak?"

That made him smirk. "Not just now."

"Refusing me again? You might as well save your coin, for I fear you waste it by visiting me here."

He lifted her fingers to his lips, planting a tiny kiss on each in turn. "I never waste my time when I spend it with you," he murmured. She smiled and leaned over to kiss his cheek.

"Come, then. Lovers know many arts." She had him slide down to the floor, resting on the soft rug, and then sat on the bed behind him. With her fingers she kneaded at the muscles of his shoulders and neck, working out the knots. He moaned at the skill of her hands, rolling his head back and forth in pleasure.

For some time they sat like that, Ebon enjoying her ministrations. With each kink smoothed, he felt his worries lessen in strength. Yet they would not vanish entirely.

The Academy must be a madhouse now, he thought. When he realized the truth, freeing Lilith had seemed the only important thing in all the nine lands. But now the Academy had a murderer on the loose yet again. He could not stop seeing Oren's body sprawled on the dining hall floor beneath a blood-spattered cloth.

"Lilith's cousin. A boy named Oren. He nearly scuffled with us in the tavern. Do you remember?"

"I do."

"It was he who was killed. He was hoisted in the air before the entire Academy and nearly throttled to death. Then the killer struck him with a flurry of knives."

Her hands stilled for a moment, and he heard her gasp. "That is awful. But that means you must have caught the murderer, have you not? Everyone would have seen the culprit."

Ebon shook his head. "They remained hidden. How, we do not know. And now Lilith weighs like an anvil on my conscience."

Adara lifted a hand from his shoulder to stroke his hair. "You did what you thought was right, Ebon. You were not the only one who thought you saw her kill a child."

He shook his head. "She was put to the question. I saw what the Mystics have done to her. It may have driven her mad. Yet this whole time, she was never to blame."

"Nor were you. Your friends acted the same. Do you blame them?"

Ebon barked a sharp, bitter laugh. "I could not if I wanted to."

She scooted over and leaned down to look at him. "What do you mean?"

"I told them, Adara. Of Cyrus, and the truth of what happened when the Seat was attacked. Kalem has not spoken to me since."

Fear shone in her eyes. "Ebon, that may not have been—"

He shook his head. "He will not tell anyone. And Theren does not think I did anything wrong."

Adara snorted. "That sounds like Theren. But Kalem is royalty."

"He will not tell anyone. You may trust me."

She kissed his cheek and leaned back to keep rubbing his shoulders. "Then I will. In all things."

"The worst of it is that I cannot deny Kalem is right. He says I should have trusted him and told him what happened from the first. I think he is right. I *should* have. He would have believed in me—indeed, he *has* believed in me, but I have not returned the courtesy. And now I know not if he will ever place his faith in me again."

"You might be right. And I wish I had not advised you otherwise. It seems I was wrong about Kalem."

He reached back and took her hand. "It was not your fault. I did the deed, and so the blame is mine."

She squeezed his fingers. "We did it together. We share all consequence. But from what I have seen of Kalem, I think his mind will change. Your friendship will be stronger for it. No longer will you have to keep everything to yourself—and to me, of course."

He pushed himself up from the floor, taking his place on the bed beside her. His heartbeat thundered in his ears, and spots danced at the edge of his vision as he clutched her hands. "There is one thing I have kept to myself all my life," he whispered, afraid to meet her eyes, "but I gave it to you the moment I saw you. My heart."

For a moment she did not answer, and her hands went still. Inside, he winced, certain he had made a mistake. They had spoken easily of love for some time, but it had been a game to her, as it should have been to him. His cheeks burned, and now the thunder of his heart was a roar, savage and angry as an ocean storm.

Their eyes met, and hers were shining. She lifted a hand to his cheek. "I have discovered myself feeling the same way," she whispered. "And it is as surprising to me as anything ever has been in this life. Sometimes love springs forth unbidden, you said, and it has for me."

His hand covered hers on his cheek. "Adara . . ."

Her mouth worked, the muscles in her jaw spasming. Then her words spilled in a rush, as though she wished to rid them from her mind. "Ebon, you may come to see me here behind the blue door—always, every day, if I had my way. Or we could see each other . . . elsewhere."

Ebon frowned. "In taverns and the like? I . . . I should love to do that again, if that is your wish."

Quickly she shook her head. "Not in taverns, Ebon. In my home. I do not mean . . . I do not mean as your lover, and you my client. I mean together. A binding of the heart, and not of coin."

The world froze about him. A voice in the back of his mind screamed *lover's words, lover's words,* and it sounded terribly like his father's. But from the depths of his heart poured unadulterated joy, and it cast aside the shadows of Oren's death and Lilith's torment like the sun burning through the clouds.

He fought for words. But he had been silent for too long, and Adara's cheeks flooded with color. She rose from the bed and walked to the side table where a pitcher of wine waited, her hands shaking. "Forgive me," she said, her words quivering and threatening to break. "It was a foolish jest—something I thought you wanted to hear. I know this is all a game, of course. I do. I—"

Ebon went to her and, turning her by the shoulders, covered her mouth with his. They melted into each other, her fingers buried in his hair, and his arm pressing her tight against him. A long while that kiss lasted, an eternity, and when it ended it left them breathless.

"It was not a game, Adara. It has never been, and it is not now. If I hid my words behind smiles and laughter, it was not because I thought them jests. I have been told of lover's words, and felt sure you were only saying what I wished to hear. I did not mind—I never could, for you are a lover, and that is what I came for. But always I wished it could be real, though I felt sure it never would be."

She seized his robes, her grip fierce, a fire burning in her eyes. "It was. It is."

Then she pushed him back upon the bed, and no more words were spoken.

It was a long while later before Ebon was ready to leave. He had certainly missed his curfew, but he would take any penalty gladly. As he cinched his belt over his robes, Adara gave him a final kiss. Ebon smiled as he looked over the room.

"It is a strange thought that I will not see this room again—or at least, not so often."

"Mayhap I will bring you back here on occasion, for the memories if nothing else."

"I will send word when I can see you next."

"And I will tell you where to find me." She smiled, a bit nervous, and clearly embarrassed. "It is strange, but I am anxious about showing you my home. It is senseless, considering how well we know each other in . . . other ways."

He chuckled and kissed the top of her brow. "I think I understand."

But then her eyes went wide, and she placed a hand on his chest. "I nearly forgot, for you were so solemn when you first arrived. Though I no longer know if it will be important. It concerned Lilith. Or rather, her family."

Ebon frowned. "The family Yerrin? What of them?"

"Her kin were under investigation by the High King herself. It seems they were already under suspicion. Apparently some scion of the house was found to be in league with the Shades—a distant aunt of Lilith's, I think. But Lilith's actions worsened their standing further, and the clan meant to disown her parents. After what you have told me, it seems likely that is no longer the case, but still I meant to tell you."

"Thank you, but I suspect you are right. Now that Lilith has been proven innocent, the family Yerrin will doubtless be . . ."

Ebon trailed off, for his mind had begun to race, and the nagging thought at the back of his mind had finally burst to the fore. Yerrin. *Yerrin.* He ran to the chair where he had put his shoes and pulled them on as fast as he could.

"I must go at once. The lovers you speak with—they have seen Mako poking about the Seat, have they not?"

"They have," said Adara, frowning.

"Please, please tell them—if they see him again, they must tell him to come visit me at the earliest opportunity. Tomorrow, if he can manage it. Tell him the usual place. He will know it."

"But—"

"Do you understand?"

"I do, my love. But why? What do you know?"

Ebon leapt up and ran for the door. But just before leaving, he stopped to kiss her again. "Nothing yet. But with Mako's help, mayhap everything."

Then he flew out the door and into the street, sprinting for the Academy.

THIRTY-TWO

When he returned to the Academy, Ebon was grateful that Mellie did not seem inclined to report his staying out past curfew. He supposed another murder lent perspective to what was truly important in the school.

He went to seek Theren and Kalem. But Theren was still at the Yerrin manor, and Ebon guessed she would spend the night. Someone in the common room said Kalem had gone to bed. For a moment Ebon considered waking the boy, but at last decided against it. Kalem was already angry, and he would surely resent being roused.

So he returned to his dormitory, but he found it impossible to sleep. Eventually he gave it up and went to the common room, where he sat by the fireplace and allowed his thoughts to spiral through his mind. Piece by piece he assembled a theory that explained all that had happened in the school thus far. Before he knew it, the blush of dawn seeped in through the common room's high windows. He yawned and stretched, suddenly feeling the sleepless hours he had spent there. But sleep could wait.

He sought Kalem in the dining hall and soon spied him among the press of students. When Kalem saw Ebon approaching, he turned the other way. But Ebon caught up and put a hand on his shoulder.

"Kalem. I must speak with you."

"I have no wish to do that, Ebon."

Ebon leaned in close. Kalem began to draw away, until Ebon whispered, "It is to find the murderer."

For a moment Kalem stood stock still. Then he looked into Ebon's eyes. "Have you discovered who it is?"

"I may have, but I will need your help to be sure."

Kalem looked back and forth, clearly uncomfortable. "What do you need my help for?"

"Not here. Will you meet me in the library this afternoon?"

Again Kalem was still. Finally he nodded wordlessly, and then made off to eat breakfast alone.

During his morning class, Ebon was a squirming ball of energy. He practiced shifting stone, and his counter-magic with Astrea. She was even more withdrawn and quiet than she had been before, but when Ebon saw it, he only gave a grim smile.

Soon this will all be over, he promised her in his mind. *Soon your nightmare will be behind you, and all of ours as well.*

He snatched a roll of bread during the midday meal, for he did not think his stomach would let him have anything more. After eating the roll, he made his way to the library and went straight to the third floor. First he went to the bookshelves and lingered there, hoping for Mako to arrive. But there was no sign of the bodyguard by the time the study period started. Ebon returned to his nook, where he found Kalem waiting.

The boy sat with arms folded, and he looked at Ebon with suspicion. Ebon sat in an armchair and leaned forwards, clasping his hands between his knees. They looked at each other a long moment before Kalem sighed and turned his gaze.

"You said you needed my help. Here I am. What is it?"

"Who stands to gain from painting Lilith as a killer?"

Kalem blinked, frowning. "What do you mean?"

"It hurts the reputation of the family Yerrin," said Ebon. "And who is Yerrin's greatest rival?"

"The family Drayden. Your kin."

"Exactly." Ebon scooted still farther forwards in his chair. "It must have been them. We know it was not—" He had been about to say *Cyrus,* but Kalem's eyes hardened, and he skipped the word. "Well, we know it was not a wizard in the Academy, and we know it was not the family Yerrin. That seems plain, now that one child of Yerrin has been killed, and the other tortured into madness. Who is left?"

Kalem shook his head. "We have already suspected this for some time. Nothing has changed."

Ebon raised a finger. "But something has. Theren had a piece of the truth, though she did not know it, nor did we. She believed Lilith was working under the control of mindwyrd. That, I think, is how my father and uncle did it. They fed a mentalist magestones and then used their mindwyrd upon Lilith, forcing her to steal artifacts and further increase their power. And by pinning the blame on her, they further weakened our rivals, the family Yerrin, and pointed all eyes upon them."

At first Kalem only pursed his lips, staring into the distance as he pondered Ebon's words, until at last he gave a reluctant nod. "That seems possible. Entirely possible. Only, wait—with Lilith in jail, how did they arrange for Oren to be killed?"

Ebon sighed. "That is the one piece I have not been able to put into place. A mentalist *must* have line of sight. That means they were in the room."

Kalem's eyes widened. "Or in the hallway just outside. They would have been behind Oren after he entered, but we would not have seen them."

"Of course!" Ebon reeled in his seat. "That is the only thing that makes sense."

Kalem smiled, but his expression soon darkened, and he stared back into his lap. "Still, I do not think this knowledge will help. We will never be able to prove it."

But Ebon only smiled. "But *that* is just what is so urgent. Now that we have guessed at the only possible truth, I have a man who can help us prove it. Wait here."

He stood. Kalem looked at him quizzically, but Ebon waved a hand. "Please, I beg of you—stay seated until I summon you. I was wrong not to have faith, for you deserved all my trust and more. But now I mean to rectify the mistake."

Kalem settled back into his armchair, though he still looked suspicious. Ebon set off towards the shelves again and ducked between two so that Kalem was lost from sight. He waited, aimlessly scanning the shelves.

"You are a brave boy, or a foolish one, to summon me as you did."

Ebon smiled and turned—but his smile faltered, for the bodyguard was uncomfortably close.

"Thank you for coming." Ebon took a half-step backwards. Thankfully, Mako did not follow.

"What do you want? Be quick, for as it turns out, I am in the family's employ, and that means I have real work that must be done."

"Yet what I have to tell you falls in with your duties," said Ebon. "I believe it concerns Halab's safety."

Mako straightened, one hand drifting to his dagger's hilt. "That is a bold statement."

"It is one I make with every confidence. But you must wait here a moment, so I can bring my friend."

"No." The word held a grim finality, and Mako's nostrils flared. "That is not how I work—nor should you. Family matters remain in the family. To do anything else is folly."

"This is not only a family matter, for many Academy students lie dead. And he is my closest friend. I trust him with my life."

Mako sneered. "I might trust him with your life as well, but not with mine."

Ebon met his gaze without flinching. "I trust him with Halab's life."

There was a long moment of silence, and then Mako rolled his shoulders. "Very well," he growled. "Bring him."

Ebon went quickly to fetch Kalem, before Mako could change his mind. But when Kalem rounded the corner with Ebon and found Mako there, he balked and tried to run.

"Kalem! Be still. He is one of my kin, and serves my family well. This is Mako—the one who warned me of the Seat's attack."

That made Kalem pause, and he swallowed hard while eyeing Mako. The bodyguard, much to Ebon's consternation, did nothing to ease the boy's mind, looking him up and down like a wolf inspecting a rabbit.

"Mako," said Ebon, pressing on before either of them could say or do anything regrettable. "I think I have at last found a link between Shay and Matami and the Academy thefts. We now know that Lilith was blameless—she killed Vali only under another's control, and may not have killed Credell at all. She stole the artifacts, but that was under mindwyrd as well."

"You speak with great certainty," said Mako. "How do you know?"

Ebon turned to Kalem. "Tell him the symptoms of mindwyrd."

The boy shrugged. "You know as well as I do, for Theren told us both."

Ebon shook his head. "I know nothing of magic. Not like you, Kalem. Please, tell him."

Kalem sighed. "Mindwyrd controls the body and the mind. As long as the mentalist maintains their control, by reestablishing it over the victim every day or so, no ill effects can be seen. But if that control slips, the victim will begin to show signs of madness. They will grow increasingly anxious, their eyes will show their insanity, and they often cannot sit still."

"That sounds very like Ebon," said Mako, baring his teeth in a feral grin. "Are you recovering from mindwyrd, boy?"

"Lilith showed these signs in the constables' station," Ebon said, ignoring the jest. "Oren showed them before he died. I even saw them in Credell. Kalem, do you remember how he came to Theren and asked her for the key to the vaults? That must have been under mindwyrd. I think Matami and my father did this, not to *build* an alliance with Yerrin, but to weaken them as rivals to our family. But they would need a mindmage. So I ask you, Mako: are there any mindmages in the family Drayden?"

The bodyguard's eyes had narrowed while listening to Ebon's theory, but at the last question they shot wide. "There is," he said slowly. "I spoke of him before: Drystan, a distant cousin of yours, who I have had no reason to suspect in any of this. Yet now that you bring him to mind, I recall something interesting: it seems he disappeared some months ago, off on some mysterious business for the family—or so Shay told me."

Ebon felt a thrill in his chest. "And where was he last seen?"

"Hedgemond." Beside Ebon, Kalem gave a start, and Mako fixed

465

him with a look. "Yes, little goldshitter. Your homeland. My work for our kin never carries me there, and so I had not paid much attention to this cousin's disappearance."

"So?" said Ebon, trying not to look too eager. "You cannot deny that this rings with truth."

Mako's frown deepened, and he stroked his chin with a thumb. "It may be something," he said at last.

Ebon broke into a grin, but he quickly composed himself. "What can we do? Can Halab intervene? Should we bring it to the constables?"

"No," Mako said. "Not that. Never. Halab may be able to act. But this is not enough evidence. We must find something irrefutable—something we can bring to her that will allow her to act without question. I know what will do the trick—but I shall need your help."

Ebon frowned. "What could you need *my* help with?"

"We will need to sneak into a place without anyone knowing we were there. You can shift stone now, can you not?"

Ebon shrugged. "I can shift it aside, but not put it back. Certainly I could not cover our tracks."

Mako moved so fast that Ebon's mind took a moment to see it. By the time he knew what had happened, he was face down on the floor with Mako's knee in his back. The man's silver dagger was pressed to his neck, the tip tickling his jugular. Kalem opened his mouth to cry out, but Mako gave him a look of steel.

"Breathe a word, and he dies," he hissed.

Kalem's mouth shut with a *snap.*

"What is this?" said Ebon, gasping from the pressure on his spine.

"Shift the stone," Mako growled.

"What?" The dagger tickled harder. "What stone?" he cried.

"The floor. Shift it. And I would advise you to be quick."

Ebon reached for his power, and the library grew lighter as his eyes began to glow. The floor rippled and twisted under his palm. The stone flew out from around his hand, creating an indent.

"Now," said Mako. "Put it back."

"I have told you, I cannot," said Ebon. Mako's grip tightened on his hair. "I swear! I have not learned it yet!" He was whimpering, but did not care.

466

"I can shift it!" said Kalem. "I can put it back. I will do what you want—only let Ebon go."

"No royalty," said Mako. "You have done your part, goldshitter. This is a Drayden matter, and a Drayden will solve it. Or—"

Ebon felt the dagger's tip nick his skin. At the edge of his vision, a red droplet splashed onto the stone.

"All right!" He tried to still his mind—not an easy thing with Mako's dagger so close—and focused on the stone. He gestured, trying to move it. But it only flew away from his hand, not under his control.

"Not good enough, boy," Mako sneered. Ebon heard his fingers tighten on the dagger's leather handle.

Ebon tried to focus. And as he did, he saw something . . . a sort of glow, surrounding the stone as it flooded like water.

The magic. *His* magic. The magic he used to shift the stone.

He focused, gripping it in his mind. The stone went rigid, molded like clay at his thought.

A long sigh escaped him. He scooped the magic back into the hole, and the stone went with it. In a moment it was done, and the hole was gone. Ebon released his magic, and the glow faded. The stone looked terrible, like a hole in a wall poorly plastered over. But it was back in its place.

"Well done, little Ebon," said Mako softly. "That will do well enough. I will come for you tonight. Be ready."

The pressure vanished from Ebon's back all at once, and he gasped. Kalem seized his arm and helped him to his feet. By the time they stood, Mako was gone.

THIRTY-THREE

AFTER MAKO'S THREATS, KALEM STRONGLY URGED EBON TO RECONSIDER working with the man, and Ebon could hardly blame him. He tried to defend the bodyguard, though he thought his arguments were made less effective by the hand he pressed to his neck, staunching the nick in his throat.

"It was only a bit of motivation," said Ebon, trying to smile. "And it worked, did it not?"

"He is a madman. I do not know what he has planned for the two of you, but I do not like it."

Ebon shrugged. "Remember, he has already saved our lives once— and mayhap the Academy. He is a hard man because he must be, but Mako means us no harm." But Ebon wondered if even he believed the words. He had heard the malice in Mako's voice.

At last Kalem gave up trying to convince him, though Ebon was certain the boy still had his doubts. He wished Theren were there. If she had been present, he doubted Mako would have made his threats. She was powerful in her magic, and could have sent Mako flying with a flick of her wrist. But also, Theren could now help him reassure Kalem that working with Mako was the only way forwards.

And it *was* the only way forwards. Ebon was certain.

The rest of their study period passed quickly, if uncomfortably. It felt odd to Ebon, sitting there and trying to read, pretending that nothing untoward was occurring. How could he read tales of history, even those of the Wizard Kings, when his life promised such danger in the here and now?

As the final bell rang, they made their way out of the library. By unspoken agreement, they passed the dining hall. Ebon had no appetite, and doubted Kalem did either. Instead they made their way into the garden, where the sun had just begun to kiss the top of the Academy's outer wall. Cool air seeped into their bodies as they walked the grounds. There was no one to be seen; everyone was inside having supper.

When the sun's final sliver vanished from sight, Ebon felt a presence and turned to see Mako lurking in the garden a few paces away. The bodyguard waved them forwards, and Ebon led Kalem into the shadows.

"Scuttle off now, royal boy. It is bad enough Ebon must see where we are going. No one else can know."

"Where *are* you going, exactly?" asked Kalem, folding his arms.

"Look at the spine this one shows," said Mako, arching an eyebrow at Ebon. "Mayhap I should rip it out, that we might see it more plainly."

"He means to lead me out of the Academy," said Ebon. "Is that right? You mean to take whatever path lets you get in and out without anyone seeing."

"Very clever, Ebon. Now tell your lover to leave us, lest I make him vanish permanently."

Kalem did not seem eager to budge, but Ebon gave him a nod. With a final reluctant look, the boy left. Mako gave him a little wave, twiddling his fingers in the air just before he was out of sight.

"Now then," said Mako. "Come and learn something you should not."

To Ebon's surprise, Mako did not lead him deeper into the garden, but instead towards the citadel. The bodyguard ran quickly from bush to bush, each time looking in every direction to ensure that no one could see.

Near the front of the Academy, the citadel joined the outer wall. There Mako went to a particular section of black granite, though Ebon saw nothing remarkable about it. He had to wait as his eyes adjusted to the shadows. In that moment, Mako did *something* that Ebon could not see. But when he was done, a section of the wall turned inwards to reveal a hidden door, so narrow that Mako could barely fit his broad shoulders inside it. But Ebon followed him in, and then Mako swung it closed behind them.

Utter darkness lay beyond. Ebon could see nothing, and could hear only his own ragged breathing. When Mako spoke, his mouth only a finger's breadth away, Ebon jumped. "Come along, little Ebon," the bodyguard whispered. "Not too far to go."

After a moment, Ebon could feel that he was alone in the passageway. But there were no footsteps, no faintest sound to follow. He was forced to put his hand on the wall and use it to guide himself along. A sudden, terrible memory gripped him: the passage beneath the watchtower on the south of the Seat, where he had followed Cyrus and Adara during the attack. It had been very much like this tunnel, and then, as now, he had been unable to see where he was going.

A slight grinding sounded from ahead, making him jump. Then Mako's hand clamped firmly over his shoulder to drag him forwards. Now, at last, there was some tiny shaft of light, and his eyes drank it in. They were in some sort of shed, with stone walls and a wooden roof. There were all manner of tools hanging on the walls—rakes, brooms, and shovels. Ebon thought they looked vaguely familiar. Then in a flash he recognized where they were.

"This is one of the outer sheds."

"Indeed," said Mako, who Ebon now saw stood just beside him.

Ebon spun to look the way he had come, but the wall was solid. "Where is the door? How did we get here?"

Mako's grin spread wider. "There are still some secrets I deem you unworthy of."

Ebon shook his head. "It is not only that. If I cannot find the door, I cannot come back to the Academy this way."

470

"Imagine the depths of my dismay." Mako's face was a mask of stone.

"Very well," said Ebon, glaring. "Let us get on with it."

Mako took him out of the shed and into the streets. The moons had not yet risen, but dusk's fading light let Ebon see well enough. Yet that was little help, for their route was so wild and winding that he was soon hopelessly lost. He searched for a landmark, such as the High King's palace towering over the buildings, but saw nothing. It seemed almost as though Mako was taking him down the narrowest streets, the tightest alleys, so that he could not hold his bearings for even a moment. And the pace soon had Ebon heaving and sweating in his robes.

"Where are we going, Mako?" he wheezed between breaths. "I cannot remain out all night. There is a curfew."

"I doubt we will be that long," said Mako, who of course was not winded. "And if we are, you can simply tunnel in through the Academy's outer wall, little alchemist."

"It does not work like that. The walls are enchanted."

Mako shrugged. "I fail to see how this is my concern."

Ebon stopped and glared. "If we do anything questionable tonight, and it is noted that I returned to the Academy past curfew, will that not level suspicion at me? And might that not be traced back to you and the family?"

He was gratified to see Mako pause before turning back to him with an appraising look. "Clever, little Ebon. Very clever indeed. Have this vow, then: if we are out past your curfew, I will see you safe inside the Academy walls. Agreed?"

"Thank you," said Ebon.

So they kept on, until stars shone bright in the sky and the faint glow of the moons at last shone from the east. Though Ebon was lost, he would have guessed they were somewhere in the city's northeastern reaches. Mako turned down a final alley to a dead end. Ebon was about to ask if they had taken a wrong turn, when the bodyguard pointed to the cobblestones.

"Now. Use your magic. Open a way through the street into the sewers below."

Ebon looked all around. "Here? Where are we?"

Mako cuffed him on the side of the head. Ebon doubted the blow had all the strength held in those brawny arms, but it still stung terribly. "I have no time for questions. Do as I say."

Glaring (and trying not to look as though it were a pout), Ebon reached for his magic. He knelt, placing his hands to the street, and soon the stone rippled away from his fingers. It piled up in little ridges around the edge of a hole that grew ever deeper. At last he reached the open space beneath, and an uneven circle of darkness gaped up from below.

"Well enough done," Mako said, and then leapt inside.

Ebon swallowed before gingerly lowering himself down. He clung to the hole's edge with his fingertips, hoping his feet would reach the bottom. Of course they did not, and he was forced to let go. He landed with a splash and a curse, before gagging as the smell of the place wafted to him out of the darkness.

"I think you should have worn more perfume, little Ebon," Mako chuckled. "Now close the way behind us."

"It is too high," said Ebon. "I need to touch it."

Mako growled, and then Ebon felt himself hoisted up by the waist. He stretched for the sewer's ceiling and put forth his power again. He remembered the way he had done it in the library, and controlled the magic itself rather than the stone. Soon the hole was sealed, and though it looked a terrible job, one would have to look closely to notice. Mako dropped him without ceremony, and Ebon splashed noisily back into the sewer water.

"Come now," said Mako. "Only a little way farther."

He set off, the muck slurping and sucking at his shoes with every step. Ebon cursed inwardly as he realized Mako had known they would go this way, but had not warned Ebon or had him bring better footwear. The bodyguard's boots kept his feet clear of the mess and the stink, but Ebon could feel the filth soaking into his shoes and staining his skin. Again he tried not to retch, and forced his mind to other matters.

The sewer itself was a grander space than Ebon had thought it would be. It was a true tunnel, round on all sides rather than the walls meeting the floor in corners. Holes in the ceiling occasionally led to gutters above, and splashing moonlight seeped through to guide the way. There were no platforms for them to walk, as in Idrisian sewers, and the walls were cut stone instead of brick. It had an ancient and unattended feel, as though forebears had laid these tunnels here in days before history, and had then abandoned them, so that now no one on the Seat even remembered they existed.

Ebon did not have long to reflect, for soon Mako stopped him. It had been some time since they had seen a gutter-hole, and only the faintest glow of moonslight allowed them to see. Mako pointed at the ceiling. "Here. Open the way for us."

"Where are we?" said Ebon.

"What have I told you about questions? Do what I brought you here to do."

Again Mako hoisted him up, and again Ebon put forth his power. When he broke through the stones into the space above, he saw the faint glow of candles. A smell burst forth into the sewer, pleasant and familiar: perfumes of all the nine lands, in a heady mix that set his mind at ease.

Then Mako shoved him up through the hole into the space above, and Ebon realized he was in a house of lovers. For a moment, panic seized him, thinking this had something to do with Adara. But he forced himself to remain calm. He might not know what part of the island they were on, but he was certain it was nowhere near Adara's blue door. However, there were two sleeping forms on the bed, and Ebon dared not come any closer to see them.

He did not have to. Mako followed him up through the hole, and in an instant the bodyguard crept towards the bed. Ebon wanted to follow, but he was deathly afraid; the fear was nameless, baseless, for he knew not what to expect, only something told him he would not like it.

Stop being a coward, he told himself. He pushed up into a crouch and crept behind Mako. One of the figures on the bed—a man—was snoring, face down, his rear end exposed. Beside him lay another, younger man, smooth chest glowing in candlelight. From the beauty of the younger man's face, Ebon guessed he was the lover.

From a pocket in his vest, Mako drew forth a piece of black cloth. This he drew over his face, covering him from nose to chin so that only his eyes could be seen. From another pocket he produced a small vial.

This he unstopped, and tipped its contents into his other hand. Ebon could see it was a powder of burnt orange.

Mako threw the powder into the lover's face. The man's eyes flew open in shock, but at once he slumped back, senseless.

Quick as a shadow, Mako stole around to the other side of the bed and reached for his dagger. Ebon's heart raced as Mako snatched the other man's shoulder and threw him over so he lay on his back.

Matami started awake, blinking hard as he tried to get his bearings. Mako brought the pommel of his dagger crashing down, knocking Ebon's uncle back to unconsciousness.

Ebon clamped a hand over his own mouth to stifle a cry. Mako took no notice, hoisting Matami over his shoulder and carrying him to the hole in the floor. Only then did he look at Ebon.

"I will go down first. Shove him in after me. I will catch him and make sure he does not break his neck."

Mako vanished into the tunnel before Ebon could nod. Terror seized his muscles, and he knew not what to do. He could only look at Matami's nude form, lying with his arm twisted beneath him.

"Ebon!" rasped Mako from below. "If I have to come back up there, I will cut off one of your ears!"

That made Ebon crawl forwards quickly. First he tried to push his uncle's shoulders, but that only made him lurch slightly to the side. Grimacing, Ebon stood, hooked his hands beneath the man's flabby stomach, and rolled him over. Matami's head sank into the hole, followed by the rest of his body. Ebon was afraid he would tumble down into the darkness. But the fall stopped abruptly as Mako caught him. Slowly the rest of Matami slithered into the darkness to join his head.

Ebon hesitated for half a moment, staring at the door of the room. He could slip outside, leave through the blue door and make his way into the streets of the city, finding his way back to the Academy. Someone might see him, but what of it? It must be better than following Mako into the dark and the stink, to who knew what end.

"Come, little goldbag." Mako's voice floated up to him out of the abyss. "If you wish to save your Academy and all your little friends, there is work still to be done."

Ebon warred with himself a moment longer. Then he sat on the edge of the hole and dropped down into the sewer.

THIRTY-FOUR

AFTER EBON HASTILY CLOSED THE HOLE BEHIND THEM, MAKO TOOK him down the sewer—but they did not go back the way they came. Instead Mako led him farther onwards, with Matami hoisted over his shoulder like a sack of flour.

More twists and turns passed, but Ebon had given up trying to determine where they were. Instead he stared at his feet while they walked, and wondered just what mess he had stepped into. When he had determined to prove Matami's guilt, and therefore the guilt of his father, he had not imagined kidnapping Matami himself. He only hoped it would not get worse—yet something inside him promised that it would.

They had been walking on a downwards slope for some time, but now the sewer opened, causing Ebon to stop in his tracks. The ceiling rose abruptly to form a chamber many paces high. The sewer's filthy, watery channel disappeared into the floor, and there was a sort of raised central platform in the center of the chamber. On that platform was an iron chair, and Ebon could see that it had been bolted to the stone floor with great spikes. Chains were nailed into the chair, and there Mako brought Matami, lashing him into place tightly so that he could not move. Around the edge of the chamber were other doorways, leading to more passageways like the one they had come from. All led upwards, and where they entered the room, their sewage flow vanished into a grate under the central platform, where Ebon could hear the sound of rushing water.

"It is the central drainage chamber," said Mako. "Or at least, it is one of them. There are several such across the Seat—though this is the most removed from the city above, and therefore the best in which to hide things."

Ebon tried to keep his voice steady. "And what are we hiding, Mako?"

The bodyguard looked at him but did not answer. Instead he went to one of the other doorways, where a torch rested in a sconce on the wall. This he took down and lit, before carrying it to the center of the room. He placed it on the floor less than a pace from Matami's bare feet. They were lashed to the chair like the rest of him and now twitched from the heat of the flame. Finally Matami woke with a jerk, eyes wild as they had been in the lover's room above. Immediately he winced at the lump blooming above his temple where Mako had struck him. He tried to raise his hand to the lump, but found that Mako had lashed his wrists behind the chair.

"Mako? What is this? What happened to—"

He stopped, eyes roving the chamber, and then down at his own naked form. His face grew a bit paler in the torchlight.

"How dare you?" he growled. "Do you have any idea of the punishment that awaits you for this? You shall be flayed, Mako. I will see the skin peeled from your—"

Mako wore leather gloves. Now he removed one, and with his bare hand, he slapped Matami across the face with an open palm. He did not put much force in the blow—Ebon could see that from where he stood—but Matami's head jerked back. It barely stopped him speaking. He looked past Mako to see Ebon lurking at the edge of the room.

"Ebon?" he sneered. "You are part of this, are you, boy? Know this, then: you are as good as dead. Your father will doubtless wish to draw the knife across your throat himself, but I fear he will not have the pleasure. I will—"

But while he spoke, Mako had sauntered around behind him and drawn his blade. He snatched one of Matami's fingers, and the man's words cut off abruptly.

Ebon watched as Mako slipped the point of the knife beneath Matami's fingernail and twisted.

Matami screamed, his voice echoing from every surface and rejoining itself in chorus, so it sounded as though an army were screeching in pain. Mako held the knife there for a moment before withdrawing it, and then stood to lean over Matami's shoulder from behind.

"Now then. We will hear no more vague, pointless threats from your fat, sniveling lips, will we?"

Matami only glared at him, pushing breath between gritted teeth. Mako waited a moment and then shrugged. He knelt and plunged the knife under a fingernail on the other hand. Fresh screams rang in Ebon's ears, and he turned his face away.

"You will not! You will not! I swear it!" Matami shrieked.

"Good," said Mako, withdrawing the blade at once. He stepped out from behind the chair and went to the torch. From his boot he produced another dagger—shorter and less ornate than the one at his belt—and left it leaning on the torch that still sputtered on the ground. Then he stepped just inside one of the passages that led out of the chamber. When he came back into view, he held another chair—this one smaller, and wooden, with thin leather upholstery on the seat. He placed it before Matami, facing the man, and then looked to Ebon. "You can find another chair there, if you wish, little Ebon. You need not remain on your feet."

Ebon only stared at him. "This is wrong, Mako. We cannot do this."

He expected Mako to sneer. Instead, sympathy filled the bodyguard's eyes. "Dear little Ebon," he said quietly. "Halab's love for you is well-placed. You have a good heart, and she treasures it. But Matami must be put to the question, or truth will never out."

"Then let him be put to the question," said Ebon. "But by the constables. The King's law. Else we are as guilty in the law's eyes as he is."

Mako cocked his head. "You know that is impossible, do you not? I am a bodyguard, Ebon, and I serve Halab. A bodyguard's first task is not to keep their master safe from a drawn dagger. Do you know what it is?"

Ebon shook his head.

"It is to keep their master from being near a drawn dagger in the first place. Now Halab is in a situation where more than daggers may be drawn against her, and Matami is at least part of the cause. To keep her safe, I must remove the danger before it grows. Do you want Halab to be safe?"

That made Ebon balk. How could he say no? Mako must have taken his silence for assent, because he turned back to Matami. The man had not stopped scowling, and now he sneered in Mako's face.

"What are you prattling about, Mako? I am no danger, and you know it."

"What have you been doing in the Academy, Matami? What have you been seeking?"

Matami's frown deepened. "You speak nonsense. I have had nothing to do with the Academy."

Mako sighed, shaking his head. He stood and circled behind Matami once more.

"I have done nothing!" Matami screamed. "I swear it! I do not know what you are talking about!"

As though he had not heard, Mako lifted a hand and plunged his dagger into the skin. He slid it sideways, across the palm just below the surface, so that Ebon could see the lump of it sliding along beneath the palm's lines. His stomach lurched, and he turned his eyes. Matami's cries were bestial, animal, horrifying things.

When Mako was done, he went to the torch, and to the dagger he had left sitting atop it. The blade was glowing red hot. He went back behind Matami, and pressed the blade to the incision where he had slipped the dagger inside. The air filled with the hiss of sizzling flesh, and Matami's screams turned into screeches and shrieks. Slowly, casually, Mako made his way back to the wooden chair and sat before Matami.

"If you waste my time, you will regret it," said Mako. "You sent a child named Lilith into the Academy's vaults to steal artifacts. Tell me why, and tell me how."

Matami had surrendered all pretense of bluster or threat. "I swear to you Mako, I have done nothing of the sort," he said, voice shaking. "I know nothing of the thefts in the Academy or the murders they say have been committed there."

Mako's hand flicked. The dagger flew from his fingers and plunged into Matami's ankle. Mako kicked out with a boot, skewing the hilt to the side and prying the flesh open. Matami wailed and tried to move his foot, but the chains held him in place.

"Claiming ignorance helps no one, Matami," said Mako, wiggling his foot casually about in a small circle, widening the gap in the man's flesh. Blood poured from the wound to pool on the ground. "Telling me you know nothing only makes me angry. Telling me you *do* know something might improve my mood."

He finally stopped kicking the dagger about and bent down to withdraw it. Again he fetched the red-hot knife from the torch and pressed it to the gaping hole. Matami screamed again, finally subsiding as Mako replaced the dagger in the fire.

"I will tell you anything," said Matami. "Anything, I swear it. But I cannot tell you what I do not know."

"Why do you persist, Matami?" Mako sadly drew out the name, the way Halab had done when she trounced him. "Why do you persist? Do you think you will get out of this by speaking your lies? I know you had something to do with the attack on the Seat."

Matami's eyes flashed, and he fell still.

Mako pointed with his dagger, making the man flinch. "There it is. What did you do?"

"Nothing," said Matami, shaking his head. "I would never participate in treason."

A moment's long silence stretched. Then Mako looked sadly over his shoulder. "Ebon, you will want to avert your eyes."

"Please!" screamed Matami. "Please, I beg of you, I knew—"

Ebon turned away quickly as Mako lunged. There was a wet, slurping, grinding noise, and Matami's throat broke as he screamed himself raw. Then came the hissing sound of cauterized flesh. When Ebon at last turned back, there was a gaping, bloody, charred hole where Matami's right eye had been.

"The attack on the Seat," said Mako. "Say on, or lose what sight you have left."

"I did not know it had anything to do with the attack. I promise you. I would never have done it. But I received messages, orders. I was the one who sent the parcel, the one the boy delivered."

Mako seized a foot and slashed his blade across the bottom. "Which boy? Say his name, wretch."

"Ebon!" screamed Matami, his raw throat breaking further. "Ebon! I sent the parcel for Ebon! The one he brought to our man. Then I gave him his orders in the castle."

"And those orders were?"

"There was someone—a guest of the High King. I did not know it at the time, but it was that man Xain, the one who is now dean of the Academy. The High King had him well guarded. Our man was meant to take the place of one of those guards, to be ready when we made a move on Xain."

Mako cocked his head. "On Xain? Why him?"

Matami shook his head. "Shay's orders did not say." Mako shifted in his seat. Matami screamed and thrashed against his chains. *"I swear they did not say!* I swear it! I was only doing what I was told. Then I received a map, showing landing points on the Seat, though I knew not what they were for, and I sent that to our agent. It was stolen from him, but I did not tell Shay, for I feared his wrath if he knew. I am sorry. I am so sorry, I should have told him. Please, please let me live. I should have told him, I see that now."

For a moment all was still. Ebon released a breath he had not known he was holding. Mako reached out and put a hand on Matami's shoulder. The man burst into racking, sobbing breaths, his chest and shoulders heaving.

"Your error was not in keeping the truth from Shay," said Mako gently. "It was in following his orders in the first place. For they have endangered all our family, and that means they have endangered Halab."

Beneath the blood from his ruined eye that covered his face, Matami grew pale. "I thought the orders were from Halab. I never thought Shay would act without her blessing."

Mako leaned in to embrace the man, an arm wrapped about his neck. He spoke so softly that Ebon could scarcely hear him. "If Halab knew about your scheming, would I be here now?"

Then he rose and went behind Matami again. Matami thrashed against the chains. "No! No, please! I have told you everything!"

"Not everything," said Mako. "What have you and Shay planned with the artifacts you stole from the Academy?"

"Nothing!" cried Matami.

Snik

Mako sliced off one of Matami's fingers. The dagger cut through the flesh and tendons like butter, and the finger fell to the floor with a wet *splat.*

"Eeaaah!" screamed Matami. *"Nothing! Nothing, I swear it!"*

Snik. Splat. Snik. Splat.

One by one Mako took them, and one by one they fell, until Matami's screams were no longer of denial, but only of wordless agony. Between each, Mako repeated the question. "What have you planned with the artifacts?" But it seemed he no longer even cared to hear the answer.

Ebon's pulse thundered in his ears, and his fists shook at his side. Mako finished with one hand and lifted the next. But then something snapped. Ebon ran forwards, reaching for his power, his eyes blazing with light.

"No!" he cried. "Mako, stop it! Stop it at—"

Faster than the eye could see, Mako drove a fist into Ebon's chest just below the ribs. Ebon's air left him in a rush, and he crashed to the stone floor, unable to breathe or move.

As though he had not even noticed Ebon's presence, Mako stepped behind Matami again. The man's screams rang out twice as loud. How could the whole Seat not hear him? Ebon felt sure that constables and Mystics and the High King's guard would all come rushing down at any moment. But no one came, and Mako kept cutting.

The last finger fell. Matami kept screaming while Mako stepped back around in front of him. But he did not sit in his wooden chair.

Instead, he straddled Matami, one hand cupping the man's cheek affectionately, the other still holding the dagger.

When at last Matami's screams subsided, he tried to speak again. At first he almost choked on the spittle and phlegm that had filled his mouth. From his one remaining eye, he gazed up at Mako in pain and terror.

"I do not know," he whimpered. "I do not know what you are asking me. *Please*."

"I know you do not," said Mako softly. "No one lasts through all ten fingers."

Then he dragged his blade across Matami's throat.

Ebon had only just begun to get back his breath. Now he flipped over and crawled to the edge of the platform. He did not make it before he retched, and his vomit splashed out across his hands. He forced his head over the brim, watching his sick pour forth into the thick, disgusting filth that seeped through the iron grate below. The smell of it made him retch again, twice as hard, and then again, until it seemed there could be nothing left inside him, and he was only a hollow shell.

Finally he pushed himself back from the edge and rolled onto his back. Flecks of vomit speckled the front of his robes, but he could not force himself to care.

He refused to look at Mako. But from the corner of his eye he was aware of the bodyguard unchaining Matami's corpse from the chair, and then dragging it towards one of the other passageways. There he dropped the body over the edge. Ebon heard it splash, and then a wet slithering as it was carried away down the channel, which must not have been covered by an iron grate like the rest. Then Mako came to stand above Ebon. He looked down for a moment, eyes sad, and then finally lowered a hand.

"Come, little goldbag," he said quietly. "It is over now. The sewer will carry him to the Great Bay, and he will not suffer any more. But we ourselves are still alive, and must go on."

Ebon stared at the hand, wondering if Mako really expected him to take it. But then he took stock of himself, and realized he was far too weak to stand on his own. So he raised his hand, and he and Mako clasped wrists, and the bodyguard lifted him to his feet.

"Let us go now. I will get you back to your Academy, and safely within the walls. But there is something we must tend to first, for killing requires drinking afterwards."

With an arm around Ebon's shoulder he set off. And Ebon hated to admit, even to himself, how heavily he leaned on the bodyguard, without whom he might have sunk into the filth and the muck to join Matami's corpse on its way to the Great Bay.

THIRTY-FIVE

THEY LEFT THE SEWERS, AND MAKO LED HIM TO A TAVERN. EBON stopped at the door, for he wanted nothing less in the world than to spend time with the bodyguard. But Mako put a hand on his back and pushed him—not unkindly—into the tavern.

As they entered, Ebon thought of how much he and Mako must stink. But though they walked among tables filled with the tavern's patrons, no one raised an eyebrow. Ebon wondered if, were he able to smell anything beyond his own stench, he might find the room's reek even worse. Certainly the tavern seemed suspect; Ebon thought it the sort of room where no one asked questions if they were not ready to die for the answer.

Mako led him to a back corner, settled him in a chair, and took a seat himself. Ebon noted that his own back was to the door, while Mako faced it. The bodyguard waved down a stout barmaid and ordered some spirit Ebon did not recognize. They waited for the drinks in silence. Mako studied him, seeming to expect something—a question, mayhap, or an accusation. But when none seemed forthcoming, the bodyguard finally spoke.

"I think that through the years, you have wondered exactly what I do for the family Drayden. Do you know now?"

Ebon shook his head. He had thought of nothing since the sewer, nothing but Matami's ruined face, and he did not care to guess just now.

Silence stretched until the barmaid returned. She did not bring them cups of wood, but two small glasses—something that seemed an uncommon luxury in a place such as this. In the glasses was an amber liquid that curled Ebon's nose when he took a sniff.

"Brandy," said Mako. "Fine stuff. Finer than they usually serve here, but they keep a stock on hand for me. I visit often. Drink."

Ebon took a sip and nearly choked. Mako downed his glass in a single gulp and then held it up towards the barmaid. She hastened to fetch another. When she came back it was not only with another glass, but with a bottle. After she had gone, Mako leaned forwards, and though no one was close enough to hear, still he dropped his voice to a whisper.

"It happens that in the course of ensuring the family's safety and prosperity, a life must sometimes be taken. When that is the case, I am the one who goes knocking on doors and tickling with my knife."

Ebon's stomach did a flip-flop. "You are an assassin," he whispered.

Mako did not flinch. "Just so. Have you never wondered how Drayden reaches such favorable trade agreements and holds such power across Underrealm when we hail from the land of Idris?"

"What does Idris have to do with it?"

"It is Idris." Mako waved a hand in the general direction of the door. "Our home, yes, and a piece of my heart will always dwell there. But it is a dry and barren landscape, and boasts few resources. Yet we have turned what little we are given into the greatest collection of wealth that the nine lands have ever seen."

"We have spices."

Mako snorted and leaned across the table once more. "Do you think we could sustain our empire on spices? No. There are not goods enough within the King's law to earn the wealth we have built. Do you think the family Yerrin could rival us, if they only sold those bolts of colored silk they pretend to fill their wagons with?"

Ebon almost asked him what they sold instead, but then he remembered what Kalem and Theren had told him: it was Yerrin who commanded the magestone trade. He turned away, and tried another sip of the brandy. It was not so distasteful as the first had been.

"Through the centuries, when some fool has stood in the way of the family, someone like me has appeared in their home at night and removed the obstacle," said Mako. "Many suspect it. None may ever prove it. I, and those few who serve me, are especially skilled."

"I want nothing to do with this arrangement. I would never ask anyone to kill for me."

Mako smiled. "You protest far too late, Ebon. All your life you have lived fat on the riches I have brought you. Your father's coin made you everything you are; it paid for your tutors, who made you wise; it placed you in noble circles, where you learned compassion and virtue; and even now it pays your way at the Academy, where you have learned your spellcraft." Mako studied him carefully over the top of his glass. "Unless I am very mistaken, it even pays for the lover who sometimes warms your bed."

Ebon slapped his hand on the table. "But I did not *ask for it!* Who knows of this? Did Matami, and my father?" A horrible thought struck him. "Does Halab?"

"Halab is the only one whose orders I obey," Mako said softly.

It was like a slap in the face. The room seemed to spin around Ebon, though that might have been the brandy. Always Halab had struck him as his family's rare exception, one bright light in the family Drayden that he might look to, when all his lineage seemed shrouded in darkness. Yet now he learned that she was the source of the shadow itself.

"Are you hurt?" To Ebon's surprise, he did not hear sarcasm or malice in the bodyguard's tone. "I can see that you are. You trusted Halab, for she has always been kind to you. And you may not trust me after tonight, but know this: you were not wrong to believe in her. I serve Halab willingly, and even with love, for I also served her father. He was the dark of a cave's deepest shadow, and she is the sun. She may be the gentlest master of the family Drayden in decades. Mayhap centuries. The number of us—we assassins—has dwindled since she took power, but we do not complain, for we have never enjoyed our work."

"You seemed to enjoy it well enough tonight," spat Ebon, and drained his brandy in one savage pull. But it was a petulant thing to say, and he knew it, for he could hear some sense in Mako's words. And it spoke to a truth he had begun to suspect: that though Halab was as kind as he had always thought her, at her core there was inflexible steel. He had seen it when Matami had tried to have him and his friends beaten, when Halab herself had struck him down.

But he could not forgive Mako so easily. He had not asked to be dragged into the sewer to witness a murder. So he reached across the table and took Mako's glass, and drained what remained of his drink. Then he held both glasses high, dangling them loosely between thumb and forefinger. "Do you mean to fill these again?"

He half hoped the bodyguard would answer in anger or accusation. Instead Mako silently refilled both glasses from the bottle. It was half empty now. "Halab is no wanton killer. Rather than order an obstacle removed by violence, she will exhaust every other possible solution. And no one is put to death unless she knows something dark about them, something the constables have never caught wind of, or at least have never proven. In the circles of power where we walk, such darkness can be found more often than not."

"And Matami?" said Ebon. "What was his darkness?"

The bodyguard lowered his gaze. "When you and I first began to suspect him, I wondered that same thing. So I had him watched, to see what might be seen. But I found nothing, and yet I was certain he had something to do with the attack upon the Seat. And so I brought my suspicions to Halab. With tears in her eyes she told me the truth— something she had kept hidden for many long years. Once, almost a decade ago, he took a man without leave."

Ebon froze in his seat. His fingers shook on the glass. "That cannot be. Halab knew of this? And did nothing?"

"He was her brother, Ebon," said Mako softly. "You can blame her if you wish. But you know better than most the bonds that can exist between siblings, no matter the circumstance. The man was well paid, and remains so to this day, tucked in a corner of Idris and supported by our coin. This Halab did in some token of repayment—and to pay for his silence, in hopes that Matami would be safe from the constables' blades."

To learn that Halab knew of such evil, and had then gone to such length to hide it . . . Ebon's heart twisted in sickness and impotent anger. Was the Drayden name so cursed that even she, his favorite, must deal in darkness and vile misdeeds?

But then his thought turned in another direction. Albi came to his mind, and then Momen. Could he have turned them over to constables, even after such a heinous crime? He wondered. And wondering, he turned his eyes back to his glass.

"So you see," said Mako. "She sat with that shame—his shame—for so long. But when she learned he and your father may have had something to do with the attack . . . it only proved to her that he was rotten through, and had suffered no momentary lapse in judgement."

"And so she ordered you to kill him."

"No," said Mako. "That was my choice. She will wonder where he has gone, of course. She may ask me, and if she does, I will not lie. But she may not. Sometimes it is easier that way—she knows, and I know, and we both stay silent in our knowledge."

"What of my father? Will you kill him, too?" Even as he asked, Ebon wondered how he would feel if the answer was yes.

But Mako shook his head. "Your father is different. He is dearer to Halab. And he is *your* father. I have no wish to cause you grief, Ebon."

"Do you think that would grieve me? To see him killed?"

Mako stared into his glass. "No child loses their father without tears. Not even the worst child. Not even the worst father."

Ebon sighed, rubbing the heels of his palms into his eyes. "I am exhausted, Mako. None of your words have changed my mind. I want nothing to do with any of this. My father has cast me out of my inheritance. I cannot say I am glad for it, but I thought I was free of his legacy forever."

"And you can be, if you wish. Yet still I must do my duty. And that means protecting Halab. Just now, it seems I am protecting her from Shay himself. Can you withhold your hand from that cause?"

For that, Ebon had no easy answer.

"As I thought. Now, we must find proof of Shay's involvement in the attack upon the Seat. And to do that, we must find the murderer in the Academy."

"How can we do that now? It seems the only one who knew anything was Matami, and he is now in the Great Bay."

"Matami knew nothing. Shay was too smart for that. He used Matami for messages, small tasks, but kept the more important ones from him. He must be using someone else—someone like your cousin, the mindmage—for the murders. He uses many hands, and none of them know the parts the others play, so that none may reveal the whole scheme. Indeed, he was foolish to let Matami know where his orders came from. But your uncle was foolish, and mayhap would not have otherwise obeyed."

"Then we are no closer to catching the murderer." Again Ebon rubbed at his eyes. "You have done nothing to make me less tired."

"That is the brandy. You must have patience. We will discover the truth. We have done much already, whether you think so or not. And you have proven your mettle, far beyond what could have been expected." Ebon scowled, but Mako raised his hands. "I speak the truth. And this, too, is true: never will I make you part of something like that again. I only thought it was time you knew the truth so that you could face it with both eyes open. Can you forgive me?"

Ebon held his scowl, but felt some of the fire die in his heart. "It is a bit early to speak of forgiveness," he muttered. "But mayhap I can understand you."

Mako smiled, and Ebon thought he looked genuinely pleased. "Good. Then let us get you back to your Academy. Curfew, I am afraid, is a long-forgotten memory."

THIRTY-SIX

THE NEXT MORNING, THEREN AND KALEM FOUND EBON IN THE DINING hall. Kalem was glad to see him safely returned. It took Ebon a moment to notice Theren—he had forgotten she had gone with Lilith. As she told him of Lilith's recovery, he gave a weak smile.

"What is wrong, Ebon?" said Kalem. "What happened last night?"

"Last night? What about last night?" said Theren.

Ebon shook his head. "I cannot speak of it now. Not here, at least."

They tried to press him at first, but he waved them off, and at last they left him alone. But as he ate his breakfast, he decided to confess that afternoon in the library. He owed them that much, at least. He would not deceive his friends again.

His morning class was torturous. Now that he had learned counter-magic, Perrin wished for him to focus on the other spells. Mists seemed simplest, and he did not have to interact with any other students, or with Perrin herself. So he sat there, spinning his mists, trying to push them farther and farther from his skin. But in fact he found his spell weaker than the last time he had practiced. It was as though he had forgotten a piece of his magic—or mayhap it was only the distraction of the night before, the way he could not stop hearing Matami's screams.

THOOM

An explosion rocked the classroom, and Ebon fell to the floor in terror. Then he realized the blast had not come from within the classroom, but from beyond the door.

He scrambled to his feet and fled the room, a dozen other students on his heels despite Perrin's shouted orders to stay. Other classes joined them in the hall, running for the entryway where the explosion had come from. Ebon wondered what they were all doing. Hearing a blast or scream in the Academy had become almost commonplace by now. Surely they all knew to run, to flee the other way. Why, then, was he racing towards the sound? Why were the others?

Then he realized—he was going to help. He was sick of the attacks, sick of the wanton death that had plagued the school for months. If the murderer was there, and wanted to strike again, let them try. Ebon was not alone: an army of students stood behind him.

Together they flooded into the front hall, and dozens of eyes blazed with magelight as students reached for their spells.

But no one stood in the hallway. There were only the forms of students and instructors, lying on the floor as they twisted and moaned in pain. They all pointed outwards from the room's center, as though a blast had thrown them towards its edges. But where the blast had come from, there was no sign, for no one was burned or singed.

Near the front, one seemed worse off than the rest—and Ebon recognized the creaking old form of Cratchett, the instructor who held the front door whenever Mellie slept.

"Help him!" said Ebon, running forwards to follow his own advice. Half a dozen others rushed forwards to do the same. The rest fanned out, helping students to their feet. The fallen students were older, all in later-year classes. He saw Nella, eyes lolling in her head as she tried to gather her bearings, and Isra, groaning on all fours. They and their classmates fought to regain their feet, helped up by the younger students who had come flooding out from the Academy.

Ebon reached Cratchett and tried to help the old man up. But

Cratchett cried out in pain the moment they tried to move him, and screamed louder when they tried again. He was old; Ebon guessed his bones were brittle, and some might have broken when he fell.

The old man's eyes fixed on his, and he tried to speak. "She . . . tried to leave," he croaked. "But when I stopped her—"

His eyes bulged in their sockets, and his body jerked like a marionette's. Cratchett flew into the air, arms twisting horribly. But he uttered no sound—even when his bones began to snap, even when an unseen hand clamped hard on his neck, crushing it to a pulp. Blood spattered Ebon's cheeks, making him flinch. The corpse tumbled back to the ground amid the students' screams.

"Back!" cried a commanding voice. "Back into the citadel!"

Ebon turned and groaned. It was Dean Forredar, ushering the students out of the front room and back into the Academy's hallways. He helped the last few of the older students to their feet one by one.

That half-heard voice screamed in the back of Ebon's mind again, warning him of something. He looked at the students who had been struck in the attack. He recognized them all—not their names, or their faces, but one place he had seen them all before. The Goldbag Society Lilith had started. Not a student present now had been absent from that assembly.

Yet someone *was* missing.

But then Xain saw him, and Ebon's attention was drawn back to the present. The dean's eyes blazed with fury, and he pushed through the teeming crowd towards Ebon.

"Drayden! Standing in the midst of another attack? This time—"

But then Perrin was there, stepping up by Xain's elbow. "I was teaching my class when we heard the explosion, Dean. Ebon was at his desk."

"Ebon!" He turned to see Kalem and Theren running out of the hallways towards him. He gave them each a swift embrace, but then turned his attention back to Xain, who still looked darkly upon him.

"What happened?" said Perrin, seizing one of the students who had regained her feet. "Who did this?"

"I do not know," she said, shaking her head. "Our instructor was bringing us for some excursion out upon the Seat."

"Upon the Seat?" said Perrin. "That is not done."

The girl frowned. "It seemed odd to me. But she was our instructor. So we made for the front hall, but Cratchett tried to stop us. He and one of the students began to argue, but then—" She shook her head. "I barely saw what happened."

"You say Cratchett argued with a student?" said Ebon. "Who?"

The girl stared vacantly, as though searching for a long-distant memory, instead of something that had happened only moments ago. "I . . . I cannot remember," she murmured, and then eyed them all in terror. "Why can I not remember?"

But Ebon scarcely heard her. For the whisper in his mind now screamed, its words ringing with clarity for the first time. He stepped back, hoping not to be noticed, and took the sleeves of Theren and Kalem, drawing them close as they turned.

"The front door," he whispered. "It is open."

"What of it?" said Theren.

"The murderer escaped."

Kalem looked uneasy. "You cannot know that. They could have remained inside."

"I know it," said Ebon. "Because I know who it was."

Theren jerked in surprise. "You do? Who?"

"In a moment. We must go after them."

Kalem groaned. "Ebon . . ."

"They are not watching us. Go . . . *now.*"

He ran for the door, and his friends came behind him. No one saw them, no one shouted, and then they were in the city, fleeing through snow to the east of the Seat.

⌒

"We will most likely be expelled now," Kalem panted at Ebon's side. "So will you please tell me, Ebon, what we are doing?"

"All this time, we have been searching for the power behind Lilith. We wondered who held her under mindwyrd—and she *was* under mindwyrd, but other times, she was not, though we believed that she was."

"What?" said Theren. "Your words are senseless. Were you struck in the head?"

494

"A moment."

Ebon stopped at the corner of a building and looked back, to where he could just see the Academy entrance many streets away. But no one had pursued them. The street was empty, and the doorway remained clear.

"They are not coming after us," he said. "That is good. I think. Come."

And Ebon ran on. They followed him, east through the streets, through alleys and busy marketplaces. At last he skidded to a stop, doubled over with his hands on his knees, breathing hard.

"Where are we?" said Theren. "Why have you stopped here?"

"To rest. But only for a moment," said Ebon. "We will not want to be winded when we round the next corner."

Theren stood before him, hands at her hips. "Enough, Ebon. What is going on?"

He grimaced. "We have no time."

She gave him a harsh look. "After we spent weeks pursuing Lilith, only to falsely accuse her, I think this time I would rather be sure before I follow you blindly."

Ebon gave a frustrated growl. "Very well. Last night, Mako took me out into the city. He said he needed my help, for he suspected my uncle Matami had a hand in Lilith's deeds. But Matami knew nothing of Lilith."

"Are you certain?" said Kalem. "What if he lied?"

"He did not," said Ebon, his voice flat. "Mako put him to the question, and in the end, he slit his throat."

Theren's face hardened. Kalem gasped and put a hand on the wall beside him to steady himself. But Ebon only shook his head.

"I know your horror," he said. "Know that I did not wish it, and tried to stop him. I will live with what I saw for the rest of my days. But that is a matter for another time. Mako thought Matami was ignorant of Lilith because my father, Shay, kept the truth from him. But Shay is not guilty of this—it was another student at the Academy."

"How?" said Theren. "We know Lilith was under mindwyrd, and so were several others. What student could have had access to magestones—except for Lilith and Oren themselves, who we know were not the culprits?"

"Not magestones. Kekhit's amulet. The book said it gave her the power to cast darkfire *without* magestones. What if that was not all it did—what if it acted as magestones for any wizard, not just a firemage?"

Theren's eyes widened. "A mindmage. They would have mindwyrd, with no need to consume the stones, and none of the evils such consumption would bring upon them."

"And their eyes would not glow when casting their spells," Ebon said softly. "For that, too, was the power of Kekhit. Do you remember what the book said? She could hide the glow in her eyes when she cast her spells. And the logbook said that the amulet's powers were hers. The wizard could have been right before our eyes, and we would never have known."

That sent them reeling. Theren paced and then balled a fist to slam it into the home's wall. A smattering of snow slid from the roof onto their heads.

"But who?" said Kalem. "You said you knew who it was."

"Adara said the lovers have seen a girl skulking about the Seat," said Ebon. "And only one girl was there during every attack."

Theren rounded on him. "Nella. Lilith's so-called friend."

Ebon shook his head. "No. Her friendship is true. She could have done it—killing Credell after trying to breach the vaults, and then Oren once he realized what was going on. But Vali, too, was killed. And that was not part of stealing the artifacts from the vaults. That was because he was Astrea's friend, and a goldbag."

"Astrea's friend?" Kalem's eyes went wide. "Sky above. Isra."

"Yes," said Ebon. "Isra. She was there every time. I thought it odd that every death was so horrifying for Astrea, and that she was there for each of them. But she was only there because Isra brought her, so that she would have an excuse for being present."

"The conniving sow," Theren whispered. "I will kill her."

"No," said Ebon. "We must capture her and deliver her to the King's justice."

"She deserves death."

Ebon lifted his chin, heart blazing with fury. "And she will find it—by the King's law."

Kalem stepped between them to interrupt. "But Ebon, I still do not understand. Why are we here, and not in the Academy trying to find her? We should help."

"Because she is not in the Academy. I was a fool, and believed what Xain wanted me to. Dasko was not helping Xain move into his new home. He was helping Xain move artifacts out of the Academy."

Kalem gawked. "Into his house?"

"Where no doubt he has all manner of magical defenses," said Ebon. "They hoped to keep them safe, mayhap thinking the thief would not know where they had been moved. But do you remember what Adara told us, about the student who had been seen lurking about the city? I think that was Isra. If I am right, she makes for Xain's house even now, to take as many artifacts as she can lay her hands on."

"That is a mighty leap of thought," said Theren.

Ebon spread his hands. "Once I realized it had to be her, I knew there must be a reason for her outburst in the front hall. She was leaving the Academy because she knew the artifacts she desired were no longer there."

"But if you are right, why did we not tell the others?" said Kalem. "The instructors, the faculty? They should be here now to help us defeat her."

"Do you think Xain would have believed me?" said Ebon, scowling. "Who knows how much time we would have wasted trying to convince him, and then Isra would have escaped. And too many have suffered because of my mistakes already. I will not drag them along with me now."

Mako's voice came from the sky. "Ebon has always been such a noble boy." Then he dropped from the roof above them, landing catlike in the street.

In an instant Theren had raised her hands, and her eyes blazed with magelight. "Who are you?"

Ebon put a hand on her arm. "This is Mako. He works for my family. How did you know to find us here?"

Mako shrugged. "I did not. I was watching the home of the Academy's new dean when I saw a girl arrive. She slew the guards as fast as blinking and entered the house, but I could not follow her, for she erected a barrier of spells. I meant to fetch you from the Academy, and yet here I find you ready to serve."

"You think we will serve you?" said Theren. "I do not know you, save that Ebon tells us he saw you murder a man last night."

Ebon quailed as Mako gave him a withering glare. "Ebon is more flap-lipped than might be wished, it seems."

"There is no time for this," said Ebon. "Even now Isra is in Xain's home, mayhap stealing artifacts as we speak. We must stop her. Mako, will you help us?"

The bodyguard shrugged. "Why not? I had nothing else to do today."

"Thank you," Ebon said earnestly. "Now come."

He stole around the corner, and the others followed. There was Xain's house—and there, as Mako had said, were the bodies of the guards Isra had slain. It had been the Mystics and High King's guard on the street, and in death they embraced one another in pairs, each with a sword buried in the other's belly. Kalem's face went Elf-white as he beheld them.

"Mindwyrd," said Ebon. "She must have made them kill each other. Mako, do not let her speak to you, or she will—"

"I know mindwyrd, boy," Mako snarled. "See to your own safety, and I will see to mine."

They reached the door. Theren rolled her shoulders. "I feel her spell. She put a barrier upon the door to keep it shut."

"Then we must find another way in," said Kalem. "If she has the amulet, her magic is backed by the strength of magestones. You cannot hope to break the enchantment."

Theren's eyes glowed. "We shall see. I think she made this barrier in haste."

She held forth a hand, reaching out with her power. Ebon saw a sort of shimmering in the air before the door, like waves of heat escaping a fire. But nothing else happened, and after a long moment, Ebon felt his sense of urgency growing.

"Theren," he muttered. "There must be a back door."

"Who is to say she did not bar it as well?" said Theren through gritted teeth. "Besides, I am almost through."

"You said she cast this spell in haste," growled Mako.

"Ebon, silence your hound."

To Ebon's immense relief, Mako actually smiled at that.

Then there was a quiet *snap,* and the glow faded from Theren's eyes.

"It is done," she said, voice weak. She cleared her throat and spoke with more force. "But it was powerful indeed. The amulet is nothing to be trifled with. Take care within."

Ebon looked at Kalem and Theren, and then at Mako. The bodyguard gave a mocking smile followed by a bow, and waved his hand towards the door. "I would not presume, little lord. After you."

"You are too kind," said Ebon, trying to sound braver than he felt. He put his hand on the doorknob and turned it. With a soft *click,* the door swung open into darkness.

THIRTY-SEVEN

BEYOND THE FRONT DOOR WAS A MASSIVE ENTRYWAY THAT STRETCHED nearly to the back of the house, a great hall where tables could be set to hold feasts of moderate size. To the left a staircase led up to the second floor, while doors split off from the main hall to either side—two to the left, and two to the right. The floor was polished wood, while the walls were plaster between bare, raw beams that held the ceiling seven paces high. Over the wood floor were laid two plush carpets of Feldemarian make, if Ebon guessed right. Broad windows were placed near the ceiling and in carefully-laid alcoves, and if their shutters had not been drawn, they would doubtless have lit the hall with the morning's warm glow. Ebon had a brief thought that if he were not so terrified, the place would have seemed warm and welcoming.

But terrified he was, and in his mind every shadow held menace. All candles and lanterns had been snuffed out, and with the windows blinded, the place was filled with darkness. They studied their surroundings in silence, Ebon trying to guess where the artifacts might be hidden.

"It is a large building," said Mako, "and we must find her quickly. Split up."

"What?" Kalem said. "No. I will not. I do not want to be here in the first place, and certainly I do not wish to wander on my own, searching for a madwoman!"

"Do you wish to stop her, or not?" growled Mako.

"Not as much as I wish to survive!"

Ebon put a calming hand on his shoulder and met Mako's eyes. "It is folly for any of us to leave Theren. Only she can hope to defend us against Isra's magic."

"I can look after myself," said Mako, sneering. "But if you three are frightened, then stay together. Look for her upstairs, and I will search this floor. If she should kill you, try to scream as loud as you may. That way I shall know I am on my own."

"Thank you for your concern," spat Theren.

Mako nodded and ducked into the first room, dagger drawn and held by his side.

Theren led them up the stairs. Ebon whispered silent thanks with every step, for not one creaked beneath his foot. On the second floor they found another hall like the one below, but narrower, with many doors, and then a pair of double doors at one end of the hallway. Ebon guessed that led to Xain's bedchamber.

"Start there," whispered Ebon, pointing. Theren nodded and sneaked in that direction.

"How are we supposed to fight her if she has mindwyrd?" asked Kalem.

"If you stay out of her sight, she will not be able to cast it," said Theren. "All mindmagic requires line of sight."

"That holds true for regular mentalists," said Kalem. "How can you know it is the same for a wizard with the power of magestones?"

Theren was silent for far, far too long a moment before she muttered, "It is an educated guess."

They opened the master bedroom's wide doors with nary a creak. Ebon tensed, ready to leap upon Isra if she was within. But he saw nothing—only a bed, more modest than he would have imagined, and two simple bureaus along the walls. A door tucked into the room's corner spoke of a large closet, while another door at the other end led to a balcony. Ebon stole across to look outside. But the balcony was empty, and he stepped back in with a sigh.

"Let us go to the next room," he said.

Then the closet door opened, and Isra emerged into view.

For a moment, they all froze in shock. Then Ebon shouted, Kalem shrieked, and Theren's eyes glowed as she struck Isra in the chest with her magic. Isra flew back through the open closet door, lank hair and dark robes fluttering about her. Ebon jumped across the bed and rolled off the other end to the floor, while Kalem ran from the room like a rat on fire. Isra reemerged a moment later, and Theren's eyes blazed as she struggled to contain the girl's magic.

Ebon sprang up and ran for the door, snatching Theren's wrist as he passed. "She has the amulet! You cannot best her!" he cried.

Theren struggled for a moment, but then relented, and made to run with him. But Isra's spell struck her, flinging her through another door into an adjoining room. Ebon went to follow, but the wall before him crumpled as Isra battered it, and he turned tail to flee the other way. He ducked into the first door he saw, slamming it shut behind him and praying Isra had not seen which way he went.

He found himself in a small antechamber, with a large wooden chest, a single bureau, and two couches of muted green and blue. He threw himself under one of the couches—or started to, but recoiled as he heard a yelp.

There, his face pressed to the floor, was Xain's son, Erin. The poor child was terrified, his eyes wide and his fingers scrabbling at the wooden floor in hopes of escape. He opened his mouth to scream, but Ebon clapped a hand across it.

"Shhh! Shush, shush," he murmured. "I mean you no harm. I am not the one who attacked your home, I am . . ." He gulped at the lie. "I am a friend of your father's. You must hide yourself."

Erin looked as though he would not scream, so Ebon carefully removed his hand. "Where can I hide?" he whimpered.

Ebon looked around the room. The couch would not hide the boy from even a cursory search, but the bureau might do the trick. "There," said Ebon, pointing. "Here, come quickly."

He helped Erin to his feet, then opened the bureau and gave his hand to help the boy in. But no sooner had he shut the bureau than he heard the latch click, and the room's door began to swing open. In a panic, he threw himself to the ground and slid beneath the couch, clamping a hand over his mouth to muffle his breathing.

The door's wooden timbers swung past, revealing simple brown leather shoes beneath black robes. The shoes took one careful step into the room, and then another. The door swung shut silently, trapping them in the room together.

"Ebon?" whispered Kalem.

A rush of air escaped him, and he pressed his face against the wood floor. "I am here, Kalem."

"Thank the sky," Kalem hissed. Ebon slid out, and Kalem helped him to his feet. "I think I heard her make for the stairs, so I came to find you and Theren."

"We are not the only ones here." Ebon stole across to the bureau and cracked open the door. "Erin. Listen carefully. You must remain here. Do not open this door for anyone, not even me. If you stay where you are, you will be safe. Do you understand?"

"Yes," came Erin's terrified whisper.

"If I open the door myself, you will know you are safe," said Ebon. "But if you hear me calling out for you, asking where you are, then I am not myself, and you must not listen to me. Tell me you will not listen."

"I will not."

"Good lad." Ebon swung the bureau door shut again. To Kalem's questioning look, he whispered, "Xain's son."

"Sky above," said Kalem, eyeing the bureau in horror.

"He will be fine if he remains," said Ebon. "Come. If Isra has gone downstairs, she may be trying to escape."

They cracked the door and peered out. The hall appeared to be empty, and so they gingerly stepped into it. But as they did, the door beside the stairs creaked open, and they froze—until Theren stepped out from the room, and they both sighed with relief.

"Thank the sky," said Kalem. "Theren, have you seen her? She—"

Theren's eyes blazed with light, and she struck at them with her magic. A spell blasted them through the air, slamming them both into the doors of the master bedroom, which buckled under their weight. They landed hard on the floor.

"What is she—" Kalem groaned.

"Mindwyrd," said Ebon, gasping as he fought for his feet. He seized Kalem's elbow and dragged him up. Another spell narrowly missed them, shattering a piece of one of the doors and sending wooden splinters through the air. They dove beneath the bed, but then it flipped up, crashing into the opposite wall. Ebon rose, only to have Theren lift him up, her eyes blazing as she pressed him against the wall.

Kalem had gained his feet. He hesitated for a long moment, unsure of what to do, before leaping towards Theren with a cry. She raised her other hand, throwing him against a dresser, where he collapsed. Ebon looked down at her in terror, gasping for breath as he felt invisible fingers closing around his throat.

"Where is the boy?" she said, her voice a flat monotone. "Xain's son?"

"Theren," he wheezed. "Theren, she is controlling you. Fight her!"

She did not so much as blink. But then Mako stepped out of the hallway behind her, and his dagger's pommel came crashing down on the back of her head.

The magic holding Ebon vanished, and he fell to the ground. At once he leapt to his feet and ran to Theren, rolling her onto her back. He felt for her heartbeat—it was there, and strong, and he could see the rise and fall of her chest.

"Come now, Ebon," said Mako, grinning. "You did not think I would kill one of your little friends, did you?"

Kalem joined them. "She has left this floor. Mayhap she fled. We might think of doing the same."

"No," said Mako. "I do not think she would leave without the artifacts. I saw a basement entry on the ground floor. I meant to investigate, but heard the fighting here."

"Then let us go there," said Ebon. "If she escapes with the artifacts, there is no telling what havoc she could unleash."

Mako motioned towards the steps. "Once more I defer to your courage."

Ebon glared at him and, after a final glance at Theren to make sure she was well, he made for the stairs.

THIRTY-EIGHT

ON THE GROUND FLOOR, MAKO TOOK THEM TO THE DOOR LEADING TO the basement steps. Ebon paused on the threshold and drew a deep breath. There were lanterns below, so that the darkness was not complete. But he could feel the empty space pulling at him, siphoning his courage like an insatiable void.

"How can we beat her?" Kalem whispered. "She has the amulet, Ebon. Only Theren could have hoped to stop her, and we no longer have her. We should flee."

"What is this amulet?" said Mako. "How does it work?"

"You know magestones," said Ebon. "The amulet gives her strength as though she had eaten them. And she may cast her spells without her eyes glowing, so that we will have little warning."

Mako frowned. "That will make her harder to kill."

Ebon held his gaze. "There will be no killing. She will be thrown before the King's justice."

"She is dangerous."

"So are you. Do you deserve death?"

Mako grinned. "Undoubtedly. But who is strong enough to deliver it?"

"Isra, if you underestimate her," said Kalem.

"That I very much doubt."

"Enough," said Ebon. He set his foot upon the first step leading down. After that, it was easier to take the next, and then the one after that. The stair only turned once, but as he rounded that corner, Ebon felt nothing in his life had ever been so hard as moving his foot. Had Kalem and Mako not been beside him, he would surely have wept like a child and fled. Instead, he forced himself to keep going.

At the base of the stairs was a wooden doorway with no knob or latch. Mako waved them back, pressing his ear to the wood. He listened, frowning.

"I can hear her. But she is far away. If I had to guess, I would say there is another hallway like the ones above. I think she is at the other end."

"How can we possibly defeat her?" said Kalem. "She will certainly see us coming."

"The hinges look well-oiled, as they are in the rest of the house," said Mako. "And the rooms are all interconnected. If we can move silently into the hallway, I think we can steal into the first rooms to the side and then get closer without attracting her attention. The two of you will go to the left, and I will go to the right. Once you reach the other end of the basement, find some way to distract her. When you do, I will—"

Ebon gave him a sharp look.

Mako grimaced. "I will *subdue* her."

"Good," said Ebon. "In that case, waiting does us no favors."

He opened the door. Just as Mako had guessed, it swung open in silence. They slipped through and ducked left, where an open doorway waited. Ebon glanced down the hall before they entered and saw Isra at the other end, kneeling before a huge iron door set into the wall. He could see the glow of her eyes, which she had not bothered to hide as she cast some spell—or, he guessed, worked to dispel some enchantment that held the door closed. But, too, he could see another glow coming from her—black and centered around her neck. It was the amulet, he realized, lending her the power of magestones.

Then they were in the room, and Isra was gone from view. On the other side of the hallway, Mako vanished behind the opposite door. Ebon and Kalem found themselves in a small storage room, with barrels and sacks stacked against the walls. Sure enough, a door led to another room closer to Isra, and then to another that was just beside her. Ebon stooped behind a barrel, with Kalem just behind. Together, they leaned over slightly to peer out.

Isra was still focused on the door, her hands working as she focused on breaking its enchantments. And then, just as Ebon was about to bob out of sight, he heard a *snap* as the enchantment was broken. A savage grin crossed her features. She stood, reached out with a spell once more, and used her magic to drag the door open. Ebon could only catch a glimpse inside, where many crates were stacked against one of the walls—the same sort of crates he had seen in the cart, the day they found Dasko loading them into the house.

From the doorway, Isra's eyes glowed as she raised a hand. She swiped through the air, and Ebon heard a sharp *crack* as every crate in the vault shattered. There came many crashes and tinkling as countless artifacts scattered across the ground.

"It is time," said Ebon.

"How are we supposed to stop her?" said Kalem.

"We are not. We are only supposed to distract her."

"How are we supposed to do *that?*"

Ebon shrugged and whispered, "When you do not know what to do, do what you know."

Then he leapt out from behind the barrel, waving his hands in the air and screaming wordlessly.

Kalem was a half-second behind him, shouting incoherent gibberish. Isra spun at once, eyes flashing as she struck with magic. Ebon only just dove out of the way in time. A barrel splintered where he had been standing. She turned to Kalem next, but he got behind one of the basement's stone pillars. Its edge shattered under Isra's spell.

"Thrice-damned little goldshitters!" roared Isra. "Can you not leave well enough alone?"

"I do not know that anything is well enough as it is," Ebon called out from his hiding place. "You have left too many corpses for that."

"*I* have left corpses?" Isra gave a horrible laugh as she stalked forwards. "How many corpses did the goldbags leave upon the Seat? And who among you faced the King's justice?"

She was far too close now, and Kalem jumped up to run. But she seized him with her power and hoisted him into the air. His eyes bugged out in terror—but she did not kill him. Instead her smile turned cruel, and power reverberated in her voice.

"Kill your goldshitting friend," she hissed.

She dropped him. At once, Kalem turned, his eyes glazed, and stumped towards Ebon's hiding place. Ebon was forced to run through one storeroom and into the next. A spell from Isra shattered the wall where his head had been just a moment ago.

"Kalem!" he cried. "Kalem, stop! You can resist her!"

Isra's voice was cruel. "You know nothing of the power of mindwyrd. Now the two of you may reenact the war your kin wage across Underrealm even now."

As if to prove her words, Kalem reached for a hammer that lay on a nearby barrel. His eyes glowed, and in his hands it twisted to a spiked orb of wood and metal. He flung this at Ebon as hard as he could, and then did the same with a metal spike. Ebon ducked behind a pillar. He grimaced at the sound of Kalem's footsteps just around the side.

"Kalem, forgive me."

He stepped out and seized Kalem's arm, even as the boy reached for Ebon with glowing eyes. He dragged Kalem in by the wrist, clenched his other hand, and drove the fist into the boy's chin. Kalem collapsed like a sack of beans, out cold before he struck the stone floor.

Before the vault, Isra snarled. "Do you think that will save you? It only means I will have you kill yoursel—"

Mako appeared behind her, silent as a shadow. He held his dagger high, and in his eyes was a killing light. He stepped towards her. But Ebon saw him, and his eyes widened. Isra saw it, and she turned at the last second. The dagger, which should have severed her spine, struck her shoulder instead, and she cried out in pain.

Ebon ran forwards to help, for Isra's eyes glowed as she looked up at the bodyguard. She lifted a hand—but nothing happened. For a heartbeat that image froze itself into Ebon's mind: Isra striking with magic, and Mako standing there unaffected.

Mako grinned as he reached down, seizing the front of her robes and dragging her up. Again he raised the dagger, already slick with her blood.

But then, in his mind's eye, Ebon saw Matami. He saw the ruined eye and the severed fingers. He saw old Cratchett, and Oren and Vali and poor, poor Credell, all of them the same—lifeless eyes staring at nothing. And he saw Cyrus, the old dean's flesh turning to stone beneath Ebon's fingers before he plunged screaming into the Great Bay.

"No!" he cried, and shoved Mako with all of his might.

The bodyguard hardly stumbled. His eyes flashed, and he struck Ebon a backhanded blow that sent him crashing to the ground.

But it was just long enough of a pause for Isra to recover. She seized a barrel and cast it through the air. It struck Mako hard, sending him flying into the next room. Ebon lay there, half-stunned, as Isra scrambled to her feet and dove into the vault. Hardly looking at what she was doing, she fell to her knees and scraped at the floor with both hands. She rose again with two armfuls of artifacts and broke into a run for the door.

"No," Ebon gasped. He struggled to stand, unable to manage it by the time she reached him. At the last moment he lunged, scrabbling to seize her arm, her robes, anything to hold her back. He missed her robes, but his fingers closed around a fine chain of silver, and as she ran it snapped off in his hand.

Ebon fell to the floor hard, grunting from the impact. But as he rolled over, he looked into his hand to see Kekhit's amulet, glinting up at him as though giving him a secretive wink. Isra reached the basement's far end, stepped through the door, and vanished up the stairs.

Mako had recovered, though his clothes were torn and ripped, and there was an ugly gash on his forehead. He made for the staircase, but he stopped for just a moment, looming over Ebon with a sneer twisting his lips. "You are a greater fool than I realized," he growled. "She will kill again. When she does, remember that those deaths are upon your head."

Then he turned and was gone.

Ebon groaned as he gained his feet. He stumbled over to Kalem, who was shaking his head as he lay on the floor. Ebon reached down a hand for the boy, pulling him up. Kalem blinked as he looked around.

"What happened? Where is Isra?"

"She caught you in her mindwyrd," said Ebon. "And now she has escaped with many artifacts. Come. We must try to catch her, if we can."

They ran up the stairs together, taking the steps two at a time, and then burst into the entry hall—and there they stopped. Mako was nowhere to be seen; but Isra stood just inside the front door. Over one shoulder she held a satchel, clanking with what were surely the artifacts. Her other arm circled Erin's neck. The poor boy's eyes were wide and frightened, and his legs shook so badly he looked as though he might topple at any moment.

"Erin, stay calm," said Ebon. "You will be all right."

"You make idle promises, goldshitter," Isra hissed. "You cannot promise the boy will emerge unscathed when you cannot even protect yourself."

Her eyes lit with magelight. Ebon braced himself, and Kalem raised his hands as though to ward off the spell. But then there was a loud *SNAP* upon the air, and Ebon heard a faltering step behind him. He turned to see Theren halfway up the staircase, leaning heavily on the bannister, her eyes glowing brighter than the moons. Her hand swung forth, trying to blast Isra. But Isra countered the spell with a strangled cry.

"Why do you throw your lot in with these pampered wretches?" she said. "They are the reason folk like you and I suffer."

Theren only glared. "The only thing I suffer from at present is the grating, hideous sound of your voice."

She blasted Isra with a spell that sent the girl staggering back. But she kept her grip on Erin's neck, and the boy yelped as he was dragged. With a frustrated shout, Isra fled through the front door and threw it shut behind her. Theren leapt down the final few steps, and Ebon made ready to run through the front door alongside her. But Theren stumbled when she reached the floor and fell to all fours on the ground.

"Theren!" cried Kalem, kneeling at her side.

Ebon reached down to help her up. Theren tried to wave him off, but it was a weak gesture. "I am still dazed," she mumbled, shaking her head as if to clear it, and then wincing as though that had worsened the pain. "Blast that man of yours, Ebon. He strikes like a mule's back hoof."

For a moment Ebon was torn. Theren could not chase Isra, that seemed certain. And without Theren, he and Kalem had no chance against her. But if they let her go . . . his mind filled with the sight of Erin, and the boy's terrified cries as he was dragged away.

Erin. Sky above, the poor boy.

They all started in surprise at the click of the front door's latch. It swung open, whisper quiet. Standing in the frame with a look of wonder was Instructor Dasko.

THIRTY-NINE

WE ARE DOOMED, THOUGHT EBON.

How could he explain this? What possible excuse could there be? The vault was breached, all of the guards were dead, and Isra was nowhere to be found, nowhere to have the blame laid rightly on her head.

And Erin. Poor Erin.

Dasko's brow furrowed. "Ebon. What in all the world are you doing here?"

"I . . ." Ebon's throat was bone-dry, and he swallowed before trying again. "I . . . I guessed that the artifacts were here," he stammered. No, that was wrong, wrong, *wrong.* "We knew the attack at the Academy was a distraction so that the murderer could steal the artifacts unimpeded. The guards were dead when we arrived. It was Isra from the very beginning—ever since Credell."

"Isra?" Dasko blinked. "The mentalism student? How?" But quickly he shook his head. "No matter. We can sort this out. I will help you, if I can, but you must come with me now. Xain and some other of the faculty are on their way here, along with many constables, and all of this can be laid before them."

Ebon felt the blood drain from his face. Over Kalem's head, Theren met his eyes. *Xain.* Xain, whose son had just been dragged into the streets as Isra's hostage. And constables, who would arrive to find three students in a destroyed home, with every inhabitant murdered.

Suddenly Dasko's eyes narrowed. Ebon looked down to follow his gaze. There in his hand was Kekhit's amulet. He almost dropped it in shock, for he had forgotten he held it.

Dasko stepped back, magelight springing into his eyes. Magic rippled along his limbs, increasing their size, and his skin hardened.

"Where did you get that?" he said, his voice deep and menacing.

"No!" cried Ebon. "I took it from Isra when we fought her. I did not take it from the vault!"

"Drop it," said Dasko in a bestial snarl.

Theren caught Ebon's eye again. She jerked her head. Ebon frowned. Then he caught a frantic motion at the bottom of his vision. Behind Kalem's back, Theren held out her hand.

Ebon swallowed and dropped the amulet into Theren's palm.

"Stop!" cried Dasko, leaping towards them.

"Be still," said Theren.

Dasko froze where he stood.

Theren stepped forwards, licking her lips. "You arrived to find the house empty, but you saw Isra running away through the streets, with Erin in tow. No one was here in the house when you investigated. You never saw us. That is what you will tell Xain and the constables when they arrive. Do you understand?"

"Yes," said Dasko, his voice utterly flat.

"Darkness below, *what are you doing?*" Kalem tried to drag the amulet from Theren's grasp, but she withheld it from him.

"The only thing we can, Kalem." But despite the determined glint in Theren's eye, Ebon could hear the quiver in her voice. "You know we would be blamed for all of this."

"We would not!" cried Kalem. He wrung his hands, pacing. "We could explain. They would believe us. They would *have* to believe us."

Theren gritted her teeth. "The only one who has to believe us is Dasko. And that is because I hold this." She lifted the amulet.

Kalem turned on Ebon. "You cannot agree. You cannot think this is the right course."

"The *right* course, Kalem? There is no right course now. This is the only way forwards that does not end in our torture and death."

They heard shouts from outside, followed by the sound of many boots tramping in the street. Theren blanched.

"We must go," she said. "Out the back door. Run!"

"No," said Kalem. "We must stay."

Theren seized one of his arms, and Ebon took the other. Theren looked over her shoulder. "Leave now, Dasko," she said. "Tell them what I told you, and forget you saw us here."

Dasko nodded. "The house was empty. There was no one here. I saw Isra fleeing through the streets . . ."

They did not wait to hear more, but pulled Kalem out the back door and into the alley beyond. They ran, boots pounding in the mud and snow, churning tracks behind them.

But they were not out of earshot before Ebon heard Xain's keening, anguished wail behind them.

Erin. Sky above. Poor Erin.

They did not stop running.

FORTY

EBON SAT OUT ON THE ACADEMY GROUNDS.

It was some days later—days that had passed like a fog while he hardly noticed. Now he had found a private bench buried in some rosebushes, and there he sat, alone. The students and faculty were in the dining hall, eating a mournful supper.

Theren had hidden the amulet somewhere safe—exactly where, Ebon did not know, and did not care to find out.

He had heard nothing from Mako.

The Academy was in an uproar. Half its faculty were on the hunt for Isra and Erin, as were the constables, and the Mystics, and the High King's guard. Yet the many hundreds of searchers had turned up nothing.

Ebon guessed they were gone. Isra had taken her ill-gotten gains from the Seat and now fled across Underrealm with Erin in tow, to bargain with if ever she was caught.

And it was his fault. At least in part. He knew Isra was mostly to blame for all that had transpired. Yet he had insisted on investigating, and had taken them into Xain's home without help. Mayhap Isra would have escaped with the artifacts, but she almost certainly would not have found Erin.

He buried his face in his hands, rubbing at his eyes. He had hardly slept since that day, for he kept seeing Erin's terrified face. Too, he saw the rage in Mako's eyes, and the unbridled hatred in Isra's. They plagued him worse than Cyrus' death ever had.

When he lifted his face from his hands, he found that he was no longer alone.

There stood Xain, framed in the arch of a hedge and blocking the rest of the grounds from view. That arch was Ebon's only escape, as he was keenly aware. His mind flashed back to last year, when Cyrus had found him in the gardens just like this. Cyrus had struck him, battering him with mindmagic until Ebon thought his body would break. Now his hands balled to fists at his side. Another dean who hated him. And now, mayhap, another attack.

But no glow came to Xain's eyes. And when he lifted a hand, it was not to strike with magic. Instead he threw a piece of cloth upon the ground. The white snow made the cloth stand out in stark relief: it was dark grey, and made of a fine silk that only a wealthy merchant could afford. A shredded cuff from Mako's shirt, ripped free when Isra had flung the barrel at him.

"I know you had something to do with this," said Xain, his voice laced with poisoned steel. "I cannot prove it yet. But I *will*. And when I do, I will end you and all of your kin. I will scour the name of Drayden from Underrealm, and when I am done, only tomes of history will remember you: a footnote scrawled in blood, scorned and spat upon by all who read it."

This was not Cyrus' white-hot rage, nor the blind hatred of Isra. This was something worse, and Ebon found himself more frightened by it than he had ever been before.

Then Xain turned and walked away, vanishing into the citadel.

EPILOGUE

Isra cinched the gag tighter and then checked the rope binding the boy to the wall. He winced with each tug on the cloth. She ignored it. He was a goldshitter like the rest of them. Let him suffer. Let him suffer the way his father and the rest of them had made *everyone* suffer.

She raised her cowl and left the room.

The stone hallways stank and made her skin prickle with nerves, and she hated them. She briskly pushed through the stench to the tunnel that led out. This was far too perilous, and she would never have taken the risk. But she must see her patron. Another outcast, like Isra herself. And the only woman who could help, now that the goldshitter Ebon had spoiled her plan.

Soon she stood before an inn. The doorman must have been warned of her arrival, for he gave no second glance despite her shabby clothes. Not Academy clothing—no, she had rid herself of that at the first opportunity. Now she had a plain cloak of brown, and nondescript clothes like any peasant. It let her go unnoticed, and it felt like a return to her roots besides.

But that brought thoughts of Astrea. She shuddered, bowing as she blinked back tears.

Poor Astrea. All alone now.

Not for long. Not if her patron had any help to offer—and she would.

Stairs at the back of the inn's common room led upstairs to rooms for rent. But Isra's patron would not be staying there. Instead Isra turned left, where a storeroom door stood slightly ajar. Inside, there was a carpet in the room's center. This she lifted, revealing a trapdoor that she opened with a flick of her wrist and a flash of magelight in her eyes. Shallow stone steps descended into the ground—but not into darkness, for the way was well-lit by many torches. Down she went, into the earth's bowels, another blast of magic swinging the trapdoor shut behind her.

A narrow corridor led to her patron's room, a guard barring the door. A mammoth man, his fists as big as her head. He had never beheld her with anything but a scowl. His skin, dark as night, only made his glaring eyes stand out the more.

"I must see her," said Isra.

The guard's nostrils flared. But from within the room came a voice. "Let her in."

A ham-sized fist reached out and opened the door. Isra slipped inside, and it closed again behind her.

The room was nothing impressive—certainly far poorer than what her patron was used to. For her patron had once been a goldshitter, just like those who Isra hated. Those who had brought this *war*. But her patron had been cast out, and had learned what Isra had known her whole life: that the true evil in the world was not Drayden, not Yerrin, but all of them at once, and more besides. It was the merchants, the nobility, those who held themselves above their fellows by virtue of coin or a throne.

"I have heard no small amount of whispers." Her patron did not sound angry. If anything, she sounded amused. "It seems plans have gone . . . *most* awry, since last we spoke. You are lucky you came to me when you did. I have business I must attend to in Feldemar, and I leave upon the morrow."

Isra nearly growled. "I lost the amulet, but gained many more artifacts during my escape."

She held up her satchel for a moment before throwing it on the floor at her patron's feet. But she received no reply. Instead, her patron regarded her over steepled fingers.

"And the boy?"

"I took him, as you asked. When can I bring him to you? He whines."

"You will keep him. I cannot have him linked to me."

Isra scowled, but said nothing.

"I thank you for holding up your end of the bargain," her patron went on. "I am a fair woman, and will help you with your aims. You needed the amulet to achieve them, did you not?"

"I did," said Isra. "Without mindwyrd, the task is impossible."

"But would you take that power another way? From magestones?"

Isra paused. Magestones were another matter. She had heard dark tales whispered about the Academy halls since her arrival.

Her patron noticed the hesitation. "I will admit, it would be a . . . different path. Far more dangerous for you. Mayhap even fatal. But it would allow the plan to work. You would have what you desire. An end to this war, and to those who brought it upon your Academy."

"Then that is everything," Isra snarled, fury raging in her gut. "But magestones are worth a fortune, and you are no longer a goldshitter—if you have been telling me true."

Her patron smiled. Then the smile turned into a laugh, and she reached into her cloak, reemerging with a brown cloth packet which she threw at Isra's feet. Isra stooped to retrieve it. Inside, in two neat rows stacked atop each other, were long black gems that she could almost see through. She gazed in wonder.

"It is true I have little in the way of coin, nor the help of my kin who have abandoned me. But I am Damaris, once of the family Yerrin, and my greatest strength has never been the weight of my purse. It is the lengths I will go to achieve my aims. What of you, Isra? Do you have the same strength?"

With shaking fingers, Isra plucked a magestone from the packet and slipped it into her mouth. With a crunch and a swallow, it vanished down her throat.

She opened black eyes, and her lips parted in a rictus.

The Firemage's Vengeance

BEING BOOK THREE
OF THE FIRST VOLUME

OF THE
ACADEMY JOURNALS

ONE

THE SNOW THAT FELL IN THOSE MIDDLE DAYS OF MARTIS DID NOTHING to chill the air—nothing, that is, when compared to the ice in Ebon's heart. The frost inside him was made of fear and dread, and if asked, he would have called it more frigid than the winds and snow that blew in his face, for the winter within kept him from noticing the winter without.

He led Kalem and Theren through the streets of the High King's Seat. His friends felt the same, he knew. Theren huddled deeper under her hood. She had not bothered to dye her hair in some time, and her dark roots showed through the blonde, though that hardly mattered since her head was rarely uncovered these days. Kalem wrapped his arms tight about himself, pale cheeks glowing red as his hair against winter's gales, and his spindly limbs shook whenever he stayed in one place too long. Yet Ebon guessed that neither of them were any more aware of the weather than he was. They had greater troubles, ones that plagued them day and night. Their studies suffered, and in the midst of conversation their thoughts drifted away. They were left staring at nothing in the middle of the dining hall, and their worries kept them lying awake in their beds late into the night.

The first was Dasko, the instructor they held in bondage, though they did not wish to. The second was Erin, the dean's son who was captive or dead. And the third was his captor, Isra, who had vanished from all sight and knowledge, a trail of corpses in her wake.

"This is a fool's errand," said Theren, bringing Ebon's mind back to the present.

"It is no errand at all," said Ebon. "We are invited."

"And why did we accept? What if something happens to Das— what if something happens back at the Academy while we are gone?"

"We cannot watch him every hour of every day, Theren." Kalem's voice held a note of careful reproach. "Indeed, we do not spend much time with him as it is."

"Yet we are always near," Theren insisted. "If our control should slip . . ."

"If we are discovered, we will be discovered," said Ebon. "Kalem is right. We cannot spend our every hour sitting on our hands, half in hope and half in fear."

"You say that more easily than I would," Theren muttered. Ebon could not tell if she had meant for him to hear it or not, but he did not blame her either way. She had the most to fear in all this untenable situation.

At long last, the black iron gate of the Drayden family's manor loomed before them. Once the guards spied the three Academy students making their way through the snow drifts, they hastened to draw the gate open. Ebon shook out his boots on the cobblestones of the courtyard, which was better swept than the streets had been. He had never spent winter in the northern lands; at home in Idris, winters were colder, but drier, and snow was an Elf-tale. To him, this type of winter seemed a deadly danger, though Theren assured him it was in fact very mild this year.

A happy shout preceded a short, plump figure bounding towards them, and Ebon recognized his sister, Albi, beneath a furred hood. She hugged him first, and he grinned as he hoisted her up off the ground. But then she embraced Kalem just as warmly, and Ebon's mouth soured. Theren she gave a more customary greeting; both hands clasped at once, she bowed. Theren rolled her eyes, but returned the greeting without complaint.

"I thought the three of you would never come," Albi said. Her voice seemed uncommonly loud after the dead quiet of the snow-covered streets, and after the anxious, hushed words Ebon had shared with his friends. "But then, it seems much later than it is, for the sky is so dark and grey. Come inside. Halab eagerly awaits you."

"We will, and gladly," said Ebon, forcing a smile. "Northern winters suit me ill."

Albi laughed and led them in. Both hearths burned in the wide front hall, and Ebon sighed in relief at the warmth of them. He cast back his hood and bent to remove his boots. They were gifts Halab had sent only recently—black to follow the Academy's rules, but lined with grey fur and laced up to just below the knee. Theren and Kalem, too, had received their own pairs, but Theren almost forgot to remove hers, and had to be reminded by a sharp word from Kalem.

Unshod, they climbed the stairs to the lounge where Halab awaited them. She rose at once and came forwards with a smile. Her dress was ochre and white, like fine-spun gold dusted with snow. Though all faces were paler now in the waning sunlight, Ebon thought she had never looked lovelier.

"Dearest nephew," she said, reaching for him. He kissed her cheeks, and then she bowed to Kalem and Theren. Kalem flushed, and Ebon knew the boy was thinking of the first time they had met, when he had kissed Halab's cheeks. Theren, for her part, did not roll her eyes so hard as she had with Albi. Ebon knew the high estimation in which she held his aunt.

"Our heartfelt thanks for your hospitality, especially in the depths of winter's chill," said Kalem.

"But that is when hospitality is needed the most," said Halab with a smile.

Dinner had been prepared already, and was brought from the kitchens to be uncovered for them. They ate ravenously, for all three of them felt their appetites could hardly be sated these days. Halab laughed as she saw them devour their meals, and quipped that the three of them must be growing. Ebon thought to himself that the likelier explanation was the oppressive cold. When snow made walking a chore, even after a small distance, he seemed to need thrice as much food just to remain upright.

After, she took them back to the lounge, where they sat and talked of small things—their classes, and their friends (only Kalem had any of these outside of present company), and the little bits of news Halab thought they might enjoy hearing. But, as happened so often in the Academy itself these days, Ebon often found his mind wandering, and he saw the same in his friends. Halab noticed it as well. Often he found her looking at the three of them, a question in her eyes, her lips pursed. At last he leaned forwards and grimaced in apology.

"I am sorry, dearest aunt. The three of us have made terrible guests, I fear."

Halab shook her head at once. "It is I who should apologize. I have taken little consideration for the troubles the three of you bear. I have heard of the Academy's rogue student, and the dean's son who she stole away. No doubt such dark thoughts are what trouble you."

Ebon studied his fingernails, not wishing to meet her eyes. She was right about Isra, of course, but she did not know just how intimately the matter concerned Ebon, nor how often he heard Erin's screams as the boy was dragged away. Mako, it seemed clear, had not told her of what transpired in Xain's home.

Kalem spoke, as Ebon did not seem to wish to. "It is a dark time for the school indeed," he said quietly. "In one sense, the danger that plagued us is gone, for everyone believes that Isra has fled the Seat. But the darkness she left behind her is not so easily cast aside."

The room fell to silence as Ebon and his friends stared at the floor. When he glanced at Albi, Ebon was surprised to see that she looked bored. But Halab wore a vaguely mournful look. She sat straighter and put her wine goblet on a side table.

"If it is not too great a request, I should like a word alone with my nephew."

Theren and Kalem straightened at once. "Not at all," said Theren, ducking her head in a sort of sitting bow. "We have troubled you long enough as it is."

"I have enjoyed your company," said Halab with a smile. "This is only a little matter, and afterwards I must leave for the High King's palace. Albi, will you please . . .?"

Albi looked burningly curious, but she sighed and led Ebon's friends away. "Come, young master Konnel," she said, holding out her arm. "Our gardens are nearly frozen over, but you and I can keep each other warm regardless." Ebon glowered as she took them towards the staircase down.

Halab gave a soft chuckle after they had gone from view. "Your sister seems very taken with young Kalem."

"I have noticed," said Ebon, mouth puckered.

Again Halab laughed, and heartier this time. "You should not worry. She is only having some amusement. Albi knows full well that Kalem's parents will never accept her as a bride."

The words came from nowhere, and Ebon sat a bit straighter in his seat. "Why not?"

"It is nothing to do with Albi herself. She will make a fine wife someday, if she meets someone who knows not to get in her way. But the royalty are . . . reluctant, shall we say, to allow us *merchants* any more power than they think we deserve." She smirked as though at some hidden joke just remembered.

Ebon frowned. "I am not sure I understand."

Halab sighed. "That is just as well. It is a complicated matter, and more so as time goes on. But Albi knows enough of it to keep her heart safe. She means only to have a little fun with Kalem. Nothing more."

In truth, Ebon was more worried about Kalem than about Albi. It seemed clear to him that Albi saw Kalem as a plaything, but Kalem did not look upon her the same way. The royal boy had had many conversations with Ebon on the subjects of love, and intimacy, and other things besides . . .

But he pushed these thoughts aside, for he doubted that Halab wished to speak with him on matters of love or matchmaking. Now she straightened and placed her feet on the floor, rather than draped along the seat, and patted the spot beside her. Ebon rose and went to her, just as she reached into a nearby drawer. From it she pulled a small iron trinket in the shape of an ankh. This she placed into his open palm.

"Here," she said. "This is for you."

Ebon was taken aback. "Thank you, dearest aunt." He looked at it curiously. The ankh was the symbol of their house, and was featured upon their crest. Yet he wondered exactly why she would give him this, for it seemed to bear little purpose. She had to know they were allowed to keep few possessions in the Academy.

Halab must have seen some of his confusion in his eyes, for she smiled and took it from him. "It is not only a trinket. Watch." She pressed the handle into the spars, and with a small *skrrtch*, sparks sprang out from the tip.

"A firestriker," said Ebon. He took it back, a bit more eagerly. "That is most cleverly made."

"Specially crafted when I was a child," she said. "It is of Calentin make. Among craftsmen, their artisans have no equal."

"Thank you," he said, and this time he meant it. "I will keep it with me always."

"That would please me," she said. Then she sighed and took his hands in hers. "This brings me to the next matter. You must know by now that your father has no intention of letting you keep your inheritance. That will pass to Albi."

Ebon stared at his lap. "She let something of that slip," he muttered.

"And I am sure you at least half-guessed it before. You have always been a wise boy. That means you will never get your mark."

The mark of their house was scarified on the skin of those who entered the family's service, on the wrist of the right arm. Father had his, and Ebon's brother Momen had had one as well. Ebon had long anticipated receiving his own mark, though the prospect lost more of its luster the older he grew.

But he forced a smile and looked at her. "Well, that is no great loss. I will be a wizard, after all. How many of our kin can say the same?"

Halab gave him a sad smile. "I want you to know," she said softly, "that if any but a parent could grant the mark, I would give it to you myself. And for those who obey me, this firestriker will serve just as well as a symbol upon your skin. You will never want for help from my house while you bear it."

His eyes stung. "Thank you, Halab. I am an even poorer guest now, for I have no gift in return."

"It is the joy of the old to provide for the young." She leaned back and took her wine goblet again. "Until very recently, I half thought I should give you a dagger. The Academy has not been a place free from peril, though it seems that danger has now passed."

Ebon's mood fell, for her words drew his thoughts back to Erin and Dasko. "I suppose it no longer plagues me, nor my friends," he said carefully. "But that does not mean there is no danger at all."

"You speak of the dean's son, yes? Erin of the family Forredar, is it not?"

"Yes. The rogue student, Isra—she took him, and no one knows where."

"Odd that she should escape both the High King's guards and the constables. I have heard even the Mystics lend their eyes to the search."

Ebon stared at his feet, fearful she would see the torment within him if he looked at her. "They say his father, Xain—the Academy's dean—is favored by the High King. I met him once. The boy, Erin, I mean. Briefly, only, yet I would not see him come to harm." He heard again Erin's cries for help as the boy was pulled into the streets. Unconsciously, his lips twisted in imitation of Isra's snarl.

"Xain Forredar has always been . . . difficult," said Halab. There was no mistaking the irritation in her voice. "To our family, I mean. Cyrus in particular earned his ire, as did your uncle Matami."

At that, the room fell to swift silence. Ebon's gaze darted about, seeking somewhere to rest. His own wine goblet sat unattended, and he took it to refill, all the while avoiding Halab's watchful attention.

The last time Ebon had seen his uncle, it had been when Mako killed him slow in the sewers beneath the city. Ebon still remembered the empty gap where Matami's eye had been, the bloodied stumps of his fingers . . .

He drank deep from his goblet and filled it once more. When at last he looked to Halab, her face was stony. But her eyes glinted with tears expertly held back. Mako had said that Halab would know, or guess, at what happened to Matami. But he had said also that she would not mention it.

Sometimes it was easier that way. That the truth be known, but unspoken.

Halab rustled her shoulders, and it was as if she shook off a cloak that had kept her mood solemn. She graced Ebon with a smile that hardly seemed forced and put her hands upon his shoulders.

"I want you to know, Ebon, that you are the closest thing to my own son, and I could want for nothing more. The pain and danger you have suffered of late weigh upon me, and I am glad such suffering has passed you by. If ever you need something from me—anything at all—you have only to ask."

Ebon's throat seized up. He had never heard such soft words from his own parents. Forgetting his manners, he seized Halab in a tight hug. "How could I ask anything of you, when already you have been my one bright light in dark times?"

She let him hold her for a moment, and then gently urged him away. "Go now, dearest nephew. I must leave, so rejoin your friends and your sister. The shadow has passed—enjoy the daylight while it remains."

He smiled in answer, and held it until she left the room. Then his face fell, and he put a hand to his forehead, remembering Matami's empty eye socket.

TWO

THE GARDEN WAS LIKE A STAGE PLAY, FOR IT WAS HUSHED AND FRESH, the white snow forming a platform waiting for its actors to arrive. The quiet of winter's air was like the audience standing in the pit below, breath held eagerly in anticipation, hearts thrumming with promise. Ebon stepped into it, and for a moment he paused there in the door. He closed his eyes, breathing deep to take in the smell.

Then, far off, he heard Albi's bright laugh. He opened his eyes with a sigh and set off down the path to find her.

She and Kalem and Theren were among the hedges, walking aimlessly along winding paths. He could see from their footprints that they had walked in many circles already. Albi still held tight to Kalem's arm, and Kalem was pressed against her side—though he flushed and parted from her slightly when he saw Ebon. Behind them, Theren had a long-suffering look on her face, and her relief at Ebon's arrival was obvious.

"You and Halab must have shared heartfelt words," said Albi, smiling at him. "I can see your eyes clouded in thought."

"We did," Ebon said quietly. "And she gave me this." From his pocket he withdrew the firestriker and held it up.

Albi tilted her head. "Why . . . why, that was Uncle Matami's. I saw him use it on the road we took here from Idris. Sometimes he would strike it absentmindedly as we drove, his thoughts wandering elsewhere, and his hands seeking something to do."

That put a sick feeling in the pit of Ebon's stomach. He looked at the firestriker anew. It had to be a message. Had Halab simply meant to tell Ebon that she knew of Matami's death? Or was it a token of forgiveness, absolving him of blame for his part in the murder?

He had been silent too long, and they were staring at him. "What have the three of you been speaking of?"

"I was telling Kalem of the caravan I will soon lead," said Albi. "I will take the wagons back home to Idris—though not directly, for that would bring us far too close to Dulmun, and there is a war on, after all. First we will sail to Selvan, there to take the King's road until it reaches the Dragon's Tail river. We will sail upon those waters until they reach the king's road again, and then drive east until we are home. I am most excited about the whole thing."

But Ebon was gaping at her. "*You* will lead the caravan? But . . . but your age."

He could almost see her hackles rise. She released Kalem's arm to put her hands on her hips, and her plump, rosy cheeks grew redder for a moment. "You think me a child? I am fourteen, Ebon—very nearly a woman grown. Our father was my age when he led his first caravan, and Halab was even younger."

Theren smirked as she looked at him over Albi's head. Kalem's eyes were wide, and he looked as though he would rather be elsewhere. "I-I meant no offense," stammered Ebon. "I was only surprised, that is all."

A thought tickled his mind: Albi would lead this caravan, not because that was what the family wished, but because Matami was no longer there to do it himself.

She lifted her chin haughtily, but some of the spark of anger died in her eyes. "Well. I suppose surprise is warranted. I half died myself, when Halab told me. But the more I have thought upon it, the more excited I have become."

"Will you not grow bored?" he said, smiling to soften the words.

Albi stuck her tongue out at him. "I will have plenty and more to do. We are not only driving the carts. We will be trading wherever we stop. That, of course, will be managed by others—I will have some oversight, but this trip is as much for me to learn as anything else. Come now, though. I am nearly frozen through. Let us go inside, and I will tell you more."

They followed her back to the manor, where they tramped the snow off their boots and removed them. She then led them upstairs to a sitting room, smaller than the one where they often met with Halab. A servant at the door stepped forwards, but Theren spoke before he could even open his mouth.

"Yes, wine, please. Something fine." She blinked and looked at Ebon as if it were an afterthought. "That is, if you do not mind. I never learned my noble graces."

"Not at all," said Ebon. With all of the news Albi had told them, he thought he could rather use a drink.

As they waited for the wine, Albi took a table and put it in the center of the couches. Then she leaned over, putting objects and trinkets at various places, naming them for the cities she would visit upon her route. And Ebon noticed that whenever she leaned forwards or back, she brushed against Kalem's arm.

"Here is Garsec, where we will land first. Then we follow the road west until it turns south and reaches Cabrus. We will stay there a little while; there is no better place to find steel in all of Selvan. Then it is a journey of many days to Redbrook, with little on the road to entertain, and that sits upon the Dragon's Tail. In each city, and mayhap some of the towns, we will stay a short while in order to trade some goods for others, or for coin. And, of course, to find new guards, if we should need them."

The wine came, and Theren drained her cup at once before handing it back to the servant. The man refilled it and then left the bottle for them. "Why should you need to find new guards?" said Theren.

"Why, if anyone should die, of course," said Albi simply. "A caravan should always travel with at least half again as many wagoners and guards as it needs. The roads are not safe in these days of war, and if

533

some of our men should be waylaid, or shit themselves to death from foreign water, who will keep our goods moving safely?"

Ebon balked, and Kalem spit up the little sip of wine he had just taken. To hear Albi speak so plainly of men's deaths . . . it made Ebon feel suddenly lightheaded, as though he had found himself in a dream. Who was this young woman who sat before him? Where was young Albi whose eyes would shine when he told her his dreams of the Academy? It seemed impossible she had changed so much in the short time he had been here upon the Seat. Yet the only other explanation was that she had ceased to be a little girl some time ago, and he was only just beginning to realize it.

Theren laughed at her frank words, while Kalem turned red. Albi saw his reaction and giggled, putting a hand on his arm.

"Do I shock you, dear Kalem? You must understand, I spent two months on wagons traveling here from Idris, and wagoners have bawdy tongues. I would guess I could teach you a thing or two of language." Then her eyes brightened, and she gently slapped his arm. "Kalem, you must make me a promise. Once you have finished your studies in the Academy, you must let me take you upon a trip. Some caravan on a long route across the nine lands. Mayhap not even to Idris. I think we might have more fun other places."

Her eyes flashed, while Kalem's grew wide and starry. But Ebon scowled in disgust. Albi's relentless flirting seemed harmless enough, most of the time, but she never left well enough alone.

Ebon stood quickly. "We should leave."

Albi frowned at him. "What? But the day is young."

"It was Halab's invitation that brought us here in the first place, yet she is gone, and we continue to take her hospitality. Besides, I have an appointment at the Academy." And that, in fact, was true. Astrea waited for him there, the way she did every day, their visits born half from Ebon's desire to help and half from his own guilt.

"Then why do you not go yourself, and leave your friends here?" said Albi.

Kalem looked like he might agree, but Ebon took him by the arm and lifted him up at once. "I am not the only one with duties at the citadel," he said, and fixed Theren with a meaningful look.

Her eyes darkened, and she rose as well. "You are right. I had hoped you would accompany me in my chores this evening, Kalem."

Kalem's mouth turned in a frown, and he lowered his eyes. In the manor, it was easy to forget about Erin, and Isra, and Dasko, but now Ebon had brought memory back to the fore. "Of course," he said quietly. "It was my pleasure to see you again, Lady Drayden."

"Albi, I beg of you. Lady Drayden sounds ever too formal for such a dear heart as yourself." She held his hand tightly in hers, until at last he kissed her fingers. Ebon gave her a brusque hug, and Theren clasped her wrists, before he could finally usher his friends out the door and back into the snowy streets.

THREE

"That seemed a bit rushed," said Kalem as they trudged on.

"I had forgotten about the time, and remembered all at once," said Ebon. It was a lie, and likely Kalem could hear it in his voice. But just now, he did not care overmuch.

They said little else before they reached the Academy. Its iron doors stood closed against the chill, but they opened easily. Without thinking, they made for one of the side halls—but a shrill cry stopped them all in their tracks.

"*Snow!*" cried Mellie. The little old doorguard thrust a spindly finger at their boots and held it there quivering. Her eyes glowed with madness, almost like magelight.

"Yes, Mellie," the three muttered in unison. They went to the side of the front door where an iron grate lay over a pit and tramped the snow off of their feet. Mellie paced behind them like a sellsword general before her troops. When they were done they stepped away—but Mellie snatched Ebon's arm and held him still, then lifted his boot up to inspect it as though he were a horse and she about to shoe him.

"Fine, fine," she muttered. "Snow! It gets everywhere, it does. Everything wet. Ugh!"

They slipped away as quick as they could, making for the stairs to the dormitories. But once again they were brought up short—this time by Jia. The instructor stepped suddenly in front of them, sandy hair pulled into its usual tight bun.

"Ebon, Kalem," she said briskly. "I must see you in the dining hall this evening. Nine o'clock. Do not be late."

That made them pause. Ebon looked to Kalem, and Kalem back at him, but each was as confused as the other. "Of course, Instructor," said Ebon. "But may I ask . . ."

But she had moved on as soon as he had agreed, and the question died on his lips.

"What could she want?" said Kalem.

"You do not think . . ." Theren let the words hang.

"She cannot know about . . . about our friend," said Ebon firmly, meaning Dasko. "If she did—if anyone did—we would be greeted by an assembly intent on capturing us. We would not be summoned to a late-night meeting. But come, we are almost late. Our 'friend' needs tending to."

"I know that," said Theren, scowling. "See to your own affairs."

"Until the morrow, then." Kalem set off towards the grounds.

But Theren did not follow him at once. "Go. I will be there in a moment." Once Kalem obeyed, she turned to Ebon. "You should not think so harshly of him."

Ebon blinked. "Harshly? What do you mean?"

"He is young, and likely cannot help the way he feels about your sister."

A moment passed before he understood, and when he did he scowled. "You think I am upset with *Kalem?* You misunderstand me. It is my sister who behaves foolishly."

Theren cocked her head. "But she is scarcely older than he is. It is the same thing."

He shook his head quickly. "I might once have thought so, but no longer. She is growing up a bit too fast, and while she has a good heart, I see too much of my family in her. She plays with him and with his affection. I am only trying to keep him from pain."

She gave him a sad smile. "That will not work forever. But do as you will. I only wanted to mention it." Then she turned and left him.

Ebon glowered as he made his way up the stairs to Astrea's dormitory. It was all well and good for Theren to dismiss the matter brewing between Kalem and Albi. If the two of them were to have a falling out, Theren would not be the one caught between a sibling and a best friend who would not speak to each other. Then again, the thought of the two of them avoiding each other had much more appeal than the present situation. Mayhap he would let things play out after all.

He had reached the door he sought, so he pushed his thoughts aside and stepped in. Among the many chairs in the common room beyond, he spied little Astrea where she sat by the fireplace. It burned low, and Ebon threw a new log upon the flames before he turned and sat in the chair beside hers. She did not so much as lift her gaze.

"Good eve," Ebon said quietly. "How do you fare?"

"The same," she murmured.

He swallowed. "I do not have as much time as I wish," he said. "Jia needs me for something this evening, though I know not what."

Her brow creased, and she folded her arms across her chest. "Very well. You do not need to come and see me if you are busy."

"I would not leave you alone. Not after . . ."

Her eyes flashed as she looked at him. He fell silent. She did not like talk of Isra, who had been like a sister to her. Ebon supposed he could not blame her. He decided to change tack.

"Why do we not take a walk upon the grounds?" he said, sitting up in his armchair. "It is cold, but in a bracing sort of way. The air might do you good. You hardly ever leave the citadel."

"I do not want to," said Astrea.

"It is not good to stay cooped up. Now more than ever. Come with me. It will be only a little walk."

She rolled her eyes, and for a moment reminded him strikingly of Albi, though the two of them could not have looked more different. "All right." She rose and followed him from the room, but he could not miss the morose stoop in her shoulders.

Outside, the air was bracing indeed. It made him gasp as it first splashed across his face, and Astrea huddled closer under her cloak.

But after a few minutes of walking, the blood began to flow, and his breath did not come quite so shaky. Astrea, despite the deep scowl she kept upon her face, began to move more easily as well. After a time she even threw back her hood. The night was dark now, but the Academy's grounds were lit by many lanterns hanging from the walls.

"How have you been feeling?" said Ebon after a while.

"I am fine," she grated. "Except that everyone keeps asking me that, or some other version of it. It is as though they think some lever will turn, and one day I will be happy again."

"My apologies," said Ebon. "It is only . . . we worry for you."

"Why should you? You see me every day in class."

"Is . . ." Ebon tried to remember how Halab had spoken to him before, so kind and gentle. "Is there any way I can help? Do you need anything?"

She looked away to hide her eyes. "I want Isra to return. I want this all to be a terrible dream."

After a moment he saw her shoulders quivering. He put out an awkward arm to drape across them. "I know she was like a sister," he said quietly. "I cannot imagine what I would feel if my own sister were taken from me this way."

"Of course you cannot imagine it," said Astrea sharply. But immediately she ducked her head. "I am sorry. I did not mean that."

"It is all right."

When she looked at him again, her eyes were wet. "She always looked after me. In our orphanage, sometimes food would be scarce. She would share hers with me so I would not get so hungry. Some other children liked to bully me, but Isra never let them get away with it. She could tumble anyone, even children larger than her. I have often become lonely here at the Academy. I have often wished I had parents to write home to, or who would come and visit me. But during the day I could always go . . . go and see Isra and she would . . . she would . . ."

She began to cry in earnest, burying her face in the front of Ebon's robes. He held her tightly, awkwardly. With one hand he gently patted her hair.

Her words echoed in his mind, giving him a feeling of vague unease. The girl Astrea spoke so highly of was nothing like the Isra he had known. He still had dreams, sometimes waking, sometimes in his sleep, of Isra's mad eyes as she tried to kill him. He still saw Vali, his neck snapped on the stone wall, and Oren, pierced by dozens of knives in the dining hall.

How could the monster who did those deeds have been so loved by this innocent, sweet girl? It seemed even the worst sort of people had some good in them. If that was so, the reverse must also be true. And so he said, not as a comfort, but as a lesson, "Even the best people have some evil in them."

Astrea pulled away from him and kept walking. "But some people do worse things, and no one calls them evil. If Isra were rich like Lilith, I think some people would help her. People might not call her a villain."

"Lilith received no special privilege because of her wealth," said Ebon. "I saw her while she was under the knives of the Mystics. It was horrible. She was like a broken creature."

The girl shook her head. Not a rejection, but a refusal to hear. Ebon almost pressed the point, but then the Academy's bell began to ring. Nine times it called out.

"Blast," said Ebon. "I am late. Jia requested me. I will come and see you again tomorrow. I swear it."

Astrea only shrugged. "Every day," she muttered. "Every day the same."

He put an arm around her shoulders and ushered her back inside through one of the white cedar doors.

FOUR

Once Astrea was on her way up the stairs, Ebon ran for the dining hall. When he reached its wide oak doors, he nearly ran full-on into Kalem, who had come from the other direction.

"At least I will not be the only one who is late," said Ebon.

"I lost track of the hour," said Kalem, wheezing hard. He had never been athletic, even for a noble-born son. "After she visited our 'friend,' Theren required some consolation."

Ebon frowned. "Is everything all right?"

Kalem's brows shot for the ceiling. "Of course not, Ebon. How can you even ask that?"

He grimaced. "Later."

They pushed open the doors and entered the dining hall. But both of them froze in the doorway, for they found they were not the only ones present. Many other students had been called, and all of them were sitting at a few tables near the entrance. Some looked up curiously to see them standing there, but most kept their eyes on Jia.

The instructor stood at the head of the little group, watching them all with a keen eye. She seemed ready to give a speech, but it did not appear she had started yet. As soon as she saw Ebon and Kalem, she waved them to the benches at once.

"Come, come. Sit, sit," she said. "There we are. Excellent. Now, I believe we may begin."

The other students began to quiet down. But Kalem whispered quickly in Ebon's ear, "Why are we here, but not Theren? What is this?" Ebon shrugged.

Jia lifted her chin. "This," she began, "is a dangerous time. Not only for the Academy, nor for the Seat, but for all of Underrealm. The High King is beset on all sides, and she requires the help of every one of us to preserve the nine kingdoms."

She paused for a moment. The dining hall settled to silence. Ebon and Kalem stared at each other. Ebon was even more mystified than before.

Suddenly Jia shook her head as if she had remembered something. "Yes, she requires our help," she went on. "But some may help more than others. Some have greater strength of arms—or spells, in our case. Some have larger armies, and some have deeper pockets. These must aid her according to their means—but it begins at the very roots, with each one of us, and not with the grand schemes of the kingdoms. Who better to defend Underrealm against its enemies than the noble families of which you are a part? A short time ago, Lilith had the wise idea to form a group of you for just such a purpose. The Goldbag Society, I believe she called it, though it is an uncouth name."

Ebon's blood ran cold. He looked at Kalem. The boy's face had gone Elf-white. A quick glance around the room confirmed it: Ebon saw no one there but the children of merchants and royalty. These were the same children Lilith had called together when she was under Isra's mindwyrd.

Jia spoke on, but Ebon could scarcely hear the words. He leaned over to whisper in Kalem's ear. "She is here."

"She cannot be," said Kalem. "How could . . .?"

"No time for wondering now," said Ebon. "Go and fetch Theren, as quickly as ever you can. And tell her to bring Kekhit's amulet."

Kalem nodded, but then gave Jia a wary look. Slowly he stood from his bench. Jia seemed to take no notice, but only continued her speech. Step by step Kalem backed away, edging towards the door of the dining hall. Some students caught the motion and stared, but Jia droned on regardless. It was as though she did not even see him. Ebon's stomach did a flip-flop. Kalem turned and ran, vanishing into the Academy's hallways.

Ebon looked about him carefully. Other than the few tables near the front, the dining hall was nearly empty. But there, at the back of the hall, he spied the doorways leading into the kitchens, which were now dark and looked abandoned.

One of the doors was ajar.

He stood from his bench and walked towards it. Jia took no more notice of him than she had of Kalem, though some of the students watched him go. He hesitated on the threshold of the kitchens for a long moment, trying to let his eyes adjust to the darkness. But when at last he could see inside, no one was in sight.

Heart thundering in his ears, he stepped into the darkness.

The dish room was empty. An oak door in the corner opened into the kitchens proper—and Ebon saw that it, too, was ajar. He crept carefully forwards, muffling each footstep as best he could.

It was darker still inside. No lanterns were lit here, and no windows let in the moonlight. He longed to reach for his power so that his eyes might help light the way, but then he might be seen. So he crept forwards, avoiding the tables around him, which might send dishes clattering to the floor if he bumped them. The air smelled of meat left out too long.

He thought he could hear a murmuring drawing near. And then, from the next room, he caught a faint glow. But something was . . . wrong about it. In its light he could see shapes, but not their color or distance. It was like an awareness rather than true sight. His mind hurt, and his eyes kept shuddering away from it.

He stepped into the doorway.

It was a storeroom, and here at last there was moonslight from a window high in the wall. There were barrels and sacks in great piles all around the place and crates stacked in its center.

In one corner sat a girl in the robes of an Academy student—only they were filthy and threadbare, and Ebon thought he could smell them from where he stood. Her hair was just as dirty, and hung lank around her shoulders.

It was Isra. The glow that shone from her eyes sent a lance of pain through Ebon's head. She was facing away from him, but it leaked around her edges like a malicious, oozing thing, a poison that sought the mouth and nose to slither in and choke the breath.

At first he could not force himself to move, or even to think. When at last he did, he grew curious what it was that she was doing. She remained hunched over, her back to him, and the feverish rasping of her voice bounced harsh off the stone walls into his ears. He took one step forwards—every moment a skipping of the heart, a fearsome clenching in his gut.

A few paces in from the door, he could at last see what it was she held in her hand. It was a lantern. At first he thought that was where the black glow was coming from—but then, looking again, he realized it was coming from her eyes.

He remembered something . . . something Kalem and Theren had told him about a black glow in the eyes. Then it came to him in a flash: *magestones.*

At once he realized what must have happened. Jia had called the assembly in the dining hall under Isra's control. Somehow the girl had got her hands on magestones, and she was using the power of mindwyrd once again.

Ebon realized he could do no good here. Quickly he backed away. He was almost to the door.

He did not think he had made a noise, but Isra stopped chanting. Her head jerked up, and then she turned around.

"Drayden," she growled.

An unseen force snatched him up. He flew through the air and into a shelf of pots, and now made up for all the clatter he had avoided while sneaking in. The dishes scattered everywhere, and after his hushed entrance it sounded like the breaking of the world. But was it loud enough for the other students to hear from the dining hall?

Isra's magic clutched him around the throat. She hoisted him up until his feet dangled helplessly above the stone floor. He gasped for breath as stars burst in his vision.

"This is a gift beyond reckoning," said Isra, walking towards him. The black glow in her eyes had increased. Now Ebon thought the sight of it might drive him mad. "I could not have planned for you to be the first to die tonight. Yet here you are, delivered as though upon a platter."

A flash of silver in the moonslight caught his eye. In Isra's hand, she still held the silver lantern over which she had been chanting. He could see something inside it: some faint and twisting light, pale and green, spinning in and around itself like the threads of a tapestry, over and over again without end. But he could hardly spare a thought for it while he hung in Isra's grip.

Then from nowhere, a blast of power rocked the kitchens, and Isra flew through the air. She crashed into another shelf of dishes, sending them flying in all directions. They were wood, and none broke, but the clatter was deafening. The magic holding Ebon vanished, but he was unprepared for it and landed hard on his hands and knees with a cry of pain.

Isra tried to find her feet, but the magic struck her again, and she flipped over backwards. Ebon heard the *crack* of her shoulder on a carving table. He looked in the direction he had come.

There stood Theren, and beside her was Kalem. The boy's eyes were alight as he touched his magic, though Ebon knew not what he hoped to do. Beside him, there was no glow in Theren's eyes at all—yet she held her hands aloft, and Ebon knew it was she who had attacked Isra. He could not see it, but he knew that beneath her robes was Kekhit's amulet, which gave her magic the strength to match Isra's.

Across the kitchen, Isra snarled as she fought her way to standing at last. Darklight flared in her eyes, and she threw a contemptuous hand through the air. Yet if she hoped to bat Theren away like some child, she was disappointed. Theren's magic met her, and it matched her. Then Ebon saw a ripple in the air, forming a wall that swept around Isra like a cage. Isra gritted her teeth as she blasted it, but the rippling air held firm.

"Are you whole, Ebon?" said Theren, though she spoke through a clenched jaw herself.

"I am." He went to stand by her. "Can you hold her? Shall we fetch an instructor?"

"She is—" But the words were cut off. Isra screamed, and Ebon felt the room shudder as Theren's barrier was cast aside. Before he could blink, Isra flung the silver lantern she had been holding at them. It clattered to the ground at their feet, but its glass did not break. Then Isra ran into the storeroom and leaped. Magic lifted her towards the ceiling, and she vanished through the high window onto the grounds beyond.

Theren made to go after her. But Ebon looked at the lamp on the ground. He saw the light within it—it was spinning faster and faster now, and blazing with a fury like the sun. Now the kitchen shone as if it were daylight.

"Down!" he cried, and snatching Kalem's collar, he tackled Theren behind the storeroom's crates.

THOOM

The air was wracked by an explosion. There were no flames, no heat. Instead it was as though an unseen battering ram struck everything in the room at once. Crates from the pile rained down atop them, but Theren batted them away with her magic. All around, sacks of flour and barrels of grain burst, coating the room in white dust and small brown kernels of wheat.

All fell silent. Slowly, Ebon got to his feet. But Theren did not hesitate. The moment she had shoved off the last crate, she jumped up and leaped through the window where Isra had vanished.

Ebon hauled Kalem up and ran through the kitchens. There was a door leading outside, and they burst through it together. Winter's air blasted them, and Kalem huddled against him on instinct. They met Theren outside, where she stood with hands raised.

But the grounds were empty. Fresh snow fell from the sky, covering everything. No one was there. No figure in a black robe could be spotted against the white. Isra had escaped.

"Darkness take me," said Theren, kicking a great fountain of snow into the air. "I thought we had her for certain."

"What is she doing here?" said Kalem. "I thought she left the Seat."

"We all did," said Theren. "It would have been the wise thing to do. I do not know what she hopes to achieve by being here."

"Do you not?" said Ebon. "She called all the goldbags together. Every merchant's child. Every royal son and daughter." He shuddered as he remembered Lilith's cold, lifeless voice saying the words, prodded by Isra's mindwyrd. "But where is Erin?" he said suddenly, as the thought struck him. "If she is here, Erin must be nearby."

"Or dead," muttered Theren.

Ebon was about to respond, but Kalem raised a hand to point. "Look," he said quietly.

His quivering voice silenced them both. Going to either side of him, Ebon and Theren followed his outstretched finger. Yet Ebon saw nothing untoward.

"What is it, Kalem?"

"The window. She jumped out the window. And yet . . ."

It took another moment. Then Theren gave a sharp hissing gasp, and Ebon saw it in the same instant.

There was only one set of tracks in the snow, and they led right to Theren. Isra had leaped through the high window above, and then had vanished without so much as a footprint.

FIVE

"We must tell the instructors at once," said Kalem. He took two quick steps, running back towards the Academy's white cedar doors. But Theren snatched his collar and hauled him back around like a mother with an unruly kitten.

"We must do nothing of the sort," she snapped. "We *can* do nothing of the sort. I hold the amulet, Kalem, or had you forgotten? How do you mean to explain that to them?"

Kalem blinked. His mouth opened and then shut without releasing words. But in another heartbeat he shook his head. "No. We *must* tell them, Theren. Everyone thinks Isra has left the Seat, but she remains here. She infiltrated the Academy itself. If they do not know they are in danger, they can do nothing to protect themselves."

"Those words come easily to you—it will not be your neck upon the chopping block if the amulet is found. We cannot afford any attention now, not while we still hold a magical artifact beyond the King's law. Not to mention that we hold Dasko in mindwyrd."

Ebon caught Kalem's uneasy look. "Theren, we cannot simply ignore this."

"What do you mean to do, then?" Theren's shout was sudden and loud, and it looked like it surprised even her. "Shall we run inside and find Perrin and say, 'Instructor Perrin! We saw Isra, Instructor Perrin, and her eyes glowed black. But I defeated her, for I wore Kekhit's amulet and used my strength of magestones against hers. Oh, yes, I should likely have mentioned that Kekhit's amulet is not in fact missing, but is about my neck.' The High King has declared martial law, Ebon. I will not receive mercy. The constables will execute me if the Mystics do not get their hands on me first."

Kalem spread his hands. "Ebon. Do you really mean to let everyone carry on in ignorance?"

It seemed an impossible question. Ebon looked back and forth between his friends but found no words to speak. In the end he shrugged. "I cannot go against Theren in this Kalem. She has the most to lose if we tell the whole truth. But Theren, neither do I think we can keep this only to ourselves."

Theren's jaw clenched. She looked up at the window, and then at the snow where no footprints showed Isra's passage. Then, all at once, the fight went out of her. Her shoulders sagged, and her head drooped. "I know," she said. "I know it. Damn her. Damn her for coming back."

Ebon put a hand on her shoulder. "We will not tell them about the amulet. Of course not. Only . . . only we must find the right lie to tell."

Kalem's mouth soured at that, but he held his peace. Theren did not seem wholly convinced. "We could tell Jia . . . mayhap we could tell her we came upon Isra by surprise—"

"Not Jia," said Ebon quickly. "She is the one under mindwyrd. We must tell someone else. Perrin, as you said. Though not the words you said, of course."

"Yes," said Kalem. Still he looked unhappy, but he gave a grudging nod. "Yes, Perrin might believe us. Especially you, Ebon."

"Then let us make our story."

Quickly they built the lie, and then they ran into the Academy and through the halls to Perrin's classroom. They found her at the front of the room, sitting at her desk. She stood at once as they burst through the door.

"What is this?"

"Instructor Perrin!" said Ebon, trying to fill his voice with panic. "We saw her. We saw Isra."

Perrin's eyes sharpened at once. "What? Where?"

"In the kitchens. She was doing . . . something, I am not sure what. We had grown hungry, and I thought to sneak in for a snack. I know that is not allowed, and I am sorry."

"Never mind that," said Perrin. She started for the door. "Where is she now?"

Ebon put up his hands to stop her, though it felt like a mouse trying to stop a bear. "She is gone. Whatever she was doing, we startled her."

"She attacked us with spells," said Theren. "I fought her off, but barely. She fled after throwing this at us."

She held aloft the silver lantern. Perrin snatched it from her hand like a venomous serpent. She went to a high cupboard, gingerly placed the lantern inside, and then locked it.

"What happened when she threw it at you?" said Perrin. "How are you . . .?"

Ebon nodded. "The explosion. I saw a light brewing within it, and something told me to run. We barely got out of the way in time." He felt a glimmer of relief—it was much easier to tell that part of the story, for it was true.

"Very well," said Perrin. "I will fetch some of the others. The three of you must go to your dormitories, immediately." She pushed past them into the hallway.

Kalem put a hand on her arm. "Instructor. There is one more thing. I . . ." he looked anxiously back and forth down the hallway. A pair of anxious tears leaked from the corners of his eyes, and Ebon marveled at his ability to act—though considering the circumstances, he likely did not have to reach far to summon the terror in his expression. "I know I should not know of this. But . . . but Theren said Isra was more powerful than she had been before, and . . . and her eyes glowed black, Instructor."

Perrin's ruddy features went pale. Carefully she removed Kalem's hand from where it rested, and then pointed at the three of them. "Into bed with all of you. Now. Do not leave for any reason. And tell *no one* of what you have seen. Do you understand?"

"But what about Jia?" said Ebon. "She is in the dining hall speaking to some other students. And she will not answer when anyone tries to speak to her. Something is wrong with her."

"Mindwyrd," Perrin whispered, almost too soft for them to hear. Then she roared, "Bed! Now!" They all jumped and hurried off as she thundered down the hallway in the other direction.

Ebon looked to his friends as they walked. "Do you think it will work?"

"The die is cast," murmured Theren. "We have no choice now but to see where it will fall."

Ebon did not follow Perrin's instructions at once, and went to his common room rather than straight to bed. There he waited a while, until the door opened again and some other students came in. He saw Nella among them and jumped up from his seat to catch her eye.

"What happened?" he said.

She stopped short and regarded him carefully. As one of Lilith's friends, Nella had never been exactly friendly with Ebon. But after the two of them fought beside each other on the day the High King's Seat was attacked, Ebon had always felt a sort of mutual, grudging respect between them.

"Several instructors interrupted the meeting," said Nella. "They took Instructor Jia away with them."

"Was she all right?"

"She fought them." Her eyes shifted away from his face. "I have never quite seen the like of it. First she screamed, and then she thrashed in their arms. She even tried to turn herself—with weremagic, I mean— but Perrin dispelled it. By the time they removed her, she was speaking nonsense. Then they told us to come straight to bed."

Her gaze fell away, and she pushed past him into her dormitory. After the door shut behind her, Ebon stared at it for a long time before his mind returned to the present. He shook himself and returned to an armchair before the hearth.

Since the moment he and Kalem had begun to suspect something was wrong, he had hardly had any time to think. Now he watched the flickering, writhing orange and red of the fire, his mind racing, unable to banish the memory of the black glow in Isra's eyes.

Why would she still be here? Wisdom would have commanded her to leave the Seat as quickly as she could. But clearly wisdom did not rule her mind now. Ebon knew little of the madness that magestones could bring, but he thought he knew enough.

Then he shot up straight in the armchair. Did this mean that Erin, the dean's son, also remained on the Seat? It would make sense.

He got up and very nearly ran from the common room. But with his hand on the door, he paused. If he had only just come to this conclusion, Dean Forredar certainly would have thought of it already. It would do no one any good for Ebon to come running to the instructors and tell them, and it might call more attention down upon him—mayhap even suspicion.

Damn the suspicion, he thought. He saw in his mind Erin's terrified eyes as Isra dragged the boy away. But another moment passed, and he let his hand fall from the door. Though it made his gut clench in self-loathing, he feared to draw any more attention than they already had.

He returned to the armchair, and there he remained until dawn's light shone through the windows. Once it did, he washed himself and made his way to the dining hall. Theren and Kalem were not there yet, and so he filled three bowls with porridge for them and himself. As each appeared, he flagged them down with a wave, and soon they sat eating quietly.

"Have you heard—" Kalem began.

"No one has heard anything yet, Kalem," said Theren.

They fell to silence again.

At last, when most of the students had assembled in the hall, the faculty came in. Ebon studied them carefully. All looked haggard, and he doubted any of them had slept a wink. At their head was Dean Forredar. His eyes looked haunted, troubled in a way Ebon could not define. It sent a shiver through Ebon's limbs. When the instructors had settled themselves into their seats, Xain tapped his cup on the table for silence. He hardly needed to; the dining hall had fallen to a quiet murmur the second the faculty had appeared.

"Students," Xain began. "Last night, there was an attack, though not a fatal one—and thank the sky for that. In recent weeks, we have tried hard to keep the rumor from your ears, but I do not doubt that you have all heard it: Isra, once a student here, is the Academy killer."

He paused for a moment, and Ebon saw his jaw twitching. What he had not said, and likely would not say, was that Isra had taken his son, Erin, as well.

When he had composed himself, he went on. "We, along with the constables and Mystics who searched for her, thought that she had fled the Seat. But last night she returned."

A hushed gasp rippled through the students. Xain did not try to shush it, but instead regarded them all carefully.

"Yes. She was here. And she tried to kill three . . . students, who came upon her in the kitchens. By sheer luck, they survived. The next time, we might not be so fortunate." Ebon heard the word twist in Xain's mouth, and it made his heart skip a beat. But Xain went on steadily. "There is something else. Another thing you should all know. What I am about to tell you goes against the ruling of past deans for many, many long years. But I was once a student here, as you are now. I know we have all heard things of which it is forbidden to speak aloud. But I will speak them aloud now, for I believe that it is more dangerous to remain silent. Isra is an abomination—an eater of magestones."

The hall burst into tumult. Some students stood from their benches in fear, while others simply sat in place and cowered. Ebon felt stunned. It had seemed dangerous enough last night when Kalem had said the word to Instructor Perrin. Now it felt as though Xain had stood before them all and spouted curses like a common dockhand. He hardly knew what to think.

Xain let the noise continue for a moment, but then he raised his hands. "Silence. *Silence!* I do not tell you this to frighten you—any more than you should be frightened, at any rate, though that may be a fair bit. I tell you this so that you know: Isra is not to be approached. She is not to be regarded with anything but fear. If you should catch sight of her, you *must not* try to fight her or capture her. She can command you with a whispered word, and you will have no choice but to obey."

"But then there is no hope!" In the middle of the hall, one student rose from her bench with a cry. Her pale skin was even paler now with fright. "We should leave. All of us should leave. How can you hope to stop her?"

"If you were to leave, no one could blame you," said Xain. "That is one reason I tell you this now. If you wish to leave the Academy for your own safety, or if you family wishes to withdraw you, I would not call it an unwise choice, and you should make it with both eyes open. But as for Isra—I said that *you* all must not fight her. I did not say that *we* would not. For magestones make a wizard powerful—but not all-powerful. Even an abomination can be stopped. Sometimes they can even be saved."

That silenced them. The girl who had spoken slowly sank back into her seat. To either side of the dean, instructors looked uncomfortably at their hands. Only Perrin kept her gaze upon him, unflinching at his words, though they bordered on blasphemy. Ebon noted that Dasko hardly seemed to be listening to the speech. His eyes were far away, and every so often his shoulder twitched as though he were flinching from something.

Xain leaned forwards, his knuckles pressed into the wooden table. "Yes. It is true. Since the time of the Wizard Kings, generations of deans have forbidden you who study here from having this knowledge. In times past, I might have understood why. But now things are different. Underrealm is at war, and magestones, though still beyond the King's law, are more common than they have been in a long while. Only knowledge can save us now. Knowledge of the good and the evil alike.

"We here, the instructors and I, will keep you safe to the best of our ability. But we cannot do it without your help. You must be ever wary and ever vigilant. You must come to us at once if you see anything odd going on—a friend acting out of sorts, or an instructor whose mind goes vacant and wandering. We can stop Isra, but not by hiding in the dark from truths that have been kept from us too long."

The dining hall was dead quiet. Someone nearby shifted their feet on the floor, and it seemed to Ebon as loud as a breaking branch.

"That is all," Xain said. "If you have questions or wish to speak to anyone of this, please see your instructors in class."

He turned and left the dining hall. The moment the door swung shut behind him, whispers burst out in the hall. But when Ebon and his friends looked to each other, none of them uttered a word.

SIX

Xain's speech was not the last time Isra and her magestones were mentioned that day. In Perrin's class just after breakfast, she spoke of it again and invited questions from the students. None were asked—the students were second-years, and most were timid, and likely few of them knew anything of magestones at all. Ebon withheld his tongue because he knew more about magestones than he wished to, and he did not want to draw any attention to himself after the events of the night before. In the library that afternoon, Kalem and Theren told him that their classes had been much the same—except in those cases, many questions had been asked. And Ebon was chilled to hear that one student had asked if they could not use magestones *against* Isra—to procure their own supply, and thus defeat her. That idea had been immediately shouted down. But the fact that it had been voiced at all . . . Ebon shuddered to think of such an idea being put into action.

Well he remembered the days after the attack on the High King's Seat, when everyone had been fearful and solemn. Now that mood had returned again, only worse. Then, they had been afraid of some enemy from far lands. Now a foe was in their very midst, and she had once broken bread with them all. She had slept beneath the same roof. And worse, no one knew where she had gone or where she might be. The weight of that terror was heavy upon them all.

"I do not understand," said Ebon. "How could she have vanished?"

"No one knows," said Theren. "They only know that she did."

"They say the Academy was searched from top to bottom," said Kalem. "But she was not found in any room. They searched in teams, and all kept careful watch to make sure that she would not trick them with mindwyrd. But they saw no trace of her."

They studied in worried silence after that. It seemed an eternity before the final study bell rang. Ebon rose from his armchair with a sigh of relief. He joined his friends in the dining hall, but found he had no appetite.

He had an appointment that evening in the city. The events of the night before had made him reconsider going out, for Isra might be anywhere. But in the end Ebon decided that Isra would hardly expect him to be out in plain sight on the streets, and would not know where he was going in any case. He would only encounter her by the most terrible of luck, and even he did not think that poorly of his own fortune. So, with blood rising to his cheeks, he excused himself and left the hall. Kalem and Theren were too preoccupied to notice his embarrassment.

Winter ran its persistent fingers up and down his skin as he stepped through the Academy's front door. He quickened his steps to get the blood flowing and headed west towards the blue door, as he had so often before—only now, he did not mean to pass through it. His heart skipped a beat, though the day's worries plagued his thoughts, and they were reluctant to leave him. He swore silently to himself that he would not spend the evening voicing such concerns to Adara. This night was about the two of them, not him alone.

When at last he reached the blue door, Adara gave him a smile and a nod. The snow dusting her mantle told the tale of how long she had spent waiting. She had chosen to wear his family's color, a golden dress with a cloak that was a few shades darker. The hood was lined with fur, which she blew into to warm herself. The moment she saw Ebon, her face lit like a kindled lantern. But then the light was doused at once, and she gave him a nervous smile. It pleased him a bit, the thought that mayhap she was as anxious as he was.

"My love," she murmured.

He took her in his arms. "Your love? I would argue that you are mine."

Her smile broadened. Then she put his arm in hers and led him away. He expected another lengthy walk—but after only two blocks, she stopped before a wooden door, this one unpainted. It stood between a tavern on one side and a building on the other that looked like a cobbler's shop. The buildings were pressed tight together so that it seemed they crowded the door to Adara's home.

"Here it is," she said breathlessly. "Would you like . . .?"

The words trailed off. She waved at the handle. Ebon tried to speak, but his throat was suddenly bone-dry, and so he gave it up.

The handle turned easily under his fingers. The hinges gently squeaked as they swung open.

There was a short staircase—short, but steep. He tramped the snow off before he climbed its steps, thankful he had remembered it and not made a slob of himself. A little railing helped him make the climb.

And then, there he was. Adara's home.

It was small, but not cramped. He guessed she did not want for more space, since many of her needs were seen to by the guild of lovers. The windows at the front of the room drew attention at once. Ebon guessed that each looked out over the front door of the tavern and the cobbler's, respectively. The evening light they admitted illuminated the room so that it did not yet need lamps. Tucked in one corner was her bed. It was nothing so ornate as the silk-sheeted thing behind the blue door, though Ebon noted with a blush that it seemed just as sturdy. On the other side of the room was a bureau, as well as a closet that stood out from the wall. Finally, before one of the windows was a small table with two chairs, behind which was a low cabinet that looked like it might hold wine (or, Ebon realized, mead, for Adara favored it). Where there was color—sashes over the windows, the bureau's trim, the bedspread—it was deep, muted blue, the perfect contrast to the dress and cloak she now wore.

Adara stood behind him now, hands clasped before her, fingers rubbing against each other anxiously. Her eyes were wide as they remained on him. It was so utterly unlike the Adara he was accustomed to. She smiled as he looked at her, though it seemed somewhat forced.

"Well? I know it is nothing so grand as my room at the guild, nor, certainly, your family's—"

"It is wonderful. It is just like you," he said quietly. Then he realized how that might sound, so he spoke hastily to correct himself. "I mean only that it is . . . it is warm, and beautiful, and does not seem to try too hard to be beautiful. Only that is not what I mean either, not at all. I . . ."

He put his hand to his forehead. She must think him an utter fool—or a caustic-tongued ass. But she smiled and took his hand, and then gently kissed the back of its fingers. "There is my Ebon. I feared to see something different in your eyes—haughtiness, or disdain, once you saw how I lived. But you are just as tongue-tied as I feel."

Ebon laughed. "That is no compliment, yet I am glad to hear it from you."

She studied his eyes. "Is it only our meeting that occupies your thoughts? I have heard some dark whispers concerning the Academy."

He sighed. "They cannot be darker than the truth." She waved him to the table before the window, and he sat. While she moved to fetch wine for him and mead for herself, he went on. "You remember what I told you of Isra. She has returned. We saw her within the Academy—Kalem and Theren and I, that is."

She froze in the middle of pouring his wine. He had to tip the bottle up to keep her from spilling it. "*In* the Academy, you say? Does that mean you are in danger?"

"I certainly do not feel safe," said Ebon, forcing a laugh. "That, along with our situation with Dasko . . ."

"Have you thought of no way out of that?" said Adara. "It must weigh terribly on Theren."

"More and more every day," said Ebon, lowering his gaze. "She will hardly even speak of it, and when she does she is short-tempered and irritable."

"Would you not be the same?"

"I do not criticize her," said Ebon. "I wish there was a way I could help her. But if she releases him from mindwyrd, it will wear off. Then we do not know what would happen. He might remember us and what we did. We know for certain that he would suffer, for the process of weaning off mindwyrd is very painful."

"Will it not get worse the longer she keeps him under control?" said Adara softly.

"It will. But we know not what else to do." Ebon's eyes began to smart, and he swiped at them, trying to make it look as though he were scratching an itch. "Forgive me. This is a happy evening, and one for celebration. Yet I have spent most of it talking about myself, as I do too often. I even told myself not to do so, just before I saw you."

"Do not trouble yourself over that," said Adara, giving him a little smile. "That is why you and I met in the first place, is it not? So that you might ease your burdens?"

A slow grin spread across his face. "I suppose that was part of the reason." But then he took her hands and grew solemn. "But now we are something more. The fact that I am here is proof of that. This is not for gold, and I do not want it to be. Tonight is not for me, but for us—or so I hope."

Her thumb rubbed the back of his palm. "So I hope as well."

He smiled and took a sip of his wine. But his eyes widened as soon as it touched his tongue, and he tilted the cup to look inside. "Stars and sky. Where did you get this?"

She waved a hand airily. "Somewhere. Sometimes I receive gifts, and sometimes those gifts are wine, for my clients do not often ask me what I prefer to drink." She gave him a secret smile, and he blushed. For a long while he, too, had assumed she liked wine, until he learned of her love for mead. "When that is the case, and when they do not wish to drink it with me immediately, I bring it here to save for a special occasion. Tonight is the first time I have opened one of the bottles I have saved."

"You must have a fine store, then."

She laughed and slapped his wrist. "You will be well sated, you drunkard."

Though he chuckled, Ebon soon fixed her with a look. "Adara . . . there is something I meant to ask you tonight, ever since you first invited me here. Only I do not wish to give offense."

"Oh?" Her eyes grew careful. "Then is it wise to ask your question at all?"

"I hope so," he said. "If I am wrong, forgive me. But . . . understand, I am overjoyed to be here. I can scarcely tell you how honored I am that you wished to bring me into your life. But . . . why? Why me, in particular?"

She softened at once. "Because I love you, Ebon. Do you not believe that?"

"You have said so, and I *do* believe you," he said. "And yet . . . I wonder why. I am nothing special. No, do not look at me like that, nor argue. I do not say this to earn words of praise. I am *not* special. I am no great man. There is little about me that is remarkable, other than my family, who few hold in very high regard."

Adara did not answer him at once, but leaned back in her chair and gave him an appraising look. Then she stood and came to him, and sat so that she was side-saddle in his lap. "A boy who is usually foolish, and sometimes wise, said that love often springs forth unbidden."

He blushed, for he remembered those words. He and Adara had whispered them often enough since he first uttered them. "But honestly," he pressed. "Have you never thought upon it?"

"I have," she said, so quickly that it surprised him. "Here is the truth. And you have begged me not to take offense at your question, so I will ask you to do the same with my answer. I did not love you from the moment I set my eyes upon you, Ebon. I think your love for me may have begun that night, but to me, you were a guest like any other. Though I saw at once that you were an uncommonly sweet one—and you were a reminder of Idris, of home, which lent you some slight favor. But when you came to see me the second time, I gave you a lover's words, as I would have done for anybody else."

She leaned in then, and pressed herself against him, and kissed him deep. "And then the Seat was attacked," she murmured. "You were an utter fool to come after me when you saw Cyrus escorting me through the streets. Yet that foolishness endeared you to me. And then you risked your life to save me after I learned of Cyrus' evil. I could not love a boy only because he was sweet. I could not love a boy only because affection made him foolish. And I could not love a boy only because he would give his life for mine. But you were all three at once, and in the same person. And love sprang forth unbidden, for you never spoke lovers' words to me."

It was hard for him to speak for a moment, and so he only held her. "But that is because I am not a lover," he finally said.

Adara shook her head. "That is not what I mean. Lovers' words go two ways. A lover tells a guest what they want to hear. But guests also lie to their lovers. The guest will speak of their lover's endless beauty, and say they wish they could be wed, and say they would buy the lover a palace if they could. But if given the chance to fulfill such whispered promises, most guests would refuse. And that is no evil thing; a lover delivers not only the pleasures of the flesh, but the pleasure of dreaming a perfect romance together, a love greater than true life will permit. Lover and guest both know that dream will never come true, but it is a precious dream nonetheless.

"The day the Seat was attacked, I realized you had never spoken a lover's word to me. You loved me in truth. I do not know when after that I knew I loved you in return. One day, I simply did."

He smiled at her. "And that has never happened before? You have never fallen in love?"

Everything about her changed at once—her posture, the look on her face, and her smile—and he saw it. Inside, he winced. Adara stood and returned to her seat. "Before I answer that, I would ask you something. Would it bother you if I had?"

Quickly he shook his head. "I am sorry," he said. "That was wrong of me to ask. I never meant to throw doubt on your feelings for me. I only . . ."

"You thought to stoke your own pride," she said with a wry smile. "To prove to yourself that you were the only one. Well, puff up your chest, my love—you are the first guest who has ever stepped into my dwelling."

He hung his head. He had made an ass of himself after all. "I am sorry, my love. You deserve someone with a smoother tongue than mine, for it trips over itself no matter my intent."

A moment's silence stretched as she drank deep from her mead. Her eyes glinted. "Your tongue is not so bad as all that."

His heart leaped—until the moment was shattered by a pounding at the door below.

Ebon was on his feet in an instant, but no faster than Adara. Their eyes met. He shook his head. "I am expecting no one," he whispered.

"Nor I."

The pounding sounded at the door again.

He ran to the left window. The sash was drawn, and he pulled it aside, trying to look down. But the angle was bad, and he could not see the street just before the door. Adara went to the other window, but from the look on her face it was clear she could see nothing more than he could.

"Hide yourself," he hissed. "I will see who it is."

"Do not be an idiot." She went to her cupboard. From its bottom drawer she pulled a long knife. "This is my home."

Before he could even try to stop her, she had pounded down the stairs and thrown open the door. Ebon was a half-step behind her as she thrust the knife out into the street.

Mako looked down at the blade and arched an eyebrow.

Ebon felt thunderstruck. For a moment he could not so much as speak. Fortunately he did not have to, for Adara did instead. "Who are you?" she said. "What do you want?"

For a moment, Mako did not answer. Then he moved, making Ebon flinch—but he only took a step back so that he did not impale himself on Adara's dagger when he gave a deep bow.

"I beg your every pardon, my lady, for this intrusion. To disturb you was my last wish. I only sought my master, Ebon, of the family Drayden. He is the boy standing there just behind you."

Ebon gawked. Adara glanced back at him. He nodded, and slowly she withdrew her dagger. Mako, seeing the motion, straightened from his bow—and then he fixed Ebon with a hard stare.

"Come with me, little goldshitter. There is work to be done."

SEVEN

After bidding Adara a hasty farewell and promising to return as soon as he could, Ebon followed Mako into the streets. The moment they had turned a corner, he seized the bodyguard's arm to pull him around. Mako gave the hand on his elbow a hard look, but Ebon did not care.

"How did you know I was there? I have not even seen you since we fought with Isra. Where have you been?"

"You have never been curious about my whereabouts before," said Mako. "I thought it was because you did not wish to know. Nor have you ever asked how I knew where you were. It is a sort of assumed truth between us, is it not?"

Mako turned and stalked off. Ebon's nostrils flared, and his hand curled to a fist at his side. But what could he do? Striking Mako would do no good—even if the bodyguard did not strike back, which seemed doubtful. He hurried to trot after Mako's retreating back.

In truth, he was terrified that Mako knew where Adara lived. But then, as he thought of it, it seemed likely that Mako had had that knowledge for some time. In fact, it would not surprise Ebon if Mako knew the dwelling of every denizen on the Seat and their families across the nine kingdoms besides. That was, after all, part of his duty. Not only as a Drayden bodyguard and messenger, but also as their assassin.

Something of Ebon's thoughts must have shown in his face, for Mako laughed at him. "You may unclench yourself, little Ebon. Your lover is in no danger from me."

"Oh? And what about from Shay?"

Mako's mouth soured in an instant. "From what we have learned of your father, I certainly will not be reporting anything to him—about Adara, or anything else."

Rather than bringing comfort, the words further darkened Ebon's mood—except instead of anger, he felt a cold fear. He saw Matami's gaping eye socket, heard his uncle's screams.

And then he remembered their fight against Isra, when the girl struck with her magic. But Mako stood untouched and leaped forwards with his dagger. Her magic had been powerless against him, and Ebon still did not know why.

"You are very silent, Ebon," said Mako. "Come. Speak. What do you wish to tell me?"

"I . . ." Ebon swallowed hard. Something, some urgent voice in the back of his mind, told him not to speak of what he had seen during the fight. "You mentioned my father. It brought an unpleasant memory to the fore."

"Does Matami still plague your thoughts? If everyone were so naive as you, there would be no more war in Underrealm."

"Never mind that now," said Ebon. "I must tell you something about Isra. Last night, in the Academy—"

"She appeared," said Mako. "I know it, boy. That is why I have come to see you in the first place. Did you think I sought to converse for my pleasure? I do not think either of us have enjoyed ourselves so far."

Ebon looked around. He did not recognize the streets they passed through. A twinge of nerves struck him. "Where are we going, exactly? You cannot know where she is already."

Mako snorted. "Of course not. You are more craven than that old instructor of yours, Ebon, and it suits you ill. I wish we *were* going to see her now, so that I could end the little girl once and for all."

"Then where?"

"You would do well to learn patience."

The next few streets passed in silence. Ebon knew only that they were somewhere in the southwest end of the city. Little construction had made its way there, and many buildings were burned or fallen to ruin. This was where the Shades had brought the full strength of their assault, and few who lived here had survived the attack. It seemed the High King did not see fit to rebuild where no one would live afterwards.

At last they came to a wrought iron fence that surrounded a wide house of nobility—wide, but not so tall as the Drayden family's manor, nor as resplendent in its design. Here and there the fence had been bent and broken, so that there were many gaps to slip through. Mako paused, fixing Ebon with a look.

"One more thing before we enter. With Isra about, you may have need of me, and your lover's messages cannot reach me quickly enough. Do you remember when I snuck you out of the Academy?"

Ebon frowned. "Of course."

"There is a piece of alabaster on the ground near that place. You cannot miss it. If ever you must tell me something, or need my help, write a note and leave it beneath the alabaster. I will come as quickly as I may."

"Very well," said Ebon. "But do you think I am in danger?"

Mako spread his hands and grinned. "A rogue mindmage is on the loose, and she has the strength of magestones within her. Do you think anyone in the Academy is safe?"

That seemed a fair point. Ebon looked up at the manor before them. "What is this place?"

"It once belonged to the family Skard." Mako looked the place over, his lip curling slightly. "They are one of—"

"A merchant family from Dulmun," said Ebon. "I know the name."

"They left the Seat just before it was attacked—and now it may be guessed that they knew of Dulmun's treachery before it happened. They have not returned since."

The sky was already darkening above them. Ebon gave a weary sigh. "What is this all about, Mako? Curfew is not far off, and I cannot be out this late."

"This will not be a long engagement," said Mako. "And besides, if you are late in returning, you will not be the only one."

He ducked in through a gap in the fence, crossed the courtyard, and entered the manor through its front door. Ebon swallowed hard, wondering what the bodyguard had meant by that comment, before he finally mustered the courage to follow.

From the street, the manor looked nowhere near as impressive as the home of Ebon's family. But when he crossed the threshold, the sight of the main hall froze him in place and robbed his breath. Far it stretched, thirty paces at least, and lined with hearths to either side. At its head was the greatest fireplace of all, where a fine mantel of marble was likely meant to hold treasures and goblets of silver and gold. The shelf lay bare now—what the invaders had not taken, looters would have stolen since. That is, if the family Skard had not taken their valuables with them when they fled.

Running the hall's length was a mammoth wooden table, wider than Ebon was tall, and a long bench to either side of it. Where the Drayden manor had little dining rooms in which the family could take their meals in privacy and comfort, this was a place for feasts, banquets for an entire clan at once, where merchants and servants alike could be seated by station, while their children and the dogs played and tussled on the rugs in the corners. Some of these still remained: those too grease-stained or ratty to be stolen. Though all the hearths lay cold, and the place was lit only by the fading daylight coming through the door, Ebon could imagine the hall filled with proud Dulmun warriors, the air ringing with their ululating songs.

Then he caught a motion at the other end of the hall, and his breath caught in his throat. But peering deeper, he saw it was Mako—and beside the bodyguard, to Ebon's great shock, were Theren and Kalem.

"What . . . Mako, what are they doing here?"

Theren glowered at him, and then at Mako. "We were summoned.

Mako told us you were in great peril, and to meet him here at once so that you might be rescued."

"And look how quickly they came, boy." Mako's smile was cruel. "We should all be so lucky to have such loyal friends."

"Ebon, what is going on?" said Kalem. Ebon could see the fear in the boy's eyes. Kalem eyed Mako's cruel knife, and Ebon knew he was thinking of the time the bodyguard had drawn blood from Ebon's throat with the tip of it.

"This sack of dung has lied to us," said Theren. "We are not your lackeys, bodyguard, to be dragged across the Seat at your whim."

Mako flicked his fingers in the air. "Isra is on the loose, and we must find her. Do you not want that? You may spurn my aid if you wish, but then you must capture her yourself."

"Do you think me incapable of it?" Theren drew up to her full height, which was only a pair of fingers shorter than Mako. "I would stand a better chance against her—one wizard against another."

"You think I have never killed a mindmage before," Mako's voice had taken on a dangerous growl. "That is the trouble with you wizards. You are used to being more powerful than everyone you meet, and so you grow overconfident. That is when someone like me arrives to slit your throats."

Theren glared back at him. But Ebon remembered Isra, and how she had blasted Mako with her magic, only to leave him unharmed. A shiver of fear ran through him.

Before Mako or Theren could utter another word, Kalem stepped between them. He held his hands out to either side, though it was ludicrous to imagine he could stop them with his diminutive frame.

"If the two of you have taken sufficient measure of each other, mayhap we could speak of whatever Mako has summoned us for? I would rather not miss curfew."

Mako's countenance shifted at once to a kindly smile. "An excellent idea, child. Here is the matter at hand: ever since last we saw Isra, something has been brewing upon the Seat, and I have not been able to wrap my fingers around it."

Theren scoffed. "Something? What does that mean? *What* is brewing?"

"If I knew that, do you think I would require your help? I am aware of how desperate I seem, coming to the three of you. But the spies I have tucked into the city's dark corners tell me nothing. When someone gets up to dark business, it sends out ripples. There have been many such ripples of late, but I cannot follow them back to the center. I thought it must have to do with smuggling Isra from the island, but now we know that she is still here."

"You are telling us, then, that you were wrong?" said Theren, arching an eyebrow.

Mako's nose flared. "Not all information is a clear as the words on one of your scrolls."

Theren nodded. "Of course not. It is easy to imagine how you might have been misled."

Ebon feared that Mako might strike her. But with great effort, he went on. "In any case, now we know she is here, and she seems to have no intention of leaving. I am bringing you into the fold on the slight chance that you may be able to help. Am I wise to do so?"

"We will do what we can, of course," said Ebon. "But I fear we know nothing more than you."

"That may be true," said Mako. "But then, you may know something *without* knowing it. Whatever buzzes within the city, it has something to do with the family Yerrin—an odd thing, for recently they have been on their best behavior."

That raised Kalem's eyebrows. "Yerrin keeping their noses clean? That is a wonder."

"They were implicated in the attack," said Mako. "The High King had half a mind to purge them from the land, and they only barely avoided that fate. They have been good little children since—but now they have begun to lurk again."

"You think they are working with Isra, then?" said Ebon.

"That is entirely possible, though not certain."

Ebon thought of Lilith. Surely if Yerrin were involved with Isra's doings, then Lilith could be of help one way or another. But even as he opened his mouth to speak, Theren caught his eye. She looked anxious, or frightened, and gave him a quick shake of her head. Ebon closed his mouth again.

The silence in the hall had stretched a moment too long, and Mako was peering at them. Theren spoke up quickly. "Yerrin, working with Isra? It seems unlikely. Her schemes brought them great suffering. Oren was murdered. Lilith was tortured, and would have been executed."

Mako shrugged. "That is hardly out of character for the Yerrins. Their thoughts and schemes stretch for years, and they are willing to prune some dead branches to ensure a healthy growth."

But Ebon was not so sure. He remembered Oren's mutilated body and the madness in Lilith's eyes. Surely even the cruelest plan could not stand by such actions. He saw the same doubt in Kalem's face.

Their hesitation seemed to annoy Mako, for he gave a little growl. "Very well, then. Let us leave the Yerrins alone for now. But to search for Isra, I must start in the right place. Tell me what happened when I left you in Xain's home—and I mean all that happened, with no detail added or left out."

Ebon stiffened in fear and saw it reflected in the faces of his friends as well. Mako saw it, and he smiled as he settled down on one of the benches at the head of the table.

"This must be an interesting tale indeed."

"As she fled, I tried to stop her," said Ebon. "I missed her, but I got hold of the amulet. Kekhit's amulet, the one she used to cast mindwyrd, and also to hide her magic."

"I remember it," said Mako. "What next?"

"When we ourselves tried to leave, she was there. She had Xain's son, and she took him prisoner." Ebon shuddered as he remembered the fear in the boy's eyes, his whimpering cries as Isra dragged him away. "She tried to kill Kalem and me, but Theren recovered and saved us."

Mako's eyes narrowed. "Why did you not give Theren the amulet? She could have stopped Isra, could she not?"

"I had not yet thought of that," said Ebon sharply. Then he stopped, and his eyes went wide.

"Yet," said Mako, his smile widening. "You had not *yet* thought of it. But you did think of it."

Theren shook. "Darkness take you, Ebon."

"He is trying to help," Ebon told her. "We will do ourselves no favors by holding back. Yes, Mako, I thought of using mindwyrd. For when Isra fled, Dasko arrived. He is an instructor at—"

"I know the man," said Mako. "And I think that now I know the rest of your tale. He found you before you could get out of Xain's home, and you were holding the amulet. You thought he would expose you— and you were right to think it. So you gave the amulet to Theren, and she used her mindwyrd to make him forget you had been there."

"Yes," said Ebon. "You have it."

Theren turned to hide her face. Kalem's head drooped, and carefully he took a seat at the table opposite Mako. Ebon sighed. To speak the truth so plainly . . . it was a relief, and yet he wished it had been to someone other than Mako.

The bodyguard was studying his fingernails. He drew his knife and began to pick under one of them. "I am no wizard. Yet it seems I have heard something of mindwyrd—that if it is not maintained, it produces a sort of mind-sickness in the victim."

No one answered him. Theren met Ebon's eyes, and he saw how haunted her expression had become.

"I take it that your silence means I am right," said Mako. "If that is so, you did not use mindwyrd upon Dasko once, and then let him be. You have been using it ever since."

"We have," said Ebon quietly. Theren turned away again.

"That is excellent," said Mako. "Your new Dean Forredar has some knowledge of Yerrin. And Dasko will be close in Xain's counsel, for he is a wise man and well respected at the Academy. Mayhap we can use Dasko to use Xain."

"What?" said Kalem, straightening at once. "We will not use mindwyrd on Dasko to control him, but only to make him forget. Keeping his memory empty is one thing. Using him to accomplish our own ends . . ."

"I will not do it," said Theren. She stormed up to the table and slammed her hands down on it. The heavy THOOM of the blow echoed around the hall, flitting about its many pillars. "I will not, and that is the end of it. He is like a puppet on strings, and I feel more of a monster every time I jerk them. Mayhap I do not suffer from magestone sickness, but this is its own kind of torture."

"We will not use him for evil," said Mako. His tone was gentle, as though he were persuading a wounded animal. "We will only collect information we cannot get ourselves. And that information could do great good. It could even save the life of the boy, Erin."

"Erin could already be dead," said Ebon. "He likely is. It has been more than a week."

"I know something of these matters," said Mako. "One does not take a hostage if one does not intend to use them. And through Dasko, we could learn something that—"

"Stop saying that!" cried Theren. "Stop saying 'we,' when you mean me. We are not committing a crime—I am. We will not be put to death if this scheme is discovered—I will."

"We are with you to the end, Theren," said Ebon quietly. "We have been there every step of the way. If the King's law learns of our dealings, we will not abandon you to die alone. And if you refuse this scheme, I for one will not argue against you."

"We cannot do it," said Kalem. "If we do, we are little better than those we hope to expose. Evil cannot defeat evil, but only strengthens it."

Mako stood suddenly from the table, and his eyes had grown hard again. "This is not a council. My duty is to see to Ebon's safety—and if you call him your friend, girl, then your duty is the same. The next time you use your power on Dasko, have him tell you what Xain knows of Yerrin, as well as anything he knows about where Isra went. I assure you, Dean Forredar will have been most earnest in his searching."

Theren did not answer him for a moment, but looked to Ebon. He gave her a little shrug. "It is your choice."

She sighed. "Very well. I will ask him—but I will not command him to go digging any further."

Mako smiled. "Good enough, I suppose—for now. In that case, the three of you had better scuttle off back home. I have heard that curfew draws near."

EIGHT

THE STREETS HAD GROWN COLDER STILL, FOR THE SUN WAS ALMOST gone. They hurried between the snowdrifts, moving quickly for warmth as well as for the lateness of the hour. Ebon waited until they had left the manor a few streets behind before he spoke to Theren.

"When I almost spoke of Lilith, you stopped me. Why?"

She gave a nervous look over her shoulder. "I wish you would not speak of her even now. I feel like that man has ears everywhere, even among us."

"He is nowhere in sight, and I am no traitor," said Kalem.

Theren sighed, and the frost of it whipped around her face as they hurried on. "I fear that if Mako knew of our closeness—well, *my* closeness—to Lilith, he might think of her as a target. Especially now that he is so interested in the doings of the family Yerrin. And I think that we have already put her through enough. We pursued her when she was innocent, and she was put to the question because of it. I wish to cause her no more harm."

"I see that," said Ebon. "Yet if Yerrin is truly a threat, and if they are behind Isra's crimes, Lilith could be most helpful. She might even help us save Erin's life."

"You sound too much like your bodyguard," Theren spat. "I thought you had no wish to be like the rest of your family, yet I hear their echoes in your words."

"Leave Mako out of it, then," said Ebon. "But we must stop Isra as quickly as we can. I have not forgotten the sight of Oren's corpse—nor Credell's, nor poor little Vali's."

"And do you think I have?" Her eyes flashed. "She has left a longer trail of bodies than that, though how can I blame you for remembering only the goldbags among them?"

Ebon stopped walking and squared his shoulders, looking her in the eye. "That is not fair."

She glared back for a moment, but then she sagged. "I am sorry. I know you do not think of it that way. It is only . . . Ebon, I am frightened."

"We all are," said Kalem. He put an awkward hand on her arm. "Who knows when Isra will appear again?"

Theren shrugged. "Who cares for Isra? I am afraid for Dasko, and for the mindwyrd I keep him under. I am afraid for all of us, and what will happen if we are discovered. And I am afraid to use the mindwyrd to pry information from Dasko's mind. I never wanted this power, and now I cannot stop using it."

They stood a moment in silence. Then Ebon tossed his head. "Come. Time stops for no one." They fell into step beside him. "I feel your fear as well. But we could at least speak with Lilith. Mayhap she can help, and mayhap not. If not, we can leave it alone, and it will never reach Mako's ears at all."

She sighed. "Mayhap. Let me think upon it. It is no decision to make lightly."

"Of course."

They reached the Academy a little while later, and no sooner had they passed through the front door than the curfew bell rang. Theren redoubled her pace, making for the white cedar doors that led out to the grounds.

"I am almost late. I will see you both on the morrow."

But Ebon increased his pace to keep up with her. "I will come with you."

"And I as well," said Kalem, who scampered along with them.

Theren did not stop moving, but she tried to wave them off. "There is no need. I can do it myself easily enough—I have the practice, certainly."

"I told you, Theren. We are in this together."

He caught the faintest quiver in her chin. "Very well," she said, her voice wavering. "Thank you both."

The grounds were as cold as the streets had been, but better lit, for the groundskeepers had already been around to kindle the lanterns. They went for the place in the hedges where they always met Dasko. He was there when they arrived, sitting by himself on a stone bench. Kalem waited at the entrance to the sitting area, standing just out of view where he could keep watch.

Dasko stood as soon as he saw them. Ebon stopped short. He had not been so close to the man in some time, a week at least. Something about him seemed . . . off. It was not just his face, which had grown a touch gaunter, nor the grey at his temples, which seemed to have spread some little way into the rest of his hair. It was a weariness, a thinness, as though the instructor were only half there, and half an Elf-dream. But mayhap Ebon was only imagining that. So far as he knew, no one else had remarked on Dasko acting strange.

Theren reached into a pocket of her robe, and Ebon knew she was holding the amulet of Kekhit. "You will not remember that you have seen us here tonight," she began. "You will return here tomorrow just before curfew and remain until I come to see you. If anyone asks, you will not tell them why you are here waiting, but will invent some excuse."

"Yes," said Dasko, nodding. Ebon shuddered at the lifeless monotone in his voice.

Kalem and Theren had explained a bit to him in the days since they had first placed Dasko under control. Theren had thoroughly erased his memories of these meetings. If they released Dasko from mindwyrd, the danger was that he might remember them. Even if he did not, there might be gaps in his memory, and he would start showing withdrawal from the control. That would prompt an investigation by the faculty, and that could lead to Ebon and his friends.

Their position seemed untenable. Often Ebon felt that they were drawing a blanket over an ever-widening hole in the floor and hoping they would not get in trouble when some unwitting child fell into it and broke their neck.

Theren gave him an uneasy look. Ebon nodded at her. "It is your choice," he said quietly.

She sighed and turned to Dasko. "Tell me what the Academy faculty knows of Isra's reappearance."

"We know nothing," said Dasko. Again his voice made Ebon shudder. It was like hearing a corpse speak.

Theren shook her head. "Tell me what the Academy faculty suspects of Isra's reappearance."

"Most think Isra must be getting help from inside the Academy," he said. "There will be an investigation to unearth anyone she may be using. We will look for anyone who shows signs of being under mindwyrd."

Theren stiffened. Ebon's heart leaped to his throat, and he spoke. "How would you find someone being held in mindwyrd?"

Dasko said nothing. Theren gave an exasperated sigh. "Tell me how you would find someone being held in mindwyrd."

"There are sometimes gaps in the memory, for Isra would not want the victim to remember seeing her," he said. "Therefore she would command them to forget the meeting."

Ebon and Theren looked at each other. "If they question him, he could lead them to us," said Ebon.

"Yes," said Dasko, surprising them both by speaking without being prompted. "In fact Dean Forredar already strongly suspects you, Ebon."

"Tell us who else suspects us," said Theren.

"No one," said Dasko. "Jia thinks Xain's suspicion is paranoia, born of his hatred for Ebon's family."

"Still, we should do what we can to hide the effects of mindwyrd," said Ebon.

Theren nodded. "I think I know how. Dasko, when you leave here tonight, you will remember being out upon the grounds, but you will remember it as if you were alone. You will not remember speaking to anyone, and you will not remember hearing anyone speak to you. You will remember all of our previous visits the same way—you have been visiting the grounds alone each night, on your own, and speaking to no one."

"Yes," said Dasko.

"Leave us now. Enter the Academy, and then forget."

"Yes." He left them, slipping out through the gap in the hedge.

Theren sank down onto the bench, her whole body going limp as though she had just run a league. Ebon quickly took a seat beside her and put a hand on her shoulder. Kalem came in a moment later, his eyes filled with concern.

"I am sorry, Theren," said Ebon. She looked exhausted. But when she lifted her head to look at him, he saw the weariness was in her eyes—a bone-sunk debility of the soul.

"It is wrong, Ebon," she whispered. "This is wrong. I know it is, and yet I cannot stop. How can I go on, committing a new evil every night?"

"We are only keeping ourselves safe for now," he said. "And we *will* come to a solution. I promise you. We will not rest until this is over."

"Of course we will not rest," she said. "I can barely even sleep these days."

Ebon stood and held out his hand. She took it and allowed him to pull her to her feet. They made their way towards the Academy with arms over each other's shoulders—not to remain upright, but merely for comfort.

Then they opened the white cedar door and nearly ran into Dean Forredar.

Xain stopped short just before they hit him, and though the children took a hasty step back, he did not move. He had eyes only for Ebon, and disgust burned in his gaze.

"Dean Forredar," murmured Kalem.

"What were you doing out upon the grounds?" said Xain. "Curfew has been called."

"It is not against the rules," said Theren. But some of her usual fire had left her voice.

"It is cold out," said Xain. "After an encounter like you all had last night, most students would wish to remain inside, where the danger seems less."

"Are we in danger upon the Academy grounds?" said Ebon, meeting Xain's stare. He was growing more and more fed up with the man's unreasoning hatred of him. "Is it not your job to protect us? I seem to remember that you made such a pledge when you first came here."

"It is my job to protect the Academy," said Xain. "From threats within, as well as without. Sometimes it is hard to tell the difference—other times it is quite clear."

Kalem quailed, but Theren drew herself up. "You have been wrong about such things before, Dean. Mayhap you see threats when none exist."

Xain stared her down. For a moment Ebon feared they might come to blows, the way they had when Xain had attacked him in the dining hall. Then, without a word, the dean stalked away.

"Darkness take him," muttered Theren.

"He is a suspicious man," said Kalem, shaking his head. "Yet who can blame him? These are dark times, and his son is missing. Come. I am weary, and I suspect the two of you feel much the same."

They made for the stairs and then up to their dormitories to sleep.

NINE

IN THE LIBRARY THE NEXT DAY, THEY REUNITED IN THEIR FAVORITE SPOT on the third floor. The place was even darker than usual. That part of the library had never been very well kept, and now the faculty had suffered losses, so that many of the lanterns stayed unlit. Kalem took one from the wall out in the main area and set it on the table beside them so that they could read by its fiery glow.

But reading did not come easy. Ebon struggled to keep his mind upon the book in his hands, a weighty tome entitled *The Conquering of Idris: A Telling of the Fall of the Tomb-Kings.* Idris was his home, and he had thought the subject might hold his attention. But too often he caught himself staring off at nothing. It did not help that the book was written in a dry and informational style, with no attempt to make the events more interesting. Not that they needed much embellishment—the magic of the Tomb-Kings of old was well renowned, and well feared. His distraction was aided by weariness, and often his head drooped towards his lap. He had spent another sleepless night in the common room of his dormitory, dozing off only in little fits and starts.

After they had sat there for mayhap an hour, Theren gave a frustrated little growl and slammed her book shut. "Enough of this. I am through pretending to study when all of us know we are doing nothing of the sort."

Kalem looked up blinking from his book, shaking his head as though he had forgotten they were there. "Hm?"

"Well, except for Kalem, I suppose." Theren folded her arms across her chest. "But I cannot even see the words on the page. Do neither of you wonder what she is waiting for?"

"Who?" said Kalem, eyes still foggy.

"*Isra*, of course, you idiot," Theren snapped. "It has been two days since we saw her. Why has she not struck again?"

"I had not wondered, for I have been thinking about Erin," said Ebon. "Where on all the Seat could she be hiding him?"

"There are many abandoned buildings upon the Seat after the attack," said Kalem. "Why, Mako himself took us to one of them."

"But that is just it," said Ebon, leaning forwards. "He must have searched out all such places by now. They would be the easiest to search. If Erin were in one of them, Mako would know something of it. Isra must be staying in some place where there are other people, and she can rely upon their secrecy to conceal her."

"Then let us catch her and throw her to the Mystics so they may put her to the question," said Theren with a glower. "Only that leaves the same mystery as before—what is she waiting for?"

Ebon shrugged. "It has been nearly two weeks since we fought her in Xain's home. She took her time to plan the attack in the dining hall. Now that we foiled it, she will likely be even more careful in her plotting—especially now that she has revealed herself."

"That will take more time that we do not have," said Theren. "Mayhap the story I planted in Dasko's mind will hold. Mayhap not. I have never had to hide—" Theren stopped short, looking about to make sure no one was close enough to hear. "I have never had to hide mindwyrd before. What if I did it wrong? What if they find us? I should throw the amulet into the Great Bay and have done with it."

Kalem's eyebrows raised. "That may be a fair idea now. Dasko would show mindwyrd sickness, but the faculty might ascribe it to Isra's doing. I would still rather we told the truth of what happened, but this is a good half-measure."

But Ebon frowned. "And what if Isra returns? She has the strength of magestones in her, and no one can resist her without the amulet. Mayhap we should leave it somewhere for the faculty to find instead. We could slide it beneath Jia's door when no one was looking. Then Xain would have it, and *he* could use it to stop Isra."

"He would not," said Kalem sadly. "The faculty would never use its powers. That would be a crime against the King's law, and punishable by death."

"I know it is!" Theren burst out, before quickly lowering her voice again. "That is why I hate this, why all my waking hours are a torment, and yet I cannot sleep. I know full well what awaits me at the end of this journey, but I cannot stop walking the road." Her arms and legs were shaking, and her knuckles were white from their grip on the arms of her chair.

Ebon looked away, for he felt her pain as if it were his own. And then, suddenly, an idea struck him. He looked at his friends, wondering that he had not thought of it at once.

"What if we find her ourselves?"

Theren and Kalem stared at him. "What do you mean?" said Kalem.

"Well, either ourselves, or with Mako's help," said Ebon. "If we capture her, and subdue her, and then *put* the amulet upon her before we turn her over to the faculty, then our problem is solved. They will assume she had it all along. Xain will have no choice but to accept that we are innocent."

Kalem frowned, and even Theren looked doubtful. Yet he watched them think on it, and saw the spark of the idea blossom to flame within their minds.

"I would still have to keep the amulet," said Theren. "At least for now."

"Yet you could release Dasko from your control, immediately," said Ebon. "You no longer need to hold him under mindwyrd."

"If she were discovered . . ." said Kalem.

"How could that happen?" said Ebon. "You have a good hiding place for it, Theren—or so I assume, since you do not carry it with you everywhere. And we can finally put this dark chapter behind us."

Theren spread her hands. "Let us say that is true. We must still find Isra, but we have no idea how."

"I think we must start with Yerrin," said Ebon. "Even Mako thinks they may know something."

Her eyes hardened. "You mean to bring Lilith into this."

He leaned forwards, counting the steps on his fingers. "If we do, everything falls into place. We release Dasko from our control. With Lilith's help—help, I say, not coercion—we track down who in her family is helping Isra. We know they must be—it is where she is getting her magestones. We capture Isra. And then we turn her over to the King's law with the amulet in her pocket. And everything will be over."

Theren looked desperately hopeful. But Kalem sat deep in thought. After a moment, he shook his head. "It is a lie, and a great risk as well. We have other resources, more than Mako, I mean. Ebon, you could ask Adara. The guild of lovers has a thousand ears, and they are always listening."

"I have hope for Mako, and I already mean to speak with Adara—this very night, in fact," said Ebon. "But Lilith may best them all, for she is closest to the source of the magestones. Yes, it means we must lie. But I am willing to bear that burden, for you and I have the least to lose as things stand. This plan helps Theren more than you or me, Kalem."

Theren studied her fingernails, and then put one in her mouth to tear at it with her teeth. Kalem and Ebon watched her.

"Let us try it, then," Theren muttered. "It cannot be worse than living this way."

"Then we must take the first step," said Ebon. "We must speak with Lilith."

"But she is still . . . Lilith," said Kalem. He shivered. "I have had difficulties enough with her in the past. Now that I am one of those who helped throw her to the Mystics' knives, I suspect she will be even less kind than before."

"We have no choice," said Ebon. "We must bring her to Mako so that she can help him in his search."

"No," Theren snapped. "Not Mako. I will not bring him anywhere near Lilith, nor will you."

"But Theren, he is the best chance we have at—"

She held up a hand to cut him off. "No. Remember your uncle Matami."

He fell silent at once, seeing Matami's brutalized corpse in his mind.

"Think on it," said Theren. "What if Mako decides that Lilith knows more than she is telling? Will he drag her down into the sewers to do to her what he did to your uncle? She is not even his kin. Do you think he will be more reluctant to kill her than another Drayden?"

"Lilith is a youth, like us," said Ebon, but the words sounded weak even in his own ears.

"I do not believe for a moment that that will save her. If we mean to work with Lilith, we will do it on our own. Mako will only put her in greater danger."

Kalem nodded in agreement, and so Ebon shrugged. "Very well."

But even as he said it, he thought of how helpful it would be to have Mako's counsel in this. He did not trust the bodyguard, exactly, or even like him very much. Yet Mako had proven his worth time and again, and had saved the children's lives more than once.

"If we mean to speak with Lilith, why wait?" said Kalem. He put his book aside and stood from the armchair. "Let us find her. Her schedule is the same as ours, and she should be in the library somewhere."

They rose together and set out to find her. Quickly they scanned the shelves of the whole third floor, but there were few students scattered among them, and Lilith was not there. The second and first floors took longer to search, for they were much more crowded, and Ebon and his friends earned several curious looks as they poked their heads in between bookshelves. But in the end they stood together on the bottom floor, and Lilith was nowhere to be seen.

"Has she returned to her dormitory?" said Kalem. "I know she has been granted special permissions to rest, if she wishes, after what she suffered."

"She has not," said Theren. In her voice was a sorrow Ebon could not place. "Come. We will have to sneak out of the library. I know where she is."

TEN

Jᴵᴬ ʜᴀᴅ ɴᴏᴛ ʀᴇᴛᴜʀɴᴇᴅ ᴛᴏ ᴅᴜᴛʏ ᴀꜰᴛᴇʀ ʙᴇɪɴɢ ᴘʟᴀᴄᴇᴅ ᴜɴᴅᴇʀ mindwyrd the day before last. Another instructor had replaced her in the library's afternoon study period. Her name was Uma, and she was short and plump, with eyes that seemed too large to work properly, and they were always blinking. One by one Ebon and his friends excused themselves to use the privies and then met each other in the hallways outside. Theren took them around a wide, looping route through the Academy's less traveled passages. At one point they climbed to the second floor, creeping among the younger children's dormitories where the space rang hollow and empty.

"Where are you taking us?" Kalem whispered.

"Hush, and you shall find out soon enough," said Theren.

They descended to the first floor again. Now they were in a part of the Academy where Ebon had seldom been. He knew some of the doors must lead to teacher's offices, and these they flew by in a rush. At last Theren stopped before a thick oaken door. It had a lock, and the keyhole was very large.

584

Theren tried the handle. "Locked," she said with a sigh of relief. "That means that Carog is not here."

"Who is Carog?" said Ebon.

"The bell-keeper," said Kalem, looking at Theren with awe. "Is this the bell tower?"

"It is," said Theren. "It is . . . well, it is where we will find Lilith."

"How can you know?" said Ebon. But she only gave him a steely look and did not answer.

Kneeling, she peered into the lock and extended a finger. From behind her he saw the glow of her eyes. A soft *click* came from within the lock, and the knob twisted in her hand. Quickly they all filed in through the door, and Theren locked it again behind them.

They stood in the base of a wide round tower with a stairwell that ran around the outer wall to the roof far above. Many windows pierced the walls, letting in shafts of light that crisscrossed each other in the air, illuminated by the dust motes that danced within them so that looking up from the ground was like seeing a honeycomb made of the sun's glow. At the very top they could see the Academy's great bell. Ebon had only viewed it from the streets of the city, where it seemed much like any other bell. From here, however, it seemed a massive thing, at least as large as a house, and its bronze glow in the sunlight nearly blinded them.

"Come," said Theren. "We should climb as fast as we may, for there is no place to hide down here if Carog should return."

"I have heard she is half blind, anyway," said Kalem.

"That may be, but she has ears like a cat. Quickly!"

She leaped up the stairs two at a time. Ebon and Kalem hastened to follow. But after only a few flights they both wheezed and gasped as they clutched at the stone handrail. Theren hardly slowed at all. When they had almost lost sight of her, she stopped and turned to look at them in disgust.

"Honestly, how do the two of you survive? Most noble children are not so frail."

"Most noble children learn to be warriors, especially firstborn," said Kalem. "They are not bookish."

"You claim that word as though it is something prideful," said Theren, arching an eyebrow.

"To some, it is."

She slowed her pace, though she kept prodding and urging them to go faster. But Ebon grew more and more uncomfortable the higher they climbed. Soon he had to press himself against the wall to their left, for he thought he might vomit if he caught sight of the floor far, far below them. He had never been overly fond of heights.

It seemed an eternity before they reached the top. When they did, Ebon and Kalem collapsed to the floor, wheezing. Ebon scooted quickly away from the edge, for though the railing between him and the open air was thick and strong, still it made him nervous. But the other direction hardly seemed better, for about five paces away was the edge of the tower, and the railing there was made of thin wooden poles. His stomach turned again, and he pressed his fingers hard against the wooden floor, as though he could catch it in his grip and hold on to it.

Theren stood there before them, dwarfed by the mammoth bell beside her, looking all around. There were a few boxes and crates of things about, though Ebon could not guess what they held, as well as many coils of rope stacked in the corners. Theren inspected them, eyes narrowed.

"Lilith?" she said softly. "It is Theren. I know you are here."

The tower was silent. Kalem looked to Ebon uncertainly—Ebon only tried not to look at the tower's edge. But after a moment they heard shuffling footsteps. Lilith stepped out from behind the coils of rope, a deep scowl embedded in her features.

Ebon was startled at the sight of her. He had not seen her plainly in some time. Even against the darkness of her skin he could see the fading remnants of bruises where she had been beaten. Her Academy robes covered most of them, but the fabric did not hide her face. And while her sleeves covered most of her hands, he spotted the pale pink of scars on the tips of her fingers, which were thin and wasted like a starving child's. And her eyes—her eyes were an animal's, filled with the futile indignation of a fox brought to bay, showing its teeth without hope.

"What are you doing here?" she snapped.

"I needed to speak with you," said Theren.

"What are *they* doing here?"

She turned eyes of fury on Ebon and Kalem, who had, without

realizing it, retreated halfway behind Theren. Ebon steeled himself and stepped forwards to stand at Theren's shoulder.

"We need your help, Lilith."

Lilith ignored him, looking only at Theren. "I *never* brought Oren or Nella into the bell tower. Never."

Theren looked as though she had been slapped. "I . . . I did not know that. But I would have brought them even if I did know. Isra has returned, and she has magestones. We think she is getting them from your family."

For a moment, whistling wind was the only sound. Then Lilith's eyes widened, and her lips twisted to a snarl.

"You think *I* have something to do with it?" she screamed. "You think I would set eyes on Isra without catching her in a blaze? She *killed* Oren. She did *this.*"

She held up her hands before her face so that the sleeves of her robe fell to her elbows. Beneath were tight underclothes of wool, proof against the cold, which she dragged down to reveal her skin.

Kalem gasped, and Ebon's stomach lurched. The scars on her fingers were not the half of the harm that had been done to her. Pink lines of torn flesh raced down the length of her arms, crisscrossing each other over and over. Some looked to still be healing.

Theren's mouth worked, but she said nothing. Ebon saw tears spring to her eyes, threatening to flood forth. He stepped forwards, drawing Lilith's baleful gaze away from Theren and onto himself.

"I am sorry," he said. "We all are. You deserved none of what you received, and Isra was not alone in the blame for it. We were just as guilty."

For a moment he wondered if she had even heard him, for her expression did not change. Finally she turned, stalking away to the other side of the bell tower.

"Go away," she said over her shoulder. "I want nothing to do with any of you."

Ebon let loose a *whoosh* of breath and heard Kalem do the same. But Theren, unmoving, only watched Lilith go.

"It was wrong of us to ask this of her," Theren murmured.

He wondered if she was right. But then he remembered Isra in the kitchens, and felt again the blast of the artifact she had tried to use to kill them. Ebon squared his shoulders, and then he took Theren and Kalem's arms.

"We are not done yet," he said quietly. "Come."

They set off along the platform after her. She had gone to sit on the edge of the tower, her feet hanging off the lip while she held on to the thin wooden railing. Ebon's stomach did a turn at that. She did not look up, even as their feet scuffed to a stop behind her.

"I do not blame you for wanting to turn us away," said Ebon. "Indeed, Kalem had no wish to come to you, for you have never been kind to him, and Theren felt the same, for we have been far too cruel to you already. I cringe at the thought of trusting you in this after the way we met. But Theren has spoken to me of you, and of the nobility she still sees in your heart. And her belief has convinced me."

Lilith turned. Her gaze locked with Theren's, and Ebon saw her expression soften at the same time he felt Theren tense beside him. But it lasted only a moment before Lilith looked away again.

"I only want to be left alone," she said, but this time softly and without malice.

Theren went forth and sat on the stone edge beside her. Ebon's gut wrenched even worse—but from the ease with which she sat there, he guessed that Theren had done this many times before.

"What was it like when Isra had you under mindwyrd?" said Theren.

Lilith shuddered beside her, and she bowed her head. "It was horrible," she said in a low voice. "Still my mind reels when I try too hard to remember it. Some things I can recall, but it is like I watched it happen to someone else. When I entered the vaults, or when Vali . . ." She stopped, remaining silent through several deep breaths. Her scarred, ruined fingers crept up to scratch at her temples. "Other things I have forgotten entirely—and there are still other memories which come and go, and when they have gone I cannot remember having remembered them. It is . . . it is like a madness."

Ebon waited a moment. Then he took a step forwards—only one, for he was still terrified of the tower's edge—and said, "That is what Jia suffers even now. Isra has had her under control. Mayhap she has others. They will all suffer the same way. I would not ask you to face Isra again. But will you help us find her, so that we may?"

Lilith glared at him over her shoulder for a moment and then turned her face out again.

"You are fools if you think my family could have done this. Oren's death and my torture prove their innocence."

"Can you be so certain?" said Theren. "From what we have heard, some scion of your house had a hand in the Shades' attack. Mayhap they are also the ones who helped Isra—and may be helping her still."

"I know of whom you speak, but she could not have acted alone," said Lilith quickly. "You are saying that others helped spit Oren like a pig. That others left me to scream as the Mystics dug their knives into my flesh."

Theren hung her head. "These are dark days, filled with dark deeds. Say, for a moment, that we are right. Would you let such deeds go unpunished?"

Lilith closed her eyes, taking a deep breath of the chilled air before letting it out in a rush.

"Very well," she said quietly. "I will ask about and see what may be learned. But I will not risk my neck for the three of you. It has been squeezed tight enough already."

"Of course," said Theren. She put a hand on Lilith's shoulder. The girl jerked away as if by instinct, but subsided almost at once. "Thank you, Lilith."

She rose to rejoin Ebon and Kalem, and they set off for the stairs leading down. Just before they rounded the edge of the bell and lost sight of Lilith, Ebon glanced back. She had not moved. Not even to watch them go.

ELEVEN

AFTER STUDIES ENDED THAT EVENING, EBON MADE FOR THE STREETS and turned his steps towards the blue door in the west. Mako had begun his search, and now they had enlisted Lilith's aid as well. Only one more resource remained to them: Adara, with her fealty to the guild of lovers. And besides that, Ebon had not been able to spend much time with her the previous night, and hoped to make up for it.

The evening was even icier than normal, and he pounded his hands against his arms. He thought at once that he should have brought a second cloak, and considered going back for one. But just when he had made up his mind to do so, he heard the scrape of a boot on stone.

Ebon froze. He had ducked into an alley, a shortcut between two busy thoroughfares, and it had appeared empty. But the sound had been very distinct, though he could see no sign of anyone behind him now.

He took one careful step forwards, and then another. Then he pressed on at a regular pace, trying to convince himself that he had imagined the sound, or that it had been an echo of the noise of his own walking. But such thoughts did nothing to still his heart, which had begun to race.

His steps quickened, though he told himself it was only to warm his limbs, and every few paces he glanced back over his shoulder casually, as though he was just looking about to see the sights of the city. Soon he had reached a main street again, and that relaxed him considerably. There were too many people around, constables and Mystics and soldiers of all the nine kingdoms, for him to worry very much about an attack in the open. The black robes of an Academy student were distinctive, and wearers of such were known to be under the High King's protection.

But the busy street did not last forever, and eventually Ebon had to turn. He reached the street and balked. Far down it he could see one trader's cart plodding its way forwards through the snow, but between him and the cart was a great stretch of empty space with no one in sight. He skipped the turn and made for the next street, but it was even more barren, with not a soul to be seen from where he stood to where it vanished in a turn behind the corner of an inn.

Ebon glanced back along the thoroughfare down which he had come. He saw nothing untoward among the crowds. No one spared him a second glance.

He swallowed hard and stepped into the street. Now his footfalls, though muffled, could be heard bouncing from the buildings again. He listened hard, but he heard no steps other than his own. And he could not be sure if he was imagining the feeling of eyes upon his back, or if they were there in truth.

At last he reached the corner of the inn behind which the street turned. Without slowing, he stopped on the spot and whirled to look behind him.

The street was empty. Or . . . or had he in fact seen the corner of a grey cloak whipping behind the edge of a nearby building?

He passed the inn, and now he made no pretense of calm. He ran. The snow clutched at his boots, dragging at him. He imagined fingers beneath its surface, like the water-wurts that dragged sailors down to their deaths. Soon he was panting like a horse on the edge of collapse. His breath clouded around his head as if he were casting mists.

Mists. Ebon, you fool. He had utterly forgotten his magic. Now he darted for the closed mouth of an alley, dark and forbidding—but small, mayhap only a pace wider than his shoulders. Ebon flung himself into its mouth and reached for his power. The alley, which at first had been pitch-black to his sight, lightened considerably as his eyes began to glow. He focused on the air touching his skin. He *saw* it. And he spun mist within it.

It sprang from him, flooding out to fill the tiny width of the alley. He was nowhere near as proficient as Kalem, but he still managed to extend it a few paces in every direction. It was thick as a stew, so that no one could see through it—but it blocked Ebon's sight not at all, for it was born of his magic. He could see the alley's walls clearly, and when it branched off in two directions he made the turn without pausing. But he left the mist where it was, moving through it while it remained at the fork. He could only hold it a moment, but by the time it dissipated, he had already turned the next corner, and the fork was out of sight.

He would have laughed if he were not afraid of being heard. Anyone behind him would be lost now. And just ahead he could see the next main street, where many carts and travelers on horseback crossed the alley's—

A blast of air struck him in the chest, flinging him backwards and robbing his lungs of breath. He tried to cry out, but only a thin wheeze emerged. Strong, wiry hands clutched his collar and dragged him upright, around the corner and out of sight of the street. The hands slammed him up against the alley's wall.

Ebon stared into the eyes of Xain, dean of the Academy.

"Good eve, Drayden. Where are you off to in such a hurry?"

Xain's voice was carefully controlled, but Ebon could hear the fury within it. He tried to answer, but Xain's hand pressed against his throat. Hot breath washed over Ebon's face, and he smelled wine.

"Ah-ah-ah. Speak not. You are a student. Listening should be your primary concern. I wanted to tell you . . ." His lip curled. "I wanted to tell you that I received your family's note."

Ebon blinked. "What?" He barely managed to croak the word.

"I will not tell them where she is," Xain growled. "I would die first. I would not let Erin die for her, but then, I do not believe you mean to release him no matter what I do. I know the note's true purpose. It is supposed to make me lash out at your family—mayhap even at you yourself—so that the Draydens will have leverage. Then they can persuade the High King to remove me. Did you think this was a clever plan? Did you think I would not see through it? You were wrong."

"I know not—"

"Do not speak," hissed Xain. He did not squeeze, but the venom in his words silenced Ebon anyway. "You are fools if you think to dupe me with the same ruse as before. Drystan played this game, and it worked for him then. It will not work again. I am wiser now—wise enough to see what you are doing. You may tell your family they have made a mistake. I will find my son. I will prove you took him. And then your names will be purged across the nine kingdoms. And if Erin has been harmed, I will not be gentle in the purging."

He snatched his hand back. Ebon fell to the ground, clutching his throat and coughing. Xain looked down on him with malice, his fingers twitching as though he longed to fill them with fire.

"Tell your kin, Drayden. Tell them they have but one hope. They may return Erin to me. Bring him to the Academy, and leave him at the front door. If it is done, I will cease my efforts to destroy them. If it is not, I will not rest until you all burn. Tell them."

Ebon raised his head to look Xain in the eyes, and despite his fear he did not waver. "I know not what you speak of," said Ebon. "I have nothing to do with your son. Isra took him. She tried to kill *me* only two nights ago. If you think we are in league with her, you are mad yourself."

Xain snarled, and blue fire sprang into his palm. He snatched Ebon's collar and pressed him to the wall again, and the blue flames swung back. Ebon flinched and cried out, pressing back against the wall as though he could sink through it and escape.

But then Xain stopped. His gaze locked with Ebon's. Slowly the magelight died in his eyes—and when they were clear, Ebon saw no fury at all. Instead he saw only a trace of doubt.

"Either you are lying, in which case, darkness take you—or you are telling the truth, and you are ignorant of your family's deeds. If that is true, then you are their sacrificial lamb. Either way, you are a walking corpse. Tell them what I have said. Tell them quick, lest they use you like bait on the end of a hook."

His eyes filled with light, and wind sprang from nowhere. It flung snow up to fill the air, thicker than mist, and Ebon had to shield his eyes against the stinging gale. When the wind died down and the snow settled back to the street, Xain had gone.

TWELVE

For a little while he stood there, every limb shaking, afraid to move, for he thought his legs might give out if he tried. But then he realized he was still in the alley and still out of sight of the street. So he forced his frozen legs to walk, and soon he was in a crowd again. He had drawn closer to the blue door, and when he saw it at last he began to shake again—though this time from relief.

The door opened easily under his hand, and the matron in the front room looked up expectantly. When she saw Ebon, her eyes filled with surprise.

"Good eve, young sir," she said. "Adara is in her room, and unoccupied."

Ebon fumbled for his coin purse, but the matron held up a hand with her palm out.

"That is not necessary. She has informed us of your new arrangement, and you no longer need bring any gold to visit her here."

Ebon pulled out a gold weight and placed it in her hand, where her fingers closed around it after only a moment's hesitation. "Take it regardless," he said. "Tonight I do not visit only for love."

He let himself through the door and made his way down the hall. His careful knock produced only silence for a moment. Then he heard her hesitant voice, almost a question. "Come in."

When he opened the door, she looked even more surprised than the matron had. "Ebon," she said. "I thought not to see you so soon."

"I thought not to visit tonight," said Ebon. "But things . . . plans have been altered, and I must speak with you."

"Has it something to do with Isra?"

Ebon looked behind him, but the hallway remained empty. Still, he closed the door and turned the lock. "It does," he said quietly.

"Come."

She patted the space on the bed beside her. He sat, and at once her hand covered his own, stilling his fidgeting fingers. He smiled up at her.

"You are shaking," she said. "What has happened?"

He remembered the fury in Xain's eyes, the wine that filled the dean's breath. But he had not come here to speak of Xain.

"I need . . . I had thought to ask you for a favor."

"If I may grant it without dishonor, then consider it done," she said. "Only, Ebon, you must tell me what is wrong."

"I . . ." But something overcame him, and he swiped at his eyes with the back of his hand. Now that he was in her presence, the whole encounter with Xain seemed at once distant and forgotten, and yet somehow more real and terrifying. But the last thing he wanted was to weep in Adara's presence, for their time together should be joyous.

Adara leaned back with an appraising look, and he flinched, thinking she scorned him. But she stood quickly and took his hands, drawing him up after her.

"Come," she said softly. "Let us retire to my home."

He had no chance to answer, let alone argue, for she led him out and down the hall at once. The matron asked no questions, but bid them farewell with a nod. It was not long before they were situated in Adara's little room again. As before, she seated Ebon at her table by the window, but she did not sit with him. Instead she went to her cupboard and drew forth two glass goblets—no, not glass, Ebon quickly saw. Crystal. Each was wrapped with a narrow gold band, and the crystal was carved in intricate, rippled diamond shapes. He marveled at them while she drew wine and mead from a cupboard.

"These must have cost a fortune," he said, distracted from his fears for the moment.

She shrugged. "I did not buy them. Another gift from a happy guest—and a wealthy one, I wager."

Ebon grew solemn. "I did not mean to take much of your time tonight, nor reduce the coin you might have earned. I can be brief, and mayhap another time we—"

Adara stopped short, and one of her fingers rose from the neck of the bottle it held. "No. It is my evening, and I will choose how to spend it. Your concern for my work is touching, but I do not lack for coin."

He smirked at his goblet. That was something he did not doubt. She came to the table with the bottles and filled both their cups.

"What do we drink to?" he said, raising his cup.

She did not raise her own, but only met his gaze for a moment. In her eyes he saw a fresh anxiety. It was the same look she had worn when first she invited him here—another wall coming down. He leaned forwards.

"To knowing more of each other," she said.

Ebon smirked. "I hardly think we could know more of each other than we do."

That earned him a wicked smile, but it quickly subsided, and her voice grew even more solemn. "I should like to get drunk with you, Ebon of the family Drayden."

He blinked, looking at the cup of wine in his hand. "I . . . I do not understand."

"Drunk. Inebriated. Overfilled with wine until our brains are addled. You cannot be a stranger to the concept."

Ebon tried to frown, but the sardonic twist of her lips softened him. "You know that is not what I meant. *Why* do you want to get drunk?"

"I have meant to ask you this for some time," she said. With a fingernail she picked at the table, scraping up a bit of its lacquer. "Even before you and I . . . before we told each other how we felt. In fact, that was how I first thought I would hear true words of love pass your lips. I thought for certain that they would never pass mine any other way."

His hand covered hers, stopping her from scratching the table further. "Adara, you need not get me drunk to hear that I love you. Have I not said it enough? A thousand times will I repeat it, and learn to say it in all the tongues of Underrealm if you wish. I will find the imps and the wurts and the satyrs in their homes, and even the centaurs where they have vanished in Spineridge, and learn to speak their words as well, if that is what you want."

"It is not," she said, rolling her eyes. "And you are a fool. Charming, but a fool. It is not the words I hoped to draw from you, for I told you that lovers' words do not only come from lovers' lips. I thought, once, that you said pleasant things we both wanted to hear, and that I might hear the truth if you were . . . disarmed, shall we say. And I feared to tell you how I myself had begun to feel, and thought mead might make the confession come more easily."

Ebon leaned back. "I see. But you know now that I speak true."

"You know the same of me," she said. "And yet."

He looked down at his hands, for he had guessed at her mind. Not long ago, he had been shocked to learn she once lived in Dulmun. Yet how could that have surprised him? He had learned nothing else of her life, and she knew little enough of his, beyond his deeds since he had come to the High King's Seat.

"To your life and mine," said Ebon. He raised his glass and looked into her eyes, suddenly aware that those sounded far too similar to wedding words. But he did not flinch.

She met his look and raised her goblet in turn. "To your life and mine," she said. "Let them be laid bare, and we the better for it."

They both drained their cups. Adara reached at once for the mead to fill hers again—but Ebon stopped her and took the bottle to pour it for her. She smiled and poured his cup in turn.

"Can you tell me now what brought you to my door?" she said. "Or must I force another goblet down your throat?"

Ebon tried to smile, but his thoughts turned dark again. "It was a little matter."

Her eyes said she did not believe him. She put her hand over his. "Tell me something else, then. A thing of yourself you have withheld until now."

598

"Withheld from you?"

"Yes. Whatever you wish. Something new."

He looked down at her hand, for he had thought of something at once. But even now he hated the thought of telling her, for it stung his eyes and put a lump in his throat. She lowered her head a bit, trying to catch his eye.

"That, Ebon. Remember. Your life and mine."

"I thought of my brother, Momen," Ebon murmured. He was afraid if he raised his voice at all, it would break. "I thought of when he died."

She waited a moment. When he did not go on, she spoke softly. "What about when he died?"

"When I heard the news, I locked myself in my room and did not come out for days. I let no one in. I know they all thought I wept. The truth is, I could not. Tears would not come, no matter how badly I wanted them to, and I was ashamed. I thought I was a monster for not weeping at my brother's death, for I loved him dearly. And I never told anyone about those days locked in my room. I know they all think I shed tears in private, but I never did."

By the time he finished speaking, his head had already begun to fog. The wine must have been strong, or else it was the effect of drinking it so quickly. Adara took her hand from his and leaned back, nodding slowly. When she answered him, her words ran together.

"I left Idris when I was only a little girl," she said. "My parents brought me to Feldemar with them, for my father had a cousin who promised him a position upon a merchant's caravan. He joined it, and was often gone on long journeys. Years he worked for the same merchant and spent more time away than at home. One day I found out my mother had taken a lover in secret, betraying him. The next time he came home, she told him what she had done and that she no longer loved him. He told her that he, too, had found another. He had met her while journeying in Selvan years before. They screamed at each other for hours, until finally I rose from my bed, slipped out my window, and ran from the house. I have not seen them since."

Ebon was frozen in his seat. He could scarcely imagine anything worse. Certainly if that had happened to his parents, he would have cared little—his father had never had love for him, and he had always thought his mother would be happier with another. But in Adara's voice he heard an aching, bone-deep sadness, and he knew at once that she had loved her father and mother both.

"Is that when you left for Dulmun?" he said quietly.

Adara shook her head. "That is another tale. And another cup. We have both told one, now. Drink."

She followed her own advice, raising her goblet and beginning to drink. Ebon drank from his as well, though not half so eagerly as last time. He could feel the drink seeping in at the back of his mind now, like a soundless ringing in his ears, an ecstasy longing to be acted upon. He refilled Adara's cup, and she filled his.

"Xain attacked me tonight," said Ebon. "Well, I say attacked . . . he did not harm me. Though I suppose he did, after all, did he not? But not greatly. Not if there is no small red mark here."

He pointed to his neck, where he vividly remembered Xain's thumb pressing into his jugular. Adara leaned forwards, blinking twice.

"There is not."

"Then he did not harm me greatly," said Ebon. "But he . . . he threatened me. He told me my family sent him a note."

"What kind of note?"

"Am I telling the story?" he said, but he grinned to soften the words. "He said . . . a note about his son. Erin, his name is. His son, not Xain—Xain's name is Xain. He said he would not tell us where she was."

Adara frowned, looking out the window. "Where who was?"

Ebon spread his hands helplessly, almost spilling his goblet. He put it back on the table, reflecting that he probably should not have held it when he gestured so. "I do not know. But he would not tell me the information he seemed to think I desired, that much was certain. And he said that if we harmed Erin, he would destroy us. All of us."

"But you do not have Erin."

Ebon shrugged. "I have told him that—or rather, I told him that tonight. I have just realized that I never told him that before. I likely should have. Not that it would have been a comfort, for he would not have believed me. And it might have sounded suspicious, defending against an accusation that had not yet been leveled."

"But if you do not have Erin, why would your family have sent him a note?"

"That troubles me. Of course, anyone could have put our name on a scrap of paper. Or left it blank, and Xain would have guessed it came from us, for his hatred knows no limits."

She looked at him in silence for a moment, and through the fog of wine he saw her eyes glint with appraisal. "You do not think Mako would have done it? Even without Erin in hand, if he thought he could gain something from provoking Xain . . ."

"The thought had not crossed my mind . . . yet you are not wrong." He scowled into his goblet. "I mean to speak to him tomorrow, for in any case I should tell him what happened with Xain. I will ask him then."

Adara nodded sagely at that, as though it were a great wisdom. Then she held up a finger. "Your last truth was a truth of the past, and I answered in kind. But the truth you have just told me is a truth of the present. So I will answer with my own. Tonight, a boy behind the blue door told me I was a fool for falling in love with you. He said you were a merchant's son, a goldbag, and that you had tricked me into giving you my services without asking for coin in return."

Ebon frowned. "But that . . . that is a lie. I—"

She stopped him with a sharply-raised hand. "I did not ask for your answer. That is the purpose of . . . this." Adara waved a hand in the general direction of the goblets and the bottles. "And besides, I gave him my answer already. I told him he was a wool-headed steer, that I had heard complaints from many of his clients about his woeful lack of expertise in our trade, and that he likely received only half of the usual rate for his work. He broke down weeping and fled through the blue door. I hope he never returns. And now we have each told another truth."

They both took their time now, sipping gingerly at their cups. But they spoke no words, only met each other's eyes. Ebon became aware of her foot atop his under the table. He twitched his leg. She moved her own in response.

"Mayhap we should finish these goblets upon the bed," he suggested.

"Are you certain?" She gave him a coy smile. "We both know wine can trouble your performance."

"That is why I suggest we move quickly," he said, standing from his chair. "Because you have never seen me well and truly drunk, Adara, and so I suggest you make use of me while you may."

She laughed easily and took his proffered hand to rise. Cups forgotten, they undressed each other piece by piece. Again she cared for him, and he for her. Then they took their cups and brought them to the bedside tables, huddling together under the warm fur blanket. But they did nothing else.

"You did not come here to speak to me of Xain," she whispered in his ear. Her hand traced the almost-absent lines of his thin, youthful chest. "He found you on your way. Why did you come to see me again so soon?"

He sighed. "I came to ask a favor, though I have no great wish to do so."

Her hand slid lower. "I am amenable to favors. What do you need?"

"We . . . I mean Kalem and Theren and I . . . and Lilith. Oh, yes. We have befriended Lilith. Not befriended, that is wrong. We are . . . in league with her. I suppose that is a poor way to put it as well. In any case, we need to know where Isra has gone. She is here on the Seat. There must be a trace of her. And you are a lover."

"Of course. I have many lovers I can turn to. Not—" She giggled, and Ebon snorted a bark of laughter. "Not lovers. That is not what I meant. Other lovers. Lovers like me, I mean."

He kissed her deeply. "There are no lovers like you."

"Be silent, flatterer. I will ask them. But I do not understand. Why were you reluctant to ask me this? It is hardly any trouble at all."

That sobered him, for the answer had been troubling him greatly. "At first my mind was taken by Xain and his threats. And then . . . I still fear for your safety, and more so the further you are drawn into all this. If Isra knew of your existence, I do not doubt that she would come for you just to hurt me. And between the amulet and our mindwyrd of Dasko, and now our investigation of Yerrin, I feel as though peril haunts my every step. And I walk well outside of the King's law now, though I hate to do it."

"But you *do* hate to do it," she said. "And that makes the difference. Now you have told me something of the future. I will do the same. One day—not soon, mayhap, but one day—I want you take me back to Feldemar, where I have not returned since I left."

He ran a finger through the hair on her temple. "Of course. I know not when, or how. But I vow that I will do it."

Her eyes shone with tears. "Dear, dear Ebon. Was that a truth? You do not owe me another one."

Ebon kissed her. "I will give you all of my truth, whenever you wish it."

To his shock, the tears broke, trickling down her cheeks. "One day I, too, may be able to do the same. I cannot yet. Not even now." Then she pushed him gently back towards the side table. "Now drink."

THIRTEEN

EBON SCARCELY REMEMBERED STUMBLING HOME LATER THAT NIGHT. He had one vivid picture of vomiting into a gutter in the streets of the city. And the next day, he did not receive punishment for staying out late, so he guessed that he must have returned before curfew. But his next clear memory was waking in his bed with a terrible headache and a stomach that felt ready to spill itself onto the stone floor. He threw on his robe and ran to the privy as quickly as he could, where he spilled his guts again. Then he simply sat there for a while, leaning to the side so that his head was pressed against the frigid stone wall.

A bell rang at last, signaling the end of breakfast and the beginning of the day's classes, and so he stumbled out and down the hall. But he made one quick diversion on his way to Perrin's room. He stepped outside and went to the place in the citadel wall where he knew Mako's secret door stood. There he found the stone of alabaster, and under it placed a scribbled note on a scrap of parchment from his pocket.

Morning's class was slow and painful. Perrin often gave him a disapproving look. Next to him, little Astrea kept leaning away. Ebon guessed he must smell like wine, and mayhap vomit. But he managed to keep some level of composure. After years beneath his father's roof, he was no stranger to drinking. And so his class passed without comment.

The moment the lunch bell rang, he was out of his seat and hurrying through the halls again. He found a bench near the secret door and sat, leaning back against the cool citadel wall. He did not have to wait long before he heard a rustle in the hedges beside him. Mako stepped out of the shrubbery and fixed him with a hard look.

"You are drunk."

"Not anymore," said Ebon, squinting in the sun. "Now I only regret being drunk."

Mako sniffed. "It smells the same. I received your note. What is it?"

Ebon stood from the bench—then swayed for a moment before he could recover himself. He crossed his arms over his chest, a perfect mirror of Mako's stance, and met the man's eyes.

"Did you send a ransom message to Xain?"

Mako blinked. "What in the nine lands do you speak of, boy?"

Ebon sighed, feeling his shoulders droop. Mako was a good liar, mayhap among the best, and so it could be that he only feigned his shock. But the look of surprise on his face was good enough for Ebon, at least in his drunken state. "Never mind. Xain came for me last night, speaking of a ransom note. He thought it came from us."

He was about to sit back down on the bench, but Mako snatched his collar and dragged him to his feet. "What note? What did it say?"

"I did not see it, Mako." Ebon made a halfhearted attempt to remove the bodyguard's hand, but he gave it up almost at once. "Whoever sent it is looking for someone—a woman—and thinks Xain knows where she is. But he said he would never reveal the secret."

Mako's eyes glinted. "Does the woman have a name?"

Ebon frowned. "Not that I know. I told you I did not see the note. Why? Do you know of her?"

A pregnant silence stretched so long that Ebon quite forgot about his headache. But at last Mako released his collar, pushing him ungently away.

"Never you mind, little Ebon. More important than the note itself is Xain's mind concerning it. He says it came from us, and I doubt anything will convince him otherwise. But if the note bore the name of anyone in the family, he would not have come to you; he would have gone straight to the High King."

"I guessed as much myself," said Ebon. "But Xain seemed most certain. Do you think this is something my father could have done?"

Mako frowned. "Once I would have said he would never be so foolish. But he has since proven himself at least that much so. It still does not make sense, though, and for one reason: Shay could never hold Erin without my knowing of it already."

"How, then, do we solve the riddle?" said Ebon. "Someone sent the note, and did so to drive a wedge between us and the dean—or, if they did not intend that, it has happened regardless."

Then Mako's eyes lit, and he snapped his fingers. "They did intend it. It is one more step in their plan. An anonymous ransom note, sent to Xain in the knowledge he would think it was from us. Sent by the one who holds Erin in their clutches."

Ebon frowned, trying to work it out. "Then . . . then Isra sent the note?"

Mako cuffed him on the side of the head, but not, mayhap, as hard as he might have. Still, it made stars dance in Ebon's eyes, and he groaned in pain. "No, little idiot. The ones *behind* Isra. Yerrin. They are the only ones who could keep Isra's hiding place from me this long. If anyone else were hiding her somewhere on the Seat—especially someone like Shay—I should have found her already."

"Do you have a way of finding where Yerrin may be keeping her?" Ebon felt a wave of guilt as he thought of Lilith. Almost he spoke on and told Mako of the conversation with her. But then he thought of Theren's insistence and held his tongue.

"There are many ways of finding out, but I cannot know which will bear fruit," said Mako.

"Then I leave you to it," said Ebon. "Only hurry, because the longer the search continues, the more energetic I think Xain will become, and if it is discovered that Theren holds the amulet of Kekhit, then we are all doomed."

Mako gave him a careful look. "I have spent some thought on that. There is a way to remove the amulet as a threat."

"There is?" said Ebon, frowning. "How?"

"We could let it be known that Theren carries it. The faculty would catch her and imprison her—but you, having revealed the truth, would face no penalty."

Ebon froze. "I . . . but Theren would be . . ."

"My duty does not bind me to protect Theren. Only you."

Rage coursed through Ebon's veins, making him shake where he stood. "You will not do that," said Ebon. "I swear that if you so much as breathe a word of it, to anyone, I will see that you suffer Theren's fate twice over."

Mako cocked his head, and a little smile played at the corner of his mouth. "How very like your father you sound just now. But I take no orders from him, either, little Ebon. My duty countermands your rage, and your threat is shorn of claws or fangs."

"But you do take orders from Halab," said Ebon. He took a step forwards, though he was aware how pathetic it must seem when the bodyguard stood a full head taller. "And if you should betray Theren, I will tell her everything. I will tell her of Matami—yes, mayhap she suspects, and wishes to say nothing, but I will not let the matter lie—and then I will tell her how you made me party to the murder, endangering me before the King's law. And finally, I will return to the Academy and tell Xain all that I have told Halab, and more besides—the truth about Isra, and the amulet, and how you fled just before Isra took his—"

With movements too fast to see, Mako spun him by the shoulder and kicked out the back of his knees. Ebon fell, his head slamming upon the stone bench, where Mako's knobby fingers held him fast. He felt the sharp prick of a dagger on the back of his neck. Even as he gasped in pain, Ebon held perfectly still, terrified to move.

"My duty is to guard you," said Mako. "And to guard Halab. But Halab comes first, always, and you have just threatened to put her in mortal peril. And all for the sake of a girl who is no kin to either of us. Sort out your loyalties, goldshitter."

"They are clear to my mind, if not to yours," said Ebon. "I trust that Halab would emerge from such a mess unscathed. I cannot say the same for you."

He heard a snort behind him, and though he could not see Mako's face, he heard incredulity in the bodyguard's voice. "You would sacrifice yourself for your friend."

"As easy as breathing."

"Be silent. I was not asking—I was seeing a truth for the first time."

The pressure on Ebon's head vanished, as did the dagger's tip behind him.

"Very well, goldshitter. If you wish to live in foolish nobility, it its yours to have. I prefer life, and power, and a purse full of coin."

Slowly Ebon rose. The motion and the impact on the stone had made his headache twice as painful, and he grimaced as he found his feet. But though Mako had thoroughly trounced him, he still felt a small sense of victory.

"Now then. It is of the utmost importance that you find Isra before anyone can discover that Theren holds the amulet."

Mako smirked at him. "I have told you already that I will use my every resource—and I have many of them. We know already that Isra must have used my secret entrance to get into and out of the Academy. I have placed a watch upon it, so that if anyone comes or goes, I will hear of it. Worry not, little Ebon. Your friend will not face the knives of the Mystics. And I will soon remove the problem of Isra from our lives."

He turned and vanished into the hedge. Ebon rubbed at the back of his neck and shuddered as he felt a little drop of blood. It felt very much as though a fox troubled his henhouse, and he had just released a lion to kill the thing. He had little doubt the fox would die—but what might the lion do after?

That night, Theren went to place her mindwyrd on Dasko for the final time. All the afternoon they spent together in the library, she bounced in her armchair. Her leg would not stop twitching back and forth, and a smile played constantly at her lips. Ebon grew irritated after a while, but how could he tell her to stop? She had borne the greatest burden of guilt out of all of them, and she deserved every feeling of elation.

When at last dinner had gone by, she led them out onto the Academy's grounds. Ebon and Kalem kept careful watch for anyone drawing too near as they went. No one did. Theren had little mind for anything or anyone other than Dasko, but Ebon was afraid that fate would play some cruel joke, and that someone would catch them in their crime even as they prepared to stop forever.

But they reached the meeting place without incident, and there they found Dasko waiting for them. He stood as they entered, and while Kalem stood lookout again, Theren went to him.

"After we are done here, you will forget you have seen us, and if asked you will say only that you went out for a walk on the Academy grounds, alone. When I tell you we are finished, you will enter the citadel. You will find Xain, and you will tell him your head is spinning, and that your memory plays tricks on you. You will tell him you saw Isra."

"Yes," said Dasko.

"He should not be so certain," said Ebon quietly. The faculty had to believe that Dasko was under mindwyrd, and therefore his memory needed to be shaky and unclear.

Theren glared at him, but turned back to Dasko after a moment. "You will tell Xain that you think you saw Isra, but you cannot be certain."

"Yes," said Dasko.

Theren released a great heave of breath.

"We are finished."

"Yes." Dasko stepped past her, making for the gap in the hedge. He was almost gone, almost out of sight, when Theren took a half-step after him and called out.

"I am sorry."

"Yes."

Then he was gone.

FOURTEEN

THE NEXT MORNING, EBON FELT HIS HEART IN HIS THROAT AS HE AP-
proached the dining hall. He found Theren within, already sitting with
a plate of food, but Kalem was nowhere to be seen. Theren had great
bags under her eyes, and her fingers were twitching. Ebon wondered if
she had slept at all the night before. Very soon now, they would learn
if the scheme had worked. Quickly he fetched his own food and joined
her at table.

"Have you heard anything?" he said.

"Who do you think I speak to, other than you and Kalem?" said
Theren irritably. She stabbed her spoon into her oatmeal. Ebon smirked
at her words—until he realized how true they were, and how he, too,
had precious little conversation within the Academy unless it was with
his two closest friends.

It seemed an age before Kalem arrived. When he did, they tried to
wave him over to the table, but he only waved back and set off to get
food. Theren gave an angry growl and made to go after him, but Ebon
urged her to remain seated.

"Let us make no more commotion than we must," he said. "Waiting a little while longer will not change the answer."

At last Kalem joined them at the table. The moment his rear touched the bench, Theren seized his arm to drag him close. "What have you heard?" she said. "Has the rumor flown yet?"

"Let go of me," Kalem groused, pulling himself from her reach. "Am I your only source of news? There are hundreds of students in the Academy."

"Pretend, for a moment, that you are indeed the only one," said Ebon. "Now speak, and quickly."

"Yes, the rumor has flown. They are saying that Dasko was found under the influence of mindwyrd, and suspicion has fallen upon Isra, as it should have."

Theren gave a happy cry, slapping her hand down on the table. Ebon quickly tamped down his own smile, leaning in to hiss at her.

"Be silent. We are trying *not* to draw attention, remember?"

Theren grew quiet, but she could not remove the smile from her face. Nor could Ebon blame her for that. She tore through her breakfast and stood at once, grinning down at them.

"I fancy a walk upon the grounds. Do either of you care to join me?"

Ebon waved her off. "We are still hungry. Go and enjoy yourself."

But just then, Lilith appeared behind Theren. Theren turned to leave and ran straight into her, forcing her to take a step back. Lilith winced and seemed for a moment as if she might fall, but Theren gripped her arms and held her upright.

"Lilith! I am sorry. Forgive me."

"It is nothing," said Lilith, turning aside as her dark cheeks grew darker still. "May I sit with you for a moment?"

Theren gave Kalem and Ebon an awkward look. "Of course. I shall see the two of you in the library."

"Actually, I meant the three of you at once," said Lilith.

"Oh! Oh, of course. Here."

Theren held out an arm, helping Lilith as she settled herself down onto the bench. She leaned forwards, prompting Ebon and Kalem to do the same from the other side of the table.

"I have visited my family—at least those who dwell upon the Seat, and to whom I may speak openly."

"And?" said Ebon. "Does anyone know aught of Isra?"

"No one seemed to," said Lilith. "Of course, I could not interrogate everyone. But if she is being held in some place owned by my kin, some would know about it. And I heard no breath of such a thing, nor saw the downcast eyes of a liar. If indeed someone in our clan is working alongside her, that truth is buried deep. Deeper than I can dig, at any rate."

"Blast," said Kalem. He leaned back, crossing his arms with a pout. "I suppose that would have made things too easy, and fate has no wish to make our lives convenient."

"I am sorry," said Lilith. "I wish I had a different answer, but I do not."

Theren cautiously put a hand on her arm. Lilith stiffened in her seat, but did not pull away. "Thank you, Lilith. You have done us a great service, and more than we should have asked of you in the first place. We will not forget it."

Silence ruled for a moment, until Theren gave Ebon and Kalem a hard look. The two of them quickly murmured their assent.

"It was the least I could do, after Oren," said Lilith. "Good day to all of you."

She stood and left the table, joining Nella, who sat a little distance away.

"That is a disappointment," said Theren.

"Indeed," said Kalem. "I suppose we must rely on Mako now. And on Adara, though I wonder if the lover's guild reaches as far as your family."

"Hm? Oh, yes," said Ebon. In truth he had barely heard them, for he was watching Lilith and Nella. The two of them sat at a table with many other students, but separated from them by a little distance. They were more than alone; they were lonely. Each fixed a somber stare upon their breakfast bowls, and when they raised their eyes to speak, their words were clipped and muted.

They looked nothing like the girls who had tormented Ebon when he first arrived. And that should have seemed like a good thing, but there was no joy in his heart. Instead he felt hollow—but likely only half so much as they did, for they had lost Oren.

He glanced at Kalem and Theren, who had kept on talking despite his distraction. What would it be like, he wondered, trying to carry on with one of them dead? He tried to imagine sitting here, eating his porridge with Kalem, or with Theren, and the third seat empty. Would he ever be able to look away from it? Or would it loom between them, vacant and filled with presence at the same time, as though a spirit sat between them, invisible and silent, watching?

Ebon shuddered, and his thoughts returned to Oren. Despite Lilith's words, he believed Mako: Yerrin had to be behind this. He wondered how a family could be so cruel, concocting schemes that led to the death and torture of their own children. The thought of Isra striking again made him quail, and he imagined her crushing the life from one of his friends as her eyes glowed black.

He could not allow it.

"Magestones," he muttered.

Theren and Kalem jumped in their seats, and both looked quickly all about them.

"Be silent, you idiot," growled Theren. "You should know better by now than to say that word aloud in this place."

"Oh, who cares for that anymore?" said Ebon, leaning forwards. "Xain himself told us all that we cannot keep hiding from the truth about magestones and their effects—though no doubt he would roast me if he heard me saying the word, unjust as it might be. I think Lilith may be able to help us find Isra after all—if she can find where the stones are coming from."

Kalem looked to Theren. "He might be right. If someone is helping her, and they are wise, they will not deal with her closely. They may funnel the stones to someone outside the family, and that person may bring them to Isra."

"I know it is a great thing to ask," said Ebon. "But it could help."

Theren's eyes shifted back and forth, and though she said no word of argument, neither did she rise at first. "She has likely taken a great risk already."

"I think she is clever," said Ebon. Theren's nostrils flared, and he held up a hand. "No, do not misunderstand me. I only mean that I am sure she can ask about such things without endangering herself. Lilith is no fool. And if she does attract some attention, it can be no more dangerous than the peril facing the Academy and all who dwell here."

Theren's jaw clenched. "We should not discuss this here. I will ask her to see us in the library this afternoon."

She rose and went to Lilith's side, leaning down to whisper in her ear. After a moment she straightened and left the dining hall. Lilith looked over her shoulder, giving Ebon a small nod.

FIFTEEN

That morning in Perrin's class, Ebon found himself endlessly distracted by thoughts of Lilith and the family Yerrin. He tried to concentrate, shutting his eyes tight to block out the buzzing of his worries.

"What are you thinking about?" Astrea's words held neither judgement nor much interest. She spoke in the same morose inflection he had come to expect from her recently.

"It is . . . well, it is all the business going on about the Academy these days."

"You mean with Isra. I am no fool."

Ebon frowned. He had not wanted to bring that up. He chose not to answer, instead looking down at the rod in his hand. Turning it from wood to stone was now as easy as blinking. But he had not yet managed to turn it the other way, though at times he felt as if he was close. Some other spells he had grown more proficient in—after the night with Matami, he could shift stone much more easily. But "transmuting up," the colloquial term for turning simple matter more complex, still eluded him.

Now he closed his eyes and took a deep breath. He pressed his fingertips to the rod, peering into it with his mind's eye. The room grew brighter with his magelight. He saw the rod, the simple parts that made up its stone, small and solid and clinging together tightly.

He changed them.

Nothing happened.

He *changed* them.

The rod rippled. A fine sweat broke out on Ebon's brow. His teeth pressed so tight together that his chin began to hurt. A little gasp burst from his mouth, unbidden.

He changed them.

Wood rippled along the rod in an instant, and with a *snap* the magelight died in his eyes.

"Yes!" Ebon crowed, leaping from his bench and holding the rod aloft. Then he froze. The whole classroom had fallen silent around him while every student stared. Near the back of the room, Perrin fixed him with a hard look—though he thought he saw some trace of amusement in her eye.

"Well, Ebon?" she said. "Now that you have all of our attention, what do you mean to do with it?"

"Nothing, Instructor," Ebon stammered. He proffered the wand. "Only I have turned my rod to wood at last."

"That is well done. And what are the rest of you staring at? Get back to your lessons."

Around the room, everyone jerked in their seats and turned their eyes back to the spells on the desks before them. Perrin murmured some final words to the student she was with and then lumbered to the front of the room.

"Well, change it back," she said.

Ebon focused, and in a moment the rod rippled back to stone.

"Good. That comes easily to you now, as it should. And the other way again, so that I can see it."

He took a deep breath, closed his eyes, and concentrated. Then he stared at the rod—no, *glared* at it, every muscle in his body tensing, his knuckles white as he gripped it. It did not take quite so long this time, but still it seemed an eternity before wood rippled down along its length, transforming it.

"Very well done indeed," said Perrin. "It took you mayhap a little longer to learn the spell than it should have, but with your skill at shifting stone, I should say you are right on course to finish this class in a year."

Ebon groaned. "I thought this took no time at all! It has not even been two months yet."

"But this is the easiest of your testing spells. You had better get to work on the next, for it will take you far longer to learn."

He slumped back down onto his bench, dejected. Perrin clapped him gently on the shoulder—gently for her, though Ebon thought she might break his collarbone.

"No need to look so crestfallen. You are a wizard just like any other, Ebon, and that is something remarkable, even if you do not have the strength of some Wizard King."

"Of course, Instructor."

"Do you remember your second test?"

He searched his mind and looked away, embarrassed. "I . . . I confess I have forgotten. I remember I have to change a stone's color, but I think that is the third one."

"Right you are," she said. "Now you must learn to turn a flower to ice without changing its shape. There is a vase of them near the front of the room. Go fetch one."

She left him to help another student while he went to do as she commanded. When he returned, he gave Astrea a rueful look. She returned only a dead-eyed stare.

"There is always another lesson to be learned, I suppose," said Ebon.

"Always," murmured Astrea. She reached out for his wooden rod, which now lay on the desk before her. With a flash of her eyes, she turned it stone—and then, with another flash, she turned it back to wood.

Ebon gawked at her. "What . . . how did you do that?"

The corner of her mouth twitched in a smile, but she crushed it at once. "You have seen me do it before."

"But not so quickly. You did it as easily as flipping a coin."

She frowned and looked about. "It came to me easily. I have said that already."

"Of course, I did not mean offense," Ebon said quickly. But he thought, *How could I not have seen the great strides she has taken in her learning? Am I so poor a friend?* "What else can you do? Have you been practicing other spells?"

Rather than draw her out, that seemed only to make her retreat further into her shell. Her shoulders hunched, and she pushed the rod away so that it rolled down the desk. "No. That one just came easily."

Guilt struck him like a blow to the ribs. He had been so preoccupied with Isra and Lilith the last few days, he had almost forgotten Astrea entirely. The girl she had once viewed as an older sister now ran amok, threatening all who studied at the Academy. How must she be suffering? She needed him now more than ever, but he was off spending his evenings with Adara instead.

"I am sorry I have not come to see you as much," he said in a low voice. "There is no excuse, for I know your heart must be greatly troubled."

"Of course it is." To his surprise, Astrea's voice had gone cold and bitter in an instant. "Everyone is troubled, but I think you are all idiots. I do not believe Isra means to hurt anyone, though it seems clear you think she does."

Ebon frowned. He knew Astrea must be angry about this, but her words were ridiculous. "Why do you think she is here, then?"

"Mayhap she has come to clear her name. Lilith cleared hers when everyone thought she was a villain. Why not Isra?"

"Lilith only had to prove her innocence *because* of Isra," said Ebon. "This is not the same thing."

Astrea gave no answer, but only turned away to hide behind her wild, frizzy hair. Ebon sighed, feeling his quickened pulse gradually slow.

"Isra tried to kill me, Astrea. My friends as well. When we saw her in the kitchen, she tried to destroy us. We only escaped through sheer luck."

She turned on him, her wild eyes sparkling in anger. "You do not know that for certain. No one can. None of you are *trying* to help her. Did you even try talking to her? Or did your friend Theren attack her on sight?"

Ebon went still, mouth open. The first thought that came to his mind was that yes, Astrea was right, Theren *had* attacked the moment she saw Isra. But that was only after they had fought Isra in Xain's home, where she had made every effort to kill them all, and had placed Theren under mindwyrd. He could not say so, however. And so he had nothing to say at all.

"I thought so," said Astrea. She turned away and buried her face in her arms where they were crossed upon the desk.

Heavy footsteps preceded Perrin's arrival. "Astrea, would you go and help Dorna with her shifting? She is not yet so proficient as you are."

For a moment Astrea only glared up at the instructor. But then she rose and went towards the back of the room, giving no answer aloud. Perrin settled down onto the bench beside Ebon, making it groan and crackle in protest.

"I know you mean well, Ebon. But you must leave off trying to convince Astrea of Isra's evil. Remember, Isra was like a sister to her."

"Yes, but Isra is also an abomination," said Ebon. "Is it not important that she knows that?"

Perrin sighed. "Is it? Imagine yourself in her shoes. Imagine your kin were dark figures who committed dark deeds, and you were but a child—not nearly a man grown, as you are now. Would it help you to know of the evil things they did in the shadows? Or would you be a happier child in ignorance?"

She fixed him with a look, and Ebon felt as though the ground had vanished beneath him. For of course, he *did* come from a dark family, and he *had* been ignorant of it when he was Astrea's age. He tried to imagine knowing the truth about his father, and Mako, and yes, even Halab, and the things she sometimes ordered Mako to do, when he had seen only eleven years. Would it have made him happier?

He knew at once that it would not.

"But . . . but this is different," he said. "I mean, this is not quite what you describe. Isra's darkness is not hidden. She wears her evil like a cloak for all to see."

"You cannot think of it that way. Astrea certainly does not. Remember, she has grown up with tales of Isra's suffering, knowing of the great injustice done to Isra's parents. You have heard the tale."

Ebon stared at his fingers. The way Isra's parents had been killed still made his gorge rise. "I have."

"None would call that anything but a grave evil. That is the Isra that Astrea knows and has heard about since she was a little girl—an even *littler* girl, I mean. And so, naturally, no matter what she hears of Isra now, she will only see this as another great injustice, something suffered but not deserved."

"But it is not," Ebon said helplessly.

"But she is *eleven,*" said Perrin. "Do not hold her to the same standards you expect of yourself. Astrea is still a child. It is the job of elders—not just parents—to keep children from the burdens of adulthood, and Astrea is overburdened already."

Perrin pushed back and stood, the bench moaning in relief. She strode off towards the next student with a hand raised, leaning down to resume another lesson. And Ebon stared at the wooden rod before him, though he did not see it, or anything else at all.

SIXTEEN

THAT AFTERNOON, LILITH CAME TO THEIR PLACE IN THE LIBRARY. Ebon saw her almost the moment she reached the third floor, for he sat where he could see down the long walkway that led to the stairs. She walked slowly, hesitantly, as though she was afraid of being spotted. When at last she reached them, she stood two paces off, hands fidgeting with each other, looking awkwardly between the three of them.

"Come, sit," said Theren. She stood and waved Lilith into the armchair where she had been sitting and then ran to fetch another.

"Thank you," said Lilith, setting herself carefully down. As Theren found her seat, Lilith looked from Ebon to Kalem. A halfhearted smile stole across her lips. "Never did I think to be sitting and conversing with the three of you here in your own little corner."

Ebon's eyebrows raised. "It is hardly ours."

Lilith waved a hand. "Do not be daft. Nearly everyone in the Academy knows this as your place, and that the three of you may be found here every afternoon."

Kalem's eyes widened, and he looked to Ebon. Ebon was just as surprised to hear they had any sort of reputation in the Academy.

"We will not keep you long," said Theren. "We need to ask you something—something we could not discuss in the dining hall. It has to do with magestones."

Lilith's eyes darkened. She crossed one leg over the other. "What of them? I know very little."

"We think we may use them to find Isra," said Ebon. "You could not find out if anyone in your family is colluding with her. But we know she has magestones. If we can find the movements of the magestones, we may be able to follow them right to her."

That made Lilith think, but after a moment she shrugged. "Mayhap, but again, I know very little. Everyone in the family—and some beyond—know we traffic in them. But details are kept from any who do not need to know them. They are especially kept from any children in the Academy. You three know as well as I do the sort of things they say about magestones in these halls—how evil they are, and how dangerous, and all that sort of talk."

"It is not just 'talk,'" said Kalem, glaring. "They *are* dangerous. Isra should be proof enough of that for you."

Lilith shrugged, and it seemed to Ebon that she barely kept from rolling her eyes. "Yes, yes, of course," she said. "Certainly in untrained hands they can be perilous."

Ebon was about to ask her just what she meant by that, but Theren met his gaze and froze him with a glare. "It seems sensible to me that your family would not let you know of their activities beyond the King's law," she said. "But is there no one who *would* know?"

"A number of people, certainly," said Lilith. "Most would not deign to tell me the hour of the day, but there might be one or two who I can trust well enough to ask for help."

"Not if it will put you in danger," said Theren.

Lilith sighed. "I know I said the same thing when you first approached me, but I have spent much thought upon it since. I decided that I am no safer keeping myself out of things than I would be if I helped you, now that a madwoman runs about the Academy drunk on magestones. At least if my kin should turn on me and kill me, they will do it quicker than the Mystics meant to."

"That is a grim thought," said Ebon. "Though no doubt it is true. How soon will word reach you, once you begin asking questions?"

"I cannot say. I have never done this before. But there is much tumult among my kin just now. You may have heard that some of us were under suspicion for collaborating with the Shades during the attack." She grew grim at that and waited for a long stretch of silence. "It has been all we can do to stave off the High King's justice, and one branch of the family has been cut from the tree. If someone has resumed collaboration with Isra, it can be assumed that they mean also to work with the Shades again, or mayhap with Dulmun. There will be many others who wish to stop such foolishness and punish those responsible. I think answers will come swift."

She stood from her armchair. The rest of them hastened to follow. Theren spoke quickly, holding forth a hand to keep Lilith from leaving. "You could study here, if you wish," she said. "I am not one for reading, myself, but this place is well suited for it. At least Ebon and Kalem lose themselves among pages here for hours on end, so it must be good."

Lilith gave her a little smile that quickly died. "Thank you," she said quietly. "But I will work elsewhere. Mayhap . . . mayhap I will join you all here, one day. I think I might enjoy that." She gave them all a nod and a glance, lingering longest on Theren, and then left.

A long uncomfortable while passed before Lilith came to them again. Ebon spent his days studying hard and his evenings keeping Astrea company. After their argument in Perrin's class, she did not wish to walk with him at first. But he apologized so earnestly that at last she agreed to speak with him in the common room, and then the next day she walked with him upon the grounds the way she used to. And for his part, Ebon did not try to speak with her when she did not wish it. He spent his time with her in silence, answering every time she asked a question, and occasionally telling her of inconsequential nothings. If she ever wished to speak of Isra again, he would be ready, and in the meantime, he would be her friend.

His latest spell gave him an entirely new difficulty. For the first day he spent all his time in class holding the flower, running his fingers along it, trying to see it in his mind's eye. When his magic flowed through him, he could peer into its substance, but he could not understand it. Its parts were many, and wild, and danced all about each other in an endless buzz of activity. Whenever he tried to change them, he could only manage stone. And if he threw the rose down, frustrated, Perrin would appear at his elbow and lecture him.

"You should not become discouraged so easily," she told him. "No type of substance is more complicated than living matter. Even the most powerful alchemists do not truly understand it, for our bodies, and the bodies of all living things, are made of more things than even the wildest rock laced with crystal and gold. You have already mastered wood—that is somewhere in between something alive and something made of stone. It is like our bones. Plants are the next step—they are soft and malleable, like flesh and skin. It will take you time to master them."

That did not seem entirely right to Ebon. He knew he could transmute living flesh down to stone—he had done it when he killed Cyrus, though he still shuddered every time he thought of that day. But turning it to ice was another matter. He could not envision ice in the first place, and so he could not make the switch.

To his surprise, after three days it was Astrea who came to his rescue. When Perrin was across the room teaching a lesson to another student, Astrea gave a quick glance over her shoulder and then leaned close to Ebon. "You should learn to master water before you try to turn the flower."

Ebon blinked. "I do not know what that means."

Astrea's mouth twisted. "Here." She took the little wooden box Ebon had been using to practice shifting stone. Then she dipped her finger into the stone, which shifted around her fingertip like water—and then, suddenly, it *was* water. Ebon gaped.

"How did you . . .?"

"I have been practicing outside of class," she said quickly, and then pushed the box into his hands. "Try to turn the water to ice. It may be difficult at first, but you will begin to learn the ways of water, the

624

parts that make it up. They are far simpler than the parts of the flower. We learned this in our first-year class: it is easier to turn a complex substance into a simple one than the reverse. Learn to turn water to ice, and then you will more easily be able to turn the flower into ice as well."

Though he hardly understood her words, he practiced day in and day out, though he had to hide the little box of water. Perrin caught him with it once and pulled it from his hands, insisting that the right way to learn was to work on the flower itself, and that water to ice was far too complicated. Thereafter he practiced on the box beneath the table, or with cups outside his normal study hours. The ice did not come easily, as Astrea had hinted it might not, but he did feel as though he had begun to understand the liquid.

When at last Lilith came to them, they were in the library. Ebon had given up on the tome he was reading—a mammoth book of Idris's early days before it joined the nine kingdoms, and written so dryly that Ebon thought he might fall asleep—and was now resting by playing with the firestriker Halab had given him. Over and over he pinched the crossbars of the ankh, sending little showers of sparks onto his outstretched fingers and making himself wince. Kalem kept giving him nervous looks, clearly frightened that Ebon would light the whole place on fire.

When they saw Lilith, they stood at once. She gave them all a nod—and then she froze for a moment, staring in surprise. Ebon followed her gaze. The chair Theren had brought for her had remained, for they had not bothered to move it away. Lilith went to it and gingerly took her seat, still smiling as though secretly pleased. Ebon caught a matching smile playing at Theren's lips.

"Good day," said Ebon. "Do you have news?"

"I might," said Lilith. "I wish to take you all with me this evening to see someone."

Ebon tensed. "Do you mean someone in your family?"

"I do. But you need not fear. She is Farah, a cousin of mine, and she is only a bookkeeper, not a warrior."

Kalem's brows furrowed. "A bookkeeper? I think I should rather meet a warrior, for they might know something more useful than one locked in a library all day."

"Not those sorts of books," said Ebon. "She means an accountant. Someone who tracks the flow of coin and goods."

"Still, what good will that do us?" said Kalem.

Theren, too, looked mystified, but Ebon and Lilith gave an exasperated sigh in unison. That made them both start, and they looked at each other uncomfortably for a moment before Lilith finally explained.

"We are not foolish enough to keep track of our magestone dealings in public record. But that does not mean we keep no record at all. That would be madness. Farah is well-placed in the family's dealings, and manages the hidden accounts that we show to no one. She would know if someone has been moving magestones."

"And she wishes to see us?" said Ebon. "Why? How can we trust her?"

"She did not ask to see you, specifically, of course," said Lilith. "But when she heard that I had been poking about after records of magestones, she came to me. I told her my purpose—without revealing too much—and she said she wished to meet those I was working with."

"You did not answer my second question."

Lilith frowned. "I was getting to it. I admit that it is a risk. Farah is my kin, but we have never been especially close. I know, though, that she is an honest sort. I have heard some whispers in the past that she disapproves of our operations outside of the King's law."

"But why must we go?" said Kalem. "Why can you not meet with her yourself?"

Theren's glare deepened, and she spoke up quickly. "Because Lilith wanted nothing to do with this in the first place, Kalem. She went searching on our behalf, and now returns with just the sort of thing we hoped she would discover. This is the least we can do, if we hope to catch Isra."

Ebon nodded. "She is right, Kalem. Besides, it is not Lilith who saw Isra. We know more about the girl's dealings. Mayhap our knowledge, combined with the knowledge of this Farah, will be enough to track her down."

Lilith smiled at him in gratitude. "That was precisely my thought. And if it calms your fears, Kalem, know that I will be there with you. If there is any danger, it will be mine as well."

Kalem frowned into his lap, but he remained silent. Ebon looked to Lilith again. "Very well. When can we see her?"

"Tonight," said Lilith. "In fact, we must. She was adamant. Plans too long in the making are more apt to be discovered, and she would rather not be found colluding with Academy students on the subject of magestones. We will go in disguise as well."

That made Ebon afraid for reasons he could not quite identify, and he looked to Theren. "Tonight? That does not give us much time to prepare."

Theren smiled. "Lilith can help us with that. She and I are old hands at this sort of thing."

Just then the Academy's bell rang, signaling the end of the day's studies. "And there is our signal," said Lilith. "What say you? Will you come with me?"

Kalem still looked doubtful, but Ebon squared his shoulders. "We will. Lead on."

They rose and made their way to the library stairs, and then down to the ground floor. As they made for the hallways, they all nodded cordially at Instructor Jia, who gave them a wan smile. She had returned only that day after being tended to by healers. Isra had not had her long under the mindwyrd, and so the aftereffects had been mild. Dasko would be a far longer time in healing, or so it was said.

Lilith took them out upon the streets of the city, and then to an inn a little ways away. It was a small place, tucked down a side street Ebon had often passed but never noticed, and no sign hung over the door. The common room seemed little used, and the innkeeper gave Lilith barely a glance as the group entered, passed through, and ascended the stairs. Kalem looked all about them with curiosity, and Ebon knew he was doing the same. Theren, however, acted as though nothing were out of the ordinary. Clearly she had been here before.

"What is this place?" said Ebon.

Lilith stopped before a door and produced a key from her sleeve to open it. "Why, this is my room."

"Your room?" said Ebon. "Why do you pay for a room here when you live in the Academy?"

Her eyes widened, and she glanced at Theren, who shrugged. "I keep it under rent for just such a purpose as this. Do you not have a room for yourself?"

Ebon flushed, for though he had never thought of such a thing, now it seemed plainly obvious that he should have. "I do not."

Lilith shook her head and led them inside. The room contained nothing remarkable—only a low, wide bed and some other plain furniture. She went to an armoire and threw it open. Within, Ebon saw many dresses and other suits of clothes of every color and make.

"Take what you will," said Lilith. "None have seen use in some time, but they are all laundered."

"I am afraid I am a little too small," said Kalem.

"True, but there is not much we can do about that," said Lilith. "I shall give you the shortest pants I have, and you can tuck them into those high boots you wear."

Theren, meanwhile, went to the rack and shucked off her Academy robes at once. Kalem and Lilith both went beet-red and turned away.

"Theren!" said Kalem.

"Your embarrassment is no concern of mine," said Theren. "And Lilith, you need not act as though this is anything new to you."

"Oh, just get it over with," said Lilith.

Ebon could not help but smirk at Kalem, and even at Lilith. "I may not be a commoner, exactly, but the two of you are too easily flustered, I think. They are only underclothes." He joined Theren in disrobing and looked over the clothes hanging before them. Several thin wooden rods ran from one side of the cabinet to the other, and on these had been hung a variety of outfits. He chose a pair of pants of dark, muted blue, and a light grey tunic under a vest of black. Theren took a dress of yellow that reminded him of his family's colors, much to his surprise.

"Could you . . .?" she muttered, turning. Ebon reached for the strings that tied it at her neck, but they were intricately laced at the back, and his fingers fumbled over them.

"Oh, let me," said Lilith. Theren hesitated only a moment before turning to let her take them. Ebon saw how Lilith's cheeks darkened still further, and she kept her eyes fixed rigidly on the strings. He could not help a secret grin.

"Mayhap . . . I think I shall wait outside," said Kalem, who sounded ready to die from embarrassment.

"Come off it," said Ebon. "Live like the rest of us, royal son, and get yourself dressed. We do not have all night."

His face was a portrait in discomfort, but Kalem did it—though he made sure to select his entire outfit before he disrobed, and did it as quickly as possible. Lilith acted much the same, and if anything, she seemed more uncomfortable than the boy was. Theren and Ebon stood back, looking at each other with raised eyebrows and little shakes of the head. But while Ebon kept his eyes studiously averted, respecting the others' discomfort, he noticed Theren's eyes continued to wander, and she swallowed hard and often.

SEVENTEEN

ONCE THE BUSINESS WAS DONE, LILITH RUSHED THEM OUT OF THE room. Their Academy robes they left strewn on the bed. "They will not be disturbed, and we will return for them," said Lilith.

They went out upon the streets. Lilith had given them all cloaks of brown—plain, but lined with fur. They drew their hoods up around their faces, and now Ebon noticed that they no longer drew the half-curious looks that Academy students did when walking about. At last he thought he saw the reason for the deception.

"No one remarks upon us," he said.

"And why should they?" said Lilith. "We could be anyone—merchants, cobblers, even beggars."

Theren snorted. "You are blinded by your own coin purse if you think any beggar wears clothes this fine," she said. "But they draw the eye less readily, mayhap, than the Academy's black."

Lilith took them north and west and made no attempt to set their trail to winding—she was not, it seemed, afraid of being followed. Ebon began to get a familiar sense, as though he had been in this part of the city before but could not place it. Then it came to him: they were very near to the inn where he had once met an agent of his family's and delivered the uniform of a palace guard. For a heart-stopping moment, he was afraid that they made for the same inn. But then he spotted the street where it lay, and Lilith passed it by. He let out a sigh of relief.

Theren glanced at him. "What is it?"

He shook his head. "Nothing."

At last Lilith stopped them before the black-painted door of a tavern. Here she paused for a moment, looking in every direction from beneath her hood.

"We will enter and move straight to the back," she said. "There is a private room there where Farah is waiting. Do not glance up or meet the eye of anyone else. The fewer who remark upon our arrival, the better."

Ebon heard the sounds of conversation and laughter from within. "It sounds a fair crowd inside. I doubt we need worry of drawing much attention."

"Let us hope you are right," said Lilith, and she pushed the door open.

They all studied their feet as they pressed into the bustling interior. Lilith led the way between the tables, and Ebon was only partially aware of the patrons they passed. Indeed, his guess seemed to be right—as far as he could tell, no one gave them so much as a first glance. Soon they had passed through the crowd and into a short hallway ending in a door. Lilith opened it without knocking and drew them all inside.

At last Ebon looked up and threw back his hood. He found himself in a small room, with every wall showing its bare wood and exposed beams above that looked to form the underside of the building's second floor. They gave the ceiling a little extra height, so that it felt less cramped than it should have considering its small size. Lanterns burned in the corners, filling the place with a warm light. There was also a window in the back wall, and though the curtains were drawn across it, he could feel a slight breeze that told him it was cracked open.

In the middle of the room was a table, and at the table was a woman. She looked similar enough to Lilith—not only the same rich, dark skin, but the pronounced cheekbones and the haughty, discerning brow. But she showed more fat than Lilith, and also she filled out her rich green dress more. She seemed less severe, and more motherly, though that was belied by the sharp glint in her eyes as she took them all in.

"Good eve, I suppose. Sit. Or do not, for it is no matter to me. There is wine."

Ebon bowed. "Well met, Lady—"

"No, no, no," said the woman, clucking her tongue. "You know my name, knew it before you came here. I know yours as well—especially yours." She gave Theren a sharp nod. "So we need not introduce ourselves, for who knows what ears may be lurking? And who knows how little time we have? Sit and take wine if you will, but let us get on with this as quickly as we may."

Kalem gave Ebon a wary look. Ebon shrugged and dragged out a chair to sit across the table from Farah. Kalem sat beside him and Theren to his left, while Lilith took the chair on Theren's other side. Farah leaned forwards and opened her mouth to speak—but paused as Theren reached for the bottle of wine. Theren noticed, and poured the wine far more slowly than she might have. It made Lilith smirk into her cup, while Farah's lips pursed in annoyance. When her cup was full to the brim, Theren turned.

"Do you care for a cup, Ebon?"

"I do," said Ebon. He snatched the bottle from her hand. "Though I will pour it myself. And you may carry on with what you meant to say, Fa—er, my lady."

Farah raised an eyebrow. "A quick study. That is good. I have little to say, but much to hear. Tell me what you have seen of the girl Isra, and what you have not seen but have heard about. The more you know, the better. The less you guess at, the better."

Ebon was about to speak when Theren took her first sip. She slurped at the cup and smacked her lips when she was done. "Mm. You goldbags drink the finest stuff."

At the word *goldbag*, Farah's nostrils flared. Kalem's glared deepened. "Enough, Theren. We all know of your disdain for the wealthy, and if our host did not know it before, she knows it now. Consider your point made."

Theren's eyes widened, and she pressed a hand to her breast. "Me? I am wounded. And besides, our host has been most clear that she wishes for no names to be used—including mine. Please, I ask that you honor her wishes."

"My apologies for my companion," Ebon interjected. "We will tell you what we know and be as thorough as ever we can."

He proceeded to tell her everything they knew of Isra—that is, the "official" version of what they knew of Isra. Of course he told her nothing about Xain's home, nor about the amulet of Kekhit. But he told her about their fight in the kitchens, painting it so that it sounded like Theren managed to catch Isra by surprise.

When he said that, Farah's eyes drew to pinholes. "Very fortunate," she said. It sounded as though she meant to say more, but she did not.

"Fortunate indeed," said Ebon, meeting her eye without flinching. Then he went on to tell her all the rumors that had floated about the Academy since—including a rumor that the faculty were investigating to see if anyone were helping Isra from within. Lilith seemed surprised at that. Of course, that was not truly a rumor, but something they had learned from Dasko.

When they had finished, Farah pursed her lips and steepled her hands. She sat that way for a little while, reaching for her wine cup every so often, her eyes studying Ebon's. Ebon tried not to look uncomfortable, though he was not quite sure he succeeded.

"Our family's particular trade goods have been on the move recently," said Farah, speaking suddenly and from nowhere, in a tone that suggested she was answering a question, though no one had asked. "They were long held in reserve, for no one wished to traffic them after the attack. Now they move again, though slowly, nowhere near so brazenly as they once did."

Theren leaned forwards. "And where are the mage—"

"*No!*" barked Farah, scowling at her. "No, we do not discuss them. They are our family's particular trade goods. That is all they are to me, and to you, or this conversation is over."

"We understand," said Ebon. He fixed Theren with a look. "And we will take that into consideration as we ask our questions."

He could see the visible effort she exerted to keep from rolling her eyes. "And where are your family's particular trade goods being moved to?"

"Here. There. It is never wise for them to move always from one place to another, for that makes them easy to find. Predictable. But someone is moving them, and some are disappearing. Those, I would imagine, are what you seek."

"Where are they disappearing *to?*" said Lilith. "I would not imagine they could simply vanish without repercussion."

"Not unless those who mete out punishment for such things know where they are going, and thus restrain their hand," said Farah. "That, I think, is what goes on here. I spotted it, of course. I saw that the numbers did not add up, that one hundred packets would leave and only ninety-five packets would arrive. But when I told them—the ones who mete out punishment for such things—they thanked me for my diligent work. And then they told me to return to it. And no punishment was meted out."

"Yet you do not know where," said Ebon.

"I do not know where," said Farah. "But that is not the right question. There are five questions, only five and always five, and one leads to the next."

"Where," said Lilith. "When, how, why, and who?"

Farah sniffed.

"Who, then?" said Theren.

"A name," said Farah. "The only name, tonight. A name banished by the family, and then reclaimed. A name that renounced another name to regain favor in the eyes of the King's law. A name that has used that favor to violate the King's law again, thereby putting our clan in danger once more, as though he did not learn the lesson the first time. Gregor."

Lilith sucked in a sharp breath. But to Ebon, the name meant nothing, and looking at Kalem and Theren, he saw they knew nothing more than he did.

"What is it?" said Ebon. "Who is Gregor?"

"She will tell you later, for we draw near the end," said Farah.

"But wait," said Lilith. "I thought he was banished, along with—"

"Only one name, tonight," said Farah. "Only one name, now, that matters."

"Very well, but in any case, he was exiled."

"He returned and threw himself upon the High King's mercy. He told her . . . things. Things that seemed of great value in the coming war. Did he tell her the truth? How can we know, unless we, too, know the truth? But it earned him forgiveness. And now, when I see one hundred become ninety-five, I see also the name of Gregor."

Abruptly she pushed her chair back and stood. "Thank you for your words, and for the meanings behind them. I hope you have found my words as valuable. But now we must leave, and I doubt we shall ever speak again."

Ebon found his feet at once. "Thank you. We will breathe no word of this."

"If I thought you would, I would not have come," said Farah. She looked hard at Lilith for a moment. "You did right to come to me. Make sure you never do it again, or both our lives may be forfeit."

She swept past them with the billowing of a green cloak and left them looking at each other around the table. Theren noisily swallowed the last of her cup and moved to pour another.

EIGHTEEN

Lɪʟɪᴛʜ ʟᴇᴅ ᴛʜᴇᴍ ʙᴀᴄᴋ ᴛᴏ ᴛʜᴇ sᴛʀᴇᴇᴛ ᴀɴᴅ ᴛʜᴇɴ sᴏᴜᴛʜᴇᴀsᴛ ᴛᴏᴡᴀʀᴅs the inn where she kept her room. The moons had risen high now, and the sunlight had almost faded in the west. They walked in a mostly silver light that reflected into their eyes from the snow. They were all silent, staring at the ground, except for Kalem, who looked at the stars. After a time, Ebon raised his head.

"Thank you, Lilith, for helping us."

She shrugged, not meeting his gaze. "It is the least I could do, I suppose. What do you plan to do now, after what you have learned?"

"I have friends who can find Gregor. They were already looking for Isra, but she must be in one of the darker holes upon the Seat. Let us hope Gregor is not so well concealed."

"He most likely is," said Lilith. "Gregor is a man of both means and wit—not the clever kind, but the cunning, ruthless kind, the kind that leaves corpses in its wake. I think he will be much harder to find than some student exiled from the Academy."

"I also have some people of means and wit," said Ebon, a little annoyed.

"Mayhap, but you do not have Gregor." Lilith shivered, though they were tramping doggedly through the snow and their blood was up. "I have heard only a very few tales of him, and yet they paint him as more of a monster than a man. Once he accompanied a caravan through the Spineridge. They were waylaid there by a storm, a freak summer snow that forced them to take refuge in a little town. Somehow, during their stay, the townsfolk discovered the magestones they were transporting. Some curious child poked their nose into the wrong wagon. When word got about, Gregor spoke to the townspeople, promising to pay them to keep their silence. The townsfolk agreed readily enough, for the Yerrin party already paid well for their food and lodging. So for a week the caravan remained in the town. The guards slept in the town's inn and drank in the town's tavern. They likely bedded some of the townsfolk.

"At last the storm abated. Gregor brought all the folk into the town hall to receive their pay. He waited until they had all arrived, for he had promised them all a gold weight, even the children. First he gave them their money. Then he locked the front door and burned the hall to the ground. He and his men stood watch to make sure no one escaped through the windows. When at last the flames died out, he made his soldiers search through the corpses to recover every bit of gold he had paid out."

Ebon did not remember when they all stopped walking, but at some point they had, and now they stood in a little circle watching Lilith in horrified silence. Now he felt sick, as though he might retch into the gutter, and he knew the chill in his bones was not from the cold air.

"That is monstrous," said Kalem. "It must be false. Surely the High King would not stand for such an act."

"What makes you think word of it ever reached her ears?" said Theren, spitting the words. "Do you think her courtiers let such troubling rumors invade the royal court? It is easier for the merchants and the royals both if they do not discuss such things. And after all, it sounds as if there were no witnesses."

"But that is not the conduct of the wealthy—it is the atrocity of a monster." Kalem sounded indignant, but he could find no sympathy in Theren's face, nor even any understanding. "You cannot think all merchants are that way. Certainly not the royalty."

"Oh, you think the royalty are exempt?" said Theren. "You know how Isra became an orphan as well as I do."

"But that . . . that is *one* king," said Kalem.

"You are no fool, Kalem, and only a fool thinks any goldbag in Underrealm has entirely clean hands."

Kalem opened his mouth to object again. Ebon spoke first. "Let it be, Kalem."

Kalem gaped at him, astonished. "You cannot say you agree with her. I know your family and Lilith's have reputations, but—"

"I said let it be." Ebon could not meet Theren's eyes, for he could almost feel the fury glowing off her. And when he once would have agreed with Kalem, that her hatred of the rich and the powerful was misguided at best and born of jealousy at the worst, now he could not put fire in such a belief.

"It grows late," said Lilith, rubbing her arms. "We should move on."

They took her advice, pressing on through the light snow that had begun to fall. Theren was the next to speak, after a long silence. The white-hot anger had gone from her voice, but Ebon still heard it smoldering—quelled for the moment, but not gone.

"Why is she waiting? She has more artifacts. We know she took them from Xain's house. Why delay?"

They kept walking in silence, for no one had an answer.

The next morning, Ebon sent a letter to Adara, asking her to search the lovers' guild for news of Gregor. He was not sure what to expect—after all, he had already asked her to seek for Isra, and that had returned nothing yet. But the very next afternoon he received a letter in response, asking him to come and see her at once in her home. It was Sunday, and he had no other demands upon his time, so he fetched his winter cloak and set out into the city. The snow that had been falling for the last few weeks had subsided at last, and though the air was still sharp with winter's chill, the sky above was a deep and pure blue. It stood in stark contrast to the snowy roofs of the city's buildings, and the sun leaped bright from every surface, so that Ebon had to shield his eyes.

Adara answered his knock almost at once and led him upstairs after he stamped his boots free from snow. She had set out a small tray of figs, cheese, and bread, and at first they ate in silence. But soon Adara leaned back in her chair, dabbing at her lips with a napkin.

"I have found your man," she said. "Yet I hesitate to tell you where."

Ebon blinked. "Why? What is wrong?"

She studied him for a moment, lips twitching towards a frown. "Why do you seek Gregor at all?"

"He is the one moving Yerrin's magestones. He is our best chance to find Isra and capture her."

"I have heard many stories of this man, Ebon. He is a fell and grim warrior, prone not only to violence, but to cruelty when he kills. The family Yerrin is known for ruthlessness, but his reputation sets him above even the rest of them."

Ebon shivered. "Well, I mean to set Mako upon him, and so I suppose we will find out who is the more terrible."

Adara shook her head. "Do not pretend that you will be free from danger in this. Why should I put you in harm's way? You are already Isra's enemy. Must you add Gregor's name to the list of those who wish harm upon you?"

That forced a grim laugh from his gut. He spread his hands. "When that list is so long, what is one more entry?"

She sighed. "Very well. He has been seen on the western end of the Seat, going in and out of the sewers that may be found there. Some whisper that the family Yerrin conducts its smuggling through some hidden port, though no one knows exactly where it may be found."

"That is good," said Ebon. "Mako knows the sewers well, and doubtless he will be able to find their hiding place. I am surprised you learned this so quickly when your connections have still been unable to find Isra, wherever she may be lurking."

Adara frowned. "I, too, have been troubled by that. Gregor has all the backing of Yerrin at his disposal, as well as their considerable coin. I cannot think how Isra has concealed herself better than he has, especially after she was spotted within the Academy itself. That should have sent word rippling through the streets, like a stone dropped into a calm lake."

Ebon thought of what Mako had said in the abandoned manor of the family Skard. "Ripples, you say. You are not the first to describe them to me. Yet she moves like a ghost, a specter already dead, and leaves no trace. And, too, she withholds her hand, though we do not know why. It has been a week since she revealed herself—more than enough time, it seems to me, to try again."

"There must be other things afoot, and mayhap Gregor has something to do with them," said Adara. "Wondering about it may do little good. Be grateful instead, and act before it is too late."

"Too much later, you mean," said Ebon. "It is already too late for Oren and Credell, and poor little Vali."

Adara nodded solemnly, and they let the names of the dead linger in silence for a while. Then she stood. "Would you have wine? It is a touch early, but when has that stopped either of us?"

He grinned. "Do you mean to get me drunk again? I am not sure I can survive another night like the last."

She laughed. "No, not that. My head still twinges with pain at that memory." She paused for a moment to look at him. "But I thank you for joining me in that. I know it was an odd request, and had its consequences, yet I do not regret it."

"Nor I," said Ebon. She returned to the table, and he took his goblet. "And I will never forget the words we spoke—nor the promises I made to you."

"I should hope not. I very much intend to hold you to them."

His smile felt somewhat forced. "Yet near the end—the end of the drinking, anyway—I remember you told me something. Something about truth, and how it came hard to you even then."

Her smile grew careful. "Did I? Mayhap my thoughts grew muddled."

The words came easily enough, but he heard the warning behind them. *Let it be. Please.* "Mayhap it was my wits that were addled, not yours," he said lightly. "You told me so many things, after all, that I had never heard before. I was honored to learn them—and would do so again, if you ever wished it."

Recognition dawned in her eyes, an acknowledgement of his unspoken invitation. "Thank you," she whispered. And then she sighed, and straightened, and the moment passed them both by. She ran a finger along the rim of her mug. "I understand you have spent much time in Lilith's company of late. More to the point, I understand Theren has, as well."

Ebon's eyebrows shot up. "And who have you heard that from?"

"The guild carries many whispers, and I do not listen only for the ones you ask me to."

He sighed. "I admit Lilith still makes me uneasy. Theren seems to trust her utterly—well, better than I do, at any rate. But I do not know how much of that stems from good sense, and how much stems from her feelings."

"She still loves Lilith, then?"

"I asked her that when Lilith was imprisoned, and she said she did not know. Yet her every action tells me that she does. It is not only the trust she places in Lilith. It is the little looks, the smiles and the half-hidden gestures. The way her hand moves towards Lilith's, as though aching to hold her. I can scarcely believe the change in her demeanor, considering how she despised Lilith when I first met her."

"Often love springs forth unbidden," said Adara. "When it does, it is rarely governed by sense."

Ebon smiled. "Do you speak of Theren and Lilith, or of us?"

She kicked him beneath the table, but gently. "I think we are more sensible about things than many. Nor do I doubt Theren's judgement in this. She is a passionate woman, governed more by her heart than by her head, yet she has wit enough to know evil from good. She placed her trust in you quickly, though she had more reason than most to despise a merchant boy. If you are grateful for that trust, return it now. After all, is Lilith not proving herself helpful?"

He frowned. "Helpful enough, I suppose. Yet it is all in the service of catching Isra, whom she hates. And I have bitter memories of her treatment when I first arrived at the Academy."

"Children may be cruel without also being evil."

Ebon mock-glared at her. "She is older than I am. Do you call me a child?"

She returned his frown, though her nose twitched as though she longed to smile. "You *are* newly come to manhood, Ebon, though you had little opportunity to ever be a child in truth."

That brought to mind a question he had never thought to ask, and he cocked his head. "How old are you?"

She smiled. "Do you see wrinkles in my skin? Have you come to regret our tryst? Do you love me only for my beauty? That cannot be, for who could call me more beautiful than any of the fine ladies you must have met throughout your life?"

He stood suddenly, and she yelped as he lifted her from her chair, holding her across his chest while she laced her fingers behind his neck. "I would call you beautiful a thousand times, though the Mystics put me beneath their knives and command me to renounce your grace. But you have not answered my question. Tell me how many summers you have seen, or I may have to draw the truth from you by every means at my disposal."

"Do your worst," she purred.

NINETEEN

THEY SPENT THE DAY DOING LITTLE OF CONSEQUENCE, AND IT WAS EVE-
ning before Ebon left her at last. The sun had almost gone down, and
he hurried through torchlight. He had time enough before curfew to
return, but he had no wish to remain in the cold a moment longer than
necessary.

The streets seemed curiously crowded for a Sunday, when many
merchants and crafters chose not to work. The Seat had become flooded with new arrivals recently. There was some vague rumors that the
High King soon meant to make her next move in the war.

Ebon soon tired of struggling through crowds and having to halt
for every passing carriage or wagon of goods. He broke away from the
press, aiming for the yawning mouth of an alley that seemed to head
the right direction. But when he reached the end, it turned north rather than south. He grumbled and increased his pace. Soon he saw the
alley's end ahead, leading to another street packed even tighter than the
last one.

He pushed into the crowds with a sigh, forcing his way across and into another side street. Here at last the way was clear, and it even headed in the right direction for a time. Ebon let loose a breath of relief and slowed.

A boot scuffed on the street behind him. He turned. The street was empty.

His heart began to race, but he scowled and fought the queasy feeling in his stomach. Xain, it seemed, was not done stalking him. He had a chilling thought: had the dean seen him leave Adara's house? But he dismissed that fear at once. No matter what Xain suspected him of, Ebon did not fear the dean would threaten Adara.

Hunching his shoulders, he pushed on through the cold. The side street led him south, but it kept turning the wrong direction as it did so. Soon he had neared the Seat's western edge, where the buildings showed more signs of damage from the fighting and the flames, and there were fewer people about. And then he came upon a street where there were no other passers-by at all.

Three quick footsteps sounded, shockingly close. But when he turned, the street remained empty.

He put his hands to his hips. "Enough of this. I can hear you, Xain, scuttling after me like some pickpocket. If you have received another note, I still know nothing about it. But come out and ask me anyway, if that is your wish, so that we may both go about our evenings in peace."

The person who stepped from the shadows was not Xain.

Ebon froze. He could see no face beneath the green hood, but the person who faced him was a behemoth—nearly as large as Perrin, and clad in mail under their cloak.

There came a *hiss* of drawn steel. A broadsword glinted in the moonlight. Ebon could not drag his gaze from its shine. Thick, heavy boots crunched in the snow, forming holes as deep as Ebon's whole leg.

"I . . . who . . ." Ebon took a step back, almost stumbling in a drift behind him.

The figure reached up to drag its hood back. It was a man, his skin almost as dark as Lilith's, and within his sallet his grey eyes reeked of death. His fist looked big enough to envelop and crush Ebon's skull. Where Ebon had often been awed by the thickness and vigor of Mako's muscular arms, this man now made Mako seem a spindly little boy,

644

a bookish scholar tucked in some dark basement away from the sun, scrawny as Kalem was. Over the chain on the man's chest was a tabard of black leather, and his fists shone with plate.

All this Ebon saw in the scant seconds it took the giant to approach him. They were only two lengthy paces apart now. But then he stopped.

"You have been seeking me." The voice from his barrel-wide chest thrummed in Ebon's lungs, deeper and stronger than Isra's voice even with the strength of magestones. And at the words, knowledge struck Ebon like a mace to the forehead.

"G-Gregor," he stammered. "You are Gregor."

There came no answer, but the man's eyes flashed. And Ebon recalled the story that Lilith had told him. In his mind he saw the hall filled with people, burning, all of them screaming. His throat seized up. He tried to take a backwards step, but his feet would not move.

"Why has your family taken an interest in me?" said Gregor. He took one step forwards, and Ebon wilted.

"I am not . . . I did not . . ."

Gregor shook his head, a single sharp jerk. "No lies. As long as your words interest me, you will live. As long as I hear the truth within them, you will live. You die tonight, but it is up to you how long you have before then."

Like a striking serpent, a hand the size of a boulder shot forth to seize Ebon's robes and haul him up off the ground. Ebon lost control of his bladder, and tears stung his eyes as piss dripped to the snow below him.

"I sought nothing," he whimpered, voice shattering to a sob. "I swear it." *A lie,* he screamed in his mind. *A lie means death.* But he could not help it. His thoughts betrayed him, for he knew now that he would die, here on this street and unseen by anyone.

But then behind Gregor, from the other side of the street, a second shadow detached itself from the darkness between two buildings. Ebon heard a soft *snik-snik,* and saw the silhouette of two daggers. *Mako,* he thought with relief.

He let his gaze linger too long. Gregor caught the look and turned on the spot, faster than such a man should have been able to move. Mako leaped, black cloak fluttering behind him. Gregor caught the daggers on his sword and shoved back with a rumbling grunt. Mako danced, shifting from one foot to the next before striking again. Again Gregor parried the blow, swinging the sword in a wide arc and slicing down with it—but Mako was already gone.

They took a step back, taking each other's measure in the darkness. Ebon wanted to step forwards, to do something, but he knew not what. He was a child in this battle of giants. What good would mists be, if he must draw within Gregor's reach to use them? And he could not help Mako by shifting stone.

Then a hand seized his shoulder to drag him back. Had he not already voided himself, he would surely have soiled his clothes again. "Come, boy," said a woman's voice. "You are of little use here."

He looked back and saw that she was clad just like Mako, and had her hair trimmed close to her scalp. Two steps he took beside her, away from Gregor, before he stopped. "We cannot leave Mako," he gasped.

"That is not Mako," said the woman. "Come."

Ebon peered closer in the darkness—and then he saw that it was the truth. The man standing before Gregor was tall enough, but not quite as broad, and his eyes glinted blue beneath his hood, instead of dark like Mako's.

Now the assassin's knives swept forwards like serpents, striking here, there, and here again in the space of a blink. But though Gregor held no shield, he used his plated arm to block one of the blows, while the others glanced from his chain.

And then his fist swung, faster than when he had seized Ebon, and crushed the Drayden man's face.

The assassin stopped moving all at once, as though a force holding him up had suddenly vanished. He held his feet for a heartbeat, though his nose was pulp and his jaw hung slack on tendons, displaying shattered teeth.

Gregor seized his head, fingers wrapping to the back of the man's skull. With the grip for leverage, he pulled the assassin onto his broadsword. Four handbreadths of blood-covered steel thrust out of the man's spine, and his legs went limp. Gregor withdrew the sword and smashed the front of his helmet into the man's face. Then he brought the man's head down with a *crunch* against his armored knee.

The Drayden man slumped to the snow, a corpse three times over.

Even as she pulled Ebon away, the woman threw a dagger with a hiss of rage. It struck Gregor in his back, but the chain shirt rebuffed the blade, which fell impotent to the snow. Gregor threw a look over his shoulder—but then Ebon was around the corner of a building and out of sight, still being dragged by the woman.

Now that he no longer beheld the giant, Ebon found he could move again, and he ran, faster even than his rescuer. After they had passed a few streets, she yanked him to face her. He looked into her hard face, wincing at the scar that ran from her upper lip through one ruined eye.

"Back to the Academy," she growled. "Stop for nothing. Look at nothing. Speak to no one. And if you value your life, do not leave again for any reason—not unless Mako is with you."

Ebon wanted to stay a moment longer, to ask her one more question. But even as he hesitated, she seized a shoulder and whirled him around. Then she planted a boot on his back and kicked hard. Ebon went sprawling to the ground, sliding along in the slush with a cry.

"*Leave,* you piss-stained steer!"

He left, scrambling to his feet and barely remaining upright. Once he started running he could not stop, but could only move his legs faster and faster. Soon he was winded, and his chest screamed at him in pain, but he only sprinted harder. He reached the main road that crossed the island east to west and pressed heedless through the people there. Many of them he struck in his flight, but he did not stop for their angry shouts.

Before long he reached the Academy's front door. Two paces away from it he stopped and doubled over to catch his breath, crying out as that sent lances of pain into his ribs. He looked back down the street. Gregor was nowhere to be seen, nor was any other threat.

The tears that had threatened now spilled forth, and bile leaped to the back of his throat. His mind burned with the image of the Drayden man falling to the ground, of the nauseating way his bones had bent the wrong direction. Falling to hands and knees he vomited. All the wine he had drunk with Adara and all the food he had eaten for supper spilled into the virgin snow.

It was a while before he could force himself to stand. His body groaned in protest when he did, and his legs were clay beneath him. But as soon as he could, he stumbled towards the front door. From the position of the moons in the sky, he had only just made it before curfew, and so he wasted no time before entering.

There in the front hall, to his great surprise, he found Theren and Kalem waiting for him. But if they saw the state of him, they did not remark upon it—and once he saw their pale faces and wide, frightened eyes, he knew that his encounter upon the streets was not the only thing that had gone terribly wrong.

"What is it?" he said. "What happened?"

"War is declared," said Theren. "Tomorrow, the armies of the High King march on Dulmun."

TWENTY

For a moment, Ebon could only stand and stare at the news. But then the pain in his side redoubled, and he stumbled.

"Here now," said Kalem, as he and Theren came forwards to take Ebon's arms. "Ebon, what is . . ." Then his nose curled. "Have you . . .?"

Ebon blinked back fresh tears. "I need a bath. Please. Help me."

They cringed, but they helped him, taking an arm each and escorting him to the bathing room, which fortunately was not far away. There he disrobed while Kalem went to fetch him water. Theren took his soiled robes and put them in a soapy basin to soak.

"What happened?" said Kalem, once Ebon had settled into the water and his friends sat to either side of him.

"Gregor found me." Ebon shuddered at the memory of the man's soulless grey eyes. "Somehow he heard that we were seeking him, and he found me out in the streets."

Theren scowled. "How did you defeat him?"

"I did not," said Ebon. He stopped and closed his eyes, for his voice was dangerously close to breaking. "I did not," he said again when he could speak. "I ran. And I only escaped because two of Mako's fighters came to my rescue."

"Did they . . . is Gregor . . .?" Theren glanced over her shoulder to make sure no one could overhear, but the bathing room was empty.

"They did not kill him," said Ebon. "He killed one of them instead, and mayhap has killed the other by now, for she turned back after she got me to safety. Gregor did not simply kill. He took the man apart. I have never seen anything so terrifying. It was worse than watching Mako put Matami to the question."

"How did he find you?" said Kalem. "What will you do now?"

"I do not know," said Ebon. "The woman who saved me warned me not to leave the Academy again, not for anything, unless it was at Mako's direction and under his guard."

"That seems wise," said Kalem, shivering. Theren glared and remained silent.

"Enough talk of that," said Ebon. "I do not wish to think of it any longer. Now tell me of your news. When did Enalyn declare war?"

They told him all that they had learned so far. That day, while Ebon was with Adara, the High King Enalyn had proclaimed that her host would go to make war upon Dulmun. What fleets she had managed to assemble would set sail from the eastern docks, while a great force of soldiers even now marched east across Feldemar to attack Dulmun's northern lands.

"What of the south?" said Ebon. If the High King's armies meant to march on Dulmun's southern reaches as well, that would take them near to Idris.

"Nothing was said of it," said Kalem. "She may be hesitant to march her armies along the north side of the Spineridge. Or mayhap she means to attack there and is keeping the plan secret, at least for now."

"That brings to mind my chief question," said Theren. "Why would she proclaim any of this? Would it not be better to strike in secret, taking Dulmun by surprise?"

Ebon had thought the same thing, but Kalem shook his head at once. "She does not hope to vanquish Dulmun by means of war. That could be costly in both lives and coin, and we are in the midst of winter. But for months now, ever since the attack, all the nine kingdoms have become mired by indecision. Only three kingdoms have openly pledged their support to the High King: Selvan, the land from which Enalyn herself came; Hedgemond, my homeland; and Calentin, whose people are so few and so far from the war that their support makes little difference either way, even if they had not sent only a token of their strength, which they have. The other kingdoms hem and haw, neither breaking their oaths nor rushing to fulfill them. By declaring this war openly and putting forth an assault, the High King means to prompt the other kingdoms to action. Now their oaths compel them to lend aid."

"And if they do not?" said Theren.

"They will be branded traitors," said Kalem. "When the war is over, and Enalyn has vanquished Dulmun, she will then turn her armies upon the kingdoms that refused to aid her. She will cast their kings down and purge their families—or exile them, if she feels merciful."

"That is a small mercy," said Theren. "But are we even certain she *will* vanquish Dulmun?"

"Of that there is no doubt," said Kalem. "Dorsea will now pledge its full strength; their king is already fearful of Enalyn's wrath, for she nearly executed him after the battle of Wellmont. And Dorsea alone would be enough. Even if the other kingdoms stay their hands—which I doubt—Enalyn will have enough backing to raze Dulmun. She knows it, and Dulmun knows it, and so she hopes they will surrender."

Theren raised her eyebrows. "You seem very certain of all this."

Kalem shrugged. "I have been taught the ways of such things since birth. Where common children learn a trade and merchant children learn to manage coin, royal children are taught the ways of power and war."

"Then Dulmun will surrender, and this war will soon end," said Theren.

"I do not think so," said Kalem sadly. "Bodil of the family Valgun is their king, and she is a warlike woman. Also, she knows that if she surrenders, her life and the lives of her close kin will be forfeit. Therefore she will fight as long as she can, if only to stave off the inevitable. I think that is another part of Enalyn's plan—she hopes to amass as much strength of arms as she can, hoping that either Bodil will surrender, or that one of her kin will rebel against her, depose her from the throne, and surrender in her place. But there shall be much bloodshed before that happens, either way."

They were all silent for a moment. Ebon thought he could almost imagine it: the great legions of soldiers marching across Feldemar, on their way to fight and die upon the soil of Dulmun, and the fleets of ships that would tomorrow speed across the Great Bay to do battle with their foe's mighty fleets. It was a chilling vision, and one not easily dismissed.

"What does the Academy mean to do?" said Ebon.

They both stared at him. "What do you mean?" said Theren. "The Academy means to do nothing, unless it is to keep training its students in the ways of magic. It is a school, not a barracks."

Ebon gaped. "So we are meant to just carry on with our studies? Going to class each day as though a war is not being waged beyond these walls? The Seat is in the middle of this fight—and I do not mean only because the High King dwells here. If Dulmun launches a fresh attack, we will be the first thing in their way."

Again Kalem shook his head. "The Seat is not in danger. It is heavily fortified, and there are many other places along the Great Bay where Dulmun would have an easier time of it. When they attacked it, it was only after luring the High King's armies away with subterfuge. Even then they struck quickly, hoping to win through surprise rather than strength of arms. Now they have lost surprise and will make their war in other ways, as long as they may." He gave a little smile. "If you hoped to escape your lessons for a time, I am afraid to tell you that Perrin will still expect you in your place every morning for your studies."

They sat in silence. It was strange: outwardly, nothing looked to have changed. Yet Ebon felt as though everything was different in some ethereal manner he could not see with his waking eyes. The objects in the room seemed fresh and newly seen, though of course he had beheld them many times before.

"War has come," he said.

"War has been here awhile," said Theren. "Now comes justice."

"I am not so sure," said Kalem. "But now, I think, must come sleep, or we shall all regret it in the morning."

Ebon sat up in the water. "Please, stay. I will be quick, but . . . after tonight, I do not want to be alone."

Kalem lowered his gaze. "Of course. I did not think of that. Forgive me."

And so they stayed, until the water was tepid and Ebon lifted himself out of it, and they all went to bed. But the moment they parted ways at the dormitories, Ebon felt a chill steal over him, and no matter how long he sat before the hearth in the common room, he could not dispel it. He went to bed at last a long time later, drifting off with his thoughts haunted by a pair of soulless grey eyes.

TWENTY-ONE

A HUSH HAD SETTLED OVER THE ACADEMY THE NEXT DAY. EBON FELT IT from the moment he woke, the way no one spoke as they dressed themselves and left the dormitory. The threat of war had hung in the air ever since the attack on the Seat; now the threat was over, for war had arrived. He did not know what they all expected to be different, for they all knew the fighting would take place far away. But he could feel the expectation, in himself as well as the other students, that *something* must happen.

They muddled through their morning classes, but by the time his lesson finished, Ebon felt the need for fresh air. He pushed against the crowds of students headed for the dining hall and went outside instead.

His steps carried him to the grounds where the alchemy students practiced their spells, and where he had once seen them stop arrows in mid-flight. A rack of weapons, all of them either dull or padded, stood against the wall. He ran his fingers over them, lifting them a bit only to let them *clank* against the rack again. How long would it be before he studied here, learning his own spells of defense? How long until he could defend himself if he landed in a fight, as he had the night before?

He heard only a single footstep on the grass behind him. Then a hand snatched his neck and whirled him around, slamming him into the granite wall of the citadel. It clutched at his throat, stifling his yelp.

"Why must you be such an abominable idiot?" growled Mako.

Ebon slapped futilely at the man's forearm. His breath came in rasps, and only just deep enough to keep stars from dancing in his vision. It was a moment before Mako released him, and Ebon fell gasping to one knee.

"If you die, I will soon follow," said Mako. "I may have no wish to see you dead, but I value my own skin more than yours. Halab is not bloodthirsty—never that—but should I fail to look after you, she will not tolerate my failure. You and I may both thank the sky that I posted guards over you."

"I am thankful," Ebon said, the words rasping from his throat. "And your gratitude seems clear as well." He got slowly to his feet.

Mako pushed him again—harder this time. "Do not be flip with me, boy. Why have you been poking about the family Yerrin? You should leave that to those who are practiced in such things, and will not draw the eye of murderers."

"We think they may lead us to Isra." Ebon paused, unsure of how to proceed. Theren had been adamant that Mako not know they were working with Lilith.

"That is another thing," said Mako. "You should not be bandying about with that Yerrin girl. They are not to be trusted, not even in the smallest of matters. Certainly not in the search for Isra."

Ebon's heart sank. Mako knew, then. It had been foolish to imagine he would not learn of it, when he seemed to know everything Ebon did. But if that knowledge now lay bare, then so be it. "You forget what happened to her," said Ebon. "Isra took control of Lilith and caused her to be thrown to the Mystics' knives. We may have no common ground with the family Yerrin as a whole, but we do with Lilith."

"You can trust no word from a Yerrin, nor can you believe they will keep your confidence. What happens if she tells someone of the amulet your little friend carries?"

That stopped him. Ebon stared at his feet. "We have not told her of the amulet."

To his surprise, Mako grinned. "Well, now. It seems you are not such a fool, little Ebon—not such a complete one, anyway."

"Mighty praise, I suppose," said Ebon. "Now, do you wish to know what we have learned, or not?"

Quickly he laid it out—what Farah had said of Gregor, and what Adara had told him about where the bodyguard had been spotted. Mako's eyes lit when he heard that. "That is something valuable indeed. Sky above, Ebon. You have fumbled your way through this dance of shadows better than I would have given you credit for. Though one of my men died in the process, and that I will not quickly forget."

Ebon lowered his eyes. "Nor will I. I will be forever grateful to his memory. Did . . . did he have a family?"

At first Mako only glared. But after looking into Ebon's eyes for a long moment, the glare softened. "It is wiser not to ask such things. But at the same time, I cannot fault you, for that is the sort of question that Halab might ask."

Ebon tried very hard not to let that compliment, small as it was, go to his head. "Very well. Now that we know where Gregor lurks, we must go after him."

"*We* shall do nothing of the sort—but *I* will, when the time is right."

"That is not good enough," said Ebon. "Every turn of the hourglass is another chance for Isra to strike the Academy, leaving more corpses in her wake."

"Do not worry yourself," said Mako. "Since last she appeared, my people have been watching every way into the citadel, the passages known and unknown. They will see her if she tries to enter."

"By the time they do, and send word to you, it might already be too late. You must search for Gregor now, without delay."

He wondered if the words sounded as hollow as they felt. They must have, for Mako looked skywards, as though trying to choose the best way to countermand the shrill yapping of an infant. But after a moment he met Ebon's gaze and shrugged.

"Very well. I will begin at once, and search for him on the west end of the Seat."

"Mayhap we should come with you," said Ebon. "Theren and her amulet are your only hope against Isra if you should come upon her."

"No," said Mako, and there was no arguing against his tone. "That would place you in danger, and that is the very thing my duties compel me to prevent."

"But what if Isra is with him, and the strength of magestones behind her?"

Mako was silent for a long moment, gazing into Ebon's eyes. Ebon felt a chill steal across him. Isra had had the strength of magestones the last time Mako had fought her, yet she could not touch the man. Ebon tried not to cringe.

At last the bodyguard spoke. "Look after yourself, and do not fear for my ability to do the same. And do not put yourself in peril chasing after secrets all on your own."

"I will not," Ebon mumbled.

"Good. I will find Gregor, and likely Isra in the same place. The Seat may be the High King's in name, but in another sense it belongs to those like me. I know its dark holes and the bodies within them, the gutters and the blood running through them. But while I busy myself with Gregor, you can make yourself useful as well: keep your eyes and ears open when you are with that Yerrin girl, and see what else you can learn of their deeds upon the Seat."

Ebon frowned. "That is not why we are working with her."

Mako grinned. "Good little Drayden boys can always do more than one thing at once."

He slipped into a nearby hedge and vanished.

Ebon heard nothing from Mako the rest of that day. It troubled him, though he chided himself, for he should not have expected Mako to find anything so soon. When he woke the next day he strode out upon the Academy grounds, even turning his steps towards the secret door in hopes that Mako might find him to report back. But the grounds were empty. Ebon left a scribbled note beneath the alabaster—*Have you found him?*—and went to class.

At his desk, he fiddled with the flower for a time, trying to see the parts of it with his mind's eye. But his thoughts were much occupied with Mako. What if the bodyguard had found Gregor already? What if something had happened to him? Ebon wished he had been able to come along. Even danger would be better than not knowing anything of what transpired beneath the streets. He pictured Mako down in the sewers, just like the night he had killed Matami. Only now the bodyguard was beset on all sides by Yerrin swords, green cloaks covering mail as they pressed him back, back into the darkness.

That made him shudder—and, too, it turned his thoughts to the night before last when he had been attacked. And he thought of the training grounds outside where advanced transmuters practiced their spells.

Ebon turned in his seat and raised his hand until Perrin came towards the front of the room to find him. "What is it?"

"I have been wondering," said Ebon. "Once, when I first came here, I saw other alchem—that is, transmuters, casting spells of defense. I saw a girl stop an arrow in mid-flight, turning it to a puff of smoke."

"Yes?" said Perrin. "What of it?"

"Could I not practice such magic? I have made little progress with my flower, and as you have said before, I might stretch my mind by turning it towards other things."

Perrin chuckled. "Other things, yes, but nothing so advanced. You are a long way off, I am afraid, from such magic. Also, you saw those spells ages ago. Why the sudden interest now?"

"No reason," Ebon said quickly. "Only . . . I have just learned to counter another wizard's magic. I thought I might learn to defend myself against other things, like a fighter with a sword."

Her brows rose. "Have you found yourself pitted against fighters and swords?"

Ebon blanched but tried to appear calm. "Not at all. It is just that, with the attack on the Seat, and now with war in Feldemar . . . it seems the sort of thing that might be useful. I am sure I am not the only one who feels the war hanging over us all."

The classroom had gone curiously quiet. When he looked about, Ebon saw that all the students had stopped in their work and were watching the two of them. Perrin looked at them all, and her stern countenance softened.

"I cannot blame you all for thinking such thoughts," she said. "It

658

is only natural that you do. But I urge you not to worry yourselves overmuch. Every member of the faculty here values your safety above all else, and we will let no harm befall you." Her look returned to Ebon. "That said, I will not hold it against you for wishing to learn spells that can keep you safe. But in ordinary circumstances, you would not even begin to learn them until your third year—if then. Know that the required spells are many, and they must be learned one after the other, and they are not easy."

"Have any of my spells been easy thus far?" said Ebon.

At that she smiled. "I suppose they have not seemed so. Very well. First learn to turn a stone to ice, and then to water. Once you master that, do the same with metal, the more difficult cousin of stone. Then learn to turn it faster and faster. In time you may be able to stop a sword even as it hacks at you. Anyone coming at you with a blade will only find themselves wet. But I say again, you will not learn these spells quickly."

"I know it, Instructor." Ebon bowed his head. "And thank you."

She trundled off towards the back of the room again, and Ebon returned to his flower. Astrea sat beside him, as she usually did. Her eyes were fixed on her own rose, and he wondered if she had paid any attention at all to what had been said. But he did not wonder long, for she spoke after a moment.

"I wonder if I could do it," she muttered. "Turn stone to water, I mean."

Ebon shrugged. "She said it was an advanced third-year trick. It would be a great surprise if you could."

Her gaze rose to the classroom and then turned to him. "I do not mean *now*, of course. I mean if—mayhap I could learn it—oh, never mind."

Ebon frowned, for her tone struck him as odd. Then he saw the flower in her hands. It was ice—crystal clear and beginning to drip on the table.

"Astrea," he said, eyes wide.

She frowned and looked down at her hands. With a cry she leaped up, away from her bench. The rose fell from her fingers and shattered on the surface of the desk.

Thundering footsteps sounded as Perrin ran towards them. "What is it?" she demanded. "What is wrong?" Then she saw the shards of ice on the table, already beginning to melt into droplets. "Astrea, did you turn the flower?"

"I . . . I suppose so," said Astrea. "I was not paying attention. I did not mean to."

"But this is no sorrowful news," said Perrin, beaming. "You are progressing fast—far faster than is normal or expected. Well done. Now fetch yourself another and see if you can do it again."

She put a firm hand on Astrea's shoulder, giving it a little squeeze before she left them again. But Astrea did not go to fetch another flower. She only resumed her seat, splaying her hands out on the desk before her, and Ebon saw that her fingers were shaking.

"Are you all right?" he asked.

"How could I do that without meaning to?" she whispered. "I did not even notice my eyes fill with light."

"It might only have taken you a moment," he said, putting a confidence in his words that he did not feel. "I know the first time I used my magic—the first time I *really* did, anyway, other than the testing spell—it came upon me all in a rush, and I hardly knew what was happening."

"Yes," she said, still in a terrified whisper. "Yes, that must be it. It must have happened in a flash."

She met his look, trying desperately to smile. But Ebon saw the dread within her and felt it mirrored in his own heart.

TWENTY-TWO

THAT DAY, EBON FELT A CREEPING SUSPICION COME ACROSS HIM. KALEM and Theren could see it in him when they sat together in the library, but no matter how often they asked, he only shook his head and held his tongue.

Before he went to dinner, he wrote a letter and placed it beneath the alabaster—where he saw that his note from that morning still waited, untouched by Mako. He took the morning's note away and left the new one, which read:

> *I fear the threat has entered the Academy again. There are strange happenings afoot. Come and see me as quickly as you may.*

He returned to the dormitories and sat long in the common room, brooding as he stared into the fire. Astrea did not act like one under mindwyrd—not exactly. But something strange was happening to her. And the last time Ebon had seen Academy students and faculty acting odd, it had been because of Isra, and then the killing had begun. He could not let that happen again.

The only thing that reassured him was that he did not believe Isra would harm Astrea. Everyone she had controlled before had been used to terrible purpose, and most of them had died in the end. But if Isra did not hold the girl in bond of mindwyrd, then what *was* going on?

Mako did not see him that evening, but Ebon thought he would hear from the bodyguard the next day. It passed, however, without word. And then most of the next day went by, and still there was no sign. Ebon spent most of the day scowling, and his mood was not improved when he went out upon the grounds at lunch and found that his letter was gone from beneath the alabaster. So Mako *had* received his message, and had not come to see him or left any message in reply. That made him irritable during their time in the library. At last Theren snapped her book shut and glared at him.

"Ebon, you are simply insufferable. I never thought I would say this, but if you cannot study in peace, go and take yourself somewhere else so that we may."

Ebon knew he was in the wrong, and so he apologized and promised to be less grim. But that only meant he sat in silence while they read and did not answer when spoken to, and so it was hardly better. The moment the day's last bell rang out, Theren leaped up and threw her book on the table between the three of them.

"I am taking you out," she said. "Let us go to some tavern, where wine and supper may ease your mood."

"We cannot go," said Ebon, aghast. "What if Gregor and his men are lurking outside the citadel?"

"Let him try to hurt you, or any of us," snapped Theren. "I have a mighty need to use my magic upon someone who deserves it in all its strength."

So he let her drag him and Kalem out into the streets, where they made their way to Leven's tavern close by and soon had lost themselves in a bottle of wine. And just as Theren had promised, Ebon soon found his mood improved tremendously. After a time he held his cup aloft, thrusting it towards Theren as if in toast.

"To my good friend Theren," he proclaimed, "who knows me for a happy drunk. And darkness below take Mako, anyway."

"Darkness below," said Theren, raising her own cup.

"That is a bit strong, I fear," said Kalem, joining them in the toast. "But I will drink regardless, for good wine makes up for dark words."

"It depends on the darkness of the words, as well as the strength of the wine," said Mako.

Ebon nearly spit out his drink. The bodyguard had appeared at the head of their table as if by magic. He pushed Ebon hard to make room and then took a seat on the bench. Across the table, Kalem and Theren were staring—and after a moment, Ebon realized why. Mako had a nasty bruise under his left eye, and the black sleeves that now covered his arms had wet spots. They could have been water, Ebon supposed, but a voice in his mind whispered *blood* instead.

"Have you met your match in some barroom brawl, Mako?" said Theren. "That seems no great surprise—you have always been boastful, and such pride often precedes downfall."

"Shut your flapping lips before I gut you," growled Mako. "I am in no mood for jests tonight, especially after you have disobeyed my order and left the Academy."

Theren almost replied, but Ebon silenced her with a stern look. He leaned close and lowered his voice. "What has happened? Have you found . . . him?"

"I have," said Mako.

"And is that what happened to . . . to you?" said Kalem, pointing to his face.

Mako sneered. "No, goldshitter. It is only that I prefer a very particular sort of lover and have just come from his company."

Kalem blinked. Ebon frowned. "You said you were in no mood for jests. Nor am I. I left you word but have not heard from you."

"I gave you a way to reach me when you had information of value," said Mako, glaring at him. "That does not mean I come to heel at your call. I obey Halab's orders, not yours."

"What have you come for, then?" said Ebon. "What happened when you—"

Mako's hand darted forwards like a snake, closing over Ebon's mouth and lower jaw. "Be. Silent. That is what I have come here to tell you, but you have yammered on like starved puppies since the moment I sat."

"Unhand him," said Theren. A glow sprang into her eyes. "Or I could make you, if you wish."

The bodyguard glared at her for a long moment, and Ebon's pulse thundered in his ears. Then Mako's fingers loosened, and his hand withdrew.

"I found Gregor, indeed," said Mako, in a voice as calm as if nothing had happened. "In the bowels of the sewers, just where your lover said he would be. But Isra is there, too, and we . . ." He scowled. "With her strength added to Gregor's, I need magic to vanquish her. Your magic." He pointed at Theren.

"You need us?" said Theren, arching an eyebrow. "Have the High King declare a holiday, for the impossible has come to pass. Mako has asked for help."

Mako slammed a fist down on the table, so hard that their cups, which were thankfully empty, overturned. "I lost two soldiers tonight," he snarled. "The black-eyed sow killed them. So spare me your smug tone. You have the amulet, and can be useful, so useful I will make you."

Theren looked around to ensure no one was close enough to overhear. "I have no wish to use the amulet openly," she said. "We know the faculty are hunting for it. What if we are discovered?"

"We will not be," said Mako. "I mean to set the constables and Mystics upon Yerrin, but not until we have done our business first. Until that happens, Yerrin wishes the presence of the King's law even less than we do."

Theren dropped her gaze to her fidgeting fingers. "Very well," she said with a sigh. "Only let us be quick about it."

Ebon nodded. "Very well. Mako, when can we move?"

"Not we," said Mako. "Or at least, not you."

That made them stop. "What do you mean?" said Ebon. "I am not staying behind."

"You certainly are, you damned fool," said Mako. "How many times must I tell you that my duty compels me to protect you?"

"I will not let my friends—or you—go into danger while I sit here in safety," said Ebon firmly.

Theren shook her head. "I can look after myself well enough. You will be no great help in a fight, Ebon—forgive me, but it is true."

"I know it, and I know, too, that you are most capable. I will not go because the two of you need me. I will go because it is *my* duty, or at least I call it so—and what else is duty, after all?"

"The same goes for me," said Kalem. "And you cannot tell *me* to stay behind if you bring Ebon, for I might actually be able to help you. Meaning no offense, of course, Ebon."

Ebon waved it off. "It is decided, then. When do we mean to move?"

Mako glared at him—but he must have seen the resolve in Ebon's eyes, for after a moment he sighed. "You will obey my every order, no matter what," he said. "If I tell you to run, you will run, even if you abandon me. If I tell you to hide, you will hide."

"I swear it," said Ebon. "When?"

"Now."

At that they balked, even Ebon. "Now?" he said. "This moment?"

"Yes," said Mako. "I have only just come from a fight with Yerrin soldiers. They will redress their defenses—they may even move their activities to some other dark hole now that we know where they are. If it is not tonight, it will be never. Are you ready?"

Ebon swallowed hard. "We are."

"Very well," said Mako, standing from the table. "Do not make me regret this. Let us go."

TWENTY-THREE

Mako led them down the street and off to a side alley until they encountered a tall gutter where a large gap led into the sewers below. He dropped to the floor and slithered into the opening like a serpent. Ebon felt a moment's trepidation, but Theren followed the bodyguard without pause, and after a moment he did the same. He dropped two paces to the floor and landed easily enough, and then he reached up beside Theren to help Kalem, for the boy's legs did not reach nearly so far into the darkness as theirs.

Though they were beneath the streets, the fading light of day still did much to illuminate the way before them, for it came through the drain holes and bounced from the light grey stones that formed the walls. Thus they were able to make their way quickly to the west where Gregor had been spotted. Ebon was grateful that this part of the sewers had platforms running along the water. The last time he had gone beneath the streets, there had been no such walkway, and so he and Mako had slogged through the muck. Now he still had to smell it, but he did not have to feel it sinking into his boots.

"How do you know where you are going?" said Kalem.

Mako did not even glance at the boy. "The sewers form a vast and intricate labyrinth—that is how Yerrin could be so busy within them without my knowing it. They are even more vast than the streets of the city itself, for there are many levels built atop one another, and each level stretches as far as the island. But there are different areas, and any who spend much time down here learn to stay close to their own territory. We rule all the levels to the northeast. The Yerrins have claimed the second level to the west. And I know we are going west because of the compasses."

He stopped at an intersection, and Ebon and his friends skidded to a halt behind him. He went to the right-hand passage and stood tall, placing one hand on the top of the tunnel. There Ebon saw an *N* had been drawn. He looked across the way and saw an *S* drawn over the opposite tunnel, and just above him was an *E*. The way they were going, a *W* had been scratched. They were dug shallow in the stone, but unmistakable all the same, if one knew to look for them.

"Clever," said Theren, sounding impressed despite herself.

"That is one thing you should always keep in mind, children," said Mako. "Scholars and those who write books often hide knowledge in pretty phrases and dust-covered parchment, for they wish to have it all to themselves and thus earn the worship of common folk. But those who build, and make, and do—they make knowledge as plain as they can and put it in plain sight, hoping to help others who come after. The artisans who built these sewers wanted them to be useful, not mysterious."

"Yet they hold a mystery nonetheless and conceal many dark deeds besides," said Ebon, thinking of Matami.

Mako shrugged, his wide smile growing cruel. "Well, they may have intended one thing for their creation—but they bequeathed it to us, and we have made of it what we wish. Enough philosophy for now. We are moving too slow."

He stalked onwards, and they had to run to keep up with him. Mako did not relax his pace, no matter the distance they covered, and not even when he stopped them and led them down an iron ladder built into the wall. Theren seemed to have no difficulty matching his strides, but soon Ebon and Kalem began to flag, wheezing and huffing as they stumbled along in the now-dark passage.

"Hurry yourselves, goldshitters," said Mako, growling. "Yerrin may have defeated me once, but they will not rest easy this night and have likely already sent for more guards. The longer we take to reach them, the harder the fight we will find waiting for us."

"I am doing my best," said Kalem, who was panting even more heavily than Ebon. "Only I am not used to such exertion."

Theren and Mako snorted in unison and then gave each other an uneasy look before pressing onwards.

It was not so long after that before Mako stopped in his tracks, holding up a hand for the rest of them to do the same. Ebon pressed himself against the wall, as did Kalem, but Theren stepped up beside Mako, body tense, eyes peering eagerly into the darkness.

"Silence your huffing and heaving," Mako whispered. "I am trying to listen."

"Do you want me to stop breathing entirely?" said Kalem between gasps.

Mako glared at him, and Kalem's mouth snapped shut. He and Ebon did their best to still their heaving chests.

At long last Mako stepped forwards again, the tension vanishing from his posture. "It is one of mine. We need not fear—at least not yet." He led them on, and in a moment a shadow detached itself from the wall and came towards them.

"The wagon has pressed on," said a voice from the shadow. Ebon thought it sounded familiar for some reason. He peered closer. Beneath the hood was a woman, the same woman he had encountered on the streets who had saved him from Gregor. She glared at him with her one good eye for a long moment and then frowned at Mako.

"What is he doing here?"

"Do not worry about them," growled Mako. "Only tell me where the wagon has gone."

"West, the same way they were headed," said the woman. "I think the witch left it at some point, but I did not wish to draw too close to make sure."

"Of course not. Well done," said Mako. "Now return to the surface.

668

I will doubtless send you a message soon, and you must act quickly when I do."

"I can stay," she said fiercely. "Let me fight." But suddenly her body gave a shudder, and she slumped against the wall. Ebon saw that one of her hands was pressed tight to her side, and he saw a dark liquid staining her fingers.

"No more battles for you tonight," said Mako. "Do as I say, or I will give you a bruise to go with that scratch."

"Then at least we would match," she said, and grunted out a pained laugh. She held forth a hand, and she and Mako seized wrists before drawing each other close for a one-armed embrace. Before she could go, Ebon took a step forwards.

"Thank you," he said. "For saving me. The other night, I mean."

She glared at him. "A fool's gratitude is of little worth."

Then she stepped into the shadows and vanished.

"Who is she?" said Ebon. "Her name, I mean. I did not get to thank her before—or I did not think of it."

"She is Talib," said Mako, "and has been my pupil for many years. She has saved your skin more times than you know—certainly more than the one time you saw her doing it. Come. We are not far now."

He crept forwards now. Ebon and Kalem no longer had to struggle to keep up. But while his footsteps were quiet as a shadow, and Theren, too, moved muffled and silent, Ebon's and Kalem's steps now seemed horribly loud, and Ebon winced every time his toes caught upon a crack in the stone with a scuffling noise. Mako glared back at him once or twice, and though he said nothing, Ebon's face burned with embarrassment each time.

But then all such thoughts were banished, for ahead they saw the orange glow of a torch, and far off, Ebon could hear the creaking of wagon wheels, a sound as familiar to him as his own breath. Too, there were tramping boots, and they moved quickly, not at some easy walking pace. Whoever accompanied the wagon, they knew they were pursued and were making good time to escape. But not good enough, clearly, for the noise grew louder.

Soon they saw the wagon: it rolled along with a deep rumble, pulled by two Yerrin guards in green cloaks, holding spars that stuck out from the front of it. Three more guards accompanied the cart, walking behind and to either side of it. Two of these held torches, lighting the way forwards.

"Fools," muttered Mako, after he had let them draw a bit ahead and out of sight. "Those torches may show them where they are going, but also serve to make the procession easy to see. And they will not spy us until we are almost upon them."

"What is in that wagon?" said Kalem, eyes wide with fright. "Are they moving magestones?"

"No," said Mako. "Only supplies to feed and care for the crew of a ship that will soon launch from their hidden dock. But upon that ship there *are* magestones, and Yerrin means to send them out across the nine lands. That is not our chief worry tonight, though. Tonight we hunt for Gregor, and mayhap Isra."

"I am more worried about Isra than Gregor," said Ebon.

"Yet you are not in command here, and should not even have come," said Mako, glaring at him. "Therefore your worries are of no consequence."

"Well, what do we mean to do now?" said Theren. "I did not see Gregor among the guards—unless the tales of his size and strength are only exaggeration. And Isra certainly was not there."

"Yet we should stop that wagon all the same," said Mako. "Anything to disrupt the family Yerrin and their criminal activities is a gift to the High King."

Kalem nodded solemnly, clearly missing the joke; Ebon rolled his eyes at the thought of Mako risking life and limb to uphold the King's law. But Mako was right in any case—to reach Gregor and Isra, they would have to get through the wagon guards. "What do you mean to do?"

Mako grinned at Theren. "Do you wish to show off that magic of yours, girl?"

Theren smiled in return.

In a few heartbeats Mako outlined the plan, and they ran forwards again in the darkness. When they came to the next corner, Ebon and Kalem stopped while Mako and Theren pressed on. They saw a flash of light as Theren's eyes glowed, for she did not bother to hide it with the amulet, and then she burst around the corner beside Mako.

The cart flipped over, slamming to the stone floor upside-down, its contents spilling all over. The wheels flew off, each one striking a guard to either side. They fell with pained cries, their torches falling into the passing flow of water and waste. The guards floundered in the sudden darkness, reaching for blades at their waists—but too slow. Theren struck again, and invisible bands of force picked them up, slamming them into the wall. Their faces were pressed into the stone so that they could not see behind them.

"Boys," growled Mako.

Ebon and Kalem ran forwards at once. The light in the tunnel increased as they reached for their magic, and then together they pressed their fingers to the stone. It flowed out and around the guards, wrapping about their wrists and ankles in bands so that they were held in place. In a moment it was done, and all three of the children released their hold on their magic. The tunnel was plunged into darkness again. They waited for their eyes to adjust to the small shafts of moonslight from above.

"We should destroy their goods," said Mako. "But I would rather not throw them into the water, in case they are carried down to where our enemies await, and they are warned of our presence."

"A moment," said Ebon. He reached into the pocket of his cloak and produced Halab's firestriker. Mako's eyes lit upon it, and he gave Ebon a hard look.

"It was a gift from . . ." Ebon trailed off, looking at the guards on the wall. They could not see, but they could hear. "Well, from family."

Many of the goods were wrapped in cloth, and he tore it up to put in piles at the wagon's corners. With a few touches of the firestriker, the cloth lit, and soon flames licked up to spread along the wagon's lengthy spars.

"That will do it," said Mako.

"And what of them?" said Kalem, pointing to the soldiers pressed to the wall.

"Do what you will to us," said one of the guards, speaking into the wall, for the stone bands still pressed her tight against it. "You will not find it so easy when you get to the end of the tunnel, wretches."

Mako grinned. "Let her down."

Ebon looked at him, aghast, but Mako only nodded. So Ebon went forwards and shifted stone again, releasing the bands that held her. The moment her boots touched the ground, she turned and reached for his throat. But Mako seized an arm and snapped it against his wrist. Ebon heard the sick *crunch* of a breaking bone, and the woman cried out. Then Mako smashed an elbow into her nose, and she fell to the ground.

"Girl," said Mako. "The amulet. Place her under your spell."

"What? I did not agree to use mindwyrd," said Theren.

"I would not ask you to make her kill herself," said Mako. His voice was soothing, though his hands jerked as he restrained the Yerrin guard, who fought to rise. "I mean to keep magestones out of the hands of rogue wizards. Only that. I promise."

Theren hesitated. But though her eyes did not glow, as she spoke again, her voice was rich with mindwyrd.

"Stop," said Theren.

The Yerrin guard stopped squirming on the floor at once. "Yes," she said, her tone dead and lifeless.

"You will not remember any of our faces," said Theren. "After you have left the sewer, you will forget seeing us, or that you were attacked at all."

"Yes," said the guard.

Theren looked to Mako. "Now what?"

"Have her go to the Mystics," said Mako, smiling. "Have her tell them where we are going and that they should go there in all haste, for they will find a hefty supply of magestones if they do."

"But they will find us," said Theren, taking a step back. "If they learn what I carry . . ."

"We will be quick, and will have vanished by the time they arrive. But they will be there to clean up the mess and deal a grievous blow to the family Yerrin." Mako gave them all a look. "You, more than others, should object to more magestones finding their way into the nine lands. We can do a great deal to stop it, now, tonight."

"Very well," said Theren. She looked at the guard again. "You will find the first Mystic you can. You will tell them of these tunnels, and what paths to follow that will lead them to the rest of your kin. You will tell the Mystics that they will find magestones here, but only if they come into the sewers, now, at once."

"Yes," said the guard.

"Go, then."

The guard turned on her heel and marched away, back down the way Ebon and the others had come. Ebon shivered, and Kalem did the same.

"We have taken longer than we should have," said Mako. "Onwards."

TWENTY-FOUR

IT WAS NOT LONG AFTER THAT THAT THE TUNNEL WIDENED AT LAST, and they came into a vast, open space. Here the walls and floor were hewn from the earth's bones, rather than built by masons, and there were many stone outcroppings all about. Mako ducked behind one of these, and the children hastened to follow.

They had reached some sort of grotto, Ebon saw. He could smell saltwater over the bitter stench of the sewer waste and surmised that this cavern must run out to the Great Bay. They had to be somewhere near the western end of the Seat, he guessed, if not at its very edge.

Where the tunnels emerged into the cavern was a narrow platform, and this joined a raised stone path that ran around the cave's right edge, with many guards posted along it. A fair distance away, the path ended at a wooden dock lined with torches that illuminated a ship.

It was no great vessel, smaller than a schooner but wider, built for capacity more than speed. Two masts it had, though Ebon saw a sail upon only one of them. He guessed it had room for no more than five crew. Two of these walked about the deck, checking lines and stowing cargo, while three managed workers on the dock. There were many crates, barrels and sacks to load, it seemed, and where they were open, Ebon could see that most of them were filled with small packets of brown cloth.

"There," said Mako, pointing at the packets. "Those are magestones, or I am a fool."

"Can it not be both?" said Theren.

Mako snorted—whether in dismissal or in a quickly stifled laugh, Ebon could not tell. "What we see here is worth more than a king's ransom. What do you say? Shall we rob them of it?"

"I do not want to steal magestones," said Kalem quickly.

Mako rolled his eyes. "Loosen your death grip upon your honor, goldshitter. I mean to destroy their cargo, not to take it for ourselves. Magestones are a toxic good to trade, as the family Yerrin is soon to discover."

"We did not come for their magestones," said Theren. "We came for Isra. Where is she?"

"I do not see her or Gregor," said Mako. "Either they have come and gone, or they are still on their way and will arrive soon. If it is the latter, we would be wise to create as much chaos as we can before they come, so that they cannot muster these guards against us. If it is the former, then we have already lost their trail tonight and should do what good we can—by which I mean, chiefly, destroying the cargo Yerrin hopes to escape with."

"Very well," said Ebon. "What shall we do?"

"I tell you again that *we* shall do nothing, and this time I mean it," said Mako. "I have taken you farther already than I should have, and it ends here. You will keep watch. If anyone else should emerge from the tunnel whence we came, you must warn Theren and me so that we are not taken unawares."

Ebon glared, and Kalem did not look entirely pleased either. But they could feel the sand passing through the hourglass—they had little time, for the Mystics would soon be on their way. "Very well. How should I signal you?"

"Squeal like a rabbit, for all I care," said Mako. "Only do not let them see you, and make sure you are not within reach. There is a little rocky shelf up there on the wall—that is where you should wait."

"What will the two of you do?" said Kalem.

"We will make this a night Yerrin remembers and regrets," said Mako. "Come, Theren."

Together he and Theren stole forwards, bent almost double in the shadows, while Ebon and Kalem scrambled onto the shelf. It was just above head-height, with the ceiling pressing down low enough above them that they had to lie down to keep from bumping their skulls.

Ebon thought that Mako and Theren would take the stone path, but Mako turned from it at once. Then Ebon saw that there were other stone shelves like the one he rested on, though not so smooth, so that the Yerrin guards avoided them. But the stone came in levels, and all of them were lower than the stone path, so that Mako and Theren could creep along unseen.

He saw them approach the first guard who stood on the path. They edged forwards until they were as close to the guard as possible, but below him and out of sight. Theren popped her head up and into the torchlight. Ebon froze and almost called out—but then Theren said something he could not hear, and the guard froze.

A few more hasty words she muttered, and then she ducked out of sight again. The guard set off down the path. He approached the next guard, who leaned unaware against the wall. The unwitting target looked only at the last moment—but too late, for the first guard smashed the pommel of his sword into the side of her helmet. She fell to the floor, senseless.

The other guards saw it, and they called out in alarm as they came running to help. There were at least a half dozen of them, and Ebon knew that Theren's mindwyrded guard stood no chance. But just as they approached, Mako and Theren struck.

Mako leaped up on the path, seizing one of the guards and planting a dagger in his throat. He fell from the path and slid down the shelf into the water. Ebon winced. Theren struck with her magic, seizing two of the guards and flinging them from the path. They fell screaming into the water and fought to keep hold of the rock wall as they tugged off their chain mail. Mako nearly killed another, but Theren struck again just in time. Her magic picked up all three guards who still stood and slammed them into the stone wall with the strength of dragon's breath. They fell unconscious to the floor.

"Come!" said Ebon, sliding down off their shelf. He helped Kalem down after him, and they ran forwards to where Mako and Theren stood. Together they ran down the path as quick as they could, for the sense of passing time hung heavy in the air. The ship's crew had abandoned their vessel, fleeing for their lives down a side passage that led in another direction.

"What of the ones who escaped?" said Ebon.

"They could not see our faces in the dim," said Mako. "The ship is all that matters now."

He leaped aboard first, and the children followed more slowly, holding tight to the rope railing of the gangplank. By the time they made the deck, Mako had already gone down a hatch and returned. "The bulk of the stones are down there," he said. "But there are plenty more on the dock. It would be best to destroy them all, but that may take too long."

"I can cast the crates on the dock into the water," said Theren.

"No good. The crates will keep them safe, and those lying in the open will simply float. Yerrin may not be able to recover all of them, but they will recover enough."

"Put them aboard, then," said Ebon. "And we can burn the ship."

Mako scowled. "Idiot. It will take longer to bring the crates aboard than it would to set them ablaze."

Ebon took quite some pleasure in rolling his eyes and gesturing dramatically at Theren. "We have a *mindmage*, Mako."

The bodyguard's eyes widened, and though it looked as though he tried to hide it, a little smirk crept into his lips.

Off to the side, Kalem muttered, "He means mentalist."

It took but a moment. Theren's eyes blazed as she lifted the crates, for she did not need the amulet's power for so simple a task. But the last few still hung in the air when Ebon heard a sharp cry and turned.

There, at the other end of the cavern, two figures stood in the entryway, silhouetted by the torchlight beyond. Gregor—and beside him, Isra.

TWENTY-FIVE

EVEN FROM ACROSS THE CAVERN, EBON SHOOK AT THE SIGHT OF GRE-
gor. Images flashed into his mind of the Drayden assassin Gregor had
killed. Next to Isra, his size seemed inhuman. The man was at least a
head and a half taller than Mako, and it seemed his shoulders were
twice as broad. His legs were like ship masts, and his arms as thick as
Ebon's torso.

"Drop that crate," Mako told Theren. "I would give both my daggers for a firemage. Boys, find torches and set blazes on the ship. Can
you stop her, Theren?"

"I have before," said Theren, her voice filled with steely resolve. "I
will do so now, and gladly."

"I hope you are not only boasting."

Mako pounded down the dock towards the path of stone. But
Theren did not bother with the dock; she ran to the ship's stern and
leaped from it. Ebon's stomach lurched—but then her magic picked
her up, and she used it to carry herself to the stone path, reaching it
even before Mako did.

Isra gave a scream of rage, and a black glow sprang into her eyes. "Kill the girl!" she cried. Gregor drew his steel and advanced down the stone path. But Mako stepped forth, and the men faced each other across the cave.

"You owe me more than one life," said Mako. "Now I will carve them from you like a boar."

"Try it," said Gregor.

Ebon realized he had been standing and staring too long. He turned to seize Kalem's shoulder. "Enough gawking," he said. "We have our own work to do."

Kalem nodded. "I will fetch one of the torches."

"No, I will see to that. Use your magic upon the ship—break parts of it up into kindling that will catch easier than boards."

As Kalem scuttled to obey, Ebon ran down the gangplank, making for the torches. But a blow struck him just as he neared the first one, a force without sound or sight. It knocked him back, nearly pitching him off the other side of the dock. The torch he had reached for was flung from its mount, falling into the water below with a sharp hiss.

"Ebon!" Kalem came running. Across the cave, Ebon saw Isra staring at him with her black-glowing eyes, and he knew it was her magic that had nearly thrown him into the water. But though her hand was outstretched still, he felt nothing more pulling at him. Theren must have countered the spell.

Kalem reached him and seized his arm, hauling him back up onto the dock. Ebon gave him a grateful smile before they stood together.

"Get another," he said, pointing to the torches.

But Isra gave another great cry. Ebon braced himself for a blow, but none came—except to the torches, which were cast down and into the water of the grotto. Now the dock was nearly pitch-black, and the cavern was only lit by the torches on the stone path. Ebon could try to take one, but it would bring him nearly within arm's reach of Gregor. Isra bared her teeth in triumph. But then Theren redoubled her assault, drawing Isra's focus.

"Darkness take her," said Ebon. "What can we do now?"

"Mayhap the ship has lanterns," said Kalem. "And you have your firestriker. Come! I will search belowdecks."

They ran up the gangplank again, and Kalem vanished down a hatch. But Ebon paused, for he had caught sight of Mako. Gregor had pushed the bodyguard well down the path now so that they were less than ten paces from the ship, and Mako was hard-pressed. A new bruise swelled on his face, and he favored his right arm, which was missing its dagger. The other seemed a poor weapon against Gregor's massive sword, and it seemed clear that Mako was no longer attacking—only trying to stay alive.

Ebon looked over the deck around him. There was an open barrel at hand, and within it he saw oranges and apples packed in straw. He seized one of the oranges, gripping it tight in his hands. Light flashed in his eyes as he felt the substance of the fruit, and then he changed it to stone. But then it was almost too heavy to hold, so he shifted some of it away to go dribbling down upon the deck. Now he took the fist-sized ball and, waiting for the right moment, he threw it.

Mako had taken a quick step back, desperate for space, and so the stone came sailing at Gregor at the perfect time. It struck metal, for he wore a helmet, but still it sent his head rocking to the side, and he stumbled. Mako lunged forwards with his dagger.

But Gregor recovered too quickly, and his plated fist smashed Mako in the gut. The bodyguard fell back, landing hard on the stone path. Ebon shouted, turned another orange to stone, and threw it. But Gregor casually batted it away, and took a step towards Mako, who struggled to stand.

Theren grit her teeth and stepped forwards. Isra stumbled against the attack, and the darklight in her eyes flamed up. But Theren broke through, knocking Gregor a pace back from Mako. With a cry she pressed still further, and Ebon saw a rippling in the air. It wrapped itself around Isra in an instant, and the girl screamed as it flung her far out into the cavern, out of the torchlight and into the water with a *splash*.

With her opponent gone at last, Theren sagged and fell to one knee. But she rose almost immediately, pushing Gregor another pace back from Mako. Ebon thought she would fling him into the water as well, but she seemed winded, and fought just to keep her feet.

There came a commotion at the other end of the cave. With shouts and tramping feet, a party of soldiers burst into the cavern, holding torches aloft. They wore mail and carried blades along with the torches, and upon their shoulders were cloaks of red.

"Mystics!" whispered Ebon. But just then Kalem emerged from belowdecks, and in his hand was a lantern. He opened one side of it even as Ebon frantically worked his firestriker, and soon the lantern was ablaze. Close at hand lay a little pile of kindling that Kalem had built. Ebon smashed the lantern down upon it, and its oil spread along the deck.

"It is time to go." Ebon turned to find Mako standing at the gangplank. The bodyguard's face was entirely covered in bruises now, and blood from his split lip dribbled down his chin.

They ran to him, and at the bottom of the gangplank joined Theren. A glance told Ebon that the Mystics were engaged with Gregor, who fended them off with huge, sweeping swings of his broadsword. They should have overwhelmed him already, but the narrow stone path kept them from engaging him more than two at a time.

Mako hurried them towards the other passage, the one the boat crew had used to escape when they first arrived. Just before they ducked within, Ebon glanced back at the ship. It was burning now, burning with a sickly black flame that rose to lick the cavern's roof. The smell of it was foul, a putrid corruption like rotting flesh or a noxious corpse. He nearly retched. Then they had gone around the corner, and the flames were lost from sight.

TWENTY-SIX

THE TUNNEL STRETCHED ON LONG AND DARK AHEAD OF THEM, AND they had to slow their pace at first. But then Theren took the lead and, eschewing Kekhit's amulet, she reached for her power. Magelight sprang into her eyes to illuminate the way. It was a poor glow, but better than nothing, and they moved as quickly as they could. Ebon heard no sounds of pursuit, but that could not last forever; eventually the Mystics must overwhelm Gregor, and then they would find this passage.

"How do we know this is not a dead end?" said Kalem.

"Because the Yerrins fled this way," said Mako. "They were afraid for their lives—they would not have trapped themselves here if there was no hope."

Indeed he proved right, for soon they emerged into another cavern. This one was much smaller and opened to the Great Bay almost immediately, letting them see by moonslight. They had come out into a small rocky shore that sloped steeply into the water.

"What now?" said Kalem, looking behind them.

"There were likely boats here," said Theren, pointing. Ebon saw that there was a spike in the rock wall and several lines trailing from it, but nothing was attached to the other end of the lines. "The crew must have taken them all when they fled."

"That means we must swim," said Mako. "Shed anything that will slow you in the water and get in."

"It is the dead of winter!" said Ebon. "We will freeze to death."

Mako scowled at him. "We can reach the shore. Unless I miss my guess, it is just around the mouth of the cave. And if you or I stay here, we will land in a Mystic prison, and the family Drayden may fall."

Ebon looked fearfully at the water. "I am not a very good swimmer."

"Come off it, Ebon," said Theren. She was already shucking off her Academy robes. Soon she stood in her underclothes, but even though she must have been freezing, she did not shiver.

Kalem and Ebon looked at each other for a moment, but Ebon knew they had little choice. They removed their robes, throwing them into the water at Mako's command so that hopefully the Mystics would not find them and learn that Academy students had been present. Their boots they kept, for those would not be a great impediment to swimming, and they would need them to run once they reached land again. Once they had disrobed, both boys hesitated at the edge of the Great Bay's water, which it looked even more frigid now.

"Oh, darkness save us," said Mako. He seized Ebon's shoulders and flung him in.

Ebon sank into the water with a yelp and nearly gasped in lungs of seawater. It was colder than he could believe. A moment later he felt the splashing of another body beside him—Kalem, too, had been thrown in. Together they fought for the surface and hung there paddling, sucking in deep breaths of air that now seemed positively warm.

Theren waded in beside them and struck out for the cave mouth. Mako was just behind her. Ebon and Kalem paddled after them but were soon outpaced.

"Wait!" cried Ebon. Then he took in a mouthful of seawater and lost his words to sputtering. But Mako and Theren glanced back from where they had almost reached the open water.

"Sky above," said Theren, swimming back. She passed Ebon and went to Kalem, who had fallen even farther behind. "Come on, then."

He clung to her back, holding on to her shoulders with a death grip. She struck out again, and though Kalem slowed her down a bit, she still passed Ebon easily. They reached Mako at the cave mouth, and he glared at Ebon as they approached.

"I am not carrying you like a suckling newborn, boy."

"I did not ask you to," said Ebon, though he had meant to, and was now secretly glad he had not.

They broke out into the open water, and Mako's earlier guess proved right. A sandy shore sank into the water a scant thirty paces away. Before they swam for it, though, Mako guided them farther out into open water, for the waves lapped against the stone cliffs of the Seat, and though the sea was somewhat calm, still it could knock them senseless against the rocks. Ebon soon fell behind again. Mako did not carry him the way Theren had Kalem, but he did reach back and seize Ebon's collar, flinging him a little bit farther along every other stroke, so that he was just able to keep up with the rest.

"Darkness take all useless goldshitters," growled Mako.

"I could not agree more," said Theren, who was now fighting against Kalem's weight to keep her head above the waves.

By the time they reached land, Ebon could no longer feel his fingers or his toes. He fell upon the shore, expecting the air to be warmer than the water. But a wind was blowing, and his shivers only redoubled.

"Get up and keep moving," said Mako. "You will not freeze to death unless you try to rest."

"But where?" said Ebon. He fought to gain his feet, but it was hard when he could not feel his limbs.

"There," said Mako. He pointed up the shore, where they could see the glow of the western docks. "There are torches for warmth, and mayhap we can steal some clothes."

So by moonlight they ran on, their steps hampered by the soft sand that grasped for their feet. Mako reached the dock piles first, and by the time they joined him he had popped his head up over the edge of the wooden planks to look.

"There are no guards nearby," he whispered. "And there is a carriage not far off that I think is unoccupied."

"You mean to steal a carriage?" said Kalem.

"No, idiot. If there is a carriage, it is because someone means to take ship. But their things are still in bags atop the carriage, and there we may find clothes. Theren, look after them and keep out of sight—I shall return in a moment."

He slithered up and into the open. Theren poked her head up to look after him, and in a moment Ebon and Kalem did the same. They saw him reach the carriage, climb up top, and pull open a travel sack. He threw it aside before opening another. This one he took up and ran back to them, avoiding torchlight wherever he could.

"Here we are," he said. "Trousers and tunics aplenty. No cloaks, but we will not be in the cold much longer."

The children hastened to don the clothing. Ebon studied Mako as they dressed. The bodyguard stood stock still with no quiver in his limbs, though his clothes still dripped seawater.

"There are clothes enough here for you, too."

Mako sneered, and the clotted blood of his lip burst, sending a crimson rivulet forth to mingle with the saltwater droplets. "I am not some weakling who is troubled by a chill."

Soon they were done. They all had trousers of brown, and Ebon and Theren had found tunics of white. But the only shirt that fit Kalem was flamboyant red with gold trim at the collar and sleeves.

"Well, this does not make me look an utter idiot at all," said Kalem ruefully, holding out his arms and shaking his head.

"Who cares what you look like?" growled Mako. "We have tarried too long. Up on the dock."

And so up they went, and once they had passed the carriage and gone a little distance on, they slowed to a walk, strolling along as though nothing untoward was happening—except for Mako, who still stole from shadow to shadow, eyes roving everywhere to watch for a threat.

"The docks seem curiously empty, do they not?" said Kalem.

"I had noticed the same thing," said Ebon.

"That may be why," said Theren.

She pointed ahead, where a large cluster of people had gathered.

There were mayhap two score of them packed in a tight little group, and all facing towards the center, except for some who looked about as though seeking aid.

"Stay away from there," said Mako. "All the better that they will not notice us."

"They will not notice us regardless," said Ebon. "They are looking at whatever is in their midst."

He pressed forwards, away from his friends and towards the crowd, ignoring Mako's frustrated growl behind him. Something was wrong. He could see it in the worried faces of the onlookers, the way they kept looking about, expecting—or hoping—for someone else to arrive, to sort out whatever lay in their midst.

The crowd was packed tight, but he pushed through them, and Theren was at his shoulder. Soon they reached the center, and there they froze. Ebon's breath left him in a rush.

Isra lay there. Dead, clearly, her sightless eyes staring up at the sky. Seawater had turned her skin dark and bloated, and blue veins stuck out in the torchlight. Fish had begun to peck at her cheeks, it seemed, for the skin was open, though the decaying flesh put forth no blood. Only a few scraps of her Academy robes still clung to her corpulent frame.

"She perished, then," Theren whispered. Ebon heard a grim finality in her voice—no trace of joy, but a steely resolve, a tone like the ending of a tale. "I did not mean to drown her. But neither am I sorry. The nightmare is over."

"Silence," said Ebon quietly. He took her arm, and Kalem's, who had stepped up beside the two of them, and drew them both back through the crowd. They pulled away from the people standing there, where Mako waited with a dark look in his eyes.

"Well?" he said. "What is it?"

"It is Isra," said Ebon. "Dead."

Mako's eyes shot wide, and he pushed past them to dive into the crowd. When he returned, his face was no less grim—in fact his scowl had deepened.

"She must have washed out of the grotto on whatever current was meant to carry that ship," said Theren. "Strange that she should have reached the docks before we did, but then, the sea is wild."

Ebon frowned, but he did not wish to speak. It was Kalem who looked up, fear in his eyes, and met Theren's look.

"No, Theren," he said. "That is impossible. Not just how quickly she came here—but she, herself. She has been dead a long time. Weeks, most likely."

Theren stared at him, uncomprehending. Her gaze shifted to Ebon, who met her eyes, and then to Mako, who was scowling off into the night, chin buried in his fist, lost in thought.

"That is impossible," she said. "We just saw her. It was less than an hour ago, and she was as alive as you or I."

Ebon shivered as he looked back towards the crowd, all of them still clustered around the body. "Yet it is the truth. I have no more explanation than you do. But Isra is more than a month dead."

TWENTY-SEVEN

THEY DID NOT KNOW WHAT ELSE TO DO, SO THEY MADE THEIR WAY INTO
the city and back to the Academy. The dock gates stood open, as constables had been summoned to inspect the corpse, and so they entered
without trouble. Before they returned to the citadel, Theren took them
to the inn where Lilith kept her extra room. Mako waited on the street
as they ducked within. At the door to the room, she produced a key
from around her neck, hanging on the same chain as Kekhit's amulet.

"I had the key before, you know," she said, looking embarrassed
and refusing to meet the eyes of either Ebon or Kalem. "Before we were
estranged. She only recently gave me one again. In case we should need
it, for something like this."

"Of course," said Ebon carefully.

She let them in and showed them where Lilith kept extra sets of
Academy student robes. Soon they had changed, and Mako led them
on through the streets. Curfew was a distant memory, and so he took
them around the Academy's east end to the groundskeepers' sheds that
housed his secret entrance.

"I must cover your eyes," he said, looking at Theren and Kalem.

Theren scowled. "Why? I can keep a secret as well as the next."

"It is not yours to know, much less to keep," said Mako. "It is bad enough Ebon knows how I get in and out. No others need the knowledge."

He took rags from the sheds and tied them around their eyes, and then he and Ebon led Theren and Kalem into one of the sheds. Inside, Mako had Ebon turn around while he pulled a lever, and the secret way opened before them. The passageway was utterly dark, and Ebon did not know how Mako could see—yet he must have been able to, for soon he opened the door at the other end of it, and they stood upon the Academy grounds.

"I suggest you rest well," said Mako. "Doubtless I shall see you all again soon."

"Thank you, Mako," said Ebon. "Though some things are unclear, it seems at least that this is all over."

Mako gave him a hard look. "I hope you are right, though I doubt it."

He left them. Ebon and his friends made their way into the Academy. It was far too late to be wandering the halls, but they encountered no instructors. Soon they had climbed the stairs to their dormitories. They stopped at Kalem's, where the common room was empty, for the younger children had gone to bed. A fire burned low in the hearth. Ebon threw two more logs on, and then they sat in armchairs around it.

"I cannot fathom all that has happened," said Kalem. "There seems no sense to it."

"Isra is dead, at least," said Theren. "I can worry about the rest of it another day."

"Is she, though?" said Ebon. "That corpse was long decayed from seawater. We all saw it, Theren."

Theren threw her hands towards the ceiling. "What, then, does it mean? Has she been a walking corpse for the last month? We have seen her alive. And tonight we saw her dead. Mayhap you guessed wrong and thought the body more decayed than it was."

"Her clothes were rotten, and fish had begun to eat her," said Ebon.

"Mayhap we are wrong in another sense," said Kalem. "Mayhap the corpse was not her, but only someone who looks like her."

"You do not believe in such a coincidence any more than I do," said Ebon. "We have seen her, studied beside her, and even fought against her. We know what she looked like—it was her body." But then a thought struck him, and he straightened in his seat. "Unless it was not. It could have been a weremage. Think of it. What if she mindwyrded a weremage to look just like her, then killed them and threw them into the Great Bay? When the body was recovered, it would cast any investigation away from her."

Kalem shook his head. "That is not how therianthropy works. When the wizard dies, they resume their true form." But now it was his turn to look up in realization. "What if the corpse from the Bay was Isra, and a weremage has been impersonating her?"

Theren looked at him with disdain. "She has used mindmagic against us, Kalem. How could she have done that if she was a weremage? No wizard commands more than one branch of magic."

The boy's face fell. "Of course," he mumbled. "I should have thought of that."

Ebon ran the facts through his mind, but he could think of none that made sense—and he knew, too, that he was less able to guess than his friends, for many ways of magic were still strange to him.

Either the corpse was Isra's, or it was not. They could not hope to guess at the truth. But either answer brought another, more urgent question: where was Erin? If Isra was still alive, doubtless she held the boy in captivity. But if Isra was indeed dead . . . was the boy now a captive of the family Yerrin? Or had she left him somewhere else entirely?

Thoughts of Erin brought thoughts of Xain, and his blood went cold.

"One thing is certain," he said at last, speaking quietly against the crackling fire in the hearth. "There will be an investigation now. And we are the only ones who claim to have seen Isra since she disappeared."

They all looked at each other. Then Theren rose from her chair and left without a word, making for the halls. Kalem left a moment later, stepping through the opposite door that led to his dormitory. But Ebon sat there until morning, staring into the fire, exhausted beyond reckoning and yet unable to even think of sleep.

It did not take long for the faculty to redouble their investigation. Ebon guessed that news must have reached the Academy during the night, for the moment he reached Perrin's class she commanded him to visit the dean.

There was no instructor in the hall to walk with him. Ebon stood there for a moment, frozen by indecision. He had a tremendous urge to turn the other way, to make for the Academy's front doors and leave forever, begging for help from Halab and Mako. They could whisk him away to some forgotten kingdom, or even, mayhap, home to Idris, there to be hidden from all knowledge.

But after a time he turned to the right instead and made his slow way towards Xain's study. He had done nothing wrong—or at least, nothing wrong when it came to Isra. He *had* seen her within the Academy. He and his friends had *not* drowned her in the Great Bay weeks ago. He must cling to that, for it was the truth. And only the truth could save him now, because outside of what he had seen with his own eyes, he was not even certain what the truth was.

Xain stood outside his office—but much to Ebon's relief, Jia was also there, as was Dasko. Dasko looked somewhat worse for wear; his face was still gaunt, and his eyes roved all about. But his hands were steady, and Ebon saw no trace of madness in him, the sickness that came over those who had long been under mindwyrd. It had faded in him remarkably fast. Ebon nodded to the instructor and received a brief jerk of the head in return.

"Drayden," said Xain, speaking through gritted teeth. "Come with us."

He stalked off down the hall. Jia and Dasko followed at a somewhat more sedate pace, with Jia holding out an arm to help Dasko along. Ebon decided to match their steps rather than Xain's, and soon the dean was forced to slow.

Ebon had had scant reason to visit the Academy's healing ward before, but that was where they turned their steps now. It lay on the bottom floor of one of the citadel's great wings, the one that stretched northwest, and there were many beds arranged in rows with tall windows that reached from waist-height almost to the ceiling. One of the beds nearest the entrance was covered, and Ebon saw the shape of a body beneath it. He could smell decay mixed with seawater.

Jia paused a respectful distance away, but Xain pushed forwards. Ignoring the healer who stood by to help, he threw back the sheet to reveal Isra's bloated corpse. Removed from the seawater, her skin had turned darker still, and her eyes had swollen into pale, milky globes, the color of which could hardly be discerned. Yet it was still clearly her, as any fool could see. She had been stripped of her clothes and cleaned up. The sight of her almost made Ebon retch.

"How is it possible," said Xain, "that Isra lies dead before us, when you said you saw her just over a week ago?" His words were calm, but Ebon heard the fire burning behind them, hot enough to melt steel.

Ebon swallowed hard, trying to remember to look shocked, as though he was surprised to see Isra dead. It was not difficult, and he thought the paleness of his skin likely helped. "I do not know," he said. "Where . . . where was she? Mayhap she died just after we encountered her."

The healer, a wizened old woman whose hair was drawn up into a tight bun, shook her head. "This corpse has been in the ocean a month at least," she said. "We inspected it most thoroughly."

Xain stalked around the bed to loom over him. "A month. A month ago is about the time she vanished from her classes. And so I ask again—how is it possible that you saw her in the kitchens, Drayden?"

"He is not the only one who saw her," said Jia.

"I am asking the boy, for it is his words that have been called into question. He can speak for himself, or he can speak with the Mystics' encouragement. It matters little to me."

"It is as Jia said," said Ebon, feeling somewhat indignant now. "I have not gone mad. My friends saw her as well."

Xain glanced over his shoulder. "Mayhap. Yet they, too, may prove false."

Ebon heard footsteps behind him and turned to see Kalem and Theren being ushered into the room by an instructor he did not recognize. Both their eyes fixed at once upon the corpse on the bed. Kalem went Elf-white, and Theren did not look much better.

"This is the body of a girl you both said you saw here in the Academy," Xain told them. "Yet she has been dead for weeks. How do you explain this? I cannot read the tale of it, unless someone in this room has been lying."

Kalem tore his eyes away from Isra at last to meet Xain's gaze. "If someone has been lying, it is not I. Not in this. We saw her. Theren fought her."

"Yet I thought you said her eyes were black," said Xain, and his baleful gaze turned to Theren. "How could you resist a wizard with the strength of magestones?"

"It is as I said before," said Theren carefully. "We surprised her. I tried to flee, but she turned and ran first."

"Clearly there is something at work here," said Jia, her voice calm and measured, and her eyes going too often to Xain. "I am certain the three of you can understand how we would be . . . confused. Concerned, even. After all, the body casts doubt upon this whole affair."

Ebon steeled himself. They stood on the brink of the hearth, now, and it seemed their only choice was to plunge headlong into the flames. "Of course, Instructor. Yet I can offer no better explanation. And after all, *someone* had you under mindwyrd, did they not? And you as well, Instructor Dasko, for longer."

Theren tensed. Xain saw her sudden discomfort, and his eyes locked upon her. "But Isra was not the only mindmage at the Academy," he said.

Feigning surprise, Ebon looked to Theren. "You mean to insinuate that *Theren* had something to do with the mindwyrd? I am only recently acquainted with magic, and nowhere near so mighty in my lore as anyone else present—"

"An understatement if ever there was one," Xain spat.

Ebon's nostrils flared, but he pressed on, though anger now burned in his breast. "—but even I know that mindwyrd is only possible with magestones. And if Theren had been using magestones, her eyes would glow black. Theren, cast a spell."

She looked at him uneasily. But a moment later he saw her reach for her magic. Her eyes glowed white, and a nearby tray lifted into the air.

"There you have it. Theren has eaten no more magestones than I have, or you yourself, Dean," said Ebon, chuckling.

"You dare to laugh?" roared Xain. Ebon flinched as the dean stepped up to him. But he did not seize Ebon's robes, nor reach for his magic.

He only loomed, his face a finger from Ebon's, until Ebon wanted to wilt and sink into the floor. "My son has been kidnapped—*my son,* you mewling, dung-licking coward—and you dare to laugh? First I am told that this girl, Isra, stole him away. Then you tell me that you saw her but did not stop her before she escaped. Now I see her corpse—and she has been dead, it seems, since she was supposed to have taken him. Laugh again. Laugh, I implore you, for it may very well break me, but I will take you with me when I shatter."

Ebon fought to reply, but pure terror had seized him. It was all he could do not to flee, and suddenly he had a desperate need for the privy. Everyone in the room stood frozen.

But it was Dasko who stepped forwards at last, still shaky on his feet but with a stern look in his eyes. He put a gentle hand on Xain's shoulder.

"Dean Forredar," he said quietly. "No one can begrudge you your wrath, nor your grief, which must be boundless in equal measure. These children are as confused as we are, certainly, and far more frightened—for to their mind, they have seen a walking corpse. Ebon was flippant in a moment of foolishness. That does not mean he is evil."

The instructor's words were gentle, his tone soothing. But Xain did not subside—rather, Ebon saw his eyes go wide. He took a step back as though he was regrouping, collecting himself.

"A walking corpse," he whispered. He turned stark eyes on Isra's body. "A walking corpse."

Ebon knew not what the words meant, what dark thing Xain thought he had discovered, but it only increased his fear. Jia stepped forwards into the sudden, awkward silence. "They should return to class, Dean Forredar, unless we have anything more for them."

Xain did not answer. He only turned back towards the body upon the bed.

"Out with you," said Jia quickly, brushing them away. They made for the door. She followed them out and around the corner, where she stopped them. Ebon was reminded of the last time she had pulled them aside to speak privately, when they had been caught sneaking into the Academy's vaults.

"I tire of repeating myself," she said ruefully. "But I must ask you to forgive the dean. None of us can imagine the pain of losing a son."

"Of course, Instructor," said Kalem politely. Theren only stared off into nothing, while Ebon was still thinking of Xain's look of dark recognition.

"I know he is angry with you, and anger may not always prompt honesty," Jia went on. "So I will ask you once more—is there anything else you know or have seen that could help? I am afraid there is little hope Erin is still alive, for we have heard nothing from his captors since he was taken. Yet we must cleave to what little hope remains."

That drew Ebon's attention. Jia must not know of the ransom note Xain had received. That meant Xain had not told the rest of the faculty. But he only shook his head and muttered, "Nothing, Instructor. I am sorry." Kalem and Theren gave soft words of agreement.

She sighed. "Very well. Then I have only one more thing to ask. Ebon, please go and see Astrea immediately. I have sent word to Perrin already. She will excuse the two of you. You seem closer to her than most, and so she should hear of this from you."

Ebon balked, looking back towards the healing ward for a moment. "I . . . I have no wish to tell her of Isra's death, Instructor."

Jia's eyes grew mournful. "Nor have I, Ebon. Nor has anyone. But would you rather she hear it from your lips, or as a rumor whispering through the Academy halls?"

He hung his head. "From me, I suppose. But I do not wish for such a duty."

She put a hand on his shoulder. "Thank you, Ebon. Your compassion has never been lacking—and that is why I keep my faith in you."

They left her then, and made their silent way through the halls. Ebon wondered if his friends, too, felt the presence of the corpse behind them long after the healing ward was out of sight.

695

TWENTY-EIGHT

EBON'S STEPS GREW HEAVIER THE CLOSER HE DREW TO PERRIN'S CLASS-room, and when at last he reached her door he stopped short. Lifting his hand to turn the latch seemed an impossible task. He very much doubted Astrea even wanted to speak with him just now, as withdrawn as she had become, and he had no wish to speak to her, either, with the news he bore.

Then he thought of her sitting in the dining hall and hearing some whispered word at her elbow. In his mind he saw her turn at the mention of Isra's name and ask a sharp question. He saw the harsh, emotionless mask of her face break down a piece at a time.

Shaking his head, he opened the door.

A few of the students looked up at his return, but Astrea was not one of them. Ebon walked past her and went to Perrin. The instructor looked down at him with sorrow in her eyes.

"Instructor," Ebon murmured. "Jia has asked me to speak with Astrea alone, if I may."

"I think that is best," said Perrin. From the pain in her expression, she must have heard about Isra, and knew how hard Astrea would take the news.

Together they approached her, and when they reached the front table Perrin put a hand on the little girl's shoulder. So great was her size that her hand nearly stretched the width of Astrea's back.

"Astrea," she said quietly. "You are excused for a moment. Please follow Ebon outside upon the grounds. The two of you must speak."

She looked up at Ebon for a moment, her fingers still fidgeting with a flower she held in her hands. Her eyes were emotionless.

"I do not want to."

Ebon shared a look of confusion with Perrin. "Come, Astrea," he said. "It will not take long, but we must speak. I have something I must tell you."

"I do not want to hear it."

"Please, Astrea," said Perrin. "It is good for us to speak of the things that trouble us, for otherwise they can fester in us like a sickness."

"I know that well enough by now," said Astrea, and grief sounded in her voice for the first time. With a sigh of resignation she pushed herself down the bench and stood, going to Ebon's side with a swish of her robes.

"Take whatever time you need," said Perrin. "And Astrea—if you do not wish to return to class afterwards, you need not."

Astrea shrugged and followed Ebon from the room. He felt suddenly uncertain, even more than he had before. He would have expected fear or grief from Astrea before she heard the actual news, for all tidings had been dark of late. He did not know how to react to this sullen indifference.

"Let us step out upon the grounds," said Ebon. "It is too stuffy in these halls."

She shrugged and followed him out through a white cedar door. Outside, students were practicing their spells in the open air, and he quickly guided her away from them, towards the hedges and the gardens that were free of any onlookers. Above, the sun shone bright in a clear sky, too clear and blue for Ebon's liking. He was exhausted after a night of shadows and death, and now he was the unwilling bearer of grim news.

"Would that I were like Dorren of old, and the skies changed to suit my mood," he said aloud. "Then the day would not be so cheery, as if it meant to mock me."

To his surprise, Astrea nodded. "I have sometimes wished the same thing. But then we would be firemages, and I am glad to be an alchemist."

"Perrin would tell you to say 'transmuter.' But I am not she."

"You said it anyway," said Astrea. Though the words came out sounding harsh, she glanced up at him from under her wild, frizzy hair and gave a little smirk. It gladdened his heart—but it also pained him, for he knew the words he must say would tear that smirk from her lips and mayhap keep it away for good.

Get it over with, he chided himself.

"Come. Let us sit," he said, waving a hand towards a stone bench. She sat with him, staring at her hands in her lap, though her fingers did not fidget.

"Have you come to tell me that Isra is dead?" she asked suddenly, even as he was taking a deep breath to speak.

Ebon deflated at once, and his mouth worked as he fought for words. She glanced up at him and must have seen the answer in his eyes. "I . . . who told you?" Ebon stammered at last. "They should have let the word come to you from the right lips."

"Who cares where the words came from?" she muttered, looking back down at her hands. "But no, no one told me. I guessed it. Why else would Perrin let you take me from class? It is not as though anyone else could have died. I have no other friends left."

He knew she must break down at that—yet she did not. She only stared into the distance.

"Are you . . . all right?" he said, uncertain of what else to say.

She only shrugged.

"Astrea—"

"What should I say, Ebon?" she snapped. "I have told you I hate it when you ask if I am all right. Do you think I *can* be all right? Isra is my sister."

"Of course I did not mean that," he said quickly. "I only mean . . . I thought you might weep. No one could blame you if you did."

698

She turned away again. "How will tears help? Mayhap I spilled them all for Credell and Vali. I cannot cry any more."

Ebon leaned over, trying to catch her gaze, but still she would not look at him. He saw the great bags under her eyes, dark and hollow, so like Isra's had been. And he saw how thin and spindly her fingers had become and how gaunt and sallow her cheeks, and he wondered if she was eating enough. Mayhap grief and anger had taken such a toll on her body that no amount of food or rest could repair it.

And then he remembered seeing eyes like hers before, and hands and cheeks as well—but he had seen them in a mirror, and they were his own, and that had been when Momen died. And suddenly he thought he understood her better. He reached out and put a hand on hers, and she did not pull away.

"I had a brother. Did I ever tell you that?" he said. "I do not like to speak of him. He died when I was very young—just your age, in fact. When I heard what had happened I went into my room, where I remained for days while everyone waited for me to stop weeping."

She turned to him, eyes flashing. "I have told you already that I do not need to—"

Quickly he raised his hands in token of surrender. "I do not mean that you should weep. For in truth, I did not. Tears would not come. But that does not mean I did not grieve. I missed him more than I could imagine. It still hurts to speak of him, though I am no closer to crying now."

That gave her pause. Her fingers fidgeted. "You did not feel bad? Because you could not grieve?"

"I felt terrible," he murmured. "Sometimes I still do. But in time I learned that I could not blame myself. We all face loss in our own way. If I could have spent less time in guilt, I would have. I suppose that in the end it was hard for me to believe he was gone. I never even saw his corpse, for he was burned in the distant land where he was killed, and there, too, were his ashes scattered."

Astrea looked down at her shoes. "That is an ill thing."

"We do not always get to say good-bye," said Ebon. "And in truth, I know it does not matter. If I had seen his body or been there when they burned it, he would not have heard my farewell. Sky above, even if

I had been there when he passed and we had whispered our parting to each other, nothing would have changed. He would still be gone, and I would still be here. Yet mayhap the pain would not be so great. I like to believe it would not."

Then he looked at her carefully. "What of you, Astrea? Do you wish to say your farewell? I could ask for it, and I doubt any instructor would refuse you. Not even the dean."

For the first time he saw tears in her eyes, though she was quick to blink them away. She shook her head quickly. "No. You said you wish you could have spent less time in mourning. I want the same thing, and I do not think that seeing Isra would help me. It would only make things worse. You had no choice in the matter—but I do."

He nodded. "Very well. Your words are wise beyond your years— but then, that is no great surprise to those of us who must suffer in class beside you, always overshadowed by your wit."

She glanced at him, and he gave her a sad smile. She did not return it, but her eyes softened, and she shook her head disdainfully.

"Do not be an idiot, Ebon."

"As well tell the sun not to shine—and we know already that that is futile. Will you walk with me?"

"If you want me to," she said. But he could hear the gratitude that lay beneath her words, and she leaped up to follow him with surprising eagerness. And the day's beauty no longer seemed so offensive as they strolled along.

TWENTY-NINE

The midday meal passed silently for Ebon and his friends, for they did not find themselves much in the mood for talking. Together they made their way through the halls towards the library and wordlessly climbed the stairs to their nook on the third level.

As they reached their armchairs, Ebon saw a note resting upon one of them—the one upon which he usually sat. It was only a brief scrawl: *Come to Leven's tavern tonight.*

Ebon looked it over and then met the eyes of his friends. "It must be from Mako."

"Truly? Do you think so?" said Theren in mock surprise, her eyes wide.

Soft footsteps made them fall silent, and they turned to look behind them. Ebon froze where he stood. It was Lilith, hands tucked into her sleeves, eyes shifting uneasily as she tried to avoid their gazes.

"Good day," she said quietly.

For a moment no one answered her, nor even moved. Then Ebon and Theren had the same thought at the same time, and both leaped towards his armchair to turn it about. But they ran into each other instead, and both stepped back awkwardly.

"I will—no, I will fetch another," said Theren quickly.

"Of course. Here," said Ebon, waving Lilith down into the chair.

She took her seat, still not meeting his eyes, while Theren fetched another armchair and placed it beside Lilith's. But she sat in it instead of offering it to Ebon, and so he was forced to take her armchair instead. Kalem had stood in silence, gawking at the proceedings with wide eyes, and it was only after all the other three had seated themselves that he started, as if waking from a dream, and took his own chair.

For a long moment, silence reigned as they all looked at Lilith in the lamplight, and she tried to avoid looking back at them.

"Where is Nella?" said Ebon, desperate to break the stiffness that had settled over them like a sheet of ice.

"We have opposite study schedules," said Lilith.

"Ah."

Again, a long quiet stretched. Ebon's fingers drummed on the arms of his chair.

At last Lilith cleared her throat. "Well," she said quietly. "I suppose there is no use trying to pretend that this is not very strange for all of us."

Theren let out a hysterical bark of laughter, too loud and too high, and then fell silent. Ebon quashed a snicker. Kalem only frowned. "Did you . . . and understand that I do not mean you are not welcome. But did you come to us for any particular purpose?"

Lilith nodded. "I had heard what happened to Isra," she said. "Is it true that the three of you saw her corpse?"

Ebon met eyes with his friends, hoping they all knew better than to say anything of the events that had transpired the night before. "We did," he said.

"Is it true she is long dead?" said Lilith. "That is what the rumors are saying."

"That is true," said Ebon. "Though we are not sure how."

"Because you saw her living, and little more than a week ago," said Lilith, nodding. "How can that be?"

"We have an idea," said Theren, sitting up.

"Theren," said Ebon.

She glared. "Lilith has not betrayed our trust thus far, Ebon. And mayhap she will have an idea for how Isra did it that we have not yet thought of." Lilith leaned forwards to listen, and Theren went on. "I have never heard of magic that could do something of this sort. My first thought was therianthropy, but if the corpse were a weremage it would not look like Isra—"

"—and if it had been a weremage in the kitchens, they would not have had mindmagic to battle you," said Lilith.

Theren slumped in her chair. "That is just what we said."

Lilith frowned, looking into her lap. For a moment Ebon hoped beyond hope that she would, in fact, know how such a feat might be accomplished. But when she lifted her gaze, she only shook her head. "I have no idea how it might have been done. I am sorry."

"It is hardly your fault," said Theren with a small smile. Lilith returned it. Kalem grimaced.

A thought struck Ebon, and he worked it around until he had thought of a question that seemed to pose no danger. "Lilith . . . have you heard aught of Gregor since last we sought him out?"

Lilith's mood darkened, and she shook her head. "I have not—not exactly, anyway. But something happened upon the Seat just last night. A fear has spread throughout my family again, just as it did when the Seat was attacked and the High King suspected us of being complicit. Now our terror is not so great, but it has certainly returned. I will try to reach out to Farah again and see if she knows what happened."

"And we will ask Mako," said Theren, giving Ebon a meaningful look. He thought he understood—they must keep up appearances that they knew no more than Lilith did.

"Will you see him soon?" said Lilith. "Mayhap I should come. We could pool our knowledge."

"No," said Theren at once.

Lilith frowned. "I do not mean to—"

Theren shook her head. "You are not the one who worries me. Mako would not be pleased to see you. You have been through enough already, and I would not bring you within arm's reach of that man, not for all the gold upon the High King's Seat."

That made Lilith subside, and she gave Theren a wry smile. "Are you certain? I wonder if you know how much gold that would be. It is a large amount. I myself would not hesitate to have a meal with Mako if I could get my hands upon it."

Theren smirked. "You goldbags. Your coffers overflow, and yet always you seek more."

Lilith giggled, and it was a sound so foreign that Ebon froze in amazement. She stood and brushed at her robes.

"I should be going," she said. "I have intruded upon your time long enough."

"It was no intrusion," said Theren. "You could stay if you wish."

"I . . . I have studies," said Lilith, looking down in embarrassment. "Jia requires a dissertation from me. Mayhap another time."

She stepped out between the armchairs—but as she did, Theren raised a hand, and Lilith took it on instinct. They held each other only a moment, but their fingers dragged against each other as they parted, as though reluctant to let go.

That night, the streets of the city seemed filled with a heightened tension—or mayhap it was only the fear in the hearts of Ebon and his friends that made it seem so. Oddly, Ebon was calmest of them all. Mayhap it was because he had faced so much danger already that he was growing inured to it.

They breathed a heavy sigh of relief when they caught sight of Leven's tavern. Together they entered as quickly as they could and tramped the snow off their boots in the doorway.

At the bar stood a broad man hidden beneath a black cloak, his hood drawn up. He turned at the sound of their entrance, though no one else seemed to pay them any mind. Ebon saw the flash of Mako's eyes beneath the cowl. He came to join them at their customary table, a bottle of wine in one hand and four cups clutched in the other.

He wasted no time on pleasantries. "Darkness take this mindmage sow," he growled. Theren sat up straighter, but he only sneered. "Not you. I mean Isra. I can find no trace of her."

"No trace but the corpse, you mean," said Kalem.

"Which we already know is not hers," said Mako, growing angrier still. "I can deceive the eye when I wish and remain unseen when I must. But even I cannot conjure my own corpse out of thin air, nor hide from every prying eye upon the Seat. When at last I get my hands on her, I will flay her slow just for the inconvenience she has caused me."

"Is it possible you are jealous?" said Theren lightly. "You seem frankly obsessed with her skill at deception, Mako."

The way the bodyguard's jaw clenched, Ebon feared he might lash out at her. But he only tightened his fist around his cup until Ebon could hear its wood squeaking.

"I find her cunning as troubling as you do, no doubt," said Ebon. "But we have another problem. We told the faculty that we saw her in the kitchens, and so the three of us have fallen under suspicion. I worry what that will mean for us, though of course we are innocent when it comes to Isra."

"Innocent?" said Mako with a cruel grin. "That is an odd word for it, and not one I would choose."

"We did not kill her, is what he means," said Kalem, as Ebon flushed and lowered his gaze.

"Well, only catching her will prove that," said Theren.

Mako pounded a fist on the table. "Yet that seems impossible, though our watch upon the Academy has been ceaseless, except for last night when I summoned my fighters to the sewers—but we know she did not infiltrate the Academy last night, for we saw her below. She is not in any of the Yerrins' usual hiding spots, and she is nowhere else upon the Seat, for I have eyes in every cranny."

"Mayhap she has used mindwyrd to send false tales to you?" said Ebon. "One of your spies might have seen her but been charmed into telling you they had not."

Mako's eyes rolled so far back that Ebon thought the bodyguard might faint. "Oh, how clever of you to think of such a thing, Ebon. If only I had thought of that immediately and taken precautions to prevent it. You should be the family's master of spies, and not I."

Theren leaned over. "I believe he means to say that he has taken precautions against such a ruse."

Ebon scowled into his drink. "It was only a suggestion."

"I do not need your suggestions," said Mako. "I need your lover."

A chill stole up Ebon's spine, freezing him in place. He glared at Mako. "Do not speak of her to me. She has nothing to do with this."

"Not yet," said Mako, glaring right back. "But she must, or we are lost. Go to her. Tell her we need help beyond our own means."

"What are you suggesting?"

"To you? Nothing." Mako threw back his cup of wine and stood. "But the words will carry weight with her. Send them along, little Ebon. Go tomorrow night—I and mine will watch your path along the streets and ensure you come to no harm. Send word to me afterwards as soon as you can."

He walked to the door and vanished into the night. Kalem and Theren stared at Ebon in wonder.

"What was that about?" said Theren.

Ebon said nothing, but only stared into his wine, his heart thundering with fear.

THIRTY

Ebon woke with guilt roiling in his gut.

After seeing Mako, he had wrestled long into the night with his feelings. The last thing he wanted was to involve Adara again. His kin had brought her enough dangers already, and though she always reassured him that her contacts in the guild of lovers would not betray her, still he worried. Though he did not understand the message he was supposed to relay, he did not doubt he would feel even more uncomfortable about it if he did.

His thoughts were in turmoil all morning. But at last, just before the bell rang for breakfast, he fetched parchment and a quill and scribbled a note to Adara, sending it along with Mellie at the front door. Isra's corpse still lay in the Academy, and the investigation would not stop simply because he wished it to. If they did not find Isra, surely it would only be a matter of time before the faculty found out about the amulet, and then they were all lost.

The day's studies went by in a blur. Ebon managed to keep up appearances well enough that Perrin did not bark at him for his wandering attention, and of course Kalem and Theren mostly left him alone in the library, for their thoughts were just as preoccupied. After dinner he set off into the streets for the second day in a row, but this time alone. He looked all about him, hoping to catch a glimpse of a black-clad assassin haunting his steps. But he saw nothing, and wondered if that should make him feel better or worse.

Though the troubles that burdened him seemed crushing in their weight, he still felt a wash of relief the moment he stepped across Adara's threshold. She came to Ebon before he reached the top of the stairs, and he heaved a great sigh as she took him into her arms. The last of his anxiety washed away like soot stains in a downpour.

"My love," she murmured. "I was overjoyed at your message, but now I wonder at its purpose. I can see that a great many things weigh heavily upon you."

"You do not know the half of it," said Ebon, "but I can fix that. Come. There is much to tell."

As quickly as he could, he informed her of all that had transpired since last he had seen her. She listened attentively, stopping him sharply when he left out a detail and threw the tale into confusion. And when he reached the end and told her what Mako had said, he saw her olive skin go a shade lighter.

"He used those words, did he?" she muttered softly. "Darkness take that man."

"What did he mean?" said Ebon. "I hear no special truth in the words, but he seemed to think they held one, and now it seems you feel the same."

"Oh, he does not speak in some code," she said. "Yet he knew that I would know what he meant. How did he learn . . ." She shook her head and stood, going to the cabinet where she kept her wine and her mead. "Never mind that. I need something to wet my throat."

"Do not—that is . . ." Ebon paused, his cheeks flushing with embarrassment. "Might I try some of your mead, instead of wine?"

She arched an eyebrow and gave him a little smirk. "Are you certain? It is an acquired taste. I doubt you will like it."

He raised his hands. "How will I ever acquire it if I do not try?"

Adara studied him for a moment and then shrugged before bringing the bottle of mead over to the table. First she poured into his cup, but only a little splash, and then nudged it towards him. "Try it. I would not waste a whole cup on you if you do not enjoy it."

Ebon lifted it to his lips and took a sniff. It did not smell . . . bad, exactly. But neither did it make his mouth water. He tilted the cup back.

The taste that slid down his tongue and into his throat was both familiar and foreign—like honey without the sweet. Too, there were herbs and spices aplenty; as a Drayden, he could not help but pick some of them out. It was not entirely unpleasant, but neither did it set him at ease the way the first good swig of wine often did.

"Acquired, mayhap," he said. "But not awful at first blush, either."

Adara seemed impressed despite herself. "Indeed? Mayhap I should have expected as much from a man whose tastes are as cultured as yours." She smirked to let him know the words were playful and then filled his cup nearly to the brim before doing the same with her own. Ebon's second sip was better than the first, and made the more pleasant when Adara settled herself sideways across his lap, draping an arm about his shoulders as she met his gaze.

"Now, tell me what hidden meaning I have brought from Mako's lips to your ears," said Ebon. "I do not like that my family's man knows something of you that I do not."

"Oh, but there are so many things you do not know about me, Ebon—and so many more things I look forward to teaching you." Though her words were light, and her tone more so, he could see the concern lurking in her dark eyes. It soon came out in a sigh. "Your man has learned—though I know not how—of a certain . . . friend I have. A friend who owes me a favor."

Ebon's jaw clenched, though he tried to hide it. He inspected his cup carefully, feigning nonchalance. "Is your friend a guest?"

She let out a slow breath through her nose, and he could hear her trying to hide her annoyance just as hard as he had tried to hide his interest. "They are not. In fact they are not interested in lovers at all, for coin or otherwise. But they are . . . well, I did them a favor once, long before I came to this life. I have waited many years for sufficient reason to ask that that favor be returned. But I wonder that I did not think of it before, for certainly I think they could be of help."

"I would not have you waste your one chance on me," said Ebon. "After all, I hardly think they could be more useful in finding Isra than Mako has been."

"You do not know my friend," said Adara, giving him a grim little smile. "You have said before that if anyone can find the girl, Mako can. That is not true. The truth is that if anyone can find the girl, my friend can."

"But that is all the more reason you should not waste such a chance on me," said Ebon. "I may not even need such help."

"Yet you may," said Adara. "And if things go ill for you without such a favor, it could mean your life. That is something I cannot allow."

She rose, leaving Ebon's lap suddenly cool. From a cupboard she drew parchment and a quill, and when she had scribbled a message she sealed it with wax using a seal Ebon had never seen before. But he could not catch a glimpse of its design before she whisked it away and down the steps. He heard her sharp whistle as she flagged down a messenger, and then in a moment she reappeared in the room.

"I must get dressed for a walk," she said. "And so must you."

"Now?" said Ebon. "Surely you cannot mean to see your friend tonight. How can you know your message will find them?"

"It will," she said. "And they will come at once. Have no fear of that. You must not be dressed in Academy robes when we see them. I have some other garments that will do."

She undressed quickly and made Ebon do the same. When his hands wandered towards her, she smirked and slapped them away. She then bundled herself up in winter clothes and gave Ebon an outfit of his own, one that was elegant without drawing much attention. As soon as they had laced up their boots, she went to him and pulled him down for a quick peck on the cheek.

"You must promise that you will not stare overmuch, nor act out of turn," she said. "And you *must not* ask me any questions. Do you understand? Mayhap one day I can explain. But not now."

"Very well," he said.

She caught his cheek and turned him to face her. She stared at him for a long moment. "Promise me."

He frowned. "I promise. Why? What is wrong?"

"Nothing is wrong," she said. "But . . . well, things are about to become very different. For both of us."

With one more kiss, she drew him out and into the snowy night.

The afternoon now wore on, and the days were shorter besides. Adara hurried as she led him along winding streets and alleys, for it would soon be dusk. Every so often he would take her hand—not out of the need for guidance or the fear of losing her in the crowd, but simply so that he could feel the warmth of her skin on his own.

They were making east now, in nearly the same direction where lay the Drayden manor. But after a time they turned off the main road that ran from the western gates to the east. They had long passed the Academy to the south, and the High King's palace loomed close above them when Adara turned aside and led him north a ways, through streets and alleys that grew narrower with every step. Soon they reached a little shop with a large red door, where Adara paused. From its chimney wafted the smell of coals and the sharp, bitter tang of molten metal. But this was no ironsmith—in the windows of the shop were set little trinkets and dishes of silver.

"Around back," Adara murmured. "It would not do for us to be seen entering the front door—and my friend would prefer it that way as well, I think."

To the shop's rear was a small door of plain, unadorned wood. Upon this Adara tapped thrice, and then twice more after a pause. In a moment Ebon heard scuttling footsteps within, and then the door creaked open. Into view came a thin little man, wild grey hair sticking out in all directions. Though the day's light waned, still he blinked at them as though a bright torch had been thrust into his eyes.

"Little Adara," he breathed. "Sky above, girl, but it is good to see you."

"And you, Aurel," said Adara. She bent to give the wizened man a kiss upon the cheek. "Are we expected?"

"I should say so," said Aurel, shaking his head. He stepped inside, waving them after him. "Between this and all the goings-on before the attack, I will be amazed if my heart does not give out before its time."

Adara took Ebon's hand and drew him inside. It took Ebon's eyes a moment to adjust to the dim. When they did, he saw a small sitting room with a stone floor, warmed by a hearth with a metal grate for a screen. Mayhap a pace from the hearth was a low, modest table with three stools. One of the stools was occupied. Aurel glanced at the figure who sat there and then at Adara and Ebon before he withdrew from the room, closing the door behind him with a soft *click*.

The figure rose. He wore a cloak of plain brown, but its unremarkable color could not hide the fine weave of its cloth, nor the work of the expert hands that had sewn its hem. The cloak covered no armor, but there was a sword at his waist—a fine thing, not the plain blade of a soldier. He lifted his hands to throw back his hood. Well-tousled, sandy hair showed a few strands of grey, and his eyes were keen as they took in Adara and Ebon. There was something intensely familiar about him, but at first Ebon could not place it. Then he saw the brooch that pinned the cloak together. It bore the royal seal. *A palace guard,* he thought—but then the truth came to him, and his limbs shook. He fell to one knee and bowed his head.

"Your . . . Your Highness," he gasped, his throat a desert.

Lord Prince Eamin, son of the High King and presumptive heir to the throne, took a step forwards and inclined his head. But Adara did not kneel, only gave a deep curtsey, and to Ebon's shock, Eamin did not seem surprised in the least.

"Well met, son. But come, and treat me no different than you would your friend Adara. Kneeling is all good for the ceremony of a throne room, but it seems a little grandiose for Aurel's little parlor, would you not say?"

Bright teeth flashed in a grin, and Ebon matched it without thinking. His heart stopped when Eamin held forth a hand. They clasped wrists, and the Lord Prince pulled him to his feet. Then, to Ebon's growing wonder, Adara stepped forwards. She kissed one of Eamin's cheeks, and then the other, the way an Idrisian greeted their close friend, or mayhap lover—though she had said that was not the case, he reminded himself.

"Your Highness," she said. "My heart is glad to see you again."

"My own mood is as I said it would be the last time I beheld you," said Eamin. "Though I am pleased to be in your company, my thoughts are solemn, knowing you would not have called except at the utmost end of need. What troubles you, Adara?"

"The same thing that troubles my friend here," said Adara, inclining her head towards Ebon. On instinct, Ebon ducked his head. The Lord Prince could not have gotten a very good look at him beneath his hood, and if Adara did not wish to speak his name, he would not speak it either. He knew nothing of the Lord Prince's politics, but would not be surprised to find that Eamin, like most of Underrealm, held no high opinion of the family Drayden.

"Well? Speak on, son," said Eamin. "We have all three of us wasted enough of a night that might be spent in merriment."

"Of course, Your Highness," said Ebon, bowing still further. His mind raced, wondering where to begin. "I . . . I imagine you know something of the Academy murders?"

Eamin's countenance darkened at once. "I do," he said softly. "Though Her Majesty was quick to send her guards to the citadel, I wish we could have done more, and more quickly. But the killer is dead now, or so they say."

"They say wrong," said Ebon. "She is alive. I do not know how. But she is alive and plotting further evil upon the Seat."

"A corpse was found in the Great Bay," said Eamin, his frown deepening. "How can she be alive if we know where her body lies?"

Ebon quailed, for he could hear impatience in the Lord Prince's voice. But then Eamin put a gentle hand on his shoulder. "Do not quiver so, son. You have not raised my ire—only if what you say is true, it is very troubling, and it has darkened my thoughts."

"It is true," Ebon insisted. "I saw her—I, and some others. It was not long ago. And when the corpse was found, they said it had been dead for weeks. That cannot be. She is out there somewhere and has found a way to deceive us all. But no one will believe us, and so we can find no help to prove it. I only want to ferret her out of hiding before she attacks the Academy again."

Eamin paused, staring into the fire. After a time he met Adara's gaze.

"Please, Your Highness," she said quietly. "Trust him in this."

713

Eamin looked to Ebon, and Ebon understood at once: Adara was in fact asking him to trust *her*. He thought the weight of her faith in him might press him into the stone floor. Slowly the Lord Prince nodded.

"Very well," he said. "I have some agents who may be trusted. I will have them search for Isra. If she is upon the Seat, they will find her—wherever she may be."

Hope quailed in Ebon's breast. Mako had been saying much the same thing for weeks. But then he realized that this was not another promise from Mako—this was the Lord Prince.

Then Eamin shook his shoulders as though waking from a deep slumber, and his mood lightened. "But so simple a request is nothing, Adara. You must not consider my debt to you repaid. Do not hesitate to call upon me again."

Adara smiled. "A small deed from a busybody weighs heavier than a great deed from the lazy, they say."

"They are fools if they call you lazy," said Eamin. "And speaking of which, I am sure the two of you have further business to attend tonight, as I do myself. If we may . . .?"

He gestured, and they hastened towards the door together. Once in the alley, Eamin made to go in one direction, while Adara and Ebon headed in the other. But just before they all departed, Eamin stopped them with a raised hand and peered at Ebon beneath his hood.

"It is good to see a Drayden on the side of right," he said softly. "Such a thing is less common than one might hope."

Ebon swallowed hard. So Eamin had recognized him after all. He felt a fool for thinking he could conceal his face so well.

"I hope my conduct may always please Your Highness so," he murmured, and took a knee again.

"Come now, I said there was no need for that," said Eamin. "Stay your course, Drayden. Though not all your kin may feel the same, I think you do your name proud. Prouder than any since . . . he would have been your brother, would he not?"

Everything went still. Ebon could not move a muscle—he even noticed that his mouth hung open, but he could not close it.

"Momen was a good man," said Eamin. "A great one, in fact, and high in the estimation of many across the nine kingdoms. Though I would not guess that your kin have told you so. He deserved better than what he got."

At last Ebon's mouth worked, though just enough to croak, "Thank you, Your Highness. But how did you . . .?"

Eamin smiled sadly. "Another time, I hope. Some tales are not worth telling if they cannot be told properly."

And then he was gone, vanishing through the gently falling snow.

THIRTY-ONE

EBON STAYED AT ADARA'S HOME AS LONG AS HE COULD, BUT EVENTUALLY he made his way back to the Academy. The next day he muddled through his classes in a fog, still overawed about the Lord Prince. He half expected some royal messenger to appear at the Academy with news that Isra had been discovered and that the threat was now over. But of course no such message came.

Kalem saw something odd in his demeanor and asked him about it. But Ebon did not wish to tell the story twice, and bid him wait for Theren. They saw no trace of her at breakfast, or at the midday meal. At first Ebon thought little of it, but when she had not appeared by the beginning of the afternoon's studies he began to grow worried. Together they conducted a quick search for her, looking through the dining hall and the hallways outside, and then even darting upstairs to seek her in the dormitories. But they found no trace of her, and so they went to the library—where they found Theren at last, waiting for them in their alcove. She was shaking, and to their surprise, she sat with Lilith.

"Theren!" said Ebon. "We looked all over for you. What is wrong?"

"I . . . they came for me," said Theren. Lilith looked up in dismay, and Ebon saw that she was clutching one of Theren's hands tightly in both of her own. "The instructors, I mean. I was called to my instructor's office—Nestor, I mean—and there I found the dean, as well as some instructors of the other branches. They sat me down in a chair, and when I tried to resist, they forced me. Then they cast . . . some sort of spell upon me, though I know not what they did. I only saw their eyes glowing and felt the itch on my skin where their magic probed me."

"Why?" said Ebon. "What were they looking for?"

"I have just told you I do not know!" snapped Theren.

But Kalem had blanched, and he sank heavily into one of the armchairs. "I know what they were doing," he said. "They sought the mark of enchantment upon you."

A glance at Theren told Ebon she knew nothing more of Kalem's words than he did. "What is the mark of enchantment?"

"Do you remember when Theren searched for Lilith's spell-sight within the vaults? It is like that. A sort of trace left upon someone who uses a magical artifact. They sought for a sign that Theren had used an enchanted object."

"But why?" said Ebon. "Why Theren? Of course *we* know she carries the amulet, but how could they?" But then he froze where he stood. His eyes went to Lilith. They had not told her of Kekhit's amulet.

"Do not trouble yourself about that," said Theren. "I have told Lilith about it already."

"You *what?*" said Kalem. He threw his hands up in the air. "Is there anyone left in the Academy who does not know?"

Theren glared at him, and he wilted. "Save us from your dramatics. I trust her. But do you not see? Xain has grown suspicious that I have been using mindwyrd. Ebon showed the instructors that I have no magestone in my blood, but Xain knows that the amulet of Kekhit has been stolen. The faculty may once have thought that the amulet was in Isra's possession, but now Xain suspects it is in mine."

Ebon slumped in his armchair. But then he had another thought, and he straightened once more. "But wait. Kalem, you told us that spell-sight is wildly unreliable, and that no one would take its signature for evidence."

"So I did," said Kalem. "And the mark of enchantment is even more inscrutable. But think, Ebon. Xain is desperate. His *son* is missing. Do you think he would withhold his hand from any method that might recover Erin? It is like we were when we were trying to prove Lilith was the Academy killer—meaning no offense, Lilith."

Lilith arched an eyebrow. "Of course. And you are correct—only Xain is more dangerous now than you were then, because his own blood is in danger, and because he has the power of the office of the dean."

Theren looked at them with fear in her eyes. "But why did they not find the mark? I have—" She cast a quick glance about them to look for eavesdroppers and then went on in a whisper. "I have been using the amulet, after all."

"I do not think the mark lasts for very long," said Kalem. "It is days since we fought Isra in the grotto. The mark must have faded."

"Then I must get rid of it before they try again."

Ebon frowned. "Mayhap you are right. It seems too dangerous now. But what if Isra should reappear?"

"I will be unable to stop her if I am in a Mystic prison with their knives digging into my skin," snapped Theren. Lilith shuddered, and her hands crossed over her chest as she turned her gaze away. "I cannot carry it with me now, in any case. Why should I not be rid of it?"

"What will you do?" said Kalem. "Will you leave it for the instructors to find? Do you not think that will raise suspicion, that it would reappear *just* after they investigated you?"

"I will throw it into the Great Bay, and good riddance," said Theren.

To Ebon's surprise, Lilith reached out and took Theren's hand. Theren looked over after a moment, and Ebon saw the sadness in Lilith's gaze as their eyes met.

"You must keep it. Only a little longer. It cannot be long before we find her," said Lilith.

Kalem leaned forwards, focusing on Ebon. "To that end—what happened last night, Ebon? Was Adara able to help you?"

For a moment Ebon hesitated, wondering if he should tell them—particularly Lilith—of the Lord Prince. But it seemed there was nothing for it, and soon he had spilled the whole of the tale. As soon as he told them of Eamin, they all went stone-still in their seats, and Ebon could see something very much like worship shining in Kalem's eyes.

"The Lord Prince," he whispered in reverence.

Even Theren's panic seemed to have diminished somewhat. "These are the first glad tidings we have heard since the Academy murders first began."

"How?" said Kalem. "I mean to say, how could Adara . . . it would be impressive enough if she knew him as a guest—that would make her a high courtesan indeed, and worthy of much honor. But outside of her business? What could possibly have brought the two of them together?"

Theren scoffed. "You make it sound as though the Lord Prince is some coward who spends all his days cooped up in the palace. He has walked upon many roads and fought in many battles both great and small. He is one of the few goldbags who even I have some measure of respect for—outside of present company, of course. Adara could have met him anywhere—and if she performed him some service, he would not forget it."

Ebon shrugged. "I do not know. I only know what she told me, and that was precious little."

But in his mind he was wrestling with the same thought that had plagued him since their rendezvous the night before. Yes, it was astounding that Adara knew the Lord Prince, and especially on such terms. But more perturbing still was the fact that Mako knew of their relationship, if so it could be called. How could the bodyguard have learned that secret, if he had only known Adara for a short time?

Mako's ever-growing omniscience had grown beyond the bounds of unsettling and was now close to terrifying. And yet the man still could not locate Isra upon the High King's Seat.

Where can she be?

Lilith loosed a sigh and shifted in her seat. "This is most comforting. If the Lord Prince himself has joined the search, it cannot be very long before Isra is dug out of whatever dark corner she has hidden herself in."

"I am not so sure," said Kalem, scowling as he put his chin on his fist. "After all, she has conjured her own corpse out of thin air. I would once have counted that impossible."

"Many things are impossible until someone of industry carries them out," said Mako.

Ebon leaped out of his chair. Kalem tried to do the same, but tripped over his own feet and went crashing to the ground. Theren leaped up with her eyes aglow, and Lilith fought to stand, but her weakened limbs almost betrayed her. She opened her mouth to scream. Mako thrust one finger at her, and his face twisted in a scowl.

"Keep your silence, and keep your life. Lose one, and lose the other."

"It is all right, Lilith," said Theren quickly. She went to Lilith and put a hand on her arm. "He is no threat. Not now, and not here, at any rate."

"What is he doing in the library?" hissed Lilith. She looked around, and Ebon did the same, for it seemed impossible that no one else could see him. But no other students were in sight, as if by chance—though of course Ebon knew it must be by Mako's design.

"He comes and goes, it seems." Ebon glared at Mako. "What are you doing here, other than frightening us all half to death by appearing from nowhere?"

"The little goldshitter is very flip for one who is sitting and taking council with a Yerrin," growled Mako, who had not taken his furious eyes from Lilith. "But that discussion must be had another time, for matters of true import are afoot. I come with news of Gregor."

Ebon felt the blood drain from his face. Kalem and Theren went very still, and even Lilith gulped before lifting her chin and fixing Mako with a defiant look.

"What of him?" said Ebon. "I thought the Mystics took him."

"They did not," said Mako. "He killed them all. He has not yet managed to flee the Seat, but he is about to. Now, in fact. We must stop him."

"Asking for help again?" said Theren, smirking through her unease. "This is truly a time of wonders."

Mako sneered at her. "The dregs of my resources you may be, but dregs are better than an empty cup. Gregor has killed most of my agents already, and those who remain still bear grievous wounds. Isra is nowhere to be seen, but I need you to contend with a firemage at Gregor's side."

"You mean an elementalist," said Kalem, by reflex. Then he froze.

Slowly, ever so slowly, Mako turned his baleful glare upon the boy. Ebon thought Kalem would die upon the spot, the boy looked so terrified.

"I am sorry," he whimpered. "It was an accident."

Mako ignored him. "Girl," he said, looking at Theren. "Go and fetch your amulet."

"No."

The bodyguard's jaw twitched. "I did not ask you a question."

"Yet I gave you an answer. They are searching for it, and they already suspect me. Besides, you said Isra was not there."

"She was not when I left," said Mako. "That does not mean she has not appeared since, or that Gregor is not making his way to her even now."

"Still I will not bring it," said Theren. "I am no good to any of us if I land in prison—and I value my own skin too highly, besides."

To Ebon's surprise and relief, Mako grinned. "That sentiment, at least, I can sympathize with. Very well—but I hope you are impressive enough without it. Meet me in the gardens as quickly as you can. You know where. Do not bring the Yerrin girl."

Before they could answer, he turned and vanished into the bookshelves.

"'The Yerrin girl,' he says." Lilith snorted. "Darkness take him. I will come if I wish."

"You will not," said Theren at once. "You have not fully recovered from your ordeal, and you have been through too much already on our account. Besides, if you come with us, I do not doubt that Mako will try to slit your throat."

"Let him," said Lilith, raising her chin. "Only a fool threatens a wizard."

"Two wizards, you mean," said Theren. "For I would not let him touch you. Yet still you should not come."

Lilith's mouth twitched, though whether towards a smile or a frown, Ebon could not say. "Do you think I trust you to look after yourself? You have failed to do so in the past. I will remain here, but I order you to come back whole."

At the word *order,* Ebon tensed, expecting an outburst from Theren. Beside him, Kalem looked between the girls uncertainly.

721

But Theren's dark cheeks flushed darker for a moment, and she stepped forwards. "Yes, my dear."

And then she kissed her.

Far too much had happened in far too short a time for Ebon to know what to make of this. He stood stock still, heedless of his mouth hanging open, unable to do so much as blink. He was only tangentially aware of Kalem beside him, teeth gleaming in a fool's grin. The moment lasted only a few heartbeats. Then Theren stepped away and hastened off, passing between the boys as she did so. She seized their elbows and dragged them after her.

"If the two of you say so much as a word, I will throw you from the balcony to the library's first floor," she hissed.

"I would not dream of it," said Kalem. But his grin said far more than words ever could.

THIRTY-TWO

THEY SLIPPED THROUGH THE LIBRARY'S FRONT DOORS WHEN JIA WAS not watching and soon had passed through the garden to the place where they knew Mako's secret entrance waited. At first the space between the hedges looked empty—but then Mako appeared, stepping out from a gap in the plants that looked far too narrow for his broad frame.

"Closer," he said. "Ebon, give me your hand."

Curious, Ebon did so—and then gave an indignant cry as Mako seized his sleeve and tore off several long strips of cloth.

"Cease your mewling," growled Mako. "Now the two of you—turn around."

One by one he used the strips of cloth to blindfold Theren and Kalem, and such was the urgency in his movements that even Theren did not complain. While Ebon turned away, Mako pushed some panel or lever, and they heard the soft sliding of stone upon grass and snow. The air within the passage was cool, cooler even than the wintry air outside. With one hand on each of his friend's shoulders to guide them,

Ebon made his way forwards through the dark, and before long Mako had them out on the streets.

"Into the sewers again," said Mako. "But not west this time."

He led them down a gutter and into the stinking passageways beneath the streets. But whether because of the chilled air or because Ebon was growing used to it, the stench was not as noisome as it had been before. Mako set a quick pace, and from the markings on the ceiling, Ebon knew they were heading mostly east.

"Where is Gregor going?" he said.

"He is trying to sail from the Seat and vanish into the nine kingdoms," said Mako. "But the western docks are watched, for the grotto was near them, and so he thinks to have better luck on the other side of the island."

"How did he overpower so many Mystics when they caught him before?" said Kalem.

Mako threw him a quick glance over his shoulder. "I did not wait around to watch the fight. But you saw his size."

"And how easily he slapped you about," said Theren offhandedly.

The bodyguard said nothing, but Ebon saw his fingers twitch as though they itched to draw his dagger.

They went on in silence for a long while, until Ebon was certain they must have traveled much, much farther than last time. Eventually Mako stopped at the intersection of two tunnels and pressed himself to one of the corners.

"We must proceed cautiously from here," he said. "We might encounter Yerrin guards accompanying Gregor to his boat. But, too, we might find more Mystics, for they have been alerted to Gregor's movements and are coming for him."

"Mystics?" said Kalem. "Then why do we not let them catch the villain, and leave ourselves out of it?"

"Because if they catch him, they are not going to ask after Isra," said Mako. "They believe that Isra is dead, for they have seen her corpse. That is why we must find him first."

"You have thrown us into the middle of a fight between Yerrin and the Mystics?" said Ebon. He straightened and folded his arms. "What happened to the man who went on and on about keeping me out of harm's way? This hardly seems a safe course."

"There are no safe courses left, you goldshitting little idiot," said Mako. "I can let you sit in comfort in the Academy, or you can get your hands dirty and keep Isra from wreaking greater evil. And in the end you will keep her crimes from being blamed on you. What happened to the boy who always wanted to stick his nose in where it did not belong?"

Ebon glared but had no answer.

"I thought so," said Mako. "Come on, then. The sooner we find Gregor, the sooner this is all over with."

But even Mako's caution could not keep them from a fight in the end. He led them around one corner and then the next, but then they had to drop down into a lower level of the sewers. The way seemed clear at first—but the moment their feet touched down in the lower tunnel, they found green-glad warriors just a few paces away. The Yerrin soldiers stopped in their tracks. Their swords came free with a ringing hiss of steel.

"Theren!" growled Mako. He threw himself into the fray.

She hardly needed his urging; two of the guards flew into the air and slammed into the walls on either side. But without the amulet, Theren's spells were not so strong as they might have been. The guards struggled back to their feet. Mako leaped upon one and drove his daggers into the back of the woman's neck. She slumped into the filth that covered the tunnel floor, her body going limp in an instant.

Ebon winced and forced his attention away. He scanned the green cloaks and the open-faced helmets, searching for one who stood above all the rest. But he could see at once that Gregor was not here.

The guards pressed forwards now, and their shock at the sudden appearance of Ebon's group faded with each passing moment. Theren struck and pushed at them each in turn, forcing those in the front back into the others. Mako danced and slashed and stabbed with his knives. Beside Ebon, Kalem's eyes glowed, and he reached into the stone wall of the sewer, pulling forth small handfuls of stone which he turned to iron and flung at the soldiers' heads. But the boy's arms were weak, and his aim was poor.

"Here, give them to me," said Ebon. Kalem gratefully handed one off. Ebon threw it at a guard's head as hard as he could. It clattered off the man's brow, making him stumble, and then Theren's magic lifted him from his feet and cast him back into his comrades. But looking over their heads, Ebon saw still more guards appear around the next bend in the sewer.

"Mako!" he cried. When the bodyguard shot him a look, Ebon pointed. Mako saw the approaching guards, and his mouth set in a grim line.

"Boy," he said, glancing at Kalem. "We must away. Use the floor."

"What is that supposed to mean?" said Kalem, close to panic.

"The *stone,* you idiot," snarled Mako.

Kalem understood at once, and he knelt. Magelight sprang into his eyes, and he pressed his fingers to the stone floor, ignoring the muck that enveloped his skin. An itch sprang to life on the back of Ebon's neck. Stone rippled under Kalem's fingers, and Ebon could almost see the magic spreading across the floor. It flowed forth like water, turning the stone to liquid, and in a blink it had spread beneath the feet of the Yerrin guards. Then Kalem lifted his hands, and the glow died in his eyes. The stone solidified again at once, and suddenly all the Yerrin guards were encased up to their ankles. They stared at their feet in fear and confusion, nearly falling over.

Mako took a step back, showing Kalem his cruel grin. "Well done, boy. Your head is not completely stuffed with wool, it seems. Come."

He ran off down the tunnel, and Ebon and his friends hastened to follow. Ebon looked back just before they turned the corner and saw the Yerrin guards looking helplessly after them.

THIRTY-THREE

"THAT WAS A WASTE OF TIME," SAID THEREN. "LIKELY GREGOR IS ALready gone by now."

"Let us hope not," said Mako. "But if we do catch him, it will not have been a waste, for he will have fewer swords by his side."

"Were those soldiers coming to reinforce Gregor, or clearing the way for his arrival?" said Ebon. "If they were behind him, he cannot still be there for us to find."

"We will know in a moment," said Mako. "Look ahead."

Ebon did, and saw a pale glow far down the tunnel. The passageway ran straight to it without stopping and with no tunnels branching off in either direction. The way was clear, and no one blocked them from it.

Mako broke into a sprint now, and Theren hastened to keep up. Ebon and Kalem were swiftly left behind, stumbling along on halfdead legs, their breath wheezing out in great gusts that misted upon the air. Mako and Theren burst out into the daylight, and the boys followed a moment later.

Everything was so bright that at first Ebon could only blink, using his hand to shield his eyes from the sun. When at last they adjusted, he searched for the Seat's eastern docks. But the great docks were nowhere to be seen. Instead there were only a few small piles in a row, to which was lashed a small, floating dock.

Everything looked intimately familiar, like a place he had visited many times before, but he could not get his bearings. He looked around, seeing high cliffs rising far above them. The feet of the cliffs ended in the small stone platform where they now stood, stretching around the edge of the Great Bay's water, which was only a few paces away. And across the little cove, steps were carved into the stone, leading up to the tops of the cliffs that stood stark and black against the bright sky above.

Cliffs.

The cliffs on the south of the Seat.

Ebon knew where they were. It was the cove—the cove to which he had followed Cyrus and Adara the day the Seat had been attacked, and where Cyrus had fallen to his death. His sense of familiarity came not from many visits in the flesh, but from the countless times he had visited the place since—in his nightmares.

His legs shook, and he clutched Kalem's shoulder for support. The boy looked up at him, brow furrowing.

"Ebon? What is it?"

Mako heard it, and looked back at them over his shoulder. When he saw Ebon's face, he smiled. "What is wrong, boy? Is this place familiar to you?"

Though Ebon tried to summon an answer, none came—and then all their thought was drawn by Theren's sudden cry. Ebon's gaze followed her outthrust finger, which pointed towards the stone steps on the other side of the cove.

Down the steps came Gregor, moving with measured haste, and beside him were a half-dozen guards. As soon as Theren cried out, he turned and saw them. He wore no helmet now, and so Ebon could see full well how his face twisted to rage, fury smoldering in his eyes.

"There," said Mako. "That is the firemage—the woman behind him." But he need not have warned them, for she stepped forwards just then, and her eyes were aglow. A bolt of flame sprang from her

728

fingers and came screaming towards them. But Theren's own magelight flared in response; an itch sprang up on Ebon's neck, and the flame died harmlessly upon the air. Theren thrust out a hand, and the firemage stumbled, but she quickly recovered.

"He means to take that boat," said Mako, pulling Ebon's attention back to Gregor and his guards. There was a small rowboat moored at the floating dock, and Gregor was making for it. "We cannot let him escape. Come!"

Around the stone shelf he ran, with Ebon and Kalem trying to keep up. But Ebon did not know what good they would be—Gregor had five other soldiers with him, and he and Kalem were no warriors, nor even wizards of a useful sort for this kind of thing, as Theren was.

But he had underestimated Theren—or he had overestimated Yerrin's firemage. For even as Theren held off the other wizard's spells, she could spare a blast or two of her own. When Gregor and his guards were still only halfway down the stone steps, an unseen forced clutched two of them and cast them over the edge. They fell screaming, not to the stone shelf, where they would surely have died, but into the water. They plunged beneath the surface and came up sputtering, fighting to reach the dock and desperate to remove the armor that suddenly weighed them down. But when Theren tried again, the firemage mustered a desperate defense and held her off.

"Your friend is worth more than she seems," said Mako. "Now is the time to prove your own worth—but stay back where you will not be harmed."

"We are no great wizards, Mako," said Ebon. "How can we help you against swords and armor?"

"Stand at my rear and throw your little handfuls of stone," said Mako. "Let Theren do her work, and do not let them get behind me."

So saying, he approached the foot of the stairs, which Gregor had nearly reached. Two of the guards came forwards first. Like Gregor, they had no shields or armor save a shirt of chain. But they had swords at their waists, and they drew them in unison.

Mako slid his own curved daggers from their sheaths, and then with a flourish he flipped them around to hold them reversed. "Come, my darlings," he said, his tone almost playful. "Come and dance with me."

They did, and for a moment that was all Mako did—he danced. The guards' swords were long and broad, but that also made them heavy, and so Mako could twist and turn around every swing and thrust. Every few moments he would slash with one of his knives—but the slashes were slow and reserved, even to Ebon's eye, meant only to make one of his opponents take a step back. If Gregor had joined the fray, it might have been different—but the stone shelf was narrow, and so he held his ground, but tried to edge around the fight so that he could approach the floating dock where his boat awaited.

Kalem bent and scooped handfuls of stone from the ground at their feet, and when he saw an opportunity, he flung them at the Yerrin guards. But Mako's dance was as erratic as it was savage, and he could rarely find an opening. But then one of the guards' boots slipped into a saltwater pool, and she slipped, and Mako struck at last. Swift as blinking he lunged, slashing the guard's throat open. She fell to her knees, gurgling her last, and Ebon's gut twisted. With one out of the way, Mako easily closed the gap between himself and the other guard, stepping inside his reach and plunging both daggers into the man's gut. To his credit, the second guard grimaced and tried to grasp Mako's throat even in death, but the daggers came out, and they sank into the man's temples. He fell heavily to the ground.

Mako stood looking at the bodies for a moment. Then he shoved his toe beneath the woman and turned her over, so that her corpse sank into the waters of the Great Bay. The man, too, he kicked into the water. Only then did he look up at Gregor.

"With that distraction out of the way—do you care to try and finish what we began the other night?"

The giant's broadsword slid from its sheath with a harsh, rattling rasp. It gleamed in the sunlight, and Gregor held it forth, pointing it at Mako as if the blade were a scepter.

"It shall not go any better for you than it did the last time."

Mako shrugged. "I did not think the last time went so badly. I still have the marks of your love to prove it." With the tip of one dagger he pointed at the bruises on his cheeks. But then he turned the dagger so that it pointed at Gregor instead. "Yet I see that you bear some of my kisses as well—and, mayhap, marks from the embraces of some of our red-cloaked friends, who arrived just at the end of our union?"

Indeed, now that Mako mentioned it, Ebon could see bruises and scrapes all across Gregor's skin. He knew Mako could not have landed all those blows when they fought in the grotto. Gregor must not have had an easy time escaping the Mystics when they arrived. Now the giant's nostrils flared, and he took a step forwards with bared teeth.

"Still your tongue and bare your steel."

"Sky above," said Mako, snickering. "There are children present."

With a roar Gregor charged. Mako danced again, but this time not so easily. Though Gregor was the larger man by far, he was lightning fast. Mako was forced to step nimbly around him, so that Gregor ended up with his back to Ebon and Kalem. They saw it at the same time, and looked at each other.

"Should we . . .?"

Ebon glanced at Gregor's broad back. Would throwing a stone even do any good? They might only anger the man, and then he would come for them. But in the grotto, Gregor had gotten the better of Mako by a wide margin . . .

"It is tempting to let him fight this battle on his own," said Ebon with a sigh. "But no. We must help him. Can you play your trick with the stone floor again?"

Kalem gave Gregor another glance, and he quailed. "I can try."

He crept forwards, hunched almost double so as to avoid Gregor's notice. And Gregor did not notice him—but the firemage on the steps above did. She cried out, and a wall of fire sprang from the stone in Kalem's very face. The boy screamed and fell back, batting at the hem of his robes where the flames had caught. Theren dispelled the fire almost immediately, but the edge of Kalem's robe still burned.

"Hold still!" cried Ebon. He seized Kalem's arm and dragged him towards the edge of the rocky platform. Taking him under the elbows, Ebon threw his legs over the edge and into the water, where the flames died in a hiss.

"There now," said Ebon, pulling him back up. "No harm—"

But Kalem looked over his shoulder, and his eyes shot wide in terror. Ebon did not even turn—he only seized Kalem's shoulder and dove. A rasping hiss sounded as Gregor's sword sliced through the air where his head had been a moment before. Now the giant loomed over them, and they fought to scramble away—but then Mako was there, forcing Gregor to turn around. And across the cove, Theren gave a shout, and her magic struck Gregor a mighty blow. He stumbled away, striking the base of the cliff hard.

The firemage was waiting. As Theren's attention went to Gregor, the woman on the steps let loose a flurry of magic. Fire shot forth, laced with thunder, and a gale behind it all. Theren threw up her arms, holding it back with a wall of pure force. But the winds broke through, and buffeted her, and then an arc of lightning struck her in the chest. She screamed and dropped to the ground.

"Theren!" cried Ebon.

He looked to Mako, hoping the bodyguard could help, though he did not know how. But Mako was not looking at Theren. He had turned towards the steps, and even as Ebon's gaze fell upon him, he threw one of his daggers. It flew through the air, straight as an arrow, and buried itself to the hilt in the firemage's neck.

She stood there slack for a moment. Her fingers probed at the dagger, while her eyes tried to turn in their sockets to see it. Then she tumbled from the edge and landed on the stone shelf with a wet *crack*.

It had taken Mako only a half-moment, but it was long enough. He danced away even as he whirled to face Gregor again, but the giant had already struck, and four fingers of his sword tip plunged into the flesh of Mako's arm before withdrawing almost at once. Mako grimaced, but did not utter a sound, not even a grunt. He sank down on one knee with the pain, and Gregor stepped forwards.

By Ebon's hand lay a sword, dropped by one of the guards Mako had killed. He snatched it up without thinking and leaped. A scream ripped from his throat as he swung it into the back of Gregor's leg. Ebon had thought the man wore only leather pants, but he must have had chain beneath, for the sword rebounded with a rending sound. Still, Gregor stumbled. He turned and sent the back of one boulder-sized fist into Ebon's face. Ebon went crashing into the stone wall.

As he lay there, senseless for a moment, he saw that his little swing had been enough. Mako was up once again, and with a savage kick he knocked the sword from Gregor's hand. It plunged into the Great Bay and vanished. Gregor reached for him, but Mako leaped over his arms and behind him. One massive arm came around, searching, but Mako caught it and wrenched it, and before Ebon could blink he had flung Gregor to the floor. He twisted the hand until Ebon thought it must surely break and put his one remaining dagger to Gregor's throat. Everyone went deathly still.

"Now then, brute," said Mako. "That is enough of your bawling. You have two choices here, and one of them sends your blood flowing into the ocean. But I will let you leave here alive—as long as you tell me where that mindmage whelp is."

"You have your own mindmage," said Gregor through gritted teeth. "Do with her what you will."

Mako sent the tip of the dagger into Gregor's throat—not deep, and almost flat, so that a half-finger of it slid *under* the skin, rather than into it. "Do not give me sass, Gregor. I do you a great honor by offering you your life, for you have killed many of my warriors. Speak now, or die."

Ebon stared at him in wonder. Would Mako really let Gregor sail away from here after all the man had done? But then he saw the hard glint in the bodyguard's eyes. And he remembered in the basement of Xain's home, when Mako had promised to let Isra live and then had tried to kill her anyway. Ebon had stopped him then, but he could not now. Mako had no intention of keeping his word and letting Gregor leave.

But neither, it seemed, did Gregor have any intention of doing as Mako wished. "Drown in your own piss," he spat. "Slit my throat if that is truly your aim, for you will get no truth from me. And you will never find Isra before it is too late."

Mako sighed and opened his mouth as if to speak. But then Ebon heard many voices from above, and Kalem cried, "Watch out!"

Mako dove without thinking, rolling away from Gregor as arrows rained down from the sky. One struck Gregor in the back, but it rebounded from his chain, and he fought to rise to all fours.

Looking up, Ebon saw many soldiers gathered at the cliff's edge, and they were beginning to come down the stairs. They were clad all in the red leather armor of constables, and his heart skipped a beat.

Gregor was up now. Ebon's limbs obeyed him at last, and he scrambled up, expecting the giant to come for them—but instead he turned and ran for the docks. He leaped into the boat there, nimble as a cat, ignoring the cries of the constables. With a dagger from his belt he cut both mooring lines, and then his huge arms pulled at the oars to launch the boat into the Great Bay.

"Time to go," said Mako, teeth bared against the pain of his shoulder. He pulled Ebon along with him, and Kalem hurried after as they ran for the sewer entrance from which they had come. Theren was there, and to Ebon's stark relief, she was up on her knees and looking about, blinking.

"What happened?" she said. "Where is Gregor?"

"Gone," said Ebon, pointing out to sea. He and Kalem took her arms to help her up.

"No!" cried Theren. She reached out, and light sprang into her eyes as she tried to clutch Gregor's boat with magic. But he did not slow, and the magelight winked out almost at once.

"He is gone now," said Kalem. "And we must leave as well." He flinched as an arrow struck the stone by them, though in truth it was not a very close shot.

"No truer words were ever spoken, goldshitter," said Mako. "Into the sewers once more."

THIRTY-FOUR

THEY HAD NOT EVEN ROUNDED THE FIRST CORNER WHEN THEY HEARD shouts at the sewer entrance and the tramp of feet behind them.

"I hope you are faster than you have shown yourselves to be, boys," grunted Mako. "Otherwise Theren and I may be forced to leave you behind, for the redbacks will surely catch you."

"You cannot abandon us down here!" cried Kalem.

"He is having a joke," said Ebon. "Though he should save his breath for running."

Mako grinned. "I know my way around these sewers like a wolf in its own den. They will not be able to track us."

But his boasting seemed a lie, for they could always hear their pursuers behind them in the tunnels. When they reached the area they had dropped down before, the Yerrin guards were gone—many ridges in the stone floor thrust through the muck to show where they had been trapped, but the stone was chipped away, and Ebon guessed that they had managed to dig themselves out. Mako helped them up the ladder and into the tunnel above, despite his wounded shoulder. There they felt sure they would lose the constables at last. But in no time they heard their pursuers anew, voices echoing with shouts and cries to halt.

I wonder if anyone ever does, thought Ebon. *Just stops in their tracks and waits to be captured.*

"How do they keep finding us?" said Kalem, voice heavy with fear.

Theren said nothing, but Ebon caught her looking at Mako. He followed her gaze and saw the blood that still flowed steadily from the bodyguard's shoulder. It ran down his arm to his elbow, and from there it splashed to the stone floor every few steps. Some of it sank into the muck in their feet, but much of it showed on the stone.

That was how the constables were tracking them. But what could they do? Ebon would not abandon the man who had saved them all so many times already.

Without warning, Mako skidded to a stop. "Here we are," he said. "The street above is just outside the Academy. The three of you must climb up and return to the citadel. I will lead the redbacks away."

"You cannot," said Ebon. "You are hurt, and they are tracking you by your blood."

"Do you think I did not spot that?" growled Mako. "Loss of blood has not yet made me a fool. But I was hampered by you and your stumpy little friends. Without you, I can finally lose the constables, as I would have from the beginning if it were not for your useless hides."

Kalem seemed taken aback by that, but Ebon only fixed Mako with a keen stare. "Very well," he said quietly. "Only do not let yourself be captured."

"Do you forget with whom you speak?" said Mako. "You need not worry yourself on my account."

"Who said I was worried for you?" said Ebon, shrugging. "I worry only that if they caught you, it would go ill for the family."

That earned him a smile. "More like a proper Drayden every day. Now shut your fool mouth, for they will be here in a moment."

He lifted them up one by one, and they broke out blinking into the light of the afternoon sun. Then he ran off again with light, springing steps. Ebon and his friends hurried away from the sewer entrance.

"Will he be all right?" said Kalem.

"Of course," said Theren. "And even if not, do you think he would spare any worries for us, if our positions were reversed?" But she could not hide the concern in her eyes as she looked back over her shoulder.

"What time is it?" said Ebon. "If it is still the afternoon study period, we should not enter the front doors."

"The sun is too low," said Kalem, pointing to it. "It must be after the bell."

"If you say so." They ran around the corner into the street just before the Academy. "I know the first place we should go, for I think we all need a bath."

Theren outpaced them for a moment and reached the front doors first. They were shut—and something in the back of Ebon's mind shouted a warning at that fact—but she had them open at once and bounded inside with the boys just behind her.

And there they stopped.

Before them were arranged almost the entire faculty. Ebon saw Jia present, and Perrin, and Dasko—Dasko who looked at them all with smoldering eyes. But Xain was at their head, and Ebon saw a look of fury upon his face—fury, and triumph.

In his hand he held the amulet of Kekhit.

For a moment Ebon and his friends stood rooted, unsure of what to do. Instinct told Ebon to run. Reason told him he would never escape before the instructors there—wizards, all of them—stopped him with spells. Terror told him to throw himself at their feet and beg for mercy, to say it had all been Theren's idea. Pride told him to hold his head high, to demand to know what they were all there for, and to deny any knowledge of the whole affair.

But no emotion won, and so he stood still.

"Drayden," said Xain. His voice was like a serrated blade in a sheath of velvet. "Do you know what I hold in my hand?"

"Dean Forredar," said Kalem. It sounded as though he were trying a diplomatic tone, but his voice cracked, ruining the effect. "The three of us were—"

"Shut up," said Xain. Kalem did. Xain lifted the amulet a little higher. "This is the amulet of Kekhit. An artifact from the Academy vaults. Stolen from them. Stolen by you."

"That is not true, Dean," said Theren. "The three of us—"

737

"SILENCE!" Xain's voice was like a bolt of thunder. The air itself crackled with the force of it. "Silence. The three of you are done talking. You have done too much of that already, and all of it has been lies. You have been behind the mindwyrd from the first. You concocted this story about Isra, when in truth you had killed her long ago and thrown her into the Great Bay. It was you who killed Credell, and Vali, and Oren. You three: a Drayden, and his accomplices."

Theren's shoulders slumped in defeat. She bowed her head, casting her hair into her eyes.

"Now you have my son. My *son.* You cannot know the lengths I have gone to for him already. And now I make you this promise: if he has been harmed in any way, there are no words for the pain I will make you endure."

Slowly Theren turned to her friends. She met Kalem's eyes first, but only for a moment before she looked straight at Ebon.

She gave him a little smile.

"I told you," she whispered. "From the first, I told you. Now run."

Ebon's brow furrowed—and then at once he understood. He lifted a hand. "Theren, do not—"

Magelight sprang into her eyes. Xain's eyes flared in defense— but she did not attack him. With a blast, she threw Kalem and Ebon through the Academy's open front door and into the street.

"Run!" she screamed.

Then with her magic she seized the front doors and flung them shut.

THOOM

Kalem got to his feet and ran for the doors, where they could hear the sounds of blasts and explosions inside. But Ebon seized the back of his collar and dragged him away.

"We cannot leave her!" said Kalem.

"We will help her!" cried Ebon. "Somehow. But we must run. We must."

They did—and every time he heard a spell hammer against the iron doors behind him, Ebon hoped it was not the sound of his friend dying.

THIRTY-FIVE

THEY FLED TO ADARA'S HOME. WHEN HE WOKE THERE THE NEXT MORN-
ing, Ebon could not remember why he chose hers, and not his family's manor. Doubtless Halab would have taken him in. Doubtless she
would have protected him. But he could think only of Adara. And by
some blessing of the sky, she had been there when they arrived, and had
ushered them in without question—though she had many questions
once they were safely within.

Ebon told her everything. Kalem added a word or two here or there,
but mostly the boy sat in the corner and wept. And when he thought
Ebon was not looking, he glared. How could Ebon blame him? The
right thing to do—the honorable thing—would have been to return to
the Academy and throw their lot in with Theren. But Ebon knew that
they would never convince the faculty of their innocence—especially
not Xain, who had hated him from the first. And mayhap outside the
Academy they could come to some solution.

Adara left once they had finished their tale, but only to put word
out through the lover's guild. By the next morning they learned that

Theren was not dead, but was in the custody of the Mystics. Ebon knew full well what that meant. His mind filled with visions of Lilith when he had visited her before, when she had languished under torture for days. To imagine that pain being visited upon Theren . . . his stomach clenched when he thought of it.

After that first night, Ebon fully expected he would have to find another hiding place. But the moment he mentioned it, Adara shook her head and insisted that he and Kalem remain with her.

"I will not turn you out," she said. "And I may be of help to you."

"So might Mako, or others in my family," said Ebon. "I should return to the manor. I should have gone there from the first."

Adara arched an eyebrow. "That would have been your death," she said. "Do you not think that that is the first place the constables and Mystics would have gone to search for you? Doubtless they have agents posted in the streets around it even now."

Ebon frowned, for indeed he had not thought of that. "But still, I only put you in danger by remaining here," he said. "Mako knew of us, and he cannot be the only one."

"He very well could be," said Adara. "Think of it—even the Lord Prince did not know until you appeared by my side, and he has his eyes and ears in every corner of the Seat."

Kalem straightened where he sat on the floor. "The Lord Prince! He must know that the constables seek for you. He could expose us."

"I have sent word. He will not intervene, though he is not happy about it," said Adara flatly. "But while he will not act to harm us, for he believes me when I say that you are innocent, neither will he help us. He will only keep trying to find Isra before she wreaks more havoc. For that is still what is most important, Ebon. Even with Theren's peril, you cannot forget that. Isra means to kill again."

"Aye, and she means to kill goldbags," said Ebon, folding his arms and slumping in his chair. "All of them, if she can. And now none of us are there to stop her, and the faculty do not even believe she is alive."

"What do you mean to do about it?" said Kalem, a strong current of annoyance in his voice.

"We must flee the Seat," said Ebon. Kalem gave an angry snort, and Adara looked at him in surprise. Ebon spread his hands. "It is the only way. What else is there? We can never prove our innocence now—not until Isra acts, and that may not be for a long while, until all this furor has died away."

"You mean to flee?" said Kalem, rising to his feet. "You would leave Theren here, suffering as the Mystics put her to the question? Often I defend your name to others, Ebon, but this is just in line with the dark tales your family seems to attract."

"Of *course* we will get Theren first," said Ebon. He felt the heat of his blood rising in his ears. "Do you think I am so faithless? Stop looking for evil in my heart, Kalem. You are as bad as Xain."

Kalem glowered, but he lowered his eyes. "How do you mean to get her out?"

"I do not know," said Ebon quietly. "We need someone who . . . can do that sort of thing. We might tunnel up from beneath the Mystics' holding cells, but it is risky, and I would not know how to get there in the sewers. I hope that Mako shows himself soon, though that is one thing I never thought to hear myself say."

"You mean to abandon the Academy, then?" said Adara. "You will let Isra kill the other children of merchants and royalty within it?"

Ebon could not meet her gaze. "I do not know what else to do," he said softly. "If we try to stop her, we will only be caught and killed ourselves. Of course I will try to help them, if we can think of a way to do it."

She rose from the table. "I will not say if this counsel is good or bad," she said. "But I urge you to think on it. We have little else to do, for a while at least."

By their third day of hiding, Ebon began to feel as if he was going mad. Adara's home was no hovel, but it was no mansion either. He could only stand so much of her four walls and coarse wood floor and Kalem's sullen glares. And of course Kalem's presence made time alone with Adara impossible, so there was not even that outlet for relief.

"You are *certain* no one will find us here?" he said, not because he was dissatisfied with her answers the previous times he had asked, but because there was nothing else to say or to do.

Adara fixed him with a look that told him she was growing annoyed. "Yes," she said. "Only the others in the guild of lovers know of our arrangement, and they will never breathe a word of it. And even if someone did, there is a hiding place beneath the floor. I will stow you there if Mystics should come knocking—or mayhap I will stow you there now and leave it locked for a while."

"I am sorry," said Ebon, and he meant it. "I only wish there was something we could do."

"I have sent word to your family as you asked, but they are . . . inscrutable. It will take time for my note to reach them."

Then, from across the room, Kalem shot up from the floor. "Alchemy!" he cried, his eyes wild.

Ebon stared at him. "What?"

"Alchemy," said Kalem, quieter this time. "That is how she did it. Isra, I mean. How she provided the corpse. She found some alchemist—and it must have been a powerful one—who took a corpse and turned it so that it looked like Isra's corpse instead. She must have done it almost the moment she kidnapped Erin."

"So long ago?" said Adara. "That shows incredible foresight. Isra may be devious, but she is only a girl."

"Likely Gregor had her do it," said Ebon, glaring at the floor. "Or whoever else in the family Yerrin commands Gregor."

"At least now we know," said Kalem. "That is one mystery solved."

"Can you prove it?" said Ebon, heart racing. "Is there some trace of her magic on the corpse that we can show to another alchemist, and thus establish our innocence?"

"Well, no," said Kalem. "But we have an answer."

"Knowledge without a course of action is useless," said Ebon, scowling. But when Kalem's hopeful expression fell, he felt guilty and tried to ease his tone. "But you are right, in that at least we have an answer. I am sorry. It is only that I am grown irritable with inaction."

"Think nothing of it," said Kalem with a sigh. "I feel much the same."

Adara stood. "It is time I was going, for the guild will need me tonight. Do not get into trouble before I return—at least not more trouble than you can get yourself out of."

Ebon rose to see her out. "We will not. Kalem, if you are still bash-ful about such things, turn away; I have been an annoyance to the love of my heart, and I must kiss her well to make up for it."

Kalem did indeed turn away, and Adara gave Ebon a wry smile. "What makes you think I want a kiss now? You have not bathed since you arrived." But she showed her words to be a lie by gripping the front of his robes and pulling him in. For a long moment they held each other. She put her lips to his ear and whispered, "We will solve this. Together. We share it, as in all things. Even peril."

"Even peril," he whispered back. "Thank you."

Then she was gone.

That left them alone for some hours. To distract himself, Ebon drank, and Kalem joined him at the table and in his cups. Ebon had tried to withhold himself from wine since he arrived; though Adara offered it to him often and insisted it was no bother, he had no wish to drain her cabinet, which he knew he might do if he gave himself free rein. And besides, who would want to sit drunk in the home of their lover for hours?

But now he and Kalem let themselves relax into one of Adara's fine vintages. When the bottle was nearly done, Kalem concocted a plan to rescue Theren that involved melting the front door of the Mystics' station, and Ebon nodded sagely that it was a brilliant idea. Then Ebon, in turn, decided that it would be better to recruit a firemage, some sellsword wizard, and have them burn the place to the ground. Some-how they would get Theren out before the flames and the smoke killed everyone inside.

He knew their ideas were beyond foolish, and he knew that Kalem knew it as well. But after two days of sitting and reflecting on their own hopeless situation, it felt good to speculate upon the ridiculous. Somehow they drank another bottle, though Ebon did not remember getting up to open it—mayhap, he reflected in the back of his mind, Kalem had done it, though he did not remember the boy rising from the table, either.

Much time passed this way before Adara returned. Ebon and Kalem were giggling when they heard the front door's latch turn, and they both stifled themselves while shushing each other heavily. But when Adara reached the top of the stairs, she was not alone; Lilith stood beside her.

743

"Lilith," said Ebon. He shot to his feet, but too quickly—he had to put a hand on the table to steady himself. The sight of her had a sobering effect on him, but not enough, for his head began to spin as soon as he stood. "What are you doing here?"

"She found me," said Adara quietly. "Theren told her you might be with me."

"Theren?" cried Kalem. He stood as well, but he handled himself even worse than Ebon had and very nearly fell to the floor. Adara took his arm to steady him. Kalem hardly seemed to notice. "You saw her? Could you speak with her? Is she well?"

Lilith glowered, and even Ebon winced at the words. "Well? She is far worse off than you two are, sitting here and getting drunk on your lover's wine."

"We did not mean for her to be caught," said Ebon, slowly, so that he could be sure to say each word clearly. "She sacrificed herself to save us."

If he thought Lilith would soften at that, he was wrong. "And do you mean to do the same for her?" she said, voice rising. "Or do you mean to sit here until you rot? It has been days since she was taken—three days, Ebon. You know what the Mystics are doing to her. You saw them do it to me. And now they are even more eager for the truth. Xain is urging them on, desperate to find his son. So how do you mean to fix it?"

Kalem looked doubtfully at Ebon, who avoided Lilith's gaze. "We . . . er . . . we have been trying to think of a way to get her out."

Lilith folded her arms, and Ebon thought she likely knew just how productive their thoughts on the matter had been. "I hope you have concocted some brilliant strategy. Because no one else will solve this unless it is us—the people in this room, and no others."

"Mako will find us soon," said Ebon. "With his help, we will find a way."

"Theren thought he would cast my life aside easily to protect yours," said Lilith. "Do you think he views her more tenderly? He did not strike me as that sort of man."

"He might surprise you," said Ebon. "In any case, I will make him help us rescue Theren—and then he will find Isra for me. If she has not fled the Seat, anyway. She might have, the same as Gregor."

744

"No." Lilith shook her head. "Gregor left to save his own skin. Isra has never cared to do that before, or she would have fled in the first place. She only wants to destroy the goldbags. And I know how she means to do it. The Goldbag Society she began—that she had *me* begin"—she paused as a shiver ran up her body—"they are having a secret gathering. An assembly. It is in less than a week. They are keeping it secret from all but their own members."

"How did you hear of it, then?" said Kalem. "I thought you no longer trucked with their sort."

"Nella told me. She was worried, though she did not know why. I urged her not to go, and urged her besides to dissuade others from going. But I fear my words, or hers, will have little effect. Isra means to gather them all together, and then she will destroy them. It will be the perfect chance."

Ebon met Kalem's eyes. "It must be what she has been waiting for," he said. "She wanted to strike them down in one fell swoop. We stopped her when she tried to do it using Jia. But that only gave her more time to ensure that *all* the goldbags will be together."

"And we are going to stop her," said Lilith. "All our efforts to find her thus far have failed, but we *know* she will be there—and we know when."

"But we cannot re-enter the Academy," said Kalem. "We will be caught and killed."

"I know you have a secret way in," said Lilith. "Or at least your bodyguard does. Find it and come. Three days hence."

Ebon met her gaze. "Very well," he said. "We will. Though Isra has magestones, and mayhap we will perish in the end. But it is the best chance we will ever have, and I will not let it go by."

Her eyes softened, and she nodded slowly. "Thank you. I told Theren, too, when I saw her. I asked her—no, I *commanded* her, to hold on until then. Because after that . . . well, one way or another, Theren's innocence will be proven."

"The same way yours was," said Ebon heavily. "Though I wish you need not have suffered as you did before then."

"I survived it," said Lilith, her voice toneless. "Theren will do the same, for she has always been stronger than I am."

She turned and made for the stairs leading out. But she paused on the top step, her hand on the bannister. "I will expect you, Drayden. Let us right the many wrongs that have been done in recent weeks."

"As you say, Yerrin," said Ebon. "And if we fall in doing so, let that right the wrongs that we could not."

Lilith gave him a final nod and left.

THIRTY-SIX

THAT NIGHT, MAKO APPEARED AT LAST.

They had gone to bed, Ebon and Adara together (but chaste) in the bed, and Kalem wrapped in blankets on the floor. Ebon thought his sleep had been deep—until he heard pounding at the door and shot awake at once. He went to rouse Kalem, but the boy was already up. His wide eyes showed their terror in the moonslight that came in through the slats over the windows.

"Into the floor, quickly," said Adara. She lifted the panel for them, and they climbed in. The space was not large, and very nearly stifled them when she put the panel back down, but they managed to still the sound of their breath.

They heard footsteps as Adara went down the stairs, and then the sound of the door opening. Almost at once, heavy boots came tramping up—but only one set. That made Ebon frown. Then he heard a growling voice from the room just above them: "Come out from hiding, boys. I may be more dangerous than the Mystics, but I am not after your blood. Not yet, anyway."

"Mako," said Ebon in relief. He pushed the panel up and emerged into the open. The bodyguard's eyes flashed as he beheld Ebon, though he did not smile. Adara had closed the front door, and soon appeared atop the stairs again, pulling her robes a bit tighter around her and cinching the sash at her waist.

"Apologies, my lady, for the lateness of the hour," Mako told her, turning and bowing low, the way he had when first they met. But then, as before, he turned to Ebon and scowled. "And what have you been doing the past few days? No doubt sitting around getting drunk, with no plan to save yourself."

Ebon lifted his chin, though Mako's words were not far from the truth. "I have had little to do, it seems to me. I was waiting for you to arrive."

"If everyone waited to be saved, the nine kingdoms would be nothing but graveyards," said Mako. "Yet here I am after all, and with a scheme. You must ready yourself, Ebon, for soon you will leave the Seat."

That made Ebon balk. "What? You have secured passage?"

"Not just yet," said Mako. "It is a tricky thing. We cannot send you in one of our own caravans, for those will be ruthlessly searched. It shall have to be with someone else. Fortunately, many of the lesser merchant families owe us favors, and I have called upon some of them to collect."

"Thank you, Mako," said Ebon. "But I cannot take that passage. Theren still rots in a Mystic prison, and we finally have a plan to stop Isra."

Mako's brows drew together. He folded his arms and said, "What plan?"

Ebon told him what Lilith had said about the gathering in the Academy and the opportunity to stop Isra. Mako listened silently, and when Ebon had finished he shook his head.

"You mean to fight her on her own terms, when she is prepared for it," he said. "The only safe course would be to find her before then and attack when she does not expect it. Yet I cannot find her, despite my best efforts—and those efforts are very good indeed." He paused and looked to Adara. "I imagine, my lady, that even your special friend has had no luck, or else I should have heard of it by now."

Adara met his gaze, her eyes betraying nothing. "If he has had any more success than you, he has not told me of it."

Mako waved a hand in her direction as though he presented a platter of sweetmeats. "And there you have it."

"We could still take her unawares," said Kalem, surprising Ebon with his vehemence. He stepped up beside Ebon and fixed Mako with a glare. "You could, if you meant to. But you do not even care if she kills students within the Academy. Nor do you care about Theren's torture."

To Ebon's surprise, Mako's scowl softened slightly. "I would not see your friend die under the knives of the Mystics," he said. "She has proven herself most . . . resourceful. Useful, even. But you *will* leave the Seat, Ebon. I will force you if I must, for I have orders from Halab."

That stopped Ebon cold. "Halab?" He had almost forgotten about her in his worries over Theren and the Academy.

"Yes," said Mako. "She is worried sick about you—terrified, even. She has not sent word home to your parents, for she fears your mother would go mad with grief and fear. Normally I keep details from her for her own safety, but she ordered me to tell her everything that has happened to you. I have never seen her this distraught. To ease her mind, there is nothing I would not do. Even kidnap you from here, if I must. But I would rather not. Ready yourself to go."

For a moment Ebon hesitated. Always Halab had been strong before him: strong and benevolent, as when she arranged for him to attend the Academy; or strong and wrathful, as when she had struck Matami down for threatening him. The thought of that strength now reduced to weakness, the steel in her eyes reduced to terror and tears . . . it struck him to the heart, making him sick.

And Mako said he would take care of it. He would stop Isra, and if she was exposed, then Theren would be pardoned.

But he thought of Theren. And he thought of how Lilith had looked when he had visited her. And he remembered Mako's words to Gregor in the cove, when he had promised to let the man live—the same way he had promised Ebon that he would not kill Isra.

He squared his shoulders. "No."

Mako's eyes narrowed. "Say again, boy?"

"No. I will not go with you. I will save my friend. And I will stop

Isra before she kills anyone else. The family may be more important to you than anything, Mako—and for Halab's sake, I am grateful for that. But I have spent too long worrying after my own safety and disregarding the consequences to everyone else. Theren would not be in prison if it were not for me. And Isra . . . well, her deeds are not my fault, yet no one else will stop her now, if I do not."

If Mako's face had indeed softened for a moment, now it hardened again, and he grew angrier than before. When he spoke it was through gritted teeth. "You are boastful, boy. I have told you I will take you from here if I must. That is no idle promise. Ready yourself or not, as you will—two days hence, you leave the Seat. And do not think to try and flee. I will know if you do, and I will track you down."

He went to the top of the stairs, but then he paused. One last time he turned and gave Adara the same deep bow as when he had arrived. "My lady."

Then he was gone.

They spent a restless day with uneasy thoughts—and then the very next evening, another knock came at Adara's door. Once again they looked at each other, and once again Ebon felt a ball of fear forming in the pit of his stomach. When she had stowed the boys under the panel in her floor, Adara answered it—but she returned almost immediately and called them out of hiding.

"It was only a messenger," she said. In her hand was a letter, the seal of which she had already broken—but Ebon saw the royal insignia upon it. "It is from the Lord Prince. He says he has exhausted all resources to hand and has found no trace of Isra. If she appears he will be notified, but for now he has done all that he can. She is not on the Seat."

Ebon sat down heavily on the bed, putting his face in his hands. "She must be. She *must* be. Darkness take her," he muttered. "How? How is it possible that she could be so invisible?"

"Still, we know where she will be," said Kalem. "We can stop her."

"Yes, but we cannot remain here in the meanwhile," said Ebon. "Mako will return here tomorrow night, and he will try to take me before we have a chance at stopping Isra."

"I can find us another place to hide," said Adara. "But Mako said he would mark our passing."

"Can you not command him to leave you alone, Ebon?" said Kalem. "No servant of my family would dare to disobey my order."

"Your family is not the family Drayden," said Ebon, shaking his head. "Halab could command him to leave me be, and he would obey her—but he will not heed my word over hers. And I have no way to send her a message and ask for her help."

Ebon gave a frustrated growl and stood to pace. He ran his fingers through his hair and then gripped it to tug at it. "None of this would have happened without me. Theren is in danger because of me. I am even the reason Isra is free, for Mako would have killed her if I had not prevented it. Mayhap that would be no happy ending, but at least the Academy would not still be in danger. And in all the time since, we have failed to find her. Where could she hide herself that no one, not even Mako—sky above, not even the Lord Prince!—can track her down?"

"It must be some magic," muttered Kalem, shaking his head. "Some dark magic, a spell unknown to us. Mayhap it is some ability granted to her by one of the artifacts she stole. I should have thought of that. Mayhap we could have searched the vault logbooks for a clue, but that chance has passed us by."

Ebon froze where he stood.

"Dark magic," he whispered.

Kalem arched an eyebrow. "Ebon? What is it?"

"Darkness take me. Kalem, I have been an idiot. We all have. And we must go. Now."

"Now?" said Kalem, incredulous. "Where?"

"To the Academy." Ebon gripped his shoulders and gave him a little shake. "Kalem, she is in the vaults. Isra is in the vaults."

Kalem's eyes shot wide. "Sky above," he whispered. Then he stammered, "We—we should summon Mako, or—or, I do not know, we should find help. Somewhere. We cannot go alone."

"When next we see Mako it will be tomorrow night, and he will try to take me from the Seat," said Ebon. "Tomorrow during the day, we cannot sneak in and find her. We can only do it now, when most of the students and faculty will be abed."

"I . . . er . . ." Ebon could see the fear in the boy's eyes.

"Think of Theren, Kalem," said Ebon quietly. "If we stop Isra—*now*—we can save Theren. Mayhap even tonight."

Kalem's eyes hardened, and he gulped. "Very well," he said, quiet but firm. "Let us go."

Ebon nodded and went to Adara. He took her by the shoulders and kissed her. "I promise I will return," he said.

She gave the barest of nods, her jaw set in a firm line. "Do not make promises you cannot keep," she said. "Promise me instead that you will be careful, for that is something I can believe."

"I promise it, then," he said. "I love you."

"And I you."

He took Kalem's arm and fled out the door with him into the night.

THIRTY-SEVEN

EBON WAS THANKFUL FOR THE LATENESS OF THE HOUR AS THEY RAN through the streets of the city. He and Kalem were in regular clothing given to them by Adara, and not in their Academy robes. But he was still wary of being recognized, and had pulled his hood as low over his face as he could. That, combined with the shadows that filled the streets, would hopefully hide his face from any curious constables or Mystics.

The cold night had driven most people indoors, and so Ebon and Kalem found the streets almost clear as they went. Soon they had reached the Academy—but Ebon passed the front door by and ran around to the side, where the scorched groundskeepers' sheds sat against the wall. He entered the one where he knew Mako's hidden entrance lay, and once Kalem had followed him inside, he closed the door behind them both.

"We must use Mako's passageway," he said. "Though I do not know how to open it, I know it is through this wall. Let us shift the stone and open the way."

Together they put their hands against the wall, where Ebon knew the door would open up for them. Ebon reached for his power, and the shed brightened as a glow sprang into his eyes. He saw the glow in Kalem's face as well, and together they pushed at the granite of the wall.

But nothing happened.

Ebon strained, trying to *see* into the stone. There it was, just as any stone or other substance he had ever shifted. Yet when he tried to command it with his magic, it would not move. And furthermore, he felt the connection to his magic slipping away. Soon the glow faded from his eyes, and he loosed a breath he had not known he was holding.

"I cannot move it," he said. "Why?"

"Enchantments," said Kalem. "Of course. The Academy is protected by many spells. Otherwise any transmutation student could slip in and out at will."

"We must find the regular way to open it, then," said Ebon. "Mayhap it is a stone to be pushed . . ."

They ran their hands along the stones, pushing on each in turn. But none moved. The wall remained solid. Ebon gave a frustrated growl and slapped the granite.

"A fine start to this adventure," said Kalem. "Should we try to sneak in through the front door?"

"No," said Ebon. "We will be spotted at once. Give me a moment to think." Then he snapped his fingers. "When you place your magic upon an object, you can see it, can you not? What if you extend your magic *into* the object? Can you search for a secret latch, or a lever, that way?"

"I can try," said Kalem doubtfully.

Magelight glowed in his eyes again, and he ran his fingers along the wall. His lips pursed, and his brow furrowed.

"Is that . . . here."

His fingers slipped into a seam between two stones, and Ebon heard a *click*. Silently, the door swung out towards them.

"Ha!" whispered Ebon. "Mako will spit with fury if he ever learns that we know his secret."

"For that to happen, we would have to survive," said Kalem with a sigh. "I am not optimistic."

"Still your tongue, doomsayer," said Ebon. "My plan has been forming all the way here. Now keep your hand on the wall to our left and probe it with your magic. We must follow the passage until we find the other door."

It was utterly dark within the wall except for the pale glow of Kalem's eyes. Fortunately there was nothing there to run into, but it was still an unnervingly tight passage. They walked on, Ebon studying the stone to their left, hoping the lever or latch would be easier to see here on the inside.

After a while he was certain they had gone too far and had missed the door, and would be lost in the passage forever. But then Kalem breathed a sigh of relief—Ebon, it seemed, was not the only one who had been frightened—and said, "Here it is."

Again his fingers found a seam in the stone, and again the wall swung open silently. A wave of fresh air washed across their faces, and Ebon drank it in deep.

They were in the Academy grounds, the same place where they had met Mako only a few days before. No one else was in sight, which Ebon was grateful for, as he could not entirely muffle the *crunch* of his footsteps in the fresh snow.

Suddenly he realized that they had made a grave error. "Darkness take me," he muttered. "We should have brought our Academy robes after all." In the clothing they now wore, they would attract as much attention as if they had set themselves on fire.

"We can take spares from the supply room," said Kalem. "Let us hope Mellie is not on duty and guarding it, or she will catch us for certain."

They found a white cedar door and slipped inside. The halls were nearly as deserted as the grounds had been, and so they were able to move quickly towards the front hall. Once or twice they heard approaching footsteps, and they quickly ducked out of sight around a corner until the way was clear again.

At last the passage reached the entry hall, and they poked their heads out around the corner. In unison they breathed a sigh of relief; Mellie was not on duty. It was some other wizened woman with salt-and-pepper hair. But she sat in her chair by the front door, and her head nodded towards her chest with sleep.

They snuck past her and into the supply room. Inside they found robes of the right size and quickly shed their street clothes to don them. Then, throwing up their cowls, they entered the halls again and made for the stairs.

"We will need Lilith's help," he whispered to Kalem as they made their way up towards the dormitories. "We will be nearly helpless against Isra on our own. And Lilith may not fare any better against magestones, but if we gain the element of surprise, she could end the fight quickly."

"You are placing an awful amount of faith in Lilith," said Kalem.

"She has placed faith in us as well," said Ebon. "And she found us in Adara's home and did not reveal us afterwards. I am willing to wager that she will not reveal us now."

Another student came down the stairs towards them. They went silent and ducked their heads at once, hiding beneath their hoods. The other student passed without comment. Soon they were outside Lilith's common room—and Ebon's. It seemed many lifetimes had passed since he had laid his head upon his pillow here, though in truth it had only been a few days.

The common room was empty, for which he was grateful, and soon they were in Lilith's dormitory. In between the rows of beds they stepped, peering through the dim light of the moons from the windows.

But before they found her, another student sat up in their bed and saw them. Her eyes met Ebon's, and they widened. It was Nella.

Her mouth opened to shout, but he leaped forwards and covered it with his hand. He put a finger to his lips, pleading with his eyes for her to keep quiet. "Please," he said. "For Oren—please, do not shout. We are not here to harm anyone."

At Oren's name she froze. He took that for a good sign and pressed on. "We know where Isra is, and we mean to stop her. Now, tonight. But we need Lilith's help to do it."

Nella's eyes widened. Slowly, Ebon took his hand from her mouth. "Please, Nella. Where is Lilith?"

Slowly she raised a hand, pointing to a bed in the other row. Looking over, Ebon saw Lilith's dark frizzled hair poking out from the covers. He met Nella's gaze and gave her a grateful nod. "Thank you."

"Wait!" she said. She stood from her bed and reached for her robe, throwing it on over her underclothes. "I can help."

Ebon and Kalem looked to each other. Kalem shrugged. "If you are willing to ask Lilith for help, I do not know how we can refuse Nella."

Nella glared at him, but Ebon raised his hands to calm her. "He only means that we did not begin on the best of terms. But thank you, Nella. I, for one, am glad for your help."

They went to Lilith and woke her with a hand over her mouth. The moment she saw Ebon she sat up, awake at once, and wordlessly dressed herself. They crept out into the common room again, where Ebon spoke to them in hasty whispers.

"Isra is in the vaults," he said. "It is the only place she can be. The only place where no one could find her—not even Mako, or . . . well, anyone else who aided us in the search."

"Sky above," whispered Lilith. "Of course. We must alert the faculty."

Ebon shook his head at once. "No. Even if they believed us—which I doubt—many could be hurt if Xain charged in there with flame and battle. But if we sneak in on our own, we may be able to stop her before she knows we are coming."

"We may be able to kill her, you mean," said Lilith. "She must die, Ebon. After all she has done, there is no other way."

Ebon could not muster an argument. But still he frowned, and his gut twisted, for the faces of Cyrus and Matami came to him. "If that must be, then it must be," he said quietly. "I do not think I could bring myself to do it, but I will not stay your hand."

"As if you even could," said Lilith. But her tone was not as fiery as her words.

"You know the vaults better than we do," said Ebon. "Will we be able to enter them?"

"There is one guard posted, but they can be subdued," said Lilith. "And I know where Egil keeps the key to the main door."

"Let us go, then," said Ebon.

They ran through the halls, ducking out of sight whenever they heard footsteps approaching. But that was rarely, and soon they had reached the vault's front door.

"The guard is inside the front office," said Lilith. "Nella, you should deal with them. Mindmagic is better for knocking someone senseless without killing them. I have no wish to catch them in a blaze."

"Very well," said Nella. She cracked her knuckles. "Open the door for me."

Ebon took a firm grip on the handle. He threw it open at Nella's nod, and she leaped inside. There was a single sharp cry, and then a *crack*. Ebon heard a body slump to the stone floor. They stole in behind Nella to find a member of the faculty—some instructor Ebon did not recognize—slumped against the far wall. She was unconscious, but her chest still rose and fell.

"I hope you are right about this, Drayden," said Nella. "I hate to think of the punishment I will receive otherwise."

"I hope I am right, too," said Ebon. When she looked at him in horror, he mustered a small smile.

"But wait," said Kalem, frowning. "If the vaults have been guarded, how could Isra have come in and out, as we know she has done?"

"Mindwyrd," said Lilith. "She still has magestones. And you would do well to remember that, or you will find yourself her unwitting slave. That is not an experience I, for one, care to repeat."

That threw a somber mood across them all. Silently Ebon opened the second door, and they entered the vaults.

THIRTY-EIGHT

ALMOST AT ONCE, EBON FELT THE CREEPING SENSATION OF MAGIC upon his skin. He remembered it well from when he, Theren, and Kalem broke into the vaults for the first time. Enchantments beyond number guarded this place, making him feel as though small creatures crawled over him, their thin and spindly legs tickling his spine.

The place was utterly dark. They were in the very bowels of the Academy and had no windows to allow moonlight. Lilith's eyes glowed as she whispered, and a small ball of flame sparked to life above her palm. It painted the place in blood, from the arched doorways to the ceiling that seemed oppressively close. Wordlessly the four of them drew closer together, eyes roving uneasily.

"Need we disable the spells?" whispered Ebon. "Jia told us there were enchantments to warn the faculty if anyone came here."

"That is a spell of mentalism," said Nella. "Isra will have disabled such magic, or else she could not come and go as she pleases."

"Should we light a torch?" said Kalem.

"My flame will do," said Lilith. "It will be easier to douse at need. We do not want her to see us coming."

Kalem nodded. For a long moment they stood there, peering into the looming blackness of the tunnel.

"Well," said Ebon.

He took the first step. The second one came easier. The others followed after a moment. Their footsteps echoed from the stone walls and mingled with the low murmur of Lilith's flame. Surely Isra could hear them, wherever she was. She must be able to. They were a chorus, an army marching with thunder.

But nothing came to greet them.

They reached a place where the hallway split. Lilith turned right. Ebon paused. "Where are you going?"

"The room where the first artifact was stolen. Its enchantments are gone. It would make sense for Isra to stay there. Anywhere else, she would have to remove the enchantments all over again."

Ebon swallowed and nodded. He had forgotten that Lilith once worked in these vaults, as Theren did. "That is sensible. Lead on."

Lilith turned them again a few paces later. But as they approached the next intersection, Kalem stopped in his tracks. He stepped away from them and went to a corner, stooping to pick something up. When he turned back, he held a cheese rind for them to see.

"Well," he whispered, his voice croaking. "If we doubted she was down here, this seems to prove it."

"Do not forget her magestones," said Lilith. "If she sees us first, we are lost. She can overpower Nella and me faster than blinking. We must surprise her."

Just then they heard the sound of leather shifting against stone down the hall.

Kalem squeaked. Lilith doused her flame. Ebon ran for the wall and pressed himself against a door, behind the stone lip of its frame. A small body struck him in the stomach, and he almost screamed in panic. But it was only Kalem.

The hallway went deathly still. No sound came to them—none but their own heavy, terrified breathing. Ebon wanted to ask Lilith for a light, but he dared not speak.

He stuck his head out. There was a glow. It was faint, just at the end of the hallway. It came from around the corner to the right. He did not know the vaults, but he would have wagered that it was the last corner before they reached the room they were looking for.

The glow was so small, he thought it must come from a candle. He tried to let his eyes adjust to it, but it was not bright enough. He could not even see Kalem pressed to the door beside him.

When he lifted a foot, its scrape sounded like a thunderclap, and Kalem went rigid. Ebon still could not see Lilith or Nella. He put the foot down again and then took another step. Bit by bit, one hand pressed to the wall, he crept forwards.

He reached the corner safely. The glow was brighter now, almost bright enough to see. When he stepped around into the next hallway, he would be able to see its source. He closed his eyes.

Sky above, protect me. And if not, then look after Albi when I am gone, and Halab, and especially Adara.

Ebon stepped around the corner.

As he had guessed, there was a candle. But the candle did not catch Ebon's eye so much as did the figure lying on the floor next to it. A small figure, partially blocking the candle's glow. Their head was laid upon the stone, and their shoulders shifted slightly moment to moment with breathing.

A hand gripped his shoulder, and he nearly died of fright. But then he heard Lilith's whisper. "It is her. Stand back. I will end this."

"No!" Ebon stuck out an arm to restrain her. "That is not Isra."

And indeed, he could see clearly that it was not. The figure was too small. And after looking a moment longer, his heart sank. Even in silhouette, he recognized the wild hair.

Astrea. Sky above.

The poor girl must be under Isra's control, left here as a guard as the older girl slept. Who knew how long she had been under Isra's command? Now Astrea's worsening complexion made sense, her increasing weariness and the heavy bags under her eyes. Ebon imagined it: Astrea returning to the vaults each night, receiving Isra's commands, and sitting in sleepless vigil in case anyone should come to capture her. Likely she only slept now because her body had given out, casting her into slumber despite all the power of Isra's magic.

"It is mindwyrd," said Ebon. Lilith looked at him. Her eyes narrowed for a moment, and then went wide as she nodded. She understood.

Kalem and Nella had approached and stood just behind them. Together they all moved forwards once more. Soon they reached the open door; Ebon recognized it from when they had come with Theren. The frame still stood bare, for no one had replaced the door after Isra had blasted it from its hinges.

Within the vault were two sleeping figures. One, nearer the back, was Isra. But there was a second, smaller figure, its shaggy dark hair sticking out in all directions, clearly unwashed.

Ebon gasped. "It is Erin!"

The dean's son lay on his back, his hands folded over his chest. For a moment Ebon feared the worst, but then he saw the boy's chest rise and fall. Quickly he stole forwards to put a hand on the boy's shoulder—and then, thinking better of that, he put his hand over Erin's mouth before shaking the boy. But he might as well have shaken a log. Erin's eyes remained closed.

"She could have commanded him to sleep," said Lilith. She whispered with her lips almost pressed to Ebon's ear, watching Isra warily. "If she did, he will not rouse until she commands him to or until the mindwyrd wears off. You must carry him out of here."

"After we . . . deal with Isra," said Ebon.

But Lilith shook her head. "No. In her death throes, she may lash out. Mayhap Nella and I can protect ourselves, but not all of you. Get the children away, and we will finish it."

Ebon nodded and motioned Kalem over. He came at once and stooped to lift Erin into his arms. Fortunately the boy was slight, and Kalem could bear the weight with only a little struggle. He trundled off down the hallway with jerky, staggering steps.

Next Ebon went to Astrea. Her mouth was slightly open, and a little drool had come out of the corner of her mouth. He hesitated. Surely she was not mindwyrded to sleep—Isra would have left her on guard. She would rouse when he tried to wake her. If she attacked Ebon with magic, could he stop her? He was not nearly as advanced in alchemy as she, but he had countered her spells before.

He gave a nervous glance over his shoulder. Lilith and Nella stood there, magelight in their eyes, looking at him. He must hasten, or Isra might wake, and then all would be lost.

Mayhap the mindwyrd had worn off already. He would have to risk it, and if not, then he must hope he was able to stop her magic. He should have kept Kalem around to help, but the boy was already out of sight around the first turn in the hallway.

Ebon slapped a hand over Astrea's mouth. Her eyes shot open. They flew about the hall wildly as she blinked in the light of the candle.

"Shh, shh," said Ebon, placing a finger to her lips. "It is me, Astrea."

She focused on him at last. Her brows drew together. But she did not lift her hands, and he saw no glow of magic in her eyes.

"That is right," he said. "It is Ebon. Are you under Isra's command?"

At first she only stared at him. His heart sank. But then, slowly, she shook her head.

Relief washed through him. "Good. Then come with me. I am getting you out of here."

He took away his hand and stood, reaching down to help her up.

Panic filled her eyes, and she screamed, *"They are here!"*

A blast of power shook the walls as Isra came awake.

THIRTY-NINE

THE CANDLE DIED—A SPELL OF LILITH'S—AND THE HALLWAY WAS plunged into darkness. Then a hand gripped Ebon's arm and dragged him down the hall. He screamed and tried to fight it off, but then he heard a growl in his ear.

"Shut up, Drayden, and run."

It was Nella. Ebon gained command of his limbs again, and followed her, though he could see nothing. She jerked left, turning the corner down another hall. The instant they reached it, Lilith threw up a ball of flame.

"We cannot let her see us," cried Lilith. "If she can see us, she can kill us." Mentalism relied upon line of sight, Ebon knew—even with magestones, Isra could not harm them if they were hidden from her view.

They heard Isra's enraged screaming behind them, and Lilith doused the light again just a few paces from the next corner in the halls. They stumbled forwards blind, and then when they turned the corner Lilith lit the way once more.

"Astrea!" said Ebon. "We have left her behind!"

"Isra had her under command," said Lilith. "She will not be harmed."

Ebon glanced back, uncertain. But what could he do, other than throw himself into Isra's wrath and surely perish?

Soon they reached the vault entrance and burst into the Academy halls. Now the place was well-lit by torches, and Ebon felt his heart in his throat. If Isra caught sight of them for so much as a second, they were lost. He saw that Nella had taken Erin from Kalem's arms and was panting heavily as she ran. Kalem was barely keeping up with them. The boy wept in fear, his breath wheezing from his near-bursting lungs.

Now they could not worry about being discovered. Indeed, Ebon hoped someone would spot them, because then they could give warning of Isra's presence. But there was no one in the halls. No instructors, no other faculty. They would have to survive on their own.

Just as they turned a corner, making for the front hall, there came a *crack* of shattering stone. Shards of granite flew through the air. One struck Ebon in the arm, forcing a cry of pain. Isra must have just caught a glimpse of them as they fled around a corner. He thanked the sky that she had not seen them in full view. But then he saw Nella and Kalem. Their pace flagged more and more with each step—Kalem from weariness, and Nella from carrying the dean's son.

Without warning he shoved them off down the next side hallway they passed. "Go!" he cried. "Get Erin to safety and get help. She will not kill all of us, at least." Then he took Lilith's arm and ran on with her. Nella cried out in protest, but she did not come after them, and soon he heard the sound of her footsteps hurrying off beside Kalem's.

Ebon and Lilith reached the end of the hall, and he pulled her to a stop before they turned the corner. Together they faced the way they had come, ready to dive out of sight the moment Isra came into view. Lilith glanced at him. "That was bravely done, Drayden," she said.

"The least I could do," muttered Ebon.

Isra rounded the corner at the other end of the hall. She was so surprised to see them standing there, facing her without running, that she skidded to a stop and nearly fell over. For half a moment she paused, too shocked even to use her magic against them.

In that half-moment, Ebon took her in. Her hair was all dishevelment, sticking out in many directions. Her clothes were filthy from collar to hem, and grime covered every bit of her skin. Hiding in the vaults had given her little opportunity to bathe, it seemed.

"Run!" he cried, and dove out of view with Lilith. Too late, a black glow sprang into Isra's eyes, and stones in the wall behind them shattered as she struck.

"She will chase us now, I think," said Ebon, breaking into a sprint.

"What wonderful news," said Lilith. They shared a grim smile.

They reached the next corner half a moment too late. Just as Ebon thought he was about to pass it safely, an invisible force picked him up and slammed him into a wall. For one moment he floated there, feeling Isra's magic crush him. But Lilith turned back, and with magelight in her eyes she struck. A blast of wind slammed into Isra. She fell to the floor, surprised by the attack. Ebon slumped, and Lilith dragged him up after her.

"It is only a matter of time before she catches us," said Ebon. Then he cried out, screaming as loud as his burning lungs would let him. "Help! Help! An enemy within the halls!"

Lilith seized his sleeve and slapped him, then shoved him on to run again. "Be silent, you fool! You will only bring more into the fray—more for Isra to kill. And I have an idea."

They were near the front hall now, but Lilith turned from it. Soon after, she skidded to a stop before a door Ebon recognized. It was the entrance to the bell tower.

He balked. "Here? But atop the tower, we will be trapped."

"Not if we can throw her from it," said Lilith. "It is the only thing I can think of." Light sprang into her eyes, and a massive ball of flame erupted from her fingers. The door exploded with a heavy *BOOM,* falling inwards as smoldering kindling.

They ran to the stairs and up, and now Ebon's lungs screamed in earnest. His pace flagged, but then he heard Isra's shrieks of rage beneath them, and fright lent his legs new strength. The stairs behind them crumpled, and one piece of railing after another exploded into splinters. Ebon raised his arm to shield himself as they pounded up the stairway. But it blocked them from Isra's view, and she could only lash out at the space around them, not ensnare them in her mindwyrd.

When at last they reached the top of the tower, Ebon fell to all fours. He forced himself to crawl forwards, heedless of Lilith when she seized his shoulder and dragged him on. Fighting to his feet seemed like the hardest thing he had ever done.

"I will hide in one corner, and you another," she said. "Whoever she finds first, the other will be behind her. If it is you, you must strike. You cannot stay your hand. Do you hear me?"

He nodded, too breathless to speak. She shoved him behind many coils of rope piled high and then ran to the same place she had hidden when he first saw her in the tower.

The place went silent. Ebon gasped and gulped, trying to control his breath, fearful that Isra would be able to hear him.

Then he heard footsteps coming up the stairs. He clapped his hand over his mouth.

Each step made the stairs creak and groan. The wood was old already, and Isra's assault had battered it so that it was now even more unsteady. But then she reached the top, and the sound of her footsteps vanished. Ebon froze, trying to press himself deeper into the coils of rope.

When a few moments had passed without a sound or sight of her, he dared to poke his head out to peer with one eye around the rope coils.

Isra came into view. The black glow raged in her eyes. She held both hands raised, ready to strike. Her frame was nearly skeletal. Her hair seemed somehow thinner than he remembered. Skin clung to her bones so that her face was little more than a skull.

A noise came from the crates where Lilith was hiding. Isra whirled. Ebon looked desperately around. There was a large metal hook on the ground, as big as both his hands. He stooped and lifted it. With a cry he jumped out of the ropes, swinging the hook at her.

She turned too quickly, and a wall of force met him in midair. It pitched him back against the ropes, which scattered in all directions. He slumped to the ground and fought to rise again. But behind Isra, he saw Lilith step out of hiding. Magelight was in her eyes, and she screamed a word of power. Isra turned and held up a hand. Lilith's magelight died. Isra seized her and threw her sideways with terrible force.

Lilith struck the stone floor ten paces away, slid under the railing, and vanished screaming over the edge.

"*No!*" cried Ebon, leaping up. He swung the hook again. This time Isra did not strike him, but seized him with her magic and lifted him into the air. Invisible fingers clutched at his throat, and it felt like two steel plates pressed his body flat. He struggled for breath, but could not even raise his hands to clutch at his neck. An image flashed into his mind of his battle against Cyrus on the southern cliffs of the Seat. But now Adara was not here to save him.

"Drayden," hissed Isra. "The goldshitter whose shit is most golden of all. I wish I had killed you in the kitchens, but it will be sweeter after waiting for so long."

Ebon tried to answer her, but he could only wheeze.

"You will not speak except to answer my questions," said Isra. She tightened her fingers closer to a fist, and Ebon cried out in pain. "Now tell me: who was the man with you in the basement of Xain's house?"

Spots danced at the edge of his vision, and for a moment Ebon could not understand her words. Snarling, she let her hand relax a bit, and the pressure on his chest relented. "Mako," he gasped. "His name is Mako. He works for my family."

"How did he withstand me?" said Isra. "I had the amulet. Even if he was a wizard, he should not have been able to stop me."

"He is no wizard," said Ebon. "I do not know why your magic was powerless against him."

She gave a frustrated shout and clenched her fist. Ebon tried to scream, but could only choke. He felt his spit catch in his windpipe, but he could not even cough it up. He began to suffocate.

The black glow increased in Isra's eyes, and her nostrils flared. "Tell me how he withstood my magic," she said. Her voice was suddenly thick and rich with power.

Ebon felt something close over his mind. It was like a fist gripped his thoughts with a force just as powerful as that which held his body. She had used her mindwyrd upon him. His muscles went slack, and he stopped his struggling. He could no longer force his vacant eyes to focus. In his mind he screamed, but his mouth made no sound. He was watching his body act now, and all thought of control had gone.

"I do not know how he withstood your magic," he said, his voice toneless. He had not summoned the words.

"You are under my command!" cried Isra. "Tell me how he did it!"

"I do not know," said Ebon. "I cannot tell you."

She bared her teeth. Trapped within his own mind, Ebon knew he was about to die. He could not give her any answers. And without answers he was of no value to her. He braced himself and readied to be crushed or thrown from the tower's edge.

But the glow in Isra's eye faltered. She shuddered, and the force clutching Ebon vanished all at once. He came crashing to the ground as Isra sank to one knee.

At once she fumbled in her robes, reaching for something in one of her pockets. "I am so close now," she muttered. "You will not stop me. You cannot stop me."

For a moment Ebon was stunned, too surprised to act. But he recovered just in time, just as she pulled forth a brown cloth packet. Just as she pulled a black, translucent stone from within it, he bore her to the ground. The cloth packet spilled from her grip, and the stones scattered on the floor.

Isra scrabbled for them, fighting him with the strength of a madwoman. But her limbs were thin and wasted, and Ebon forced her hands away. One of his hands went to cover her eyes so that she could not use her magic against him. The other went to her throat. Almost unbidden, he felt his power flow into him, and the tower grew brighter as his eyes began to glow.

He *saw* her. All the tiny parts of her that made up her skin, and the flesh beneath, and the blood that flowed through it all.

Almost, he changed it. Almost, he turned it to stone. But he froze at the last second.

He saw Cyrus plunging into the Great Bay. And he heard Matami's screams in the sewers beneath the city.

She will kill you, he thought. He remembered Lilith pitching over the tower's edge, and his jaw clenched.

He *changed*—

A glow flooded Isra's eyes, and she flung him off with desperate strength. He flew back, landing flat on his back on the stone, and all his breath left him. Even as he gasped, he saw Isra scoop one of the black stones off the floor and shove it between her lips. Her whole body spasmed, back arching and then curling in on itself. She screamed, but the scream turned into a laugh, terrible and long and cruel. The black glow returned to her eyes, and she rose to her feet on the strength of her magic alone. Once more her teeth showed in a skull's smile.

"Now die, you Drayden shit," she growled.

Ebon flinched—and then flames erupted all over her body, and she fell to the ground, screaming.

He looked past her. There, beyond all hope, was Xain. The dean stood at the head of the stairs, and a mighty glow was in his eyes. His teeth were bared in a grimace just as terrible as Isra's, and he screamed dark words as the flames leaped higher on Isra's skin.

But Isra had the strength of magestones, and she recovered herself before he could press the advantage. She snarled, and the flames upon her skin winked out in an instant. Still smoking and smoldering, she turned and battered him with spells. Xain tried to fend them off, but she overpowered him and he fell back, landing hard on the stone floor. Still he raised a hand, warding off a blow that might have crushed his head to a pulp.

Somehow Ebon found the strength to rise. He tackled Isra from behind, and again he covered her eyes with his hand. Crying out, he tried to press harder, digging into her eyelids. But her fingers gripped his, and with terrible strength she began to pry off his grip.

"Ebon! Get away from her!" cried a voice.

The shout dragged up his gaze. Lilith knelt at the tower's edge. Fury was in her eyes, and her lips spasmed in anger.

He rolled off and away. Almost before he was clear, Lilith sent forth a bolt of lightning. It flew straight and true, and struck Isra straight in the eyes.

Isra screamed, a scream so terrible that Ebon feared his eardrums might burst, and her head struck the stone as she flew back. She thrashed back and forth, clawing at her eyes, but between her fingers Ebon could see the damage: beneath her brow was a ruined pulp, a mix of burned and melted flesh and flowing blood.

Lilith stepped forwards, lifting her hands again. Her screams matched Isra's own, as full of fury as the mindmage's were of pain. Flames sprang to life on Isra's body again, white-hot, so that Ebon had to shield his face from them. He scrambled away from the roasting fires and the sudden sounds of melting, popping, sizzling flesh. Lilith did not relent. The flames grew in strength, rising higher and higher. Even when Isra stopped moving at last, Lilith kept the fires blazing, kept screaming, tears streaming from her glowing eyes as the corpse turned to slag upon the floor.

FORTY

The tower faded to silence. The only sounds were the crackling of the flames on Isra's remains and Lilith's ragged, heavy breathing. Her hands began to shake. She looked at them, fear dawning in her eyes. Quickly she shoved them into her sleeves and huddled her arms against herself as if for warmth—and indeed, now that the terror had begun to leach away, Ebon was again aware of how cold the air was. Outside the tower, a light snow had begun to fall, and it skittered in little eddies around the belfry.

Behind Lilith there came a groan, and Xain struggled groggily to his feet. Ebon's heart skipped a beat as the dean straightened and looked at him. When Xain walked towards him, Ebon fought to crawl away— but Xain only reached down a hand to help him up. Ebon stared at it a moment before reaching up to take it. They clasped wrists, and in a moment Ebon was on his feet.

"Are you all right?" said Xain gruffly.

Ebon tried to speak, but did not know what to say. In the end he shook his head.

Xain snorted. "Fairly said."

Lilith was now shaking where she stood. Ebon stepped past Xain and went to her. Just before he reached her, her knees gave way—and to his surprise, she clutched his shoulders and held him in a sort of embrace. His hands hovered in the air, unsure of what to do, before he gingerly placed them on her back. It lasted only a moment, and then she stepped away, refusing to meet his eyes. But she left a hand on his arm, gripping him tight for support.

"She threw you from the tower," said Ebon.

Lilith's brow furrowed. She pointed to the edge over which she had been thrown, and together they went to it. Just below the edge, Ebon saw one of the great hanging banners with the Academy's sigil upon it.

"I caught hold of the banner," said Lilith. "If I had not, I would be dead."

They turned to see Xain staring at both of them. Ebon could read nothing in his expression.

"You found her in the vaults," said the dean. There was no question in his voice. "How?"

Ebon shook his head. "Ever since we saw her in the kitchens, my friends and I have been searching for her—and my family as well. Even when the corpse was found. But our best efforts turned up nothing, and we thought she must not be on the Seat. It was only tonight I realized that the vaults were the one place on the island she could hide where no one would find so much as a trace of her."

But thought of the vaults reminded him of Astrea. His eyes went wide. "In the vaults, hiding with her, we found—"

Xain raised a hand to stop him. "Astrea. She is in the healing ward now, and under Jia's care. My son is with them."

His voice grew thick at that, and he blinked hard as he looked away. It was a moment before he went on.

"Kalem found me almost at once, for I had been roused by the sound of your flight. Then I followed the trail of destruction here to the belfry."

His eyes fell upon Isra's corpse—or what remained of it. Ebon did not even wish to look at the body, it was so twisted by the flames. Xain recoiled, though Ebon saw it was not from the sight of melted flesh. He had focused instead on the black stones scattered upon the ground.

"The magestones," he said. "Gather them."

Ebon glanced at Lilith. She nodded and released his arm. Ebon went to do as he was bid, scooping the magestones up into the brown cloth packet from which they had fallen. Some had been caught in the flames that had consumed Isra, but Ebon saw that they had not been burned.

"Destroy them," said Xain, once Ebon had gathered them all up.

Ebon raised them before his eyes. "Should I . . . should I crush them?"

Xain shook his head at once. "No. Not here. Not where we can . . . not here."

"Shall I throw them from the tower, then?"

"*No,* you fool," snapped Xain. "Some student will find them and go mad, or worse, someone *else* will find them, and then all the Academy will be purged as abominations."

Annoyed now, Ebon thrust the packet forwards. "Fine, then. Destroy them yourself."

Xain recoiled as though Ebon had thrown an adder in his face. "No! Get them away from me. Fire. Only fire will do it."

Ebon pointed to Isra's corpse. "They were caught already in the flames. It did not harm them."

"Not magical fire," said Xain. "True fire."

The belfry's torches were all cold. Ebon thought for a moment, and then with a flash of realization, he reached into his pocket. His fingers closed around Halab's firestriker. With a few quick squeezes, he cast a flurry of sparks upon the brown cloth packet. It caught like parchment, blazing with surprising heat and forcing him to step back—but the flames were dark and twisted, and seemed to reach for him.

Xain quivered, his whole body shaking as a long and ragged breath slipped from him. He closed his eyes for a moment, and Ebon thought he saw the dean sniff. When his eyes opened again, they were clear, and fixed upon Ebon's.

"Thank you," he said quietly. "Now, the two of you should come with me. We must fetch your friend Theren from prison, where she should never have been in the first place."

Ebon's heart thundered in his chest. "We are pardoned, then? I thought you might not, for we held the amulet in secret."

Xain fixed him with a look. "Because you knew you would need it against Isra," he said quietly. "And because you knew she held my son. Words will be had—with the King's law, as well as between us. You are not free from all penalty, Drayden. But I will not let the mindmage girl suffer any longer when she only tried to save my own blood. Come."

Lilith took Ebon's arm again, and he felt her hands trembling. He helped her make her shaky way down the bell tower steps after Xain.

FORTY-ONE

THE REST OF THAT NIGHT PASSED LIKE SOME NIGHTMARE, A MEMORY IN reverse of when Ebon had gone with Theren to fetch Lilith from the hands of the Mystics. Only this time Theren had not suffered so greatly, for she had not suffered under mindwyrd as Lilith had.

They all returned to the Academy, and there Lilith helped Theren to bed. But Xain took Ebon aside and brought him to his office, demanding to know everything.

For the first time, Ebon spoke freely of Isra. He told Xain what had happened in the dean's home and how Erin had been stolen away in the first place. He told Xain of how Theren had used the amulet of Kekhit upon Dasko, and repeated the tale of how they had seen Isra in the kitchens, and now Xain believed him. He said nothing of Mako, of course, nor his uncle Matami, nor anything to do with the family, for some secrets were not his to tell. Neither did he mention Adara, but when he came to that portion of the tale, he only spoke of going into hiding somewhere in the city. Though Xain's eyes flashed with interest, he held his peace. And at last Ebon told him how he guessed where Isra must be hiding, and came to find her.

When he had finished, Xain stared into the candle on his desk for a long while. In the end he said only, "I see."

Ebon's brows raised. He tried to hold his tongue, but as another silence stretched he felt compelled to speak. "Is that all?"

Xain's mouth worked as though he were chewing upon his own thoughts. "I understand what you have done, Drayden. I even understand why you did it, and your motives were nowhere near so dark as I thought. Yet you have committed crimes—crimes that can carry with them grave punishments."

Ebon tried to hold his head high, but he could feel himself shaking, and knew Xain must see it. "Will those punishments be meted out?"

Xain shook his head, and Ebon's heart leaped—but when the dean spoke, his hopes were dashed. "I cannot say. At least not now. This is a matter for the morning."

He stood and bid Ebon to return to his dormitory and sleep. Ebon obeyed—or tried to. He lay awake for hours before giving up and going to the common room, where he stared at the flames until morning light showed through the windows. The moment they did, he rose and traversed the Academy's halls, making for the western wards.

Jia sat in a chair outside the door to the healing ward when he arrived. She sagged in her seat, her head drooping, but the moment she spotted him coming she straightened and stood.

"Ebon," she said, nodding stiffly. "I am glad to see you well."

He stopped before her, lifting his chin and giving her a formal half-bow. "And you, Instructor. I much prefer our meetings when you are not trying to throw me before the King's law."

Jia's nostrils flared. "I prefer it when you and your friends are not holding a member of the faculty under mindwyrd."

His face fell, and his mouth worked for a moment as he fought for words to say. In the end, the only thing he could muster was a strangled "I spoke only in jest."

She softened, but only a little. "I know why you did it, Ebon. But sky above . . . what were you thinking? How could you be so foolish? Do you have any idea what it did to Dasko?"

Tears sprang into his eyes as he turned from her. "I do," he said. "I wish I had not . . . that I had not asked Theren to . . ." He stopped before his voice broke.

Jia let the silence rest for a moment. "We can reflect on what we might have done," she said at last. "But that is of limited use. Look to your future instead. You must be better from here on. If you are truly sorry, then you must never be so foolish again. And you must do what you can, now, to make it right."

He swiped his sleeve against his eyes. "I will, Instructor," he whispered. "I promise."

She waited until he met her gaze, and he saw that her eyes shone as well. "I believe you."

Then the door to the healing ward opened, and by unspoken agreement they looked away from each other. A plump older woman stepped out into the hallway and fixed Ebon with a look.

"You are the transmutation student, I imagine?" she said, frowning.

"I am," he said. "Is she all right? I have come to see her."

The healer's eyes widened. "Not likely. She needs rest and time. The madness of mindwyrd was set deep within her, for she wished to believe the lies she was fed. She will not be ready for visitors for a while yet."

Ebon frowned—but over the healer's shoulder, he saw Jia trying to catch his eye. As soon as he looked at her, she nodded and took the healer by the shoulder. "Freya," she said. "I have been working on a poultice that I wanted your opinion on. Could you come and take a look at it for me?"

Freya turned to Ebon a final time and said, "Come back once a week has passed, hm? We will see if she is ready to see anyone then."

"Oh, yes, ma'am," said Ebon, nodding quickly. He meandered off down the hall in the other direction, but slowly, while Jia led Freya away. Once the two of them were out of sight, he stole back towards the healing ward's door and slipped inside.

He saw Astrea at once, for all the other beds in the ward were empty. She glanced at him as he came in. If she was surprised to see him, she did not show it. Indeed, her face did not show any emotion at all. And when Ebon approached her bed, she turned away towards the tall windows that covered the far wall. The pink light of morning painted her face in its glow.

"Hello," said Ebon quietly. "How are you feeling?"

She gave him no answer.

Ebon sighed. "You . . . you have heard what happened by now, I suppose. Or you can guess it."

"Isra is dead," said Astrea. "You killed her."

"I did not—" But Ebon stopped himself and bowed his head. "Yes. I did, in part. I beg you to believe me when I say that she would have killed me if we had not stopped her."

"You do not know that," whispered Astrea.

Again he wanted to answer, but again he held his tongue. Instead he asked another question. It had run through his mind endlessly in the common room as he stared into the flames.

"When I saw you in the vaults," he said. "I asked you if you were under her mindwyrd. You said you were not. That was not a lie, was it?"

Slowly she turned until their eyes met. The silence between them stretched into a chasm.

Ebon's eyes fell away first. "I do not blame you," he said softly. "I have wanted so badly to believe in people before. It is not your fault, what Isra did. It is *not.* Do you understand?"

"She did nothing wrong," said Astrea.

Ebon let that hang there for a moment. Then he said the other thing on his mind. "An alchemist created Isra's corpse," he said. "The one they found in the Great Bay. That alchemist was you."

Astrea's nostrils flared, and for the first time her eyes filled with fear. "Yes," she whispered.

"How?" said Ebon. "How could you do it? You are only a second-year student. Kalem said he did not even know of an alchemist in the Academy who could accomplish such a feat."

Astrea shrugged. "I . . . Isra helped me. There was a black glow in her eyes, and she . . . she *told* me to. And I did. I could. I obeyed her without even knowing how."

Ebon shivered, though he tried to hide it. But just then, the door to the healing ward creaked open. Ebon shot to his feet, expecting a tongue-lashing from Freya. But instead, Xain appeared in the doorway. Ebon's stomach did a somersault.

"I . . . I am sorry for sneaking in," he said. "I only wanted to see—"

Xain cut him off with a wave. "Stay your fear, Drayden. I am not here about that. But a matter needs tending to."

Something in his tone made Ebon quail. "What matter?"

To his surprise, Xain grew solemn. "The matter of punishment," he said quietly. "Come."

Ebon's feet seemed suddenly to be made of lead. He turned back to Astrea upon the bed. "I will come and visit again," he said. "As soon as I can. Be well, and rest."

She turned away once more and gave him no answer. He forced his limbs to move, and followed Xain out the door.

Xain led him through the halls and towards his office. Ebon wanted to ask him what this was all about, but he also feared to speak, and that fear kept him silent.

When Xain opened the door, Ebon's heart sank still further. Within the room were Kalem, Theren, and Lilith. But there, too, was Instructor Dasko. The man sat in a chair, leaning heavily upon the armrest, his chin buried in his fist. He looked up as the door opened, and his eyes fixed on Ebon, and narrowed.

After he had ushered Ebon in, Xain moved around behind his desk and sat. Ebon took his place beside Theren. She was seated in the other chair and had her arms clutched about herself. She had been cleaned up considerably after Ebon had seen her the night before, but bruises still stood out angrily on her cheeks, and she pulled her sleeves low to hide the cuts and scars on her arms. Lilith stood on Theren's other side, her hands folded as she studied the floor. Kalem was looking all about the room, licking his lips nervously. Theren's eyes stared straight ahead—not at Dasko, nor at Xain, but somewhere in between them, and seeing nothing.

"Now then," said Xain. "In accordance with my duty as the dean, a matter of punishment must now be resolved. I speak of crimes committed by students in this room, against a member of the Academy's faculty also present."

Silence stretched. If Xain expected Dasko to say anything, he was disappointed, for the instructor only kept his eyes on Theren. Upon the arm of the chair, his fingers had begun to twitch.

Xain cleared his throat. "For a period of many days, you, Theren, held Instructor Dasko under mindwyrd. You forced him to obey your commands, and through him you spied upon the Academy's investigations into Isra. You did this to hide your own involvement in the events that took place in my home, in which Isra stole many artifacts that were under the care of the Academy. Those artifacts are yet to be recovered, and are likely lost. Ebon, Kalem, and Lilith—you all knew of the mindwyrd, though Lilith learned later than the rest. You are complicit in the crime, though your punishment, if there is one, will be less."

"If there is one?" said Theren, her voice a weak croak.

"Yes," said Xain. "Your knowledge of the stolen artifacts is an Academy matter, and therefore under my judgement. In light of the punishment you, Theren, have already received, and your aid in rescuing my son from Isra's clutches, I have decided to pardon those crimes. But your use of mindwyrd is another matter. Instructor Dasko was your victim, and so it is for him to decide whether you will be punished for using it against him."

Ebon's breath seeped from him in a quiet sigh. But then he saw Dasko's eyes. The Instructor regarded him with cold scorn. Now he sat straighter in his chair, like a king about to pronounce judgement from his throne.

"I do not pardon them," he said. "They will be punished. All of them."

"What?" said Ebon. "Instructor, you cannot."

"I cannot?" said Dasko. His hand shook where it gripped the arms of his chair. "Do you even know what your schemes have done to me, Ebon? She was inside my mind. My memory is in shambles. Sometimes I forget where I am—I have forgotten *who* I am, on occasion. I will never remember all the times the three of you dragged me into the garden, when you wiped away my very thoughts, where you took away my will. *My mind is not my own,* even now. And you tell me that I cannot?"

Ebon could say nothing. He tried to plead with his eyes, but Dasko's own were hard and vicious. Silent tears leaked from Theren.

Xain's jaw clenched. "Mindwyrd can carry the penalty of death," he said softly. "Withholding knowledge of it may bring banishment. Do you wish to press for these punishments?"

The office fell utterly silent for a moment. Ebon's heart stopped. *He will do it. He will sentence Theren to death.*

But though his mouth twisted, Dasko grated out. "No. She need not die for this. But she will be banished from the Academy. They all will."

Ebon felt as though a hammer had struck him between the eyes, casting him out of his own body so that he was watching events take place from afar. He could not feel his skin. He could not feel the breath in his chest. Theren's tears dried at once, as though she had moved to a place beyond grief. But Kalem took her place, casting his gaze into his hands and weeping openly. Even Lilith's dark skin had gone a shade paler.

This meant least to her, Ebon knew. She would return to her family, almost a full-fledged wizard already. Kalem had many more years of schooling ahead of him, but he, too, would return to a family who would welcome him, and mayhap they would even find him a private tutor to continue his training. If not, he had gotten far enough in the Academy that he could continue practicing, and mayhap come to the height of his power in time.

But Theren. Ebon wanted to weep as he saw her there, trying so hard to sit straight in her chair, trying so hard not to let the pain shine through in her eyes. Theren would suffer more than any of them. She would be forced to go home to a patron she hated and who disdained her, and would make her perform mind-numbing toil in court for the rest of her days.

"No," said Ebon, softly.

Dasko's eyes snapped to him. "You think to countermand me?" he said, voice nearing a shout. "You think that after—"

Quickly Ebon shook his head. "I did not mean that, Instructor," he said, his words growing in strength. "I know your anger is justified. But I beg you: do not turn it into punishment against the rest of them. Your mindwyrd was my idea. From the very first. Every day, Kalem argued against it. I had to drag him from Xain's house the first time we took control. Theren begged me—*begged* me, Instructor—to stop, to throw the amulet into the Great Bay. She did not suffer as you have suffered, but she suffered enough. And now the Mystics have had days to play their knives across her skin. I put the plan into motion, and I ordered it to continue. Banish me. Punish me even further than that, if you want. But spare the others."

That stunned the room to silence. Theren did not look at him, but Kalem did, and Ebon saw tears shining in the boy's eyes. Lilith showed her gratitude in a small nod, while Xain leaned back as if appraising him. But Ebon's heart sank as the fury in Dasko's face only doubled.

"I believe you," said Dasko quietly. "I believe you, and I call myself a fool for not seeing it earlier. I came to you before because I thought you might be like your brother. He was a good man, and sought to escape the darkness of your family name. But now I see that he was alone in that. You are a schemer, a trickster, and vile as any of your kin. If the headsman's axe hovered over your neck instead, I would jump upon it with both feet. But I will not spare your accomplices. Let them learn what it means to follow the will of an evil man."

Before Ebon could reply, Theren spoke up. "Followers we might have been, but not equal in sharing the blame," said Theren. "It was I who controlled you, Dasko. I will vouch for the truth in Ebon's words—Kalem urged countless times for us to stop, until even I wearied of it. And Lilith has known of it for all of a few days. Punish Ebon, and punish me. The mastermind, and the lackey who did the deed. Spare the others."

Dasko's nostrils flared. He studied her for a long moment, until Ebon was sure he would refuse. At last he shot to his feet and sniffed.

"Very well," he said. "The boy and the Yerrin girl may stay. But I hope never to lay eyes upon the other two again."

Dasko swept from the room, even as a high whine sprang up at the edge of Ebon's hearing, like a scream in his mind.

He was banished.

He was banished from the Academy.

FORTY-TWO

No one in the office moved for a long while. Theren was the first to stir. She fought to gain her feet, and Lilith quickly came forwards to help her. Ebon, too, took an arm. When at last she had risen, she met his eyes.

"I am sorry," he said. "This only happened to you because of me."

Theren pursed her lips, and then shrugged. "I could not have long remained in any case. But you are right, it would not have happened if not for you."

She took a halting, lurching step, aided by Lilith. Ebon held her as best he could, though she did not put much weight upon him. "I am sorry, Theren. Please. There must be something I can do. Mayhap my family . . ."

He trailed off as she shook her head slowly. "No. No, let your family be. This is not their doing—not for the most part, anyway." He knew she was thinking of Mako. "Only be better in the future, Ebon. Remember this, and remember that the false path never leads to a good end."

Ebon drew back. But she softened her words by taking his arm, and pulling him close for an embrace. "I do not hate you, Ebon. And I am not leaving tomorrow. We will have time to speak again. But now I must rest."

Lilith helped her hobble out the door. Kalem stared at it for a moment. Then he burst into tears and fled into the halls. Ebon meant to go after him, but Xain raised a hand and spoke.

"A moment, Drayden. I am sure your friends need tending to, but you and I must speak first."

"I . . ." Ebon looked to the door. He considered ignoring Xain's words and running after Kalem.

"Give them time," said Xain, but gently, as if he had heard the thought in Ebon's mind. "Come."

Xain rose and guided Ebon out of the office. He led the way through the halls and out a white cedar door onto the Academy grounds. The hour was still early, and their breath misted in the air. Ebon rubbed his arms against the chill.

"Allow me," said Xain. He whispered as his eyes glowed, and a small ball of flame sprang up before them and between them. Ebon held his fingers out towards it.

"Thank you," he said softly.

Xain nodded. Then he sighed, as though preparing himself for a most unpleasant task. "I am not skilled in such things, and so I will be brief: I was wrong to think so poorly of you simply because of your family name. I treated you worse than I ought, and that was my error. It does not excuse what you did, but mayhap my own ire made things worse than they might have been."

"Worse than you ought?" said Ebon, arching an eyebrow.

Xain's jaw clenched. *"Much* worse, I suppose."

But Ebon only shrugged. "In all honestly, I am rather used to such treatment by now."

His words earned another sigh. "I suppose you are right. Many of us, it seems, are accused of crimes these days in which we were blameless."

Ebon gave him a look. "You mean what happened between you and Drystan, and Cyrus as well," he said.

Xain's easy look darkened: not, Ebon felt, out of anger at him, but rather at a memory. "I suppose everyone here knows something of that, do they not? I do not know if you had any love for Cyrus, but I—"

"I killed him."

Xain went very still. He stared at Ebon for a long moment. "Say that again."

"I killed Cyrus," said Ebon. "It was the day the Seat was attacked. I saw him sneaking off through the streets. I followed him to the cliffs on the south of the island, and there he attacked me. I turned his feet to stone, and then I cast him into the water, where he drowned." Tears stung his eyes, and his breath came short in his chest.

"If that is true, why would you not tell the King's law?" said Xain. "If you defended yourself—"

"I do not fear the King's law," said Ebon. "But do you think my family would feel the same?"

The dean's lips twitched. "You should not be telling me this. Why would you?"

"Because I need you to understand," said Ebon, his voice cracking. "I could have stopped Isra when we fought her in your basement. And I could have stopped her last night, before you arrived. Only . . . only every time she was at my mercy, and I could have taken her life, or allowed it to be taken by another—I saw Cyrus, I heard his screaming, the way I do in my dreams, over and over again—"

He broke off, for his voice would not last much longer, and he turned away so that Xain could not see the tears in his eyes.

Now you have done it, you fool, he told himself. *Now Xain will reveal you, and your life will be forfeit.*

Let it.

"It was my fault your son was taken," he whispered. "I thank the sky that he survived, but he might not have. Because of me."

He still faced away from Xain. But behind him, he heard the dean sigh.

"It is no ignoble thing to stay the hand from killing," said Xain softly. "I have taken my share of lives. My share and more. Yet someone wiser than I am reminded me in recent days that it is not for the living to lightly mete out death."

When Ebon looked again, Xain's eyes were far away. "Then you will reveal my crime to the constables? I would not blame you."

Xain snorted. "Your murder of Cyrus? Hardly. I knew the man—likely better than you did. I am not so reckless about killing as I once was, mayhap, but I will not mourn his passing."

Shaking, Ebon let loose a long sigh. "I am . . . relieved to hear it."

"I imagine you are," said Xain, fixing him with a stern glare. "But your relief may not last long. For I heard what Theren said to you, and I agree with her. If you seek redemption for what you have done, you cannot look to your past, but to the future. And not just your future—but the future of all of Underrealm."

The air had grown thick with tension, so thick that Ebon found his breath coming shallow. "What do you mean?" he said.

"You must leave the Academy, yet I do not think you wish to return to your home of Idris," said Xain. "What if I could arrange for you to stay here upon the Seat? I could even arrange for you to have a private tutor—an instructor who would continue your training in magic."

Ebon's heart thundered in his chest. "You would do that?" he said, managing little more than a whisper.

"Yes. But not for free."

"What, then? I would pay a hefty price for such a gift."

Xain shook his head. "I do not want your coin. Rather, I want what your coin has secured: your family's influence and power across the nine kingdoms."

Ebon blinked. "I do not understand. What do you mean?"

Xain hesitated. "I only share this with you because you have proven yourself to be . . . something nobler than your kin. I know the Drayden name and the darkness that surrounds it, and you do as well. Yet as a Drayden, you have access to resources I could never hope to muster on my own."

"I thought you were favored by the High King herself."

"So I am, and we work together in this," said Xain. "Yet the High King Enalyn walks in the light of her own laws. The Draydens often dip into the darkness beyond those laws. That is where I think you might help me. All sanctioned by the High King. You will face no blame for any help you give us."

Fear thrummed in Ebon's chest, and he felt himself standing on the edge of a precipice. "You do not make this sound like any light matter, Dean."

"Nor is it. You are about to learn something known only to a handful of people across Underrealm. You are going to help me find the Necromancer."

EPILOGUE

HALAB LOOKED UP FROM HER WINE AS MAKO OPENED THE DOOR. HE stepped into the drawing room and then stood aside, holding the door open.

Nella stepped into the room. Her gaze flew everywhere, and Halab could see at once how the girl was overwhelmed by the finery. Not a merchant child, though Halab had heard she was friendly with the Yerrin girl.

Mako closed the door with a soft *click.* "Tell her what you told me," he said gently.

The girl looked up in fear, meeting Halab's eyes for the first time. Halab smiled at her. Nella gave a little smile back, seeming to draw some comfort from the gesture.

"I . . . I told him about the day the Seat was attacked. I saw Ebon slip away from the other students."

"This has reached my ears already," said Halab. "Did he not run off trying to help a student who had become lost, only to discover she was a handmaiden from the palace?"

"That is what he told everyone when he came back," said Nella, nodding. "But it is not the truth. He and I were fighting together. We battled those—the grey-and-blue clad warriors, the ones they call Shades. So when he ran off, I ran after him a pace or two before I turned back. And I saw where he really went."

Halab took a sip of wine. Then she shook her head. "Sky above, forgive me, girl. My manners have fled me. Would you like a cup of wine?"

Nella swallowed hard. "I might. I can finish the story first, if it pleases my lady."

"Oh, I am no woman of nobility," said Halab, smiling graciously. "And there is no hurry. Mako, pour her a cup. You may take the chair beside me, girl."

The girl nodded and came forwards to sit in the chair. Mako had a cup in her hand in the space of a heartbeat, and she sipped at it. Her eyes widened, and she took another, deeper sip.

"That is the best wine I have ever tasted," she said.

Halab's smile grew. "We keep fine vintages on hand. Now, please continue."

"Well—and now, understand, I only glimpsed them for a moment—I saw Cyrus. Cyrus of the family—well, your kin. He was the dean before the new one, that man Xain with the dark eyes."

The room went quiet. Halab looked from Nella's face over to Mako. The bodyguard's expression betrayed nothing.

Nella felt the tension in the room, clearly, for her next sip of wine was timid. "That . . . that is who Ebon went after. Not some palace woman. He went after Cyrus. What happened to them both after that, I do not know."

Halab had not taken her gaze from Mako. "Does this mean what it sounds like it means?"

Mako shrugged. "Mayhap. Cyrus is dead; that much we know. If he were not, I would have found him. Ebon might have killed him."

Pursing her lips, Halab stared into her cup. She took another sip. Beside her, Nella's eyes had gone saucer-wide. She drank a heavy gulp of her own cup.

"Halab." Mako's tone had become worried, reluctant. "This throws everything into disarray. Cyrus should have died in the fighting, so that others would think he perished heroically upon the Seat. The fact that everyone thinks he fled has been a serious blow to our standing, and now, to learn that Ebon might have killed him . . ."

She flung her glass goblet into the fireplace. The glass smashed, and the wine hissed in the flames. "Do not lecture me about what this means," she snapped.

"Of course," said Mako, bowing his head.

"How could this happen?" she shouted, letting the fury show in her voice. It was rare that she let it out, for she had learned long ago that rarity gave it strength. "How could we not have learned this already? It is your job to know such things."

"I learn what I learn in just this way," said Mako quietly. "From the right questions put to the right people. I could not have known that I should have asked this exact girl this exact question. Meaning no disrespect, of course." He inclined his head towards Nella.

Nella still sat frozen in her seat, looking afraid to move. At Mako's words, she shook her head quickly.

"If Cyrus knew of our involvement with the Shades . . ." said Halab.

"He did not," said Mako at once.

"Pardon me if I do not put complete faith in your word just now," spat Halab. "What if he did, Mako? What if he told Ebon?"

Another long moment of silence passed. Mako sighed. "I can . . . I can remove the danger of this situation."

Halab glared at him sharply. "We have already had to kill one of Shay's sons. We will not kill the other. We *will not*. Do you understand me? Ebon may yet be molded. And I love him, Mako. He is not Matami. Am I completely understood?"

Mako bowed again. "Of course, Halab."

Now Nella's face was covered in sweat, though she still feared to move. It was as though she thought that, if she only remained still, they would forget she was there. But as the silence now stretched for longer than ever before, she at last mustered a small, squeaking voice. "Should I remove myself?"

Halab sighed and put her hand over the girl's. "Child, no one must know about what we have spoken of here. You understand that."

Nella's eyes filled with tears. "Of course I understand that. I will never breathe a word of it."

Slowly, sadly, Halab shook her head. "We both know that that is not what I meant."

Mako drew his dagger across the girl's throat. Halab withdrew her hand before the blood could splash upon her fingers.

ADDENDUM A

———

A GENERAL DESCRIPTION
OF THE MAGICAL BRANCHES

THE MAGIC OF UNDERREALM

Less than one human in a hundred is born with the gift of magic. There are rumors that things are different in other parts of the world. Tales speak of the lands far to the east of Idris where entire populations are gifted with magic, but in small degree, and nothing so impressive as the blasts of an elementalist. But these people are understandably wary of their western neighbors, and thus little is known about them.

Elves, of course, are in full command of all magics, but seem to use mentalism above the other schools. They also possess a magic that has been little studied, since it never manifests in humans, and Elves of course are far too perilous to inspect. Scholars have somewhat ineptly labeled it "soulspeech," and it may be likened (again, ineptly) to an advanced form of telepathy. To the knowledge of Underrealm's best scholars in the time of Ebon of the family Drayden, no human has ever displayed this skill—though that knowledge is not, in fact, correct.

Of the one-in-a-hundred people who can use magic, less than a quarter are born with abilities that anyone would consider impressive. But many with weaker magical abilities are able to use them in very clever ways. The infamous wizard Auntie, for example, who was the bane of Theren's youth and who also tormented the Nightblade, could change her skin color, hair color and appearance—handy for one who was both a thief and a murderer.

Though one is born (or not) with magic, it is not hereditary, and therefore the magical percentage of the population never varies to any great degree. Wizard Kings would sometimes engage in selective breeding policies, trying to create more wizards for their armies, but all these attempts failed. Some were so horrific that they formed part of the brutal basis for the Fearless Decree, which barred any wizard from taking a throne.

It seems that whatever force has bestowed magic upon the world does not wish to see it wax or wane in power.

Magic is always an innate ability one is born with, but beyond that, the branches differ in their application.

OF ELEMENTALISM

If one were to ask any child in Underrealm what magic a wizard can perform, they would likely hear about feats of elementalism. Called "firemagic" by the uneducated, elementalism is perhaps the most visibly impressive and certainly the best-known branch, and powerful elementalists have been the stuff of legends since the time before time.

Common folk and early scholars in the subject often bear the simple opinion that elementalists can control fire, lightning, water, and air. While this is certainly true, it ignores the true heart of this branch. Elementalists, in fact, control energy.

With fire, they generate combustion in the material to be burned—or in the air itself, though this is far more difficult, and when a wizard does so, an outside observer knows little of the internal strain on their psyche.

Lightning is much easier to summon, but far more difficult to control. Painful or damaging electrical shocks are common among burgeoning elementalists, and it is one of the chief duties of their instructors to prevent such accidents, for just as with any branch of magic, elementalists are far from immune to their own powers.

When it comes to water and air (or, indeed, any gas or liquid), elementalists control the highly volatile potential motion energy of these substances. The more energy that already exists, the easier it is to control. This is why it is less strenuous for elementalists to redirect the flow of water or wind than to create such a flow in the first place. Inertia plays a large role in the powers of an elementalist.

A strange quirk of elementalism is that the presence of life is a complete block to the wizard's powers. While elementalists can easily manipulate the energy of the physical universe, their influence ends when it comes to a living body. Thus an elementalist cannot boil the blood in a person's veins, nor ignite a small fire in their belly.

This has always been a mystery to scholars of magic. Life, of course, is one of the most energy-abundant forces in the universe. It would seem, at first glance, to be the perfect playground for a wizard who can control energy. But life is anathema to elementalism, and it always has been. Even plants resist their magic.

The clever elementalist can find ways around this restriction, however. It is not necessary for them to set a fire in an opponent's skin—they can create fire from the air, and their foe will burn all the same. They may not be able to create lightning from the energy of an enemy's body, but a bolt summoned from the sky will have much the same effect.

Elementalists require verbal commands to cast their spells. Their commands may be given in the common tongue of Underrealm, but they are far more powerful when given in an ancient tongue, the origins of which have long been lost to history. No one fully understands why this ancient tongue seems to hold so much more power than modern speech, but it appears to have always been so. Many elementalists also use hand gestures as a mental crutch to help visualize their spells, though this is not required.

The most effective way to neutralize elementalists is to gag them—or, for a permanent solution, remove the tongue.

OF MENTALISM

The branch of mentalism is perhaps less visually impressive than elementalism, but it is no less useful. Indeed, to those who have a simple understanding of magic, elementalism and mentalism are commonly held to be the more "powerful" branches, and wizards of either branch are much sought after by kings and lesser lords to serve them or fight in their armies. This view, of course, grossly undervalues the complex and subtle powers of therianthropy and transmutation.

A mentalist is able to affect their surroundings by envisioning force and then exerting that force. This force can go in any direction, and its strength (or lack thereof) is limited only by the mentalist's own abilities.

As with elementalism, this magic can be present in greater or lesser strength. There are (very rarely) mentalists who can break down a castle wall if it has not been enchanted, and then there are mentalists who can barely lift an apple off a table. It is not that the weaker mentalist cannot envision the force required, but only that the gift has manifested itself in them less strongly.

Mentalists require line of sight to their target. They must see an object and visualize the force they would place against it. This is what prevents them from casting their spells inside a body, for example, although very powerful mages can obviate the problem by forming knives of pure will and slicing the target open—at which point, further internal damage hardly seems necessary.

This restriction presents some very interesting challenges to the mentalist. They can, with very little training, push an opponent away from them, but it requires some very clever thinking to *pull* an opponent forwards, since the mentalist cannot usually see their back in order to place force against it. Different mentalists solve this in different ways: Theren, for example, often grips the front of her foe's clothing, which she can see, and uses that to pull them towards her; Isra, before she perished, would grip their hands or face.

There are other restrictions that can make mentalism difficult. A mentalist can exert force against a door, but they cannot manipulate a latch on the *other* side of a door to open it quietly. For this reason, it is common to see castle and city fortifications with locks that are blocked from outside view, to prevent a mentalist from trying just such a trick.

Blindfolding a mentalist will cut them from the source of their power. When the King's law sentences a mentalist to have their magic removed permanently, the eyes will be put out.

OF THERIANTHROPY

Therianthropy, or, inexplicably, "weremagic" to the common folk, allows the wizard to alter the form, size, and coloring of their own body. Some advantages of this branch are immediately apparent: the therianthrope can alter their appearance to avoid detection when being hunted; they can turn into a great beast to overpower a foe; they can turn into a bird and travel great distances at speed. But as with its sibling branch, transmutation, therianthropy has many subtler and potentially more powerful applications.

In stark contrast to transmutation, color is one of the first things a therianthrope learns to control. In fact, when Academy testers work with children, they search for this branch by testing for response to a stimulus. If the child's eyes are blue, for example, the Academy staff will say, somewhat forcefully, "I did not know your eyes were brown." If the child is a therianthrope and does not expect the statement, their eyes will shift from blue to brown at once.

The next easiest thing to control is size, and after that, form. Even very early in their education, a therianthrope can easily grow or shrink in height. But to change the form of their entire body is something that takes years of skill and practice.

One restriction on therianthropy is the pain associated with the wizard's changing body. When turning to a bird, for example, the therianthrope's very skeleton is rearranged—some bones fuse together, while entirely new ones grow in other parts of the body. If one recalls the growing pains experienced in youth, and then imagines all those pains coming together at once in the space of a few heartbeats, one can imagine the pain of a weremage's transformation.

Therefore, when learning to change size and form, a therianthrope must learn how to deaden the pain in their own body. This is done by changing the structure of the nervous system—something the therianthrope must learn to reach out and feel inside their own flesh. Such magic is complex and difficult, but once it is mastered, therianthropes can make all sorts of transformations while applying the same basic principles.

The transformed body—or the "destined form," as instructors call it—provides another challenge. One cannot simply turn into a dog, for example, without learning just how a dog's body is formed. The results of an inexpert transformation can be nightmarish, causing the therianthrope to panic and lose control. This will cause their body to revert to its natural form, but without the benefit of the pain-deadening techniques that require extreme mental focus, such reversion can be painful enough to cause permanent damage or madness.

Therefore therianthropes must study their destined form rigorously. They practice changing one part of their body at a time before they can master the full transformation. It is thus common to find that each therianthrope has their own repertoire, a selection of beasts or forms that they have mastered, and to see them using only those forms while they study other forms that might be useful. Instructor Jia, as an example, transformed into a bear during the battle of the Seat, while Instructor Dasko turned into a lion. These are the forms they have mastered for battle. In order for Jia to turn into a lion, she would have to learn an entirely new transformation, and the same would be true for Dasko turning into a bear.

Therianthropes use their powers like flexing a muscle, just as any person does to smile, frown, or draw their eyebrows together. Clouding a weremage's mind or knocking them unconscious is the only way to prevent them from using their powers, and there is no method of permanent power removal—if a weremage's crimes are too great, they are simply executed.

OF TRANSMUTATION

Transmutation is held by many to be the weakest of the four branches of magic; Ebon of the family Drayden himself often voices this opinion. Yet in so saying, he only reveals his ignorance of the vast complexity and potential of this most peculiar branch.

Unlike elementalism, transmutation works on life as well as inert matter (although living flesh is much more complex and requires greater skill). Unlike mentalism, transmutation works on objects the wizard cannot see. And unlike therianthropy, transmutation does not cease to work the moment the wizard drops their concentration on the magic.

The simplest description of this branch, of course, is that transmutation allows the wizard to change and shape matter external to their own body. But the full ramifications of this magic are rarely grasped. Sometimes even transmuters themselves underestimate their abilities through a simple failure of imagination.

As Ebon learned very quickly, there are held to be three classes of substance. Kalem of the family Konnel described these as flesh, wood, and stone, for the sake of simplicity, but they would more aptly be called flesh, plant, and matter.

Matter is the inert stuff of the world around us: stone, metal, and mineral. It also includes the gases and liquids of the physical universe. It can be complex, but it is, as a class, the simplest stuff that the universe has created, and therefore it is the simplest to alter.

"Plant" encompasses all plant life. The material found in plants is far more intricate than that of matter, and yet it has not taken on all the properties of flesh. Life has begun to work on otherwise inert materials, transforming them into something less active, but still teeming with complexity.

Flesh is the living stuff of all creatures that can move about the world of their own free will—humans, animals, and all the various creatures in between, such as satyrs, imps, carrocks, and so on. Flesh is immensely complicated, for life has developed combinations of matter that even the most advanced chemist could scarcely dream of. A transmuter's abilities are therefore restricted by life (though not forestalled, as in elementalism) because the wizard must always understand, or at least begin to grasp, the substance they seek to transform.

Each branch has its great restriction, and for transmutation, that restriction is referred to as reversion. Transformed matter, if it is not magically turned back to its original form and composition, will decay with time. If a transmutation student were, for example, to bore a hole in a stone wall, the shifted stone would eventually crumble to dust. Depending upon the skill of the transmuter, this can take more or less time. Very powerful transmuters can change matter that will remain changed for centuries, but even so, it will eventually decay.

Thus it is not uncommon for early transmuters to go about the Academy creating crumbling holes in walls. The Academy's tuition pays for the repairs of such damage, and repeat offenders are punished as well.

Transmutation, of course, may be used in some limited medical capacities. An alchemist could seal a wound closed to prevent a patient from bleeding to death, or they could close the skin over a broken bone jutting forth. Attempts at more permanent repairs are ill-advised, however, because of reversion. While permanent healing could theoretically be achieved by a powerful transmuter, it is incredibly delicate and tricky work, and only the very highest-level transmuters would even attempt it, and then only in the gravest need.

Extremely advanced transmuters may be inducted into the High King's Medicas. These healers are without peer in their transmutation, and it is only they who will attempt permanent healing with magic—but they will only do so when absolutely necessary, for mistakes can happen, and the effects of decaying flesh are horrible to behold (and experience). More commonly, they will use their spells to stop catastrophic injuries from killing the patient before their healing and apothecarial arts can save them.

But the High King's Medicas serve another purpose. There are in Underrealm, just as there are in all places where humans dwell, individuals born into bodies that do not suit who they truly are—a child whose parents assume she is a boy, only to learn of their mistake when she is older, for example—and of course the same is true for some boys, and those who are neither, who are called in Underrealm the twixt.

In any case, the High King's Medicas will help such people assume the form they were always meant to have. This service has existed as far back as Underrealm's historical records reach, but in more recent times, it has become an official duty of the Medicas. The Medicas are well-practiced in this procedure, to the point that they can usually ensure the flesh will not begin to decay for more than a century, at which point the patient, of course, will no longer care, having died already. If a patient ever begins to notice ill effects, they can revisit the Medicas to have any issues addressed. But their bodies usually take very well to the procedure, as though the spirit knows the body is finally the way it always should have been.

Since antiquity, such people have been called in Underrealm "ander," and if they ascribe themselves to either identity, an "ander man" or an "ander woman."

The High King who preceded Enalyn was a man named Trenter. Trenter was not a good ruler, but his failures came from ineptitude rather than cruelty. And one of his most enduring legacies was also one of his best.

While Enalyn was still young, she visited the High King's Seat, and in their conversations together, Trenter learned that she was ander. But her noble family had fallen upon hard times and lacked the coin to pay the Medicas the fee required to transition.

Trenter had not realized until that moment that the Medicas even required payment for such treatment, but the moment he learned it, he abolished the practice at once and made their services available to any in Underrealm who wished for them. Medicas have long been stationed in all the great cities of Underrealm, there to oversee the health of all the High King's citizens as best they can. And for near to a century now, any citizen of Underrealm may travel to see their local Medica and receive this service, or, if they cannot make such a journey, send a letter, at which point the Medica will visit them.

It can be a lengthy process or a simple one, depending, but the Medicas are there to serve. Sometimes the ander requires many treatments, for their body can only withstand a little change at a time, but the necessary changes are substantial. This was the situation with Enalyn. In such cases, the Medica will meet with the ander and consult with them on the way they feel their body ought to be and gently guide them to the state that they can currently accept. After the first spell, the Medica will always revisit the patient to ensure that they are doing well and to see if any more work is required. In this way, many spells might be worked, one at a time, and never more than the ander can handle.

Of course, sometimes a little change is all that is required, as in the case of Perrin of the family Arkus. She retained her considerable size and great mass of shaggy hair, only requiring a few minor modifications to achieve an appearance she found satisfactory.

(It must be mentioned here, though it has little bearing on transmutation, that of course there are ander who are perfectly happy with the state of themselves, thank you very much, and are able to achieve their desired appearance with only clothing and careful grooming—or lack thereof.)

Enalyn, for her part, never forgot Trenter's actions, and though his rule was startlingly buffoonish in most ways, she refused to hear anyone speak ill of him. The two became fast friends (though Trenter always ignored Enalyn's sensible advice in the running of the kingdom), and on his deathbed, Trenter recommended that she be chosen as the next High King. So it came to be, and of course Enalyn continued the policy that Trenter had put in place when it came to the Medicas and the ander.

Transmuters must touch with their hands the thing they wish to turn. Once contact has been made, they can extend their magic through the object and even into other objects touching the first. A very, very powerful transmuter can extend their power from their hand through the rest of their body, so that they could work upon the floor with their feet, for example, but this degree of skill has not been seen since the time of the Wizard Kings.

A transmuter can be restrained by binding their hands with silk covers, as silk is highly resistant to transmutation. For a permanent removal of magic, the hands are cut off.

ADDENDUM B

CALENDAR OF UNDERREALM
AND A TIMELINE OF EVENTS

THE CALENDAR OF UNDERREALM

There are 363.5 days in an Underrealm year. In their calendar, these are divided into 12 months of 30 days each. To reconcile the extra days, at the end of each year there is a three-day holiday called, appropriately enough, Yearsend. It takes place in the middle of winter when the world is coldest, and after which the world "comes to life" again. Yearsend is often a time of celebration, when people of all the nine kingdoms take to feasting and revelry, bidding farewell to the year that has ended and readying themselves to greet the year that approaches.

Even-numbered years have leap days, placed in the middle of Yearsend, so that it is four days long in those years.

For the sake of ease, the twelve months of the Underrealm calendar have been given their Latin names from the Gregorian calendar. However, they are arranged in the original *order* of the Gregorian calendar, with Martis being the first month of the year, as follows:

Martis — WINTER
Arilis — SPRING
Maius — SPRING
Yunis — SPRING
Yulis — SUMMER
Augis — SUMMER
Septis — SUMMER
Octis — AUTUMN
Novis — AUTUMN
Dektis — AUTUMN
Yanis — WINTER
Febris — WINTER
Yearsend* — WINTER

Martis comes just after Yearsend. As with any calendar, the "assignment" of seasons is arbitrary, and the people of Underrealm saw no reason to make them fit the calendar symmetrically. Therefore winter stretches from Yanis to Martis. Spring is Arilis to Yunis. Summer lasts from Yulis to Septis, and autumn is from Octis to Dektis.

In the strictest sense, then, the seasons do not truly fall where they are delineated on the Underrealm calendar. However, this assignment was seen as a neater solution than having the seasons begin and end in the middle of months, which would of course be chaotic and confusing to everyone involved.

* Yearsend is included for the purpose of showing its order in the calendar, though of course it is a three- or four-day period and not truly a month on its own.

THE COUNT OF YEARS

"The Year of Underrealm 1" is held to be the year Roth, the first High King of Underrealm, ruling from the city of Rothton on the island capital of Dulmun, declared the nine lands to be under his dominion. Though some scholars enjoy debating the exact count, it is generally accepted to have occurred 1,311 years before the Shades attacked High King Enalyn on the Seat.

(This is, however, an inaccurate counting, since Roth laid claim to Underrealm some eighty years before his granddaughter would mark the start of the Underrealm calendar. But this truth has long been lost to history.)

Years are notated as, e.g., *The Year of Underrealm 1312.*

WEEKS

The twelve months of Underrealm are further divided into three weeks of ten days.

As we have done, the days were named for planets that the denizens of Underrealm could observe. But this presented a problem: only six planets were visible in the sky. These were named Taya, Yuna, Kina, Marama, Dal, and Kasay in the time before time, and gave Underrealm the day-names of Tasday, Yunsday, Kinsday, Marsday, Dalsday, and Kasday. Two more days were named for Underrealm's twin moons of Enalyn and Merida, giving them Lynday and Meriday. The Sun led to Sunday, as it did for us, and that was also the Underrealm day of rest.

It is said that before humans came to Underrealm, the tenth day (which always preceded Sunday) had various names among different peoples. And so, when the first High King of Underrealm, Roth, founded the nine lands, he named the tenth day after himself, calling it Rothsday.

Thus the days are, in order:

LYNDAY
MERIDAY
TASDAY
YUNSDAY
KINSDAY
MARSDAY
DALSDAY
KASDAY
ROTHSDAY
SUNDAY

THE YEAR OF UNDERREALM 1312

OCTIS

22 Octis: Ebon and his parents set out from their home in Idris, making for the High King's Seat.

NOVIS

27 Novis: The Draydens arrive upon the High King's Seat, seeking the High King's favor to establish a new trade route traversing Dorsea's western reaches.

DEKTIS

1 Dektis: Ebon of the family Drayden visits Adara for the first time.

2 Dektis: Halab takes Ebon for a tour of the Academy, against his father's wishes.

3 Dektis: Halab tells Ebon he will be attending the Academy before she and his parents depart the Seat. Ebon arrives and meets Mellie and Jia, and later Isra. Lilith of the family Yerrin encounters him in the common room and torments him for starting his training so late.

4 Dektis: Ebon attends Credell's class for the first time and is later tormented by Lilith again. He meets Kalem of the family Konnel in the library. Kalem shows Ebon the book of the Wizard Kings and agrees to teach him alchemy. That night they leave the Academy to celebrate and meet Theren in a tavern. Lilith arrives to harass Ebon, but Theren defends him. Ebon, Kalem, and Theren spend the night drinking together.

5 Dektis: Theren helps Ebon get revenge on Lilith by embarrassing her in front of the other students in Ebon's common room.

23 Dektis: Mako appears in the library and tells Ebon his father needs him to deliver a parcel. Ebon sneaks out of the Academy and encounters Theren on the streets of the Seat. Together they go to the Shining Door and deliver the parcel to a man within.

24 Dektis: Kalem tells Ebon of magestones. Mako visits Ebon and warns him not to involve Theren or Kalem with his schemes again. Ebon visits Adara for the second time.

25 Dektis: Halab returns to the High King's Seat. When the dean tries to speak with her, she refuses to see him. All communication from the family Drayden to the dean ceases.

4 Yanis: Jia confides her worries about the war in Wellmont to Ebon. Kalem teaches Ebon to spin mist, the first spell he has learned since the alchemist's testing spell.

12 Yanis: Ebon, Theren, and Kalem sneak out of the Academy and back to the inn where they delivered the parcel. They discover the parcel contained the uniform of a palace guard. The Shade arrives and frightens them off, but Theren steals his map of the High King's Seat.

15 Yanis: Dean Cyrus Drayden, after not receiving any letters from his family for some time, attempts to ply information from Ebon.

16 Yanis: Halab visits Ebon and spends a day visiting with him in the city. Together they watch the armies marching forth. Halab tells Ebon to do whatever Mako asks him to, and to honor his father.

20 Yanis: Dean Cyrus attacks Ebon, convinced Ebon has information about the family Drayden's plans. Theren tells Ebon the truth about why she is still at the Academy.

21 Yanis: Ebon sneaks out of the Academy with Theren and Kalem, investigating the map they have found. They find nothing on the eastern docks, and are nearly discovered before they can reach the southeastern tip of the island. They retreat and head back to the Academy, but stop at a tavern first. There, Ebon has a brief conversation with a girl in a black cloak and green eyes that shine with a curious light. The Shade from whom they stole the map sees them and tries to kill Ebon, but Mako murders him without Ebon being any the wiser.

23 Yanis: Lilith tells Ebon that her family is taking her on a surprise holiday. Ebon soon learns that the same is true for all the Yerrin children, and some of the other wealthy merchant families as well.

24 Yanis: Mako tells Ebon to leave the Seat at once. Theren realizes the Seat will be attacked, but Ebon does not believe her. He brings her and Kalem out of the Academy to prove it. Together they head towards the southeastern corner of the island where the small boat was drawn on the map. But as they reach the eastern docks, the kingdom of Dulmun attacks the Seat. Ebon and his friends assist the Academy in evacuating the students. Ebon sees Dean Cyrus running off with Adara and pursues them. After Cyrus attacks him, Ebon turns the dean's feet to stone and casts him into the Great Bay. Together, Ebon and Adara escape the Seat in a boat.

FEBRIS

4 Febris: The students return to the Academy. Jia informs them that with the dean gone, the High King has appointed Xain Forredar as the new dean. Xain gives his first speech to the students, pledging his commitment to protecting them.

13 Febris: Ebon passes his first-year class and joins Perrin's second-year class. He receives a letter from his sister, Albi, that the Draydens will soon visit the Seat. Rumors fly through the Academy that something has been stolen from the vaults. Credell's throat is cut in the Academy halls.

15 Febris: Ebon visits Adara, who advises him not to tell Kalem or Theren about Cyrus. The High King posts her own guards in the Academy. Mako informs Ebon that the Draydens will arrive the next day. Ebon discovers that the stolen item is the amulet of Kekhit, though he does not know what that is. Lilith tries to get Ebon and Kalem to join her goldbag society. In a rage, Theren convinces them to infiltrate the vaults to try to prove Lilith's involvement in the theft.

16 Febris: Perrin shows Ebon a spell of invisibility. Jia asks Ebon to recount what happened to him the day the Seat was attacked, and Ebon repeats his lie, omitting any mention of Cyrus. Ebon goes to visit his family in their manor, where he reunites with Albi and grows suspicious of his uncle, Matami. Ebon learns that his father, Shay, has disinherited him. Ebon takes Mako's counsel that Matami and Shay may have had a hand in the attack upon the Seat, and that they now work with Lilith. Theren guesses that Cyrus, not Shay, is behind Lilith's scheme.

18 Febris: Ebon sneaks into the vaults with Kalem and Theren. They discover the empty vault, but Theren's spell-sight reveals no trace of Lilith's involvement. They are caught by Xain and Jia and nearly expelled.

21 Febris: Ebon comforts Astrea over Credell's death, but then her friend Vali says he never wishes to see her again, dismaying her utterly. Theren and Lilith nearly come to blows in the dining hall.

23 Febris: Ebon practices shifting stone and spinning mists in Perrin's class.

26 Febris: Ebon begins to learn counter-magic by practicing with Astrea.

30 Febris: Kalem finds a book about Kekhit, and Ebon learns of the amulet's ability to cast darkfire without magestones. Ebon, Kalem, and Theren have supper with Adara, where she tells them some Academy student has been seen lurking around the streets near the Drayden family manor. Mako finds Ebon and shows him a torn page from the logbook with that day's date, revealing that another theft is about to take place. Ebon brings the page to Jia, but is too late to stop the attack. Before everyone's eyes, Lilith appears to kill Vali with her magic and is taken into custody. In a fury, Isra lashes out at Ebon with her magic, but he declines to have her punished.

YEARSEND

1 Yearsend: Ebon learns that more artifacts were stolen from the Academy the night before, but no one has been able to find out where Lilith hid them. Ebon, Kalem and Theren visit the Drayden manor. Ebon searches for the stolen artifacts in Matami's wagons, but finds nothing. They see Dasko, cloaked, escorting wagons to Xain's new residence, where crates are being loaded in. Xain finds them lurking and warns Ebon that he is watching the Draydens' doings. Dasko tells Ebon of his history with Momen, Ebon's brother.

4 Yearsend: Ebon and his friends encounter Isra outside of Leven's tavern. Inside, Adara tells them the Academy student has still been seen skulking about, even after Lilith's capture. Oren tries to recruit Ebon and Kalem into the goldbag society once again.

5 Martis: Ebon and Theren visit Lilith, who is seized by madness. Lilith insists she did not kill Credell. Theren tells Ebon that she and Lilith were once lovers.

11 Martis: Oren confronts Ebon, asking after Lilith. He nearly attacks Ebon with his magic, but stops himself in horror.

12 Martis: Ebon learns to counter Astrea's magic. Dasko pulls him from Perrin's class, asking after Lilith. Dasko seems to think Lilith may be innocent, though he does not explain why. Later, Theren comes to Ebon and says she thinks Lilith acted under the mindwyrd of Cyrus. Ebon is forced to confess to his murder of Cyrus. Kalem grows upset and stops speaking to him.

13 Martis: Oren rages at Ebon in the dining hall and is murdered by an unseen mindmage using magestones. Lilith is released from prison, her innocence proven. Theren and Lilith's parents escort Lilith to her home. Ebon goes to Adara for comfort. She invites him to her home to break their bond of coin. Ebon realizes that his family must have another mindmage and leaves in haste, telling Adara to ask Mako to see him.

14 Martis: Ebon tells Kalem of his suspicions. Mako visits them in the library and hears the same thing. He tells Ebon he can find proof of Matami's involvement, but he will need Ebon's help. Together they sneak through the sewers and abduct Matami from a house of lovers. In the sewers, Mako tortures Matami to death trying to learn of his involvement with Lilith and the attack on the Seat. After, he tells Ebon he leads the Drayden order of assassins.

15 Martis: Ebon decides to tell his friends what happened, but before he can do so, the front hall is attacked. Ebon realizes that Isra has been behind the attacks, and together he and his friends pursue her to Xain's manor. There they are joined by Mako, who helps thwart Isra's attempt to steal all the artifacts, but she manages to escape and take Xain's son, Erin, hostage. Dasko arrives and sees Ebon holding the amulet of Kekhit.

Theren takes the amulet and mindwyrds Dasko to lie and say they were never there.

17 Martis: Isra approaches her patron, Damaris of the family Yerrin, and acquires a packet of magestones to continue her plans.

20 Martis: Xain approaches Ebon and gives him the torn cuff of Mako's shirt. He says he knows Drayden abducted his son, and he promises to annihilate them.

30 Martis: Ebon and his friends visit Halab in the Drayden manor, and she gives Ebon his firestriker. Ebon learns that Albi will soon be taking the caravans back to Idris. Ebon visits Astrea, who is grief-stricken by Isra's betrayal. Jia summons Ebon and Kalem to a meeting, where she encourages the growth of the goldbag society. Ebon discovers Isra in the Academy kitchens and is rescued by Theren before he can be killed. They tell Perrin they have seen Isra, and they give Perrin the lantern artifact that Isra carried.

ARILIS

1 Arilis: Xain announces to the students that Isra is the Academy killer, and that she has magestones. Ebon visits Adara's home for the first time and confesses his worries about Dasko. Mako takes him to an abandoned noble manor where Theren and Kalem await. They decide to use mindwyrd to draw information from Dasko and expose Yerrin's collaboration with Isra. Dasko reveals that the faculty think Isra has help inside the Academy, and Xain suspects Ebon.

2 Arilis: Ebon and his friends decide to catch Isra on their own, planting Kekhit's amulet on her and absolving Theren of guilt. They visit Lilith in the Academy's bell tower and get her agreement to find who in Yerrin is helping Isra. On his way to Adara that night, Ebon is accosted by Xain, who says he received a ransom note from the Draydens. Ebon visits Adara and asks her to help find Isra, if she can.

3 Arilis: Ebon confronts Mako and asks about the ransom note. Mako guesses it was an anonymous note from Yerrin meant to turn Xain against the family Drayden. Theren conducts her final mindwyrd on Dasko, commanding him to tell Xain he has been under mindwyrd so that the faculty will assume Isra has been controlling him.

5 Arilis: Ebon passes his first test, turning a stone rod back to wood. He and Astrea argue about whether Isra is evil. Ebon, Theren, and Kalem ask Lilith to trace down the magestones, hoping to find Isra's supplier. She agrees.

6 Arilis: Lilith brings Ebon and his friends to meet Farah. Farah tells them Gregor is supplying Isra.

8 Arilis: Ebon sends word to Adara, asking her to seek Gregor using the lovers' guild.

9 Arilis: Adara tells Ebon she has found Gregor in the sewers on the western end of the Seat. On his way back to the Academy, Ebon is attacked by Gregor. A Tabarzin (a Drayden assassin) named Talib saves him, though another Tabarzin dies in the process. Theren and Kalem inform him of Enalyn's declaration of war against Dulmun.

10 Arilis: Ebon informs Mako of Gregor's whereabouts, and Mako promises to bring the Yerrin bodyguard to justice.

11 Arilis: Ebon asks Perrin to teach him defensive magic, and she tells him the spells he must master. Astrea turns a rose to ice by accident.

13 Arilis: Theren drags Ebon to a tavern, where Mako finds them. He brings them to the Yerrin grotto where they set fire to a ship carrying magestones. Mako battles Gregor. Isra is flung into the water and later appears to have been found drowned upon the western docks of the Seat, but her body is too far decayed for the time she spent in the Great Bay.

14 Arilis: Xain resumes the investigation into Ebon and his friends, accusing them of lying about Isra. They are able to prove their innocence, but barely. Ebon informs Astrea of Isra's death, but she is curiously calm. Mako commands Ebon to ask Adara for help "beyond their means," though Ebon does not understand the message.

15 Arilis: Ebon relays Mako's words to Adara, who sends a message and then takes him to see the Lord Prince Eamin. Eamin promises to use his resources to find Isra upon the Seat. He reveals that he knew Ebon's brother, Momen.

16 Arilis: Xain and the faculty search Theren for the mark of enchantment, but they find nothing. Mako approaches them in the library and tells them Gregor means to flee the Seat. He takes them to the cove where Ebon killed Cyrus, and there they battle Gregor. Theren is hurt, as is Gregor, and they barely escape before being caught by the Mystics. Upon returning to the Academy, they are confronted by Xain and the faculty, who have found Kekhit's amulet. Theren allows herself to be captured so that Ebon and Kalem can escape. They hide in Adara's home.

19 Arilis: Lilith finds Ebon and Kalem. She urges them to rescue Theren and tells them when Isra means to strike: in three days' time. Mako appears later and tells them that he means to remove Ebon from the Seat, and he will not hear of any schemes to stop Isra. He gives Ebon two days to prepare.

20 Arilis: Kalem realizes that Isra mindwyrded an alchemist to create the false corpse. Ebon realizes that Isra is hiding in the vaults. Together, he and Kalem sneak back into the Academy and confront Isra with the help of Lilith and Nella. They find and rescue Erin, who is mindwyrded, and Astrea, who is Isra's accomplice. Lilith kills Isra. Xain at last accepts Ebon's innocence and hears the whole of his tale.

21 Arilis: Xain and Dasko confront the children. Dasko tries to banish all four of them, but Theren and Ebon convince him to spare Lilith and Kalem. Xain takes Ebon aside and asks for his help to defeat the Necromancer.

22 Arilis: Mako brings Nella before Halab. She reveals that Ebon was with Cyrus the day the Seat was attacked. Halab has Mako kill her.

ADDENDUM C

FAMILIES AND FIGURES OF THE ACADEMY JOURNALS

THE FAMILY DRAYDEN

Of the powerful merchant families in Underrealm, the family Drayden has the darkest and fiercest reputation. They may not yet hold the power and the long, storied history of the family Yerrin, but they are nonetheless feared beyond all others.

To all outside appearances, the family Drayden deal in spices. This has been the case for many centuries. The kingdom of Idris has few green lands suited for the growing of pepper and other such plants, but these were all acquired by the Draydens centuries ago through a long process of purchase and political machination. While Feldemar has a similarly forgiving climate for these crops, it is also often battered by storms and monsoons that make farming more difficult, and the political turmoil of that kingdom has always made it difficult for a thriving trade to take root. Therefore the Draydens have a hold on the greater portion of the spice market across the nine kingdoms.

However, it was only in the relatively recent past that the family Drayden began to amass their true power and their current fearsome reputation, and they did so through much darker methods.

In the Year of Underrealm 1094, a new matriarch came to rule over the family. Her name was Idia, and it was she who first formed the Tabarzin.

The Tabarzin are an order of assassins. The arranged murder of political opponents is, of course, as old as human civilization. But it is naturally condemned, and the penalties for any attempts made along this line can be severe. Idia realized that assassination, like any tool, must be used correctly. Kings and lords would try to use it like a hammer, pounding a foe into submission by trying to cut off their head. But Idia knew that murder could be used more like a surgeon's knife.

Therefore the Tabarzin have never been used for something so foolish as attempting to assassinate the High King—a nearly impossible prospect in any case, and one that would throw Underrealm into such turmoil that no one could reliably hope to gain power or coin from the situation. Instead, the main work of the Tabarzin is the collecting of information. When the family Drayden encounters a problem, the Tabarzin are sent to investigate and find a linchpin to remove that will send the problem crashing down.

If the Selvan king, for example, does not want the Draydens to trade in their kingdom, the Tabarzin will find out why. They might find that the king has a cousin who purchases Drayden spices in Wadeland and sells them in Selvan for much higher prices. The cousin is still too close to the king to be targeted without retribution. So the Tabarzin will investigate further, only to discover that the cousin's trade relies upon a caravan directed and managed by a grizzled veteran of Dorsean wars.

The Tabarzin kill the veteran. They arrange for the blame to land on Dorseans. The caravan languishes. The king's cousin can no longer trade spices in Selvan. And the king is suddenly much more amenable to the Draydens' terms.

In this way, the Draydens have been expanding their power for many years. Some suspect the Tabarzin's existence, of course—it is not difficult to see the number of times the Draydens have benefited from someone's untimely and unexpected death. But the truth is that the Tabarzin are responsible for many more deaths than have ever been laid at their feet—and even when they are suspected, no one can prove anything.

The power of the family Drayden took a great leap forwards when Mako joined the Tabarzin some decades ago. His arrival to the order is, of course, shrouded in mystery, but it was not long afterwards that Halab became the family's new matriarch, and together she and Mako have amassed more political gains for the family than it has seen since the Tabarzin's inception. This is due in equal part to Halab's mastery of political strategy and Mako's uncanny ability to gather information—an ability that no one has yet been able to explain.

THE FAMILY KONNEL

The noble family of Konnel has held its place of honor in the kingdom of Hedgemond for generations beyond counting. Their scions have held places of prestige in the courts of the High King, they have done deeds worthy (and subject) of legend, and they have always shown themselves to be the most stalwart and loyal of allies.

They are also, as a rule, honest to a fault, and this has greatly hampered their position in Underrealm's political hierarchy—not that any member of the family would be very bothered by this fact.

During the rise of the Necromancer, there were two Konnels of particular note.

The first, of course, was Kalem of the family Konnel, who became the best friend of Ebon of the family Drayden.

Kalem and Ebon's friendship was very unusual for their time. Both boys were quite oblivious of the growing schism between noble and merchant families across the nine kingdoms. The details of the divide are too numerous to expound here, but in summary, the merchant families had begun to grow hungry for greater power than they could acquire merely through bags of gold. Independently across the nine kingdoms, as if word had passed among all of them—and in several instances, this was indeed the case—the merchants began taking steps towards securing some of the hereditary power that the nobles had enjoyed since High King Roth himself.

The noble families were aware of this, of course, but they could take little direct action. Taxes on the merchants were their greatest source of income. They did, however, stymie the merchants' attempts to gain power whenever they could. The primary method of denial was the rejection of politically expedient marriages. Where once the nobles had been happy to arrange for their successors to marry wealthy merchants, now they were almost universally averse to the practice. And the nobles carefully crafted images of the merchants as grasping social climbers and fed these tales to their children.

Thus, interestingly, it became far more usual for royal children to marry commonfolk than merchants, and several families with no erstwhile claim to nobility suddenly found themselves in positions of elevated power. This went poorly in some cases, though there were also many accounts of commoners raised to nobility who began to make their lands far more just than they had ever been before.

But Ebon of the family Drayden had never been permitted to participate in the inner workings of the Drayden family, so he did not know that Kalem was not *supposed* to want to be his friend. And Kalem, of course, was young and impressionable, and immensely happy to find an older student at the Academy who knew far less than he did. If Ebon had carried himself with the haughtiness and self-assurance common to his kin, it is certain that Kalem would never have befriended him.

The second Konnel of great importance during these times was named Hollen. She became Lord Chancellor of the Mystic Order shortly after the Battle of the Seat. By almost cosmic chance, the former Lord Chancellor was a Drayden named Qarad—a strange parallel of the Drayden and Konnel families being so closely entwined that would play itself out in Ebon and Kalem's relationship.

After Qarad's death in battle defending High King Enalyn against the Shades—and, in particular, against Rogan, chief among the Shadeborn—Hollen of the family Konnel replaced him. She had formerly been a chancellor of the Mystics, but in the northern kingdom of Feldemar, not in her homeland of Hedgemond.

Hollen's deeds would have a great impact on the war with Dulmun—and, indeed, on the fate of the Mystic order. But that tale is best told elsewhere, and in connection with Ebon's friend Theren, who would end up being far more concerned with such matters.

XAIN FORREDAR

There exist in all the events surrounding the Necromancer no person more varied in manner, deed, or intent, than Xain of the family Forredar.

The tale of Xain's youth has been told elsewhere, but some small mention of it must be made here. In his youth, Xain saved the life of the Lord Prince Eamin after Eamin had been kidnapped by bandits. The bandits had hoped to extract a ransom from High King Enalyn, but in the end, Xain and Eamin slew them all. In return for Xain's heroism, Enalyn promised him that she would do her utmost to arrange his marriage to anyone in Underrealm he wished.

Ultimately, Enalyn's best efforts were not good enough.

Xain's heart belonged to Trill of the family Adair. Trill's father, Damba, was a vengeful and spiteful man, but he doted on his daughter, and so she loved him. Before Enalyn could make a move, Damba convinced Trill to marry another—for the good of her family, or so he said. Though it broke her heart to sunder herself from Xain in this way,

Trill obeyed her father, and so Xain's deepest desire was torn from him forever.

His one consolation was that Trill was already with child before she wed, and after the birth of the boy, Erin, Trill sent him to live with Xain. Damba was more than glad to be rid of the boy, a constant reminder of Xain, whom he loathed.

Damba had less than noble intentions in marrying Trill off. He arranged for her to be wed to a daughter of the family Yerrin. This alone was highly unusual, since, as has already been said, the noble families of Underrealm are most reluctant to join the merchant families in marriage. But Damba needed a worthy suitor, one who he could convince Trill would be a great benefit to the family. The Yerrins' seemingly limitless gold reserves fit this requirement very nicely. A suitor of nobility might have served just as well, but a noble would have been reluctant to arrange such a marriage, since it was well known that the High King desired to arrange Trill's marriage to Xain. Thus the Yerrins provided the perfect answer in both respects.

But Damba's spite ran even deeper than that. The family Adair had long feuded with the family Forredar, who also hailed from Hedgemond. Their lands bordered each other for some leagues, and the exact borders had never been drawn to either family's satisfaction. Thus the two families often came to blows over the contested lands, a microcosm of the border squabbles between Dorsea and the other northern kingdoms. The union of Xain and Trill might have done much to mend this rift, but it was not Damba's wish to heal the wounds of generations of fighting.

And Damba had another, much darker reason for binding himself to the family Yerrin. But that is a tale for another time.

ADDENDUM D

A SELECTION OF
DOCUMENTS OF NOTE

HIGH KING ENALYN'S DECLARATION OF WAR

The Year of Underrealm 1313, in Arilis, upon the Ninth Day
By the Authority Of and Recorded From the High King Enalyn, who is The Just

It is in darker times the dutiful burden of the High King, who, though they desire always the health and safety of all their people, and that none of them should perish in the flames of war, yet recognize that some number of their subjects threaten the greater population through base treachery, to declare those subjects Enemies of the land, thanks to no actions but their own, and to order their immediate subjugation and purging from history's great and storied annals. No one with any wisdom granted to them by the sky above can find it in them, even if their deceit is boundless, to deny that we now find ourselves unwillingly cast into just such times.

Among the mighty and wise who dwell today in Underrealm, where are gathered the mightiest lords humankind has yet put forth and the wisest scholars to ever become learned in matters of power and of history, there is no trace to be found by even the most stringent and adamant search of any known tome of lore, not even if the searcher plumbed the depths of every library from the Academy for Wizards to the Tomb-Keeps of Idris, of any betrayal more unjust or more vicious than that which has been visited upon their rightful liege-lord, unless they endeavored to cast their thought into a time so deep and so dark that any righteous mind would shy away from it in terror and disgust, and witness in the bloodiest pages of the past the betrayal of Roth, the first and righteous High King, whose rule has passed to me in line unending since almost the Time before Time, by his daughter Renna, who is the Blackheart. Only by such correlation and in experiencing the bone-deep revulsion it entails, which springs from all that is righteous and honorable in the deepest part of the natural human spirit, may the intrepid mind assume the proper attitude with which to view those evil affairs which have cast upon Underrealm its current pall of enmity, distrust, and war.

To the meanest and the simplest folk of the nine kingdoms, wherever

829

they may dwell and howsoever often they may encounter or fail to encounter some knowledge of the wider world, it is even to them now known that a vicious and foul attack by boat and by sword and bow, and by magic, and which was unwarranted, unlooked for, and unprovoked in every measure, was, during the Year of Underrealm 1312, in Yanis of that year, upon that month's ninth day, carried out with the utmost malevolence upon the High King's Seat, where have sat the preceding High Kings in a line unending to the High King Andara, mother of the High King Andriana, who is exalted as the Fearless, and who before dwelt, as did the High Kings before her, in Rothton upon the great island Landfall in the kingdom of Dulmun, and that this duplicitous and cowardly attack was carried out by two separate forces of great size and fell nature, from two directions, so that by their treasonous deceit they hoped to envelop and entrap the righteous and loyal forces who serve me, as is their duty and their privilege.

It is further known even to them, as was made clear by their ruthless and malignant actions, that the ultimate aim of these traitors was my own death, for they drove forwards towards my palace and besieged it, and there were my forces brought to bay, and many heroic and loyal soldiers perished in the fighting there, which was both tragic and needless. And it is further known even to them that one of these fell armies sailed across the Great Bay from the east, and that they set sail originally from the kingdom of Dulmun, where declared Roth his dominance over Underrealm at the very start of this nation, and thus he brought an end to the time before time, though his mighty gift to all of us has now been squandered.

Therefore I now declare, as is the right that has been handed down to me through ages beyond counting and in unending line of succession:

—That the kingship of Dulmun, which is a great honor and one that many nobles in Underrealm would seek most avidly, and would not squander or spurn as she has, is removed from Bodil of the family Geyun, who took the crown with false and evil intent, and who is a traitor so vile that no good-hearted person in the nine kingdoms will speak her name without hatred and contempt;

—That the nation of Underrealm, which is as eternal as the sky above, and as merciless towards its betrayers as the darkness below, is now engaged in a just and unending war against Bodil of the family Geyun, and that

this war, the righteousness of which none can contest, shall not cease until she is destroyed, and her name and her likeness cast from any record of honor or place of power that may exist in her kingdom;

—That because they, too, have acted in betrayal of me, who is their rightful liege lord, any of the generals, soldiers, servants, retainers, or any citizens of Bodil of the family Geyun who, knowing her evil and treacherous nature, yet elect of their own volition stand or fight by her side, are likewise traitors to the nine kingdoms, and their names shall be counted as dishonorable as her own, and they shall be put to death by any servant of the High King;

—That every rightful king of Underrealm, who have taken their kingships with honor and with loyalty, and who have not failed for generations beyond count to stand beside their rightful ruler, and who shall now lend aid in the destruction of Bodil of the family Geyun shall, after her death and erasure from any claim to nobility or righteousness, receive from me and from the bounty gained in such war, gifts commensurate with the quality, the plenteousness, and the expediency of the aid they have lent.

I, Enalyn, who am the High King, do therefore now command with all the authority of my crown, which holds dominance over all the nine crowns, and my throne, which sits higher than all the nine thrones, the rightful kings of Underrealm, who are in their subservience and their loyalty, lesser in authority than I, and yet no lesser in honor and righteousness, to send by land and by sea, and by all means at their disposal and whatever the cost to their own treasuries might be, such strength of arms, be it in wizards, soldiers, weapons, beasts of burden or of war, or supplies as they can afford, while not endangering or starving their own people, to aid in Bodil's justified destruction, in accordance with and obedience to the oaths they have sworn and continue to uphold, binding their nine thrones to the service of mine.

I so decree, in sight of the sky above, which is eternal, and in fear of the darkness below, which is merciless.
High King Enalyn

—It was universally acknowledged by scholars of the time that for all Enalyn's great strengths as a ruler, she was an abysmal writer. Though they often put it more politely in their letters to each other.

MOMEN'S FINAL LETTERS

The Year of Underrealm 1307

12 Maius

Dear Eboniya,

Mother tells me you have been unhappy since I left. Try not to be. I miss you, too, but let us be honest with each other: my stories were growing stale. Do you not realize that when I return, I shall have a thousand and one incredible tales of my journeys to tell you? All of your favorite stories have come from past caravan trips just like this one. I must go out and have more adventures to tell you about.

I wish you could see the lands the caravan has traveled through already. We rode into Wadeland and are following the Zanbibi river south. You have never seen a land so green. The mountains reach for the sky like spears. I have heard that centaurs live there, but we have not seen them.

I do not want to be away any more than you want me to be. I hope you will not spend much time moping. Work hard at your lessons. Enjoy your reading when you can slip away from Tamen, and do not worry too much about what Father says. And please take good care of Albi. She is young yet, and she needs an older sibling to look after her—just as I have always looked after you.

Until my return brings us both joy,
Momen

* * *

To Father,

The caravan progresses quickly. We have faced no obstacles upon the road. There is no word of bandits in the area, but then, we did not think there would be.

Mako left us yesterday. He claimed he had urgent business from Halab. I thought it was strange that this would not have been mentioned to me before we left, but then, Mako is Mako.

I will send you another letter when we reach Selvan. That should be in a week or so.

Your son,
Momen

* * *

16 Maius

Dearest Halab,

I must thank you once again for placing upon me this highest of honors. You shushed me every time I said it back home, so I will tell you now, when you cannot forestall me: I vow to bring honor to you and to the family by seeing our goods safely to their destination. I swear I will make you proud.

Speaking of which, I can hardly restrain my eagerness to see dear cousin Filip again. I am sending a letter ahead to him, but to see him in person will be a joy beyond description. As you have asked, I will give him your love.

Kanlena is every bit as glorious as you hinted. It is nowhere near so grand as the meanest city in Idris, of course, but it is so . . . exotic would be the word, I think. Once again I find myself blessed by your belief in me.

I am pushing our tradesmen to fetch only the best prices for the pepper, as it appears to be in high demand. The other goods will achieve a less lofty return, of course, but ours are of the highest quality, and I think we shall still do well here.

If it is no trouble, I hoped to bring a small matter to your attention. Mako left the caravan yesterday, telling us you had given him some task to perform. Mayhap I misheard or forgot, but I did not remember such a detail being discussed when we planned this journey. I only mention it, of course, to inform you that Mako did as you no doubt asked him to do. If you require anything further from me in this matter, you know you have only to ask.

I will write you again soon to inform you of our progress. All my gratitude for your faith in me.

Your nephew,
Momen

* * *

Flip, you monkey,

Two weeks! Two weeks until we see each other! I can hardly stand it!

I snuck into my father's cellar before we left Idris and stole the best bottle of wine I could find that was not locked down. The very first thing we must do when we see each other is retreat from all watchful eyes and get drunk as piss. I hope you will have something similarly fine to share, because just one bottle may not do the trick. And I hope you have been sampling all the blue doors near you, because I will accept nothing but the best.

And afterwards, I mean to speak with you about that matter we have only spoken lightly of before. I will admit it here, so that you may lord it over me when I arrive: you were right, and I was wrong. There is *something strange going on back home. I can see it, now that I am looking for it after you mentioned it. It is just as you said—no one says anything, but it is the* way *they do not say anything that gives the game away.*

But I have no more idea what is happening than you did when last we spoke. I only know that—well, that a certain dark watcher, *whom we have discussed before, seems to be involved. (He has vanished, by the way, but still I cannot shake the fear that he will read this. What a foolish thought.)*

But I can feel it, Flip. I can feel the weight off my shoulders now that I am no longer under my father's roof. What a feeling this is. If only I could remain gone forever, roaming with this caravan—or better yet, free from it, riding with you from city to city and kingdom to kingdom. I never want to go back home, Flip. To Idris, yes, perhaps, but certainly not home.

If you write me back before I see you, do not say a thing about the Seat. I do not want to know even the smallest detail. I want to see it all in person.

Two weeks, cousin! Ready yourself!

Until then,
Momen

* * *

Dear Eboniya,

Well, this shall certainly make for a tale of adventure. You will not believe what has happened. The caravan's navigator vanished in the night—and he took our maps with him!

Now, I can imagine you staring at this letter in horror right now. But fear not. We are many, and we have much food and many coins. And we are in Selvan—all we must do is head north until we reach the Great Bay or west until we reach the Dragon's Tail, and we shall know where we are again. Fear not for me, but be prepared for a thrilling tale of adventure when at last I return.

That return will be somewhat delayed, however. I am sure you understand.

Are you taking care of Albi, as I asked? Tell her an exciting story about her brother Momen wandering the landscapes of far distant kingdoms—and make it sound better than it is, for in fact I am fat and happy.

I miss you, little brother. Kiss Mother for me. I will see you soon, though later than I would like.

With love,
Momen

* * *

22 Maius

Dear Flip,

I do not know what under the sky is happening.

I know I am only an apprentice. I know I am not in charge of the caravan. But you have done this before. Please, if you can, offer me some advice—or at least some reassurance!

Our navigator has vanished, and his charts are gone with him. The caravan head, darkness take her, insists on taking us farther west, but I <u>know</u> we should be heading north. That is where you are, for one thing. But also, we are supposed to travel from Garsec, and from there to the Seat. The caravan head wants to take the road north through Cabrus and then south of the Birchwood. Why add weeks to our journey? She is a fool, and the navigator is not here to tell her otherwise.

Where in the dark below did that fool go, anyway?

I would be lying if I told you I was not worried, but then again, this is hardly the worst fate that can befall a caravan. It seems we must wait quite some time before our reunion, but I still have that bottle of wine.

If you have any wise words, send them as quickly as you may. Otherwise, watch out for me.

Yours,
Momen

* * *

Father,

You know I would not write you like this unless it was urgent, so please, listen to me.

Something is wrong. We are in strange, backwater lands in the southeast of Selvan. The caravan leader is leading us west for reasons I do not understand. We should be heading north towards the Great Bay, not deeper into Selvan. And it is not as though she has looked up a better route; as I am sure you have been told, our navigator and all his maps are gone. We have not seen a city for days, only meager little towns where we can leave letters like this one, hoping a King's messenger arrives sometime soon to carry it your way.

There is something afoot, but I do not know what. The caravan head is behaving most oddly. Could she have been paid off by one of our enemies? I do not know. All I know is that we are in more danger the farther we proceed on this reckless course. I have tried to speak my mind in this matter, but Halab only made me an apprentice. The caravan head will not listen to me, and I cannot strip her of her authority.

I know you will think me weak, but I will admit it: I am frightened, Father. Something is wrong, and it is a problem I have never been trained to solve.

I do not know what you can do, but if you have any ideas, please. Help me. Mayhap you can send Mako to investigate, if that dark-damned man has reappeared—we still have not seen him.

Your son,
Momen

* * *

Dearest Halab,

Our ability to send letters has been hampered, and I do not know if you have received any word of the caravan's progress for the last few weeks. In any case, I must write you now, and urgently. Something has happened. The caravan was attacked.

These were no bandits. We do not even know if they were human. They came in the night, but they bore no torches. It was like they could see in the dark. They slew the caravan head and two of her guards, and then they vanished again. No, that is not entirely true—they destroyed the wheel pins of three of the wagons before they left.

Do not think I am in despair. I am now in charge of the caravan, and as is my duty, I am simply informing you of what happened. We mourned our caravan head, burning her and her guards after wrapping them in muslin. I beg of you, deliver my heartfelt sorrow to their families until I can return home and do it myself.

I have decided to abandon the crippled wagons. I will transfer as much of our goods to the other wagons as I can, but I must save our people. We are too far west—a matter I tried to resolve with the caravan head, but could not. I will say no more, for I wish to speak no ill of the dead.

I know my duty, dearest aunt. I will not shirk it. I will save every life I can, as well as every coin for the family. I mean to lead us east again and then north once we have cleared the mountain range, making for the Great Bay as we were supposed to do in the first place.

You will see that your faith in me was not misplaced. I swear it.

With love,
Momen

* * *

Father,

We have been waylaid in eastern Selvan. I cannot say exactly where, for the maps are by now a distant memory.

Last night was the third attack so far, though I have no doubt they will strike again—whoever they are. No, I do not say <u>whatever</u>, but <u>whoever</u>. It was a human, I am certain of that. They moved in the darkness. There were few of them—I think, in fact, one.

Father, I cannot write more plainly. But you must send aid to us, now, at once. And you must do it yourself. I am certain that by the time this reaches you, the family will have mobilized to come to our aid. Do not rely on them. I cannot tell you why, but <u>you</u> must come. Please, if you value my life at all, if you ever have, trust me.

We have taken shelter atop a hill just a few leagues away from the main road. There are many standing stones and trees behind which to take cover. We have enough supplies to hold out almost indefinitely, and I have set a constant guard.

I am sending this letter with a messenger and hoping they survive the journey. If you receive this, do not wait. Come as soon as you can.

And if you are too late, please try to find out what happened. Do not stop searching. Our family has the means. Use them, and see what results.

A final request, if indeed this letter does not save us, as I fear it might not. Look after Ebon for me. I know you too well to ask you to be kind to him. But see to his safety, if nothing else. He may be in danger, just as I am, and it may threaten him from anywhere.

Your son,
Momen

* * *

Dear Filip,

Do you despair to see me use your real name so formally? Well, I am about out of concern for such things.

Flip, I think I am doomed. And I think our family is to blame.

Your words to me have never rung more true in my memory. Something dark has taken root in the family Drayden, and it is that darkness that circles me now, that I fear will claim me in the end.

If this letter ever reaches you, it will have been seen by no one else. So I will speak plainly to you, when I could not do so in my last letter to my father.

Mako is here.

It is he who has been attacking the caravan, darkness take him. I caught only a glimpse of him, but it was enough. There may be others with him, other members of the Tabarzin, but Mako is here for certain.

I will do my best to survive. We are taking every precaution to hold out until rescue can come. But you know the Tabarzin as well as I do—perhaps better. I have little hope left.

But Flip, there is something more. Something I am only just now coming to realize: Mako cannot be acting alone. It is impossible. The shadowed messages we have both caught wind of, the strangers who appear in our homes only to vanish before daylight, all of it. All this could not be carried out by the Tabarzin without help.

Halab has something to do with it.

I am sorry, Flip. I know she is your mother. I am certain of my guess, though I wish I were not. Everything we have seen—and all the things we have only begun to suspect—they are happening by Halab's orders.

I think that if I die here, you will come to pay your last respects. If you are reading these words, then I have succeeded in hiding the letter in such a way that only you will be able to find it. If I did it right, then heed my advice, dearest Flip: run. Leave the family and never look back. You owe them nothing. Neither of us ever did. Make for yourself the life you have always wanted—that we have both always wanted.

Do it for me.

Love,
Momen

* * *

Dear, dear Ebon,

If you are reading this . . . well, I do not need to tell you what has happened.

I would do anything to see you one last time. But we are under attack, and I am not likely to survive. These things happen to caravans, little brother. This is part of our life. A life I hope will be gentler to you than it has been, in the end, to me.

I find myself in the odd position of having to give you one final piece of advice. It is unfair. You are so young, and I do not know the sort of man you will grow up to be—what advice you will need the most. And I am so young myself. How can I tell you how to live a good life, when mine has been cut short so soon? I am no wise old man with an abundance of wisdom to share. So take what I have to say and use it, or not, as you see fit.

But Ebon, I do not think you are suited for the life our family has laid before you. You are too fond of books, and not fond enough of numbers; too interested in peace, and quiet, and friendship, and not interested enough in travel and adventure.

You have a gift, Ebon. I will write to you of it freely now, though neither of us was permitted to speak openly of it when I was at home with you. That gift should not be squandered. And if you get the chance to use it, you should. You are a wizard. Be a wizard. Be a learned master of lore, be an alchemist of renown. Do not waste your days driving caravans across the nine kingdoms.

But above all, be who you wish to be. You have a better heart in your breast and a better head atop your neck than I do—or, I should say, I did. I think you know, in your heart, what sort of man you should grow up to be.

I only wish I could see it.

You have all my love, even from the darkness.
Momen

* * *

Listen here, you sow.

I know the truth. I know what you have done. I know that Mako is coming to kill me—to kill all of us—and that he is doing it on your orders.

I am sickened to think of how I always trusted you. How Ebon still trusts you, and Filip. We idolized you. And now you have cast me away, because—because what? Because I had begun to suspect the truth about you? Because I had caught some faint inkling of what you and Mako were up to? And because you feared I would tell what I knew to Filip? I do not know for certain, but that would be my guess.

Well, you have won. Filip will never hear what I have to say about you. He will never learn the truth. He will continue to idolize you, and that will make you very happy, I am sure.

I know Mako will come for me. It may be tonight, it may be days from now. I will wait for him. And before he slits my throat, I will give him this letter for you. I will _make_ him give it to you, so that you know I see you for what you are—worthless, faithless, and deserving of nothing but the deepest scorn and dishonor. Know it, and remember it always.

I will also give Mako another letter. It will be for Ebon. You _will_ see to it that Ebon receives the letter. You will _not_ withhold it. Do not worry—I will tell Ebon nothing of what has happened, of what I now know to be true about you and Mako and the whole sorry, rotten heart of our family.

But I am Ebon's brother. He always needed me, with the way Father treated him. And you will not stop me from doing the most I can for him, even now.

You will follow me into death, one day. That is the only thing that comforts me as the sun sets on what might be my final day. And in the darkness below, I will torment you forever.

Momen

—It should be noted for the reader that Halab did not, in fact, prevent Ebon from reading Momen's final letter. But Shay, Ebon's father, did.

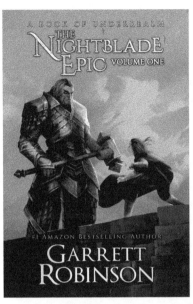

KEEP READING

More books in The Academy Journals are coming. But this is not the only tale of Underrealm. The Nightblade Epic tells the story of Loren of the family Nelda, known to many as the Nightblade.

Either series is complete on its own—but together, they form a greater part of the tapestry of Underrealm.

Contained within the Nightblade Epic are answers to many of the mysteries laced throughout The Academy Journals. Just why did the Shades come to the High King's Seat? Where did Xain come from, and why does he hate magestones so?

And just how does Mako know as much as he does?

Find out in The Nightblade Epic volumes, which contain dozens of pages of bonus materials just like you found in this book.

Get them here NOW:

Underrealm.net/Nightblade-Epic

THANK YOU TO MY PATRONS

Even before I started writing the books of Underrealm, I had the support of many incredible people on Patreon. Through the good times and the bad, they have been my constant, and I am incredibly grateful. If you want to join them, please visit:

Patreon.com/GarrettBRobinson

STUDIO EXECUTIVES

Hayley Marsden, Kris Nieder, Kristen, Mark Monroe, Monica Leonelle, Old Man Smithers, Sean Platt, Sybil R. Case

SPONSORS

Michael O'Neal

INNER CIRCLE

A Howard, Amy Teegan, Cathy Pelham, E.L. Drayton, Eric Ugland, Felipe Avila, Felix , Gin Hollan, Hank Green, James Stonesmith, Kakirtog , Karl J. Leis, LupineKing , Matty Franklyn, Maureen Army, Ophir Ronen, Ryan Starbloak, Sam Reeves Writes, Tommy Donbavand, Violet Rodriguez

PATRONS

Aidan McCormack, Chad Kukahiko, Colby R. Rice, Damon , Diane Campbell, Doctor Woo, Donovan Scherer, Draconicrose , Graham Brown, Jessamine Haak, Kj Caston, Kristen Ho, Kyle Hamman, Lars Leonhard, Luke Kondor, Mr. C, Rosie Reast, Sara Langworthy, Simon Cantan

CONNECT ONLINE

FACEBOOK

Want to hang out with other fans of the Underrealm books? There's a Facebook group where you can do just that. Join the Nine Lands group on Facebook and share your favorite moments and fan theories from the books. I also post regular behind-the-scenes content, including information about the world you can't find anywhere else. Visit the link to be taken to the Facebook group:

Underrealm.net/nine-lands

YOUTUBE

Catch up with me daily (when I'm not directing a film or having a baby). You can watch my daily YouTube channel where I talk about art, science, life, my books, and the world.
But not cats.
Never cats.

GarrettBRobinson.com/yt

THE BOOKS OF UNDERREALM

To see all novels in the world of Underrealm, visit:
Underrealm.net/books

THE NIGHTBLADE EPIC
NIGHTBLADE
MYSTIC
DARKFIRE
SHADEBORN
WEREMAGE
YERRIN

THE ACADEMY JOURNALS
THE ALCHEMIST'S TOUCH
THE MINDMAGE'S WRATH
THE FIREMAGE'S VENGEANCE

TALES OF THE WANDERER (COMING SOON)
BLOOD LUST
STONE SKIN
HELL SKIN

CHRONOLOGICAL ORDER
NIGHTBLADE
MYSTIC
DARKFIRE
SHADEBORN
BLOOD LUST
THE ALCHEMIST'S TOUCH
THE MINDMAGE'S WRATH
STONE SKIN
WEREMAGE
THE FIREMAGE'S VENGEANCE
HELL SKIN
YERRIN

ABOUT THE AUTHOR

Garrett Robinson was born and raised in Los Angeles. The son of an author/painter father and a violinist/singer mother, no one was surprised when he grew up to be an artist.

After blooding himself in the independent film industry, he self-published his first book in 2012 and swiftly followed it with a stream of others, publishing more than two million words by 2014. Within months he topped numerous Amazon bestseller lists. Now he spends his time writing books and directing films.

A passionate fantasy author, his most popular books are the novels of Underrealm, including the series The Nightblade Epic and The Academy Journals.

However, he has delved into many other genres. Some works are for adult audiences only, such as *Non Zombie* and *Hit Girls,* but he has also published popular books for younger readers, including The Realm Keepers series and *The Ninjabread Man*, co-authored with Z.C. Bolger.

He now runs a publishing company, Legacy Books, dedicated to uplifting the voices of those authors traditional fantasy publishing has often ignored.

Garrett lives in Oregon with his wife Meghan, his children Dawn, Luke, and Desmond, and his dog Chewbacca.

Garrett can be found on:

BLOG: garrettbrobinson.com/blog
EMAIL: garrett@garrettbrobinson.com
TWITTER: twitter.com/garrettauthor
FACEBOOK: facebook.com/garrettbrobinson

CPSIA information can be obtained
at www.ICGtesting.com
Printed in the USA
LVHW110729260720
661548LV00008B/98/J